David Clarkson

The Practical Works of David Clarkson

Vol. 1

SALZWASSER
VERLAG

David Clarkson

The Practical Works of David Clarkson

Vol. 1

Reprint of the original, first published in 1864.

1st Edition 2022 | ISBN: 978-3-75259-163-7

Verlag (Publisher): Salzwasser Verlag GmbH, Zeilweg 44, 60439 Frankfurt, Deutschland
Vertretungsberechtigt (Authorized to represent): E. Roepke, Zeilweg 44, 60439 Frankfurt, Deutschland
Druck (Print): Books on Demand GmbH, In de Tarpen 42, 22848 Norderstedt, Deutschland

NICHOL'S SERIES OF STANDARD DIVINES.

PURITAN PERIOD.

THE

WORKS OF DAVID CLARKSON, B.D.

VOL. I.

THE PRACTICAL WORKS

OF

DAVID CLARKSON, B.D.,

FELLOW AND TUTOR OF CLARE HALL, CAMBRIDGE.

VOL. I.

M.DCCC.LXIV.

CONTENTS.

SERMONS, &c.

PREFATORY NOTE.

RESPECTING the personal history of David Clarkson, a volume of whose works we now submit to the reader, we regret that almost no information has been handed down to us. The following particulars are gleaned from a Memoir by the late Rev. John Blackburn, prefixed to a volume of his Select Works, published by the Wickliffe Society, the contents of which have been kindly placed at our disposal.

David Clarkson was born at Bradford, in Yorkshire, in the month of February 1621–2. He was educated at Clare Hall, Cambridge, and became fellow and tutor in that College in 1645. He gave up his fellowship in 1651, on his marriage with a Miss Holcroft; and he was afterwards Rector of Mortlake, Surrey, from which he was 'ejected' by the Act of Uniformity in 1662. After this he spent his time in retirement and study, until, in 1682, he was chosen as colleague to Dr John Owen in the pastorship of his congregation in London. On the death of Owen, in the following year, he became sole pastor of the congregation, and discharged his duty faithfully until his death in 1686.

This is really all that is known of the personal history of our author. Perhaps it is not rightly matter of surprise, however much it is to be regretted, that we can obtain so little insight into the particulars of the every-day life of most of the Puritan Divines. We are not sure that it would be possible to ascertain many particulars of the lives even of distinguished ministers who died forty or fifty years ago, unless special memoirs of them were written immediately after their death; and, of course, the difficulty must be greatly enhanced when the stream of two hundred years has rolled over the sands upon which a man has imprinted his footmarks. And then it is to be remembered that our researches refer to a time when the periodical press had no existence.

If Owen be admitted to be, as by common consent he seems to be regarded, the 'David' of the Puritan host, and Howe, and Baxter, and Thomas Goodwin to be the 'first three' of its worthies, we believe that the second trio must include the name of David Clarkson, associated probably with those of Charnock and Sibbes, or perhaps Flavel. It is manifest, however, that such a statement is to be taken only in a very general sense. In some respects, Sibbes is as much superior to Goodwin, as in others Goodwin is superior to Sibbes; while in some most important particulars, and especially in respect of clearness and liveliness, Owen himself is unquestionably below all the seven others who have been named, and many others who might have been mentioned. From the very nature of the case, the question of precedence amongst writers cannot be determined but in a vague and general way. No man would ever think of asking the question whether Shakespeare or Bacon were the greater genius, the better writer; or even the more limited question, whether Hume or Gibbon were the better historian, Addison or Johnson the more accomplished essayist. And in the domain of Christian and theological literature, the qualities of different writers are manifestly incommensurable. There are diversities of gifts; and it may not be determined whether the possession of a larger measure of one gift, and a smaller measure of another, be more or less valuable than that of a greater degree of the latter, and a less measure of the former. The clear eye of one may be as precious as the fine ear of another; the delicate touch of one as the firm standing of another; and the eye may not say to the ear, I have no need of thee, nor yet the hand to the foot, I have no need of thee.

It is, however, unquestionable that, in respect of the qualities of a theological writer, Clarkson occupied a very high place amongst the divines of the Puritan period. His vigorous and clear mind, his extensive and varied learning, his fervent piety and zeal for the glory of God and the good of men, enabled him to produce writings remarkable for soundness of reasoning and fervency of appeal, and adorned with the graces of a tasteful eloquence. There can be no difference of opinion as to the propriety of including in the present series, at least the non-controversial portion of these writings—the theological and practical, as distinguished from the ecclesiastical portion; and we do not doubt that many readers will regard them as, upon the whole, the most valuable, as they will certainly be found to be among the most generally attractive, of all the works of which the series is to be composed.

His first appearance as an author was in the publication of a sermon which he preached at one of the Cripplegate Morning

Exercises. Its title is, 'What Christians must do, that the Influence of the Ordinances may abide upon them.' His next publication was another Morning Exercise sermon, on the thesis 'The Doctrine of Justification is dangerously corrupted in the Romish Church.' This was followed by a quarto volume on 'The Practical Divinity of the Papists, discovered to be destructive of Christianity and men's souls,' a work of great research and candour. His next publications related to the episcopal and liturgical controversy. They were a treatise entitled, 'No Evidence for Diocesan Churches,' and another under the title, 'Diocesan Churches not yet Discovered in Primitive Times.' His sermon on the death of Owen was also published. We find also allusions to anonymous tracts of which he was the author, but it is probable that these are irrecoverably lost.

His posthumous works were, 'Primitive Episcopacy stated and cleared from the Holy Scriptures and Ancient Records,' and on the 'Use of Liturgies,' a 'Discourse on the Saving Grace of God,' and a large folio volume of sermons.

These sermons, which will occupy the greater portion of the three volumes which it is intended to include in our series, are thirty-one in number. They are of very various lengths, and, as we venture to think, of very various degrees of excellence. Some of them may be ranked amongst the finest sermons in our language, while others are of little more than average merit. They have the disadvantage which is incident to all posthumous publications, that they contain some things which their author would probably have cut out, and do not contain some things which he would have put in, had he prepared them for the press, or contemplated their publication. Even the fullest of them contain many passages which are evidently only heads and notes for fuller discussions, which were doubtless supplied in the delivery, and which would have been inserted had he revised them for publication. There are also some things which we venture to think he would have omitted. We cannot believe, for example, that so ripe a scholar as he evidently was, would have allowed to pass an argument which he founds on a Hebrew word in the sermon on Original Sin. The root יחם signifies *to be warm;* and by a very obvious process has the two secondary meanings, *to conceive,* and *to be angry.* But Mr Clarkson founds upon this coincidence an argument that the *anger* of God rests upon man from the instant of his *conception.* By a slip of a similar character in another sermon, referring to the prodigal's coming to himself, he makes repentance to be a recovering from madness, rather than a change of mind, as if the composition of the Greek word were μετ' + ἄνοια, and not μετα + νοια. These things any man might write off-hand, but we cannot think that a scholar like Clarkson would have published them.

But with a few slight drawbacks of this kind, Clarkson's sermons, as a whole, are exceedingly valuable. They appear to us, in respect of style of thought and language, to be in advance of many of the writings of the period. They contain no plays upon words, no grotesque similes, no verbal or logical conceits; but an earnest, strong vindication of great gospel truths, and most affectionate and fervent appeals to sinners to embrace the offered salvation. There is often a considerable resemblance to the matter of some of Goodwin's works; occasionally the same arguments employed in continuance. And we have no doubt that Clarkson was well acquainted with such of Goodwin's writings as were published up to the time when he wrote.

The doctrine of Clarkson is very decidedly Calvinistic, and is occasionally somewhat harsher than that of most of the puritan Calvinists. There is, for example, an argument respecting the divine sovereignty (p. 380 of this volume) which, the author tells us, 'clears up the absolute dominion of God, and those difficulties which concern it, very much to his own satisfaction.' It is in subtance that God might, on the ground of absolute sovereignty, righteously deprive even a sinless creature of 'being or well-being.' This is, to say the least of it, harsh doctrine. We do not think that anything like it is to be found in Calvin, and we are sure that something very unlike it is to be found in Goodwin. We venture to recommend the reader to compare the sentiments of Clarkson and Goodwin, the one in the passage referred to, the other in the treatise 'Of the Creatures, and the Condition of their State by Creation,' Book II. Chap. i. (Goodwin's Works, Vol. VII. p. 22–27).

It is hoped that three volumes of our Series may contain all the extant works of Clarkson, with the exception of those on Episcopacy and Liturgies.

The reader will be interested by the perusal of the following tract, entitled, 'A Short Character of that Excellent Divine Mr David Clarkson, who departed this life 14th of June 1686.' This tract Mr Blackburn unhesitatingly ascribes to Dr Bates, who preached Mr Clarkson's funeral sermon. To us it does not appear that his reason is at all sufficient, it being only that he has seen a copy of it bound up with that sermon.

'Although the commendation of the dead is often suspected to be guilty of flattery, either in disguising their real faults, or adorning them with false virtues; and such praises are pernicious to the living: yet of those persons whom God hath chosen to be the singular objects of his grace, we may declare the praiseworthy qualities and actions which reflect an honour upon the Giver, and may excite us to imitation. And such was Mr David Clarkson, a person worthy of dear memory and value, who was furnished with all those endowments that are requisite in an accomplished minister of the gospel.

'He was a man of sincere godliness and true holiness, which is the divine part of a minister, without which all other accomplishments are not likely to be effectual for the great end of the ministry, that is, to translate sinners from the kingdom of darkness, into the kingdom of God's dear Son. Conversion is the special work of divine grace, and it is most likely that God will use those as instruments in that blessed work, who are dear to him and earnestly desire to glorify him. God ordinarily works in spiritual things as in natural; for as in the production of a living creature, besides the influence of the universal cause, there must be an immediate agent of the same kind for the forming of it, so the divine wisdom orders it, that holy and heavenly ministers should be the instruments of making others so. Let a minister be master of natural and artificial eloquence, let him understand all the secret springs of persuasion, let him be furnished with learning and knowledge, yet he is not likely to succeed in his divine employment without sanctifying grace. 'Tis that gives him a tender sense of the worth of souls, that warms his heart with ardent requests to God, and with zealous affection to men for their salvation. Besides, an unholy minister unravels in his actions his most accurate discourses in the pulpit; and like a carbuncle, that seems animated with the light and heat of fire, but is a cold dead stone, so, though with apparent earnestness he may urge men's duties upon them, yet he is cold and careless in his own practice, and his example enervates the efficacy of his sermons. But this servant of God was a real saint; a living spring of grace in his heart diffused itself in the veins of his conversation. His life was a silent repetition of his holy sermons.

'He was a conscientious improver of his time for acquiring of useful knowledge, that he might be thoroughly furnished for the work of his divine calling. And his example upbraids many ministers, who are strangely careless of their duty, and squander away precious time, of which no part is despicable and to be neglected. The filings of gold are to be preserved. We cannot stop the flight of time, nor recall it when past. *Volat irrevocabile tempus.* The sun returns to us every day, and the names of the months every year, but time never returns. But this servant of God was faithful in improving this talent, being very sensible, to use his own words, "that the blood of the soul runs out in wasted time." When deprived of his public ministry, he gave himself wholly to reading and meditation, whereby he obtained an eminent degree of sacred knowledge, and was conversant in the retired parts of learning, in which many who are qualified to preach a profitable sermon are unacquainted.

'His humility and modesty were his distinctive characters wherein he excelled. What a treasure was concealed under the veil of humility! What an illustrious worth was shadowed under his virtuous modesty! He was like a picture drawn by an excellent master in painting, but placed in the dark, so that the exactness of the proportions and the beauty of the colours do not appear. He would not put his name to those excellent tracts that are extant, wherein his learning and judgment are very conspicuous. He was well satisfied to serve the church and illustrate the truth, and to remain in his beloved secrecy.

'In his conversation a comely gravity, mixed with an innocent pleasantness, were attractive of respect and love. He was of a calm temper, not ruffled with passions, but gentle, and kind, and good; and even in some contentious writings, he preserved an equal tenor of mind, knowing that we are not likely to discover the truth in a mist of passion: his breast was the temple of peace.

'In the discharge of his sacred work, his intellectual abilities and holy affection were very evident.

'In prayer, his solemnity and reverence were becoming one that saw him who is invisible: his tender affections, and suitable expressions, how melting and moving, that might convey a holy heat and life to dead hearts, and dissolve obdurate sinners in their frozen tombs.

'In his preaching, how instructive and persuasive to convince and turn the carnal and worldly from the love of sin to the love of holiness; from the love of the earth, to the love of heaven! The matter of his sermons was clear and deep, and always judiciously derived from the text; the language was neither gaudy and vain, with light trimmings, nor rude and neglected, but suitable to the oracles of God. Such were his chosen acceptable words, as to recommend heavenly truths, to make them more precious and amiable to the minds and affections of men; like the colour of the sky, that makes the stars to shine with a more sparkling brightness.

"Briefly, whilst opportunity continued, with alacrity and diligence, and constant resolution, he served his blessed Master till his languishing distempers, which natural means could not remove, prevailed upon him. But then the best Physician provided him the true remedy of patience. His death was unexpected, yet, as he declared, no surprise to him, for he was entirely resigned to the will of God; he desired to live no longer, than to be serviceable: his soul was supported with the blessed hope of enjoying God in glory. With holy Simeon, he had Christ in his arms, and departed in peace to see the salvation of God above. How great a loss the church has sustained in his death is not easily valued; but our comfort is, God never wants instruments to accomplish his blessed work."

The following documents, detailing some portions of the Christian experience of two of Mr Clarkson's daughters, will form an appropriate conclusion to this note.

'*The choice experience of* Mrs Rebecca Combe, *eldest daughter of the late* Rev. Mr David Clarkson, *delivered by her on her admission into fellowship with the church, late under the care of the late* Rev. Mr Thomas Gouge.

'In giving an account of the dealings of God with my soul, I desire truly and sincerely to represent the state of my case; I am sensible it will be in much weakness, but I hope my end is, that God may have the glory of his own work, which he hath wrought on so mean and unworthy a creature as myself.

'I had the advantage and invaluable blessing of a religious education, both my parents being eminent for wisdom and grace. Under the instructions of my good mother, I had early and frequent convictions, though these impressions lasted not long, for I wore them off, either by a formal engaging in some religious duties, or else by running into such diversions as were suited to my childhood. But my convictions being renewed as I grew up, and it being impressed on my mind that this way of performing duties, by fits and starts, merely to quiet an accusing conscience, would not satisfy the desires of an immortal soul capable of higher enjoyments than I took up with; this put me on serious thoughtfulness what method to pursue, in order to bind myself to a more stated performance of those duties which, I was convinced, the Lord required of me.

'Accordingly, I made a most solemn resolution to address myself to God by prayer, both morning and evening, and never on any occasion whatever to neglect it, calling the Lord to witness against me if I broke this solemn engagement. But, alas! I soon saw the vanity of my own resolutions, for as I was only found in the performance of duty through fear, and as a task, and, having once omitted it at the set time, I concluded my promise was now broke, and from that time continued in a total neglect of prayer, till it pleased the almighty Spirit to return with his powerful operations, and set my sins in order before me. Then my unsuitable carriage under former convictions, together with my breaking the most solemn engagements to the Lord, wounded me deep. Indeed, I was tempted to conclude I had sinned the unpardonable sin, and should never be forgiven.

'Yet, in my greatest distress and anguish of spirit, I could not give up all hope, having some views of the free and sovereign grace of God, as extended to the vilest and worst of sinners, though I could not take the comfort of it to myself. My sins appeared exceeding sinful. I even loathed and abhorred myself on account of them, and was continually begging a deeper sense and greater degree of humiliation. I thought I could have been content, yea, I was desirous, to be filled with the utmost horror and terror of which I was capable, if this might be a means of bringing me to that degree of sorrow which I apprehended the Lord expected from so vile a creature. The heinous nature of my sins, and their offensiveness to the pure eyes of his holiness, were ever before me, insomuch that I thought I could not be too deeply wounded, or feel trouble enough.

'This put me on a constant and restless application to God through Christ, from whom alone I now saw all my help must come. I had tried the utmost I could do, and found it left me miserably short of what the law required and I wanted. I was convinced that an expectation of some worthiness in myself, as the condition of my acceptance before God, was that which had kept me so long from Christ and the free promises of the gospel; and therefore, as enabled, I went to the Lord, and pleaded those absolute promises of his word, which are made freely to sinners in his Son, without the least qualification to be found in me. I was enabled to urge those encouraging words, Rev. xxii. 17, "Let him that is athirst come, and whosoever will, let him take the water of life freely;" also Isa. lv. 1, "Without money and without price;" with many more of the like nature, which would be too tedious to mention. I desired to come to Christ, unworthy as I was, and cast my soul entirely upon him, for I clearly saw that all I had heretofore done profited me nothing, since my very prayers, considered as a sinner, were an abomination to the Lord. There was nothing left therefore for me to take the least comfort and encouragement from but the free grace of God in Christ Jesus, which I continued to plead with much earnestness, and found my soul enlarged beyond whatever I had experienced before.

'Soon after, I providentially opened a manuscript of my father's, and cast my eye upon that part of it where he was shewing what pleas a sensible sinner might make use of in prayer. Many things were mentioned which were very reviving. I was miserable, and that might be a plea. I might also plead his own mercy, the suitableness, the largeness, and the freeness of his mercy. I might plead my own inability to believe, of which I was very sensible. I might also plead the will of God, for he commands sinners to believe, and is highly dishonoured by unbelief. I might likewise plead the descent of faith, it is the gift of God, and the nature of this gift, which is free. Yea, I might plead the examples of others who have obtained this gift, and that against the greatest unlikelihood and improbabilities that might be. I might and could plead further, my willingness to submit to anything, so that I might but find this favour with the Lord. Moreover, I might plead Christ's prayer and his compassions; the workings of his Spirit already begun; that regard which the Lord shews to irrational creatures; he hears their cries, and will he shut out the cries of a poor perishing sinner?—in short, I might plead my necessity and extreme need of faith, a sense of which was deeply impressed on my soul.*

'On reading these pleas I found great relief, yea, they were to me as a voice from heaven, saying, This is the way, walk in it. I was enabled to go and act faith upon a Redeemer, and could give up my *all* to him, and trust in him alone *for* all. I was now convinced by his Spirit that he would work in me what was well-pleasing and acceptable to God, and that he required nothing of me but what his free rich grace would bestow upon me. Now was Christ exceeding precious to my soul, and I longed for clearer

* See the sermon in this volume, on 'Faith in Prayer.'—Ed.

discoveries of him, both in his person and offices, as prophet, priest, and king.

And oh, how did I admire his condescending love and grace to such a poor, wretched, worthless creature as myself! I was greatly delighted in frequent acts of resignation to him, desiring that every faculty of my soul might be brought into an entire obedience, and could part with every offensive thing, and would not have spared so much as one darling lust, but was ready to bring it forth and slay it before him. In short, I could now perceive a change wrought in my whole soul; I now delighted in what before was my greatest burden, and found that most burdensome in which I before most delighted. I went on pleasantly in duty; my meditation on him was sweet, and my heart much enlarged in admiring his inexpressible love and grace, so *free*, and *sovereign*, to so *wretched* a creature, which even filled my soul with wonder and love.

But this delightful frame did not long continue, for I was soon surprised with swarms of vain thoughts, which appeared in my most solemn approaches to God, and such violent hurries of temptation, as greatly staggered my faith, which was weak. Hereupon I was ready to give up all, and to conclude that I had mocked God, and cheated my own soul; that these wandering thoughts, and this unfixedness of mind in duty, could never consist with a sincere love to the things of God. I thought my heart had been fixed, but oh how exceeding deceitful did I then find it! which greatly distressed me, and made me conclude my sins were rather increased than mortified, insomuch that I was ready to cry out, "Oh, wretched creature that I am, who shall deliver me from the body of this death!" and in consideration of the power and prevalency of indwelling corruptions and daily temptations which I had to grapple with, I was ready to say, "I shall one day fall by the hands of these enemies."

'But these discouragements were fully removed by reading some of my father's writings, where it was observed that a person had no reason to conclude his sins were more increased merely because they appeared more, and became more troublesome, since this arose from the opposition they now met with, from that principle of grace which now was implanted. Hence I learned, that before the flesh reigned *quietly* in me, and therefore I perceived not the lusts thereof, but now all the powers and faculties of my soul were engaged against them, they gave me the *greatest* disturbance, and struggled more and more. Also these words were impressed on my mind with an efficacious power, 2 Cor. xii. 9, "My grace is sufficient for thee," which gave me peace in believing that it should be to me according to his word.

'Thus, after many conflicts, comforts, and supports, I determined to give myself up to some church, that I might partake of the Lord's Supper, and have my faith confirmed in the blood of that everlasting covenant, which I hoped the Lord had made with me, since he had given me his Spirit as the earnest thereof. I accordingly was joined to a church, and in coming to this ordinance, found great delight: my faith was strengthened and my love increased from that sweet communion I then enjoyed with my Lord by his blessed Spirit, who often filled me with joy unspeakable and full of glory. Thus I walked under the sweet and comfortable sense of his love; and whilst in the way of my duty, I was thus indulged with such sights of the Redeemer's glory, and such a taste of his grace, I frequently wished that I might never more go back to the world again.

But after all these manifestations, oh wretched creature! God in his providence calling me more into the world by changing my condition, this new relation brought new afflictions and new temptations, which, being too much yielded to, insensibly prevailed, and brought me into such perplexing darkness that I want words to express it. I lost the sense of the love of God, and hence my duty was performed without that delight I had once experienced, the want of which made me often neglect it, and especially in private, while I attended on public worship with little advantage or pleasure.

The consideration of this decay in my love, and the loss of those quickening influences of the Spirit which I used to experience in duty, increased my darkness, and I had doleful apprehensions of my state. And my inordinate love to the creature, and want of submission to the will of the Lord, in disposing of what I had so unduly set my heart on, prepared me to look for awful things, in a way of judgment from the righteous God, which I afterwards found; his hand was soon laid on that very object by which I had so provoked him; for a disorder seized him, under which he long languished, till it ended in his death.*

'This was a melancholy stroke, and the more so as I saw his hand stretched out still, for I continued in an unsuitable temper, and without that submission which such a dispensation called for. The Lord still hid his face from me, and it is impossible to give a particular account of those perplexing thoughts and tormenting fears which filled my mind. Everything appeared dreadfully dark both within and without. Oh, were it possible to describe it to others as I then felt it, they would dread that which will separate between them and God! I expected, if the Lord did return, it would be in a terrible way, by some remarkable judgment or other; but oftentimes, from the frame I was in, I could see no ground to hope he would ever return at all.

'But was it to me according to my dismal apprehensions and fears? Oh, no! my soul and all that is within me bless and adore his name, under a sense of his free and sovereign grace, who manifested himself unto thee as a God, pardoning iniquity, transgression, and sin. This was the title by which he manifested himself to Moses when he caused his glory to pass before him, Exod. xxxiv. 6, 7. And it was in the clear apprehension, and powerful application of this by the almighty Spirit that I was brought to admire so greatly the free grace of God, thus discovered to me in so extraordinary a manner, that it even transported my very soul with love

* Her idolised husband died of a consumption at Hitchin, Herts, but in what year is not known.

and thankfulness, beyond anything that I had experienced in the whole of my past life.

'The beginning of this wonderful alteration in my frame, was hearing the experience of one which I thought very much like my own, when the Lord first began to work on my soul. I concluded that this person was the subject of a real and universal change; on this occasion, I determined to consider *my* former experience, in doing of which I found the blessed Spirit of all grace assisting me, and witnessing to his work upon my heart, insomuch that, ere I was aware, my soul was like the chariots of a willing people; I was wonderfully enlivened in duty, and enlarged in thankfulness to God for thus manifesting himself, and directing me to those means which he had so inexpressibly blessed, beyond my expectation.

'Thus the Lord drew me by the cords of love, and lifted up the light of his countenance upon me, so that in his light I saw light, which scattered that miserable cloud of darkness that had enwrapped my soul so long. Yea, he dispelled all those unbelieving thoughts which were apt to arise, on account of that low estate out of which he had newly raised me. It was suggested to me that this was not his ordinary way of dealing with such provoking creatures as myself, but that they are usually filled with terrors, and brought down even to a view of the lowest hell, &c. Thus Satan endeavoured to hold me under unbelieving fears, but the blessed Spirit, by taking of the things of Christ, and shewing them unto me, prevailed over the temptation.

'I had a discovery of the glory of the Father's love, as unchangeable, free, and eternal, which was discovered in pitching on me before the foundation of the world. And the glory of the Son as proceeding from the Father, and offering a sacrifice of a sweet-smelling savour, and in bringing in an everlasting righteousness, which by his Spirit he enabled me to rest wholly and alone upon, as the foundation of every blessing which I have received, or he has promised, for the whole of my acceptance before God, for my justification, sanctification, and full redemption. On this foundation he has enabled me stedfastly to rely, which greatly enlivens and enlarges my soul in its addresses to the Father, through the Son, by the assistance of the Holy Spirit, for pardon and strength, against those powerful corruptions which still remain in my heart.

'Oh the love, the infinite, condescending, and unchanging love of the Father! and oh that fulness of grace which is treasured up in my Redeemer, to be bestowed on me by his promised Spirit, of which so much hath already been communicated, that my soul is even overwhelmed under the sense and consideration of it! The Lord appears to me as resting in his love, and joying over me with singing, as it is expressed, Zeph. iii. 17, which scripture, with many others, has been so opened and applied as makes my approaches to him exceeding delightful. And this sense of his love lays me low in the views of my own vileness and unworthiness, and constrains me to love him and live to him, and to give him all the glory of that change, which of his own free and sovereign grace, he has wrought in me. There was nothing in me to move him to this, yea, what was there not in me to provoke him to cast me off for ever? But thus it hath pleased him to magnify his grace and mercy on a creature the *most* unworthy of any that ever received a favour at his hands.

'I know not where to end. He has recovered me from amongst the dead, and he shall have the glory of it whilst I live; yes, I will praise him, and tell of the wonders of his love to others, that so he may be honoured, and none may distrust him. He has filled me with his praises, though he has not given me that natural capacity which some have been blessed with, to express what I feel and find, of his work on my soul. But this I can say, I have found him whom my soul loves, he hath manifested himself to me, and there is nothing I dread so much as losing sight of him again. His presence makes all his ordinances, and all his providences, and everything delightful unto me. It is impossible to express the joy of my soul in sweet converses with him, with a sense of his love and the experience of his presence, under the influences of his Spirit, whose office it is to abide with me, and to guide, direct, and comfort me for ever.

'It is from a sense of my duty, and a desire to follow the direction of that blessed Spirit, that I request fellowship with you of this church. Amongst you my Lord has been pleased to discover himself to me, and to make the ministry you sit under exceeding useful and comfortable to my soul; by it I have been built up and settled on the right foundation, the righteousness of Christ, that rock that shall never be moved. Your order likewise appears to me very beautiful and lovely, being, as I apprehend, most agreeable to the rules of my Lord. Hence I desire to have communion with you, that so by your example and watchfulness over me, and the other advantages arising from church-fellowship, I may find what I expect and earnestly desire in communion with you, namely, that I may experience fellowship with the Father and the Son, through the eternal Spirit, whilst I wait upon him in the ways of his own appointment.

'REBECCA COMBE.

'*December* 17. 1697.'

'*The remarkable experience of* MRS GERTRUDE CLARKSON, *second daughter of the late* Rev. MR DAVID CLARKSON, *given to the church with whom she lived in communion.*

'MY education has been very strict. The constant instruction and example of my parents had so early an influence, that it is hard to tell which was my first awakening. Ever since I can remember anything of myself, I have had frequent convictions of the danger of sin and an unregenerate state, attended with fears of the punishment due to it; therefore was desirous of an interest in Christ, by whom I might be pardoned and saved from the wrath of God. This made me very fearful of omitting duties, or committing known sins; and, though these convictions wore off, yet they often returned, and rendered me uneasy, unless I was praying or learning scriptures, or something which I thought good. In these exercises I was well satisfied, though it was my happiness to be under the most careful inspection and judicious helps for the informing of my judgment.

'Before I apprehended what it was to rely upon an all-sufficient Saviour for righteousness and strength, I remember my notion of things was this, that I was to hear, and pray, and keep the Sabbath, and avoid what I knew to be sin, and then I thought God was obliged to save me; that I did what I could, and so all that he required; and I further conceived, that if at any time I omitted secret prayer, or any other duty, yet if I repented it was sufficient; and, on this consideration I have often ventured upon the commission of sin, with a resolve to repent the next day, and then, having confessed the transgression, my conscience has been easy, and I was well satisfied. Indeed sin, at that time, was not burdensome. I truly desired that my sins might be pardoned, but thought the ways of religion hard; and, though I durst not live in the constant neglect of duty, yet I secretly wished that I had been under no obligation to perform it. When I reflect on the thoughts and workings of my heart and affections in these times, and the confused apprehensions which I then had both of sin and grace, I am fully persuaded that, through grace there is a real, and in some measure an universal, change wrought in my soul.

'After my father's death, I was reading one of his manuscripts, wherein both the object and nature of saving faith were described, and the great necessity of it pressed, &c. The plain and clear definition there given of the saving act of faith, caused other apprehensions of things than I had before.* I then began to see how short I had come in all my performances of that disposition of soul which the gospel called for, and how guilty I was while depending upon these performances for acceptance with God, not casting myself wholly and alone upon Christ, and resting on his righteousness *entirely* for pardon and justification. The concern of my mind was very great, that I had lived so long ignorant of those things which related to my eternal welfare. I was sensible, the means and helps I had been favoured with for improvement in knowledge were beyond what is common, but I had refused instruction, the consideration of which was very terrible to my thoughts, fearing lest I had sinned beyond all hope of forgiveness.

'But in the most discouraging apprehensions of my case my heart was much enlarged in the confession of sin, and in bewailing my captivity to it, which was attended with earnest wrestlings with the Lord for pardoning and purifying grace. Those absolute promises in the 36th chapter of Ezekiel, of "a new heart and right spirit," were my continual plea, together with Mat. v. 6, "Blessed are they who hunger and thirst after righteousness, for they shall be filled." I found longings and pantings of soul after that righteousness, and saw that it could only be received by

* This is the same discourse that was useful to her sister Rebecca, and is the third in the volume, entitled 'Faith,' and based on Mark xvi. 16.

faith; this faith I earnestly begged, and that the Lord would pardon that *great* sin of unbelief which so provoked and dishonoured him, and that he would by his own Spirit enable me to embrace Christ as freely held forth in the gospel.

'About this time I was much affected with the consideration of Christ's offices, as prophet, priest, and king. And though I durst not claim an interest in them, yet was often meditating upon them, admiring that infinite condescension which is manifested therein. I thought whatever my condition was in this world, yet if I might be under his powerful and effectual teachings as a prophet, and have the benefit of his atonement and intercession as a priest, and be entirely subject to him in every faculty of my soul, as *my* Lord and King, then how satisfied and happy should I be!

'I was under these strugglings a long time before I came to any comfortable persuasion that I was accepted. Sins against light and love deeply wounded me, and the many aggravating circumstances which attended them were so represented by Satan, that I could not tell how to believe such iniquities as mine would be forgiven. But in the midst of these distressing thoughts I found in that manuscript of my father's, that none but *unworthy sinners*, who are empty of all good in themselves, were the objects of pardoning mercy, that the whole needed not the physician, but the sick. This encouraged me to plead with hope that the Lord would glorify the freeness of his own grace in my salvation, and to urge that Christ called "weary and heavy laden to him with a promise of rest," Mat. xi. 28.

'I found my soul was extremely burdened with sin; it appeared more exceeding sinful than ever before; sins of thought as well as words and actions were then observed with sorrow, and lamented before him. Yea, even the sins of my most holy things, those swarms of vain thoughts and wanderings of heart and affections of which I was conscious in my secret retirements, and most solemn, close dealings with God. In short, my own soul was my intolerable burden, which made me often question whether there were not more provoking sins in me than God usually pardons. Oh, I found every power and faculty were depraved, and that I could not do the good I would!

'It would be tedious to relate the many particular discouragements and temptations I laboured under, sometimes pouring forth my soul with some hope in his free mercy, sometimes only bewailing my condition without hope, till it pleased him whose power and grace no impenitent heart can resist and prevail, to put a stop to my unbelieving reasonings, from the unlikelihood of such sins being pardoned, sins so aggravated and so provoking as mine, by giving me an awful sense of his absolute sovereignty from those words, Exod. xxxiii. 19, "I will be gracious to whom I will be gracious, and will shew mercy on whom I will shew mercy." Also Isa. lv. 1, 'For my thoughts are not your thoughts, neither are your ways my ways, saith the Lord." These considerations were so impressed on my mind, and struck such an awe upon my spirits, that I durst not any longer give way to my carnal reasonings; I thought I could commit myself to his sovereign pleasure, let him do with me as seemed him good.

'After some time my mother, perceiving my concern, conversed very freely with me, and asked if I was not willing to accept of Christ to *sanctify* as well as to *save* me? I told her I desired this above all things. She then said he had certainly accepted me, adding, that it was Christ who had made me willing to close with him, and that he never made any soul thus willing, but he had first pardoned and accepted that soul. I shall never forget with what weight these words were impressed on my heart. I thought it was a pardon sent immediately to me. I could not but say, I was above *all* things desirous to be entirely subject to Christ in every power and faculty of my soul, that every thought might be brought into subjection to Christ, and nothing might remain in me contrary to him, but that there might be a perfect conformity to his image and will in all things.

'After this conversation I found great composure in my mind, believing that the Lord had created those desires in me, which nothing but himself, and the enjoyment of himself could satisfy, and that he would answer them *with* himself: "That he would not break the bruised reed, nor quench the smoking flax," Mat. xii. 20. My delight now was in nothing else but meditating upon, and admiring of the *free* and *sovereign* grace of God in Christ, which distinguished me from many others who had not so highly provoked him, having called me out of such gross darkness which I had been long in, and given me any glimmerings of the light, of the knowledge, of the glory, of his grace. My desires greatly increased after further discoveries, and clearer light into the deep mysteries of the love and grace of God in Christ Jesus; and all diversions from these meditations were a burden.

'Oh, I then thought, "all old things were passed away, and everything was become new!" I experienced a universal change in my mind, will, and affections; the bent of them was turned another way. The ordinances, which were once irksome, were above all things pleasant, and the return of Sabbaths continually longed for. I was very thankful it was my duty as well as privilege to set apart the *whole* day for the worship and glory of my Lord. I bewailed much that I could love him no more, that there was so much sin remaining in me, and which I found mixed with all that I did, and that I was not wholly taken up in those blessed and delightful employments without the least interruption. Oh I longed for that state wherein all these fetters should be knocked off, and my soul set at liberty in the worship and praise of my God, being freed from corruptions within or temptations without!

'My soul was thus delightfully carried out for some time, in which I heard a discourse from these words: John xxi. 17, "Thou knowest all things, thou knowest that I love thee." The scope of this sermon was for a trial, whether *our* appeal could be made to him who knows all things, that we loved him? Under this discourse I found my heart greatly carried out in love to Christ in all his ordinances, and the discoveries made of his will therein. These subjects concerning the love of Christ, and his people's love to him, being long continued, one sermon after another, I found I sat under the word with great pleasure and enlarged affections.

'At this time my mother was persuading me to join in communion with some church, which greatly startled me at the first. I could by no means think of that, not apprehending myself to have come so far yet. I thought there must be something more in me, or I should eat and drink damnation to myself. But being better informed both as to the nature and end of the ordinance, and that it was intended for the increase of grace and strength, and that it was a positive command of my Lord, with whose will in all things I was very desirous to comply, I was at last prevailed with to venture on that great ordinance, and was much refreshed and satisfied in my renewed resignation and enlarged expectations of receiving all needful supplies from him who is the head of the church. Oh the condescending love and grace of my Redeemer, represented to me in these transactions, how greatly did they delight and affect my soul! I wished I might have been always thus exercised, expecting with great pleasure the return of those seasons wherein I might hope for further manifestations and larger communications of grace and love.

'But after some time my affections began to cool. I had not such sweetness and enlargement in my approaches to God in public as I used to find. I thought the preaching more empty, and came short of what I found I wanted. This deadness continuing, filled me with no small concern, fearing I should fall off. I was very far from charging the ministry I sat under, but my own *wicked wavering* heart. I have often gone to the house of God with raised expectations of receiving those quickenings I used to be blessed with, but found sad disappointments. This frame of spirit as to public worship was matter of continual mourning and bewailing in secret. I was often examining my heart as to its *aims* and *ends* in my public approaches, and could not but conclude my desires were above all things to glorify my Lord in all his appointments, and to receive those blessings from him which might enable me so to do.

'The missing of the Lord's presence under the means, in the use of which he had commanded me to expect it, and which he had heretofore in some measure vouchsafed, was very grievous. I earnestly begged a discovery of every sin that might be hid from me, which might be the cause of this withdrawing. But the decay of my affections still remaining, it caused great misgivings of my heart, that things were not right with me. Yet still I had supports in my secret applications to God, that his grace would be sufficient for me, and that I should be kept by his almighty power, through faith unto salvation, which encouragements kept me still waiting with hope, that he would yet return and bless me.

'After some time, being providentially brought to this place, I found the preaching of your pastor so suited to my case, that I was greatly enlarged in thankfulness to God, who had so directed me. Those sermons upon

Gal. vi. 3, "For if a man thinketh himself something when he is nothing, he deceiveth himself," though I had heard your minister before with great satisfaction, brought me to a resolution of sitting under his ministry. I do not question but you remember what unusual and deep-searching discourses they were to me. They razed me again to the very foundation, and discovered the many secret holds Satan had in my heart, which before I thought not of, and how many ways I was taken up in something which was nothing. I wish I could express what they were.

'These discourses caused deep humblings of spirit, and enlarged desires after further enlightenings. Oh I found these things reach me! I needed to be led into the depths of my own deceitful heart, and thereby observe that secret proneness there was in me, to be laying hold on something in *self* to rest upon and expect from. In short, I now saw that utter insufficiency and weakness in myself, and everything done by myself to satisfy the cravings of my immortal soul, which I had not so much as once thought of before.

'I have been also led more to that fulness from whence only I can receive what may render me acceptable to the Father, and have never found so much sweetness and solid satisfaction in my access to God as when most sensible of my own unworthiness, and entire emptiness of anything agreeable to him in myself, and all my performances, and when most apprehensive of that infinite fulness and suitableness of grace laid up in Christ Jesus, from whence I am commanded and encouraged to be continually receiving fresh supplies. Oh those infinite, inexhaustible treasures! Nothing, nothing less can satisfy the restless cravings and pantings of my soul! By *this* preaching I have been continually led to this fresh spring that never fails, and have experienced great quickenings in my applications to Christ, and comfortable rejoicings in him. Notwithstanding all those miserable defects and failures in my poor performances, this gives me comfort, that there is perfect righteousness wrought out of me, which I may receive *freely* by faith, and therein stand complete before God for ever.

'The insisting on such truths as these, which have a direct tendency to lead from self to Christ, by opening and unfolding the mysteries of grace laid up in him, so admirably suited to answer all the necessities of poor, helpless, guilty creatures, I find above all things encourages me *to*, and enlivens me *in*, duty. My low improvements under these suitable instructive helps fill me with mourning to think there should be no greater establishment upon the sure foundation of a Redeemer's righteousness, on which I hope I have been enabled to build.

'At times I can apprehend with some clearness that this righteousness was wrought out for me, and can apply to him with confidence and joy as the "Lord my righteousness and strength," and gladly hope that through *that* strength I shall be more than a conqueror over every disturbing corruption and temptation; yea, that I shall see him shortly as he is, in the full displays of the glory of that grace and love which I cannot now comprehend, and by the transforming sight be made like him. But oh how short, how seldom are these interviews! my unbelieving heart *still* returns to its former darkness and distrust, and gives me frequent occasions to bewail the fluctuations of my weak faith. Oh that it was stronger, that it was more stedfast! But blessed be his name in whom I put my *entire* trust, there is grace in him to help me under all decays and failings, through weakness. It is from hence I receive strength to elevate and excite the acts of faith and love when sunk so low that I cannot raise them. Yea, it is from the same fulness I receive grace to regulate the actings of grace, and to set my soul from time to time in a right way of improving the grace I received, and for obtaining pardon for all my defects, as well as for the removing all my defilements.

'These are truths that feed and support my faith, and without these were set home with power on my soul I must give up under the great aboundings of indwelling corruptions. I desired a submissive waiting for further manifestations of his love in his own time and way. And although I have not those constant shines of the light of God's countenance, with which some of his people are blessed, yet I humbly adore him for the little light he hath afforded me, and beg your prayers that I may be kept close to him, and have such constant discoveries as may strengthen my faith, by a close adherence to him, and firm reliance on him without wavering. But I am sensible that I am too apt to be looking off from the only support and foundation of my faith and hope, and to be depending on, and expecting from, the frame of my own spirit, and workings of my affections towards spiritual things.

'Oh the unsearchable deceitfulness of my heart, which is so *many* ways betraying me into an unbelieving temper of spirit! I find I need greater helps than those may who are more established, and I dare not neglect those helps which my Lord has provided for his church. I need to be watched over, and excited and encouraged under difficulties from those experiences which others have of the dealings of the Lord with them. I have been wishing for these advantages for a considerable time, being fully convinced that those who are members of his church should be building up one another. I bless the Lord that he has discovered his will to me in this point, and that he hath provided greater helps than what I had been before acquainted with for my furtherance in my progress to heaven. Accordingly, I would cheerfully and thankfully fall in with his will herein, and so take hold of his covenant in this church, expecting the blessing promised to those that are planted in his house.

'GERTRUDE CLARKSON.'

SERMONS, &c.

OF ORIGINAL SIN.

Behold, I was shapen in iniquity; and in sin did my mother conceive me.—
PSALM LI. 5.

THE end of the ministry of the gospel is to bring sinners unto Christ. Their way to this end lies through the sense of their misery without Christ.

The ingredients of this misery, are our sinfulness, original and actual; the wrath of God, whereto sin has exposed us; and our impotency to free ourselves either from sin or wrath.

That we may therefore promote this great end, we shall endeavour, as the Lord will assist, to lead you in this way, by the sense of misery, to him who alone can deliver from it.

Now the original of our misery being the corruption of our natures, or original sin, we thought fit to begin here, and therefore have pitched upon these words as very proper for our purpose.

They are part of the psalm which is styled 'a Psalm of Repentance.' In the beginning whereof you may observe the expressions and the grounds of David's repentance.

The expressions are, petition and confession; that in the 1st and 2d, this in the 3d verse.

The grounds of it are, 1, the object of this sin; 2, the fountain.

1. The object against which his sin was directed, ver. 4: that is, God.

2. The fountain from whence his sin sprung; *i. e.*, his natural corruption. He follows the stream up to the spring head, and there lays the ground of his humiliation, ver. 5.

Obs. The ground of a sinner's humiliation should be the corruption of his nature. Original sin should be the rise of our sorrow. I shall not attempt a full and accurate tractation of original sin, but confine myself to the text, and the scope I aimed at in the choice of it.

And that I may open and confirm it more clearly and distinctly, I shall take the observation into parcels, and present it to you in these three propositions: 1, The corruption of nature is a sin; 2, We are guilty of this sin as soon as we are born, as soon as we are conceived; 3, This sin, thus early contracted, must be the ground of our humiliation. This we shall confirm, and then add what is practical, so representing this natural corruption in some particulars, as may humble us, render us vile in our own eyes, and drive us to Christ, who can deliver you from the guilt and power of this pestilent evil.

I. Natural corruption is a sin; so it is styled twice in the text, both עון perverseness, iniquity; and חטא, sin. That is sin which the Lord peremptorily forbids. The apostle's definition of it is unquestionable, 1 John iii. 4. No greater transgression than this, since it transgresses all at once.

We are commanded to be holy; so the want of holiness is forbidden, which is the privative part of this sin. We are commanded to love the Lord with all our hearts; so the heart's inclination to hate God is forbidden, which is the positive part of this sin.

A nonconformity to the whole law of God is a transgression of the whole law; and this being such, it is not only a sin, but all sins in one.

The apostle Paul was more able to judge what is sin than any papist, Socinian, &c., and he calls it sin five times, Rom. vi.; six times, Rom. vii.; three times, Rom. viii.

The apostle's description of it, Rom. vii., is very observable; for therein you may find near twenty aggravations of this sin. I will point at them, and leave the enlargement to your own thoughts.

(1.) It is that which is not good, ver. 18. Why did no good thing dwell there, but because nothing dwelt there but this corruption, which is wholly evil.

(2.) And that we may not mistake it for an evil of suffering, he calls it sin, as elsewhere, so ver. 20, sin, and so the greatest evil.

(3.) And that it may not pass for a sin of an ordinary size, he styles it, ver. 13, ἁμαρτία ἁμαρτωλὸς, nay, καθ' ὑπερβολὴν, excessively hyperbolically sinful. Here is a real, not a verbal hyperbole: for as in a verbal hyperbole the expression exceeds the reality, so in this real hyperbole, the reality exceeds the expression; it is so sinful, as scarce any expression can reach it.

(4.) It is a condemned, a forbidden evil, ver. 7, that we may not question, but that it has the formality of a sin.

(5.) It is a positive evil: ver. 17, 'No more I that do it, but sin.'

(6.) A perverse evil; grows worse by that which should make it better, ver. 8.

(7.) A debasing evil; made and denominates him carnal, ver. 14.

(8.) An intimate inherent evil, ver. 17, sin in him, in his members.

(9.) It is a permanent evil, οἰκοῦσα ἐν ἐμοί; a fruitful evil, ver. 8, all manner of lusts; a deceitful evil, ver. 11, ἐξηπάτησέ; an imperious evil; a law, ver. 23, gives law; a tyrannical evil, αἰχμαλωτίζοντά, ver. 23, a rebellious, conflicting warlike evil, ἀντιστρατευόμενον, ver. 23, an importunate and unreasonable evil, ver. 15, forces to do that which he hates; a watchful evil, ver. 21, is present, παράκειται; a powerful evil, ver. 24. Who shall deliver me? A complete evil, ver. 24, a body furnished with all members of unrighteousness; a deadly evil, ver. 24, the body of death; a miserable evil, ver. 24, above all things made him wretched.

Obj. If it be objected, this can be no sin, because it is not voluntary,

Ans. 1. That rule, whatever is not voluntary is not sinful, is not universally true, nor is it admitted by our divines, without limitation; no, not when it is applied to actual sin, much less in this case.

Ans. 2. But admit this rule. Natural corruption is voluntary, both *à parte ante*, in respect of Adam, and *à parte post*, in respect of us; or, as Augustine, *sive in opere, sive in origine.*

(1.) In respect of Adam, he contracted this evil voluntarily, and we in him. He is not to be considered as one man, but as the root or representative of all men. *Omnes eramus ille unus homo:* we all were that one man, and therefore his will was the will of all men. All being included virtually in him, what he voluntarily consented to, that was voluntarily consented to by all.

(2.) *A parte post*, in respect of us. It is voluntary, in respect of after-consent. All who are capable of humiliation have actually consented to their natural corruption, have been pleased with it, have cherished it by occasions of sin, have strengthened it by acts of sin, have resisted the means whereby it should be mortified and subdued, which all are infallible evidences of actual consent. That which was only natural is thus become voluntary, and so, by consent of all, sinful.

II. *Proposition*. We are tainted with this sin from our birth, from our conception, while we are formed, while we are warmed in the womb, as the word is. Natural corruption is not contracted only by imitation, nor becomes it habitual by custom or repetition of acts, but it is rooted in the soul before the subject be capable either of imitation or acting. It is diffused through the soul as soon as the soul is united to the body. And if we take conception in such a latitude as to reach this union, there will be no difficulty to conceive how we are capable of this sin in our conception.

The prophet upbraids Israel with this, Isa. xlviii. 8, 'And wast called a transgressor from the womb,' and so may we all be called, though the expression be inclusively, not only from the time of our coming out of the womb, but from the time of our being formed in it.

If I would step out of the way, I might here inquire how this sin is conveyed unto us in the womb. But the curiosity of this inquiry is handsomely taxed by that known passage of Augustine. A man being fallen into a pit, one spies him, and admires how he came there. Oh, says the fallen man to him, *Tu cogita quomodo hinc me liberes:* Be careful, cries he, to get me out; trouble not thyself to inquire how I fell in.

Thus should we be disposed as to our natural corruption, not so curious to inquire how we came by it, as careful to know how we may be rid of it. And one way is pointed at in the next particular, the third proposition, which is this:

III. *Proposition*. This sin should be the ground of our humiliation. I might confirm this with many arguments, but I shall content myself with one, which, with the branches of it, will be sufficiently demonstrative it should be ground of our humiliation, because it is the foundation of our misery. Our misery consists in the depravedness of our natures, our obnoxiousness to the wrath of God, and our inability to free ourselves from either. But this is what has depraved our natures, or rather is the depravation of them; this makes us obnoxious to the wrath of God, &c.

1. The depravedness of our natures consists in a privation of all good, an antipathy to God, and a propensity to all evil. And these three are not so much the effects, as the formality of this sin.

(1.) It is a privation of all that is good. In that soul where this is predominant, there is neither seed nor fruit, neither root nor branch neither inclination nor motion, neither habit nor act, that is spiritually good. No spark of holiness; no relics of man's primitive righteousness; no lineament of that image of God, which was at first fair drawn upon the soul of man: Rom. vii. 18, 'In my flesh,' *i. e.*, in my nature considered as corrupted. Man's soul is left like a ruined castle; the bare ragged walls, the remaining faculties, may help you to guess what it has been; but all the ornaments and precious furniture is gone. Is not this ground of humiliation? Thy ruined soul can never be repaired, but by him who brought heaven and earth out of nothing.

(2.) There is an antipathy to God, and the things of God; to his ways and image. 'The carnal mind,' Rom. viii, 7, the mind overspread with natural corruption, usually called flesh, is not only an enemy, but 'enmity.' In enmity there is hatred, malice, despite, mischievous thoughts and contrivances. This is the temper of thy soul till thou art born again; thy heart is full of enmity, malice, &c. Oh, is not this ground of humiliation, that a poor worm should swell big with malice and enmity against the great God, should be an utter enemy to him, in whom alone are his hopes and happiness! A natural man will not believe this. But here is a demonstration of it from another fruit of this corruption; and that is an antipathy to the holy ways, spirit and heavenly employments, to the image of God, to holiness itself. Naturalists write of a beast that will tear and rend the picture of a man if it come in his way; and this is taken as an argument that he has a stronger antipathy to man than is in any other beast. And does it not argue as strong an antipathy to God, when men will tear his image, vent their malice in jeers and reproaches against holiness? Does it not argue an antipathy to holiness, when holy employments and exercises are most tedious and burdensome? Oh the sad issue of our depravedness, when it possesses with enmity against God! Is it not a ground of humiliation?

(3.) There is a propensity to all evil. I say not, an equal propensity in all to every sin, but a propensity more or less in every one to all sin. 'Folly is bound up,' Prov. xxii. 15. This folly is the sin of our natures; all sin whatsoever is wrapped up in this natural corruption; actual sins are but the unfolding of it.

As all men are said to be in the first virtually, *in primo cuncti fuimus patre*, so may all sins, in respect of this propensity to all, be said [to be] in this first sin, the sin of our births and natures. The Seventy render sin and iniquity in the text plurally, ἐν ἀνομίαις, ἐν ἁμαρτίαις. There is a plurality of sins in our natural corruption. It is all sin virtually, because it disposes and inclines the soul to all.

And is not here ground of humiliation, when, by reason of this corruption, we are not only destitute of all that is good, but disposed to all that is evil?

2. Another part of our misery is our obnoxiousness to the wrath of God. And natural corruption is the foundation of this also, Eph. ii. 3. Why by nature, but because there is that in our natures which is the proper object of God's wrath? 'Children of wrath;' born to it, because born in sin. Children, this is your portion, wrath is your inheritance; the writings and evidences for it are the curses and threatenings of the law. These make it sure, by these wrath is entailed on you and yours. From the word in the text, which we read *conceived*, and in the margin, *warmed*, comes the word which we render indignation; חֵמָה. As soon as we are warmed in the womb, the Lord's indignation is kindled against us. The corruption of our natures is its fuel. Oh what ground is here of humi-

liation, that by reason of this sin of our natures we are exposed in our conception, birth, life, to the wrath of God!

3. Another part of this misery is your inability to free yourselves from this sin and wrath. This is evident from hence: those that are born in sins and trespasses are 'dead in sins and trespasses,' Eph. ii. 1. Till ye be born again, ye are dead. There must be a second birth, else there will be no spiritual life. Every one, since death entered into the world by this sin, is born dead; comes into the world, and so continues, destitute of spiritual life. And what more impotent than a dead man? You can no more repair the image of God in your souls, than a dead man can reunite his soul to his body; no more free yourselves from that antipathy to God, and inclination to wickedness, than a dead carcase can free itself from those worms and vermin that feed upon it; no more free yourselves from the wrath of God, than a dead man can raise himself out of the grave.

Into such a low condition has this corruption of nature sunk the sons of men, as nothing can raise them but an infinite power, an almighty arm.

Nay, so far are men, in this estate, from power to free themselves from this misery, as they are without sense of their misery. Tell them they are dead; it is a paradox. They will not believe the report of Christ; they will not hear, till a voice armed with an almighty power, such a voice as Lazarus heard, do awake them. Till then, they are without life, and so without sense. Here is the depth of misery: to be so miserable, and yet insensible of it. Yet thus low has this sin brought every sinner.

Nay, if they were sensible of their misery, and of their own inability to avoid it, yet can they not, yet will they not move towards him, who only can deliver them. They are without life, and so without motion. 'No man comes to me except the Father draw him,' John vi.

They lie dead, putrefying under this corruption, under the wrath of an incensed God, without motion or inclination toward him who is the resurrection and the life.

This is the condition into which this sin has brought you; and can there be a condition more miserable?

Is there not cause to be humbled for that which has brought you so low, which has made you so wretched? Should not this be the chief ground of your humiliation? I need say no more to demonstrate this truth.

IV. Let me now proceed, in the fourth place, to make this truth more practical. And this I shall endeavour, by representing this sin to you in some particulars, which tend to humble you, to make you vile in your own eyes, and drive you to Christ, who only can save you from this sin, and the woeful effects of it.

1. Its unnaturalness. This corruption is incorporated into our natures. It has a real being in us, before we have a visible being in the world. It is conceived in us at our first conception, Ps. li., 'in sin.' The old man is furnished with all its members, before we are formed, shapen; quickened, before we are alive; and is born before we come into the world.

This makes us evil in God's eye, before we have done good or evil; and by virtue of it, we are born heirs apparent to eternal wrath: Eph. ii. 3, 'By nature children of wrath;' we are born to it; this is our title. Though men use this to excuse their sin, It is my nature; yet this is the greatest aggravation of it. We can better endure a mischief, when it comes accidentally, than one who is naturally mischievous. Would this be a good plea for one who has plotted treason, to say, I am naturally a traitor; it is my nature to be treacherous, murderous? This would make him more odious: such a man would not be counted fit to live a moment.

Why do we hate toads, but because they are naturally a poisonous vermin? That which is so accidentally, we rather pity than hate it. The Lord has a stronger antipathy against natural corruption, than we against the most poisonous vermin. A toad is good physically, *sub ratione entis*, as a creature; all the works of his hands are good; but this corruption is both physically, morally, and spiritually evil; and the worse, because it is natural.

2. The sinfulness of it. It is more sinful than the most grievous actual sin that ever hath, or ever can be committed. It is in some sense more sinful than all actual sins put together.

(1.) An actual sin does but directly violate one command of God; but this is a violation of all God's commands at once, a transgression of the whole law, a contrariety to every part of God's revealed will. For this corruption is forbidden in every commandment; because *cum prohibetur effectus, prohibetur causa*, when any sin is forbidden, that which is the cause it cannot be avoided, is forbidden. *Cum prohibetur actus, prohibetur inclinatio ad actum*, when any sin is forbidden, all degrees of it are prohibited. Now this is the cause of the inclination to all sin; and so it is forbidden in every precept; and therefore this is a breach of every precept.

(2.) Sin cannot be always actual, and therefore the law is but sometimes broken by actual sins; but this is a violation of the law at all times. We are not actually sinners before we are born; but in respect of this, we are sinners in our mother's womb. Infants, before all use of reason, do not actually sin; but even when we are infants, we are sinners, transgressors of the law, by natural corruption, Rom. v. 14. Death reigned over infants; therefore infants were sinners, though not actually, as Adam. Acts are transient, this is settled, continuing against God.

(3.) Actual sin does but break the law in being, the time it is in acting. But this is a continued violation of the law without any interruption, without the least intermission, from the instant of the soul's conjunction with the body to the hour of our dissolution. There is no *lucida intervalla*, no good fits, no cessation; well may the apostle call it καθ' ὑπερβολὴν ἁμαρτωλὸς.

3. Its causality. It is the cause of all actual sin. Every sinful act in us derives its descent from this. This is that loathsome spawn to which all this abhorred vermin owe their original, James i. 15, ἐπιθυμία συλλαβοῦσα, &c., *i. e.*, original concupiscence, as it is ordinarily called by the ancients, or natural corruption; having conceived, τίκτει, brings forth actual sin, is its mother in both. This is actual sin as it were in the egg, worse than those of the cockatrice, which by Satan's incubation is hatched, and brings forth the serpent's cursed and poisonous issue.

There was a tree of life in the garden of Eden; and so there will be in the paradise of God, Rev. xxii. 2, whose leaves will be for the healing of the nations. But since man was cast out of paradise, a tree of death, a root of bitterness, has grown in every soul, bearing all manner of cursed fruits; and every leaf, every bud, tends to the death of mankind. It is a vine, as Deut. xxxii. 32, worse than the vine of Sodom, and of the fields of Gomorrah. Its grapes are grapes of gall, its clusters are bitter; its wine is the poison of dragons, &c. By these allusions the Lord declares the cursed nature both of tree and fruit: Mat. xv. 19, 'Out of the heart,' *i.e.*, corrupt heart, or natural corruption in the heart. If you pursue these filthy streams to their first rise, you will find the spring head to be this corruption. Actual sins are nothing but this native corruption multiplied, as an hundred is but one multiplied so many times, an hundred units. It is the cause of all. If we must repent of the effects, much more of the cause.

4. Its habitualness. It is not a transient act, nor a moveable disposition, nor a dull slow-paced faculty, as all faculties are till they be habituated; but an habitual evil, both in respect of permanency and facility in acting.

(1.) Its permanency. A habit is χρονιώτερον and μονιμώτερον, more permanent, more durable than any other quality. So is this; it will continue while the union betwixt soul and body continues. It is ἁμαρτία οἰκοῦσα, an inhabitant which will never be removed till the house be pulled down where it dwells. The power of grace may cast it down, but it will never be cast out. Some streams may be dried up, but we can never in this life dry up the spring; we may lop off some branches, but it will sprout again; we cannot root out this root of bitterness. It is like such a fretting leprosy in our earthly tabernacles as is described to be in the Israelites' houses, Lev. xiv. Though some infected stones be removed, and the house scraped, and the walls plastered, ver. 41, 42, yet the plague will break out again. No perfect freedom from this spreading incurable plague till the house be quite pulled down. It will reign in those that continue unsanctified, till eternity; it will dwell in the best, till this earthly tabernacle be dissolved; a constant occasion, do the best they can, of repentance.

(2.) Facility in acting. It is the property of habits, *facile operari*; it makes the faculty nimble, quick, and freely active. All habits do so; but above all natural habits, because the faculty hereby has a double advantage. Such is natural corruption. Hence it is that we sin so freely, find no such backwardness, reluctancy to evil, as to good: 'Evil is present,' Rom. vii. 21, παράκειται, it is at hand, ready to further and facilitate sinful acts. Hence where this is predominant, sinful acts proceed as freely from it as water runs down a precipice from an overflowing spring. This being born with man, he is born not only to sorrow, but to sin, as freely as the sparks fly upward; as freely, as heavy bodies move downwards towards their centre; they need no outward impulse to enforce their motion; their natural gravity is sufficient, if nothing interpose to stop its course. If God should withdraw restraining grace, this corruption would carry men on to act all wickedness with greediness. Every man would turn to the most desperate wicked courses, even as freely, as eagerly, as the horse rusheth into the battle, Jer. viii. 6, need no other spur but his native wickedness, which is secretly bent to all evil, without external enforcements. Here is great cause of repentance.

5. Its pregnancy. It is all sin virtually; all sin in gross, which is retailed out in sinful acts. All in one; as he of Cæsar, *in uno Cæsare multi proditores*. All treasons, disobedience, rebellions against the sovereign Majesty of heaven, are to be found in this. It is the nursery, the spawn, the seed, the womb; every sin that is possible to be committed is in this womb; so conceived, formed, animated, brought to the birth, as there needs nothing but a temptation, occasion, opportunity, to bring it forth. Those several crooked lines, sinful acts, which are scattered in any man's life, as in the circumference, do all meet in this as in the centre.

The guilt of all abominations whatsoever are complicated, wrapped up in this one. And in respect of this we are guilty of all sin, how great soever, even of those that we were never actually guilty of.

It may be thou never embruedst thy hands in thy brother's blood, as Cain did. Thou art not actually guilty of that horrid murder, but thou art habitually guilty. In respect of thy corrupt inclination, thou art as apt to do such a bloody act as he. All the difference is, and all the reason why thou doest it not, is because the Lord restrains thee; like temptations and occasions are not offered thee. No difference, but from without; corrupt inclination is equal, thy nature as bloody.

It may be thou didst never commit adultery, incest, or such abominable uncleanness; thou art not guilty of this actually, but thou art guilty of this in respect of thy inclination; these sins are in thy heart.

It may be thou didst not set cities on fire, dash out children's brains, rip up women with child; thou art not actually guilty, but these sins are in thy heart, though they were never acted by thy hands. Hazael was angry that the prophet should tell him thus much, 2 Kings viii. 12, 13. But he acted that afterward, when king, which he seems here to detest, so far as though he should never be guilty of them, except transformed into a dog. He was not acquainted with the desperate corruption of man's heart, which habitually inclines him to the most barbarous and bloody acts.

It may be you detest Herod, Pilate, and the Jews as bloody monsters for swearing, wounding, crucifying our meek and innocent Saviour. Ay, but this very sin, though the most horrid act that ever the sun beheld, is in your hearts. And he is a stranger to the corruption of his nature, who will presume he would not have done as they did if he had had the same temptations, and no more restraint from God.

There was no sin ever was, nor ever can be committed by evil men on earth, but it is in every man's heart, and every one, in respect of habitual inclination, is guilty of it. If men believe this, sure there would need no arguments to shew the necessity of repentance for this corruption. But no wonder if it be not believed, since the heart, as it is 'desperately wicked,' so it is deceitful;' the prophet joins them: Jer. xvii. 9, 'Deceitful above all things,' and will not be known; 'desperately wicked,' so wicked as it cannot be known; natural corruption is so great, so pregnant, there is so much wickedness, so many sins in the heart, as we may despair of knowing them. But what we are able to know we should be willing to bewail. They are deceived who think they are not cruel, unclean, because not actually so; they are inclined to all, though not equally to all.

6. Its extent. This contagion has overspread the whole man, and seized upon every part. Therefore, Heb. xii. 1, *εὐπερίστατον*, it is the old man, and some member of it is stretched forth in every faculty. It is a world of wickedness, and this little world man is full of it: 'from the crown of the head to the sole of the foot,' Isa. i. 6, man wholly corrupt, both in body, and soul, and spirit. There is an ocean of corruption in every natural man. And as the sea receives several names from several coasts, so does this from the several parts and faculties. In the mind it is enmity, Rom. viii. 7; in the thoughts, vanity, Ps. xci. 7; in the apprehension, blindness, Eph. iv. 18; in the judgment, evil good, darkness light, error truth; in the will, rebellion, 'we will not,' &c.; in the consience, searedness; in the heart, hardness, Ezek. ii. 3, 4; in the affections, carnalness; in the memory, unfaithfulness, Jer. ii. 32; in the fancy, folly; in the appetite,

inordinancy; in the whole body, vileness. Every part, faculty, is naturally corrupted, and wholly corrupted in all acts.

The mind, in its apprehensions, blind; in its judgments, erroneous; in its reasonings, foolish; in its designs, evil; in its thoughts, vain.

The will, as to its elections, perverse, chooses evil, less good, seeming; in its consent, servile, overruled by corrupt judgment, base appetite; in its commands tyrannical, without, against all sanctified reason; in its inclination, wicked; in its intentions, obstinate; in its fruitions, furious.

The memory, apt to receive what is evil, to exclude what is good; to retain that which should be excluded, to let slip that which should be retained; to suggest that which is wicked, to smother what is good.

The conscience, corrupt in its rules and principles, in its injunctions and prescripts, in its accusations, in its absolutions, in its instigations, &c. So the affections.

The enlargement of these particulars would require many hours' discourse. I am forced to do as geographers, give a view of this world of wickedness in a small map; but, if you will seriously study it, you will see cause enough of repentance, if there were no actual sin in the world. As it is extended over the whole man, our whole life, so should the extent of our repentance be.

7. Its monstrousness—the monstrous deformity it has brought upon the soul. The mind of man was the candle of the Lord, but hereby it is become a stinking snuff. The soul, as it proceeded from God, was a clear, lightsome beam, brighter than any ray of the sun, but hereby it is become a noisome dunghill. It was one of the most excellent pieces of the creation, next unto the angelical nature, but hereby it is transformed into an ugly monster. Why do we judge anything a monster, but for want, defect, or uselessness; impotency, dislocation, or misplacing of integral parts? And, by virtue of this corruption, there is a concurrence of all this in the soul, answerable, and in some proportion to what we judge monstrous in a body.

A child born without eyes, mouth, hands, legs, we judge a monster. There is a defect of such powers in the soul as are analogical to these parts in the body: there is no eye to see God naturally, corruption has put it out, born blind; there is no arms to embrace Christ, though he offer himself to our embraces; there is no mouth to receive spiritual nourishment, no stomach to digest it; there is no feet to move towards God, he must renew these organs before any spiritual motion.

All those parts are impotent which are in the soul. Though there be something instead of eyes (an understanding), yet it sees not, perceives not the things of God; though there be something in the room of hands (the will), yet it inclines not to, it acts not for God; something in place of feet (the affections), yet they walk not in God's ways; if they move, it is backward, either like the idol, without motion, eyes and see not, &c., Ps. cxxxv. 16, or monstrous motion; if look, it is downward, grovelling; if walk, it is backward from God, &c. The soul, ever since the fall, is halt, maimed; all its parts broken or unjoined. *Cecidit è manu figuli.* Man's soul, framed by God according to his likeness, fell out of the hands of the potter, and so is all broken and shattered. Man's soul, wherein the Lord had exquisitely engraven his own image, and writ his own will and law with his own hand in divine characters, did cast itself out of God's hands, and fell, as the tables of stone, God's own workmanship, fell out of the hands of Moses, and so is broken into shivers; nothing is left but some broken, scattered relics, some obscure sculptures covered with the mud of natural corruption, so as it is scarce visible. That which appears is woeful ruins, such as shew what a glorious creature man was, though he be now, to his spiritual constitution, a monster.

There is a dislocation. What remains in man's soul is monstrously misplaced. We count that birth monstrous where parts have not their due place, when the head is where the feet should be, or the legs in the place of the arms, &c. The soul's faculties are thus monstrously dislocated; that which should be highest is lowest; that which should rule is in subjection; that which should obey does tyrannise. Passion over-rules reason, and the will receives law from the fancy and appetite. The will was sovereign, reason its counsellor, the appetite subject to both; but now it is got above them, and often hurries both to a compliance with the dictates of sense. A spot, a blemish in the face of a beautiful child, when it comes but accidentally, does grieve the parents. How much cause then have we to bewail that natural, universal, monstrous deformity which has seized upon our souls!

8. Its irresistibleness and strength. Nothing but an infinite power can conquer it; none but the almighty arm of God can restrain it. Not the power of nature in men, for that it has wholly subdued; not the power of grace in the saints, for then Paul had never been captivated by it. He was, in all outward opposition he met with in the world, more than conqueror; but by this he was led captive. He triumphs over them, but he sighs and complains of this.

All the cords of love, all the bonds of afflictions, cannot restrain this. It is Satan's strongest champion; it breaks them all, as Samson did the new ropes, Judges xvi., it breaks them off like a thread. All mortifying exercises, moral persuasions, spiritual restraints, can never utterly quell this. See how the Lord describes leviathan, behemoth, and the warlike horse, Job xxxix.–xli., and by analogy you may collect a description of the strength and fury of untamed lust. Nor judgments, nor mercies, nor threatenings, nor promises, nor precepts, nor examples, nor resolutions, nor experiences, are, without a higher concurrence, sufficient to restrain it. What then? Nothing but that which sets bounds to the raging sea. None but he who shuts up the sea with doors; he only, who says, 'Hitherto shalt thou come, and no further; and here shall thy proud waves be stayed,' Job xxxviii. 8–11; Isa. lvii. 20, 'The wicked is like the troubled sea;' and no wonder, since this is a raging sea of wickedness in them, which he can only bound and rule who gives decrees to the sea, and lays his commands on the waters, Prov. viii. 29; he only, whom the winds and seas obey. No limits to the rage of lust but almighty power, this bound it cannot pass, Jer. v. 22.

9. Its devilishness. There is nothing in the world that has so much of the devil in it; nothing more like him, nothing better liked by him. It is his issue, the first-born of the devil, πρωτότοκος τοῦ διαβόλου; he hatched it. It is the seed of the serpent, that which he begot and nourishes. It is his work, his master-piece, that wherein he applauds himself and glories, John viii. 44. Why is he the father of natural men, but because he begot corrupt nature? It owes its original to him.

It is his strumpet, is prostituted to him; if any *succubus* in the world, this is it. There is a carnal, though invisible conjunction betwixt it and Satan; the issue of it is all the sins in the world; numerous and deformed issue.

It is his image. The image of Satan succeeded the image of God. Those black, hellish characters, which are legible in the soul, are of his own impression. As face answers to face, so does man's corrupt nature answer the nature of the devil. It has all the essential parts of it. The divine image is razed out in it, so it is in him. In it there is an averseness to all spiritual good, so in him. In it a propensity to all evil, so in him. If any ask whose image and superscription is that which is now imprinted on the soul? he does not answer truly, who does not say it is Satan's.

It is his throne. By this he rules in the children of disobedience; and here is the palace, the place where Satan dwells. This keeps him up, this advances him. By this he keeps possession of the soul; so long as any of this remains, he will have some footing.

It is Satan's correspondent. It maintains secret, constant intercourse with man's mortal enemy; it is a treacherous inmate, ready upon all occasions to betray the soul to him who seeks to devour it. This encourages him to invade, make inroads into the soul; knowing he has a strong party within that will not fail him. His fiery darts would not be so dangerous, but that there is this matter to kindle on. He would in time be weary of assaulting, but that this innate domestic enemy is so ready to open to him, John xiv. 30. There was no natural corruption in Christ for Satan to work upon, no such inbred traitor to open, no secret friend of his to give entertainment; and therefore, after three or four attempts, he quite leaves Christ, desists from his enterprise, despairing of success; but he will never want encouragement to assault us so long as natural corruption continues in us.

This should be a great occasion of sorrow, that we are so near akin to hell, have such intimate correspondence with the devil; that we have so much of him within us; that which makes us so unlike him, affords him so great advantage against us.

10. Its brutishness. It hurries the soul on, in a blind fury, to such acts and motions as right reason would highly condemn, and an apprehensive soul would tremble at; and in respect hereof man is compared to irrational creatures, brute beasts—to the horse and mule, Ps. xxxii. 9; to the wild ass, Jer. ii. 23, 24; to an untamed heifer, Hos. iv. 16; nay, worse, Isa. i. 3, Jer. viii. 7, the brute beasts will know, will own and take some notice of their benefactors. But this makes men kick against God, wound Christ, expel the Spirit in its motions, bellow out reproaches against his servants, those whom he sends to feed and nourish their souls, Prov. xii. 1. They have an inclination to that which is good, which tends to preservation and continuance of health, strength, life. But this makes men averse even to their own happiness, and all the spiritual means that tend to it; a strong antipathy to holiness, the way to life, and the most opposite to those ways that are most strictly holy. They are, Jer. x. 21, afraid of what is destructive to their life and being; but this pushes men on in the ways of death, the paths that lead to destruction, makes them love death, and make haste to ruin their souls. An appetite to drink in sin, more deadly to the soul than any poison to the body, as greedily as the fish, &c., Job [xl. 23]; delight to wound, mangle their souls unto death, Ezek. xxi. 31, the reason of this desperate fury Job gives: Job xi. 12, 'Man is born as a wild ass's colt,' brings into the world a nature more wild, fierce, untamed, than any beast of the field.

11. Incorrigibleness, perverseness. It becomes worse by that which

should amend it. It takes occasion to grow more wicked from that which God has appointed to restrain its wickedness, Rom. vii. 8; the more sin is forbidden, the more exceeding sinful will it be; because wickedness is threatened, therefore it will be more wicked, ver. 13; even as a dunghill, the more the sun shines upon it, it sends forth greater plenty of filthy vapours, and infests the air with a more noisome smell. There is such a malignant humour in it, as when the holy law of God is applied to it, its rage and fury breaks forth with more violence. It is exasperated by that which should tame it. When the law would restrain it, it rages like a wild bull in a net, Jer.* The heathen could observe this rebellious inclination, *nititur in vetitum*. That is a desperate evil which grows worse by that which should cure it, but such an evil is this.

12. Its vileness. Take a survey of heaven and earth, and your eyes can fix upon nothing so vile as this. There is not anything so vile, base, contemptible in the world but has some degree of worth in it, as being the work of the great God; only natural corruption, and its corrupt issue, has not the least scruple of worth in it in any sense. It is purely vile, without any mixture of worth, vileness in the abstract. The Scripture holds forth its vileness under many notions, no one being sufficient to express it. At present take notice of one, that which is its common name. It is ordinarily called flesh, Gal. v. 16, 17, 19. Hereby is held forth the vile degeneracy of man's soul since this corruption seized on it. By creation it was pure, heavenly, spiritual, akin to the angels, as like to the nature of God as a creature could be; is now as it were transformed into flesh, mind carnal, &c.; as great a debasement as if heaven should be turned into earth, an angel into a beast, or the sun into a cloud. Nor is it flesh only, there is too much worth in that to be made a resemblance of our vile natures; it is dead flesh: Rom. vii., a 'body of death;' so vile as it is ghastly. Nay, it is deformed, leprous flesh. Leprosy was but an emblem of it, it is so vile as it is loathsome. Nay, it is putrified flesh. The old man is corrupt, Eph. iv. 24, full of putrefied sores, full of loathsome vermin; that which is more loathsome to God, exhaling filthy vapours, noisome, more offensive to God than what is most to us. Therefore man, who in integrity was admitted to intimate communion and converse with God, as soon as ever he had corrupted himself, the Lord could no longer endure him: Gen. iii. 24, 'He drove out the man.' Corrupted flesh is not fit to have so near converse with God, a Spirit.

It is both *formaliter* and *effectivè* vile. As it is so in itself, so it has made man vile. No creature so debased as man, being in this respect become viler than any creature. There is no such depravation in the nature of any creature, except in the diabolical nature. No creature ever razed God's image out of its nature, but only man. There is no aversions to the will of God, no inclination to what offends him, in any creature on earth but man. Man, then, who was once the glory of the creation, is become the vilest of all creatures, for that is vilest which is most contrary to the infinite glory, but so is our nature—Ps. xlix. 12, 'Man being in honour, abideth not'—is now like the beasts that perish; nay, worse than they, if the greatest evil can make him worse. Man was made a little lower than the angels, crowned with glory, advanced to be lord and governor of all the works of his hands; and all creatures in this world were put under his feet, Ps. viii. 5, 6. But by this natural corruption he that was but a little lower than angels is now something below the beasts.

* Qu. 'Isa. li. 20'?—Ed.

He was to have dominion, but is made baser than those over whom he rules. They were put under his feet, but now he is as low as they. This is the sad issue of natural corruption. It is a lamentation, &c.

18. Its propagation. All parents do propagate their natural corruption to their children. A woeful necessity is hereby brought upon mankind, so as none can be born without it. It is a sad consideration that parents should convey such a deadly evil to their children, but so it is. If man had continued uncorrupted, he had begot children after the image of God, and with his own similitude had conveyed lovely representations of the divine nature; but being corrupted, he begets children after his own image, which is now little better than a draught of Satan's, John iii. 6, Job xiv. 4: Job xxv. 4, 'How can he be clean that is born of a woman?' An unclean nature can have no other than unclean issue. Your cursed natures makes your children cursed. You convey spiritual death to all the children that have life from you; convey to that you most love that which makes them hateful to God. They have from you lovely bodies, but monstrous souls. Even those who are renewed cannot convey renewed natures to their children.

It is a most sad consideration that this evil is so communicative, as it does not only abide in us, but will pass to all that proceed from us; that we should convey an evil so sinful, so permanent, irresistible, deadly, devilish, to children. Take a view of natural corruption as spread before you in these considerations, and it will appear as Ezekiel's roll, 'writ within and without, lamentation, mourning, and woe,' Ezek. ii. 10.

OF REPENTANCE.

Except ye repent, ye shall all likewise perish.—LUKE XIII. 3.

IN the former verses you have the occasion and cause of what is said in this.

Verse 1, The occasion, Pilate's cruelty.

Verse 2, The impulsive cause, 'Suppose ye;' to correct, &c., a false and injurious supposition.

Jesus answering. He answered, though not to their intention;—that might be to ensnare him, whether approve or reprove,—but for their advantage. If his answer was not for their purpose, yet for their profit. If not what was expected, yet what was most expedient. He makes excellent use of that relation, and directs them how to improve that sad accident.

Obs. We should labour to make good use to ourselves of God's judgments on others. Why? God expects it; this is the way to prevent the execution on ourselves. How?

1. 'Learning righteousness,' Isa. xxvi. 9; faith, seeing him execute threatenings; fear, beholding his severity; obedience, sure want of that is the cause; love, whilst we escape.

2. Forsaking sin: 'Sin no more,' John v. 14. All sin, because every sin is pregnant with judgment; therefore it summons to search and try, &c., especially those sins which brought wrath on others. Observe providences; use means to discover what is the Achan, &c.

Use. We have great occasion to practise this. Wrath is kindled and burns, &c.; the cup of indignation goes round; the sword has had a commission, &c.; the scars and smarting impressions continue in bodies, estates, liberties. Let us learn to believe, to tremble, to love. Let us forsake sin, our own; the sins that have unsheathed the sword, mixed this bitter cup. What is that? In all probability contempt of, disobedience to, unfruitfulness under, the gospel. This ruined the Jews, ver. 6, 7, 34, 35, captivated before for it, 2 Chron. xxxvi. 15–17 with Jer. xxv. 7–9, &c. Probably it is the greatest sin, that brings the severest judgment. But what greater than this, more heinous than the sins of Sodom, therefore more tolerable for them, &c., Mark vi. 11, and if this be not it, what is the reason those parts who enjoy not the gospel escape better, Turkey, Tartary, Persia, &c.? Oh take heed, sure this is the Achan! Bewail it, avoid it!

Make not this warning ineffectual with the Jews' supposition. Rather hear, believe, apply what Christ says, Except I repent, &c.

The words are monitory. In them we have, I., the admonisher, *I;* II., the admonition. In which, 1, an ἐπανόρθωσις, nay; and, 2, a διόρθωσις, except ye repent. Ye must repent if ye would not perish.

I. From the admonisher, Christ, in that he teaches repentance.

Obs. Repentance is an evangelical duty; a gospel, a new-covenant duty. This should not be questioned by those who either believe what the gospel delivers, or understand what it is to be evangelical; but since it is denied, let us prove it. And first from this ground.

1. Christ taught repentance. But he taught nothing but what was evangelical. Is he who was the sweet subject, the blessed end, the great mediator, the glorious preacher of the covenant of grace and gospel, a legal teacher? He begins with this, it was his first sermon, Mat. iv. 17, Mark i. 16; and he ends with this, it was his last sermon, Luke xxiv. 47; leaves this to his disciples as their directory for preaching. Christ indeed answers the young man asking what good things he should do, &c., legally, according to his question, If thou wilt go to heaven by doing, no better rule than the commandments, Mat. xix. 17; but his intent was evangelical. He endeavours to convince him this was not the way to life, shewing the impossibility of fulfilling the law by enjoying* that which he would not, could not do, ver. 21, and so makes use of the law to serve the gospel. All his teachings were evangelical, but he taught repentance.

2. It is excluded by the covenant of works. There is no place for repentance there. Nothing but death after sin; no *tabula secunda post naufragium*. That enjoins not repentance; nothing but perfect obedience. Nor does it admit repentance; it promises nothing but to perfect obedience. It prescribes no means, leaves no hopes for sinners. They understand not the law, what the covenant of works is, who make repentance legal. There is nothing in it, but the mandate and the sanction. But the law neither commands it, nor does it reward the presence or practice; nor does it threaten the absence of repentance. It admits not of pardon; that comes in by virtue of another covenant. And where there is no pardon, there is no place for repentance. It requires only perfect obedience directly and expressly, and offers life to no other condition; but Adam hereby being obliged to obey God in all things, was by consequence and implicitly engaged to obey whatever God should require in any other way or covenant and upon any other terms, and so to repentance, which the gospel commands. These are the privileges of the covenant of grace.

3. It is required in the gospel, Acts xvii. 30. *Now,* in the times of the gospel, after the Messiah is come; now, when the covenant of grace comes forth in its last and best edition; now, when free grace appears in fairest and largest character; now, when the covenant commences new; even 'now he commands all,' all that will be saved, have any benefit by the Messiah, enjoy any blessings of the new covenant, to repent.

4. It was preached by the apostles. Christ makes it one of their instructions, puts it in their commission, Luke xxiv. 47. And they who found grace to be faithful, observed their instruction. It is the principal point in Peter's first sermon recorded after the ascension, Acts ii. 28, and of his second too, by which we may conclude of the rest, Acts iii. 19. John gives sweet encouragements to it, 1 John i. 9. If ever there was an evan-

* Qu. 'enjoining'?—ED.

gelical preacher in the world, sure Paul was one; and he solemnly professeth it was his constant practice, Acts xx. 20, 21, and xxvi. 20. It is express of all, Mark vi. 12.

5. It was the end of Christ's coming, Mat. ix. 13, to call sinners. He had no end in coming, but purely evangelical. He came to confirm the covenant of grace, which was established in the room of the covenant of works, by which no sinner could get any benefit. He came not to establish, to require anything legal; therefore, repentance is not legal.

6. It was purchased by Christ's death. But the privileges that he purchased were evangelical: Acts v. 31, 'Him has God exalted,' &c. What he bestows in his exaltation, he purchased by his humiliation. We owe the purchase of evangelical mercies to his satisfaction, the application to his intercession. If he had procured anything legal, he would have purchased life for us upon personal performance of perfect obedience; for this is the sum of the covenant of works. But this he procured not. That which he merited, was the blessings of the new covenant, whereof repentance is one, therefore evangelical.

7. It has evangelical promises. And these are not made to any legal duty: Prov. xxviii. 13, 'Whoso confesseth.' Confession is the sign, and forsaking an essential part of repentance. This is an evangelical promise, though in the Old Testament. As there is something legal in the New Testament, so much that is evangelical in the Old Testament. And these are sure characters, whereby we may distinguish gospel from law. Wherever we meet faith, repentance, confession, forsaking of sin, pardon, or mercy, those are gospel strains. The covenant of works disowns them, Mat. v. 4. Blessedness and comfort entailed upon mourning, a principal part of repentance.

8 It is urged upon evangelical grounds. It would be incongruous so to urge it, if it were legal; this would be to put new wine into old bottles, &c. So John Baptist, Mat. iii. 2, so Christ, Mark i. 14, 15, where is a definition of evangelical preaching. 'Kingdom of heaven,' that is, the heavenly and spiritual kingdom of Christ to be erected, with all the honours, privileges, duties of its subjects, are to be purchased by his satisfaction, and offered and declared in the gospel. The infinite goodness and love of God in sending Christ; and the wonderful love of Christ in undertaking the redemption of forlorn sinners; and the precious fruits of that undertaking, should be grounds of and motives to repentance; but these are evangelical, *ergo*, it is.

9. It is the condition of the prime evangelical mercy. God offers, gives remission of sins, upon condition of repentance. What Christ commands us, himself does practise, Luke xvii. 3. If he repent, forgive him. So Acts iii. 19, and ii. 38. The way Peter prescribes to Simon, Acts viii. 22, hence they are frequently joined, Luke xxiv. 47, Acts v. 31. A condition, not *quoad rigorem*, in point of exact performance, as though he required to repent by our own strength, and would not pardon till the condition were so performed. For such are legal conditions, and proper to the covenant of works; whereas, though he command, requires repentance, yet he promises it, Ezek. xi. 19, and gives it. But largely, and in respect of the necessity of its presence, he does not, he will not, pardon till we repent. No remission without it. In this sense repentance is propounded as the condition of forgiveness, 1 John i. 9; confession is an appendix, if not a formal part of repentance.

10. It is confirmed by the seal of the covenant of grace. Baptism is

the seal of repentance. Hereby God engages himself to begin, or increase and continue it in his elect; and the baptized engage themselves to practise it. Hence it is called 'the baptism of repentance,' Acts xiii. 24; John baptized to repentance, Mat. iii. 11. But baptism being the seal of the new covenant, confirms, signifies, exhibits, nothing but what is evangelical.

11. It is a fundamental of Christianity, Heb. vi. 1. But nothing legal can be such a fundamental. The covenant of works is so far from being the foundation of Christianity, as it is inconsistent with it. True Christians are quite freed from it. 'Ye are not under the law,' Rom. vi. 14, Gal. v. 18.

12. It is the way to life, Acts xi. 18. But there is no other way but that of the gospel. The way by the law, or covenant of works, was shut up by sin. Justice, like the angel, guards the passage in paradise; none can enter, that are sinners, by that old way, nor ever any enter. If the Lord had not found out a new way by the covenant of grace, no flesh had been saved. Repentance is part of this way. The convinced Jews ask the way, Acts ii. 37, he shews this. This is the way not to perish, 2 Peter iii. 9, so in the text.

Nor should this seem a duty of too sour and unpleasing a complexion, to be evangelical. There is more joy in godly sorrow, than in the choicest worldly pleasures. The heart, if not seared and void of sense, even in laughter is sorrowful, Prov. xiv. 13. But in the midst of this sorrow the heart rejoiceth. Those that have had experience will bear witness to this. And what heart so sad and mournful, into which that promise will not convey a stream of joy? Blessed, &c., Mat. v. 4. Godly sorrow not only rejoices the heart on earth, but causeth joy in heaven, Luke xv. 7.

Use 1. It reproves those who reject this duty as legal. Certainly those who find not this in the gospel, have found another gospel besides that which Christ and his disciples preached. But let them take heed, lest, whilst they will go to heaven in a way of their own, that way prove a by-path, and lead to the gates of death, instead of the place of joy. No way but Christ will bring to heaven, and that has three stages, faith, repentance, and obedience. He that will sit down at the end of the first, and never enter upon the other, will never reach heaven. Indeed, he that walks not in all, walks not in any, he is deluded, misled by an *ignis fatuus*, a false fire; and if the Lord do not undeceive him, will fall into the bottomless pit.

Use 2. Exhort. To practise this duty evangelically, that is most congruous. Directions:

(1.) Undertake it for evangelical ends. The end gives nature and name to the action. If your aims be legal, mercenary, the act will be so. Go not about it only to escape hell, avoid wrath, satisfy justice, remove judgments, pacify conscience. Ahab and Pharaoh can repent thus, those who are strangers to the covenant of grace. How then? Endeavour that you may give God honour, that ye may please him, that you may comply with his will, that you may never more return to folly. Confess, to give honour, as Josh. vii. 19, get hearts broken, that you may offer sacrifice well pleasing.

(2.) Let evangelical motives lead you to the practice of it. Act as drawn by the cords of love. The goodness of God should lead you to it, Rom. ii. Horror, despair, terror of conscience will drive Cain and Judas to strange fits of legal repentance. The remembrance of sins against electing, distinguishing love, against redeeming, pardoning mercy, against the free grace of the gospel and offers of it, should lead you to it. So should your dealing unfaithfully in the covenant of grace, sinning against the blood of Christ, wounding him, grieving him, who became a man of sorrows. Piercing, Zech. xii. 10, that you have hated him who loved you; grieved him who would have comforted you with unspeakable comforts; dishonoured him who thought not his own glory too much for you; provoked him who would see his own Son die, rather than you should perish; undervalued him who thought not his life too dear for you.

(3.) In an evangelical manner, freely, cheerfully, with joy and delight; not as constrained, but willingly. As those that are *amici legis*, in love with the duty—for so are pardoned repenting sinners, *justificati amici legis efficiuntur.** Christ's people in covenant with him are 'a willing people,' Ps. cx. 3, as ready to mourn for sin as for worldly crosses, sufferings; to hate it as to hate a mortal enemy, forsake it as freely as forsake an infectious disease, go against their lusts as David against Goliah: 1 Sam. xvii. 32, 'Thy servant will go fight with this Philistine.'

(4.) Repent that ye can repent no more. This is an evangelical temper, to be sensible of the defects and failings of spiritual duties; be grieved that you can grieve no more for sin; abhor yourselves that you cannot hate it with a more perfect hatred; count it your great affliction that sin and you are not quite divorced; count the relics of sin which you cannot drive out, what the Canaanites were to the children of Israel, Num. xxxiii. 55, as pricks in your eyes and thorns in your sides, continual vexation. It is a repentance to be repented of, as it is defective, though not as it is our duty.

(5.) Think not your repentance is the cause of any blessing: it is neither the meritorious nor impulsive cause; it neither deserves any mercy, nor moves the Lord to bestow any.

To think it moves him to give any mercy is an impious conceit, because it makes him changeable, who is without variableness. To think it deserves anything at God's hands is a legal conceit. Perfect obedience performed by Adam in the state of innocency had not been meritorious, could not deserve eternal life, *suâ naturâ*, in its own nature, for it was but his duty; nor was eternal happiness due to it in justice, as the nature of merit requires, but only by virtue of the promise, *vi pacti;* much less can our imperfect repentance. It does not procure blessings one way or other casually.† The Lord pardons sin, loves us, blesses us *when* we repent, not *because* we repent; it is *via*, not *causa;* a duty, not desert; a means, no merit; a qualification, necessary *ratione præsentiæ*, not *efficientiæ*.

(6.) Think not that your repentance can satisfy God, or make any amends for the wrong sin has done him; do not imagine that it is any recompence for the injury sin has done him, or any reparation of that honour which is violated and defaced by sin. Every old corrupt heart is so far legal as it would have a righteousness, a satisfaction of its own, and not rely upon another for it; so proud is corrupt nature, as it is loth to deny its own, to depend only upon another's satisfaction. And therefore we are apt to think that our acts of repentance do satisfy God and appease him, and thereupon, after the exercise of them, will speak peace to ourselves, and stop the mouth of an accusing conscience with such performances, resting on them as though thereby we had satisfied the Lord.

But we must consider that no satisfaction is sufficient to make amends for sin but that which is of infinite value, since the injury sin has done is infinite, having disobeyed, displeased, dishonoured, an infinite majesty.

* Ambr. † Qu. 'causally'?—ED.

And such a satisfaction no finite creature can make, not the most perfect saint, not the most glorious angels; much less can such vile, weak, sinful creatures as we, by such imperfect acts of repentance.

(7.) Ye must depend upon Christ for strength, ability to repent; all evangelical works are done in his strength. Repentance is an act above the power of nature, and therefore we cannot practise it without power from above. Ye must depend on, seek to Christ for this power. Adam's condition in innocency required not so much dependence, for he was empowered with sufficient grace to perform all that was required; but his not improving that sufficiency has left all his posterity destitute of all ability to do anything supernaturally good. We want both habits and acts before we can repent; Christ must both give us soft hearts, hearts that can repent, and must teach them by his Spirit before they will repent. Except he smite those rocks, they will yield no water, no tears for sin; except he break these hearts, they will not bleed. Repentance is his gift, his work, Acts xi. 18, 2 Tim. ii. 25. We may as well melt a flint, or turn a stone into flesh, or draw water out of a rock, as repent in our own strength. It is far above the power of nature, nay, most contrary to it. How can we hate sin, which naturally we love above all? mourn for that wherein we most delight? forsake that which is as dear as ourselves, right hand, eye? It is the almighty power of Christ which only can do this; we must rely on, seek to him for it, Jer. xxxi. 18, Lam. v. 21; that which ye do in your own strength you do legally, and so ineffectually, to no purpose. The gospel beats us quite out of self; live by another life, Gal. ii. 20; act by another strength, and satisfy by another's righteousness, Philip. iii. 9; and do all that we do graciously, by the grace of Christ. I laboured, 1 Cor. xv. 10. Therefore Bernard prays *quid efficiamus, operare*. And Augustine, *Da domine*, &c., according to his principle, which is truly evangelical, *Certum est nos facere quod facimus*, &c. *In nobis, et nobiscum, ut operemur, operatur*. He works our works in us and for us.* Go into your closet, and pour out your requests: Lord, thou commandest me to repent, and I see the necessity; but I have a hard heart, opposite; and Satan and the world, &c.

(8.) Ye must expect the acceptance of your repentance from Christ. No evangelical service whatsoever, or by whomsoever performed, can be well pleasing to God, either in itself or as it comes from us, but only in Christ. Not as it comes from us, for our persons must be accepted before our services can be capable thereof. But how can sinful persons please a holy God? We must either be righteous in ourselves or in another, or else the righteous God will loathe, must punish us. No flesh can be justified in his sight, Ps. cxliii. 2, till Christ cover its deformities, and clothe it with a robe of his righteousness; nor in themselves, for so the best are sinful, in regard of many defects, &c., not fit to be looked upon by him who is 'of purer eyes,' &c., Heb. iv. 13; only acceptable through Jesus Christ, 1 Peter ii. 5, Eph. i. 6.

Adam indeed, under the covenant of works, might have been accepted without a mediator; the purity of his person and perfection of his services would have found acceptance immediately; but for us so to expect it, is both legal and irrational. We sinful persons, with sinful services, having no speckless righteousness to present to God but that of Christ, must either appear in that, or hide ourselves from the presence of him who sits on the throne. No appearing for us but in and by our advocate. God

* Concil. Arans.

will take nothing well from us unless we take our surety with us. No blessing can be obtained except we come to God in the garments of our elder brother: Isa. lxiv. 6, *De se, non de impiis*, all our righteousness, &c.; *de bonis operibus, non solum de lapsibus*, till they be cleansed in the blood of the Lamb, Rev. vii. 14, Job xxix. 14. If we put on any other robe but that of Christ's, it is *vestis belli, magis quam pacis, ubi adhuc expugnatur*, &c.*

(9.) Think not your repentance obliges God to the performance of any promise, as though he were thereby bound, and could not justly refuse to bestow what he has promised to the penitent; for he is not obliged to fulfil it till the condition be perfectly performed. Imperfect repentance is not the condition; God requires nothing imperfect. If he accomplishes his promise upon our weak defective endeavours, it is not because he is by them engaged, but from some other engaging consideration. No man is obliged to perform a promise but when the condition is perfectly fulfilled. If it be defective in quantity or quality, not so much nor so good as the agreement required, he is not engaged, he may refuse; *e. g.*, Ephron promises Abraham a field for four hundred shekels of silver, current money, Gen. xxiii. 15. Now if Abraham had but brought him three hundred, and that not current, wanting weight, or mixed with dross, none will say Ephron had been obliged to give him the field, or unjust for refusing.

The Lord promises such and such mercies upon condition of repentance, but it is perfect repentance, for he promises nothing to that which is defective, else he should promise to that which is sinful. But this rather brings us within the compass of threatenings, Gal. iii. Perfect performances are still required. The gospel remitteth no part, no tittle of the substance of the law, which commands perfect obedience in duties, whether expressly or implicitly, and by consequence contained in it, as repentance is. If it were not still required, why should we strive after perfection, and bewail the want of it? The obligation is eternal, founded in our natures, due from us as we are creatures, &c. The condition therefore of the promises is perfect repentance.

Now our repentance is defective, both in quantity and quality, measure and manner, neither so great nor so good as is required. Our sorrow not so hearty, constant, ingenuous, &c., and so does not engage.

Why then does God perform? How is he obliged? Why, it is Christ that has obliged him; he makes good the condition. When we cannot bring so much as is required, he makes up the sum; he adds grains to that which wants weight. He has satisfied for our defects, and they are for his sake pardoned, and therefore are accepted, as though they were not defective; *omnia mandata Dei facta deputantur, quando quicquid non sit ignoscitur.*† Christ's undertaking makes good the condition, and so the promise is obliging. Hence, 2 Cor. i. 20, he is so obliged by Christ's undertaking as, except he will be changeable or unfaithful, he must accomplish. Hence he is called the Mediator, Heb. ix. 15, and surety, chap. vii. 22. God had promised an eternal inheritance upon conditions, but we broke the conditions, and were not able to make satisfaction, are all bankrupts. God therefore lays hold on our surety, and gets satisfaction of him, and hereby the agreement is made good, and God obliged. God abates nothing of his first proposal; perfect conditions are still required, only he dispenses with personal performance. That which we could not do, Christ has done; his satisfaction is accepted, Rom. x. 4, the end, the accomplishment. His fulfilling is the believer's righteousness. *Per-*

* August. † Aug. Retract. cap. 19.

*fectionem legis habet, qui credit in Christum.** Christ has procured pardon for all defects. And in this sense our repentance is as it were perfect, because the defect thereof shall not be imputed. Hence it obliges the Lord, not by virtue of our performance, but of Christ's satisfaction. It is not we, but Christ for us; not what we do, but what he did, suffered, that engages the Lord to perform any promise. Even as when one engaged to conditions, fails in performance, if his surety make other satisfaction, it is the surety that obliges to the accomplishment. It is not our defective, imperfect repentance that engages God to perform promise; for he never promised to imperfect performances, but Christ making the Lord satisfaction for our defects and imperfections. And so they being not imputed, are not in themselves, but by virtue of this satisfaction, no less obliging than if they were perfect.

(10.) Expect a reward, not from justice, but mercy. The Lord rewards repentance, and other evangelical services, under the covenant of grace. That the reward is not of debt, but of grace; not *merces debita*, but *gratuita*; not κατ' ὀφείλημα, but κατὰ τὴν χάριν. It is a recompence, but a gracious recompence. He is not obliged *ex debito justitiæ*, but bestows it freely, of mere bounty and mercy.

It is true Adam, under the covenant of works, whilst he kept his integrity, might have expected something in justice; for the eternal life was not due to him *ex dignitate operis*, but *vi pacti*; and so is *debitum improprie*, and not *ex ordine justitiæ*,† because there was no proportion betwixt it and his services; and so far as the reward exceeds the value of the service, so far it is of grace and favour. He deserved not eternal life. Yet perfect obedience, if performed, would have deserved justification. It had been but just, that he who was perfectly righteous, should have been pronounced and declared so, if there had been occasion. This was due, Rom. iv. 4.

But to think that any blessing is due to us for our best services, that our repentance makes God in our debt, is a legal apprehension.

It is much is due in justice to the obedience of Christ, for he is worthy. But nothing due to us. It is mere mercy, that what Christ has merited should be bestowed on us. It is mere mercy that we are not consumed. Oh what mercy is it that we are pardoned, reconciled, saved! It is mercy that our repentance is not punished, much more that it is rewarded. It is mercy that we escape the greatest suffering, much more that the Lord vouchsafes to pardon, bless, enhappy us. All is grace, from the foundation to the topstone.

II. Thus much for the admonisher, 'I tell you.' Proceed we to the admonition. And in it, 1, the correction, 'nay.' Hereby he corrects two mistakes of the Jews: (1.) Concerning their innocency. They thought themselves innocent, compared with the Galileans, not so great sinners, ver. 2. (2.) Concerning their impunity, grounded on the former. Because not so great sinners, they should not be so great sufferers, nor perish as they in the text. From the first.

1. (1.) *Obs.* Impenitent sinners are apt to think themselves not so great sinners as others; to justify themselves, as Pharisees in reference to others; like crows, fly over flowers and fruit, to pitch upon carrion; say as Isa. lxv. 5, 'Stand by thyself,' &c.

[1.] Because never illuminated to see the number, nature, aggravations

* Ambr. † *Vide* Baron. p. 388.

of their own sins, how many, how sinful; examine not their hearts and lives; judge of sins according to outward appearance, not secret heinousness.

[2.] Self-love. They cover, extenuate, excuse their own; multiply, magnify others. A κάλυμμα for their own, a glass for others.

[3.] Ignorance of their natural sinfulness. In which respect they are equally sinful as others. Seed-plots of sin; have a root of bitterness, an evil treasure of heart; a disposition to the most abominable sins that ever were committed, such as they never thought of, nor will ever believe they should yield to, 2 Kings viii. 11, 12; want nothing but temptation, a fit occasion. Their heart as tinder; if the Lord permit Satan to cast but a spark in, they will be set on fire of hell, break forth into the most hellish wickedness, &c. Apt to think natural sinfulness an excuse, whereas it is that which makes us most sinful, odious to God, &c. Would you take it for a good excuse if a servant that has robbed you should tell you he has a thievish nature? This will make you hate him far more.

Use. Take heed of this. It is a sign of impenitency. Paul counts himself the chief of sinners: 'If you judge yourselves,' &c., 1 Cor. xi. 31.

(2.) From their conceit of impunity.

Obs. Sinners are apt to flatter themselves with the hopes they shall escape judgments. If they can believe they are not so great sinners, they are apt to conclude they shall not perish: 'Put far from them the evil day,' Amos vi. 3, threatened, ver. 7; cry Peace, &c. Satan has blinded them. He seeks their ruin, and would have them perish in such a way as there should be no avoiding, and therefore would not suffer them to entertain the least thoughts of their danger lest they should think of preventing, Prov. xxii. 3. Lest they should do so, he puts out their eyes, lulls them asleep, that they may perish unavoidably before they be aware; uses them as Jael did Sisera, lays them asleep that justice may strike through their souls while they slumber, that they may go down quick into pit, and not awake till in hell.

Use. Beware of this. It has been the ruin of millions. Those perish soonest who think they shall longest escape, Amos vi. 7, 1 Thes. v. 3; 'be not deceived, God is not mocked,' &c. Believe the Lord threatening rather than Satan promising. Delude not yourselves with conceits of mercy. There is no mercy for impenitent sinners. To imagine the contrary is a great dishonour to God, an high affront to Christ, makes the gospel a nullity. Satan says, Though thou sin, yet God is merciful, he may save thee. Christ says, 'Except ye repent, ye shall all likewise perish.' Now, whether will you believe? Satan says, Though ye do continue to sin, &c., ye may have peace; but the Lord says, Deut. xxix. 19, 20, he will not spare him, &c. Think not to say within yourselves, We are not so great sinners; the least sin, not repented of, is enough to destroy you for ever, to bring the curse of God upon soul and body, Gal. iii. 10. He says not, he that continues in some, or in the greatest, but all. If ye so keep all the precepts of the law, as to fail but in one, that one failing will cause all the curses of the law to fall on you. This is the sad condition of every sinner, whatever his sins be. And there is no relief for any, but by the covenant of grace; and you can be assured of no relief thereby without repentance; for Christ, who is truth, has said it, 'Except ye repent, ye shall perish.'

2. So we come to the other part of the admonition, viz., the direction.

Obs. Those that will not repent shall perish. Whosoever. Though as many privileges as these Jews had, and as few sins as they thought they had, yet without repentance they must perish. No salvation without it. It needs no confirmation, since Christ himself does twice affirm it.

It is implied, 2 Peter iii. 9, they must needs perish that never recover themselves out of the snare of the devil, 2 Tim. ii. 25, 26, and never are weary of treasuring up wrath, Rom. ii. 5.

Repentance has such a relation to, such a connection with, life and salvation, as this cannot be expected without that; for though it be neither merit nor motive, yet consider it as it is, an antecedent and sign, qualification, condition, or means of life and salvation, and the truth will appear.

An *antecedent*. So there must be no salvation till first there be repentance. Sown in tears before reap in joy.

Sign. A symptom of one being an heir to salvation. And so life belongs as to all, *πάντι*, so only to him, *μόνῳ*, that repents.

Qualification. To fit for life. He that is in love with sin, is not fit for heaven. No unclean thing enters there. Neither will God himself endure him to be there.

Condition. For that is *ἄνευ οὗ ἀνεὺ οὐχ*, without it, never see God: 'Except ye,' &c. This is the condition, without which ye shall not escape.

Means and way to life: *via regni*, Christ's highway. 'Repentance to life,' Acts xi. 18. Peter directs them to this, Acts ii. 38.

1. What is it to repent? 2. Why must they perish that do not? For the

1. To repent, is to turn; to return from former evil ways; Ezek. xiv. 6, 'Repent, and turn yourselves.' One explains the other: Acts xxvi. 20, 'should repent and turn to God.' Μετάνοια in the New Testament is תשובה in the Old Testament, *à* שׁוּב.

Now in turning, as in every motion, there are two terms, *à quo* and *ad quem*, *ἀποστροφὴ* and *ἐπιστροφὴ*: something *from* which, that is sin; something *to* which, that is God or righteousness. Hence Athanasius gives this account of the word, *quæst. id.*, *διὰ τοῦτο γαρ λέγεται μετάνοια, ὅτι μετατίθησι τὸν νοῦν ἀπὸ τοῦ κακοῦ πρὸς τὸ ἀγαθόν*. Because hereby the mind is turned from evil to good.

I suppose it principally consists in turning from evil, sin; though he be never truly turned from sin, that turns not to God, &c. Yet that belongs properly to another grace. Repentance especially is turning from; and therefore I shall insist on this. In this turning, there are three acts, as it were so many steps: sorrow for sin, hatred of it, resolution to forsake it. He that does not mourn, &c., shall perish. This is Christ's meaning: 'Except,' &c.

1. Sorrow for sin. To repent, is to mourn for sin, 2 Cor. vii. 9, 10. The Lord exhorting Zion to repentance, expresses it thus, Joel ii. 12; and Peter's repentance is expressed by this, Mat. xxvi. 75. Though there may be sorrow without repentance, yet no repentance without sorrow. It is not every sorrow, for there is a sorrow unto death; nor every sorrow for sin, for Judas was sorry he had sinned, Mat. xxvii. 3, 4. What sorrow then? how qualified? It must be hearty and godly sorrow.

(1.) Hearty, such as greatly affects the heart. Not that of the tongue, which is usual, I am sorry, &c.; nor that of the eyes neither, if tears spring not from a broken heart; not verbal, slight, outward, superficial, but great, bitter, cordial humbling; such sorrow as will afflict the soul. The Israelites, in their solemn day of repentance and humiliation, were commanded to afflict their souls, Lev. xvi. 29; and the want of it is threatened, chap. xxiii. 29. Such a sense of sin, such sorrow for it as will be a soul affliction.

When the heart is truly sorrowful for sin, sin is a burden to it; such penitents they are whom Christ invites, Mat. xi. 28, there will be such pain and anguish in the heart as when it is pricked, wounded. So were Peter's penitents, Acts ii., as if it were rent and torn; so Joel ii. 13, as if it were broken and crushed. A penitent heart is a broken heart, as David calls it in his penitent Ps. li. 17. He regards no sorrow but this which issues from a contrite heart, Isa. lxvi. 2.

It must be a great, a bitter mourning, and therefore is compared to that which is caused by the greatest outward afflictions. So is the sorrow of the Jews at their conversion prophetically described, Zech. xii. 10, 11; such sorrow as Sarah would have made for the loss of her first-born, her only son Isaac; or Hannah for Samuel, the son of many tears, of so strong desires.

Sorrow is proportionable to the cause. Now what more bitter affliction than the loss of a child, especially to the Jews, who counted children a greater blessing, &c.? To lose a child, a son, an only son, first begotten son, Oh what sorrow, what bitter lamentation would this have occasioned! Even such should be the sorrow for sin; a bitter mourning, a great mourning, ver. 11, like that for the untimely death of that blessed prince Josiah; as the inhabitants of Hadadrimmon for Josiah, slain in the valley of Megiddo.

A hearty sorrow, not confined to the heart, but if the natural temper afford them, breaking forth in tears, sighs, and sad complaints, the ordinary companions of a sorrowful heart. Such must be sorrow in some degree of sincerity, or else perish.

(2.) Godly sorrow, 2 Cor. vii. 9, 10, sorrow for sin, as it is against God; not as it is against yourselves, prejudicial to you; as it brings judgments, exposes to wrath, makes you obnoxious to justice, brings within the compass of curses, and in danger of hell. Not as it withholds temporal blessings, so Esau; nor brings temporal judgments, so Ahab; nor as it excludes from mercy, so Cain; nor as it brings hell into the conscience, so Judas. This sorrow is carnal, worldly, unto death. But as it is against God, his authority, mercy, glory, blessedness, holiness, power, sovereignty, truth, justice, being.

His *authority:* as a disobedience of his command, violation of his righteous law, as opposite to his blessed will.

His *mercy:* against him who is unwilling to destroy, willing to pardon, ready to be reconciled, gave his Son, sends his Spirit.

His *glory:* that which dishonours him, casts unworthy reflections on him, crosses his design, and robs him of the glory due to him.

His *blessedness:* displeases, grieves, wearies, burdens; causes him to complain, repent.

His *holiness:* contrary to his pure nature, the greatest deformity, that which he cannot endure to look upon.

His *power* and *truth:* as that which questions whether he is able to execute his threatenings, or whether he will be as good as his word in executing; sin is an implicit denial of these.

His *sovereignty:* as open rebellion against him, 'Who is the Lord?' &c., and as it makes us unserviceable to him; treason.

His *being:* as that which denies him, would depose, dethrone him, cause the holy one to cease; 'This is the heir,' &c., Mat. xxi. 38.

His *excellencies:* prefers self, vanity, Satan, sin, before him.

2. Hatred of sin. This is an act of repentance, and that indeed which is

principally essential to it. It is described by this 2 Cor. vii., ἀγανάκτησις. Where no indignation, no hatred, there is no repentance. And Job joins these, Job. xlii. 6, so Ezek. vi. 9, chap. xx. 43, and xxxvi. 31, loathe themselves as sinful, for sin; therefore loathe sin more than themselves. They would not be loathsome but for sin.

It is not enough to dislike it, be displeased at it, angry with it, no nor sorry for it. He that repents will hate it. Be so affected to sin as we use to be towards that which we most hate. We may make use of that sinful hatred amongst men to discover the nature of this gracious affection. When you hate one you wish his ruin, rejoice when any evils befall him, and be ready to do him a mischief when occasion is offered, join with any that would undo him. He that repents will so hate sin as to seek its death, to crucify, mortify it, rejoice when it is wounded, love that word which smites it, have his heart rise at the approach of it, manifest an antipathy against it.

(1.) This hatred is *well grounded*. He will hate it, because it is hateful, loathsome in the eye of God, and every eye that is opened. It stinks in his nostrils, therefore would destroy it. So Jacob, Gen. xxxiv. 10, 'Ye have made me to stink,' I shall be destroyed. Hate it, because he looks upon it as a mortal enemy to God, to his soul, to all that is good. David gives this account of his hatred: Ps. cxxxix. 21, 'I count them mine enemies.'

(2.) An *universal* hatred. All sin. He that hates not all does truly hate none at all. He that hates sin, as it is sin, will hate all, and he that does not hate it as sin, does not repent of it. It is not enough to hate some sins, in the sense of others, or those that are commonly hated amongst men, as perjury, murder, nor to hate those sins that you have no great occasion to love, those that are not pleasing, profitable, but even that which ye have most loved, had most delight and advantage in, secret as well as open, spiritual sins as well as carnal, small and great. Repentance is inconsistent with love to any sin, Ps. cxix. 104.

(3.) *Irreconcileable*. He doth hate it so, as never to be at peace, amity with it; not fall out with it by fits, in some good mood, but return again to folly, be friends again with sin, and use it as kindly, act it as freely as ever. This is not to repent, but to mock God, and delude your own souls, and make your condition worse than before, Mat. xii. 43–45. When the soul returns to sin, the devil returns to the soul, and brings with him seven worse than himself. Relapses give the devil more possession. He never truly hated sin who hates it not always. It must be perfect hatred, as extensive, and intensive, so persevering.

3. Forsaking sin. In resolution never to sin more. To repent is to turn; and how turn from sin if not forsake it? It is impossible; as to leave a way, and walk in it; a contradiction. All the characters of repentance, 2 Cor. vii. 11, include this carefulness. Fear, vehement desire, zeal, imply strong resolution. Every resolution is not sufficient; not future, weak, partial; it must be *de præsenti*, forsake sin presently. Not enough to say, I will do it hereafter, when I have had a little more pleasure, reaped a little more profit by my sins. He that will not forsake it presently, to-day, while it is called to-day, has no true resolution, is far from truly repenting.

Effectual, strong. Such as will put you upon the use of all means to perform it, and make good your resolution to avoid all occasions, company, place, &c.; make you watchful against temptation, stand guarded, careful to remove the cause, original corruption; stopping up the puddle, the spring; not only lop the branches, but strike at the root; diligent in the use of mortifying duties, &c. Where repentance is, there is ἐκδίκησις, a resolution to be revenged for the wrong sin has done to God, to the soul, &c.

Impartial. Forsake all. He that repents, must not say, I will forsake my former ways, so many, so great; I will forsake all but one; the Lord be merciful to me in this. This is but a little one, let me escape with it, and let my soul live in it. All these things I will do, all these sins I will leave, only let me be spared in this. I know not how to live, how to subsist without this. I shall have no comfort of my life, no credit with my neighbours, if I leave this. This is not the voice of a penitent, but of a hypocrite. The best of the sheep and oxen Saul spared, and destroyed the rest, the vile and refuse, when God had enjoined him to destroy all; and then he comes to Samuel with a justification of himself: 1 Sam. xv., 'I have performed the commandment,' &c. But what says the Lord? how does he resent his partial obedience? See ver. 23. So will the Lord deal with those who, pretending repentance, yet will destroy, forsake none but the vile and refuse, unprofitable, unpleasing sins, &c. He that forsakes not all, forsakes none at all, James ii. 10: *Eâdem pœna afficietur, atque si omnia violasset.* If the rest of the body be cured, yet leave but a gangrene in the least part, it will be the destruction of the whole: *Per hujus solius peremptionem, etiam illa integra trahi ad mortem.** Sin is the snare of the devil; by repentance we escape it. *Quomodo passer, etsi non toto teneatur corpore, sed uno solo pede, est in potestate aucupis,*† &c., 2 Tim. ii. 25, 26. One leak neglected may sink a ship as well as a thousand. Herod did many things, so he avoided many sins; but Herodias he would not part with, and so he perished. It is not enough to forsake almost all; Agrippa was *almost* persuaded, &c. They are but almost resolved who are not resolute to part with all, Ps. cxix. 6. He that has 'respect to all commands' must respect no sin. That repentance which makes not resolute to forsake all sin is a repentance to be repented of, you must be ashamed of; notwithstanding it, you may, you shall perish.

Reas. 1. Christ has said it. There is reason enough in his word. That is the best ground we have, or can have, for any truth in the world. He has said it, and lest we doubt, he speaks it twice, ver. 3. and 5. He speaks it to the Jews. If any people in the world might think to escape without repentance it was they, having received such great privileges, such special favours; yet these he tells, 'Except ye repent, ye shall perish.' He speaks universally, admits no exception, no limitation. Ye shall all, whether your sins be small or great, whether greater sinners than the Galileans or not, 'except ye repent,' &c. He says it, who is truth itself, and so speaks undoubted truths; who is God himself, and therefore cannot lie; who is judge of quick and dead, and therefore cannot err in the sentence; who is the great prophet, of whom it was prophesied many thousand years since, that whoever would not hear, that is, believe him, should be cut off; he whose word is more firm than the foundations of heaven and earth: 'Heaven and earth shall pass away, but this word shall not pass away.' They shall be dissolved, turned into nothing, sooner than this saying of Christ shall be convinced of the least falsehood. No firmer truth in the world than this, 'Except ye repent, ye shall perish.'

Reas. 2. Christ never died for impenitent sinners. They must needs

* Aug. † Chrysost.

perish for whom Christ never died; but he never died for such. Those sins must be punished in hell to eternity which are not expiated by Christ's blood, but it was not shed for final impenitency. Christ gives repentance to all for whom he died, Acts v. 31. Those who do not will, ask, seek, receive it; those who put it off, defer, have no ground to believe that Christ died for them. And till there be some ground to believe this, there is no hope to escape, no way for such, but they perish. Christ only died for those whom his Father gave to him, John vi. 37. But impenitent sinners were not given to Christ; for those who are given to him do come to him, return; those who continue impenitent, run from him.

Reas. 3. Unpardoned sinners must perish. For whom the Lord does not pardon he will punish eternally, but impenitent sinners are unpardoned. Repentance and remission of sins are usually joined in Scripture, and the Lord will never suffer them to be separated. No repentance, no pardon. It is not the cause, but it is the condition, without which no remission. Solomon would not ask pardon but upon this condition, 2 Chron. vi. 26, 27, nor does the Lord answer him but on the same terms, chap. vii. 14, *conditionalis nihil ponit in esse.* Those who turn not from sin while they live, must die in their sins when they die; and who so die, die eternally. The Lord, who is of purer eyes than to behold iniquity on earth, will not endure it in heaven. Ye shall sooner see the most holy of the saints cast into hell than an unpardoned sinner admitted into heaven.

Reas. 4. Those whom the Lord hates must perish. But he hates impenitent sinners, Ps. v. 5, 'Thou hatest all workers of iniquity.' Now, who are so properly workers of iniquity as those who are so eager at it as they will not leave this work though they be in danger to perish for it? Christ puts it out of doubt. The workers of iniquity must perish, Luke xiii. 27. Those whom the Lord will tear in his wrath must perish with a witness; but those whom he hates, he tears, &c., Job xvi. 8. What more due to such impenitent sinners than hatred! what more proper than wrath, since they treasure up wrath! Rom ii. Will he entertain those in the bosom of love whom his soul hates? No; destruction is their portion, Pro. xxi. 15. If all the curses of the law, all the threatenings of the gospel, all judgments in earth or in hell, will be the ruin of him, he must perish. If the Lord's arm be strong enough to wound him dead, he must die: Ps. lxviii. 21, 'He will wound,' &c.

Reas. 5. He that is not, cannot be in the way of life, must perish. But can he escape death and ruin who will never leave the paths that lead thereto? Can he come to life who never sets foot in the way? There never were but two ways to life, the covenant of grace, and the covenant of works; and impenitent sinners are out of both. The way by works is quite blocked up to all; for there are three things in that covenant: all, as creatures, are under the precept; all, by nature, are under the penalty; but none of all are under the promise. None can enter into life by virtue of that, because none can perform the condition. No sinner can come to life this way. Lest, therefore, no flesh should be saved, the Lord was pleased to open another way to life; that is, the covenant of grace. Jesus Christ, by virtue of his satisfaction, is become a new and living way; but to whom? To those only who believe and repent: John viii. 24, 'If ye believe not,' &c.; Acts xi. 18, no life now without satisfaction for transgressing the former way. Christ has made satisfaction; but none shall ever have benefit thereby but those that repent; till then, the threatening of the first covenant is in force, nothing but death.

Resolution of some cases:

Case 1. Whether does this belong to those that have already repented? Whether may this truly be applied to them? Except ye repent, &c.

Ans. In some respects it may; in some it may not.

In respect of those sins for which they have repented it belongs not to them.

But in respect of future sins, such as they may commit, or have committed, and not repented of them, to them it must be applied, 'Except ye repent, ye shall perish.' For though those sins be pardoned at first repentance, yet but pardoned conditionally, so that the sentence shall be revoked if the condition be not performed. Now the condition is repentance; and therefore, in this respect, this is applicable to them, Except ye repent, ye shall perish.

For the understanding of this, observe three proportions:

1. All sins are pardoned upon the first act of faith and repentance. All past, present, to come, are actually pardoned, Rom. viii. 1. If any sin were not forgiven, there would be some place for condemnation; for the least unpardoned makes liable to condemnation. Hence divines say, *Justificatio est simul et semel:* a sinner is justified, pardoned, but once, and all at once. But though all be then pardoned, yet not all alike. Therefore, observe,

2. Sins past and repented of are pardoned absolutely, because the condition is present; and where the condition is present, that which was conditional becomes absolute. A thing is only conditional when the condition is not present but future. The guilt of those sins would not return, no, not upon supposition of an impossibility, if the conditions which give or shew his right to pardon should be lost. If a man could lose the grace of repentance he should perish, not for his sins formerly repented of, but for his after-impenitency, which would not be true if former sins were not pardoned absolutely.

3. Future sins, or sins unrepented of, are but pardoned to a believer conditionally. Because the condition of pardon is not in being, is future; he has not yet repented for those sins; and if he utterly fail in performing the condition (though the Lord's engaging for performance, by honour and promise, makes this impossible), yet if he should not repent, the former sentence of absolution and general pardon would be revoked, would be a nullity, of no force as to these sins, and consequently he should perish; so that, in respect of these sins, it may be said to those that formerly have been the greatest penitents under heaven, Except ye repent, ye shall perish.

From hence we see how dangerous it is to conceive that, after we are assured of pardon, there is no need of repentance. They must perish that are not absolutely pardoned; but these are not absolutely pardoned till they repent; therefore except they repent, they shall perish.

Case 2. Since we must repent of all sins, then it is necessary for sins of ignorance; but how can we repent of these? It seems hard we must perish for not repenting of those acts which we know not to be sins.

Resolution of this will be to shew what sins of ignorance must be necessarily repented of, so as except we repent we shall perish; and also how we may so repent of them as we may not perish.

To this end observe, 1, some distinctions; and, 2, some propositions resolving the use.*

1. Ignorance is either voluntary or involuntary.

* Qu. 'case.'—ED.

[1.] Involuntary; when one is ignorant, because not able, or not obliged to know. Either negative, when one is not bound; or invincible, when one cannot know such an act is unlawful.

[2.] Voluntary ignorance is either affected, or out of negligence: affected, when one will not know what is sin, because he has a mind to continue in it, unwilling to leave it: *libenter ignorant, ut liberius peccent;* out of negligence, when one does not know his sins, because he neglects the means of knowledge, when not diligent to find out whether such an act be sinful.

[3.] Repentance is in act or in purpose: actual, when repentance is presently practised, and the acts of it put forth upon present occasion; in purpose, when there is a disposition, intention, and resolution to exercise repentance, whenever just occasion shall be made known and offered.

[4.] Repentance is implicit and general, or express and particular: particular, when sins in particular are confessed, bewailed, forsaken, every sin punctually and singly by itself; general, when sin is bewailed, not expressly in particulars, but implicitly and in the gross.

2. This premised, for understanding of what follows, take the resolution in six propositions:

(1.) No man shall perish for not repenting of such ignorances as are altogether involuntary. The Lord expects not repentance for such. For sin only is the object of repentance. But such ignorances as are purely unwilling, that is, such as we neither can nor ought to know, are not sins. It is possible an act may be unlawful in itself, and yet no sin to the actor; *v. g.*, it is unlawful in itself for a man to know one who is not his wife; but Jacob knew Leah, who was not his wife, yet sinned not, because he knew not, nor could in an ordinary way discover that she was not his wife. Jacob might be sorry for this as his affliction, but was not bound to repent for it as his sin; but such ignorances are rare.

(2.) Every man must perish that does not repent of those sins whereof he is affectedly ignorant. He is bound to repent of both; for the ignorance is a sin no less than the act; it argues love to sin, unwillingness to leave it, which is a sign of an impenitent heart, of one that gives himself up to live in sin. There can be no true repentance, where such ignorances are not repented of. He that does not repent, both of that ignorance, and of those sins whereof he is so ignorant, must perish.

(3.) He is deservedly in danger to perish who repents not of those sins which he is ignorant of, through carelessness, negligence. For though there may be true repentance, where there is some degrees of negligence, where all possible diligence is not used, for getting the knowledge of those sins which are to be repented of, yet such repentance is dangerously defective, and in that respect must be repented of, except ye will perish.

Therefore, when ye go about this great work of repentance, you must use all diligence in surveying your lives, and searching your hearts, and viewing both in the glass of the law, and desiring the Lord to make clear and full discoveries of sin, that so, if your repentance be defective, it may not willingly be so.

(4.) Because, after all diligence we can use, multitudes of sins will not be discovered, since they are so many as they pass knowledge, Ps. xix. 12; though it be required under penalty of perishing, that we repent in particular of every known sin; though we must confess and bewail particularly, and singly by itself, every sin that we do or may know; yet for sins that we cannot know, a general repentance will be accepted; we may wrap up such unknown sins in gross, as David, Ps. xix. 12. But this consideration that your sins are so infinitely many, that you cannot repent of them in particular, as you should do, must increase your sorrow for, and add to your hatred of, this fruitful monster, and beget resolutions of more watchfulness, &c.

(5.) Though no more be expected for present, than such a general repentance for unknown sins, yet withal there must be a particular repentance in purpose: *i. e.*, there must be an intention, a disposition, a resolution, to repent of every of those now unknown sins, particularly and punctually, when discovered; and where this is, the general implicit repentance will be accepted, as though it were particular; for in this case the Lord accepts the will for the deed, according to that 2 Cor. viii. 12. Where there is this purpose of particular repentance, there is a willing mind to repent particularly.

(6.) A man shall not perish that repents of sins altogether unknown, though he do not reform them. Some acts of repentance will be sufficient for these, though all be necessary for known sins. One may truly mourn for these, though he do not usually forsake them; for a man may bewail unknown sins in general, though he have not a distinct knowledge of them; but he cannot reform them, except he know particularly that they are sins. Sorrow for all sin, known and unknown, is necessary; but there cannot be actual reformation of sins altogether unknown; therefore, instead of actual reformation, a resolution to forsake whatever the Lord shall make known to be a sin, is in this case sufficient. So it was with the holy men before Christ, in reference to polygamy; they repented for all sin in general, and so for this: but they did not reform this, because they did not know it was a sin.

There must be actual reformation of every known sin, else ye perish; but for those which ye cannot know, repenting in general, mourning, confessing, prayer for pardon of all in general, with a stedfast purpose to forsake, reform, whatever shall be discovered to be a sin, will be sufficient.

Quest. Is repentance necessary after first conversion? And how?

Ans. It is necessary in respect of sins before conversion, of sins after, and of that sin which is both before and after, natural corruption.

1. In respect of sins before conversion. That is not denied by any. You may as well deny there is any such thing as repentance, as deny these are to be repented of. Those grant it necessary for these, which deny it for the other.

2. In respect of sin both before and after, natural depravation. I have suggested many grounds why this is to be repented of, and they equally concern all. An abiding sin, so superlatively sinful, is a constant ground of sorrow, hatred, self-abhorrency, and endeavours to be rid of it.

3. In respect of sins after conversion. From the ground formerly expressed, repentance for these is the condition of pardon of these sins; they are not absolutely pardoned till the condition be fulfilled, and so, not till they be repented of.

That it is the condition of pardon as to these sins is evident, because it has all the ingredients that are in any evangelical condition—all that is to be found in anything which the gospel calls a condition. And therefore, if anything in the gospel be a condition, repentance is so in reference to the remission of these sins. It is,

(1.) *Promissioni annexa*, added to the promise of pardon, as a condition, which civilians call *res addita negotio*. Promise of remission runs conditionally, 2 Chron. vii. 14; here is a promise to pardon the sins of

God's people (therefore sins after conversion) upon condition of repentance, 'if they humble themselves and turn.'

(2.) *A promittente postulata.* It is required, commanded by God to his people, after conversion; so a condition, for that is *res postulata*, &c. To waive instances in the Old Testament, as those against which the opposites, though most vainly, except, see how often Christ himself requires it of his people in the Asian churches; of Ephesus, after much commendation of her graces, manifested both in doing and suffering for him, Rev. ii. 4, 5; of Pergamos, for tolerating heretics amongst them, ver. 16; of Sardis, for her imperfections, Rev. iii. 3; of Laodicea, for lukewarmness, ver. 19; yet there he intimates his will that they should repent. Paul required this of the Corinthians, and rejoiceth in their compliance therewith, 2 Cor. vii. 8, 9. All commands of repentance concern such sins; *non est distinguendum ubi lex non distinguit.*

(3.) *Necessaria ad impletionem*, necessary to performance. *Conditio est res sine quâ non.* This appears from the premises. If the Lord would pardon absolutely without it, why does he peremptorily command it to converts? Why adds he this, in form of a condition, to the promises of pardon? Prov. xxviii. 13. This must be extended to sins after conversion, because there is no reason to restrain it.

That it is necessary, appears further thus:

It is a part of regeneration, an infused grace: therefore it does not vanish after its first acts; that is contrary to the promise: nor does it continue idle, unexercised in the habit, till death; for that is contrary to the nature of grace: it will be active, fruitful—active, when there is occasion. Sin, when committed, is an occasion to exercise repentance, or else there can be no occasion for it. Can an instance be given of any other grace, whose exercise is never required, but immediately after its first infusion? Must all graces else be exercised all our lives, repentance only excepted? Who can imagine this without evident ground from Scripture?

That which is not fruitful, active, is not from the Spirit. There may be some intermission, but no total cessation. It may be sometimes winter, but not all the year, all a man's life.

That is no tree of righteousness which brings not forth fruit in its season; no plant of our heavenly Father's planting, but that which must be cut down.

Is it not absurd to make this rod of God blossom upon our first implantation into Christ; and then immediately wither, and continue in the soul as a dead stick, without leaf or fruit, without act or exercise? Does the Lord give a soft heart to continue always, to shew itself only at first conversion? It is too absurd for any rational mind to close with.

Besides, the acts of repentance are necessary, in respect of sins after conversion; therefore repentance itself. It is necessary we should hate, forsake, bewail sins, after conversion; *ergo*, necessary to repent of them.

1. Hatred of those sins is necessary: for if continuance in the state of grace be necessarily required to the continuance of pardon, then hatred of these sins is required to the pardon of them. But the former all grant, and the consequence is clear, because want of hatred to sin, or, which is all one, love to sin, is inconsistent with the state of grace, Ps. lxxix. 10. He that hates not evil, those evils, loves not the Lord; and he that loves not the Lord is not in the state of grace, 1 John iii. 14. with chap. v. 2.

2. Forsaking of those sins is necessary to pardon, for the same reason.

Pardon is not continued, but to those that continue in the state of regeneration; and those that live in sin are not in that state, 1 John iii. 9 and v. 18. As he commits not sin like others, so he continues not committing it as others. Where no forsaking of these sins, no regeneration; and where this is not, there is no pardon; *ergo*, without forsaking these, no pardon.

3. Sorrow for these sins is necessary to pardon: for he that is not sorry for these sins, takes pleasure in them; and he that takes pleasure in sin is in a state of condemnation, therefore not pardoned, 2 Thes. ii. 12. Besides, if it were not necessary, why should the saints afflict themselves with it? Why did Peter weep bitterly? Why David? If they were not necessary, they were works of supererogation.

Quest. Whether must sorrow, required to true repentance, be as great as our sorrow for outward afflictions, loss of relations, estate, liberty, credit, hopes, &c.? If thus much be necessary, I fear I am in an impenitent state, &c. I never felt my heart so sensibly affected, so heavily affected with sin, as with these.

Ans. 1. Not only as much, but more sorrow for sin, is necessary to repentance, than for outward afflictions. He never truly repented, who has not been more grieved for his sins than for his sufferings, Mat. x. 18; Luke xiv. 26, hatred, a less degree of love; he that loves not these less than me, &c. Now sorrow is a sign of love, proportionable to it. He that mourns more for the loss of these than losing, dishonouring Christ, loves these more than Christ. And such are unworthy of Christ, are in a state incapable of any benefit by Christ, an impenitent state. Thus no true repentance, where is not more sorrow for sin, than for any affliction has befallen, or you can imagine may befall. But lest you may mistake it for less, or but equal, when more, observe,

2. There may be a greater sorrow in a soul truly penitent, than sorrow for sin when it is there alone, viz., when sense of affliction and sense of sin both lie upon the soul at once, and the heart is sorrowful for both. This double sorrow may exceed sorrow for sin, when single. When these two streams meet, the tide of sorrow will be higher. Therefore it is no ground to conclude against the truth of repentance, because there has been greater sorrow than sorrow for sin alone; except when both these have seized upon the soul together, sorrow for the affliction has exceeded the sorrow for sin. David mourned both for his sin and the loss of his child at once; there was more sorrow in his soul than if there had been but one occasion of grief: yet his repentance was true, because his sorrow was more for his sin than for the loss of the child. There may be greater sorrow in the soul than sorrow for sin alone; yet sorrow for sin may be the greatest.

3. Sorrow and grief for afflictions may seem greater than sorrow for sin, when it is not really so. It may seem greater, because many times it is more sensible, more passionate, makes greater noise, vents itself more in outward expressions, tears, &c. That sorrow which is most passionate, is not always greatest in God's account. How passionately does David bewail his loss of Absalom! Yet was his sorrow for sin greater, upon a just account, else he had never been approved as a sincere penitent. There may be true repentance, not where grief for sin is less, but where less outward, less sensible, passionate, &c. It may be greater in other respects, more necessary to repentance, more acceptable to God, though less in these respects. Therefore observe,

4. Sorrow for sin may be greater than sorrow for outward sufferings, though it seem not so in many respects.

(1.) *Objectivè*. Because this sorrow for sin has more objects. He mourns for more sins than afflictions; therefore this sorrow is more for sin than for sufferings. He is grieved, sorrowful for all known sins, but these infinitely exceed sensible afflictions in number, and therefore his sorrow for these is greater. If his grief for some particular sin should be exceeded by grief for some special afflictions, yet sorrow for all sins, being so many, will exceed sorrow for sufferings, being so few. But supposing that it is not sufficient to true repentance, that sorrow is in this sense greater for sin, &c., because indeed we should be more grieved for any one sin than for all afflictions; yet with others it will be sufficient to it.

(2.) *Subjectivè*, in respect of the subject. Sorrow for sin takes up more of the soul than sorrow for afflictions, &c. This is a passion, and is principally in the sensitive appetite; but the will and understanding have more influence upon sorrow for sin.

[1.] There is more of the will in grief for sin, &c. *Quoad voluntatem* more; for this is voluntary, that is natural. This is of choice, that seizes upon the heart unavoidably. This is comfortable, that is an affliction, part of the curse. A true penitent would choose this sorrow, rather than freedom from outward affliction.

[2.] Every affection, every act of the will, contributes something to this sorrow for sin, and so makes it more. A penitent desires he could mourn more; wishes his head were waters, and his eyes fountains of tears, &c.; that all sorrow were turned into sorrow for sin; loves a broken heart, and that word which melts it; hates the relics of hardness, counts it the greatest judgment; is ashamed he mourns so little for that which deserves so much; and so is more afraid of a hard insensible heart than of outward affliction; delights in tenderness, when his heart will melt, bleed, &c.; and is sorrowful because sorrow is so small. So it is *quoad affectum* more.

[3.] The understanding makes sorrow for sin more, by several acts.

First, A man judges sin the greatest cause of sorrow; the least sin a better ground, a juster occasion for the greatest sorrow than the sharpest affliction of the least; thinks afflictions a slender ground in comparison of sin.

Secondly, He judges he can never sorrow enough for sin, though too much for afflictions: thinks tears of blood would not be too great an expression of grief for sin; rivers of tears not sufficient.

Thirdly, He judges and censures himself for the defects of this, for the excess of that. Counts it his sin, his misery that he mourns so little for sins, so much for afflictions: so more appropriative. Though sorrow for outward crosses be more passionate, yet if he can find grief for sin greater than it, in respect of will, affections, judgment, according to the tenor of the particulars expressed, no reason to conclude against the truth of repentance, especially if greater.

(3.) *Interpretativè*, in respect of endeavours. He that labours to grieve more in God's gracious interpretation, does grieve more. A true penitent will aggravate his sins to the utmost; will entertain such thoughts and considerations as may humble him, and increase his sorrow for sin; will be importunate with the Lord to take away the heart of stone; will be often looking upon Christ crucified; will be diligent in the use of all means which are appointed to break, humble, affect his heart with sin; endeavour to mitigate his sorrow for afflictions, as that which is unprofitable, dangerous; but to increase sorrow for sin. So it is *quoad conatum* more.

(4.) *Terminativè*, in respect of the termination of his sorrow. When he mourns for afflictions, his sorrow is terminated in sin. He grieves for them, because they are the issues of sin; would not think them worthy of his sorrow, but only because they are the effects of sin. If the effects be so grievous, Oh, what is the cause? If I had never sinned, I had never suffered, therefore I have more reason to grieve for sin. This is the spring, they are but the streams that flow from it. This is that root of bitterness, they but branches. This pulls down God's hand to scourge me, they are but rods. Oh let me not be so foolish as to grieve at the rod, but at that which procured it! He that grieves for afflictions, principally because they come from sin, grieves more for sin than them.

The papists say they do not worship an image so much as God, because they do not terminate their worship in the image; but though this evasion will not excuse them from idolatry, because they should not worship an image at all, yet it is true in this case; he that grieves for afflictions, but terminates his sorrow in sin, grieves more for sin; so that, if when you mourn for crosses, if principally because for sin, and for sin the cause, no reason to conclude against the truth of your repentance.

(5.) *Effectivè*, in respect of the effects. Sorrow for sin in a penitent has this issue, he had rather suffer any affliction than commit the least sin. And this is a sign, an evidence, that sin is more grievous, that his sorrow for it has been greater. He looks upon it as an object more full of sorrow and misery than any suffering. Where sorrow for sin has this effect, there is no reason to conclude that sorrow for affliction has been greater. He that would suffer anything rather than sin in the least, may be assured that he is grieved more for sin than afflictions. Yet this is its effect in true mourners, sincere penitents.

(6.) *Ratione oppositionis*, in respect of the opposition. We find it true in other things, that which seems a little, because much opposed, is really more than what seems much when no opposition. Sorrow for sin is strongly opposed by Satan, the world, sinful nature; it inclines naturally to happiness, and thinks sorrow contrary to it; it loves sin, and will not be brought to mourn for it. But sorrow for affliction has no such opposition. Satan is a friend to it, nature resists it not, for it is natural; and therefore that which may seem no great degree of sorrow for sin, yet if it be sincere, may be accounted greater than passionate grief for afflictions.

(7.) *Habitualiter*, and in respect of continuance. That is the greatest sorrow, which is of longest continuance. What it wants in height of passion and sensibleness is made up in duration, it is permanent. A land-flood fills the banks on a sudden, and more water is visible at that time than all the year; and yet there is more water conveyed there in an ordinary stream, because the current is constant. So sorrow for some unexpected, grievous affliction may make his sorrow rise and swell like a land-flood; yet sorrow for sin, continued in a constant exercise of repentance, is greater than it, though it make not so much noise, because it is of longer continuance, more durable.

Sorrow for affliction is worn out with time, and often quickly over; but sorrow for sin in a true penitent doth never cease, always manifests itself upon occasion.

He that truly mourns for sin will never be comforted in respect of the offence of sin, though is always comforted in respect of the guilt of sin.

He is always grieved when he remembers how his sins have offended, dishonoured God, and so he refuses to be comforted. He need not be sad for the guilt, for the danger of his sin, to which it exposed him, because it is removed; no condemnation in reference to the guilt. The Lord says he sees no iniquity, &c., Num. xxiii. 21. Nor need a penitent any more to see it so as to be afraid, dejected, grieved for the punishment deserved by sin; for he is as safe from that as though he had never sinned, and so may rejoice and be glad in this respect in the midst of his sorrow, be comforted in the midst of his mournings.

But in reference to the offence it is with true penitents as it was with David, Ps. li. 3, his sin ever before him; and whenever it was in his eye, grief was in his heart. Can never consider what injury sin has done to God, but the soul will mourn, the heart grieve. When the Lord has once opened a spring of sorrow in the heart, it is never quite dried up till he come to heaven, if there. So it is more, because it continues longer.

If your sorrow for sin be in these respects greater than for afflictions, it is greater upon all accounts that are necessary, and so no reason to conclude against the truth of repentance.

Quest. Whether may we mourn for sin in reference to those effects of it which concern ourselves? Whether may sin be the object of our sorrow, as it exposes to wrath, makes us miserable, excludes from mercy, brings in danger of hell? Whether do they repent who mourn for sin because of these effects?

Ans. That this may be resolved, we must distinguish the effects of sin that concern us. Some of them concern us only, seem alone prejudicial to us; as that it brings judgments on us, deprives us of outward mercies, exposes us to eternal miseries. Some of them concern both God and us, and so it is injurious to both. Such are its defilement, it makes the soul deformed so as it cannot please God. Impotency makes it unserviceable, so as it cannot obey God; contrariety sets the soul in opposition to God, contrary to his nature, will, designs, so as it cannot honour him; nothing but dishonour, displease, and disobey him.

This premised, take the resolution in four propositions.

1. We may mourn for sin in respect of those effects that concern us only. That sorrow is not unlawful in itself which has these for its objects. It is lawful to mourn for things less grievous, for outward temporal afflictions, such as are common to all. The Scripture forbids not this sorrow, but only limits it; bids us mourn moderately, as not without hope, &c. The Lord requires not we should be stocks, without sense of sufferings, 'without natural affections.' No; ἀστόργοι are reckoned amongst the greatest of sinners, Rom. i. 31. Now, if we may mourn for smaller evils, much more for greater; if for those of this life, then for those that concern eternity; if for bodily afflictions, then for soul judgments; if for loss of estate, friends, then for loss of God, of happiness. It is not unlawful.

2. This kind of sorrow, if only or principally for these effects, is no act of saving repentance. It is rather, if alone, 'the sorrow of the world, which worketh death.' It is not that which worketh repentance unto salvation. The cause of such sorrow may be, and is, self-love, not love to God; the issue may be death, the companion despair; the subject may be a reprobate. Such was the sorrow of Cain, Judas, Ahab, Esau. It is true the Lord often works such sorrow in vessels of mercy before he bestows grace, and therefore it is called by many a preparation for grace; and so it may be called in some sense; but so understand it as that it has

no necessary connection with grace. He that goes no further, as divers do not, shall never arrive at grace. He who sorrows no otherwise for sin, does not 'sorrow after a godly sort,' does not 'sorrow unto repentance,' 2 Cor. 7.

3. Sorrow for sin, in reference to those effects which concern both God and us, is not only lawful, but necessary. It is an act of true repentance to mourn for those sad issues of sin; to bewail sin, because it has made us deformed, impotent, contrary to God. David, when he repented, was affected with the defilement of sin; he was humbled, mourned for sin, in this respect. Hence it is his prayer: Ps. li. 7, 'Purge me,' &c., 'wash me.' Paul bewails his impotency, Rom. vii. 18, 19; and ascribes it to sin dwelling in him, ver. 20; and in sense of both cries out, ver. 24. Such sorrow, since it is for sin, not only as it is prejudicial to the sinner, but principally and ultimately as it is injurious to God, is, and should be, accounted godly sorrow.

4. Sorrow for sin, the more it is for sin as it is against God, the more ingenuous, the more evangelical, the more genuine act of saving repentance. The more it is for sin, as sin is prejudicial to us, the less ingenuous, &c.; and a less evident, a less comfortable, sign of repentance unto life. There are two sure characters of ingenuous, gospel sorrow: when it proceeds from sense of God's love to us, *non potest agere pœnitentiam, qui non sperat indulgentiam;* and when it proceeds from our love to God, when we mourn for offending him, because we love him. Now, these are not, or not so visible, in any sorrow for sin as that which mourns for sin as it is against God. The other springs rather from self-love, when we bewail sin because it is against us, hurtful, dangerous, damnable, Ezek. vi. 9. This was not the temper of David's sorrow, it was of a more evangelical strain: Ps. li. 4, 'Against thee,' &c. Why, David had sinned against himself, not only against God. He had sinned against his friend, against his own body, soul, estate, family, and involved all these in great dangers, exposed all to grievous sufferings. It is true David knew it, but he takes no notice of that. That which grieved, affected him was, that his sin was against God; and his sorrow so much respects this, as though he had sinned against God alone, as though his sin had been only injurious to him. This is the genuine temper of godly sorrow.

Therefore, though sorrow for the effects of sin may have its place elsewhere, yet when we would sorrow to repentance, we should look at the nature of sin, not at its effects (except such as concern God only, or him principally, him more than us); sin, in its nature, is more against God than in its effects. For the effects of sin are not directly against God, but when one sin is the effect of another.

That is most properly godly sorrow, which is for sin as it is against God. But sin in its nature is most against God, a violation of his law, disobeying his will, contempt of his authority, &c. That sorrow which arises from the consideration of the nature of sin, is most ingenuous, and the most certain evidence of sincere repentance.

Quest. Whether the hatred of sin, which is required to true repentance, may consist with any love to sin?

Ans. 1. All hatred of sin is here imperfect. No perfection in this life, but sense of imperfection. Both graces, and gracious affections, want many degrees of perfection. Grace is but of a child's stature, it has perfection of parts, but not of degrees. A child has all the parts of a perfect man, but wants many degrees of man's perfection. And as with grace, so with this affection; it is not perfect, either *ratione objecti;* sin is not hated as it should be according to its hatefulness; nor *ratione facultatis,* so much as it is possible for the heart to hate it; not raised to such high degrees of hatred, as it may be will be.

Ans. 2. A less degree of hatred may be called love. He that hates sin less than he should do, may be said in some sense to love it. A less degree of love is called hatred, Luke xiv. 26. And so a less degree of hatred may be called love, though not properly and strictly. For that imperfect hatred should be called love, as it is not according to the ordinary rules of art, so it is not according to the constant tenor of Scripture expressions. I remember no place but this to ground it, and this but by consequence.

Ans. 3. He that truly hates sin, though but imperfectly, cannot be properly said to love it. He that hates all sin, and hates it above all that the world counts hateful, and abhors himself that he can hate it no more, and mourns for the imperfection of his hatred, and strives in the use of appointed means to perfect it, does truly hate it.

In the same subject there cannot be contrary affections to the same object. We count it impossible to love and hate the same thing or person. In immediate contraries, *positio unius* is *sublatio alterius.* He that hates does not love, &c. It is as impossible, as for the same thing to be both black and white; the same water to be at once both hot and cold. It may be neither, but it cannot be both; if one, not the other. So here, and though hatred be but in us in a remiss degree, imperfectly, and it may be supposed the imperfection arises from the mixture of the contrary affection, yet that which is predominant gives the denomination. He that hates sin more than he loves it, may be said simply absolutely to hate it. We say not water is cold if it be hot above lukewarmness, though it be not hot in the utmost extremity. We say not that he loves sin who hates it truly, though not perfectly. If he be overpowered to act it, surprised with some pleasure in it, this argues not love. For he abhors himself acting, mourns bitterly for delight in it, as Paul, Rom. vii.

Ans. 4. He that truly repents, does truly hate sin; so hate it, as he gives no occasion, upon any just ground, to say he loves it. And by consequence true repentance is inconsistent with love to sin, it may be without perfect hatred, but it cannot be with any degree of that which may be properly called love, &c.

Quest. Whether must we repent of original sin?

That this may be more clearly propounded and resolved, observe a distinction, the non-observance of which occasions much darkness, both in men's apprehensions and discourses of this subject.

Original sin is, 1. Imputed, 2. Inherent.

1. *Imputed,* is Adam's sin, that which he actually committed in eating the forbidden fruit. Called original, because it was the first sin, and committed at the beginning of the world, when the first foundations of man's original were laid. Imputed, because Adam representing us and all mankind, what he did, we did in God's account, he looks upon us as sinning by him, Rom. v. 19, 20.

2. *Inherent,* is that natural corruption which cleaves to us, dwells in us, consisting in the privation of original righteousness, and propensity to all unrighteousness; the sad issue and effect of the former sin. Adam receiving this original holiness for himself and his posterity, lost it for himself and them; and holiness being gone, a proneness to all sin necessarily

followed. It is called *sin*, because it is a state opposite to the will and law of God; the absence of that which it requires, the presence of that which it forbids. *Original*, because we have it from our birth, from our original. *Inherent*, because it is not only accounted ours, but is really in us. Of this Gen. vi. 5, and viii. 21, Job iv. 5, Ps. li. 7.

Quest. Whether must we repent of Adam's sin, that which is but imputed to us, that which was committed so many years before we were born?

Ans. This must be repented of with such acts of repentance as it is capable of, confessed, bewailed, hated. As to avoiding, forsaking of it, we need not be solicitous, because there is no danger it should be recommitted. But we must acknowledge, aggravate, mourn for it, abhor it, hate the memory of it. So I conceive (though I meet not with any that determine this), on this ground.

1. We are bound to repent and mourn for the sins of others, much more for those that are any ways our own. This *à fortiori*. This has been the practice of holy men formerly: David, Ps. cxix. 158, so Jer. xiii. 17. Sins of fathers, Jer. xiv. 10, many hundred years committed before. It is prophesied of the Jews, that when the Lord shall convert them, they shall mourn for the sin of their forefathers who pierced him; so Dan. ix.; and Moses's ordinary practice. If repentance prevent judgment, then it might prevent those that are inflicted for sins of others, progenitors. The Lord often punishes for their sins; if we would not suffer for them, we should repent of them. And if of others' sins, then of that which is ours; and this is ours by imputation. And justly is it imputed to us. For by all human laws, children are charged with their fathers' debts, the father's treason taints his posterity.

2. We are bound to rejoice in imputed righteousness, and therefore to mourn for imputed sin. Adam's sin is ours, the same way as Christ's righteousness, viz., by imputation, Rom. v. 19, and *contrariorum contraria sunt consequentia*. If we must rejoice in Christ's righteousness, we should bewail Adam's sin. And indeed great cause of joy in that it is the marrow, the quintessence of the gospel; the most gladsome part of those εὐαγγέλια, those glad tidings which are published in the gospel; the sweetest strain of that message, which, the angel says, was 'good tidings of great joy to all people,' Luke ii. 10. Imputed righteousness is that blessed design which the Father from eternity contrived, which Christ published and performed, into which the angels desire to pry, that lost man, who could not be saved without righteousness, who had no righteousness of his own to save him, should have a righteousness provided for him, whereby he is freed from wrath, and entitled to heaven. Sure this is, this will be, an occasion of eternal joy; and if so, imputed sin is a just ground of sorrow.

3. As long as the Lord manifests his displeasure against any sin, so long we are called to mourn for it The Lord is highly provoked, if, when his hand is stretched out against any place or person for sin, they will not see it, so as to repent of it, and be humbled under it. He interprets this to be a contempt, and this highly exasperates. It has been the practice of holy men, when wrath was either executed, or threatened, to mourn for the sins that occasioned it, though committed by others, and long before. See it in Josiah, 2 Chron. xxxiv. 31. There he takes notice of forefathers' sins; and see how he is affected therewith: ver. 27, 'his heart was tender, he humbled himself.'

We are called to mourn for sin, whenever wrath is manifested against it; but the wrath of God is still revealed from heaven against that first unrighteousness; his displeasure is still legible in the effects of this sin, the dreadfullest effects that ever any act produced, no less than all sin, and all misery. That threatening, Gen. ii. 17, is still in execution, and the execution is terrible; every stroke is death, spiritual, personal, temporal, eternal, take it in the most extensive sense. Adam's soul was struck dead immediately; and by virtue of that sentence, all his posterity are dead men, born dead in trespasses and sins. Personal death, death of afflictions; all the sorrows and sufferings of this woeful life, they flow from this cursed spring. Temporal, in Adam all died; it he had not sinned, all had been immortal. Eternal, all must die for ever that repent not. Great cause then to repent of this sin.

Quest. Whether must we repent of that original sin, which is inherent; that natural corruption, the loss of original holiness; and that innate propensity to evil? It may seem not to be any just occasion of sorrow, because it is not voluntary, but natural; having, without our consent, seized upon us unavoidably.

Ans. This is principally to be repented of, as that which is the mother sin, the cause of all actual sins. Nor should the supposed involuntariness of it hinder us from making it the object of our sorrow.

For, 1, every sin is to be repented of. But this is a sin exceeding sinful, indeed, all sins in one. For, what is sin, who can better determine than the Lord himself? And he in Scripture determines, that whatever is a transgression of the law is sin, whether it be voluntary or no; not only that which we actually consent to, but that which he peremptorily forbids. The apostle's definition of sin is unquestionable, 1 John iii. 4, ἁμαρτία ἐστὶν ἡ ἀνομία; but no greater transgression than this, since it transgresses all at once. We are commanded to be holy; so the want of holiness is forbidden, which is the privative part of this sin. We are commanded to love the Lord with all our hearts; so the heart's inclination to hate God is forbidden, which is the positive part. Was not the apostle Paul more able to judge what is sin, than any papist, Socinian, &c.? He calls it sin five times, Rom. vi., six times, Rom. vii., three times, Rom. viii., yea and *his* sin, though he then consented not to it.

2. Suppose (that which is false) no evil is to be repented of, but what is consented to, this should not hinder any from repenting of this sin; for all that are capable of repentance have actually consented to their natural corruption, have been pleased with it, have cherished it by occasions of sin, have strengthened it by acts of sin, have resisted the means whereby it should be mortified and subdued, which are all infallible evidences of actual consent. That which was only natural, is to us become voluntary; and so, by consent of all, sinful; and therefore necessarily to be repented of.

3. The necessity of it is grounded upon unquestionable examples of saints, both in the Old and New Testament. Instance in two of the holiest men that the Scripture mentions. David, in that psalm, which is left as a public testimony of his repentance, to the world, he bewails, acknowledges this, Ps. li. 5. Paul does acknowledge, aggravate, bewail it, as one heavily afflicted with it, Rom. vii. His description of it is very observable: as that which is *not good*, ver. 18; *in me, i.e.*, in the unregenerate part, that which is not good, that which is evil, ver. 20, sin, six times; the greatest evil, a condemned forbidden evil, ver. 7; a sinful evil, ver. 13, καθ' ὑπερβολὴν ἁμαρτωλός; a private evil, ver. 20, hinders him from doing good; a positive evil, ver. 17, *no more I that do it, but sin;* perverse evil, grows worse by that which should make it better, ver. 8; debasing evil,

made and denominates him carnal, ver. 14; intimate, inherent evil, sin in him, ver. 17, in his members; a permanent evil, οἰκοῦσα ἐν ἐμοί, ver. 17; a fruitful evil, ver. 8, all manner of lust; a deceitful evil, ver. 11, ἐξηπάτησέ; an imperious evil, a law, ver. 23, gives law, commands as by authority; a tyrannical evil, αἰχμαλωτίζοντά, ver. 23; sold, ver. 14; a rebellious conflicting, war-like evil, ἀντιστρατευόμενον, ver. 23; an importunate, unreasonable evil, ver. 15, forces him to do that which he hates; a watchful evil, ver. 21, is present, παράκειται; a powerful evil, ver. 24, 'who shall deliver?' &c.; a complete evil, ver. 24, a body furnished with all members of unrighteousness; a deadly evil, ver. 24, body of death, θανατώδης, ver. 11; slew me, ver. 9, I died; a miserable evil, ver. 24, above all things made him wretched.

Paul suffered as many calamities in the world, as any we read of in it; see a catalogue, 2 Cor. xi. 23–28. But all these sufferings could never extort such a passonate complaint from him, as this corruption. He could glory in those; but sighs, complains, exclaims, in the sense of this. You see how large he is in aggravating this. Here is above twenty aggravations of this. His sorrow was proportionable. No sin, no suffering, for which he expressed so much soul-affliction. And if he saw so much reason to bewail it, it is our blindness if we see it not. The more holy any man is, the more sensible of natural corruption. The more they get out of this corrupt element, the more heavy it is. Those who feel it not, are drowned in it. *Elementum non gravitat in proprio loco.* Sin is their proper element, who are not burdened with natural sinfulness.

If it was such an intolerable evil in him who was regenerate, how much more in the unregenerate! If it made him account himself wretched who was so happy, how much more miserable does it make those who have no title to happiness! If it was such an impetuous evil in him who had extraordinary powers of grace to weaken it, how prevailing in us, in whom grace is so weak! If he had cause to complain, bewail, repent of it, much more we!

Quest. Who are impenitent sinners? How shall we know them? How may I discern whether I be in that number, in that danger?

Ans. I shall propound several things whereby ye may know this.

1. He is an impenitent sinner, who does not leave sin at all. Repentance is a turning from sin; he that doth not turn from it at all, does not repent at all. He who lives in sin, does so act it, as he makes it evident that he is a worker of iniquity; does not only ἁμαρτάνειν, as a true penitent may do, sin sometimes by surprisal, without deliberation, full consent, unwillingly, &c., but ποιεῖν ἁμαρτίαν, sins constantly, when he has occasion, as though sin were his trade; is constant in sinning; not that he is always acting it visibly, but that he always acts it, seldom forbears when he is tempted; will swear when provoked, be drunk when he meets with company, profane the Sabbath when he has business, though not necessary, disobey the word when it doth not please, revenge injuries when he has opportunity, lie when advantage, deceive when unperceived. When the chief reason why he sins not is because he wants occasion, temptation, opportunity, he is impenitent. He who acts sin in every scene of his life,—in his particular calling, is covetous or careless, negligent of God, to think of, depend on him; in his general calling, frequent omissions, or heartless performances; in his family, ignorance or profaneness, not instruct, not pray for and with them; to neighbours, envious, contentious; in discourse, profane or graceless; in dealings, deceitful, disingenuous; when some sin

reigns in every part of his conversation,—if thus, it is clear as the day, if there be any light in the Scripture, he is impenitent.

2. He that leaves not all sin. Repentance is a turning from all sin. He that turns not from all does not at all repent. Where true repentance is, there is an equal respect to all commands. Leaving off sin must be like the Israelites' departure from Egypt, there must not a hoof be left behind, Exod. x. 26, the least sin must not be retained, reserved. That is hypocritical repentance, which, like Saul's obedience, kills only the vile and refuse. It is not enough to reform one part of your conversation, to make clean one corner; the whole will be reformed where true repentance is. If carriage to others be reformed, it is well, but not sufficient, except thou amend thy deportment to God. It may be thou wilt not be drunk, but if thou swear, that is enough to shew thee impenitent. It may be not swear, but profane the Sabbath, &c., it may be attend the ordinances; well, but if not obey, if not pray with heart; if conform to public worship, it is well; but if serve him not in family; it may be left many sins that formerly reigned; but if there be any thou thinkest too pleasing, too profitable to part with, thou art not a true penitent. Turn from all, Ezek. xviii. 21.

3. He that leaves sin only outwardly, excludes it out of his conversation, not out of his heart. Repentance is a turning with all the heart, Joel ii. 12; it is not only a turning from all sin, but a turning of all the man, the whole man, inward and outward, from all sin. He that abstains from all sin outwardly and visibly may pass for a penitent with men, but it is not so in God's account, unless sin be turned out of the heart as well as out of the life. Man judgeth according to outward appearance, but the Lord judgeth of repentance by the heart. There is no true repentance where the life is not reformed; but there may be an unblameable conversation, a life outwardly reformed, where there is no true repentance. Paul professes that he had lived in all good conscience, &c., until that day, Acts xxiii. 1; and therefore, since he lived so all his life till that day, he lived so before he repented, unblameably, in good conscience outwardly before God, in the account of others, and in his own account; he lived so before he had truly repented, as neither others nor his own conscience could accuse him for outward sinful acts, Philip. iii. Therefore abstinence from sin outwardly is not sufficient. If sin be regarded in the heart, there is no true repentance though the life be freed from it. Men judge of the heart by the life, but God judges of the life by the heart. He hears every prayer of a penitent soul, Isa. lvii. 15; yet David says, Ps. lxvi. 18, 'If I regard iniquity in my heart, the Lord will not hear me.' Whatever his life was, God would not respect, regard him as a penitent, if he did regard it in his heart. If ye do not break out into gross acts of sin, yet if your hearts entertain them, if you act uncleanness, revenge, covetousness in your thoughts, you are in a state of impenitency.

4. He that leaves sin because he cannot commit it. Repentance is a voluntary forsaking of sin; but sin rather forsakes him than he it. He that is not unclean, because his strength is spent; is not contentious, because he wants means to prosecute suits; wrongs not his neighbours, because he sees them wise to prevent, or able to hinder him; gives not himself to drunkenness, voluptuousness, because not rich enough to maintain himself in such intemperate courses. The heart may be most desperately hard and impenitent, and yet may these abstain from sin; nay, there is such a forsaking of, and abstinence from sin in the devil himself, he can forbear when he cannot help, when there is necessity.

He that sins not because he cannot would sin if he could; and because he would sin, it argues him as much impenitent as if he did. He that rewards the will for the deed in that which is good, condemns and will punish the will for the deed in that which is evil.

5. He that leaves sin only out of sinister respects, by-ends, because it would deprive him of some advantage, or expose him to some loss, if committed, of friends, credit, profit, in respect of God or men; gives not himself to intemperance, because it is expensive; to uncleanness, because it is a sin shameful in the account of the world; avoids oppression, revenge, because civil laws lay penalties; wholly omits not ordinances, lest he should be accounted an atheist; he that leaves sin only thus does not repent; for true repentance is 'repentance toward God,' Acts xx. 21. It makes a man forsake sin out of respect to God, because it offends, dishonours him, as Joseph, Gen. xxxix. 9; but this is to abstain from sin out of respect to himself.

6. He that leaves one sin for another; divorces one and engages himself to another; puts away one, and entertains another in the room of it; will not be prodigal as formerly, but grows more covetous; will not be superstitious, but grows profane; not omit duties, but is hypocritical in performance; runs away from one extreme to another; such a reformation is no act of repentance. It is but like Jehu's, 2 Kings x., who destroyed Ahab's Baal, but set up Jeroboam's calves, ver. 29; this is not a turning from, but unto sin; as the Pharisees, casting out devils by Beelzebub, one cast out another.

7. He that leaves sin but for a time; leaves sin, and resolves to leave it while some judgment lies upon him, whilst under affliction, when upon a bed of languishing, in fear of death, apprehensive of hell and the last judgment. This, in discourse, could make Felix tremble, and almost persuade Agrippa. Many at such times will resolve to abandon such and such sins, and to reform their lives if God will prolong them; but when God's hand is removed, they prove the same men, by following their former courses. When life is restored, hopes of life revive, they return with the dog to their vomit, &c. This is not to repent, but to mock God, and delude your souls; this is not to escape out of the snare of the devil, but to ensnare your soul ten times more. Ephraim in affliction would seek God, but after-revolts made their case desperate, Hosea vi. 4.

True repentance is never repented of. But those that return to sin hereby shew they are sorry, repent of their shows of repentance, Hosea vii. 16. This is returning, but not to the most High. Such are like a deceitful bow, break, or return to their unbent posture before they have delivered the arrow; unbend their resolutions before they come effectual. God looks upon such as guilty of impenitency in a high degree; such as are so far from repenting of sin heartily, as they are sorry they entertained any thoughts of it; for this is the language of after-returns. This was Pharaoh's repentance; while the judgment of locusts was on Egypt, he confesses his sin and desires pardon, Exod. x. 16, 17, but the locusts and his repentance vanish both together.

8. He that leaves sin, but does not endeavour to subdue it, will be content it should be confined, but not crucified; restrained, but not put to death; will have the fury and rage of it curbed, that it do not break out so openly, but will not starve it; kept under, not rooted out. He that will not avoid the occasions of sin, those that nourish it, have drawn him on to act sin formerly. He that truly repents of drunkenness will avoid that

company which has tempted him to it. He that repents of uncleanness, will, as Job, make a covenant with his eyes. He that repents of profaneness in words, will set a watch before his mouth. He that repents of Sabbath breaking, will so dispose of his affairs before, as he may have no occasion to profane it, to absent himself from the public worship. He that repents of wanderings in prayer, will be watchful against distractions, drive them away. He that turns not from occasions turns not from sin, and so is no true penitent. He that is not diligent in the use of mortifying duties to weaken sin, will not apply that word to his conscience which wounds his sin; casts off searching words, words of reproof and terror, as too sharp, painful corroding plasters for his sore; rather be exasperated against him that speaks them, as one that rails, is too strict.

He, the strength of whose prayers is not against the strength of sin, can pray affectionately for worldly blessings, removal of afflictions, and it may be for pardon of sin, but wants heart, feels an ebb, a coolness in his affectionateness, when he should pray against the strength of sin, either leaves this out of his prayer, or his heart leaves his prayer when he should desire this; can be content to set apart days for private fasts, when some judgment is near or upon him, but never looks upon the power of sin within him as a sufficient, a necessary occasion to humble himself before God by extraordinary mourning and fasting. When such means are not used constantly, as are appointed by God in ordinary for subduing of sin, and extraordinary too, when there is occasion,—a dangerous sign of impenitency.

The heathens, many of them, went far in a way of outward reformation, but came short of repentance, because they endeavoured not the destruction of the inward power of sin.

Without this there is no true repentance; for that is a turning from sin wholly, with the whole heart, not only in respect of sin in its guilt and outward acts, but power and dominion. There is an ἐκδίκησις, which is the companion of repentance, 2 Cor. vii.

9. He that so turns from sin as he does not turn to God. This motion cannot be perfect without its *terminus ad quem*. If it be not essential to, it is inseparable from repentance, Isa. lv. 7. So forsake sin, as embrace Christ; so hate sin, as love holiness; so grieve for it as delight in God's ways; steer the conversation to a quite contrary point. Not only cease to do evil, but learn to do good, Isa. i. 16, 17. It is not sufficient not to profane God's name; he that repents will glorify it; not only not omit holy duties, but perform them in a holy manner; not only not pollute the Sabbath, but sanctify it; not only not dishonour profession, but adorn it; not only abstain from sin, but exercise grace. There are fruits of repentance which John requires, Mat. iii. 8, and Luke iii. 8. That repentance which brings not forth fruit is not sound, no plant of God's planting; the doom of it you may see, ver. 9.

Would you think it a sufficient evidence of a good vine, that it brings forth no wild grapes? No; if it be an empty vine, though it have no bad, if it bring not forth good grapes, it is good for nothing. Negative righteousness will never evidence true repentance. It is not enough to say with the Pharisee, Luke xviii. 11, 'I am not as other men,' &c.

The apostle joins these, repent, turn to God, do works, &c., Acts xxvi. 20. Those that would approve themselves clear in this matter, who would give clear evidences to the world and their own consciences that their repentance is to salvation, and that they sorrow after a godly sort, must produce all the effects of repentance which he inquires after, 2 Cor. vii. 11; not only indignation against sin, clearing themselves from vice, but carefulness to express the contrary virtues; not only fear of offending God, but vehement desire to please and honour him; not only revenge for dishonouring God by wicked courses, but zeal for his glory in all the ways of holiness. A fruitless repentance is rejected.

10. He that never had a full, clear discovery of sin. Repentance begins here. The first step is illumination; the Lord causes a light to shine in the soul to discover the hidden things of darkness, sends the Spirit to convince of sin, makes him believe those acts, &c., to be sins which he accounted innocent.

Discovers sin in its number, multitude of abominations; carries him, as the Spirit carried Ezekiel, from one part of his life, from one corner of his soul to another, and still shews him greater and greater abominations, brings those sins to his remembrance which it may be he never thought of since they were committed. Though the work begin at some master sin, and the heart may be affected with one more than the rest, yet it is sensible of all, each adds something to increase sorrow.

In *weight*. Makes him feel the burden of sin, shews how they are gone over his head, Ps. xxxviii. 4.

In the *aggravations*. Such a sin against mercy, under affliction, after conviction, reproof, when conscience checked, &c.

In the *effects*, what it has done, and what exposed to.

In the *evil* of it. The sinfulness of it. More evil in it than ever he imagined, than ever he thought he could have believed; more evil in it than in anything he ever acted or suffered.

There must be first knowledge of it before repentance. How can ye repent of that ye never knew? When God gives repentance he first 'opens the eyes,' Acts xxvi. 18, 'turns from darkness to light.' As a man who has walked through a way in the dark, full of serpents, snares, pits, when he passes through it again with a light, and sees his danger, he wonders that every step was not his death. He that wondered before that any should make so much ado about sin, that so much sorrow, so much mourning should be pressed; he that was apt to think that they were hypocrites, who talked of their humiliation, tears, and secret mourning for sin, to imagine that whatever was pretended, there was no such thing in reality, will now change his opinions; sees so much evil in sin as he can never sufficiently bewail; wishes he could command back all that sorrow which he has misspent upon his sufferings in the world, that he might spend it upon sin as that which most deserves it; thinks all his time little enough, his constitution cannot afford tears enough to bewail it; so many, so sinful enormities, he wonders that any sin should be counted small, πολὺ ἁμάρτημα, &c.

11. He that has not some sense of the corruption of his nature. He that repents, bewails actual sins, and he that sees and feels the evil of the members, will have some sense of the body. He that tastes bitterness in the fruits, will disrelish the root of bitterness. Those who are persuaded their natures are good, will be angry at any that shall tell them they have wicked, perverse, naughty natures; never saw cause to complain, as David, of their birth-sin; nor to cry out with Paul, 'O wretched man!' Those that think themselves innocent enough, but for some outward gross acts, find no other reason why God should be displeased with them, why they should be excluded from heaven or communion with God; take no notice

of inward averseness to God, proneness to evil, so as to make it an occasion of sorrow, humiliation, self-abhorrency; are apt to excuse sinful acts from their natures. Where there is not in some degree a sense of inbred corruption, there the heart is hard, impenitent.

12. He that is loath his sin should be discovered. A penitent is thankful to those that will convince him of any sinful practice. He desires the Lord to search him if any way of wickedness. It is his petition to God: Job xxxiv. 32, 'That which I see not, teach thou me; if I have done iniquity,' &c. He would not hide his sins from God; he knows this is opposed to repentance, Prov. xxviii. 13; nor would have the Lord hide his sins from him. As he would have the Lord discover them, so he is not unwilling men should manifest them. He that repents looks upon sin as a close traitor; and who would not be glad to have a close traitor discovered? If an enemy lance the imposthume of his heart, whatever be the intention of the actor, he will be glad at the event of the act. He that would have sin hid, is in love with it. He that is unwilling to have sin detected in any practice, delights in it. None hide wickedness under their tongue, but those in whose mouth it is sweet, Job xx. 12, 13, he would spare it. He counts them his best friends who will discover such a dangerous enemy. How thankful was Saul to the Ziphites for a discovery of a supposed enemy? 1 Sam. xxiii. 21. He will be as thankful for discovering sin, as David was to Abigail for preventing sin, 1 Sam. xxv. 32. He will be so far from taking this for an occasion of enmity, as he will make this a motive to friendship, and consult with the discoverer how he may destroy that which is discovered.

It is a sign he has no mind to turn to God, who will not endure to be told when he is out of the way.

13. He that will not endure a reproof. Those that cannot abide their sins should be reproved, either by public ministry or private, will be ready to 'lay a snare for him that reproveth,' Isa. xxix. 21, and count him their enemy who tells them of sin, though he tell the truth, as Paul complains. Be ready to do him a mischief, as wicked Ahab did Micaiah, 2 Chron. xviii. 25. Whatsoever Joash was, the Holy Ghost leaves an eternal brand upon him for his severity against Zechariah reproving his sin, 2 Chron. xxiv. 22. Those who break out into reproaches against those that reprove them, say as those against Jeremiah, chap. xviii. 18; or if they break not out into acts, words, yet boil inwardly with rancour and malice. Those who, instead of reforming the sin reproved, fall upon an inquiry after the failings of the reprover, that they may retaliate. Hatred of reproof is a sign of a scorner, Prov. ix. 7, 8; and scorners are placed in the highest rank of sinners, Ps. i. Those are furthest from repentance. Hatred of reproof and repentance are two such contraries as can never meet in the same subject; quite contrary things are ascribed to them. Repentance leads to life, this to death, Prov. xv. 10. That is to salvation, this to destruction, Prov. xxix. 1. You may as well say the same man shall both go to heaven and hell, as say that man is a penitent who hates reproof. You may know the temper of a humbled soul in David, Ps. cxli. 5. He is in love with sin who will not endure reproof, says to ministers, as David to Joab concerning Absalom, 2 Sam. xviii. 51, 'Deal gently for my sake,' &c. He that hates it will have it roughly handled, will penitently bear all the evil that can be spoke against it; and not only against sin in general, but against his sin. That word pleases him best which represents it most hateful, most dangerous. He desires not the ministers should speak soft

and pleasing things, to flatter him in his evil ways, but welcomes reproof for sin, though they be like the words of David's enemies, sharp as swords; the sharper the better, the more healthful. He would not have this dangerous sore skinned over, before it be thoroughly searched. He knows reproofs for sin, how sharp soever, are 'the reproofs of life,' Prov. xv. 31, 32.

Use 1. Terror to impenitent sinners. Hear the doom in the text: 'Except ye repent,' &c. Those that do not, will not repent, must perish, shall perish. There is no way without repentance to avoid perishing, and these will not repent, mourn, hate, forsake sin. What will become of them? Christ, the righteous judge, gives sentence, they shall perish, certainly, universally, eternally.

1. *Certainly*. For Christ has said it. He speaks peremptorily; not they *may*, but they *shall*. Here is as much assurance that they shall perish, as any saint ever had that he should be saved—the word of Christ. It is as certain as if one from the dead should affirm it; and Dives desired, though an unbeliever, no more certainty. It is more certain than if an angel from heaven should speak it; for, behold, one greater than the angels, higher than the heavens, has said it. As sure as Christ is true, as sure as Christ is God, if there be any truth in truth itself, then this is certainly true, those that repent not shall perish. *Si Christus loquatur*, &c.

2. *Universally*. All, and every one, without exception, whatever he be, have, do, or can do, 'Except,' &c. Christ speaks to the Jews, and to all without exception—all perish. If any people in the world had any ground to plead exemption, sure it was the Jews; no people ever in greater favour, none ever had greater privileges. Whatever you can plead why this should not concern you, they had as much ground to plead.

Are you outwardly in covenant with God? So were they; to them belonged the promises: Rom. ix. 4, 'To whom pertain the covenants and promises.'

Do ye profess yourselves to be the children of God? So might they; to them pertained 'the adoption,' a peculiar people.

Do ye enjoy those inestimable pledges of his favour, the gospel and ordinances? So did they; 'to them were committed the oracles of God,' Rom. iii. 2.

Are you baptized, sealed to be his? So were they circumcised, received circumcision, &c., Rom. iv.

Has the Lord vouchsafed you such privileges as no people under heaven enjoy besides; so did he to them, Ps. cxlvii. 19, 20; but all these would not secure them from perishing without repentance. Even them Christ tells, 'Except ye repent,' &c. No more will they secure you; except you repent, you shall perish; all, every of you.

Nay, these are so far from exempting you from repentance, as these should lead you to it. The impenitent heathen, that never knew God, shall more easily escape than you. 'Except you repent, you shall perish.'

3. *Eternally*. Soul and body, here and hereafter, now and for ever, must perish without redemption: For who shall redeem from it but Christ? and Christ cannot do it except he will act against his own word, except he will deny himself. The sentence is passed, and none in heaven will, none in earth can, recall it. Men and devils cannot; angels and saints dare not; God himself will not. This sentence is like the decrees of the Medes and Persians, that can never be recalled. Christ has pronounced it, and he will not fail to be as good as his word, except his power fail. Nothing shall save impenitent sinners from perishing eternally, if Christ have power

to punish them with everlasting destruction. And is not Christ able to destroy you? Why, all power is given to him, Mat. xxviii. 18; power to save and power to destroy. And how he will exercise this power he here tells us; viz., by saving eternally those that repent, and by the eternal destruction of the impenitent: 'He that has the keys of hell and death,' Rev. i. 8; Rev. iii. 7, 'shutteth, and no man openeth.' That which Christ has here spoke with his mouth, he will at the last day execute with his hand; he will thrust impenitent sinners into hell, and lock them there for ever: for when he shuts, no man, no angel, no, God himself will not open. What his hand doth, none will undo for ever, and he will do what he has spoken; and that which he speaks is plainly this, impenitents shall perish eternally. It cannot be meant of temporal ruin only (though that also be included) for divers of the Jews to whom he spoke (as we may presume) did not perish, like those Galileans, temporally; therefore either eternally, or else not at all, which cannot be if Christ be true. Perish eternally; eternal torments is the proper portion of such, it is only theirs. Who are those that must 'suffer the vengeance of eternal fire,' but those who have been 'treasuring up wrath'? &c., Rom. ii. And who are they but impenitent sinners? Who is he that must be 'cast into outer darkness,' &c., but the 'unprofitable servant'? Mat. xxv. 30. And who more unprofitable than he who will neither do his Master's will, nor shew himself truly sorry for not doing it? And who is this but an impenitent sinner? Who are they that must 'depart into everlasting fire'? &c. Christ tells, Matt. xxv. 41, 'ye cursed;' and who are these but impenitent sinners? Other sinners are cursed by the law, but these are cursed both by law and gospel; and this is it which makes their misery eternal. He whom the gospel curses can never be blessed. If the law only cursed, if God only, there might be hopes in the gospel, in Christ; but he whom Christ curses shall be eternally cursed. But Christ curses the impenitent, therefore they shall perish eternally.

Use 2. Exhortation 1. To the practice of this duty.

Christ urges it, and under such a penalty. These should be sufficient enforcements. But there are many more considerations to stir up to this duty. I shall reduce them to three heads; some concerning, 1. Sin to be repented of; 2. Christ that urges repentance; 3. Repentance itself, the duty urged. 1. Concerning sin.

(1.) No creature ever got, nor can get, any advantage by sin. Whatever gain seems to be in sin, is but an imagination; and that conceit is put upon men by a cheat, viz., by the deceitfulness of sin, the deceitfulness of their hearts, and the cunning device of Satan. There is neither pleasure, profit, nor credit to be got by sin, nor ever was. Satan, when he presents sin, makes a show of these; but he merely cozens poor sinners, that he may ruin them. There is no sinner in the world that can pass a right judgment, take a true estimate of his incomes by sin, but must say his losses are real, great, many; his gains a mere show, an empty delusion.

Men seem to gain by sin, when they get or increase their estates by lying, oppression, immoderate cares, with neglect of their souls; but let such consider, the curse of God accompanies whatever is so gotten. And while they gather some heaps of earth, they treasure up wrath, and lose their souls; and then let them tell me what they gain. 'What will it profit,' &c.?

Men fancy pleasures in uncleanness, drunkenness, &c. But this will be bitterness in the end, and such bitterness as will raze out the memory of all former imaginary delight. Such pleasure in sin ends in the bitterness of death, when it brings hell into the conscience, or brings the soul into hell; it is like poison taken in a sweet potion, pleases the palate, but conveys death into the inward parts; it inflames, swells, tortures, and destroys the soul.

Ask Daniel* what advantage he got by sin. He might fancy delights in those unclean, unfaithful enjoyments; so he might think, while Satan's witchcraft prevailed. But when he is come to himself, then ask him, and he will tell you it was an act as full of bitterness as ever man acted; it broke the bones of his comfort, and made him go with sorrow to his grave.

Ask Saul what he gained by disobedience. He imagined no small advantage in reserving the best spoils of Amalek; but really what did he gain? Why, for a few sheep and oxen, he lost a kingdom, 1 Sam. xv. Indeed, this is all the gain in sin: lose a kingdom for some cattle.

Ask Ananias and Sapphira what advantage they got by sinning. They thought to have gained a part of their estate by a lie; but did they gain by it? No; they lost their estate, and their lives, and their souls too. Oh woeful gain!

Nay, ask the devil himself what he got by it. If he would tell the truth, he must say he is the greatest loser in the world by sin. It tumbled him down from the height of glory into the nethermost hell. Sin cast him out of the glorious enhappying presence of God into everlasting burnings, where he is reserved in chains of darkness.

This is confirmed by a general suffrage of all creatures: none ever was a gainer by sin. And this consideration may be a sufficient motive to repent.

(2.) The least sin is infinitely evil. When I say *infinite*, I say there is more evil in it than the tongue of men or angels can express, than their largest apprehensions can conceive. When I say infinite evil, I understand it is a greater evil than the greatest in the world besides it. A greater evil than any poverty, greatest torment, loathsome sickness, dreadfullest death, nay, than hell itself. Gather up in your thoughts whatever on earth or in hell you count evil, and put them all together, and the evil that is in the least sin will far outweigh them all. It is inconceivably more evil than all in the world together. To be infinitely evil, is to be evil above all we can speak or think. Infiniteness is not ascribed usually to any but two: God, the greatest good, and sin, the greatest evil. God is infinite essentially; sin is infinite objectively: infinitely evil, because against him who is infinitely good, because injurious to an infinite God; an offence of infinite majesty, a contempt of infinite authority, an affront to infinite sovereignty, an abuse of infinite mercy, a dishonour to infinite excellency, a provocation of infinite justice, a contrariety to infinite holiness, a reproacher of infinite glory, an enemy to infinite love.

Oh consider what ye do by continuing impenitent. You harbour an evil in your souls that is unspeakably worse than hell; and act that frequently which it was better ye should die ten thousand times than act once. What greater occasion of sorrow, than sin the greatest evil! What fitter object of hatred, than that which is infinitely hateful! Eternity is little enough to bewail such an infinite evil. Oh think not much to employ some of your time in bewailing it.

(3.) The least sin deserves infinite punishment, *i.e.*, greater than any can endure, express, or imagine. The Lord has engaged himself never to let any sin go unpunished, Ex. xxxiv. 7, and his justice requires that the punishment should be equal to the offence: render to every one according

* Qu. 'David'?—ED.

to his deserts. But the offence is infinite; and therefore God's justice is obliged to punish every sin infinitely, to inflict as much as is consistent with the creature's being; and what wants in degrees, to make it up in duration. Eternal punishment is the wages of every sin, Rom. vi. 23; eternal death (as the opposition betwixt death and eternal life does evidence) is as due to every sin as wages to a hireling, as a penny to those who wrought all day in the vineyard.

Oh then, what do ye, while ye continue impenitent? By every word, thought, act, draw down eternal vengeance on your heads, and treasure up infinite wrath; such wrath as, though it will be expending to eternity, will never be quite spent, nay, will never be diminished. After a thousand millions of years' expenses of wrath upon sinners that are impenitent, this treasury will be as full as when first opened.

Oh then, make haste to repent, that your sins may be blotted out; for if the Lord come to reckon with you, and find any one sin on the score unblotted out, your payment must be eternal torments.

(4.) The least sin cannot be expiated without infinite satisfaction. Nothing can satisfy God for the injury of the least sin, but that which is infinite, *i. e.*, such as no creature, no man, no angel, can tender to him; no, nor all the creatures together, by all that they can do or suffer while the world endures. God is not satisfied till sufficient amends be made. No amends is sufficient, but that which is equal to the injury. The injury is infinite; therefore, nothing can satisfy for it, but that which is infinite.

He that will satisfy the Lord for the least sin, must bring him that which is of more value than heaven and earth, than men and angels, than all the creatures.

'Without blood there is no remission,' Heb. ix. 22. No remission without blood of an infinite value. If all the creatures on earth, if all the glorious saints in heaven, if all the glorious angels in the presence of God, should offer to sacrifice their lives for the expiation of one sin, it would not be accepted, it could not be sufficient; for their lives, being finite creatures, are but of a finite value. Only the blood of him who, being God, derives an infinite value upon his blood.

(5.) It is the cause of all the evils that we count miseries in the world. Whatsoever is fearful, or grievous, or hateful, owes its birth to sin. Were it not for sin, either no evil would be in the world, or that which is now evil would be good.

Is poverty a burden? Sin should be much more burdensome; for there had been no poverty but for sin.

Is the cruelty of men, the crossness of friends, the contention of neighbours, the unkindness of children, an affliction? We should be much more afflicted with sin; for there had been no such grievance, no self-seeking, revengefulness, jars, &c., were it not for sin.

Is there vanity and vexation of spirit in all outward employments? Oh how then should you be vexed at sin, which has embittered all!

Do ye complain of pains, languish under bodily distempers, sicknesses, &c.? Oh rather complain of sin, for this breeds all such miseries; it is the sting and anguish of pain; sickness had never seized on the body, but that sin seized on the soul.

Is the wrath of God a terror to you? Oh let sin be more terrible; for we had never known any such thing as wrath in God had it not been for sin, nothing but smiles, promises, mercies.

Are you afraid of death, that the king of terrors should apprehend you?

Be more afraid of sin; the sons of men had never known, had never feared death had it not been for sin.

Do ye tremble at the apprehension of hell, those everlasting torments? Tremble more at the approach of sin; for there had been no hell, no devil, but for sin. It was sin that prepared both tormentors and torments; it was sin that digged that bottomless pit, and overshadowed it with darkness, and filled it with tortures; it was sin that kindled the wrath of God, which, like a river of brimstone, nourishes, continues those torments to eternity. There had been no poverty, crossness, vexation, sickness, &c., but for sin. We hate, we avoid, we mourn for these; much more should we hate, avoid, and mourn for sin, which is the cause of them.

(6.) It is the soul's greatest misery. Those evils which sin has brought into the world are lamentable, but the miseries wherein it has involved the soul are much more grievous.

[1.] It consumes the soul, weakens it, eats away its strength insensibly; a dangerous consumption, leaves no power to act, suffer, bear, resist, move, help. So the state of sin is described to be a state of impotency, Rom. v. 6.

[2.] It impoverishes the soul, steals away its riches, its ornaments, those riches which are more valuable than all the treasures of the earth, those which make the soul rich toward God. When sin broke into the soul it robbed, spoiled, ransacked it, left it poor, empty, naked. The state of sin is a state of poverty, nothing to cover it, nothing to feed it, nothing to lay out for its own necessities. No such beggar on earth as one poor in soul; nay, after the Lord has in part repaired these losses by communicating the riches of grace, yet even then the more sin the more poverty, Rev. iii. 17.

[3.] It defiles the soul, deprives it of its beauty, lustre, comeliness, deforms it with ugly spots, besmears it with loathsome pollutions, such as make it hateful in the eye of God, angels, &c.: 'Ezek. xvi. 6, 'polluted in blood.' Hence sin is called 'uncleanness,' Zech. xiii. 1; and 'filthiness,' 2 Cor. vii. 1; Ezek. xxxvi. 25, compared to things most filthy in the world. Hence, before the Lord will suffer sinners to come near him, he bids them 'wash,' &c., Isa. i. 16. *Corruptio optimi est pessima.*

[4.] It enslaves the soul to the body, to Satan, to itself, a worse, a viler tyrant than either; no galley-slave in the world so miserable as a soul enthralled to sin, led captive by Satan, &c. No thraldom so woeful as spiritual soul slavery.

[5.] It confines the soul to itself, to the dungeon of the world, gives no liberty to have any converse with God, Ps. cxix. 82; it loads it with chains of darkness; those invisible irons enter into the soul, the weight of them presses it down to the earth, yea, towards hell. It is bowed down under the pressure of them, so as it cannot lift up itself to God; and thus it lives till Christ set it free; and even then sin is ready to entangle it with new yokes of bondage, to encompass it with new fetters, Heb.*

[6.] It straitens the soul, contracts it. As it deprives it of what it had, so it makes it uncapable of receiving what it wants, blocks up the passages whereby grace, comfort, &c. should be conveyed; so that nothing but infinite mercy will relieve a sinful soul; so nothing but infinite power can make it capable of relief, Acts xvi. 14.

[7.] It blinds the soul, deals with it as the Philistines with Samson; not only fetters it, and makes it grind in the prison-house, but puts out its eyes, Judges xvi. 21.

* Qu. 'Gal. v. 1'?—ED.

[8.] It wounds it, makes wide gashes, deep and bloody furrows in it, and in every part of it, the pain whereof, when felt, is intolerable, Prov. xviii. 14, and when not felt is most dangerous; leaves it as the thieves left the man, Luke x. 30.

[9.] It murders the soul: it was so from the beginning, has murdered all mankind; all are 'dead in trespasses,' &c., Eph. ii., *i. e.*, dead of this. This is that mortal disease which never seized upon any soul but it deprived it of spiritual life. What the pestilence is to the body, that sin is to the soul, a deadly plague.

Oh look into your souls, see what a lamentable spectacle sin has made them, and you will need no other motive to mourn! If you would avoid misery, and hate that which makes you miserable, sin above all things is to be hated, to be avoided, as that which involves in greatest, *i. e.*, in soul miseries. Every sinner may cry out, Have you no regard, &c.? 'See if there be any misery like my misery,' wherewith sin has afflicted me. And the sorrow for sin should be answerable to the miseries of sin; no misery like that, no sorrow like this.

(7.) It is God's greatest adversary; it has done much against the world, more against man's soul; ay, but that which it does against God is most considerable, as that which should move us to hate, bewail, abandon it, above all considerations. It has filled the world with fearful evils, the soul with woeful miseries; but the injuries it does to God are most horrible.

The injury of one sin is equal to the ruin of heaven and earth. Christ says it is better these should pass away than that his law should not remain inviolable; but sin violates it, and would have it quite abrogated.

It is so injurious as the Lord complains of it. We never find he complains of anything but sin; but of this he complains as a burden to him, an oppressing burden, that which wearies him, Isa. xliii. 24, Amos ii. 13; and shall not that be a burden to us?

It provokes, angers, highly offends, kindles his wrath, &c. And why, but because it is unspeakably injurious to him?

In sin there is some *contempt* of God, low unworthy thoughts. No man durst sin if he did apprehend God to be what he is.

Some *sacrilege*. Sin robs God, and robs him of that which is dearest to him, as precious as the apple of his eye, more dear to him than our lives to us, his honour.

Some *idolatry*. The heart gives more respect to something else than God.

Something like *witchcraft*; an implicit compact, an agreement with Satan, for some pleasure or profit, &c., and to do that which is most injurious to God, 1 Sam. xv. 23.

Some *treason*. Sin is high treason against the most high God, a conspiracy with the Lord's greatest enemies against him.

Some *rebellion*; making use of members and faculties as weapons of unrighteousness to fight against God.

Some *blasphemy*. Sin has a secret language which the Lord hears, though we take no notice of it. It speaks proud and blasphemous things against God; denies him to be what he is, so holy, just, severe, true; makes him to be what he is not, ignorant, careless; ascribes that to others which is only his, goodness, happiness, pleasures, &c.

And is sin thus injurious? &c. How should this consideration make us tremble, that we deferred repentance so long! and ashamed, that our sorrow for, hatred of sin, is no more. A wonder the Lord will grant any time for repentance after the commission of such a provoking act as sin is! Great reason to make haste to break it off by repentance.

(8.) Consider the multitude of your sins. If any one sin be so infinitely evil in itself and in its effects, oh how evil is he, what need to repent, who is guilty of a multitude of sins! And indeed so many, so numerous are our sins, as it will be hard to find an expression which may help you to conceive how many they are. I cannot better shew how numerable they are, than by shewing they are innumerable.

And this will be evident, if ye consider that before repentance, every act, word, thought, is a sin; you can do, speak, think, nothing but sin. A bad tree cannot bring forth good fruit. A soul, till implanted into Christ, can bring forth nothing that is good, nothing but sin. And one of the first-fruits after this implantation is repentance; till then nothing but wild grapes. Now if every act you did since you were born be sin, put all those acts together, and into what a multitude will they swell! They are without number, beyond knowledge. He that takes the strictest survey of his life and actions that is possible, cannot give an account of 'one of a thousand,' Job ix. 3. Let him be as diligent as can be, yet where he takes notice of one, a thousand will escape his observation. Those that we know are not the thousand part of those we know not. The stars in the heavens, the hairs of our head, are far more easily numbered than our sinful acts. They are like the sands on the sea-shore, which cannot be numbered. And if sinful acts be innumerable, what account can we take of our words! They are more than innumerable, as being innumerably more than our actions; ay, and our thoughts more than both. What then? How many are all put together? Ask man, ask angels; both will be nonplussed: Ps. xix., 'Who knows the errors,' &c., Ps. xl. 12.

We lose ourselves when we speak of the sins of our lives. It may astonish any considering man to take notice how many sins he is guilty of any one day; how many sins accompany any one single act; nay, how many bewray themselves in any one religious duty. Whensoever ye do any thing forbidden, you omit the duty at that time commanded; and whenever you neglect that which is enjoined, the omission is joined with the acting of something forbidden; so that the sin, whether omission or commission, is always double: nay, the apostle makes every sin tenfold, James ii. 10. That which seems one to us, according to the sense of the law, and the account of God, is multiplied by ten. He breaks every command by sinning directly against one, and so sins ten times at once; besides that swarm of sinful circumstances and aggravations which surround every act in such numbers, as atoms use to surround your body in a dusty room; you may more easily number these than those. And though some count these but fractions, incomplete sins, yet even from hence it is more difficult to take an account of their number.

And, which is more for astonishment, pick out the best religious duty that ever you performed, and even in that performance you may find such a swarm of sins as cannot be numbered. In the best prayer that ever you put up to God, irreverence, lukewarmness, unbelief, spiritual pride, self-seeking, hypocrisy, distractions, &c., and many more, that an enlightened soul grieves and bewails; and yet there are many more that the pure eye of God discerns, than any man does take notice of.

And besides, every one of these many sins manifest themselves in every duty many several ways, and every way sinful.

Now if so many sins be discernible in the best duty, and many more in every unlawful act, and the acts themselves be innumerable that have such a numberless multitude of sinful attendants, what do ye think will the total arise to? Even such a sum, as all the arithmetic of men and angels cannot give an account of. If one sin, being so infinitely evil, deserve infinite punishment, being so horridly injurious to God, being so dangerously mischievous to the soul, call for shame, sorrow, indignation, hatred, &c., oh what then does such a multitude of sins, numberless even to astonishment, call for!

2. Considerations from Christ, who enjoins repentance.

If our sins were occasion of sorrow to him, great reason have we to mourn for them. But so it is; our sins made him a man of sorrows. The cup which he gives to us, he drank himself; he drank out the dregs and bitterness, the wormwood and gall, wherewith this sorrow was mixed. That which he left to us is pleasant. The cup which Christ gives us, shall we not drink it? Nay, the cup which Christ drank, shall we refuse to taste?

Our sins made him weep and sigh, and cry out in the anguish of his spirit; and shall we make a sport of sin?

Made him weep, express his grief in tears, Heb. v. 7; disfigured by sorrows, and made him a reproach, Isa. liii. 2–4; shall not we grieve?

Made him sigh. The weight of our sins made his soul heavy, heavy unto death, Mat. xxvi. 37, 38. Why? Isa. liii. 6, 1 Pet. ii. 24, our sins were that deadly weight, &c.

Made him cry out to heaven, 'My God,' &c., Mat. xxvii. 46. To earth, 'Have ye no regard, all ye,' &c. He was afflicted by our sins, and shall not our souls be afflicted? 'He was wounded for our transgressions,' and wept not only tears, but blood; Oh, shall neither our eyes nor hearts shew sorrow?

3. Considerations from repentance, the duty enjoined.

That is the time when all happiness begins, when misery ends, the period of evils; the time from whence ye must date all mercies. Till then, never expect to receive the least mercy, or have the least judgment, evil, removed without repentance. Till then,

(1.) Whatever ye do is sinful. 'Without faith it is impossible to please God;' and where no repentance, no faith. Whatever ye think, speak, act, is a provocation. Every thought; for what is said of the old world is true of every unrenewed man, not renewed by repentance, Gen. vi. 5. Every inward act, every word; for 'out of the abundance of the heart, the mouth speaks,' Luke vi. 45. Now there is nothing in the heart but wickedness; therefore the words must be so; good words cannot be brought out of the evil treasure. Every action: as soon gather grapes of thorns, and figs of thistles, as good actions from an impenitent: Luke vi. 44, 'He that is born of God, sinneth not'; but till then, he does nothing but sin. Till repentance, no man is born of God; for that is one of the first vital acts.

(2.) All your enjoyments are cursed. All the curses of the law are the portion of an impenitent sinner; and there are curses for himself, and every thing that belongs to him, Deut. viii. 16, 17, &c.; Deut. xxix. 19, 20.

A penitent has an undoubted title to all the promises; but to an impenitent sinner the curses belong. He that repents not is not within the covenant of grace, and therefore under the law; which, since it was broken, speaks nothing but curses to all under it. The penitent hear nothing but from mount Gerizim, the impenitent nothing but from mount Ebal, Deut. xi. 29.

(3.) All sin is unpardoned. The handwriting of ordinances, which is against sinners, is not cancelled till then, Acts iii. 19. They remain in God's sight, as writ with a pen of iron, Jer. xvii. 1. The Lord will never speak of pardoning till then; and then, though their sins be as scarlet, they shall be as white as snow, &c., Isa. i. 18. Sin remains, John ix. 41. Impenitence makes other sins unpardonable; that which is small, shall never be pardoned.

(4.) All ordinances ineffectual, uncomfortable, hurtful, damnable. The word, the savour of death: till the heart be broken, the seed is rejected in stony ground. The sacraments, seals of damnation, 1 Cor. xi. 26. Death in the pot, poison. Prayer an abomination, Prov. xxviii. 9. No sacrifice acceptable without a broken heart, Isa. i. 15.

(5.) God is an enemy. No communion with God till agreed; no agreement without repentance. Will God count them friends who fight against him, will not lay down their arms, their weapons of unrighteousness? He dwells in a penitent heart, Isa. lxvi., Isa. lvii. 15. But he is so far from dwelling in an impenitent heart, as he will not endure his word should be in their mouth, Ps. l. 16, 17. 'He will wound the head of his enemies,' &c., Ps. lxviii. 21. Never expect smile, promise, mercy, till you repent.

(6.) Justice is unsatisfied. No satisfaction without compensation; none can make that but Christ: nothing will be accepted but his λύτρον, that which he paid as the price of redemption. But to whom is he a redeemer? Isa. lix. 20, to them that turn from transgression. Justice is your adversary; no agreement without repentance; nothing but such a dreadful process, Mat. v. 25, to be cast into prison.

(7.) Wrath is unavoidable. That is the attendant of unsatisfied justice. No way to escape without this. Who has warned? Mark iii. 7, 8; Rev. xvi. 11, vials are poured out on those that repented not. Jer. xv. 7, destroy, because they returned not.

(8.) Death is terrible. Better to die than live impenitent; but better never live than die impenitent. Death comes to them like the king of terrors, not as a messenger of peace; armed with a sting, repentance only charms it; comes as an officer of justice, to drag the soul to execution; Christ's pursuivant, to bring before the dreadful tribunal of an incensed judge, before the judgment-seat of Christ, to receive the sentence of eternal condemnation. The penitent long for his appearance; these will call to mountains to fall on them, &c.

(9.) Hell is certain. It was prepared of old for these. Every tree that brings not forth the fruits of repentance shall be cut down, &c. They cumber the ground, are unfruitful, and hinder others: Rom. viii. 13, 'If ye live after the flesh, ye shall die.' It is, as was said of Judas, ἴδιος τόπος; none but they, and all they, have that place for their portion.

(10.) Hopes of heaven are delusions, expectations of happiness dreams, vain groundless fancies, which Satan begets and nourishes, that he may more securely ruin impenitent sinners. The apostle asserts it peremptorily, Gal. v. 21. Though it be long since you did these, yet till repentance, you are still doing, still continue in them. There is not only the word of an apostle, but the oath of God; he swears, hardened sinners shall not enter into his rest, Heb. iv. 3.

Obj. God is merciful, infinitely so; will not be so strict as many make him. He may save me though I be not so penitent, though sorrow be not so great, &c.

Ans. This is an ordinary conceit, suggested by Satan; and the matter of it is unreasonable, false, blasphemous, perverse.

1. It is infinite mercy that God will save any sinner that repents, that he will vouchsafe life upon such terms. It is infinite mercy that any one is saved, that all are not cut off in the height of sin. It would be infinite mercy that sinners might be admitted to life upon terms more harsh, chargeable, difficult. Oh what mercy to have life upon terms so easy, equal! Would not that traitor think himself graciously dealt with, who, having acted treason a great part of his life, should be admitted to favour, honour, if but sorry and reform? Who would expect such easy terms for rebellious sinners? Oh, what would the damned do and suffer to have such an offer! It is unreasonable to think God will save without repentance because merciful, whenas it is mercy we may be saved upon our repentance.

2. Infinite mercy will not save an impenitent sinner; it is a false conceit, and very dangerous to entertain it. It has been the ruin of millions to presume on mercy without ground. The Lord does plainly exclude all such from all hopes of mercy, Deut. xxix. 20.

3. To think mercy will save impenitents is a blasphemous conceit, that which makes God unjust, untrue, unfaithful. He has said, and sworn; he has engaged justice, truth, faithfulness for the ruin of impenitent sinners. To think he will be so merciful as to save them, is to make God a liar, think he will deny himself to save you, trample upon his own glory to advance you, and so make an idol of God.

4. Mercies should lead to repentance, and not be turned into perverse disputes.

Obj. I will repent hereafter, it is time enough; I am so full of business, I cannot attend it now.

Ans. The matter of this objection is groundless, false, and desperately dangerous; for,

1. This is the devil's suggestion, which he proposes with a cruel intention to destroy your soul. He would have you defer repentance that you may perish. It is the great design which he now drives on amongst you; by yielding thereto you join with your greatest, most deadly enemy, against God, Christ, the Spirit, your own souls. He is loath you should escape out of his snare.

2. You presume without ground that you have time enough. You know not how soon death may seize on you, how soon Christ may summon, what watch the Master will come. You have no security for one hour, for the time is uncertain, and comes upon most when they expect it not; and why not so to you? And if so, if death come before repentance, oh it will be a sad hour, a day of blackness and thick darkness! You would be loath to leave anything you value in the world at such uncertainty, and will you leave your souls so? Will you leave that in continual danger every moment to drop into hell?

3. If your lives should be prolonged, yet you will have time little enough to repent though you should begin presently. Man's life, if longer, affords not time sufficient to bewail sin, if sorrow should be proportionable to what sin calls for. No pardoned sinner can ever think he bestows too much time in mourning for sin. Besides, there are daily occasions for continual exercise of repentance. The work is long, and life is short; no room therefore or reason for delay.

4. Business and designs in the world should not hinder; for if they be

worth following, repentance will not hinder them. No man ever lost anything by obeying God in this. This is the way to make the business succeed, your designs prosper. Repent, and all things shall be well, those which seem worst; but till then, never expect but all will be either crossed or cursed. You should rather argue thus: I have much business in the world, therefore I will make haste to repent, because I have so little time. It is a perverse inference, and savours of hell, where all such are forged, I am too busy to repent.

5. When you say you will repent hereafter, you imagine you may repent when you will; but herein you delude your souls; it is not in your power to repent. It is the gift of God; 'If so be,' &c., Acts v. 31. He gives it when and to whom he pleases. You can never hope to have it till he give; and when have you any ground to hope he will give it, but when he calls for it? But now he calls for it, 'now he commands all men to repent,' Acts xvii. 30. 'This is the accepted time,' &c., 'To-day, if ye will hear his voice,' &c., Heb. iii. 15. To-day is the Lord's time, to-day is your time; who knows what to-morrow may bring forth? To-morrow the door of mercy may be shut, the Lord's hand may be closed, the Lord's patience may be terminated. To-morrow it may be too late, and then, alas! where are you? You may defer it till it be too late; for there is a time when the Lord will not be found, when repentance will not be found, though ye seek it with tears, Heb. xii. 17; and if you now neglect to learn to obey the Lord's voice, you may swear that hereafter will be too late. God will not hear them hereafter, that will not hear him now, Prov. i.

6. The longer ye defer repentance, the harder it will be to repent. You will be every day the less able; the longer you neglect to get your hearts softened, the more will ye be hardened through the deceitfulness of sin, Heb. iii. 13; the longer ye live in sin, the more ye will be in love with it; the longer ye continue in the snare, the faster you will be entangled. Oh, make haste while there is hope to escape. It must be done, it is necessary; either repent, or perish. Resolve to do it then, while ye may do it with most ease, before it become too difficult, impossible.

7. Ye judge such delays madness in outward things, much more is it here; nothing of greater consequence, of more present necessity. You apprehend a present need of rain, and would censure him as void of sense or reason, that would say rain will come time enough a month, a year hence. But, oh, is there not more need of relenting hearts! You may lose a year's fruits by the intemperate drought of the season; ay, but you may lose your soul's happiness, not for a year, but for eternity, by hardness of heart. If your house should be on fire, would any but a madman say, it will be time enough to quench it to-morrow? For why? It may be consumed to ashes before to-morrow. The least delay may undo you: Why, so it is here; your souls are on fire though you feel it not, the wrath of God has kindled on them, and it will burn to the bottom of hell, burn and not be quenched till repentance be. Oh, make haste, while there is hope, before it be too late, before your souls be quite consumed. The Lord, to impenitent sinners, is a consuming fire.

If one be stung with a serpent, will he say it will be time enough to mind the cure hereafter? None but a mad, a desperate man will say so. The poison is diffusive, will spread, and, if not prevented, seize upon the vitals, and so become incurable. No poison like the poison of sin; it is like the cruel venom of asps. This serpent has bit the soul; if it be not prevented, it will be mortal to the soul; no cure for it but the balm of

Gilead, the blood of Christ; and this is never applied without repentance. Oh, defer it not, delay is dangerous, it may cost the life of your souls.

8. This has been the ruin of thousands. Ask those wretched souls that are cast into outer darkness, what is the reason they are now in that place of torment? They will tell you, because they deferred repentance. It is this that shipwrecked so many souls in that lake that burns with fire and brimstone; and will you run your souls upon the same rock? You have a whole world of warnings in one. Ask the old world why the Lord brought the flood upon them? why, by a deluge of waters he swept them into a deluge of fire, and destroyed them in such a terrible manner, twice at once? They will tell you, it was because they repented not at the preaching of Noah. If the men of Nineveh had no more regarded the preaching of Jonah, calling them to present repentance, they also had been certainly destroyed here and hereafter.

Use. Exhort. Does the Lord command it, and presently? Take heed of deferring repentance. Disobedience will be like the sin of witchcraft. You have had warning for some years together; you have had sin discovered, and the danger of it; ignorance, drunkenness, profaneness, Sabbath-breaking, neglect of worship, resisting holiness, contemning the gospel; sins of place and persons. If you will still continue in these sins, when the Lord commands now to repent; take heed he who now commands do not the next moment threaten, do not next moment execute.

Take heed, if there be any regard of your souls; take heed of continuing in any sin, of hardening your hearts in any evil way; take heed of it, it infinitely, it eternally concerns you. It is matter of life and death, and that of your souls, and that eternal. This is it I have been doing, and which the Lord employs his messengers to do. Take it in Moses's words, and mind it, as if it were the last thing ye should hear: Deut. xxx. 19, If ye repent, turn now when the Lord requires, you choose life; but if you will live in sin, scorn holiness: I call heaven and earth to record this day, and the God of heaven and earth will call me to witness against you at the last day.

Obj. The thief on the cross repented when he was dying; and so may I. Why should I then trouble myself with repentance, while I have health, strength, &c.?

Ans. His repentance at death, is no ground to defer repentance till death. It is dangerous to rest upon it. For,

1. It is but an example, and that is no ground of hope, that you either shall or may find place for repentance then. If you had either permission or precept to defer it till then, or promise that the Lord would then give or accept it, you might defer, in hopes you might then repent. But it is quite contrary. He is so far from tolerating such delay, as he declares against it, commands it now; so far from promising, &c., as he threatens, Luke xxi. 34, 35, and xii. 19, 20, and xvii. 27; 1 Thes. v. 2, 3; Mat. xxiv. 38. An example added to these would be an encouragement; but without these, is no ground at all. Your hopes, without other ground, are delusions; and this example will prove a broken reed, break under those that lean upon it, pierce their souls, and suffer soul and body to sink. It is desperate madness, to leave your souls without any hopes for eternity, but what this will afford.

2. It is but one example. The Bible, a history of near four thousand years, affords but one instance of one saved by repentance at death. Whereas, if we could search the records of eternity, we might find many

thousands instead of those, who have eternally ruined their souls, by deferring repentance till death.

All that can be argued from this one example is, that it is possible to repent when dying. Nay, if there were a multitude of examples, they would but make it probable. A probability might satisfy in matters of small concernment; but in that which concerns the eternal state of your souls, nothing less than certainty is sufficient. But here is no certainty, here is no probability! If you defer repentance till then, it is ten thousand to one you will never repent. And what then? It is ten thousand to one you will perish. It is deperate madness to be satisfied with a possibility; whenas, if for anything in the world, certainty is here necessary.

It is astonishing, to have your souls in such a state, which will not afford so much as a probability of being saved. You should make your salvation sure; but, relying upon one example, you make it not probable.

Roman history affords us one instance of Horatius Cocles, who maintained a pass against a whole army; but will any state therefore trust their safety with one man? Will any, invaded by a numerous army, employ none but one man to resist it? Would not all that hear of such madness, judge such a people besotted, that they might be ruined? Yet there is as good ground to do this, and expect victory, as for any to defer repentance, and expect salvation. Here is but one example for this, and no less for that.

Mithridates affords an instance of one that could take poison without danger; will any therefore eat deadly poison, and hope for life, because he did? You may as well hope for long life, though ye eat poison, as hope to be saved by repenting at death; there is as good ground for the one as the other; one example.

Jonah was cast into the sea, and was preserved by a whale; but will any cast himself overboard, in hopes of such an escape? You may as well cast yourselves into the sea, with hopes of such a preservation, from the example of Jonah, as defer repentance, in hopes of repenting on your deathbed, from the example of the thief.

3. It is an extraordinary example. Now there is no reason to draw a rule from an extraordinary instance. This was little less than miraculous, we see it placed in a crowd of miracles; would you have the Lord work miracles to save you? It is high presumption, to expect the Lord should save you at your death, if you wilfully neglect the ordinary means of salvation all your lives.

Would not you think it strange madness for one to expose himself to death, in hopes to be raised again to life by the wonder-working power of Christ, because Lazarus was so raised. And why? But because that was extraordinary. It is no less madness to defer repentance till death, in hopes you shall then repent, because the thief did then repent and was accepted. For this was extraordinary. The Lord will rather shew extraordinary severity in punishing such mad presumption.

4. It is an impertinent example. It was not intended it should, and it cannot in reason be used to that purpose for which you apply it. It may be he never heard of Christ before. It may be he did not enjoy the ordinary means of repentance in his life. It is probable he never deferred it, in hopes to repent at his death. The case is not alike. However, it is certain the Lord never intended it to be an encouragement for any to live impenitently. He left such an example, that no penitent should despair; not that any impenitent should presume. They may fear, the Lord

never intends them mercy, who abuse this to that purpose that he never intended it.

Obj. But repentance is harsh and unpleasing; if I should take notice of sin, to mourn for it, crucify it, I should make my life sad and uncomfortable.

Ans. 1. Suppose there be something unpleasing in repentance, as there is to corrupt nature; yet there is infinitely more bitterness in impenitency.

What is there in repentance so grievous as slavery to sin and Satan; so burdensome as Satan's yoke and tyrrany? But while you continue impenitent, you are his slaves.

What evil so lamentable as madness? But impenitents are, in Scripture phrase, in God's account, madmen. The prodigal, when he returned to his father, *i. e.*, repented, it is said, he 'came to himself.' He was besides himself before, and so are all impenitent sinners. Μετάνοια comes from ἄνοια, *amentia;* he that turns not from sin is a madman.

What so terrible as death? What bitterness in repentance comparable to the bitterness of death? But impenitents are dead in sins and trespasses.

What in repentance like the curse of God! What like the guilt of sin, so much, of so many! What like to the wounds of a terrified conscience! What like the lashes of vengeance, revenging justice! What like the scorchings of incensed wrath! What like to hell, everlasting fire, the gnawing worm that never dies, weeping and gnashing of teeth to eternity!

He that will expose himself to these miseries, rather than displease his corrupt nature by the practice of repentance, is like one who had rather continue all his life in a burning fever, than endure a chirurgeon to breathe a vein. Or like one who, having drunk poison, will rather die a painful death, than take an unpleasing potion to prevent it. If there were any bitterness in repentance, there is incomparably more in impenitency.

Ans. 2. It is false that repentance is unpleasing. It is not so in itself; it is not so to any but those whose palates are distempered; to those whose minds the god of this world has blinded, so as they cannot judge; call bitter sweet, and sweet bitter. It is not so to those who have had experience of it, and none else are competent judges. Oh if ye would but practise it, if ye would but taste and see what joys, what comforts, what delights are in repentance, you would soon change your judgment, and cry out upon Satan as an impostor, and your hearts as deceitful, for representing it unpleasing. How can that be but comfortable upon which the Lord has entailed so much comfort, to which he has made so many sweet promises: 'Blessed are they that mourn,' Mat. v; 'Those that sow in tears shall reap in joy,' Ps. cxxvi. 6, and xcvii. 11. No great distance between seed-time and harvest. Who can think that unpleasing on earth which occasions joy in heaven? Luke xv. 7. While your hearts mourn, bleed for sin, bemoan it, Jer. xxxi. 18, the Lord's bowels yearn toward you. While your spirit is sad in the remembrance of sin, the Spirit of joy and glory rests on you. When you are confessing sin, Christ is speaking peace: John xvi. 20, 'Sorrow shall be turned into joy.' While you are returning, nay, but resolving to return, to repent, the Father is running to embrace you. And oh what joy will there be in such embraces! What joy to see the Father falling upon your neck and kissing, giving such sweet intimations of his love, as men use to do by such affectionate expressions! Oh, let the world judge what they will, let Satan suggest what he will of repentance, those that have had experience of it will count it pleasing, comfortable, delightful.

Ans. 3. It is not so only positively, but comparatively. There is more sweetness in repentance than in all the pleasures of sin. All the ways of Christ are 'ways of pleasantness,' Prov. iii. 17; *i. e.*, most pleasing, superlatively so, beyond comparison. And this is one reason why Moses chose rather affliction, Heb. xi. 25. And why but because more desirable, and really more delightful, whatever they seem? The pleasures of sin are short, like the light of a candle, quickly spent if it burn till consumed, but often put out, Job xxi. 17. The pleasures of repentance are like the sun that shines more and more, Prov. iv. 18. Those are mixed; the heart is sad in the midst of laughter, Prov. xiv. 13; like John's little book, Rev. x. 9, 'sweet in the mouth, but bitter in the belly;' like Belshazzar's feast, Jael's entertainment. These are ure,pspring* in heaven.

Those are brutish, sensual, have little pre-eminence above the pleasures of a beast; these are spiritual, heavenly, glorious, 1 Peter i. 8.

Those are groundless; in fancy, when there is real cause of sorrow; like joy in a frantic man, or a malefactor led to execution; lamentable joys, such as deserve pity; joy when most cause of sorrow. The end in sorrow, will be bitterness in the end; for a moment's joy, eternal sorrows; for a few pleasures, many sorrows, Ps. xxxii. 10.

This sorrow ends in joy; a moment's sorrow, endless joy, everlasting joy; it is a well of water springing up to eternal life; a small stream, but leads to the ocean.

Now, judge what ground for this objection, what reason to be hindered by a conceit of unpleasantness, since the hardest part of repentance has such comfort attending it here, and such joys rewarding it hereafter.

* So in text; perhaps 'These are re-upspringing.'—ED.

OF FAITH.

He that believeth, and is baptized, shall be saved; but he that believeth not shall be damned.—MARK XVI. 16.

THESE words require as serious attention as any that ever were spoken to the sons of men; for they are the words of Christ, the words of one from the dead.

The last words of Christ, of our departing Saviour. The last instructions of a departing friend, whom never like to see more in the world, they make deep impression.

Why here is the last words of Christ upon earth, the last will of Christ, our husband, our friend, our elder brother. When he had said this, he said no more that the evangelist relates; for, ver. 19, 'after he had spoken these words, he was received up into heaven.'

They are of greatest consequence, the sum of the gospel, the whole epitomised in two sentences; the whole covenant of grace. As much in this verse virtually, as in the whole gospel. Life and death, and the conditions of both; the terms of eternal happiness or misery. If a malefactor at the bar should see the judge going about to declare to him upon what he might expect life or death, how diligently would he attend! All sinners are malefactors. The Judge of heaven and earth declares here, upon what terms we may live, though we be cast, found guilty, and condemned. It is not a matter of credit or estate, but a matter of life and death, of the life of our souls. It is no less than eternal life or eternal death, that these words concern. And therefore,

The condition of life is double: 1, principal, faith; 2, accessory, baptism. Accessory, I call it, because it is not absolutely necessary to life, as faith is. *Non privatio, sed contemptus damnat.* And therefore it is left out in the latter part. It is not, he that is [not] baptized shall be damned, but he that believes not. Faith is so necessary, as he that believes not, though he be baptized, shall be damned.

Doct. Salvation or damnation depend upon faith and unbelief. No salvation but by faith. Nothing but damnation by unbelief.

Faith is the principal saving grace, and unbelief the chief damning sin. No sin can damn without this, and this will damn without any other sin: John iii. 18, 'is condemned.' The law, which threatens death for every sin, has already passed sentence of condemnation upon all, because all are sinners. This sentence is so peremptory as it admits but of one exception, which the gospel brings in. All are condemned, and shall be executed, except they believe. So that where there is not faith, the sentence of condemnation is in full force. An unbeliever so continuing is as sure to be damned, as if in hell already; as sure to be cast into outer darkness, as if he were tormented in everlasting burnings; as sure to bear the eternal, insupportable wrath of God, as if he had now fellowship with the devil and his angels.

We say of a man that has the symptoms of death, he is a dead man. Unbelief is the symptom of eternal death. There is nothing but death to be expected where this continues; no hopes of eternal life if he persevere in unbelief. He is dead while he lives; in hell while he is on earth.

The great physician of souls gives him over. He that healed all manner of diseases cannot cure him, cannot prevent his eternal death who continues in unbelief. When the plague-sore appears in a person, we conclude him dead, shut him up, debar him of society with living men, write *Lord have mercy* upon his door. Unbelief is the sore of an eternal plague, of that plague which is incurable. While unbelief continues, he is shut up amongst the dead, but in this more miserable, as there is no hopes of life, so no hopes of mercy; he must die without mercy. There is neither life nor mercy for an unbeliever. When we see a condemned malefactor upon the scaffold, with his neck upon the block, and none to plead for his pardon, nor hopes of prevailing if there were any to plead, we may conclude he is a dead man.

In such a condition is an unbeliever, he is condemned already, the instruments of death are ready. There is none in heaven or earth will plead for his pardon; nor would the Lord pardon him, so continuing, if all in heaven and earth should become intercessors. No hopes for him, except he believe, he must die the death, he is condemned already, the mouth of the Lord has spoken it.

Now if faith be so necessary, and unbelief so dangerous, it concerns us to know what it is to believe.

It comprises, 1, knowledge; 2, assent; 3, dependence, or relying on the Lord Jesus Christ.

1. *Knowledge.* Faith is expressed by knowledge, Isa. liii. 11. If knowledge be not faith, yet there can be no faith without knowledge.

That blind faith of the papists is good for nothing but to lead them into the ditch. That ignorance is the mother of devotion, is one of the principles of the father of lies. Sure it is the nurse of unbelief. It is Satan's muffler, which he makes use of to lead sinners blindfold into hell; it brings them there before they know where they are. Ignorant persons are like the Syrians, struck with blindness, 2 Kings vi. 20. They thought they were going on a hopeful design, but when their eyes were opened, they found themselves in the midst of Samaria, in the midst of their enemies. The first step to conversion is to open the eyes, to scatter darkness, Acts xxvi. 18. He begins the new creation as he did the creation of the world: 'Let there be light,' Gen. i. The first thing he produces is light. There is a dawning of the day before the day-star arise; some light goes before the sun rising. Such a dawning of knowledge there is before the Sun of righteousness arise, before Christ dwell in the heart by faith; some light from the law discovering sin and misery; some light from the gospel discovering Christ's excellency and all-sufficiency. There is a competent knowledge of the mysteries of the gospel, a knowledge more distinct, more convincing, more affecting, than that which he had in the state of unbelief.

2. *Assent.* As to the principles of the doctrine of Christ, so especially to these two truths: 1, that he has a necessity of a Saviour; 2, that Christ is the only all-sufficient Saviour.

(1.) There is an absolute necessity of a Saviour, which the Scripture declares upon three grounds: 1, the sinfulness of a natural man; 2, his misery; 3, his inability to free himself from it.

There must be a full and effectual assent to, and belief of, what the Lord declares concerning his sinful, miserable, impotent state.

3. *Recumbence*, relying upon Christ. To rely upon Christ alone for salvation is saving faith.

It is not to believe him, but to believe *on* him; which the New Testament expresses by a peculiar phrase, not used by heathen authors: *πιστεύειν εἰς τὸν Χριστὸν*, Acts xix. 4; *εἰς ἐμὲ*, Mat. ix. 42; *ἐπὶ τόν*, or, *ἐπὶ τῷ*, Acts xvi. 31, *ἐπὶ τὸν Κύριον*; Rom. ix. 33, *πιστεύων ἐπ' αὐτῷ*; Mark i. 15, *ἐν τῷ εὐαγγελίῳ*; Rom. iii. 25, *ἐν τῷ αἵματι*; Gal. iii. 24, *εἰς Χριστόν*; Eph. i. 15; *εἰς τὸ ὄνομα*, John i. 12, &c.

It is not to give credit to him, but to rely on him; it is to trust in him. To trust in him is more than to believe him, to assent to his word as true. It is, as Lombard explains it, lib. 3, dist. 23, *credendo in eum ire, credendo ei adhærere*, to adhere, depend, rely on him; not *credere*, but *fidere, fiduciam ponere*.

This is the essence, the formality of saving faith. There cannot be justifying faith without knowledge and assent, but there may be knowledge and assent without it; these are as the body to faith, this relying is the soul; without this, knowledge and assent are but a carcase. The devils and hypocrites may have more knowledge, and they may have as firm an assent, but this act is above their reach, and they never attain it.

Now because there is some difference amongst divines about the nature and essence of faith, some placing it in assent, some in assurance, &c.;

And because there are mistakes amongst ordinary Christians, many concluding they rely on Christ when indeed they do not;

And because mistakes are here dangerous, it being a matter of life and death eternal, of salvation or damnation,—faith being the first stone on which the structure of salvation is raised, and an error in the foundation threatens ruin to the whole;

It behoves to be diligent in inquiring what this faith is, what the nature of this dependence and relying on Christ.

Now, the best way to find this out will be to discuss those words and phrases whereby the Holy Ghost in Scripture expresses faith. From these we may get light sufficient to discover the nature of this act; and these are various.

1. To believe is to come to Christ, so it is expressed in the New Testament; to betake ourselves to him, so in the Old Testament. And both express this dependence, this relying on Christ; for to betake ourselves wholly unto one is to rely on him. To say, I betake myself to you alone, is as much as I rely only on you.

So מסך, used in the Old Testament for trust, relying, &c., signifies also to approach, to draw near, Ezra xxiv. 2,* answerably the apostle, Heb.

* This sentence is evidently incorrect. There are not twenty-four chapters in the Book of Ezra, and מסך does not mean either to *trust* or to *approach*, but to *mix*. Perhaps it ought to be, 'So חסה, used in the Old Testament for trust, reliance, &c., signifies also to draw near, *Job* xxiv. 2.' In the next paragraph, חסה is three

x. 22, Προσερχώμεθα ἐν πληροφορίᾳ πίστεως, let us come with full sail, with all haste, as a ship when it makes all its sail; or if we take it as it is rendered, full assurance of faith, such a confidence as faith is in its full growth and strength; yet there is also a beginning of our confidence, Heb. iii. 14. The first intent motion of the soul to Christ is ἀρχὴ τῆς ὑποστάσεως,[1] faith in its infancy. But to come to the words whereby it is ordinarily expressed under this notion:

To believe is to come to Christ, John vi. 35; here, to come is to believe. The same may be evidently collected from ver. 64 and 65. We see this in the prodigal; he is an emblem of a sinner both in his fall and in recovery by faith: Luke xv., 'He went into a far country,' ver. 13. A sinner in unbelief is a stranger to Christ, lives at a great distance from him, without God in the world. His employment base, ver. 15; baser is the employment of a sinner; he is sin's drudge, he is Satan's slave, serves them in a cruel bondage; though he gratify Satan, and provide for his lusts, yet he starves his soul, ver. 16. The lusts of the flesh, the vanities of the world, are the husks that a sinner feeds on; no wonder if his soul pine and languish at the gates of death. All this while he is in a swoon, sin has stupified him, he has lost his senses. Though he be ready to perish, he apprehends it not; he comes not to himself till he think of coming to Christ, ver. 17. Till the Lord awaken the stupified conscience by the ministry of the law, till he prick the heart, drop wrath into the soul, make some impressions of terror on it, he remains senseless as to the condition of his soul; but then he comes to himself, he comes to his senses, feels the burden of sin, sees hell ready to swallow him, apprehends himself ready to perish. And then, not till then, he resolves, ver. 18, 'I will arise,' &c., and he pursues his resolution, ver. 20, he came; *i. e.*, he believed. The word in the Old Testament is חסה; Ps. lxiv. 10, 'The righteous shall be glad in the Lord, and' חסה בו 'shall trust in him.' It signifies to fly, to betake one's self to a place of safety; as the chickens, in danger to be seized on, fly under the wings of the hen: Ruth ii. 12, 'Under whose wings thou art come to trust,' לחסות. The helpless bird pursued by the kite, in danger to be devoured, runs under the wing of the dam. Thus it is with a sinner at the first working of faith, he apprehends himself pursued by wrath and judgment; he knows if they seize on him he must perish without remedy. Oh the sad condition of such a soul! Oh, but he sees Christ spreading his wings ready to secure perishing sinners; he hears him inviting in the gospel to come under his shadow. Oh, how sweet is that voice to him (however, while senseless he neglected)! He hears, obeys, and runs to Christ for shelter, and so he is safe: Ps. xxxvi. 7, 'How excellent is thy loving-kindness, O God! therefore the children of men put their trust under the shadow of thy wings.'

To believe in Christ is to fly to him as to a stronghold, a refuge, a sanctuary, Nahum i. 7. The Lord is good, a stronghold, he knoweth them חסי, that trust in him. And hence it is that from this root come some words, חסות and מחסה, which signifies a refuge, a place of security, a hiding place: Ps. xci. 2, 'I will say of the Lord, He is my refuge and fortress: my God; in him will I trust;' Isa. xxx. 3, 'They trust in the shadow of Egypt;' Ps. xiv. 6, 'The Lord is his refuge.'

It is with the sensible sinner as it was with the man-slayer under the law; if the avenger of blood overtook him before he recovered the city of

times printed for חסר: but the correction is put beyond doubt by the references. Indeed, every Hebrew word in this sermon is misprinted.—ED.

refuge, he was to kill him. The awakened sinner perceives that he is pursued by revenging justice, it follows him as Asahel did Joab, pursues him close, he turns not to the right hand nor to the left, and if he overtake him, the sinner dies without mercy, he dies eternally. Now there is no city of refuge for the sinner but Christ only; he is discovered, he is set open in the gospel, and he that gets into him is safe, revenging justice cannot touch him. And therefore the poor sinner makes haste, he flies as for his life, the life of his soul, he knows he is but a dead man if justice reach him; he casts off sin, which clogs him in his flight, he looks not aside to the world, he puts forth the whole strength of his soul, and makes out to Christ with all his might, and never rests till he get into him. This vigorous motion of the soul towards Christ is faith. Those dull and sluggish souls, who have no motion to Christ but some wishes, some faint inclinations, know not what faith is. So eager was the apostle in his tendency to Christ, as he cast off all things as dung, how precious soever they had been to him before; he threw away all as loss and dung that might hinder him in his way to Christ, Phil. iii. Be found in him as in the city of refuge. Joab knew that he was obnoxious to justice; he heard Adonijah was put to death for a crime that he was guilty of, he expected nothing but death except some extraordinary course were taken to prevent it. Now what course he takes you may see; 1 Kings ii. 28, 'he caught hold on the horns of the altar.' Answerably, a sensible sinner, he apprehends his guilt, his provocation, he has received the sentence of death within himself, he knows there are thousands in hell for those very sins whereof he is guilty, and he concludes his soul will be in hell ere long, it may be the next hour, if he take not some course to secure himself from justice. Now there is no sanctuary for a guilty soul but Christ only; therefore he flies to the tabernacle of the Lord, and so takes hold on the horns of the altar; he flies to Christ, lays hold on him, resolves if he die he will die there. There he is safer than Joab in his sanctuary; for Christ is that strong tower to which the righteous fly and are safe, Prov. xviii. 10. This making out to Christ with all the strength of the soul for refuge is faith. To believe is to come, fly, Heb. vi. 18.

2. To believe in Christ is to lean upon him, to stay and rest on him. The word is שען, and it is used when Saul is said to lean upon his spear, 2 Sam. i. 6. Hence comes משען, which signifies a stay, a staff whereon we lean to support ourselves. So the Lord is called: Ps. xviii. 18, 'The Lord was my stay.' Thus, to lean upon Christ is to trust in him, when we stay on him as the only staff and support of our souls. So the word is rendered, Isa. x. 20, when we rest on him. So we have it, 2 Chron. xiv. 11, 'Help us, O Lord our God, for we rest,' &c. More especially, Prov. iii. 5, 'Trust in the Lord,' &c.; Isa. l. 10, 'Let him trust in the name of the Lord, and stay himself,' &c.; where to trust and to stay, בטח and שען are all one, one is explained by the other.

Now this leaning does most significantly express this act of faith we call relying; and so the word is rendered 2 Chron. xiii. 18, 2 Chron. xvi. 7, 8.

There is another word of the same signification, by which the Holy Ghost expresses faith in the Old Testament, and that is סמך, which signifies to lean or stay upon: Isa. xlviii. 2, 'Stay themselves upon the God of Israel,' נסמכו, which is explained to be trusting, Isa. xxvi. 3; סמוך, whose mind is stayed, because he trusteth בטוח. So 2 Kings xviii. 21, 'Thou trustest upon the staff of this bruised reed, on which if a man lean' (יסמך), &c.

Now these words give us great light to discern what this act of saving faith is. A sinner, before the Lord stir him up to believe, is in a dead sleep; and there he dreams of heaven, and who surer of it than he? But when the Lord awakens him, he finds that he has been all this while sleeping on the battlements of hell; all his former hopes and persuasions prove but fancies and delusions. He thought himself safe enough, but he finds that he stands upon the very brink of the bottomless pit; has no sure footing neither; he stands in a slippery place; and the very weight of his sins is enough to carry him down headlong into that place of torment. Sin is a fall, παράπτωμα; and it is a wonder that every sin is not a fall into hell. One sin was heavy enough to cast many hundreds of angels from the height of glory into the lower hell. And alas, then, says the sinner, what shall become of me, who have the weight of so many thousand sins upon my soul! How shall I stand under so many, when they were sunk by the weight of one! Oh what sad thoughts will assail the soul of a sinner, when he is fully apprehensive of his danger! Ay, but this is not all; he not only stands on the ridge of destruction, in such a tottering condition, but Satan is pushing at him, and incensed justice is ready to tumble him down. And what if a tempest of wrath should arise, if the Lord, in just indignation, should come upon him as a whirlwind? what would then become of him? Had he not need to look out for some support, for something to stay his soul on, which otherwise is every moment in danger to tumble into hell? He has nothing at present that keeps him standing but the patience of God. Oh but this is abused, provoked; this is no sure support, he is not sure of it an hour; it may withdraw the next moment, and then where is he? What then can stay the soul from falling into everlasting burnings? Why, none but Christ. Unless he stay his soul upon him, he falls, he sinks, he perishes without remedy. This he hears and believes, and makes out to Christ for support. Not being able to stand under the weight of sin, under the pressures of wrath and justice, he leans upon Christ. The burdened sinking soul rests upon Christ, and so is established, Ps. cxii. 7, 8.

3. To believe in Christ is to adhere to him, to cleave to him, cling about him. The two words last instanced in, rendered to trust, do also signify a close adhering: Numb. xxi. 15, 'Lieth upon the border of Moab,' runs close to it. We may get some sparks from this word to light us in this search. A man that has suffered shipwreck is left to the mercy of the waves; has nothing in his reach to secure him but some planks or mast. How will he cling to it! how fast will he clasp! He will hold it as if it were his life, 2 Kings xviii. 5, Deut. iv. 4. He knows he is a dead man if he leave it; and therefore if any wave drive him off, he makes to it again with all his might, and clasps it faster. He knows there is no way but sink and perish if he part with it.

A sinner, when the Lord begins to work faith in him, apprehends himself in a gulf of wrath; all the billows and waves go over him, and the depths are ready to swallow him up. Now in this case he sees no other security but Christ; he is the only *tabula post naufragium*, the only plank that is left (after our miserable wreck in Adam) to bring a sinner to shore; and therefore he cleaves to him; his soul clasps about him; he holds him as he would hold his soul ready to leave him, if it could come into his embraces. He knows, if he part, he sinks for ever; and therefore if any apprehension of wrath, of sin, of unworthiness, would drive him off, he clings closer to him, or he sinks eternally.

4. To believe in Christ is to roll, to cast ourselves upon him. The word is גלל, rendered by trust: Ps. xxii. 8, 'He trusted in the Lord,' גל אל יהוה, he rolled himself upon the Lord; so Ps. xxxvii. 5, Commit thy way,' גול על־יהוה, roll thy way upon the Lord; and what that is, the next words shew, בטח, it is to trust in him; so Prov. xvi. 3, 'Commit thy works unto the Lord,' גל, the same word, roll thy works upon, &c. The expression is explained by another word, שלך: Ps. lv. 23, 'Cast thy burden upon the Lord,' &c., a metaphor taken from one ready to fall down under a heavy burden; he casts it upon one more able to bear it.

Now sin is a heavy, a most grievous burden; the Lord himself complains of the weight of it, Amos ii. 13. The weight of sin, though Christ had none of his own, made him sweat, and sweat blood; made his soul heavy. It is burdened with the wrath and heavy indignation of God; it is clogged with the curses and threatenings of the law, so called frequently. No wonder if one sin be as a millstone about the neck of the soul, able to sink it into the bottom of hell.

But though it be so burdensome, yet the sinner, till conversion, finds no weight in it. No wonder, since he is dead in trespasses. Cast rocks and mountains upon a dead man, he feels them not.

Ay, but when the Lord begins to work faith, and brings the sinner to himself, then he feels it burdensome indeed; he wonders at his former stupidness, he groans under the weight, he apprehends himself even sinking under the burden; and if he be not eased of this burden, he feels it will press him into hell. He lies grovelling under the weight, and cries, Help, help, or else I sink, I perish; and who is there that can help the soul in this sad condition?

If he should call to the angels, they know it is too heavy, they dare not come near it; they can remember since the weight of one sin sunk some thousands of their companions into the bottomless pit.

If he should call to the saints, they have enough of their own burden, Ps. xxxviii. 4.

If he should call to the inferior creatures, they need help as well as he. It is the weight of sin that makes the whole creation groan and travail in pain, Rom. viii. 22. Let the oppressed sinner cry out to whom he will, they will all answer, as the king to the woman, 'If the Lord do not help,' &c.

Why, then, must the burdened sinner perish? Is there no remedy? Yes, the Lord has laid help on one that is mighty. Christ is willing, and he is only able to ease the burdened soul. He invites him to come; he will take the burden on himself, rather than the soul shall sink under it. Now, the sinner hearing this, it is glad tidings indeed to him: he closes with Christ, rolls himself, casts his burdened soul upon him, and so believes. For a sinner thus burdened, thus sensible of the weight of sin, to roll himself upon Christ, is to believe in him.

5. To believe in Christ, is to apply him. It is an intimate application, such as that of meat and drink by one pinched with hunger, and fainting with thirst. Hence faith is expressed by eating, John vi. 51, 53, 54, 56. To eat there, is to believe. It is not sacramental eating, as some mistake it; for then all that partake not of that ordinance should be damned (no infants should be saved), and all that partake of it should be saved; whereas this is against experience, that against charity, both against truth. But it is a spiritual eating, that is, believing, as we are led by the coherence to expound it, verse 35. That which is eating here, is there

coming (fiducial coming); and that which is drinking here, is there believing. So in the Old Testament, סמך, ordinarily rendered to trust, rely, or stay on one, does also signify to nourish, to refresh and comfort, as one fainting is refreshed with wine: Cant. ii. 5, סמכוני, 'Stay me with flaggons;' and the only other word untouched, which the Old Testament uses for faith, אמן, signifies in Kal *nutrire*, in Hiphil *fidere*. This is enough to evince that faith is an application, such an application of Christ as that of nourishment to one that is hungry. And this tends something to discover the nature of this act, which we shall make evident by a Scripture allusion, Gen. xxi. The state of Hagar and her son in the desert resembles the state of a sinner in unbelief. They are for their insolency cast out of Abraham's family; they wander, and lose themselves in the wilderness; and, which is worse, their provision is quite spent, and nothing is to be looked for but a miserable death. Nay, death is already seizing on Ishmael; he faints, and she not enduring to see him die in this extremity, withdraws herself, lifts up her voice, and weeps, verse 16. Now the Lord, pitying them in this forlorn condition, shews her a well of water. Oh with what great eagerness, do ye think, with what greediness, does she apply this water, to save the life of her dying child! Thus it is with a sinner; he is cast out from the presence of God for his rebellion; he wanders, and loses God, and then loses himself. In this sad condition his provisions are spent, he has nothing to support his soul, nothing to feed on but wind. His soul faints and languishes, and lies gasping even at the gates of eternal death. This is his sad condition, and this he apprehends when the Lord begins to work faith; and oh with what anguish does the apprehension thereof afflict him! Nothing can save his soul from death but a draught of the water of life, a taste of Christ. The Lord in this extremity discovers Christ, opens his eyes to see the fountain of life opened in the gospel. And when the sinner, in sense of his dying condition, applies Christ for life, then he believes. When the soul takes in this water of life as greedily as the hunted hart, who in danger of death, both from burning thirst within, and the eager pursuers without, pants after, and plunges himself in the water-brooks: when the soul, in sense of such extremities from the indignation of God on all sides, takes in this water of life as he would take in life itself, then he believes, Ps. xlii. 1, 2.

6. To believe in Christ is to receive him, John i. 12. Receiving is explained by believing; so that to receive is to believe on him, Col. ii. 6, 7. As faith has taken root by this first act of receiving, so let it grow strong and fruitful. Sometimes the object of it is otherwise expressed; so that to believe in Christ is to receive his righteousness, and to receive remission of sins. And these expressions give light to discover the nature of this act, as we shall improve them by a similitude or two.

A poor man over head and ears in debt, who owes more than he can pay, if himself and all that he has were sold for payment. The serjeants arrest him, and hale him to prison, and there he is like to spend all his days miserably in a dungeon; while he is afflicted with the sad apprehension of his misery, and even at the prison door, and one offers him a sum that will discharge all that he owes, oh how will the poor man be transported with such an offer! how joyfully will he receive it, though it were upon condition that he should be his benefactor's servant all his life!

The case is parallel. Sinners are debtors to the great God. Sins are called ὀφειλήματα, Mat. vi. 12. The least sin is such a debt, as the sinner's body and soul is not of sufficient value to discharge it. But justice must be satisfied, and in default hereof, the sinner is every moment in danger to be cast into hell, and must not come out till he have paid that which he can never pay, the utmost farthing.

Now while the sensible soul is dejected with these apprehensions, Christ in the gospel offers him his righteousness, of such value that it will satisfy the utmost demand of justice.

Now when the sinner receives this with such an open heart, such a transported soul, as a debtor dragged to prison would receive a jewel able to satisfy all his creditors, when he thus receives it, he believes, Rom. v. 17. This gift of righteousness is that which is elsewhere called our λύτρον, the price of our redemption. To receive this, is to believe. For that which is receiving the gift of righteousness, ver. 17, and receiving the atonement, verse 11, is styled, being justified by faith, verse 1.

To believe, is to receive remission of sins, Acts xxvi. 18. And this affords another simile, to illustrate the matter in hand.

A condemned person upon the scaffold, all the instruments of death ready, and nothing wanting but one blow to separate soul and body, while he is possessed with sad apprehensions of death, one unexpectedly comes, and brings him a pardon. Oh how will his heart welcome it! How will his hands receive it, as though his soul were in his hands! So here.

A sinner, while in unbelief, is condemned already, he has received the sentence of death in himself; and there remains nothing but a fearful expectation of judgment, and the fiery indignation, nothing but an expectation of execution, but a step betwixt him and the eternal death. He hears the gospel in this condition offering mercy, and proclaiming a pardon through the precious blood of our Lord Jesus Christ.

Now for the dying soul to revive at these glad tidings, to welcome Christ, to receive him for the remission of sins, as the condemned person with his neck upon the block would receive a pardon, is to believe, Acts x. 43.

7. To believe in Christ, is to apprehend him, to lay hold of him, to embrace him: Rom. ix. 30, 'have attained to righteousness.' The best Latin translators render κατέλαβε, by *apprehenderunt*, have apprehended, have laid hold on the righteousness of faith, *i. e.*, the righteousness of Christ, who is the Lord our righteousness, the proper object of justifying faith. Now what it is to apprehend the righteousness of Christ, or Christ who is our righteousness, we are taught, verse 33. So that to believe on him, and to apprehend his righteousness, is all one.

It is to embrace Christ, Heb. xi. 13; ἀσπασάμενοι; they had not yet received the promises, *i. e.*, the things promised. Christ was not yet exhibited, he was afar off; but he was offered in the promise, there they embraced him, *i. e.*, believed on him. For there the apostle is giving an account of the several acts of faith, whereof this is the principal, to embrace Christ in the promise.

And this we may improve to discover the nature of this saving act, Mat. xiv. 29–31. There Peter was so bold, as to come out of the ship and walk upon the waters. But when the tempest grew strong, then his heart fails him, and then he begins to sink, and sinking he cries out, Lord, save me! Christ, seeing him ready to perish, stretches out his hand, or, as some render it, takes him by the hand, and so cures him. Answerably here.

To walk in the ways of sin, is to walk as it were upon the waters; there is no sure footing, how bold soever sinners are to venture. If patience were not infinite, we should sink every moment. The sensible sinner, he begins to see his danger, patience will long ere withdraw, it will not be always abused; a tempest of wrath will arise; nay, he finds it grow boisterous, it does already ruffle his conscience, he is as sure to sink, as if he were walking upon the waves. Nay, he feels his soul already sinking; no wonder if he cry out as a lost man, as one ready to be swallowed up in a sea of wrath.

But now Christ stretches out his hand in the gospel. Now for the soul in sense of its sinking state, to stretch out itself to lay hold on that everlasting arm, that only can save him from going down into the bottomless pit, this is to believe, Cant. iii. 4, *apprehendi eum*;* to hold him, as one falling from a steep place, in danger to be dashed in pieces, holds a branch, a bough that he meets with, that he catches at in his fall; to hold Christ, as that only which can stay him, when he finds himself falling into hell and eternal destruction; to embrace, as he would embrace life, glory, happiness.

This may be sufficient to discover the nature of faith. But for further evidence, observe what is included in it, as appears by the former.

1. Sense of misery. It is a sensible dependence. Faith presupposes sense of misery. When the Lord brings a sinner to believe, he makes him thoroughly apprehensive of his miserable condition by reason of sin and wrath; he not only assents to it, but is sensible of it.

A man that has read or heard much of the sad effects of war, he may assent, believe that it is a great misery to be infected with war. Ay, but when the enemy is at his door, when they are driving his cattle, and plundering his goods, and firing his houses, he not only assents to it, but he sees, he feels the miseries of it; he has more sensible, more affecting apprehensions of it than ever. A sinner that continues in unbelief, hearing the threatenings, the wrath denounced against unbelievers, he may assent to this, that unbelievers are in a miserable condition; but when the Lord is working faith, he brings this home to himself; he sees justice ready to seize on him, he feels wrath kindling upon him. He now not only believes it, but has a quick sense of it. He has often heard of the misery of such a condition by the hearing of the ear, but now his eye sees it, and he sees it so as his eye affects his heart. He has often heard of the burden and danger of sin, but now he feels it. He apprehends himself at the point of sinking under it. He has often heard how terrible the wrath of God is, but looking on it at a distance, it did no more affect him than a painted fire; ay, but now he feels the heat of it, it begins to kindle in his soul, and scorch his conscience. He has heard of dreadful threatenings and curses denounced against such and such sins, but he looked upon them as at a distance, as discharged at random; ay, but now he sees them levelled at himself, his soul in the butt, the mark to which those arrows aim and are directed, and the poison thereof drinks up his spirits. He reads and hears the terrible things denounced against sin, as though he were another man, and is affected with them as though they were not the same things. He wonders at his former stupidness. This thunder is not afar off, but it startles him, as though he were even in the thunder-cloud. Till it be thus in some degree, he will not believe, will not come to Christ, till they not only enter his fancy and understanding, but prick his heart. The physician is neglected, while the patient thinks himself in health. The whole, *i. e.*, those that think themselves whole, see no need of the great physician. Till the sinner apprehend himself, his soul sick unto death, Christ is not

* Meroir.

looked after. The malefactor will never sue for a pardon to purpose, till he be (or apprehend himself in danger to be) condemned. No flying to this stronghold, till there be some fear of pursuers. There will be no flying to Christ, no believing in him, without some sense of misery. . Lot would never have fled to the mountain, but that the country was all in a flame, Gen. x. 28.

2. A rejecting of other dependences, other supports. It is a sole depending, a relying upon Christ alone. While the sinner depends upon anything else, in himself, or without himself, for safety, he believes not on Christ, he stands no longer upon* his own legs. While the sinner stands upon his own bottom, his own righteousness, his good meaning, good nature, good deeds, his charitableness or religiousness, his being better than others, or not so bad as most, and upon this raises hopes of pardon, he is far from faith, he is but in the condition of the unjustified Pharisee. But when he looks upon these as no greater securities than tow or stubble would be, to shroud him from a consuming fire, then he will look out for a better screen to interpose betwixt his soul and that fiery indignation that his sins have kindled.

When the soul, feeling the flame of wrath kindling on her, cries out as one that is already perishing, None but Christ, none but Christ, then he is in the highway to faith.

If the dove which Noah sent out could have found rest for the sole of her feet elsewhere, she would not have returned unto the ark, Gen. viii. 12. Such an averseness there is in our natures to Christ, as he is the last thing a sinner looks after. If he can rest in anything else, if he can find rest in his friends, in his boon companions, in his accommodations, in his worldly employments, in his religious duties, in his good accomplishments; if he find rest to the sole of his foot here, the ark is forgotten, he returns not to Christ. But when he sees a deluge of wrath overwhelm him, when the waters of God's wrath rise so high as nothing appears but the ark, nothing to rest on but Christ, nothing but drowning and perishing in the common deluge, except he get into the ark, then he rests not till he gets into Christ, then he flies to him as for his life. See faith thus working in Ephraim, Hosea xiv. 4. They reject all foreign dependences: 'Asshur shall not save us;' they reject all dependence on themselves: 'we will not ride,' &c. They reject all that they had formerly idolised, and that by relying on them, they knew that this was the high way to mercy. None but the fatherless, τὸ ὀρφανόν. Till the sinner apprehend himself as an orphan, without strength, without counsel, all his supports dead which were a father to him, he will not betake himself to Christ as his only guardian; till he thus betake himself to Christ, he believes not.

3. Submission. Faith is a very submissive grace. Sin and wrath lie so heavy, as the soul is bended to what the Lord will. If he will but pardon me, says the humbled sinner, if he will but forgive me, let him deal with me otherwise as seems good in his eyes. If he will but shew mercy, let the Lord do it when and how he pleases. Ps. xxxvii. 7, 'Rest,' that is, trust; but the word is דום, 'be silent to the Lord.' That is the temper of faith, whatever the Lord says or does, the believing soul is silent. He is sensible of so much sinfulness and wretchedness, as worse cannot be said of him than he is, worse cannot be inflicted on him than he deserves; and therefore let the Lord say of him, and do with him what he pleases, he puts his mouth in the dust, and is silent. Only let his life be given

* Qu. 'stands upon'?—ED.

him, the life of his soul, and however otherwise the Lord proceeds, he will not reply. If the Lord say, he shall continue upon the rack of terror, he submits; only, says he, Lord, save my life, let me have that for a prey. If the Lord say, though he pardon him, yet he will make him exemplary by sharp afflictions, that the contagion of his example may not spread, O Lord, says he, only spare my life; whatever is not hell is mercy to such a wretch as I am.

The sinner has been battered by the law, justice does besiege him, wrath is ready to assault, he sees himself reduced to extremity, he stands not upon terms, indents not with the besieger, but yields at discretion, will be at the mercy of the conqueror, cautious for nothing but his life, stands upon nothing but his soul, that this may not perish for ever. Whatever is not death, whatever is not eternal wrath, is infinite mercy to such a rebel as I have been. If the shipwrecked man can get to shore, can save himself from drowning, he regards not the wetting of his clothes, the spoiling of his goods; a greater matter is in danger; so it is with a sinner, in whom faith is working. His soul is in a sea of wrath, he is ready to sink; if he can but reach Christ, get to shore, he is content, though he come there naked, stripped of all that was otherwise dear to him. For why? His soul is in danger; if the Lord let that escape, come what will come else, he submits, he is silent.

4. Resolution to persist in his dependence. It is a resolute dependence, he is resolved to keep his hold whatever the event be. He knows justice is incensed, and the wrath of God is kindled against him, and whether or no the Lord may proceed to destroy him, he knows not; but he apprehends withal that there is no other way to pacify the Lord, no other way to escape wrath, but by casting himself on Christ, and therefore he resolves to persist in it.

It is with him as with Esther in her undertaking for the Jews, Esther iv. 16. If she should go, and the king not hold forth the golden sceptre to her, she was but a dead woman; but then if she did not go there was no other way to save her and her nation from ruin, and therefore she resolves, 'I will go in unto the king, and if I perish, I perish.' So here, if I go to Christ (thinks the trembling sinner), and take sanctuary in him, it may be justice may pursue me thither; Oh, but if I go not, then there is nothing for me but certain destruction; thereupon he resolves, I will go to Christ, I will lay hold on him, and if I perish I will perish there; if wrath seize on me, it shall find me in the arms of Christ; if I die, I will die at his feet.

When Joab had fled for refuge to the tabernacle, and caught hold of the horns of the altar, Benaiah, sent to execute him, bids him leave his sanctuary: 1 Kings ii. 30, 'Thus says the king, Come forth.' 'Nay,' says Joab, 'but I will die here;' if there be no mercy for me, no remedy but I must die, I will die here.

Thus the humbled sinner when he has taken sanctuary in Christ, and laid hold of Christ; when Satan or his own guilty soul tell him that he must come forth, there is no mercy for such a traitor, such a heinous offender; nay, says the believing soul, but if I must die, I will die here; if justice smite me, it shall smite me with Christ in my arms; though he kill me, yet will I rely on him; here will I live, or here will I die; I will not quit my hold, though I die for it.

This his resolution as to his former evil way. He will not quit his hold of Christ, to return to his former courses, though he die here. As the three children, Dan. iii. 17, 18, 'The Lord on whom I rely is able to deliver me; but if not,' I will never serve my lusts any more.

5. Support. It is an establishing dependence. The heart that trusts, that relies on Christ, is in some degree or other fixed, more or less established: Ps. cxii. 7, 8, 'His heart is fixed, trusting in the Lord.' His heart is established, סָמַךְ, rendered to *trust*, to *lean*; transitive signifies to *underprop*: Ps. lxxi. 6, 'By thee have I been holden up from the womb.' A man cast into the sea scrambles up to a rock to secure him; the rock is firm enough, able to support; ay, but the apprehension of his late danger has left impressions of fear on him; he is still timorous; though he be above the water, he knows not but a storm may blow him off, or a wave may wash him again into the deep.

Christ is the rock of ages; he that stays on him stands firm; he cannot but have some support for the present, though he has little confidence, no assurance. He cannot yet say, The Lord will shew me mercy, I shall have pardon, he will be reconciled, I shall be saved; he cannot conclude this certain. Though there be *certitudo objecti*, yet not *certitudo subjecti;* though it be sure he shall not perish, yet he is not sure, he is not fully persuaded of it. Only this he has to support him, it may be the Lord will pity me, will shew mercy. He has that which was Benhadad's support in his great extremity, 1 Kings xx. 31. The Lord is a merciful king, and this is the only way to find mercy, peradventure he will save my life. Who knows but the Lord may be reconciled? Who can tell? Jonah iii. 9. This bears up the heart at present, and by degrees he finds more and more support. It is with him as with the lepers, 2 Kings vii. 3, 4: 1, he may; 2, he will; 3, he has.

6. A consent to accept Christ on his own terms. This is included in the phrase of coming to Christ, and receiving him, whereby faith is ordinarily expressed. For we must not understand by coming, any corporal motion, but a motion of the soul. Now the will is *animæ locomotiva facultas*, the soul's moving faculty, the organ whereby it performs this motion; it moves to an object by consent, and from an object by dissent. When it consents to take Christ, it comes to him; it is included in the phrase of receiving Christ; for this is an act of the soul too; and the will is the soul's receptive power; it is as the hand of the soul, which closes when it dissents, and opens when it consents. The will is naturally closed against Christ, but consent opens it; and when the will is open to receive him, it always receives him; when it opens, it consents; when it consents, it receives, *i. e.*, believes.

II. Of the object. Having largely opened the act of saving faith, it remains that I declare what the object of it is; for virtues, as other habits, being defined by their acts and objects, as being their prime essentials, the essence and nature of this saving faith will be apparent when to the explication of its acts I have added a declaration of its object.

Now, this I shall endeavour, 1, in general; 2, more distinctly in some particular propositions.

1. In general. The object of justifying or saving faith is Christ; it is he by and in whom faith seeks pardon and salvation. For this purpose to him a believer flies, on him he leans and rolls himself, to him he cleaves and clings. It is Christ he applies, receives, apprehends, and embraces when he would obtain pardon and life. I should rehearse to you a great part of the gospel if I should allege all those testimonies which the Scrip-

ture gives to this truth, Gal. ii. 16, Acts xvi. 31, Rom. ix. 33, Gal. iii. 26, 1 Peter ii. 6, John iii. 16, 18, 36.

2. More particularly.

(1.) The whole word of God is the adequate and general object of faith, when faith is taken for assent. Saving faith believes the histories, the precepts, the threatenings; but as it believes these, it is not saving; for those that shall not be saved, viz., the devils and reprobates, may believe as much. Justifying faith assents to the whole, but it does not justify as it assents to the whole, but as it rests on Christ; even as the hand which feeds the body hath many offices, to work, to receive, to defend; but it feeds not, but as it conveys nourishment to the mouth. As the rational soul has many powers and acts besides the power to understand,—it remembers, and wills, and fancies, but it understands not but as it apprehends the truth of its object,—so justifying faith has many acts besides that whereby it justifies: it believes the threatenings, yields to the commands, assents to the historical relations of the word, but it justifies only as it respects Christ. So that the whole word of God is not the proper and specifical object of saving faith.

(2.) The mercy of God is but a partial object of faith. A partial, I say, because this alone is not enough to give faith any hold. Faith can find no mercy to pitch on but in and through Christ, nor is there any mercy for a sinner out of him. Therefore Christ must be added before mercy can be an ample object for faith to fix on. Christ is the only mercy-seat of faith. Would it find mercy? it must seek it where it is to be found, where it is seated: Rom. iii. 25, *ὃν προέθετο ὁ Θεὸς ἱλαστήριον*, whom God has placed as a mercy-seat; the same word, Heb. ix. 5, *κατασκιάζοντα τὸ ἱλαστήριον*. The mercy-seat in the tabernacle was a type of Christ; and the posture of it is no more mysterious than comfortable, Exod. xxv. It was the covering of the ark, above it were the cherubims of glory, the seat of the divine Majesty; and therefore he is said to sit betwixt the cherubims, Ps. lxxx. 1. Under it were the tables of the covenant, or of the testimony, as it is called, Exod. xxv.; *i.e.*, of the law, which bears testimony against sinners, which accuses, curses, condemns. Christ the mercy-seat is interposed betwixt the judge and the condemning law. Take away Christ, and nothing can be expected from the Judge but the law in its rigour, law without mercy. As the law will shew no mercy, that is all for justice, so the Lord will shew no mercy but on the mercy-seat, none but through Christ. Christ must be added to make mercy a complete, a fit object for faith. Without him it is but a partial object, if any at all. Mercy through Christ is faith's object. If faith pitch on mercy without him, it will pitch upon that which will not support it.

(3.) The promises of the gospel, they are the less principal, the subservient objects of faith. The promise is as the dish wherein Christ, the bread of life, the manna from heaven, is set before faith, and presented to it. Both are served up together; but faith feeds not on the dish, but on the manna, the bread of life in it.

The promise is as a glass, a prospective, wherein the Day-star, the Sun of Righteousness is discerned. When we make use of a glass to discover a star, we look upon both; but our sight is not terminated in the glass, the use of it is to be subservient to a farther discovery, to be helpful to our sight to discover the star, which is the principal object. So faith, 'with open face,' does, in the promise, 'as in a glass behold the glory of God,' take a view of Christ who is the brightness of his Father's glory.

The promise is but subservient to that happy, that delightful sight of Christ. And therefore I call it a subservient object, a mediate, less principal object.

(4.) The proper and principal object of faith is the person of Christ; not the promise of Christ, not the benefits of Christ, but the person of Christ; not the promise, as we shewed before. Faith is not an assent to a proposition affirmed, but affiance in a Saviour offered; not the benefits firstly and principally. Faith unites the soul to Christ; it is the bond of our conjugal union. Now, we marry not the dowry, but the person.

That faith respects Christ himself in the first place, appears by the notions of faith, which we may collect from Scripture.

Faith is the *hand* of the soul; so it receives Christ himself, who is the gift of God, John iv. 10.

It is the *arm* of the soul; so it embraces Christ, Cant. iii. 4.

It is the *eye* of the soul; so it looks upon Christ, as the stung Israelites upon the brazen serpent, John iii. 14, 15.

It is the *mouth* of the soul; so it feeds on Christ the bread from heaven, John vi. 32–34.

It is the *foot* of the soul; so it comes to Christ, Mat. xi., John vi.

It is the *lips* of the soul; so it kisses Christ, Ps. ii. In all it has an immediate respect to Christ, to his person.

(5.) The person of Christ, as invested with his righteousness, is the formal object. Not the person of Christ barely considered, but as clothed with a righteousness qualifying him to a Mediator, a Saviour; as one that has fulfilled the law and satisfied justice in whatever it could demand on our behalf. As Christ without this would not be a Saviour, so without this he cannot be the object of saving faith: Rom. iii. 25, 'Through faith in his blood;' where blood, being the most signal part of his satisfaction, is put for his whole righteousness. Here is in this verse whatever is assigned as a special object of faith. Here is Christ and his righteousness expressly the formal object; faith in his blood, called ἀπολύτρωσις, ver. 24, through the redemption, *i. e.*, through the satisfaction of Christ, who paid a satisfactory price (a λύτρον) that captive sinners might be delivered. And that price was his righteousness, here called his blood: *ut significetur fidem non aliò quam ad Christi sacrificium ferri.*

The person of Christ, the principal object, in the particle ὅν, Jesus Christ, whom, &c.

The gospel, the subservient object, intimated in προέθετο, whom God has set forth; as in the decree and in his understanding, so in the gospel, now seen, Rev. xi. 19.

The mercy of God the partial object, to be a propitiation, a mercy-seat, and this by his blood: *ut per hostiam corporis sui hominibus propitium faceret Deum.** Faith does, in the business of our justification, embrace whole Christ; but it is properly terminated in his blood.† That is the proper (as I take it), the formal object of saving faith, that righteousness by virtue of which Christ is a Saviour.

(6.) The benefits of Christ are but the secondary objects of faith, Rom. viii. 32; they seem more properly to be the end of faith. We depend not upon pardon or salvation, but upon Christ for pardon and salvation; and that not as having obtained, but that we may obtain them.

* Origen.

† Fides totum Christum amplectitur, et proprie in ejus sanguine terminatur.—*Pareus.*

Faith at first relies on Christ, not as one that has pardoned sin, but as one through whom alone pardon is to be obtained. The persuasion that sin is pardoned is a consequent of justifying faith, it is not the justifying act.

III. How does the Lord work faith? That is the next thing we undertook to shew, in what manner, by what steps and degrees, the Lord ordinarily proceeds when he brings a sinner to believe. Having giving an account of the act and object, let us see how the Lord brings the act and object together.

But, 1, we shall not attempt to shew how this is wrought in infancy or those of unriper years, for that is a secret; the Scripture seems reserved in this case, and secret things belong not to us.

And, 2, there are some extraordinary cases wherein the Lord proceeds not in the ordinary method. He ties not himself to one track. He is a most free agent, and works as when, so how, he pleases. We shall only follow him in the ordinary, the beaten road, where his footsteps are visible by Scripture and experience.

And, 3, in ordinary cases there is great variety in respect of circumstantials; it may be as much variety as there is in faces. Now, as no limner will undertake to draw a piece that shall exactly resemble every face in every feature and lineament, though, without any curious inspection of particulars, he may draw one that will easily distinguish a man from any other creature, so we will not undertake to give such a discovery as will exactly answer every one's experience in circumstantials, but such as may be sufficient to distinguish a saving work from that which is but common to those that are not sound believers. And this will be very useful, both for discovering faith where it is, and for direction where it is not, to shew what way they must walk in who would attain it. To proceed then.

The Lord, when he works faith in those that enjoy the gospel, and are capable of improving it, doth ordinarily proceed by these steps, and brings them to believe by these degrees.

1. A discovery of sin, which the Lord makes by the law and by the Spirit, Rom. vii. 7. The law of God is a light. A sinner, while he continues in unbelief, he shuts it out as an unwelcome guest; hates the light, John iii. 20; but now the Lord brings it into the soul and conscience, and this discovers sin to purpose. In the dark great things seem small, and small things are not discerned; while in security, great sins are extenuated, neglected, and small sins are not at all taken notice of, but this makes a discovery of great and small.

The Spirit of God concurs with the law. It is his office, and one of the first he performs to the unbelieving world, John xvi. 8, ἐλέγξει. Before he convince of righteousness, he shall make evident their sin, give them a demonstration of it, make their sin manifest. That is the import of the word, ἔλεγχος γάρ ἐστι λίαν δηλῶν,* a clear manifestation.

This is the first thing he works by the ministry of the word, when it is effectual, Acts xxvi. 18, to open their eyes, before he turn them to God, before they receive forgiveness of sin, before they have faith to receive it: He opens their eyes, &c. They were as blind men before, but now they see sin in its colours. Their apprehensions of sin now differ as much from those they had of it formerly, as the conceits which a blind man has of colours differ from his apprehensions of them when his eyes are opened. He apprehends his sins in their number and danger, guilt and stain, weight

* Chrysost.

and heinousness, in their dishonouring and incensing quality as to God, in their defiling and damning power as to himself.

The Spirit of God removes all excuses which he made use of to extenuate sin, make it seem light, and keep the weight of it from his conscience; now he looks on it as aggravated, as exceeding sinful, exceeding damnable.

And though this discovery begin with some one particular sin, which the Lord sets home to the conscience, as the apostle first convinced the Jews of their sin in crucifying Christ, Acts ii., yet usually it rests not in one, but proceeds to more. As a man run much in debt is first arrested for one sum, but when he is clapped up, then one action is laid on him after another, till he be charged with the whole debt; so after the sinner is under this arrest of the law, when one sin has seized effectually on the conscience, the rest (as David said of his enemies) like bees, &c., he can say with a sad heart, 'Lord, how are they increased that trouble me.'

As the Lord led Ezekiel from one place to another, and the further he went the greater abominations he discerned, Ezek. viii. 6, from the door of the court, ver. 7, to the door of the gate of the Lord's house, ver. 14, and from thence to the inner court, ver. 16; so the Spirit of the Lord leads the sinner from one part of his house to another, from one room, one faculty of his soul to another, and still discovers greater, more and more abominations; leads him from the profaneness of his ordinary conversation to the sins of his religious duties, and from the sins of his life to the sins of his heart, from the streams of sin in his actions to the spring of sin which bubbles up continually in every part of his soul, Job xiii. 26. He brings to mind the sins that he has forgotten, makes him possess the sins of his youth, of his youngest years; though he had let them slip out of his mind, yet the Lord takes a course to retain them, he seals them up in a bag, Job xiv. 17. And now the bag is opened, and the sinner sees what he is to reckon for, he cries out as the prophet's servant: 2 Kings vi. 15, 'How shall we do?' and as David, Ps. xxxviii. 4, 'Mine iniquities are gone over mine head: as an heavy burden, they are too heavy for me.'

2. Application of the desert of sin. The Lord convinces him that all those dreadful things which are denounced against sin belong to him, so that he applies them in particular to himself. He not only apprehends in general what is due to sin, the curses and threatenings of the law, the sentence of condemnation, the wrath of God, &c., but he applies these in particular: I have sinned thus and thus, and these are due to my sins, and therefore these are my portion.

Heretofore he looked upon these in general without any personal application; or if he applied them it was to others: Such and such a notorious sinner, these will fall heavy upon him, but I am not so wicked, mercy will keep off these from me. Oh, but now these are laid at his own door; his conscience tells him (as Nathan did David), 'Thou art the man.' So he takes it to himself: I am the man whom the Lord threatens, whom the law condemns, whom justice pursues, whose portion is the wrath of God, who am sentenced to death. He looks not upon the tempest of wrath as afar off, as that which may spend itself before it reach him, but he feels it beat upon his own vessel, ready to sink it; the sea of wrath works and is tempestuous about him, and his conscience speaks, as Jonah i. 12, 'I know that for my sake this great tempest is come,' it is I, that vengeance follows; it is I, that in justice and sentence of law stand condemned to eternal death.

He comes not to the assizes as formerly, to be a spectator, to see others tried and condemned. He sees himself now at the bar, himself arraigned and indicted, he cannot but plead guilty. He is clearly cast in law, and he hears the sentence of condemnation as though his name were writ in the Scripture, as though the Lord did by name pronounce sentence against him.

This is the work of the spirit of bondage, of which, Rom. viii. 15, where observe the order and opposition.

The *order*. The spirit of bondage goes before the spirit of adoption; again, intimating plainly, they had received the spirit of bondage formerly, viz., before they had received the spirit of adoption. They had fearful apprehensions of wrath, before they had the assurances of a Father's love.

The *opposition*. These two spirits are opposed in their works. The work of the spirit of adoption is to witness together without our spirits, the spirit of believers, that they are the children [of God]; and, therefore, the work of the spirit of bondage is to witness together with the spirits, the consciences of unbelievers that they are the children of wrath.

And as the spirit of adoption works this comfortable assurance by way of a practical reasoning, in like manner does the spirit of bondage give in the contrary testimony by way of a syllogism. 'Cursed is every one that continues,' &c. But I have continued in practices quite against the law, *ergo*, I am cursed. 'The wages of sin is death;' but thousands of sins lie upon my charge, *ergo*, eternal death is due to me. 'The wrath of God is revealed from heaven,' &c. But I am guilty of so much ungodliness, so much unrighteous; *therefore* what remains but that the wrath of God should be revealed from heaven against me? The Lord Jesus shall be revealed from heaven in flaming fire, taking vengeance on them that know not God, and obey not the gospel of our Lord, 2 Thes. i. 7, 8, but I have disobeyed the gospel, and, *therefore* (unless salvation come by the Lord Jesus Christ), I shall be punished with everlasting destruction from the presence of God, verse 9. 'He that believes not is condemned already,' John iii. 'The wrath of God abides on him;' but I have continued in unbelief, *ergo*, I am condemned, the wrath of God abides on me, and (unless some gracious provision be made for my perishing soul) I shall be damned. This application, &c., is another step to faith. And though the condition of a sinner under these convictions seem sad, yet is far more hopeful than the state of those who continue secure and senseless, because they are in the way, they are upon the anvil; and though the law be a hammer to them (as the word is called, Jer. xxiii. 29), and the strokes thereof be terrible, yet this is the way to be polished, to be made fit stones for Christ's temple, for the New Jerusalem; whereas secure sinners are as stones in the quarry, far off from that which is but a preparative to faith and salvation.

3. Compunction. The soul is wounded with the apprehensions of sin and wrath; the weight of them lie heavy upon his conscience, they enter as iron into his soul: Acts ii. 37, 'When they heard this,' when their sin was applied particularly, ye have crucified, verses 36 and 23, and apprehended what was due in particular for such a horrid act, 'they were pricked at the heart,' κατενύγησαν, it pierced their hearts as though they had been run through with a sword or a spear. So the word is used ΙΛ. Ο. νύσσοντες ξίφεσιν τὲ καὶ ἔγχεσιν. Such acute anguish, such piercing grief, did wound their souls, as though a sword had lanced their very hearts, Jer. vi. 4. It is a rending of the heart elsewhere, Joel ii. 13, a ploughing up of the heart. The law armed with wrath makes deep furrows in the heart. Now what anguish will follow such a rending, a wounding of the heart, we may imagine; but our thoughts and our words will come short of the sinner's sense.

The issue of such a particular application of wrath must needs be fear, horror, anguish, and fearful expectations of judgment. The very discourse of this made Felix to tremble, Acts xxiv. 25, much more might the gaoler tremble, who had the sense of it, Acts xvi. 29.

The Lord sometimes makes use of outward providences, the sight or report of some fearful judgment, or the quick apprehensions of death, to startle the sinner, and likewise to bring him to the sense of his misery. These may be subservient to the word, to begin or increase this consternation of the soul, as we see the earthquake was to the gaoler, verse 28.

And the Lord, when he makes his word effectual, he fixes the eye of the soul upon these sad things, holds it to them. This is grievous to nature, the sinner will be inclined to shake off these sad thoughts, and Satan will be ready to offer him diversions enough, to draw him to his jovial companions, that he may drown or sing away these cares, or to engage him in deep worldly business, that the noise of the world may drown the cries of his conscience. He will tempt him to shake them off, as Felix did when he began to tremble at Paul's preaching of judgment, 'Go thy way for this time; when I have convenient season I will call for thee,' ver. 25. Or carnal friends, &c. Ay, but when the Lord intends hereby to fit the soul for Christ, he prevents this diversion, he holds the iron in the furnace until it be malleable; he fixes the eye upon sin and wrath, so that whithersoever he turns, his sin is with him, and hell before him; the cry of sin, and the curse of the law, is ever in his ears, Ps. li. 3. The pillar of fire leaves him not till he be on the borders of Canaan, till it leads him to the Lord Jesus Christ.

He continues him under the spirit of bondage, where work is fear, Rom. viii.; he abides under these fears, this anguish, hanging as it were by a thread over the bottomless pit, till he be fit for the glad tidings of the gospel.

But hence observe, the Lord is very various in this dispensation, both as to the continuance of those fears and terrors, as also to the measure and degree of them. Some lie long upon the rack of terror; to others he does but as it were shew the torture. Some lie long under the pangs of the new birth, their throes are strong, and many others have a more quick and easy delivery. The apprehensions of wrath seize upon some as an earthquake, which makes the foundations of the soul to shake, and with violence breaks or unhinges the door of the heart; in others, the door is unlocked, the bolts knocked off with a blow or two, and the heart opened to Christ in a gentler way. Some are led through these dreadful visions of wrath, even to the pit of despair; others have a door opened, when they are newly come into this valley of the shadow of death.

It is the Lord's design in all upon whom he thus works, to make them sick of sin; but in some it is a burning, a raging fever; in others it is but as a stomach sickness, which makes them loathe sin, and vomit it up as bitter and nauseous.

But though this humiliation be in some more, in some less, both as to time and degree, yet in all, when the Lord draws to believe, there is so much as to drive them utterly out of themselves unto the Lord Jesus.

4. Inquiry, how he shall avoid this misery, what he shall do to be freed from that burden of sin and wrath, which is ready to sink him; what he shall do to pacify that wrath that burns like fire, and is ready to devour; how he shall satisfy that justice which pursues, and is every moment ready to smite him dead; what course he shall take to escape those everlasting burnings, into which he is in danger to fall every hour? When Peter's sermon had wounded the Jews with sense of their sin, this is the imme-

diate issue of it, Acts ii. 37, 'What shall we do?' So in the gaoler; when the apprehension of his misery shaked his soul, even as the earthquake shaked the prison, Acts xvi. 30, it puts him upon this inquiry, 'What shall I do to be saved?' Nor does the sinner in this case inquire as upon the bye, carelessly, indifferently; but his whole soul puts itself forth in this inquiry. As a man run through with a sword has present death before his eyes, would inquire for a chirurgeon,—Oh for a chirurgeon, or else I die! or as one whose house is on fire, and the flames all about his ears, would inquire how he may quench it; or as a man upon the sea, when the waves and storms beat the ship upon the rock, when he apprehends the vessel broke, and the waters breaking in upon him, would inquire what he should do to escape death and drowning,—he inquires as for his life. He is not as one that comes to a shop to cheapen a commodity, indifferent whether he have it or no, unless he can get an extraordinary pennyworth; but he inquires as one that resolves to have it, whatever it costs him. He inquires of the way, as a soldier after a route inquires after a stronghold: he is pursued by the enemy, death is at his heels; he resolves to press in, if he can find the way, whatever danger or difficulty encounter him, Luke xvi. 16. John was the messenger of the Lord, sent before Christ to prepare the way for him, 'to prepare the way of the Lord,' &c. And this he does by declaring their sins, and the wrath of God coming upon them for sin, Mat. iii. 7, 10. Now when they were effectually possessed with the sense thereof, they press. The straitness of the gate, the crowd of impediments wherewith Satan, the world, their lusts stop up the way, shall not hinder them; they resolve to press through, to put their whole strength and might, as a man that would break through a thick crowd. An inquiry thus resolved is another step to faith.

5. A renunciation, a renouncing of all unsafe ways, all indirect courses, to procure peace. When the sinner comes to inquire what course he shall take, he may meet with many counsellors, and he does not always at first pitch upon the best. Satan and his carnal acquaintance will advise him to return to his former sinful courses, those that have been so delightful to him formerly, that in them he may find ease. If he follow this counsel, he is lost; but if this seem too gross, too dangerous, if the flame already kindled be so terrible as he dares not add fuel to it; if he be convinced that this is not the way to quench the fire, but to make it flame higher: it may be one more specious may be suggested; he will betake himself to hear and pray, to wait upon the ordinances, to reform some things amiss, and think hereby to pacify God, who seems so angry, to satisfy justice, which is so incensed, and so to get ease to his afflicted conscience. Ay, but if he rest here, he will never come to faith; and therefore when the Lord intends a saving work, he will not suffer him to rest in these. These are good in themselves, and necessary; but, if rested in, they are pernicious. The Lord will convince him that these are the way, not the end. To rest in them upon these terms is to make them saviours, not the way to a Saviour. He will shew him that these amount not to the least mite, whereas he owes ten thousand talents. He will shew him the sinfulness of them, that they are so far from satisfying, as that thereby he runs further upon the score; that these are so far from saving him, as that he needs a Saviour when he has done his best, lest the sins of his best deeds should condemn him. He knocks down these rotten pillars, on which the soul would find an unsafe support; so that he falls flat down under the sense of his sinfulness and impotency. He sees, for all that he has, or all

that he can do, he must perish, unless help be laid upon one that is more mighty. He empties him of all opinion of his own righteousness, of his own sufficiency. He spreads his net in the gospel to catch this lost sinner, that will else be a prey to Satan. Now, as fishermen, when they would be sure of a good draught, they beat the sides of the river; they know if the fish can lie secure in any hole, they will never come into the net; thus the Lord drives the sinner out of conceit of himself, out of every lurking-place, that he may run straight to Christ.

Faith is a flying to Christ. Now in this motion there is something from which, *a terminus à quo;* this is not only his own wickedness, but his own righteousness. This is the stronger hold of the two, and usually holds out longer. To drive him out of it, the Lord shews him the vanity and weakness of it, that it is but like those, Nah. iii. 12. The least blast of the Lord's displeasure will make them fall, as ripe figs in a storm of wind; that they are but as broken reeds, if he lean on them they will break under, pierce him rather than support, and let him fall into hell besides. He says to him, as Rabshakeh to Hezekiah, 2 Kings xviii. 21, 'If a man lean on it, it will go into his hand and pierce it.' And so he brings him to the apostle's opinion, who, Phil. iii. 8, counted his own privileges, righteousness, but as loss and dung. And now he is in the highway to Christ; there is but a step betwixt him and faith.

A soul in this distress, like a drowning man, will catch at every twig to save his life; but if the Lord intend to bring him to shore, he will not suffer him to trust to that, that will let him sink and sink with him; not trust to his own righteousness, performances, &c. He takes him not off from performing these, but from resting in them. Oh! alas! says the humbled soul, if I have nothing else to save me, I perish for ever. He sees these are but a refuge of lies: Isa. xxviii. 17, 'The hail shall sweep away,' &c. It is a deceitful refuge; I shall have nothing of what I expect from it. It is such a shelter, as a storm will beat down about my ears and sweep it away. If I take sanctuary in my duties, righteousness, these will not secure me. Justice will pluck me from the horns of these altars, and slay me. And therefore he looks further.

6. Revelation of Christ. When the Lord has brought him out of these by-ways wherein he would lose himself, he shews him the true way, the only way to pardon and life. When he has diverted him from his deceitful refuges, he shews the distressed sinner a city of refuge opened in Christ.

He shews him the glory and excellency of Christ, represents him as 'fairer than the children of men, the chiefest in ten thousand, and infinitely loving and lovely.'

He shews the sufficiency of Christ; that there is nothing can be required to deliver and enhappy a humbled sinner, but it is to be found in him; that he is able to save to the utmost, Heb. vii. 25.

He shews his necessity of Christ, that there is 'no other name,' &c. Acts iv. 12. No other sanctuary will secure, no other price will discharge him, and no other surety will be accepted.

He shews him a possibility that Christ may save and pardon him; he has pardoned such and such, whose sins were so great and so many; he came to save what was lost, and why not him?

He shews him a certainty of it in case he will believe, that he will cast off none that come to him; that he will lose none, suffer none to miscarry, that cast themselves on him.

The sinner has heard these things, it may be, often before, but he heard them as though he heard them not. He was like the Jews when the veil was upon them; seeing, he saw, but perceived not; hearing, he heard, but understood not. Not because they were not clearly revealed, but because of his blindness, unbelief, carelessness; his carnal heart was not moved with spiritual discoveries, looked on them as not so much concerning him. He heard of this as a man with a full stomach hears of a feast; or as one that thinks himself above the fear of justice hears of a pardon; he finds no need of it, and so little regards it. Thus he heard of Christ before. Oh but now he hears these things as though he were another man, as though he had another soul. The report of Christ is glad tidings indeed. He hears of Christ as one in the executioner's hand, ready to die, hears of a pardon. He looks on Christ as one that has been all his days in a dungeon would look on the sun: 2 Cor. iv. 6, the discovery of Christ is to him as a glorious light shining on a sudden upon one in darkness. He was before in Satan's dungeon, as the apostle was before the revelation of Jesus Christ, verse 4; his eyes was put out. And besides, the object was veiled; he saw no more beauty in Christ than the Israelites saw glory in Moses's face when the veil was upon it, verse 8. But now his eye is opened, the veil is removed (for to that the apostle alludes), and he sees a glorious light, a glorious beauty in the face of Christ.

7. Hope. Though he despair as to himself, yet the Lord keeps him from despairing as to Christ. Though he have no hope in himself, yet 'there is hope in Israel,' there is hope in the gospel 'concerning this thing.' Though he be ready to sink under the pressure of sin and wrath, yet the discoveries of the gospel keep his head above water. He continues trembling under the apprehensions of wrath and misery, yet the Lord keeps him from falling quite down. The discoveries of Christ afford so much hope as somewhat strengthens the feeble knees, and yields some support to the trembling soul. He continues in a fluctuating condition, sometimes up, sometimes down, according as the impressions of law or gospel prevail, sometimes more, sometimes less. His feet are sometimes quite gone, his hold is lost, and he is ready to say, My hope is perished from me. Yet the Lord has made such provision in the gospel that though he fall, yet shall he rise; though he sink, yet will the Lord bring him up again. Some twig or other the Lord helps him to in the gospel, and holds him by it till he bring him to shore. He apprehends justice pursuing him, he hears it crying out to an incensed God, Shall I smite him? shall I smite? and he is in dreadful expectations of the fatal blow. Oh but he hears withal there is a sanctuary, there is a city of refuge set open in the gospel if he could but reach it; if he could but get into it, there is hopes for him, there he might be safe, there he might be secure from revenging justice. It never seized on any sinner that was fled thither for refuge.

He feels that sin has stung his soul; the sting of that fiery serpent is deadly, the poison thereof drinks up his spirits, he feels it even seizing upon his vitals; it has brought him even to the gates of death, all the art of men and angels cannot cure the wound. Oh but he hears withal there is a brazen serpent lifted up in the gospel, there is a healing, a sovereign virtue in Christ, there is balm in Gilead, there is a physician there, one that can heal a dying soul with a word, with a touch, nay, with a look. If he might have but a sight of him, might be admitted but to touch him, though it were but the hem of his garment, there is hopes. Though I were dead, yet should I live; no poison too deadly, too strong for that sovereign virtue that is in Christ.

He apprehends the waves and billows of God's indignation ready to go over him, ready to sweep him out of the land of the living; he knows not how soon he may be buried under those waves, under that wrath; he lives in a fearful expectation of it, and here the waves grow higher and higher. Oh but he hears withal there is an ark able to save him from that deluge, if he could but reach it; if he could but get into it, he might be safe; if Christ would but put forth his hand and take him in, he should be above that dreadful flood.

Wrath is due to thee, says the law, it is coming, thy damnation sleeps not; it is swift destruction, wrath will come upon thee speedily. Oh but, says the gospel, there is a Jesus, a Jesus that delivers from the wrath to come. Oh how sweet is that sentence to the sensible sinner, Jesus who delivers!

Alas, says the sensible sinner, I am but a dead man, the sentence of death is passed upon me, I am condemned already; I am now in the hands of justice, ready for execution. Oh but does not the gospel speak of a pardon? There is a pardon out for some that are condemned, here is some hope for me; though the sentence of condemnation be passed, yet it is not absolute; though I be cast in law, and judgment passed against me, yet if I could but believe, execution might be stopped. There is life to be had for some who have received sentence of death. My condition is not hopeless, unless my unbelief make it so, 1 John v. 11, 12. There is life for condemned wretches if they believe. Though wrath has so far seized on me as to proceed to sentence, yet wrath will not abide on me unless I abide in unbelief; there is some hopes if I could but believe. Thus the sensible sinner is helped up from sinking; hope keeps his head above the waves, or brings him up again when he is already overwhelmed and seems quite gone.

When he is even oppressed by the powers of darkness, and the dismal apprehensions of wrath and misery, the Lord opens some crevice, lets in some glimpse of hope. The discoveries of Christ in the gospel are as 'a door of hope opened to him in this valley of Achor,' Zech. ix. 11. Here is the state of a lost sinner represented by the state of the Jews captivated in Babylon: where you may see the misery of it, 'in a pit'; the helplessness of it, 'no water'; the hopes of it, though prisoners, yet 'prisoners of hope'; the grounds of those hopes, wholly out of themselves, in the blood of the covenant, and this stronghold.

Their misery, which sinners in the way to faith are sensible of, they are in a pit, a dark pit; the state of nature is a state of darkness, it is Satan's dungeon, not a spark of saving light; and therefore when brought out of it they are said to be 'turned from darkness to light, and from the power of Satan to God,' Acts xxvi. They are bound, fettered in this dungeon; and therefore the Dutch render it 'thy bounden ones;' they are loaden with fetters, with that which is worse than fetters and iron, the bonds of iniquity. They are in no capacity of themselves to scramble out of this dismal condition; nay, the mouth of the pit is closed, the Lord has shut it up, and shut them up in it, Rom. xi. 32, συνέκλεισε. And as of themselves they cannot get out of it, so they cannot live in it, they have not so much as water to live upon; a pit wherein there is no water, no succour, no comfort, no refreshment, nothing to refresh or sustain their souls for a moment. He apprehends the misery of it, a pit wherein there is no succour, destitute of all remedy. So he now finds it, he must look out if he mean to live.

But as it is helpless, is it hopeless too? No; a sensible sinner, though a prisoner, yet a prisoner of hope, he hears there is a refuge, a stronghold for him; though he be now sunk into this pit, though there be no water to keep him alive in it, yet there is the blood of the covenant to bring him out of it. This is it which makes him a prisoner of hope; an eye of hope, in this forlorn state, upon this stronghold, upon this blood of the covenant, is one step out of the pit, one step towards faith.

8. Self-abhorrence. This springs from the former. Hopes that he may find mercy with God, and probability that he may have pardon through Christ, fill him with indignation against sin, and himself for sin; makes him condemn himself and justify God, though he should proceed against him with the greatest severity. When the soul is cast down low, under dreadful apprehensions of wrath and misery, and then raised up, though but a little, to some hopes of deliverance, it makes a great impression upon the heart. And is there hopes for me, says the sinner, who have so much, so long, so highly offended God? for me, who have so shamefully abused mercy, so vilely contemned Christ? Is there hopes for me, who might have been now in hell, in a hopeless condition? for me, when so many less sinners than I are without hope? for me, who have done all I could to make my condition desperate? Can the Lord be inclinable to shew me mercy? Can Christ entertain any thoughts of peace concerning me? Is this possible? Is there hopes after all? Oh then what a wretch am I, that have so dishonoured such a God! that have so affronted, so wounded such a Saviour! Oh there is no hell too grievous for such a wretch as I am, no wrath too heavy for such a rebel as I have been, no vengeance too severe for such injuries, such sins as mine. How few are there in hell, who have more deserved hell than I! I am, I hear, in a way to mercy, in a way of hope, when so many better than I are in that place of torment, shut up in a despairing state for ever. And is it that God whom I have so provoked, so dishonoured, that has made this difference? Has all those millions of provocations been levelled against that God, against that God that gives me hopes of mercy? Oh what a monster am I! Oh how exceeding monstrous are my sins! Nothing in earth or hell so vile as I! No sins so abominable as these of mine! The provocations of devils and damned souls are not worse than mine. They sin not against a God that gives hopes, as I have done. The sinner thus affected, apprehends he cannot speak bad enough of himself and of his sins.

This makes him abhor himself, this makes him sick of sin. That which was before as a sweet morsel, it is now nauseous to his soul, it lies heavy on his stomach, he is sick of it, Mat. ix. 12. The sinner will not come to the physician, nor will the great physician undertake his cure, till he be, more or less, in some degree or other, thus sick of sin. This nauseating of sin, this loathing of it, and himself for it, is another step to faith.

9. Valuing of Christ. He has far other thoughts of Christ than heretofore. When he is brought so low in the sense of his own vileness, sinfulness, misery, impotency, and sees the excellency, the all-sufficiency of Christ discovered in the gospel, his thoughts of Christ are raised. He that heard before of the blood and righteousness, of the satisfaction and intercession, of the love and bounty of Christ, as common things, words of course, of which he had but common thoughts, he finds a strong, a strange alteration as to his apprehensions of the value, worth, and necessity of them. Discourses of Christ are not tedious now; he thinks he can never hear enough

of them; they do not pass out as they come in; they do not glide through his mind, without leaving any impression. He finds his thoughts of Christ raised by every word. He was before in a soul lethargy, as, alas! the most are. Tell him of cure, he minds it not, he is insensible. Ay, but now he has such thoughts of Christ, as one tortured with the stone has of that which he hears may give him ease and cure. He prizes Christ, as one ready to die with thirst and heat would prize a well of waters, as Samson, Judges xv. 18, or Hagar. He prizes Christ now, as one in cruel, miserable bondage in Turkish slavery would prize a ransom. So does he value this λύτρον. He looks on Christ now, as one that has been long in a dark dungeon would look upon the light, if a beam of it should break in on a sudden upon him in that dismal place, Mal. iv. Suppose a man born blind should have his eyes opened on a sudden, and see the sun rising in its glory, what thoughts would he have of it! Such thoughts has the sensible sinner now of Christ, when, his eyes being opened, he sees him revealed in the gospel.

He wonders at his former blindness and stupidness, that his apprehensions of Christ should be so low, when he has been so clearly revealed in the word. Where Christ is truly preferred before all things, there are the seeds of faith. But I suppose this high esteem of Christ is in order of nature, though not in order of time, before actual faith. For till Christ be thus valued, the sinner is not willing to accept of Christ on his own terms; till he be the pearl of great price, he is not willing to sell all for him, to renounce all, that he may cleave only to Christ for pardon.

10. Strong desires after Christ. It is the goodness of a thing which makes it the object of our desires; and the more excellent that goodness is apprehended to be, the more ardent are our desires. The more necessary it is apprehended, the more restless, and importunate, and insatiable are our desires, and the more easily will we yield to any terms upon which it may be obtained.

Now the discovery of the sinner's misery and impotency, makes him apprehend an absolute necessity of Christ. The discovery of Christ's all-sufficiency, as able to save and relieve him to the utmost, makes him apprehend a transcendent excellency in Christ. Hence his desires after Christ are ardent, importunate, such as make him ready to stoop to anything, so as he may have Christ.

His desires are ardent. He longs for Christ as Rachel for children, Gen. xxx. 1. Oh give me Christ, or else I die. Wrath will overwhelm me, justice will seize on me, hell will swallow me up; there is no way but I must perish, without Christ. Give me Christ, or else I die.

His heart is carried after Christ, as David's was to that which he calls the law, the word, the testimony of God; he longed, he breathed, he panted after them: Ps. cxix. 40, 'I have longed after,' &c.; ver. 20, 'My soul breaketh for the longing that it hath,' &c. His heart was so far stretched out in longing desires, as it was ready to break. Now indeed that which he thus intensely desired was Christ, veiled under the expressions, law, &c., for we cannot by the law here understand the covenant of works (for what is to be desired in that?) but life. Now life, upon the terms of that law or covenant, is become impossible; and that which is impossible, is not desirable. The object of desire is a possible good. It is not the doctrine of the covenant of works. What then can it be, but the doctrine of the covenant of grace, since the whole doctrine of the Scripture is referred to one of these covenants? That law, &c., which he longed for, was that which is contained in the covenant of grace. And what is the sum of that but Christ? This is it which he longed for. And indeed Christ was as fully and sufficiently held forth in the Old Testament as in the New, though not so clearly and perspicuously. They had the gospel under that administration, which we call the law or Old Testament, sufficiently, though not so evidently as we. And therefore Paul, who preached the gospel as purely and fully as ever it was preached in the world, professeth that he preached nothing but what was contained in the law and the prophets, nothing in the New but what was in the Old Testament, Acts xxvi. 22.

David had the doctrine of the gospel of Christ, of salvation by Christ then. And this was it his heart was so drawn out after; and so he expresses it, Ps. cxix. 81, 174. The law wherein he delighted was the doctrine of salvation, and so the doctrine of Christ, in whom alone salvation is to be found; and Christ is called salvation, Luke ii. 28. That which Simeon saw David longed for; he longed for it ardently. And so does the sensible sinner long for Christ as for salvation, when he finds himself in such danger to be damned; longs for Christ as for life, when he sees death and hell before him, and no hopes of life without Christ.

This makes his desires importunate. Nothing else will satisfy him; he will not be put off with any else. If the Lord would offer him a world in this case, it would not satisfy. Alas, says he, what would a thousand worlds avail me, if, after a momentary enjoyment of them, I must go to hell for ever! What will these profit me, so long as the Lord's wrath burns against me! What will all the pleasures and riches of the world avail me, so long as I am but a condemned person, and in danger every hour to be led forth to execution! Oh no; let me have Christ, whatever I want. Let me have him who can procure a pardon for a condemned soul; let me have him who can make my peace with an incensed God; let me have him who can save me from the wrath to come. Oh Christ, or nothing. Alas! whatever else I have or the world can afford, they are woeful comforts, miserable comforts to a perishing soul. A Jesus, a Saviour for a lost soul; none but Christ.

Effectual desires. Such as make them stoop to any terms, submit to any conditions, so he may have Christ. He will not now capitulate with Christ; but so as he may have himself, he may make his own terms. He is ready to do anything, to suffer anything, to part with anything, so he may gain Christ. So it was with the apostle, Philip. iii.; those things which were gain to him, of which he thought to make the greatest advantage, he would part with them as loss, as freely as a man would part with that which he were like to lose by, as that which is like to undo him. And those things which he counted his glory before, he would part with them as σκύβαλα, as dung, as freely as one would cast dung out of his lodging. And why? That he might gain Christ; that he might be found in him. Ask the soul now (who was resolved before to keep such and such a sin, notwithstanding all that Christ could do or say in the ministry of the gospel), Wilt thou part with such a lust, that which has been so gainful, brought in such a revenue of pleasure, profit, or applause? Oh, says he, it is loss now; it would undo me if I should not quit it; I should lose Christ, I should lose my soul, if I live in it; I'll part with it as freely as I would part with a mortal disease, as with that which would ruin me.

He desires Christ, as Esau longed for meat when he was ready to faint and die for hunger; if Jacob would but give him meat, he might make his own terms for it, Gen. xxv. 30–32: 'Sell me thy birthright,' says he.

Here was hard terms; for the birthright concerned the office of the priesthood, a pre-eminence over the brethren, and a double portion of the father's estate. But though this might seem hard, yet Esau's necessity is so great, his appetite so strong, that he sticks not at it, ver. 32. So the sinner hears what he must part with, if he will have Christ; and when Satan or his corrupt heart would persuade him it is a hard bargain, yet he finds his extremity so great, death so near him, he will not stand on it. Behold, I am at the point to die; there is but a step between me and eternal death; my soul is ready to drop into hell; and what will these riches, these pleasures, these lusts do to me? I shall die, if I had ten thousand times more of the best of these, if I have not the bread of life, if I have not Christ. And therefore he resolves as firmly as if he were tied by Jacob's oath, that he will quit all, if he may but have life, if Christ will be life to him. He longs for Christ, as Shechem did for Dinah, Gen. xxiv. 8. He would give anything, if he might but obtain his desires, ver. 11, 12. Oh but they stand not upon dowry; they propound terms of another nature, ver. 15. He and his people must be circumcised, if he meant to have Dinah; and to be circumcised was painful, it was perilous too, and it is like at that time reproachful to the heathen. But yet so was his heart drawn out after her, as even these hard terms pleased him, ver. 18, 19. It pleased him so as, how grievous soever it might seem, he deferred not to do it.

Thus it is with a sinner in this case; he is so taken with Christ, he does so long for him, that if the match may be but made up, whatever terms Christ will propound shall please him, even the reproach of Christ, even dangers and sufferings for Christ shall please him, so he may but enjoy him. Whatever stands in the way shall be cut off, though it be as dear to him as his own flesh, as a right hand or right eye. Even his heart shall be circumcised, since Christ would have it so; how painful soever it seem, yet it does please him, he will not defer to do it, so as Christ may be given him.

And when it is come to this, the seeds of faith (which are in the heart when Christ is so highly valued, as I shewed in the former head) begin to sprout forth. Such an ardent, importunate, effectual desire after Christ is a sprig of faith; but yet he is not come to cast himself on Christ, to that actual dependence on him, whereby the Holy Ghost seems most frequently to represent faith unto us, one step further he must go before he come to this.

11. A persuasion that the Lord would have them to believe that Christ is willing they should rest on him for pardon and life. Not only that he will receive those that come to him, but that he is willing they should come; not only that he will not fail those who rely on him, but that he is willing they should rely on him. He convinces the sensible sinner not only of the necessity of faith, that unless he believe, there is nothing for him but wrath and condemnation, no way but this to avoid hell and eternal death. Not only of the excellency of faith, and of the certain advantage which may be got by believing, that if he could believe, the storm would be over, justice would be satisfied, wrath would be appeased, pardon, and reconciliation, and life would be his portion, but also that it is a duty, yea, his duty to believe, and to believe now. Many times the sensible sinner sticks at this, he finds a difficulty here not easily mastered. Though he be satisfied it is a duty to some to rest on Christ, and apply the promise, those who are deeply humbled, and fitly qualified, yet he questions whether it be *his* duty, at least whether it be *yet* his duty. He doubts whether Christ's

invitations and commands be directed to him for this purpose. He eyes not the authority of Christ so much as his mercy in such injunctions, and doubts that he is not yet a fit subject for such mercy. He looks upon believing as a privilege rather than a duty, a privilege that he is altogether unfit for, unworthy of. He is not yet sufficiently prepared, not humbled enough; he is too sinful, too unworthy, to have anything to do with Christ and the promise. It may be a duty to others, but it would be presumption in him to lay hold on Christ in the promise. That is bread for children, he cannot presume that a crumb of it belongs to him. Will the Lord invite such a woeful prodigal as I have been to return to his house? May such a rebel as I have been have access to the King of glory? Will the golden sceptre be holden out to me? Does Christ stretch out his arms to such a sinful piece of deformity? May I come into his embraces? Oh, it is no easy matter to persuade a humbled soul of this. But yet he waits upon the Lord in the use of appointed means, and in the use of them the Lord lifts him above this difficulty, and satisfies his doubts, removes his scruples, persuades him that it is his will, even that he should believe. And indeed, as faith of assurance comes ordinarily by the application in particular of a promise, so the soul comes not ordinarily to this faith of dependence but by the particular application of Christ's commands and invitations, till he be persuaded that the general command to believe concerns him, and is, as it were, directed to him in particular.

When he hears these gracious invitations, 'Come unto me, all ye,' &c., 'Ho, every one that thirsteth, come,' &c., and 'let whosoever will, come,' Why, says he, it seems Christ would have me come to him; I am the person, how unworthy soever, whom he invites, importunes, beseeches. When he hears the command, 1 John iii. 23, he takes it to himself, as though he were named in it: It is the will and pleasure of Christ that I should believe; he directs his command unto, and lays it to me. When he hears that to believe is to give glory to God, Rom. iv. 20, Why, says he, though I have so much dishonoured Christ, he will count himself glorified by my believing in him. When he hears that he that believes not makes God a liar, 1 John v. 10, If I should not believe, says he, I should cast this dishonour on him; my keeping off from Christ puts this affront on him; either I must believe him or give him the lie. Oh, I have dishonoured, affronted him too much already, shall I add this to all the rest?

12. He resolves to comply with the Lord's invitation, to obey his command, and so casts himself upon Christ, cleaves to him, rests on him, embraces him, and holds him fast.

Though I be the unworthiest sinner that ever had access to Christ, yet since he delights to glorify the freeness and riches of his grace in admitting those that are most unworthy, and since he expresses it by inviting me, shall I not hearken to him? shall not I comply with his gracious invitations?

Though I be unworthy to come, yet is not he worthy to be obeyed? I am cast away for ever if I cast not myself on Christ; and now he stretches out his arms to receive me, what can I desire more? I perish if I come not; and now when he invites me to come, shall I refuse? shall I defer? shall I destroy myself and dishonour him both at once, by forbearing to do what he commands me, when I am damned if I do it not?

The invitation of Christ encourages him, but his own extremity forces him to roll himself on Christ; it forces him, &c.

It is with the sinner in this case as it was with those four lepers, 2 Kings vii. 3, 4. Thus says the sensible sinner within himself, Why stay I in this state of unbelief till I die? What course soever offer itself, there is but one way to escape death, and that is by running to Christ. If I say, I will enter into the city, if I return back to my former evil ways, whether of profaneness or formality, the wrath of God beleaguers that state, a famine is there, no relief can come into it, my soul will certainly perish there; but if I sit still here in the state where I am, without venturing on Christ, why, here I shall surely die, I am every moment in danger of eternal death. Now therefore, come, let me fall into the hands of Christ; if he save me alive, I shall live, and if he kill me, I shall but die. There is hopes I may live by coming to him, but if I go not, there is nothing but certain death. Nay, the humbled soul has more encouragement here than the lepers. There is not only provisions for life enough in Christ's all-sufficiency, he has his invitation to come to him for life; nay, he has his promise, that if he will come, he shall live.

Upon this, the soul resolves, and ventures, renouncing all other ways and supports, resolving to submit to Christ's terms, whatever they be; he casts his perishing soul into the arms of Christ, and there he rests.

Now, when the Lord has brought the sinner thus far, he is actually arrived at that faith which is saving and justifying. I have explained this act at large before. I need add no more, only a brief account of some of the consequences of this act.

13. The Lord discovers his faith to him, possesses him with an apprehension that he does truly believe. The former is the direct act of faith, this is a reflex act; when he has acted faith, to know that it is faith which he acts.

And sometimes it is a good while before the believer knows that he believes indeed. As a man fallen into the water, in danger of being drowned, yet drawn out to land with much ado, through the fear and amazement that is on him, though he be safe, yet for a while knows not where he is, &c. As it is the power of the Spirit that works faith, so it is the light of the Spirit that discovers faith when it is wrought, 1 Cor. ii. 12.

14. This makes way for assurance, that assurance which we call discursive; wherein the Spirit of God witnesses together with the spirit of a convert, that he is a believer; by consequence brings him in this testimony, that he has everlasting life. He that believes has everlasting life; but I believe, *ergo*, I have, &c.

There is another kind of assurance, from an immediate testimony of the Spirit, without such an application of Scripture grounds.

But whether this assurance be intuitive or discursive, if it be an act of faith, it is not the justifying act; indeed, it seems rather an effect than an act of that faith, and that which follows after it, and sometimes at a great distance, Eph. i.

15. From this assurance proceeds sometimes peace, sometimes comfort, sometimes a joy, triumph, and glorying in God. Peace, freedom from fears and terrors; comfort, a degree above peace; joy, which is comfort in its exaltation; peace, which is the hushing of the storm; comfort, which is as the breaking out of the sun; triumph, joy, which is as the sun shining in its full strength, Rom. v. 1–3.

Use 1. Information. See here the misery of unbelievers. Here is a dreadful representation of this in these words, we need go no further. Here is the handwriting of God in the text, as terrible to unbelievers as that handwriting on the wall was to Belshazzar, Dan. v. 5, 6. Methinks the countenance of every unbeliever, that sees or hears these words, should be changed. 'He that believes not shall not see,' &c. Particularly here is misery negative: 'He shall not see life;' positive, 'the wrath of God,' &c. We have here an epitome of hell as the portion of an unbeliever. The miseries of hell are no more than *pœna damni*, and *pœna sensus*, and both these are entailed upon unbelievers: 'He shall not see life;' here is the pain of loss; the pain of sense: 'The wrath of God abides on him.' An unbeliever is so far in hell upon earth as hell can be upon earth. He is without life; he is dead spiritually; he has not the least degree of spiritual life, no breathing, no motion truly vital and spiritual; he is dead legally; the law has passed sentence of death on him, he 'is condemned already,' ver. 18, and the sentence is so far executed, as that the wrath of God does now actually abide. He is without God, the author of life; without Christ, the purchaser of life; without the covenant, the promise of life, and without hopes of heaven, the seat of everlasting life; without grace, the beginnings of life; without hopes of this; so far he is from it, that it is out of sight; nor shall he ever see it, or hopes of it, till he believe. Distinctly,

(1.) He is without Christ, the fountain of life. It is faith by which the soul is contracted to Christ. An unbeliever is a stranger, an enemy to Christ, whatever friendship he pretend. And so is Christ a stranger, an enemy to him. It is faith by which the soul is united to Christ. An unbeliever is as far from Christ as earth is from heaven; you may as well mingle and join heaven and earth together as join an unbeliever to Christ, Eph. ii. 12.

It is faith by which Christ dwells in the heart, Eph. iii. 17. Christ dwells in the heart by faith. Satan dwells in the heart by unbelief. The heart of an unbeliever is the place where Satan has his throne. The heart of a believer is the habitation of Christ. The heart of an unbeliever is the habitation of the devil, Rev. viii. 2. Christ has possession of a believing soul, but the soul of an unbeliever is possessed by the devil. The strong man armed keeps that house, there he dwells, there he rules, Eph. ii. 2, υἱοῖς τῆς ἀπειθείας, the children of unbelief, so rendered, Rom. xi. 32. He rules there, not only in hell, but on earth; not only then, but now, νῦν ἐνεργοῦντος, now, and will do for ever, till Christ come by faith to put him out of possession.

An unbeliever has nothing to do with the person of Christ; that I have shewed; nor has he any rights to the purchase or benefits of Christ. Instance in two, which comprise the rest: the blood of Christ, or the righteousness performed on earth; the intercession of Christ, continued in heaven.

An unbeliever has nothing to do with the *righteousness* of Christ; for this is the righteousness of faith, Rom. iii. 22. Nor with the *intercession* of Christ, John xvii. 9, 20.

Now, being without Christ, it follows necessarily they are without life, 1 John v. 11, 12. And who is he that has the Son? Ver. 10, he that believeth.

(2.) He is without the covenant, the evidence of life. An unbeliever is not at all specified in the covenant of grace; it no more belongs to him than the writings, the evidences of another man's lands belong to you, who were never thought of, never mentioned in the drawing of them up. Believing is our first entering into covenant with God; how can he that never entered into covenant be in it?

Unbelievers are strangers to the covenant, Eph. ii. 12. The covenant of grace is called the law of faith, Rom. iii. 27, as the covenant of works is called there the law of works.

Now as Adam, not performing perfect obedience, which was the condition of the covenant of works, could have no benefit by that covenant, no more can he who believes not have any benefit by the covenant of grace.

Unbelievers are not in covenant with Christ; their league is with hell, their covenant is with death. Christ looks on them as confederates with Satan, that cursed league is inconsistent with any confederacy with Christ, and that league is never dissolved till ye believe. Your pretended renouncing of sin and Satan is but a deluding of your souls, a mocking of Christ; you never break your league with Satan, never enter into covenant with Christ till ye believe.

An unbeliever has nothing to do with the promises; for the promises are but as so many articles of the covenant, and so it is called a covenant of promise, Eph. ii. Now what has he to do with the articles of a covenant that never entered into it? Rom. iv. 13. The promise is through the righteousness of faith; and, ver. 16, it is of faith. It is of faith that we have a right to any promise. The promises of life and pardon are all to faith: 'If thou believest in the Lord Jesus, thou shalt be saved;' 'He that believes has everlasting life.' The promises are a sealed fountain to an unbeliever, it is open to nothing but faith. It is children's bread, and we are the children of God through faith. An unbeliever has neither a hand, nor a mouth, either to gather or to eat any crumb of this manna.

And as nothing to do with the covenant, so neither with the seals of it. What right has he to the seals of your writings or evidences, who has nothing to do with the writings and evidences themselves? The covenant is evidence for heaven, under the hand and seal of God; a deed of gift under the seal of heaven. How does the seal belong to him, who has nothing to do with the deed?

Indeed, the seals of the covenant are, as Augustine, *verbum visibile, visibilis promissio*, visible promises. Now he that has no right to the audible promise, that which offers pardon and life to the ear, has no right to the visible promise, which offers pardon and life to the eye, since the very same thing is tendered in both. As we must not apply the audible promise to an unbeliever, so must we not apply the visible promise; there is the very same reason for both. The promise belongs to believers and their seed, both visible and audible promises, for they should never be separated. Neither of them belongs to unbelievers, nor their seed, for they are not the heirs of promise. And to make over the inheritance, or the seals and evidences of it to them, would be to give the heir's inheritance, in its sealed evidences, to pretenders and intruders, to those to whom Christ in his will and testament never bequeathed it,—an injustice that we should use all our care to avoid. While a man is visibly in unbelief nothing can be sealed to him but condemnation, because he has no evidence for anything else. So the seal is either set to this, or nothing.

(3.) Without grace, the beginning of life. He that is an unbeliever, whatever fine show he make in the flesh, whatever he pretend, profess, or practise, how specious soever his deportment be, whatever outward conformity he shew, either to the rules of law or gospel, he is a graceless person. How finely soever the sepulchre is painted and beautified without, if faith be not within, there is nothing but dead bones and rottenness; nothing but what is as loathsome in the eye of God, as the rottenness of a dead carcase is to us. For it is faith that purifies the heart, Acts xv. 9. Till the heart be purified by faith, nothing is pure, either within or without, Titus i. 15. There is not the least degree of holiness or sanctification, till faith; it is that by which we are sanctified, Acts xxvi. 18. Faith is a root-grace; there is not, there cannot be, a spring of holiness, till faith be fastened in the heart.

No degree of spiritual life without faith: Gal. ii. 20, 'The life that I live is by faith in the Son of God;' by faith uniting Christ to the soul as the principle. Till then the soul is dead, even as the body is dead when not in conjunction with the soul. This is his state, he is dead in sins and trespasses, and so are his actings; all his works are dead works, till there be faith in Christ, as appears by that connection, 'repentance from dead works.' And,

(4.) He has no title to heaven, which is everlasting life. No title; for how should he come by it? The Lord never ordained heaven for unbelievers; 'he has chosen the poor, rich in faith.' He has prepared hell for unbelievers, Rev. xxi. 8. Christ never purchased that for them. He is 'become the author of eternal salvation to those (only) who believe.' Those that contend most for the extent of Christ's death, will never say that the blood of Christ ever brought any unbeliever, so persevering, into heaven. He was given, and gave himself only for this end.

He was never promised to them. Nay, all the threatenings, in law or gospel, are the portion of unbelievers. Take one for all, and that from the mouth of Christ, who speaks mercy and life when there is any to be had; and they are part of the last words he spoke in this world, Mark xvi. 16.

They have no right by adoption. They were never adopted. Unbelievers are not the sons of God, but the children of the devil. No sonship but by faith, Gal. iii. 26; those that are not so by faith, are not so at all; for all that are sons, are so by faith.

(5.) They are far from life; so far, as they never come in sight of it, never see life. And if they can never come in sight of it, what hopes can they have to enjoy it? Hope of heaven without faith, is a castle in the air, a structure without a foundation. Alas! how can they hope to enjoy it, whom the Lord calls off from all hopes ever to see it! While ye are without faith, ye are without hopes, in that forlorn condition of the Ephesians, before they believed, Eph. ii. 12.

(6.) All this is certain, as sure as the Lord is true. For it is he that speaks it, and he speaks it peremptorily. He does not say, possibly he may never see life; or probably he may never see life; but he *shall* never see it. As sure as the Lord will not lie, as sure as he is able to make good that word, so sure is this, he that believes not shall not see life.

This is the sentence of the gospel. If it had been a sentence of the law, that is not so peremptory, that admits of an exception, the gospel may relieve one against the sentence of the law. Ay, but this is the sentence of the gospel, the final decision of this case, which admits of no exception, against which there is no relief, neither here nor hereafter, the last declaration of God's will concerning a sinner, that if he believes not he shall certainly die, and that without any further hopes of mercy or remedy; he shall never see life.

Here is the negative misery of an unbeliever. Oh that this might stir you up to search your hearts, to examine seriously, as becomes you in a business of such consequence, &c.

Come we to his misery expressed positively. 'The wrath of God abides on him.' Every word is dreadful, and big with terror. It is *wrath*, and the wrath *of God*, and the wrath of God *on him*, and the wrath of God *abiding* on him.

(1.) *Wrath*. It is not anger or displeasure only, though that be dreadful; but wrath, sublimated anger, anger blown up into a terrible flame. This is it which kindles upon unbelievers, a consuming fire, the furnace made seven times hotter. This is the portion of unbelievers, their lines fall in this place; they are children of wrath, and this is their heritage. There is no quitting of this woeful relation, but only by faith. 'Who can stand before thee when thou art angry?' Is there no abiding of it then? Who then can stand before it, when it flames forth into wrath? Isa. xxxiii. 14, 'Who can dwell,' &c.

(2.) It is the wrath *of God*. It is not the wrath of a king, though that be as the roaring of a lion, at which all the beasts of the field do tremble; it is not the wrath of all the kings of the earth; it is not the wrath of all the men on the earth, or all the angels in heaven put together. What then? It is a wrath infinitely more dreadful; it is the wrath of that God, in comparison of whom all the men on earth, all the angels in heaven, all the creatures on earth, are as nothing. All their wrath put together is as nothing compared with the wrath of God. Theirs would but be as the breath of one's nostrils; whereas the wrath of God is as a whirlwind, such a one as rends the rocks, and tears up the mountains, and shakes the foundations of the earth, and shrivels up the heavens like a scroll, and causes the whole fabric of heaven and earth to stagger like a drunken man. Oh, 'who knows the power of his wrath!' Their wrath is but like a spark; his wrath is like a river, a sea of kindled brimstone, Isa. xxx. 33. This wrath, this wrath of God will be thy portion, if thou believe not.

(3.) It is the wrath of God *on him*. He says not, it is near him, or coming towards him, but it is on him. Not that all the wrath of God is on him already, for there are vials of wrath that will never be emptied, never emptier, though the Lord be pouring them forth to all eternity. It is compared to a river, and that is continually running; and when it has run some hundred years, there is as much to come as if there were none run by already; it will run on thee to eternity, unless by believing thou stop it, divert the course of it in time.

But it is all on him as to the sentence. He is adjudged to all the wrath of God already, and execution is beginning, though the beginning be small in comparison of what it will proceed to hereafter. The first fruits of wrath are reaped now, but a full harvest is coming; and the longer thou continuest in unbelief, the riper thou art for that dreadful harvest. All that thou hast from God now, thou hast it in wrath; for as all the ways of God are mercy to the believer, so all his ways are wrath to the unbeliever. The execution is begun now, and the Lord is ready, if thou prevent it not, for a farther, a full execution. He does 'whet his sword,' Ps. vii. 12, 13. If you continue in unbelief, you are likely to be the butts of the Lord's indignation; his arm, his sword will fall upon you.

(4.) It is *abiding* wrath. If this wrath were but for a moment, it were more tolerable, but it is abiding wrath; it is not on and off, but always on him without intermission; and there, unless he believe, it will abide for ever, wherever he is, whatever he does, wherever he goes. The curse and the wrath of God are in effect the same thing; and what the Lord denounces against the Israelites concerning the curse, holds true against unbelievers as to this wrath of God: Deut. xxviii. 16, 17, 'The wrath of God is on him in the city,' &c. The wrath of God is on him in every place, in every state, in every enjoyment, in every undertaking.

This is the woeful, the miserable condition of every unbeliever.

Quest. But who are unbelievers? Are there any amongst us in this dreadful case?

Ans. 1. He that has no other faith than a bare assent to the truths of the gospel, a belief that all that is declared concerning Christ is true, all that is delivered in the Scripture is the truth; he that has no other faith than this is an unbeliever, for the devils have as much as this comes to, James ii. 19. If he go no further, he shall no more see life than they.

Ans. 2. He that goes on in any known sin of omission or commission; whether it be an acting of what God forbids, uncleanness, intemperance, profaning of God's name or day or ordinances, worldliness, idleness, injustice, covetousness; or neglect of what God requires, neglect of hearing the word, prayer, meditation, self-examination, &c.

When you hear this or that condemned as a sin in the word, and yet will continue in it, here is enough to evidence you are unbelievers. The apostle speaks of 'the obedience of faith;' they are inseparable, children of disobedience who are children of unbelief; the apostle uses one word for both, Eph. ii. 2; Rom. xi. 32. 'Faith purifies the heart,' Acts xv. 9; when that is purified the conversation will be purified; where it is not, there is no faith. If you go on, allow yourselves in any unlawful thing, this is your portion.

Ans. 3. He that finds not an universal change in himself. He who finds he did love any sin, and does not now hate it, did delight in it, or make light of it, and does not now bewail it, count it his burden and affliction; he that did scorn purity, or at least slight holiness, and is not now in love with it, that durst once venture on sin, and does not now fear it; he that has had low thoughts of Christ, and does not now highly value him, so as to part with all for him, so as to prefer him before his chief joy; he that did neglect Christ, and does not now hunger and thirst after him; he that did immoderately follow the world, and does not now contemn it; he that did gratify the flesh, and does not now strive to crucify it; he that did count the word and prayer a burden, and does not now count them his delight; that has been careless, heartless in holy duties, and does not now stir up his soul, and strive with his heart to get it raised to God in them,—he that does not find such a change is an unbeliever; for when the Lord works faith, he works such a change.

If this be thy case, all the dreadful things are thy portion. Apply them as you love your souls, put not off conviction; for you are never like to come to faith till convinced of unbelief.

Use 2. Exhortation. This should excite sinners to mind this duty, as that which is of greatest concernment. This I shall direct to sinners that are secure: these should never be at rest till they find their hearts willing to accept of Christ upon his own terms; sensible sinners, those who are willing thus to close with Christ, should never rest till they be brought to depend on Christ, to rest theirselves on him for pardon and life. Here are two sorts of sinners, and two acts of faith. I think this distinction necessary, the conditions of these persons being so different, they must be led to a different act of faith; for a secure sinner, not yet sensible of his sin and misery, not yet willing to leave all for Christ, not yet resolved to come under the government of Christ, &c., for such a one to depend on Christ for pardon and life, is not believing, but presumption. He must first be brought to this, to be willing to accept of Christ as he is offered; till then he has no ground to expect pardon and life from Christ; till then he has no encouragement to rely on Christ for it; till then we cannot press it on him as his duty.

But for the sensible sinner, who is already brought thus far, who is burdened with his sin, abhors himself for it, who prefers Christ before all, who has such ardent, importunate, effectual desires after Christ (as I explained to you), it is his next duty to cast himself on Christ for life and salvation. This is that the gospel calls him to, to which, in this use, I shall encourage him, propounding some motives, removing impediments, answering objections, and giving some directions distinctly, in reference to these different states, as the case shall require.

For motives I shall go no further than the text. Here is the weightiest duty propounded, with the weightiest motive in the world: believing the duty; everlasting life the motive. Every word contains the strongest attractive. Here is *life* for him that will believe; here is *everlasting* life, and here is this *at present*, 'hath everlasting life.' 'He that believes hath everlasting life.'

1. Here is life for him that believes. And what more sweet, more necessary, more desirable, than life, especially to him who is in apparent danger of death! A man that is sentenced to death, that is condemned already, that is every moment in expectation to be led to execution, what would not he do that he might have life? Why this is the condition of every man by nature, not one in the world excepted; he is a child of wrath, a son of death; the great Judge of the heaven and earth has passed the sentence of death on him. It stands on record in his righteous law; you may find it everywhere in the Scripture. The mouth of the Lord does there pronounce it, Thou art condemned already, ver. 18; every moment in danger of eternal death. And in this condition thou remainest, till that almighty power, that raised Jesus Christ from the dead, work this great, this difficult work, which is beyond the power of men or angels, faith in thee. Now if there be any sense of thy condition, if sin and Satan have not quite stupified thee, wilt thou not cry out for life? Is not life desirable? Why, there is no way but one to save thy life. This is the only way, and this is a sure way. Believe, and thou shalt have life; otherwise thou art a dead man. All the world cannot save thy life: no way but this. Unless thou believe, thou art never like to see life, never like to feel any thing but the wrath of God.

2. Here is everlasting life to him that believes. A condemned man would be glad of a reprieve; he would do much for that. Ay, but here is not only a reprieve, but a pardon, if thou believest. Here is not only a respiting of the execution, but a revoking, a nulling of the sentence of death. Here is not only a reprieve, not only a pardon for a malefactor, a rebel; but the highest advancement and preferment. A son of death becomes an heir of life and glory; 'heirs of God, and co-heirs with Christ.' He is not only brought from his dungeon and fetters unto light and liberty, but brought to a crown, to a kingdom; not only raised from the dunghill, but set amongst princes, those that are heirs apparent of the crown of life and glory; a kingdom that cannot be shaken, a crown that fadeth not away, that which he shall enjoy, that which he shall wear for ever, everlasting life.

Oh what a motive is this! Everlasting life is a big, pregnant word. There is more in it than the whole world will hold. There is more in it than in all the kingdoms of the earth and the glory of them put together. There is all in it that the eternal decree of love does grasp. There is all in it that the precious blood of Christ could purchase; that sum, that price, in comparison of which (so rich, so valuable is it), that all the treasures of the earth amount not to a mite. There is all in it that the covenant of grace and the everlasting gospel can hold. There is more in it than tongue can express, than heart can imagine, than angels can comprehend. All this is in it; and all this will be thine, if thou believest: nay, all this is thine.

3. Here is everlasting life at present for him that believes. 'He that believes,' ἔχει. He does not say he *may* have it, as though it were only possible or probable; he does not say he *shall* have it, as though it were merely future; but he *hath* it, it is his own at present. Whatever is comprised in this pregnant word, he hath right to it all at present, and he hath something of it in possession; and he is as sure of the rest as if he now had it, and as if he were actually possessed of it. And here I shall come to open this more fully.

(1.) He hath it in the decree of God. The Lord purposed from eternity to bring his chosen to everlasting life by faith. Faith is an effect of that eternal purpose, such an effect as is an evident and infallible sign of its cause; a certain evidence of those that are comprised in that purpose of love, an infallible character of an elect soul, and therefore called 'the faith of God's elect,' Titus i. 1.

The purpose of God is secret: it runs under ground till faith, and then it breaks forth, then this secret comes to light when the soul believes. Faith is the first saving appearance of it: he that believes may conclude that he is elected to life. He has eternal life by an unchangeable decree, a purpose as unchangeable as God himself, that can no more be changed than that God who is 'without variableness or shadow of changing.'

Upon this account the apostle speaks of those that believe, as having already obtained the inheritance of life, Eph. i. 11, 12, he speaks of himself and others then on earth as having obtained. And how had they obtained it? he adds, being predestinated; and who are these that had obtained it by this purpose? Why, those that trust in Christ. Believe then, and that great question, *Am I elected?* will be no more a question, there need be no more doubt of it. Believe, and you have everlasting life by the decree of heaven.

(2.) He hath it by the purchase of Christ. It is bought for a believer; it is bought and paid for; and what is more his own than that which is so purchased for him? Everlasting life is a purchased possession, Eph. i. 14. The purchaser is Christ; the price was his blood; a price of such value as did fully satisfy him of whom the purchase was made. But for whom did he purchase it? Why for all those, and only those, that believe. Christ had no need to purchase any thing for himself, he wanted nothing; he purchased for others; and who are they? ver. 16. Believe then, and eternal life is as much thine as that which is bought and paid for in thy name, and for thy use. The Lord is engaged, not only in point of mercy and favour, but as he is just and righteous, to let thee have it, it was purchased for thee.

(3.) He hath it by the sentence of the gospel. As an unbeliever has the sentence of death passed against him by the law, so a believer has the sentence of life passed for him by the gospel; both in chap. iii. the former, ver.

18, the latter in the text; so John i. 5; and this latter supersedes the former. If a man who has received sentence of death from the law, can appeal to the gospel, and there plead that he believes, the gospel will quit him, and declare him an heir of life, by virtue of the sentence of God himself, pronounced and recorded in the gospel. The sentence of death is of force no longer than the sinner continues in unbelief. As soon as he believes, from that time forth he hath everlasting life. If any question his right to it, he has the verdict of the gospel, the sentence and judgment of the Lord of life; that is sufficient to decide all controversy, and put it out of question that he has everlasting life.

(4.) He hath it in title. He is born to it, 1 Pet. i. 3–5. Those who are kept through faith unto salvation, are begotten again to an inheritance incorruptible.

Faith is one of the first acts of a new-born soul, a sure evidence that he is born again, that he is born of God; and he that is born of God is a child of God, and all his children are heirs, Rom. viii. 16, 17. Believe, and you are sons of God, and then this is your portion. Everlasting life is as much yours as the portion bequeathed to you by your father. Believe, then you are heirs, and this is your inheritance; you have this life as your patrimony.

(5.) He hath it by covenant. The covenant of grace is a covenant of life; the Lord therein engages to give everlasting life to those that enter into covenant with him. Now faith is our first entrance into covenant with God. When the soul consents to accept of Christ upon his own terms, the match is made up. The day of believing is the day of espousals; Christ becomes his husband, and everlasting life is his dowry, it is made sure to him. Now a dowry is appointed and made sure to a woman; though she have not the full possession and disposal of it while her husband lives, yet none will deny but she has a jointure. So, though a believer have not the full possession of heaven now, yet there is no reason to deny but he hath eternal life; for it is a dowry made sure to every one that believes, 1 Cor. iii. 22, 23. A believer has the word of Christ for it, his promise, Rom. iv. 16. He has it under the hand of Christ, a written evidence, John xx. 31. He has it under the seal of Christ, sealed evidence, Rom. iv. 11. He has it under the oath of God, Isaiah liv. 9, 10, Heb. vi. 17, 18.

(6.) He hath it in possession in some respect. He has possession of it in his head. Believe, and you are united unto Christ; united to him as really, as intimately, as inseparably, as head and members are united. Christ and believers make but one body. The union is so near, as both head and members have one name; both are called Christ, 1 Cor. xii. 12. The Lord Jesus and believers make but one Christ. Now, Christ is in possession of everlasting life; and therefore they are, because Christ and they are but one. The best, the principal part of a believer, his head, is in possession, and therefore he is said to be in possession. Hence it is that believers, as though they were in heaven already, are said to sit in heavenly places, even while they are on earth, Eph. ii. 6. Christ and believers being so much one, what is ascribed to Christ is ascribed to them; what is suffered, done, enjoyed by him, is said to be done, suffered, enjoyed by them. Because Christ was crucified, they are said to be crucified, Gal. ii. 20. Because Christ is risen, therefore they are said to be risen, Gal. iii. 1. Because Christ is set at his right hand in heavenly places, Eph. i. 3, and set down together there, Eph. ii. 6. But how can this be?

They are still on earth. Why, it is true in respect of Christ, it is in Christ Jesus; he is their head, and he is in possession, and therefore the best part of them is in possession already. Christ is their husband; he is gone before to take possession of heaven in their name, on their behalf: 'I go to prepare,' &c. And what is in the husband's possession belongs to the wife. Believe but this, and thou art in some respect in heaven already.

(7.) He has the beginning of everlasting life now. That life which will last for ever, is begun as soon as ye believe, Eph. i. 13, 14. They have the earnest of this inheritance as soon as they believe; and it is such an earnest as does not only make sure the bargain, the contract, but is part of payment, part of the purchase. That light which they have now from the Spirit of truth, is the same in kind, though not in degree, with that which they shall have in that inheritance. That joy which they have now from the Comforter, is the same in kind, though not in degree, with the joys of heaven, John xiv. 16. That glory which they have now from the Spirit of glory resting in them, is part of that which heaven affords, though short in degree, 1 Pet. iv. 14. That holiness which they have now from the Spirit of holiness, is the same in kind, though in less degree than in heaven, John iv. 14. The same water of life that overflows in heaven, is springing on earth in the heart of a believer. It springs not so fast now, nor does it rise so high; but it is the same well, and it is in him now, and all the powers of darkness cannot hinder it from springing up to everlasting life. He has everlasting life now as in a well, there he shall have it as in a river.

(8.) He has everlasting life for his use and advantage upon all occasions. He is not only a proprietor, and in part a possessor of it, as appears before, but an usufructuary. He may make use of heaven for whatever he needs, and whenever he has occasion.

He may have access to the throne of grace, the best place in heaven, whenever he will. Faith sets open the door; he may come with boldness and confidence, Eph. iii. 12, Heb. iv. 16. And coming in faith, he may come with full assurance that he shall have whatever he asks, 1 John v. 13, 14.

(9.) All this is sure. He is sure of all that is present. He is sure of all that is not yet in possession; as sure of it as if he had it already. This the expression imports, *he hath*. He is as sure of heaven as if he were in heaven. Nay, he is surer of heaven than his mere being in heaven could make him; for the fallen angels had a being once in heaven; but that was no assurance of everlasting life to them there; the event proves that a believer on earth is more sure of everlasting life in heaven, than those angels were when they were actually in heaven. But how come they to be thus sure? Why, it is partly through faith, 1 Pet. i. 4, 5. Through faith. Oh, but may not their faith fail? No, so long as Christ has any interest in heaven, so long as he has any power to prevail with his Father, who will easily be prevailed with for those whom he eternally loves. Now he has prayed to this purpose, Luke xxii. 32. But was not this peculiar to Peter, wherein others share not? No; for he adds, Strengthen thy brethren. When thou findest the benefit of this prayer, securing thy faith, strengthen thy brethren with this encouragement. Now what encouragement had this been to them, if Christ did not pray for them as well as him? John xvii. 20.

2. Impediments that hinder men from believing, that keep them short

of saving faith. These must be discovered, and removed. I shall endeavour both together.

The impediments are many. Satan uses his utmost craft and power to multiply and enforce them. I shall insist on some, that I apprehend to be the principal, most common, and most dangerous.

(1.) A conceit they have faith already, when really they have it not. This is Satan's great engine, whereby he destroys heaps upon heaps (as it is said of Samson), ruins multitudes of those that live under the gospel. When the light of it discovers the necessity of faith so clearly as there can be no gainsaying, he comes up with his reserve to secure the hold, and make good the ground that he has in a sinner, when his forlorn of atheism is routed. What, says he, though there be no salvation, no life, without faith, yet trouble not thyself, thou hast faith already. Hereby he keeps off conviction, renders the word ineffectual, hardens the sinner in his unbelief, and makes him secure there, without looking out for faith in the use of those means whereby faith might be attained. This conceit is as a great stone rolled to the door of the sepulchre, to make the soul, who lies buried in a state of unbelief, sure from starting. It is such a mistake as if a physician should judge the disease of a man desperately sick to be quite contrary to what it is, and should prescribe him physic accordingly. The patient [is] in this case under a double mischief, both which are mortal. He not only wants that which is proper for the allaying of his distemper, but he has that applied which feeds and heightens it. So the sinner, under his mistake, avoids that which is proper to his distemper, rousing and convincing truths, threatenings, and representations of the misery of unbelief. He puts away these as belonging to others, and applies the promises and sweetnesses of the gospel as his portion, presuming he is a believer; whenas, considering the true state of his soul, these are as deadly to him as poison; Satan makes use of these to destroy him. These to a believer are the savour of life; but to him, being but a believer in conceit only, they are the savour of death.

Now this mistake arises from another. He mistakes the nature of true faith, and so takes himself to be a believer, when he is not. He takes an historical faith for a justifying faith, or a temporary faith for a saving faith, or a presumptuous credulity for sound believing. Satan, concurring with a deceitful heart, can put a counterfeit faith into the habit of that which is saving, as Rebekah dressed up Jacob like his elder brother; and so far delude a credulous soul, one that is willing to have it so, as he blesses himself, takes the blessing as his portion; whenas indeed he is under the curse, and the wrath of God abides on him.

Now to remove this, the counterfeit must be uncased, the imposter must be discovered; the vizard must be taken off, that the true face of that glorious faith or presumption may be discerned, which is most commonly mistaken for that which is saving and justifying.

A sinner is thus deceived sometimes with an historical, a temporary faith, sometimes with a credulous presumption. For the former,

[1.] He believes the Scripture, that all is true, and orthodox and divine truths. He believes all the articles of the Christian faith; he does not doubt of or question any of them. He believes that all that is related in the Bible is true; that all the commands are just and good, and ought to be obeyed; that all the threatenings are true and righteous, and will be executed; that all the promises are true and gracious, and will be fulfilled. And he that believes all this, is not he a believer? Is not this faith? He believes that Christ is the Saviour, a Saviour of sinners, those that believe; the only Saviour; that there is no salvation in any else. Hence he concludes that he has faith, and he is a believer, and shall be saved. And if any should tell him he has no faith at all, then he would wonder at it, and tell him he is very uncharitable; his faith is as good as the best.

For the discovery and removing of this dangerous mistake, take notice, that this faith comes far short of that which is saving. Though it be necessary to believe thus much, yet to believe thus much is not sufficient to salvation. There is no saving faith without this; but all this may be, and much more, where yet there is no saving faith. This is a common faith, common both to elect and reprobates; it is not that special faith which is saving, called the faith of God's elect. And to convince you of this, take some testimonies of Scripture.

Hypocrites may have such a faith as this, and apostates too, such as shall never see life. Those hearers of the word, which are compared to the stony ground, those in whom the word had no saving effect, had yet such a faith as this, Luke viii. 15. They received the word, and received it with joy, and believed too, and yet fell away, turned apostates, whereas saving faith never fails.

Reprobates may have this faith, even such as Simon Magus the sorcerer, Acts viii. 13. He believed, and continued with Philip, attending on the word which he believed, and was so affected as he was filled with wonder and admiration; and yet Peter tells him he had neither part nor lot in the Holy Ghost, in that which was saving. If he had any faith at all in reality, it could amount to no less than this; and yet his heart was not right in the sight of God, though he seemed to be right in the sight of Philip and the rest, else they would never have baptized him. Yet it was not so in the sight of God; for all his faith, and for all the show that he made of more than this, yet he was in the gall of bitterness, ver. 23. Those that are in a damnable state may have this faith.

Nay, those that are in a state of damnation actually, even the devils, may have this faith, James ii. 19. The devils know as much of the nature and attributes of God as men can know, and much more; and they know it so clearly, with evidence and conviction, as they cannot but believe it; they believe it so effectually, as it makes them tremble. Now, the truth of God is one of his attributes, so that knowing the Scripture to be the word of God, they cannot but believe that it is universally true; relations, assertions, promises, threatenings, they believe all; that which they would least believe, the threatenings, these they so believe as it makes them tremble. They believe not only natural truths, such as the light of nature can discover, but supernatural truths, such as depend upon divine revelation, the truths of Christ and the gospel.

That Christ is the Son of the living and true God, is a truth not known but by revelation, Mat. xvi. 16. Here seems to be much in Peter's acknowledgement and belief of this; yet the devils do acknowledge and believe this, Mat. viii. 28, Luke viii. 26, Mark v. 7, 8.

They believe the gospel to be the doctrine of salvation, the preaching of the gospel to be the way of salvation. This appears sufficiently by their opposing of it; but there is a plain testimony of it, Acts xvi. 16, 17. It is well if some amongst us did not come short of the devil in this. If they believed it indeed to be the way of salvation, methinks they should be more in this way. The spirit of divination, which was a devil, believes and acknowledges that Paul and his companions were the servants of the Most High, and the gospel they preached the way of salvation.

Thus, you see, the devils believe the gospel; and there is no article of the Christian faith but they believe it, these being contained in the gospel. So that those who have no more faith than this, have no more reason to conclude they have saving faith than that the devils have it. You must have another kind of faith than this, else you shall no more see life than those that are in hell already.

Oh, but, says another, I have more than this; I not only believe that Christ is a Saviour, but I trust he will be my Saviour. I have hopes of heaven and salvation, and I hope in Christ for salvation, and I hope in Christ alone for it. Now, this is it which the devils can never attain to, though they have some kind of faith; yet their faith has no confidence, they are without hope.

For removal of mistakes in this, consider that all this may be no more than presumption. Though faith be not without some confidence, yet there may be great confidence where there is no true faith at all. Faith is not without hope; but hope there may be where there is no faith. Job speaks of the hypocrite's hope,—a hope that is not saving, that is in those who shall never be saved,—a hope like the spider's web, Job viii. 13, 14, which, together with those that rely on it, will be swept down into destruction. We have a clear instance of it in the parable of the virgins, Mat. xxv. The foolish virgins, when the door was shut, yet they come to the door, which they would never have done but that they had some hopes to be let in. They had some confidence they should be admitted into the marriage chamber as well as the rest, and they hoped in Christ the bridegroom for it; and that makes them call upon him to open, ver. 11. And it seems they hoped in him alone for it, for they apply themselves to him only; and yet this was but vain presumption, Christ shuts them out, and will not own them, ver. 12.

For a fuller discovery of this mistake, we shall lay down some grounds by which presumptuous hopes and confidence may be discovered from true faith, shewing the difference betwixt faith and presumption in some particulars which the Scripture affords us. They differ,

[1.] In their rise; *vide* Sermon on James.

[2.] In their object. Faith pitches upon whole Christ, presumption will but have part of him. Christ is so precious in the eye of faith, it cannot endure he should be divided; he cannot spare, he cannot be without any of him. He will not have the Lord Jesus separated; he will have him as a Lord as well as a Jesus, as his Lawgiver no less than a Saviour. That is the voice of faith in Thomas, John xx. 27–29, as a Lord to rule him as well as a Jesus to save him.

He embraces Christ coming by water as well as blood. He would have him for purity as much as for pardon, for sanctification as much as for satisfaction. Pardon will not satisfy him without purity; heaven will not please him without holiness; he sees something of it in holiness. He would have complete redemption. He would be redeemed not only from hell, and death, and the wrath to come, but from that which might give Christ any distaste at present, he would be redeemed from a carnal temper within, from a vain conversation without. He counts it but the one half of salvation to be saved from hell hereafter, and the powers of darkness.

His lusts are an affliction, a torment to him, if he were freed from other tormentors. A carnal, worldly temper, corrupt temper of heart, is a misery something like hell to him. He would have Christ to save him, to save him from these, or else he cannot count himself happy. He would have Christ to be his King in all his royalties. He is welcome to him, not only with his crown for glory and happiness, but with his sword and sceptre. He would have Christ come with his sword to circumcise his heart, to cut him off from carnal, worldly interest, to wound his lusts, to put to death his dearest corruption. The sceptre of Christ is lovely and glorious in his eye. He would have him come into his soul with the government upon his shoulders. He desires nothing more than to be brought fully and unreservedly under the government of Christ. He would have Christ reign in him here in holiness and righteousness, as much as he would reign with him hereafter in glory and happiness. Here is the proper genius and the true strain, the genuine character of saving faith; and he would have all Christ, and this above all.

But now presumption would have Christ divided; it can be content with part of him. It shews itself to be presumption in that it will pick and choose something in Christ it likes, something in Christ it dislikes; it will take what it likes, and leaves the rest. A presumer, he would have Christ's righteousness to satisfy justice, procure him a pardon, and purchase him heaven; but he cares not for Christ's holiness. When he looks upon that, he sees no beauty in it, nor comeliness that he should desire it. Such strictness, such holiness, such purity, he hopes he may be saved without that; however, he will venture it. He has no mind to the strait and holy ways of Christ; that is a yoke too grievous, it is a burden too heavy; he hopes Christ will be so gracious as to dispense with him here: The Lord be merciful to me in this, I cannot digest it! As much of Jesus as you will, but as little of him as Lord; or if as Lord, yet not really, universally, or solely.

Not really. He will call him Lord, profess and acknowledge him to be his Lord as well as the best. So the foolish virgins, Mat. xxv.; and those presumptuous hypocrites, Mat. vii. 21, 22. This was verbal, not real; but while his tongue confesses him, his heart does not stoop to him.

Or if they yield to him in some things, yet not in all; if they admit him as their Lord, yet not as absolute Lord; they submit but in part, not universally. Some things they may do, yea, many things, in compliance with Christ, but not all; something or other seems too precise, too difficult, too hazardous; it entrenches too much upon their ease, or pleasures, or carnal humours, or worldly interest; the sceptre of Christ must waive that.

Some sins they will leave, yea, many sins; but some or other is too pleasant, and too gainful, and that is the reason they cannot part with it; the sword of Christ must not touch it.

Here is presumption indeed! If they entertain Christ, either he must come without his sceptre, or else his sceptre must be broken; they will not come under the entire government of Christ. Either he must lay aside his sword, or else it must be only unsheathed at their discretion. He must spare what they cannot part with, and do execution only where they will appoint him, and yet they will hope to be saved by him. Can presumption appear in more lively colours? Alas, how apparent is this in most of those who say they hope in Christ for salvation! And how many, in whom it is not so apparent, yet in their own consciences, if they would look there impartially, they might read this presumption put together with all their hopes, or indeed made up of nothing else, so that if this presumption were subtracted from them, the hopes remaining would be a cypher, and stand for nothing, except it be to delude them.

[3.] In the grounds. Presumption properly is a confidence without ground. Then he presumes, who is confident he shall be saved, when his confidence has no bottom; either no ground at all, or that which is as good as none. The grounds of presumption, such as they be, are either without or within him. Without him, such as these, God is merciful, he delights not in the death of sinners, he would have all men to be saved, &c. Christ is a Saviour, he died to save sinners, &c.

These indeed, when there is a special reason for a particular application, are grounds of hope, but to one who is yet in impenitency and unbelief, they afford no more hopes than to Cain or Judas; for why might not either of them draw this conclusion from the premises as well as such a one? Yet if Cain, or Judas, or the like, should conclude thus, God is merciful; Christ died for sinners, *ergo* I shall be saved, who would not say this is presumption?

The grounds within them are ordinarily their own righteousness, their good meaning, purposes, inclinations; they mean well, whatever fault be found with them. They do no man wrong, give every one his own, are not so bad as others, nay, much better than many about them. Upon such grounds did the presumptuous Pharisee raise his confidence, Luke xviii. 11, 12; or their outward conformities and enjoyment of ordinances, such as theirs, Luke xiii. 37, &c.; or upon their performances, doing much in an outward formal way of religion. So theirs, Mat. vii. 22, 23. But now a true believer grounds his confidence and hopes of heaven upon something which the Scripture assigns as proper and peculiar to the heirs of heaven, which can be found in none but those that are in a saving state. He draws not his conclusion but from such premises as are confirmed by the Spirit of God. He concludes his interest in mercy and salvation, because he finds the first fruits of salvation, the effects of special mercy, in his soul, he has the earnest of the Spirit in his heart, this makes sure the contract for eternal life, Eph. i. He concludes Christ died for him, because he finds the saving effects of his death produced in his soul. He has lively hopes, because he is alive to God, he is born again, he is begotten to these hopes, 1 Peter i. 3. His hopes of glory arise from Christ within him, Col. i. 27. He finds Christ dwelling in him, Eph. iii. 7, working in him, acting him by his Spirit, and thereby testifying to him that he is a son, and so an heir. He concludes that he is in Christ, because he is 'a new creature,' 2 Cor. v. 17. He finds 'old things passed away, and all things become new.' His old vain, carnal, wanton imaginations are passed away. His old secure, benumbed, unfaithful conscience is passed away. His old perverse, stubborn, rebellious will, he has a new will. His old strong, sensual, corrupt, unbelieving, impenitent heart is gone; he has a new heart, a heart of flesh, bearing the image of Christ. His old disordered, misplaced, inordinate affections, &c., his old vain, sinful conversation is altered, he has a new life, all things are become new. He has new thoughts, new inclinations, new intentions, new designs, new resolutions, new desires, new delights, new employments, new conversation, all suitable to the state and hopes of a new creature, becoming one who is renewed in the spirit of his mind, which has put on that new man, which after God is created in righteousness and true holiness, as the apostle speaks, Eph. iv. 22–24. He can say, he was sometimes darkness, but now he is light in the Lord, Eph. v. 8; sometimes carnal, but now in some measure spiritual; sometimes worldly, but now in some degree has his conversation in heaven; sometimes profane, but now in part holy. There is such a change, as in the Corinthians, 1 Cor. vi. 9–11.

[4.] In the effects. As faith and presumption do differ in their nature, so they produce different effects, and these effects may be referred to three heads. They respect Christ, or sin, or the persons themselves.

First. The effects of faith, in reference to Christ, are a high esteem of him, strong desires after him, unfeigned love to him.

Presumption does not transcendently value Christ so as to prefer him before his chief joy; nor effectually desire him, so as to part with all for him; nor sincerely love him, so as to cleave to him only. Something takes place of Christ in his mind and heart, though it may be self-love (which is very strong in a presumptuous confident) does so blind him as he does not perceive it, will not believe it. But of these effects of faith I have spoken sufficiently in the explication.

Secondly. The effects of faith in reference to sin are fear of it, hatred of it, sorrow for it. Faith sets the heart fully against sin, as that which is dreadful, hateful, and most grievous, whereas presumption slights sin, at least some sins, makes no great matter of them, cleaves to some, and is indifferent as to others; presumes it shall go well with him though he go on in this or that evil way.

First. A true believer fears sin; faith makes him afraid of it as of a dreadful evil, Heb. xi. 7. Where faith is in the heart, the heart is moved with fear, this makes such an impression on him, all the scorns of the world will not prevail with him to neglect a duty. Though he see not the effects of sin, though they be future and at a great distance, as the flood seemed to be, yet being warned of God, he is moved with fear. His own experience is enough to render sin fearful to him. He has felt the burden of sin oppressing his soul, he is afraid to add more weight to a pressure that he has found too heavy for him. While the Lord was working faith in his heart, he found his iniquities going over his head, Ps. xxxviii. 4. He has felt sin straining his conscience. He remembers the anguish of a wounded spirit, he is now afraid of it as of a serpent. His soul has been scorched with sin, he remembers that it kindled wrath in his soul, and now he dreads the fire, is afraid of coming near the flame; whereas presumption is bold and venturous, will play with the flame, will be tampering with some evil or other, though it singe him, and at last he drops into hell, as the moth, making too bold with the candle, at last loses her wings, and falls down lame or dead before it.

The voice of faith is that of Joseph, 'How shall I do this great wickedness, and sin against God!' but the voice of presumption is like that of Lot concerning Zoar; he says of this or that sin, 'Is it not a little one?' my soul may live in it and be secure.

That which seems to be a great sin to faith seems a little one to presumption; that which faith trembles at, this makes bold with it. He presumes that the Lord is not so strict and severe as to condemn him for not straining at such sins as he counts but like a gnat, presumes he may come to heaven though he be not so strict and precise as the word would have him. To be so precise, is to be over righteous in his conceit, he will make bold to gratify himself in one or other forbidden path, whatever come of it. Presumption is a bold, a venturous humour; he blesses himself, and says, I shall have peace, though he walk after the stubbornness of his own heart.

Secondly. A true believer hates sin. He is not only angry at it, displeased with it, but he hates it, pursues it to the death, seeks its ruin, would have it utterly destroyed, root and branch, the body of death and all its members, would have the whole crucified, and shews his hatred by diligence in use of all means to get it mortified. He hates all sin, every false way, even those that he has most loved, wherein he has most delighted. His hatred is universal and impartial. Faith in Christ is always accompanied with a dear love to Christ, and love to Christ always attended with hatred of sin: Ps. xcvii. 10, 'Ye that love the Lord, hate evil.' Being so much in love with Christ, and knowing there is nothing so contrary, so injurious, so hateful to Christ as sin, he cannot but hate that which is so contrary to him whom his soul loves, Ps. cxxxix. 21. Every sin is hateful to Christ, and therefore he hates every sin. But self-love is predominant in the presumer; he hates sin no further than self-love leads him, no further than it is contrary to his own humours, inconsistent with his own interest, or disagreeing with his temper.

Hatred springs from some contrariety betwixt the person so affected and the object hated. Now a believer has a new nature, to which sin is as contrary as darkness is to light, John i. 11, 12. Now as in the natural birth, so in this supernatural, there is a new form, a new nature; he is renewed after the image of God in holiness. Now sin and holiness are as contrary as hell and heaven, as filthiness and purity. Hence it is, that there is in every true believer an antipathy to sin, as being contrary to that new nature. That divine nature which he partakes of, he comes to partake of it by the promises, and so consequently by faith, without which the promises afford us nothing, 2 Pet. i. 4; and by this escapes the pollutions of the world through lust. This divine nature puts him upon this, by all means to flee to Christ, make an escape from the pollutions of sin, as that which is hateful and contrary to him.

But there is no such principle in a presumer, and therefore no such act. He may be angry at sin, and so may avoid it, and put some restraint upon it, so as he may seem to have escaped the pollution, but he hates it not; he contents himself to restrain it, that it break not forth into outward acts, but he seeks not to ruin it. Or though he may hate some sin, as being contrary to his temper, or inconsistent with his credit, profit, safety, or other interests, but he does not hate all sin; there is one or other that he is always in love or league with; and if he would deal faithfully and impartially with his soul, he might discover it. But presumption is a blind, hood-winked boldness, which, as it will not see that which is hateful in a beloved sin, so it will not see, will not believe that he loves it. Or if this cannot be avoided, rather than his presumptuous heart will yield to conviction, he will presume that the sin which he loves and lives in, is no sin, or at least, no such sin as will keep him out of heaven, or argue a damnable state.

Thirdly. Sorrow for sin. A believing heart is a new heart, a heart of flesh, a heart that receives deep impressions from the love of Christ, a heart that will melt and bleed when he remembers the injuries, the unkindnesses that he has offered to Christ, Zech. xii. 10. When the soul looks upon Christ with the eye of faith, when he sees what he has done, and against whom he has done it; when he sees Christ pierced, and pierced by him, and willing to be wounded, that the soul that was thus unkind, thus cruel to him, might have life by him, oh this makes him mourn, and mourn greatly, and mourn bitterly, as they mourned for Josiah at Hadadrimmon, a place in the valley of Megiddon, where that peerless prince was slain.

The soul looks upon Christ, represented in this posture in the gospel, set forth there, as if he were pierced and crucified before his eyes. His eye sees, and so sees this spectacle of love and wonder, as his eye affects his heart. Oh, says he, what have I done? what have I been doing all this while that I have lived in sin? Have I been all this while piercing Christ? Has every sin (when I am guilty of so many) wounded Christ? Have I been all this while crucifying him, and put him to an open shame? Have I been piercing him who loves me, who so loved me as to be willing to die for me? And does he now love one who has been so unkind, so cruel to him? Will he pardon me after such provocations? Will he think thoughts of love and peace to one that has thus used him? Will he embrace one who is covered with such bloody sins? Why, yes; behold he offers love to such a wretch; he stretches out his arms to embrace me who have pierced him; he will make no other use of those wounds that I have given him, but to heal me by them. Oh the wonders of Christ's love! Oh the bloody guilt of my sins! Oh these thoughts enter deep into a believing heart: it melts him, he is all dissolved into sorrow. The rod of Moses did not smite the rock more effectually when the waters gushed out of it, than this thought, this sight of a pierced Christ, strikes and pierces the heart. He now tastes in his sins the bitterness of death, the bitterness of Christ's death; no wonder if he mourn bitterly.

But now a presumptuous heart is a hard heart; it is a heart of stone. It melts not, it bleeds not, when it sees Christ set forth bleeding and dying. The love of Christ makes no deep impressions on it; it glides off, as water from a stone. There is no such heart-meltings, no such passionate relentings, no such breaking reflections on Christ or upon sin, no such great or bitter mourning.

Presumption is impudent. He hardens his face, and will not blush in secret for all his unworthy dealings with Christ. His heart is hardened; it will not bleed, though he sees Christ pierced before him. Indeed, how can it be that his heart should break into sorrow for that which his heart loves and delights in?

Thirdly. The effects, in reference to these persons, are humility and watchfulness in the believer, pride and security in the presumer.

First. A believing heart is a humble heart. Faith lays the soul low, in sense of its own vileness, emptiness, impotency; in sense of former sinfulness, present unworthiness; in sense of its many wants, weaknesses, distempers, corruption. As nothing more exalteth Christ, so nothing more debaseth man. As it advances man high in the account of God, so it lays him low in his own eyes. The Lord, having a design to display the riches of his grace, made choice of faith as the fittest instrument, as that which gives all to God, and nothing to man. It is the soul's going out of himself, as having nothing but sin and misery, unto Christ for all. It has a double aspect: one to himself, there it sees nothing but guilt, weakness, emptiness; another to Christ, and there it sees righteousness, strength, all-sufficiency.

Faith empties a man of himself, self-conceit, self-sufficiency, self-confidence, makes him seem nothing, that Christ may be all in all. Where the strongest faith, the greatest humility, Mat. viii. 7–10; judges himself unworthy of the least favour, counts himself the greatest of sinners, less than the least of all mercies, thinks better of others than of himself, patient of reproofs, and ready to stoop to the meanest service that Christ shall call him to; ascribes all he has to Christ and grace.

Whereas presumption is proud and haughty, swells a man full, and raises him high in his own conceit. It is attended with self-conceit and self-confidence; thinks well of himself, and stands upon his own bottom; counts himself fit for services above him, and is impatient of reproofs, contradictions, and what he judges undervaluings. Some strains hereof are visible in that presumptuous Pharisee, Luke xviii. 11, 12.

Secondly. A holy jealousy and watchfulness over himself, Rom. xi. 20. Because he stands by faith, therefore he is not high-minded or self-confident, but wary and watchful; careful that he may not receive the grace of God in vain; fearful lest he should make unworthy returns; jealous over his heart, as knowing it to be treacherous and unfaithful; watchful over his spirit, that it do not start aside from Christ; careful that no mercy may slip his notice, that no rod or affliction may speak in vain; keeps a strict hand over his soul in all his ways, especially in ordinances of worship; trembles at the word; and in a word, works out his salvation with fear and trembling. Easy to be convinced of miscarriages, thankful for such discoveries, such smitings are acceptable to him, when he is himself; and ordinarily his own heart smites him first, and more than others.

But presumption is careless and secure, gives the reins to his heart. The temper of his spirit is loose and negligent, even in acts of worship; bears up against conviction in miscarriage, staves it off, and is stubborn against the word when it crosses him.

We may see this in the deportment of the Jews, the presumptuous part of them, under the ministry of Christ himself.

[5.] In their properties. True faith being a form far differing from presumption, the properties that flow from it are far different.

First. It is a purifying faith. The confidence, which is either the act or attendant of it, is a lively hope, that will be working out all impurity of flesh and spirit. As a living spring will not long continue mudded, but is still working out the mud and impure mixtures which defile it, 1 John iii. 3. *Vide* sermon on Mat. vii. 21. 1. He makes it his work. 2. It is his beauty. Impurity is an eye-sore to faith; this looks upon sin as its deformity and defilement, as that which is nasty and loathsome. Now as one that affects beauty will not endure anything upon the face, the seat of beauty, which is nasty and loathsome, will use all means to wash off such a defilement, to remove that which is looked upon as an ugly defilement, so does he who has this hope labour to purify himself from the defilements of sin, to free himself from it, as that which he knows is most loathsome to Christ, in whose eye he would be lovely. And Christ is his pattern. 'He that hath this hope in Christ, purifies himself as Christ is pure.' He sets the holiness of Christ before him as his pattern; he would have that purity copied out in his soul; he would be holy, as he is holy; he would have 'the same mind to be in him which was in Christ.' And though he knows, when he has done his best, he shall come far short of this high example, yet since the Lord has set it before him, he will strive to come as near it as he can. He will be following of Christ, though it be *haud passibus æquis*, though it be at a great distance, through the weakness of the flesh. Though he come far short of him, yet he will strive to keep Christ in his sight, Heb. xii. 1, 2. Though he cannot make so large steps as his glorious forerunner, yet he will be careful to make straight steps to his feet; he will not step out of that holy way wherein Christ is gone before him; he will not turn aside to the right hand or to the left, into by-paths of sin and vanity; but endeavours to follow Christ fully, fully, though weakly. Other examples, even the greatest, he will not follow further, or otherwise, than they follow Christ, 1 Cor. xi. 1, 1 Pet. ii. 21. He will not encourage himself, by the sins and failings of the most eminent saints, to grow loose, or take liberty to do the least thing that may be offensive. They did thus and thus formerly, they do so and so now. Well, says he, be it so, but they are not my pattern. Would Christ do so and so? I must follow him.

Ay, but presumption writes not after this copy. This will make bold to waive Christ's footsteps, where the way seems cross, or rugged, or deep, or difficult; especially if he see any, who have the repute of holiness, go before him herein. He copies out the blots of God's saints, those characters in their lives which agree not with the original. He encourages himself by their sins and failings; his hopes feed upon their corruptions, and nourish themselves thereby. Noah, Lot, David, Peter, these and these sinned thus and thus, and yet were saved. My sins, says he, that I fall into now and then, are not worse, are not so bad as these. And therefore though I continue in this or that evil, why should I doubt of salvation? Here is the true face of presumption without any mask.

A true believer abuses not his hopes, so as to grow more loose, to sin more freely, to make more liberty to himself in things doubtful or suspicious, to be negligent of more purity, careless of an increase in holiness, higher degrees of grace. He argues not thus: My condition is safe, I am sure of heaven, therefore I need care for no more; if I should take liberty in such and such things, to decline a little from the strictness of the rule, it would cut me off from salvation; and therefore why should I not gratify myself herein? He contents not himself with such a degree of purity, such a measure of holiness, as will be sufficient barely to bring him to heaven. No; but because he has this hope, therefore he is more careful to avoid sin, therefore he purifies himself more and more, therefore he would be more heavenly, therefore he strives after more holiness. Hope spurs him on in the way that is called holy; hope makes those ways pleasant and delightful to him; hope quickens his endeavours, makes him unwearied in the pursuit of holiness, engages him cheerfully against all difficulties, incumbrances, opposition, that would hinder his growth and proficiency in holiness.

Those hopes that encourage a person to sin more freely, to walk more loosely, to count strictness and preciseness more than needs, to count purity and holiness in the strength, life, power, exercise, and daily increase of it needless, any degree of holiness or righteousness too much, they are no better than a damning and deluding presumption.

These hopes put a man upon an universal purity; purifies himself, all that is in himself, both inward and outward man, and that especially which is most himself, his heart and soul, Acts xv. 9. Faith purifies both heart and life, but it exerts its purifying virtue first in the heart. That is the spring of impurity; and the streams will never run clear to purpose in the conversation, till the spring be cleansed. 'A good man, out of the good treasure of his heart, brings forth good things,' Mat. xii. 33. Till the heart be good, nothing is good; till that be purified, all is defiled. Even that which makes the greatest show of purity, that holiness which is not minted in the heart, and brought out into the life from thence, as out of a good treasury, however it glister, it is but counterfeit coin, it is not current with Christ, however it may be with men. When he brings it to the touch-stone, it will be found but dross, or gilded wickedness. It is not of the stamp of heaven, if it bear not the impression of that precious faith which purifies the heart. A true believer will not content himself with outward purity, with visible holiness, a refined conversation, though he has all care of that; but if he could converse in the world like an angel, as to outward purity, holiness, innocency, yet, so long as he find vain thoughts lodge in his mind, so long as he feels sinful, impure notions stirring in his heart, though they should never break forth into outward act, nay, though they should never procure full inward consent, yet this he accounts an impurity, a defilement not to be endured. Those secret motions of sin, which no eye sees but the eye of God, are his burden and affliction. Faith makes him restless, industrious to get his heart and mind purified from these. These buds of that root of bitterness, his natural corruption, he is cropping them off, casting them out as that which defiles him. He is daily striking at the root itself, that by degrees his heart may be cleansed from that mass of corruption.

But now presumption rests in an external purity, satisfy themselves with an outside holiness, consisting in avoiding gross sins, and the outward acts of religion and righteousness, and presume upon this they shall get to heaven, whoever be excluded. In the mean time they trouble not them-selves with inward purity, to get their minds and hearts purged; sinful thoughts, impure motions are tolerated. The body of sin is no burden. The stirrings and actings of natural corruption are winked at. All is well enough, if it break not forth into open acts. If the outside be clean, they look no further. This they take as a sufficient evidence for heaven. They will scarce believe that there are any who do more. This was the very temper of the presumptuous Pharisees, who were so confident of heaven, as though it had been reserved alone for them. Thus does Christ describe them, while he pricks their swelling confidence with those sharp menaces, Mat. xxiii. 25–27.

I have insisted the longer on this head, because the particulars in it are very plain and distinguishing; so as, if you would deal faithfully with your souls, in applying them, and examining by them, you might be able to discern whether the hopes of heaven be the issues of a true faith, or of a vain presumption.

1. The presumer makes not holiness his work, it is not his great business to purify himself. He minds it not seriously. If he mind it at all, it is but upon the by. There is something else that is more his design, which has not only more of his time and endeavours, but more of his heart.

2. Holiness is not purity to him. It is not an ornament, a beauty in his eye. He is not in love with it. The face of it is not so lovely, that he should be at so much pains to wipe off, to wash out the spots which are contrary to it. As the judgments or fancies of some persons are so depraved by custom or example, that they count a spotted, a patched, a painted face beautiful, so these confidents please themselves with their bespotted souls, yea, and presume that the Lord is pleased with them; so well pleased with them, as that he will admit them into heaven, though they be not cleansed, purged, purified. And, which heightens this presumption, they will believe this in contradiction to what the Lord has plainly and positively declared, that 'without holiness no man shall see the Lord,'

and that the pure in heart are blessed by God, and shall alone be admitted to see him.

Secondly. True faith is working faith. Presumption is an idle fancy. Saving faith is operative, Gal. v. 6, ἐνεργουμένη. It worketh, and it 'worketh by love.' It worketh, and therefore called effectual, Philem. 6, and 1 Thes. ii. 13. There is an effectual working in those that believe. It is effectual to make them walk worthy of God, verse 12. How that? Why, as the apostle, verse 10. Where this is rooted in the heart, it grows up and spreads itself in all the branches of obedience, and is filled with the fruits of righteousness. It makes a man active for God, and thereby shews it is a living principle, a lively faith, a lively hope, 1 Peter i. 3; whereas the hope and faith of presumers is dead: no breathings after Christ, no vigorous motions towards him, no lively actings for him. No wonder, for it is dead, and hereby appears to be so, James ii. 17; verse 20, he says it again, it is as a carcase, a body without a soul. Not that good works are the soul of faith, but because they are the vital acts of it. Where there is no vital acts, there is no soul; because the soul where it is will be acting, will shew itself by acts of life. Even a new-born infant, though it cannot walk and work as a grown man, yet it cries, and breathes, and moves, and sucks; and hereby shews it is alive, that there is a soul, a principle of life in it. Whereas a child coming into the world, if it do not put forth some of these acts, if it do not cry, move, or breathe at least, we then conclude it is still-born, it is already dead. Not because these acts are its life, but because they are the signs of life.

So that the apostle makes good works to be the vital acts of faith, whereby a living faith may be distinguished from a dead. Presumption, if it do not cry after God, move towards him, breathe after him, cling to him, as the child to the breast, act for him in a lively manner, according to the proportion of strength received, it is but a mole, a lump of flesh, not informed with a living soul. Though there may seem to have been some conception, some tumour, yea, some travail too, some legal pangs like those of the new birth, yet that which is brought forth is but a dead thing, if it want these vital acts which the apostle calls works. It is but a picture of faith, how much soever it resemble it. Though it have the colour, the features, the lineaments, the proportions of a living child, yet these are no more than you may see in a picture. Without these acts it is but a painted faith. If you would make it appear to be alive indeed, you must do it by the acts of obedience, by good works.

Quest. But you will say, May not presumptuous hypocrites do good works? May not they abound in them? in good works of all sorts, works of charity, and works of righteousness, and works of piety and religion? Did not the Pharisees exceed in works of piety? Was not that a notable work of charity in Ananias and Sapphira, when they sold their estate, and brought the greatest part of it to be disposed of for the relief of those that were in want? Did not those presumptuous hypocrites, Mat. vii. 22, do many wonderful works? If good works be common to both, how can this be a distinguishing character to know the one from the other?

Ans. Presumption may be attended with good works, and a presumer may go as far in this respect as a true believer. He may do the same works, if you look only to the outside of them; but if you look in the inside of those works, there is a great difference; and such a one as a man, if he will faithfully and impartially examine, may discern in himself, though he cannot discern in another.

This difference is intimated by the apostle James, ii. 23; he wrought for God as a friend, and so the Lord accounted him. His works were acts of friendship to God; they proceeded from love to him; not out of love, or fear of punishment, or hopes of reward only; but because he was a friend, and loved him. A true friend, though he have no fear to lose any thing, nor hopes to gain any thing by what he does, yet he will appear and act for his friend. Why? Because he loves him. Thus it was with Abraham, and thus it is with every true believer. If there were neither heaven nor hell, neither hopes of the one, nor fear of the other, yet he would do what is well pleasing to God; he would be acting for him because he is his friend, he loves him. Where there is love, there will be acts of love; and the acts of this love and friendship to God is obedience, John xiv. 15, and xv. 14.

But this difference, which is but intimated by James, is plainly expressed by Paul, Gal. v. 6, 'Faith works by love.' Presumption works by something else; he has some other principle or motive that sets him a-work. The papist works that he may merit heaven. The Pharisee works that he may be applauded, that he may be seen of men, that he may have a good esteem, a good report with them. The slave works lest he should be beaten, lest he should be damned. The formalist works, that he may stop the mouth of conscience, that will be accusing, disquieting him, if he do nothing. The time-server works, because it is the custom, the fashion, the way to stand or to rise, to gain his own ends, or secure his own interest. The ordinary professor works, because it is a shame to do nothing, where so much is professed; the temporary, because he is in a good mood. These are all presumers in their kind, or as bad as presumers. But the true believer works because he loves. This is the principal, if not the only motive, that sets him a-work. If there were no other motive within or without him, yet would he be working for God, acting for Christ, because he loves him; it is like fire in his bones.

But presumption works not by love. Either it is idle, or it is acted by some other principle. Some of the fore-mentioned motives, or some other of like nature, set him a-work, when he betakes himself to any work that is good. If he acted by love, it is not love to Christ, but self-love. Indeed, the presumer makes himself his centre: all the lines in the whole circumference of his life, all his acts and works that have a show of goodness, are drawn from hence; and here they all meet and are united. He loves himself so well, as he would be happy, he would not be damned, he would be applauded and esteemed, he would not be disquieted by a clamorous accusing conscience, he would avoid reproach and shame, he would compass his own ends. And these, or the like, are the weights that set all the wheels on motion when he seems to move for God; if these were taken off, all would stand still. Love does not sway him. Faith is active, and works for God, because he loves; and presumption is idle, or else works for himself, being acted by self-love.

Thirdly, True faith is precious; it is like gold, it will endure a trial. Presumption is but a counterfeit, cannot abide to be tried, 1 Pet. i. 7. A true believer fears no trial. He is willing to be tried by God, Psa. xxvi. 2, cxxxix. 23. He is willing to have his faith tried by others, he shuns not the touchstone. He is much in trying himself. He would not take anything upon trust, especially that which is of such moment. He is willing to hear the worst as well as the best. That preaching pleases him best which is most searching and distinguishing, Heb. iv. 12. He is loath to be deluded with vain hopes. He would not be flattered into a good conceit of his spiritual state without ground. When trials are offered, he complies with the apostle's advice, 2 Cor. xiii. 15.

But presumption takes things upon trust, will not be at the trouble to try, and is loath to be troubled with searching truths. That teaching pleases him best, which keeps at a distance, comes not near his conscience, makes no scrutiny in his soul. Such a man as would convince him that his hopes are but delusions, his confidence presumption, he takes him for an enemy, though he do but tell him the truth, and that truth which is most necessary for him. When he is called to trial in the ministry of the word, and means offered whereby his heart might be searched, he keeps off, as a cheater would keep off from the touchstone with his counterfeit coin. Why, would you drive me to despair? says he; trouble not me with so many scruples; I trust my faith is as good as those who make a greater show: however, God is merciful, and I will trust him with my salvation without more ado. And thus he is willing to delude himself; ay, and will be deluded. Those that do pity him, and would undeceive him, are suspected, or scorned, or hated.

Fourthly, True faith is growing. It comes not to its full stature at once, but by degrees. There is a growing from faith to faith, Rom. i. 17, a passing from weakness to strength, and from one degree of strength to another, and in the way a conflicting with doubts, weaknesses, discouragements, opposition. So it passes from acceptance to dependence, and from dependence on him for pardon and life, to a life of dependence, a resting on him for all things; and from dependence to assurance, and from a weak assurance to a full assurance. The beginnings of it are small and weak, and there is a sense of this weakness, and strivings after increase. 'I believe,' &c., Mark ix. 24. A true believer is apprehensive of his weakness, and feeble as his faith is, finding unbelief strong, is struggling with it, complains of it, bewails it, diligent in the use of all means to get faith encouraged and strengthened, and grows up accordingly.

But now presumption starts up on a sudden, and comes to its full growth and maturity in a moment. There is no such sense of weakness, meets with no such opposition, finds no such cause to complain of unbelief, no such wrestling with doubts, no such need of diligence for increase. His faith, *i. e.*, his presumption, is as strong at the first, as it is after many years' standing; sensible of no increase in the use of means.

Fifthly, In the extent. True faith, in its actings, reaches both to the things of eternity and the things of this life. Presumption trusts God only as to his soul and salvation; things which he less minds than temporal things. A true believer trusts God with all. A presumer hopes, or, as he says, trusts that God will be gracious to his soul; but as to the things of the world he trusts himself; he will rely upon his own wit, or prudence, or industry, or friends, or parts, or interest. That which we mind not, value not, we can be more free to leave to the care and in the trust of others; but that which is above all dear to us, we are cautious in trusting any with it but ourselves. This is the truth of the business. Those that ordinarily presume so much of heaven, the things of this life are dearest to them, and most valued by them, therefore they will take care of these themselves; but the things of eternity they much mind not, and therefore they leave these, as they say, to God's mercy. So that their trusting God with their souls is no more than this in plain English, they do not much mind them. And this appears, in that they think no industry and pains too much, all care little enough for their estates or posterity, little fear lest their care should be immoderate, lest it should intrench too much upon that care and time that is due to their souls; little or no scruple lest the means they use, the courses they take, should be irregular. Or if there be any scruple, yet if they see the same used ordinarily by others, that will be a sufficient *salvo*, a sufficient warrant to proceed therein.

They make haste to be rich or great, or get from under the cross, poverty, disrespect, &c. They will take nearer ways than God sets open to them; they will not stay to take God along with them, or to see him going before them (as those that trust him will do), they will not be hindered by busying themselves much about their souls, they are in haste: and hereby they shew plainly they believe not in God; for he that believes will not make haste, Isa. xxviii. 16. He that truly trusts in him, will stay God's time, and use God's means, and walk in God's way, though it seem about; they will not neglect their souls for haste; they know this would be to make more haste than good speed. Nor would they step out of the way, the way that is holy and righteous, though they may escape a loss, an affliction by it, though they might gain some desirable advantage by it. True faith goes leaning upon God, and therefore will keep his way, Ps. xxxvii. 34. He that will not be liberal for the promoting and honouring of the gospel; he that fears poverty or affliction more than he fears sin; he that is more careful for the things of the world than for his soul; he that takes indirect or suspected courses, to get, or increase, or secure his estate; he that is not jealous or watchful, lest his cares for the world (when he is much engaged therein) should be immoderate,—it is plain he does not trust God with his estate; and he that does not trust God for his estate, whatever he think or pretend, he does not trust God for his soul, for his salvation; his hopes of heaven and salvation are but presumption.

Thus I have given you an account of the differences betwixt faith and presumption; and hereby, if you deal faithfully with your souls, you may be able to discern whether you truly believe indeed, or whether you only presume. This may be sufficient through the Lord's concurrence to discover mistakes in this weighty business, and so to remove the first impediment which keeps men from faith, viz., a conceit they have faith, when in truth they have no such thing.

2. Impediment. A conceit that faith is a business of no great difficulty. Men wonder why any should make such ado about believing; they think it an easy thing to believe, and so trouble not themselves much about it, make it not their business to look after it. This conceit being so common, it is a plain evidence there are few who have it. Those who think it such an easy matter to believe, shew plainly they never did believe, nay, they do not so much as know what it is to believe indeed. And as it is a sign they want it, so it is an impediment that keeps them from it.

To remove it, consider what the Scriptures declare concerning faith in opposition to this conceit.

(1.) It is the gift of God. It is not the work of man's hand, or of his head, or of his heart. It is something without him, not in him naturally; something above him, out of the reach of nature, though improved and raised to the height. It must be reached down by the hand of God, otherwise man can never come by it: Philip. i. 29, 'To you it is given,' &c. It is not a gift of nature, nor a gift acquired by the improvement of nature's abilities, but a gift supernatural, a gift of grace, Eph. ii. 8. Both salvation and faith are of grace; neither of them of ourselves, both the gift of God. What Christ said to Pilate in another case, is true here, John

xix. 11. There is no seeds of it, no propensity to it in nature, it must come from a foreign hand; nay, there is no power in nature to receive it when it is offered; the hand is full, and *intus existens*, &c.: 'How can ye believe?' John v. 44.

(2.) Man is naturally unwilling to receive it. Not only without it, unable to procure it, but unwilling to receive it, John v. 40. Coming is believing. Now, though Christ, who is truth itself, told them this was the only way to life, yet, though their life lay on it, they were not willing to come, they were resolved not to come at him, not to believe. Is not he unwilling to receive a thing who will die rather than receive it? Oh but though they were unwilling to come to Christ, yet suppose Christ should condescend to come and offer himself to them, could they be then unwilling? Sure then we should see them willing to receive him. No; not then: 'He came to his own, and his own received him not,' John i. 11. Those who challenged the Messias as peculiar to themselves, those to whom he was promised, those who had so long expected his coming, yet when he comes, they receive him not. So the Lord complains: 'Israel would none of me.' Christ takes up the complaint, Mat. xxiii. 27. They would not be gathered by him, when he would have gathered them; they would not receive him, when he offered himself to them. They were so far from receiving him, as they hated the sight of him: 'Light is come into the world, and men love darkness rather than light,' John iii. 19. Here is not only a bare unwillingness, but an averseness rising up into hatred, Isa. lxv. 2. Here is not only an unwillingness, but a rebellious opposition. And such an opposition to faith, to Christ, there is in the heart of every man till born again. Ye do but flatter and delude yourselves if you think you are better disposed than the Jews. It is thus with every man, all men, though no natural man will believe it. The Jews could think better of themselves than they were; this is not only the delusion of these days, Mat. xxiii. 29. They would not believe they should have opposed the prophets, as their forefathers did, and yet even then were they opposing Christ himself, the prince of prophets. No wonder if men will not believe now they oppose Christ and faith, even when in the ministry of the word they do daily resist and oppose them. But however you delude yourselves, this is the truth of God; there is a desperate opposition in every unregenerate heart against faith, against Christ himself.

(3.) This opposition is so strong as it requires an exceeding mighty power to overcome it.

The power of nature cannot master it. Indeed, this is wholly employed for the strengthening of unbelief, to enforce the opposition against faith. The stronger a man's parts are, wit, memory, judgment, reason, affections, the more vigorously does he oppose faith. That is evident in the scribes and Pharisees, men amongst the Jews of greatest parts; and those most heightened and improved, in them the opposition was strongest.

The power of divine institutions alone cannot master this. What more powerful than the word? Yet this alone cannot prevail: 'The weapons of our warfare,' 2 Cor. x. 4, 5, 'mighty through God;' ay, but in themselves too weak for unbelief; too weak, though managed by an apostle, the greatest of the apostles. 'Paul may plant;' ay, but all this is labour in vain without a higher, a mightier power, 1 Cor. iii. 5–7; too weak, though managed by an angel, as you may see in the ministry of the angel Gabriel to Zacharias, leading him to a particular faith, a business one would think of less difficulty, the circumstances considered, Luke i. 11, 19, 20.

Too weak, though managed by Christ himself. How little did his ministry prevail against the opposition of the unbelieving Jews! So little, as he complains: 'I have laboured in vain,' Isa. xlix. 4. Oh the wonderful power of unbelief! the incredible strength of this opposition! that the power of the word in the ministry of Christ himself, yea, the power of miracles, wherewith his ministry was enforced, could not prevail against it, John xii. 37, 38.

Nay, the power of God does not master it when it is put forth only in a common way; for a common concurrence is always vouchsafed; without that we cannot move nor breathe, yet we see unbelief is seldom overcome, this opposition to faith seldom mastered.

But the power of God, the almighty power of God, must be put forth in a special manner to prevail against this opposition. That almighty arm must be made bare, and stretched out; it must be put forth in the infiniteness of its strength, that a sinner may be made able or willing to believe, Isa. liii. 1; that the report of Christ may be believed, the arm of the Lord must be revealed, it must be made bare, Isa. lii. 10; alluding to the gesture of men, who setting themselves to some special work in good earnest, that they may use the force of it with less encumbrance, strip the arm up to the elbow. Such a power is required to raise sinners out of the grave of unbelief as was requisite to raise Christ from the dead. Thus the apostle pregnantly expresses it, Eph. i. 19, 20.

3. Impediment. A conceit that the terms of Christ are hard. This keeps off a sinner from closing with Christ as he is offered. Satan, who seeks by all means to hinder the match betwixt Christ and a sinful soul, he represents the conditions hard; and the heart, which is under the power of Satan's suggestions, does easily believe him. Oh, says he, if I accept of Christ as he is offered, I must leave my sins, I must be deprived of my ease, my former stolen pleasures, my former sweet delights; I must abandon such a course that has been so gainful, so advantageous to me, that which has upheld my credit and repute, that which has been such a solace, a refreshment to me; I must relinquish such a practice to which I have been so long accustomed, which is so endeared to me; Christ declares it offensive to him, he will not tolerate it; I must enter into that way which is so strait and holy, that path which seems so sad and melancholy, which is jeered and derided by others, and which has been so distasteful to me. Oh, this seems a hard saying, this keeps him off from giving his consent to Christ. He sees something desirable in Christ, he sees some reason to close with him, he sees some necessity of him, there is no salvation without him. Oh, but if he yield to Christ, his beloved sin, his Benjamin must go. This seems hard, he cannot yield to it, and so when Christ has been long treating with him in the ministry of the word, the match is broken upon this account; Christ stands upon too hard terms, thus he apprehends. This is the true cause why the ambassadors of Christ prevail so little in their treaty with sinners; the main cause why Christ being offered to so many, is accepted by so few. The greatest part do not like Christ's terms, they seem too strict, too hard.

It much concerns us therefore to endeavour the removing of this, it being the great stumbling-block, the great rock of offence upon which so many fall and split ther souls. For this purpose consider,

(1.) The terms of Christ are easy, whatever Satan or a corrupt heart suggest to the contrary. They are as easy as possible can be, as easy as the nature of the matter can possibly admit of, as easy as can be desired with any reason. They could not be easier without the greatest absurdity and contradiction imaginable. They are such as those who object against them would in a like case count them easy enough in all reason. Satan knows them to be so; and those wretched souls who are now damned for not accepting, without doubt do now acknowledge them easy and reasonable, though they would not see it till it was too late. That this may not prove the sad case of any of you, I will make it plain to you; so plain, as if any will not close with them, as they will certainly perish, so they will perish without all excuse. Suppose a man should offer to restore sight to another upon condition he would not wilfully shut his eyes, is it possible he should have his sight upon any other terms? Or could he desire his sight upon any easier terms? Would it not be absurd, unreasonable, impossible for him to desire to see, while he is resolved to shut his eyes? The case is like here; Christ offers to discover to a sinner the things that concern his peace, if he will not shut his eyes, if he will not give himself up to be blinded by Satan. He offers to discover himself to him, if he will not turn his back on Christ when he is presented to his view. Could he have this happy sight upon any other, upon any easier terms? Is it possible to have it upon other? Is it reasonable to desire it upon easier terms? A prince offers to adopt a man for his son, and to admit him to the state and privileges of a son, upon these terms, that he do not wilfully continue in the state of a slave. Could this be done upon other, upon easier, terms? The Lord offers to adopt a sinner for his son, to admit him into the state and privileges of that blessed sonship upon these terms, that he do not wilfully continue in the slavery of sin and the service of Satan. Now, can this be done upon any other easier terms? Are not these two states inconsistent? Is it not utterly impossible that a man should be in the state of a son and of a slave both at once? Is it not a plain contradiction? Would it not be absurd to desire it, to think of it? Christ offers to restore sinners to the glorious liberty of the sons of God, if they be but willing to leave their dungeon, to have their fetters knocked off. Is it possible they should have liberty while they are resolved to continue in their fetters? Your sins are your fetters; hence they are called the bonds of wickedness, the bend of iniquity. It is a most absurd contradiction, a most unreasonable thing, to desire to be at liberty and in fetters both at once. Can ye have liberty upon easier terms than to leave your fetters?

Christ offers to be reconciled to you, to delight in you, to make you beautiful and lovely, if you will but part with your leprosy, your deformity, sin, which makes you nasty and loathsome to him. Now, would you have Christ to be in love with deformity? Would you have him delight in that which is nasty and loathsome? Can any have beauty upon easier terms than to part with their leprosy, their deformity? Nay, is it possible to have it upon any other, upon any easier terms? Can Christ pardon you when you will not lay down your weapons? Or would you have him heal you while you will not part with your disease? Is not this a plain contradiction; to be cured, and not part with the disease?

If a physician should undertake to secure his patient's life in case he will not drink poison, is it possible he should do it otherwise? Why, sin is the poison of the soul; sinful words are called the poison of asps, sinful practices are called the poison of dragons, Deut. xxxii. 33. Now, Christ will secure the life of the sinner if he will not drink in this poison, if he will not drink in iniquity, &c. Would you not think him a madman that would have life upon any other terms besides these terms? What, live and not leave this deadly poison!

Suppose a man having wandered from home and lost himself, should meet with one that would lead him home, but upon these terms, that he would leave that path which leads him directly further and further from it; would you not think him void of all sense and reason that would be brought home upon other terms, that would go backward and forward, north and south, at once? This is the case. The sinner has lost himself, lost his soul, lost heaven, lost the way to it. Christ meets the sinner, offers to bring him home, to bring him to heaven; but it is upon these terms, he must not still walk on in the path that leads directly to hell, for these lie quite contrary, as north and south. And are these terms hard? Or rather must not he bid defiance to all reason, that would think of coming to heaven upon any other terms? If a man were to make his own terms, would any be so ridiculous, so absurd, as to say, I will come to heaven in that way that leads directly to hell? Would you have Christ, by making other terms, to make himself more absurd, more ridiculous, than any man that has the use of reason would be? Oh, the unreasonableness of sin! the absurdness of a deluded soul! May not the Lord say, 'Are not my ways equal? O house of Israel, are not your ways unequal?' Could I have stooped lower to sinners? Could I have condescended further? Could I have devised terms more easy, more equal, for a sinner's happiness? Those whose hearts now quarrel with them, will hereafter be so confounded with the clear apprehensions of their equity, that they will be struck dumb and speechless when they shall stand before the judgment-seat of Christ, when he shall then demand why they refused him when offered upon terms so easy, so equal; the sense hereof will strike them dumb and silent. This is so clear as I doubt not but it is seen even in the darkness of hell. I question not but the apprehension does wound those damned souls with more anguish than any pang of death, when they remember that they refused Christ when he was offered upon such easy, such equal, terms.

This is the first consideration, the terms of Christ are easy. Not as easy is opposed to difficult, for there is difficulty therein to corrupt nature, but as it is opposed to that which is harsh, rigid, or unequal. So they are most easy.

(2.) The grounds upon which thou thinkest the terms of Christ to be hard, are false and delusive. He is a cheater that suggests them to thee; there is a design therein to cheat thee of heaven, to cozen thee of thy soul. Examine them a little, and this will be plain. If thou closest with Christ, says that deluder, thou losest thy ease, thy pleasures, thy gains, thy friends and boon companions, &c. These are the grounds upon which Christ's terms are judged to be hard. Well, but inquire a little further, what ease, pleasures? Christ will abridge thee of no ease but that which is unlawful, of no pleasures but those that are impure and sinful, of no gain but that which is unjust and unrighteous, of no friends but those that are unworthy of the name of friends, those that are indeed enemies to Christ and thy soul. When all is cast up, if thou close with Christ, thou losest no more than these by the bargain, and then thou losest nothing that is worth the keeping. To lose these is indeed the greatest gain. Thou art lost, undone if thou quit them not. Would any man be loath to part with that which will undo him? Shall the match betwixt Christ and thy soul be broke upon such terms? Wilt thou judge Christ's terms hard because he would have thee part with that which shall certainly and eternally ruin thee? Wilt thou break with him upon this? Wilt thou suffer thy soul to be thus cheated? Consider of it a little better, and view those things more distinctly, and do it seriously. Be mindful that I am by the appointment of Christ in a treaty with thee about thy soul, the issue of it will be life or death to thee for ever.

[1.] Thou art at ease now, neglecting thy soul, and [not] troubling thyself much about thy eternal estate. But if thou accept of Christ, this spiritual sloth must be shaked off. Now, thou art loath to forego thy ease, and art ready to forego Christ rather than thy ease. And is Christ indeed so little set by? Is thy soul of so small value with thee that thou wilt not trouble thyself about it? Well, but this is not the way to avoid trouble, this is not the way to enjoy thy lasting ease. Believe it, for it is certain truth, this ease will end in endless torments. Oh, that is a woeful ease that has such a woeful issue! Woe to them that be at ease! So soon as that fool in the gospel had said, 'Soul, take thy ease,' the tormentors take his soul; this night, Luke xii. 19. If thou break with Christ for thine ease, thou art no wiser than that fool, nor wilt thou fare any better. Torment for ease, intolerable torments for a little ease, eternal torments for a moment's ease! O foolish, deluded soul, wilt thou make such a bargain? wilt thou break with Christ for a little ease? Well, take heed thou dost not find it a 'little-ease' indeed when it will be too late to repent.

[2.] For sinful pleasures. Thou now eatest, drinkest, and art merry; carnal mirth and jollity is that which makes thy life desirable to thee. Thou givest the reins to thy sinful appetite, usest no curb to thy receptions.* Thou singest away care, and drinkest away sorrow, and laughest at those that would restrain thee, or are so precise as not to follow thee in these excesses. Or if thy excesses be not open, yet there is some secret sin which thou hidest under thy tongue, and pleasest thyself with it as with a sweet morsel. There is some forbidden fruit or other on which thou feedest with much delight. Now if thou shouldst close with Christ, all the sport would be spoiled. And so it would indeed, so far as it is sinful, and in things unlawful, so far as it is immoderate and excessive in things lawful. And wilt thou break with Christ for this? Are sinful pleasures of more value with thee than Christ, than thy soul, than heaven, than life? It may be so, but then they are taken upon the devil's report. But will you behold them, and judge of them, as Christ represents them? Methinks those that profess themselves Christians should be as ready to believe the Spirit of Christ as the father of lies. Why, then, the pleasures of sin are worse than the bitterest affliction. The Spirit of God testifies that they were so to Moses, Heb. xi. 25. The bitterness of death is in the pleasures of sin, and they will prove such bitterness in the end. If Christ be put off for these, and the way of holiness declined as a sad, uncouth, melancholy path, that which is pleasant to the palate will be torture to the bowels, Rev. x. 9. Lazarus's sores and poverty is far better than a fulness of such delights; and so Christ propounds it in the parable, and so he found it who fared deliciously every day; being in torments, he could see it. 'And in hell,' says the text, 'he lift up his eyes.' He could see it then, though he would not see nor believe it before, Luke xvi. 23: 'Son, remember,' ver. 25. Oh that is a sharp memorandum; it cuts deep. Remember thou hadst thy pleasures. Thou hadst them; but

* Qu. 'affections'?—ED.

now they are gone, they are vanished; nothing remains but the remembrance of them; and this does more torture him than ever the enjoyment delighted him. Thou hadst thy pleasures. Oh, but what has he now? Why, now thou art tormented. Ay, thou art, and thou wilt be. This will be true in every moment of an endless eternity, thou art tormented. And as sure as these are the words of Christ, this will be thy condition, who wilt not quit thy sinful pleasures to close with Christ. Oh that you would now remember it, before the time come, when it will be too late to remember it, before you be in that place where it will be a hell to remember it. Have you not seen a distracted man skip, and dance, and laugh, and sing, as though he were the merriest man alive? But have you not, withal, pitied that mirth, as being the issue of madness and distraction? Such is the mirth of those who will not quit their sinful pleasures to follow Christ. It is the mirth of madmen; their jollity and pleasures are the acts of spiritual frenzy and distraction. It is said the prodigal 'came to himself' when he resolved to come to his father, when he was upon his return to Christ. Before, while he run in his way of pleasures, he was beside himself, Luke xv. 17. So is every sinner, till he leave all to return to Christ. He is beside himself, his mirth is but frenzy, his delights are the issues of distraction. Oh, lamentable mirth! If he knew his condition, it would soon damp all his joy; his laughter would be turned into mourning, and his joy into heaviness. But he is beside himself; and what clearer symptoms of madness than this? He will forego Christ rather than his pleasures.

[3.] Unlawful gain. Whether it be got in an ungodly way, by laying out those thoughts, that time, those endeavours, for the things of the world, which should be employed for the things of heaven; or whether it be got in an unrighteous way, by unjust or indirect courses in word or deed. Take the apostle's estimate of such gain, and then judge whether the relinquishing of this be any just ground for to count Christ's terms hard, James v. 1–3. To hoard up such gain is to hoard up sorrows; it is for a man to make a bed of thorns for himself, which will make him weep and howl, and pierce him through with many sorrows, to heap up racks, to heap up miseries. It is not a heap of precious things, but a mass of corruption. It is not a treasure, but a canker, a consuming rust, which will not only consume the rest of his substance, but himself, and that in a grievous manner, as with fire. This is gain with a witness; but it is such as will bear witness against him, and cast him in the day of judgment. Ye have heaped up, ye think ye have heaped up treasure; true, but it is a treasure of wrath, and so you will find it at the last day. Now sum up this together, and then judge whether you will lose anything by quitting this for Christ. Such gain is a hoard of sorrows, a heap of miseries, a mass of corruption, a consuming rust and canker, a devouring fire, a condemning witness; and, if this be not enough, a treasure of wrath. And will any man count it a loss to be rid of such a horrible evil as this? And are they not miserably cheated who will be persuaded to quit Christ rather than to quit such a dreadful mischief? This may be sufficient to clear this second consideration.

(3.) Christ will make up what you seem to lose by accepting him with real gains, and that in abundant measure, in a transcendent manner. Though, by closing with the terms of Christ, you lose nothing that is worthy the keeping, you lose nothing but what it is a gain to lose, as appears by the former consideration. Yet he will make up that seeming loss with better things, such as are incomparably, unspeakably, inconceivably, infinitely better.

For carnal ease, you shall have spiritual rest; rest from the intolerable and cruel slavery of sin and Satan; rest from the troubles of a disquieting conscience, 'Come unto me,' &c., Mat. xi. 28; rest from the vexations of the world, 'In the world,' &c., John xvi. 33; eternal rest, 'There remains a rest for the people of God,' Heb. iv. 9; 'Blessed are they that die in the Lord; for they rest,' &c., Rev. xiv. 13.

For sinful pleasures, the comforts of the Holy Spirit, 'I will send the Comforter;' for fading pleasures, everlasting joy, Isaiah lxi. 7; for unsatisfying pleasures, satisfying delights: Ps. xxxvi. 8, 'abundantly satisfied;' for pleasures that are not worthy the name of pleasures, unspeakable joys; for impure pleasures, glorious joy, 1 Pet. i. 8; for embittered pleasures, fulness of joy; for the pleasures of mad men, the Master's joy, Mat. xxi. 21, John xv. 11; for the pleasures of sin, the joy of Christ.

Set these things together, and see if there be any comparison.

For unlawful gain, the riches of Christ's purchase; for uncertain riches, an inheritance immortal, undefiled, &c.; for riches on earth, treasures in heaven; for a little gain on earth, the unsearchable riches of Christ; for thorny pricking enjoyments, a rich crown of glory; for a little gain, that which is as good as nothing, that which amounts to no less than all things, 1 Cor. iii. 21–23, 'will I give to inherit all things.'

For carnal friends that ye may lose, the Lord will admit you into an inward friendship with himself, with his Son, with his Spirit, with the glorious angels, with the spirits of just men made perfect, with all that are excellent upon earth; such a friendship, as all together shall have one heart, and one spirit, and one interest, and one habitation; all these joined in one blessed league, to promote one interest, even that interest which is thine, and Christ the head of this league. Oh what is the league with death, the covenant with hell, the confederacy with the greatest carnal men on earth, to this league! Oh, if men be not wholly given over to the spirit of delusion, the terms of Christ will never be counted hard.

Compare the terms upon which you give up yourselves to sin and Satan, with the terms of Christ, and see then if they be hard. Till you accept of the terms of Christ, while you close with those of sin and Satan, what is your state, your employment, your reward? By these you may judge of Satan's terms.

As to your *state*, you are slaves, slaves and drudges to the vilest of creatures, to the most unmerciful tyrant in the world, 'led captive by Satan at his will,' at his lust.

Your *employment* is to fight against God, and to wound and destroy your own souls. This you do continually; you are slaves upon no better terms. Your lusts are weapons of unrighteousness, and Satan continually sets you on work thus to use these weapons against God, against your own souls. And lest sinners should be unwilling to do this, if they should see what they are doing, he puts out the eyes of these wretched slaves. He deals with you as the Philistines did with Samson when they had taken him captive, Judges xvi. 21.

And what *reward*, what encouragement, may they expect for this hard, intolerable service? Why, 'the wages of sin is death.' Here is all; when the poor sinner hath spent himself, soul and all, in their service, and comes to look for a reward, behold they put him to death. Here is no other reward for him but eternal death.

These are the terms upon which you serve sin and Satan. These are the terms which you count better than the terms of Christ. Christ's terms are hard, but these are easy to you. And is it so indeed? Or are not sinners blinded and bewitched, who call bitter sweet, and sweet bitter; darkness light, and light darkness; hard easy, and easy hard? If the Lord open your eyes, and undeceive you, this may be sufficient to remove the third impediment.

4. Impediment. Is a man's resting in his own righteousness. While a man rests in himself, he will never rest on Christ. While he stands upon anything in himself, he never rolls himself upon Christ. He will never rejoice alone, rely alone upon Christ Jesus, who has any confidence in the flesh. The apostle including his own righteousness in this word flesh, directly opposes these, Phil. iii.

But are there any such? Alas! nothing more common amongst the Jews, who professed so much confidence in the Messias. Nothing is more ordinary now amongst those who profess that Christ is their only Saviour, than to neglect him, and rest on their own righteousness. How common is it for men to state their righteousness thus. They hear the word, desire the ordinances, pray in public and in private; they mean well, are charitable to those in want, deal honestly, do no man wrong, keep the commandments as well as ever they can, hope their hearts are as good as the best; fall into no great sins, or when they are overtaken with sin, they are sorry for it; and for this they trust that God will be merciful to them, and will save them, whatever become of outrageous sinners; for this they hope to find pardon, to procure acceptance with God; and here they rest, and ground their hopes of heaven.

Now this is one of Satan's strongest holds, whereby he keeps sinners safe and sure from coming to Christ. Against this did Christ and the apostles bend the force of their ministry. For you may see the apostle Paul in travail with this design, especially in his Epistle to the Romans and Galatians. He knew Christ would never be formed in them, till they were cured of this tympany, this false confidence and conceit of their own righteousness. Against this did Christ direct that parable of the Pharisee and Publican, Luke xviii. 9. This was the great stumbling-block of the Jews, upon which they fell and split their souls. Instead of resting on Christ, Rom. ix. 30–32, chap. x. 3, they placed and established their own righteousness in the outward conformity to the law; and because they did outwardly observe it, for this they concluded that God was pleased with them, would pardon, and bless, and save them. They thought this righteousness sufficient, stood upon it, and would not stoop to any other; submitted not to the righteousness of God, and so came short of the righteousness of faith, never attained it. Such a block was this in their way, as the Gentiles found righteousness sooner than they. The Publicans, who had no such thing to rest on, were more easily persuaded to cast themselves on Christ, than the confident Pharisees.

To remove this, let me shew how groundless and dangerous this is.

(1.) You have, as you suppose, some righteousness; but have you not withal some sin? You can recount several religious, charitable, righteous acts, but is there no one act of sin you are guilty of? I hope there is none so brutishly stupid, as to have such a thought. If this be acknowledged, then further ye may be assured, that all your supposed righteousness will not countervail one sin, and that either in reference to the honour of God, or to thy own salvation.

All thy righteousness does not so much honour God, as that one sin does dishonour him. He gets not so much by all thy righteousness, if it were far more than it is, as he loses by that sin. 'Heaven and earth shall pass away,' &c. So tender is the Lord of his law, as he had rather heaven and earth should pass away, than that this* part of the law should be abolished. Now every sin would abolish that part of the law, against which it is directed; every sin would do that, which the Lord had rather heaven and earth should perish, than it should be done. And the Lord knows the tendency of it, and accordingly resents it. The injury that is in sin, considering against whom it is directed, is infinite; but no finite creature, no finite righteousness, can infinitely honour him. One sin will do more to condemn thee, than all thy other righteousness can do to save thee. For the least sin is such a wrong, a dishonour to God, as he cannot in justice admit the sinner into heaven, or into his favour, till he be satisfied for it. Now all thy other righteousness cannot satisfy the Lord for that one sin; nay, all the righteousness of men and angels cannot make amends for that one sin. For when they are perfectly righteous, they are no more than they ought to be; they do no more than they owe, therefore they cannot thereby satisfy for that one sin. For the payment of one debt does not discharge another.

So then, all thy righteousness vanishes at the appearance but of one sin. One sin renders all thy other righteous acts unavailable to salvation. What then will it do, when thou art guilty of many millions of sins? If one sin will dash all thy righteousness out of countenance, and quite deface it; where will it appear before so many swarms of sins, as the Lord may charge thee with? Alas, poor deluded sinner, thou leanest upon a shadow, a shadow already vanished, when thou restest on thy own righteousness.

(2.) The righteousness that you rest upon is no righteousness; and therefore when you rest upon it you rest upon nothing: you hang the weight of salvation and your souls upon nothing.

This will appear if you grant but that one supposition, which every one but he that is stark blind will acknowledge. Grant but that you are guilty of one sin, and the apostle will thence infer that you are guilty of all, James ii. 10. The parts of the law are so linked together, that he who transgresseth one part thereof, does in some way and degree or other transgress the whole law. Now, he that is a righteous man is an observer of the law; therefore, he that is a transgressor of it is not righteous, and consequently has no righteousness, except in his deluded fancy and imagination. What righteousness has he then, who continually transgresses the rule, who seldom or never observes it as far as he can, who, to be sure, never observes it as far as he ought? And is not this your case? And does not every one see it, whose mind the God of this world has not blinded? The church's acknowledgment is observable, Isa. lxiv. 6. We have no more righteousness to rest in but what is indeed no righteousness at all, no more than filthy rags are clean.

Farther, that observance of the rule of righteousness which is not done in a due manner, and for sincere ends, is no part of that righteousness which is according to law. That which is not done in a due manner, wants the form, is but the carcase of a righteous act, wants that which is the soul of it, and therefore is no more a righteous act than that lump of flesh is a man, which wants a reasonable soul.

* Qu. 'the least'?—ED.

And that which is done out of sinister respects is not a righteous act, but an act of hypocrisy. Now whosoever rests in his own righteousness, he never did anything in a due manner, never anything with a sincere aim; and therefore, how confident soever he is of his righteousness, the truth is, he never did any righteous act in his life; and so when he rests upon his righteousness, he rests upon that which he never had, upon nothing, upon that which is not, nor ever was in being.

Moreover, there is no righteousness but either that which is legal or evangelical; but this self-confident has neither. Legal righteousness he has none; indeed, there is none now in the world; for the law acknowledges no righteousness but that which is absolutely perfect. And he is not only without righteousness, but without sense and reason, that will arrogate to himself such a perfection.

Nor has he any evangelical righteousness; for that is the righteousness of God, of Christ, of faith, as the Holy Ghost calls it. But he that rests in his own righteousness has none of these; for his own righteousness is not the righteousness of God, nor of Christ, nor of faith. Nay, by resting on his own, he makes himself altogether incapable of this righteousness; that must be renounced before this can be received, as the apostle shews by his own practice, Philip. iii.; so that the righteousness which he rests on is no righteousness that the Scripture will acknowledge, and therefore none at all; so that trusting to this, thou trustest upon nothing, layest the stress of thy soul and salvation upon nothing.

(3.) Inquire a little farther, and we shall discover the righteousness which men rest on is indeed unrighteousness; that seeming righteousness which they rest on is really unrighteousness. That this may be evident, take notice that the righteousness of a self-confident is made up of acts which he conceives to be righteous. Now acts are specified by their end, a true rule in morality, which holds true in divinity. It is the end that gives both name and nature to the act. If the end be not good, the act, whatever the matter of it be, is stark naught. If the end be ungodly, the act is ungodly, though for the matter it be one of the highest acts of divine worship. If the end be unrighteous, the act is unrighteous, though for the matter it be one of the highest acts of justice. Now he that rests in his own righteousness is an unbeliever, and he that is an unbeliever has no good principles, his heart is not purified, his mind and conscience is defiled, Titus i. 15. Now he that has no good principle can have no good end in anything that he does. An unholy heart cannot have an holy end, for the streams rise no higher than the spring. The fruit can be no better than the tree. It is Christ's own reasoning, Mat. vii. 15–17. Then, since his end cannot be good and righteous, it must be evil and unrighteous; for there is no medium, no third thing in this case. And his end being unrighteous in all his acts, all his acts must needs be unrighteous, so that the righteousness which he rests on is all of it unrighteousness. It is a plain case; all the ends and purposes of these self-confidents are perverse and wicked, and tend some way or other to the promoting (though they will not discern it) of some other iniquity, so that the acts of righteousness which they rest on, when they are sifted, will be found no better than instruments of iniquity, weapons of unrighteousness. To conclude then, that which they rest on under the notion of righteousness is really and indeed unrighteousness. The matter, when it is searched to the bottom, appears to be this: they trust that for their righteousness God will accept them, be well pleased with them, and admit them into heaven. Now, whether this be a greater madness or a greater wickedness is not easy to determine; sure it is in a high degree both.

(4.) Those that trust in their own righteousness are enemies to all righteousness. Their righteousness is not only no righteousness, it is not only unrighteousness, but their resting on it bears upon it the brand of an high enmity against all that is righteous. They are enemies to the righteousness of God, of Christ, of the law, of the gospel.

If you rest in your own righteousness, you are enemies to the righteousness of God; for the righteousness of God consists principally in his truth and justice. Now this confidence rises up against both, for his truth is engaged that no man shall come to heaven without a righteousness that can satisfy his justice, and justice has declared that it will not be satisfied with any imperfect, sinful righteousness. Yet this self-confident believes and rests on it, that his own righteousness will please and satisfy God, and that, however it appear to be sinful and unrighteous, it will make his way to heaven notwithstanding, so that to trust in this is indeed to trust that God is unrighteous, that God is no God; for he is no God if he be not true and just, if he be not a righteous God, and he is not righteous if he be not true and just.

If you rest in your own righteousness, you are enemies to the righteousness of Christ. This confidence in self-righteousness thrusts Christ's righteousness out of doors, leaves no place for it, no use of it. It counts the blood of the covenant an unholy thing, a thing of no use or value; tramples upon the blood of Christ as an useless, a fruitless thing; counts Christ to have done and suffered so many things in vain, Gal. ii. 21. Now the self-confident says he has a righteousness that comes by the law, by some outward works and acts which the law requires; places his righteousness in some outward observance of and conformities to the law, and so would make Christ to have died in vain; for why did he die, but that lost man might have a righteousness to bring him to heaven? If men have this in themselves, Christ's undertaking, and his sufferings too, were vain and needless. In vain did he take upon him 'the form of a servant,' in vain was he 'made under the law,' in vain did he 'fulfil all righteousness,' in vain did he become a 'man of sorrow,' in vain did he bear the wrath of God, in vain was he wounded, scourged, and crucified. All this was needless and waste if men have a righteousness of their own to be rested on. Oh, what a horrid reflection does this cast upon Christ! What a monstrous provocation is this! No imagination can fathom the depth of it.

If you rest on your own righteousness, you are enemies to the righteousness both of the law and of the gospel, for by thus doing, you give the lie to both. The law says, there is no life to be had without perfect obedience; the self-confident says, he shall have life, though he have neither such an obedience, nor faith to be justified from the defects of it. The law says, 'Cursed is every one that continues not in all things,' &c., Gal. iii. 10; he says, he shall be blessed, though he continue not in all things, no, nor any thing, as it is prescribed in the law, though he rest not only upon him who only can free a sinner from the curse.

It gives lie to the gospel too; for that says, 'By the works of the law shall no flesh be justified.' But he says, he shall be accepted for his works, for his righteous acts, and his observance of the law therein. The gospel says, no sinner shall come to heaven but by the righteousness of Christ, the righteousness of faith: he trusts he shall find acceptance and life for his own righteousness. See here what it is to rest in your own righteousness. View it in its own colours, and then judge whether it be not a horrid provocation, since it is no better than this when unmasked, than to trust he shall have acceptance and life, and procure it by such a horrible wickedness, as this appears to be. If there be any fear of God, any respect to Christ, any regard to your own souls, let this consideration fright you from resting on any righteousness of your own.

Thus much for the removing of the impediments, which keep insensible sinners from believing.

I now proceed to answer those objections which are ordinarily made by sensible sinners; those that are convinced of their sin and misery, who are apprehensive of the weight and burden of sin and wrath; who not only see, but feel an absolute necessity of Christ; who highly value Christ, and prefer him above all; and whose souls are drawn out in strong and restless desires after him. These are they indeed whom Christ invites to come to him, and rest their weary souls on him. But several discouragements there are ordinarily cast in their way by Satan and unbelief, which hinder them from complying with Christ, and closing with the promise. These I shall endeavour to remove, but briefly; because, considering how small the number is of humbled and awakened souls, in comparison of these who are secure and insensible, I fear it will not be so generally seasonable. Some few I shall touch on.

1. One objection wherein humbled souls are ordinarily entangled is drawn from election. Oh, says the soul, I fear I am not elected; and then what ground have I to believe in Christ, to rest on him for pardon and life? Faith is peculiar to chosen vessels, it is called 'the faith of God's elect.' If I knew that I belonged to the election of grace, then I might believe indeed; but till then, I cannot, I dare not; till then, I cannot think that Christ or the promise belongs to me. To this I answer,

(1.) It is impossible to know election before faith; therefore to desire this, is to go about to compass impossibilities. This was never done, nor ever will be. If this had been stood upon, there had been no faith in the world, no soul had ever believed in Christ; for it is not possible for any to know he is elected till he believe. This is to desire to see thy name is writ in the book of life, written in heaven, before thou hast an eye to see it. It is the eye of faith that only sees this, that alone can read this; it is impossible you should see it without an eye, without this eye.

It is impossible you should read this in the book of life till that book be opened; now it is a book shut and sealed till faith open it. Election is a secret, it runs under ground till faith. When the soul believes, then it first breaks forth; then, and not till then, is this secret made known and brought to light. When you desire assurance of it before, you desire to know that which cannot be known, to see that which cannot be discerned.

(2.) It is preposterous. To attempt this, is to set the cart before the horse, to desire to be at the end before ye are in the way; as if a man would be at a good distance from him,* before he set a foot out of his own door: as if the Israelites would have been in Canaan, that pleasant land, before they were come out of Egypt.

This is to have a conclusion proved without any premises, without any good medium to prove it by. You must first have the ground and medium before you can reason and draw the conclusion. If ever you would conclude on good ground that you are elected, faith must be the ground on which you must conclude it. I believe, therefore, I am elected; that is

* Qu. 'home'?—ED.

the method wherein the Lord would have you reason. First, make that sure, I believe; and then this conclusion will be easy and certain, I am elected. This is the apostle's method, 1 Thes. i. 4, first the work of faith, and then the election of God.

The work of a sinner's salvation is like Jacob's ladder; it reaches from earth to heaven, and so has many rounds: the highest round is election, that is as high as heaven; the lowest round is faith, that is on earth. Now would ye be at the highest round before you have set foot on the lowest step? No; be not unreasonable, invert not the order that God has set. If you would get up to this great height, and mount this heavenly ladder, begin at the bottom; begin at faith, that is the lowest step, and so you will ascend by degrees towards election, the knowledge and assurance of it.

(3.) It is impertinent to trouble thyself about this. It is a secret, and so the Lord will keep it till thou believest. It is not his will that it should be known to any before faith. To inquire into it before is to pry into God's secrets. Indeed, if a man were certain that he were not elected it were another case, but as it is not certain that thou art elected, so it is not certain that thou art not elected. Thou hast no means to know either the one or the other till faith certainly; till then the Lord reserves it in his own breast as a secret. Now 'secret things belong to God,' Deut. xxix. 29. The Lord shews here what belongs to him, and what belongs to us, that we should mind our duty, and not busy ourselves with impertinencies. Whether thou art elected or no at this time is a secret which the Lord never discloses to an unbeliever, and therefore till faith it belongs not to thee. But that thou shouldst believe is no secret; that is a revealed duty; the law, the gospel enjoins it. The law of faith is a known law; this is it which belongs to thee, to do all the words of the law. Thou wilt not believe, lest it should be too much boldness, being uncertain whether thou art elected; but is it not a greater boldness to pry into God's secrets? Thou thinkest it would be presumption to believe, though God reveals it to be his will; but is it not greater presumption to inquire into that which it is his will thou shouldst not know?

Observe the apostle's order, 2 Pet. i. 10. Both belong to thee, but not both together, but one after the other, as the Holy Ghost has placed them. First make thy calling sure: till then it belongs not to thee to seek assurance of election; till then thou wilt seek in vain, never find it. The duty that lies upon thee, and which must first be looked to, is to make sure thy calling. The Lord calls thee now to believe; answer his call by believing, and so thy calling will be sure. This being assured, thou art in the highway to assure thy election. Thy diligence will not miscarry, because thou takest the way, and followest the method that God prescribes thee. But to follow thy own way, and give diligence in that which belongs not to thee, is not the way to prosper. Believe in the Lord, and so shalt thou prosper; but unless thou believest, thou wilt never be established as to thy election.

(4.) You think it needless, unreasonable, to pry into God's decrees before you apply yourselves to other undertakings; and it is as unreasonable here. When you are dangerously sick, and the physician tells you unless you take such a course of physic, your case is desperate, do ye use to reason thus: If I knew that God had decreed my recovery, I would take that course that is so like to restore me; but till I know that God has decreed my recovery, I'll take nothing. Sure we should think such a reasoner not only sick, but distracted. Thus it is here. The sinner is ready to perish; apply thyself to Christ, says the Lord, cast thyself on him, apply the promise; there is no other way to save thy life. Oh, says he, if I knew the Lord had decreed my salvation, I would venture on Christ; but till I know this, I must not believe. Oh the unreasonableness of unbelief! Satan's suggestions make poor creatures act as though they were distracted. This is as if an Israelite, stung with the fiery serpent, should have said, If I knew that the Lord had decreed my cure, I would look upon the brazen serpent; but till I know this, though there be no other way to save my life, I will not look on it. If all the stung Israelites had been thus resolved, it is like they had all perished.

Or as if one pursued by the avenger of blood, should have set him down in the way to the city of refuge, when he should have been flying for his life, and said, If I knew that the Lord had decreed my escape, I would make haste for refuge; but till I know this, I will not stir, till I die for it. Would not this be counted a wilful casting away his life, with a neglect of that provision which God had made to save it? Was it not sufficient that a way was made for his escape, and a way feasible enough, the city of refuge always open? Even so are the arms of Christ always open to receive a humbled, distressed, perishing sinner flying to him for refuge. And wilt thou destroy thyself, by suffering Satan to entangle thee with a needless, impertinent, and unreasonable scruple? If there be no way but one, and any encouraging probability to draw men into it, they fly into it without delay, never perplexing themselves with the decrees and secrets of God. This is thy case, Christ is thy way; there is no way but this one, fly to it as for thy life; and let not Satan hinder thee, by diverting thee to impossibilities and impertinencies. Do thus, and prosper. When the disciples were inquiring after an impertinent secret, Acts i. 6, 7, Christ takes them off, and directs them to the duty that then lay upon them: 'It is not for you to know,' &c.

Obj. 2. Oh but I am unworthy to come near Christ, unworthy to have anything to do with the promise. Will Christ entertain such an unworthy wretch as I am? I have not only no merit, but no motive, nothing to engage, nothing but what may disoblige him, most highly engage him against me. Oh the sense of my unworthiness sinks my heart, and does utterly discourage me.

Ans. 1. Christ never excluded any upon this account, because they were unworthy. Christ never laid this as a bar to keep thee out; why shouldst thou make use of it to bar thyself out? He has always shewed himself ready to entertain a humbled returning sinner, how unworthy soever. Christ makes this no exception; why dost thou make it one? He never spoke word of discouragement to this, and why dost thou make it a discouragement? Who more unworthy than the prodigal, either really, or in his own apprehension? How unworthy he was really, you may see in the former part of the parable; how unworthy in his own apprehension, you may see by his own expression. Yet does not this hinder him from returning, nor did it hinder the father (who there represents Christ) from receiving and embracing him. When he returns, filled with shame and sorrow, burdened with the sense of his former unworthy carriage, see how freely, how affectionately, how joyfully he entertains him. See it, and never let the thought of unworthiness discourage thee more. Methinks the sad heart of a humble, dejected sinner should revive and leap within him to see this affectionate passage. When this worthless wretch is afar off, he runs and meets him; when he comes at him, he falls about his neck and kisses him; when he has brought him home, he has the kindest entertainment that love can make him, thinks nothing too dear, nothing too good to welcome him, who in the mean time is thinking nothing so vile, nothing so bad, so base and unworthy, as himself. He rejoices in him as one would do who receives a dear child from the dead. He rejoices himself, and he calls heaven and earth to rejoice with him. Oh see here the tender compassions, the wonderful kindness, the overflowing affections of Christ to the unworthiest of sinners, when he does but really return to him. As sure as that parable is Christ's, so sure will this be thy welcome, thy entertainment, poor dejected soul, if thou wilt but return to him. Thou hast unworthy thoughts of Christ, if the thoughts of thy unworthiness do discourage thee from coming to him. Will that hinder Christ from receiving thee, that never hindered him from admitting any?

Ans. 2. None that were worthy did ever believe. None such ever came to Christ, nor did Christ ever receive any such; and wilt thou have that before thou believest, which none ever could have? There are none, there never were any, really worthy; and those that think themselves worthy, will not believe, cannot cast themselves on Christ; or if they should come, yet would not Christ receive such. It is not his way, it stands not with his honour. Look over all those thousands or millions that have trusted in Christ, thou canst not find one amongst them all that were worthy. If thou canst find any thing in them that will bear the name of worth, they brought it not to Christ, but received it from him; they had it not before faith, but received it by faith. And wilt thou be such a one before thou believest, as never any one will be after thee? If none had believed but those that were worthy, there had never been a believer in the world, there had been no faith on earth, there had been no soul in heaven. And wilt thou be such a one as neither heaven nor earth will afford? If thou wilt never believe till thou art worthy, thou wilt never believe while thou hast a being. If thou must either believe while thou art unworthy, or not at all, why does unworthiness hinder thee, unless thou intendest to continue in unbelief for ever?

Oh it is true, you will say, none are worthy, all are unworthy! but I am more unworthy than any, there is none like me for that. Well, suppose this were true, which is not so likely, yet consider,

Ans. 3. It is most for Christ's honour to receive those which are most unworthy. It suits best with his greatest and dearest design; it tends most to promote that which he most aims at, when he graciously receives those that are most unworthy. And therefore thy unworthiness should not discourage thee, nay, it should rather encourage. For will not Christ do that freely, which most advances his own great and glorious design? You doubt not but an intelligent man will do that freely, which is most for his own interest. Why, it is the interest of Christ to receive those that are most unworthy; and will he not freely do it? Do ye think he does not know his interest? Will ye make him more ignorant than the sons of men? Or do ye think he will neglect his interest? Can he be guilty of negligence? To make unworthiness a discouragement, accuses Christ of both, casts those unworthy reflections of ignorance or negligence. Sure to do thus, is as great an unworthiness, as that which you object. Though you be worthy to be neglected, yet sure Christ will not neglect himself, his own great design and interest. This is Christ's design in admitting sinners, to make his freeness and riches of his grace most conspicuous, to make his grace glorious, Eph. i. 10–12; ii. 7–9. This is his counsel, his purpose, his design, his interest; to shew the exceeding riches of his grace. Now grace is most rich, grace is most grace, when it is most free. That is plain to any who understand what grace is; and grace is most free when it is shewed to those that are most unworthy, those who have nothing in the world to boast of. Then it appears in its lively colours, then it shines forth in the riches of its glory. Well, then, thou art unworthy, thou art most unworthy; thou art greatly afflicted, deeply humbled under the sense of thy utter unworthiness; and does this discourage thee from coming to Christ? Dost thou think for this he will reject thee? Why, thou art the person in whom, above others, Christ may meet with that which he most aims at; thou art he on whom Christ may make himself, his grace, most glorious. Thou art the fittest subject for Christ to accomplish his great design on. And why? Because thou art, and art sensible thou art, most unworthy. Lo here, that which thou objectest as a discouragement to keep thee from him, from believing in him, proves a great encouragement to hasten thee to him.

Ans. 4. Christ, in pursuance of his gracious design, does, as it were, pick out those that are most unworthy. Who is more worth? he that can bring money and a price, something of worth to Christ; or those that have nothing? Now Christ will have those to come that have nothing, Isa. lv. 1. Who are worthy? Those that are rich and full, or those that are hungry and empty? Why, these will Christ choose, while he rejects the other: 'He fills the hungry,' &c. Who are more worthy, the righteous or sinners? Why, Christ calls the unworthiest of these: 'He came not to call the righteous, but sinners,' &c. Who are more worthy, the wise or the foolish? the mighty or the weak? the noble and honourable, or the base and despised? those that are something or those that are nothing? Why, Christ pitches most on the more unworthy, 1 Cor. i. 26–28. If thou wouldst be more worthy, thou wouldst be among those whom Christ is wont to reject or pass by; while thou art more unworthy in thy own apprehension, thou art one of those whom Christ is wont to choose and pick out for himself. And is unworthiness a discouragement? Thou hast more encouragement now than thou wouldst have, if thou wert in thy own sense more worthy.

Ans. 5. Unworthiness does rather qualify you for Christ than otherwise, and therefore should rather encourage you to come to him than keep you from him. The Jews plead ill for the centurion, when they allege that he was worthy, Luke vii. 4. He pleads better for himself, and there is more truth, more ingenuity in his plea, that wherewith Christ is more taken, ver. 6, 7; not worthy that Christ should come to him, not worthy he should come to Christ. But does he fare worse for this? No; he obtains all that he desires, and a transcendent commendation besides. No subjects so capable of Christ and his benefits as unworthy creatures; not only in reference to Christ's honour, of which before, but in respect of their necessities, those that render them unworthy. If they were not such, they were not in such a capacity of a Saviour. Are you such in a spiritual sense, as you find Luke xiv. 21? Why, these are they whom God invites to the marriage of his Son. Are you in Laodicea's state? a condition unworthy enough, Rev. iii. 15. Why, Christ offers the riches and treasures of his purchase unto such, ver. 18. None else are so capable of them. Art thou poor, afflicted with thy soul-poverty? Why, who else should Christ enrich but such? His treasures would be slighted by, and thrown away upon others. Art thou blind, afflicted with that darkness that covers thy soul? Who else should Christ restore to light but such? His eye-salve others will count needless. Art thou naked? Hast nothing to hide thy soul defilements, nothing to cover the shame of thy inward nakedness? Why, who else should Christ clothe but the naked? The white raiment will be useless to others. Art thou halt and maimed, thy soul out of joint, and discomposed? Why, who else should Christ cure but the maimed? The more desperate thy case seems to be, the more will it be for his credit and honour to undertake and effect the cure. The whole need not the physician, but the sick. Art thou wretched and miserable? Who else should Christ enhappy but those that are miserable? Art thou sinful, exceeding sinful, ashamed, grieved, burdened with thy sinfulness? Why, who else should Christ pardon but sinners? Art thou over-spread with soul-pollution? Who else should the blood of Christ cleanse but those that are polluted? For whom was the fountain opened? Art thou empty? Who else should Christ fill but the empty? To what end else did it please the Father that in him should all fulness dwell? Can he fill those who are full already? Are they capable of it? Art thou lost indeed, and in thy own sense? Who else should Christ seek but those that are lost? Should he seek those that never went astray? He came to seek them that were lost. Art thou a captive to sin, to Satan, weary of it, groanest under it? Who else should Christ redeem but the captives? Art thou nothing, less, worse than nothing, in thy own apprehension? To whom else should Christ be all in all? To whom else can he be so? Can he be all in all to those who are something in themselves?

Take a view of whatever makes thee worthy* in thy own apprehension; and being sensible of it, afflicted with it, and it renders thee more capable of Christ; so far is it from being a discouragement to keep thee from him.

Ans. 6. To believe is not only a privilege, but a duty. (*Vid.* Serm. on James.†)

Ans. 7. The longer you continue in unbelief, the more unworthy you will be to come at Christ. Whatever tends to make you unworthy is hereby increased. Is it hardness of heart? Your hearts will be daily more and more hardened through the deceitfulness of sin. Is it inability to be serviceable to Christ? You will be every day more unfit, more unable to do him service. Sin is every day wounding and weakening your souls. You lose time too, wherein you might do him much service, you lose both ability and opportunities. Is it sinfulness? You will grow every day more and more sinful. Is it the defilement and loathsome pollution of your hearts? Your souls will every day grow more and more loathsome; no stepping out of that puddle of sin, till you come out to Christ. You will still wallow more and more in it till you believe, still more besmear yourselves with that which renders you loathsome and hateful in the eye of Christ. Is it the multitude of your sins? You will find them grow more and more numerous; that horrid heap will rise higher and higher, swell bigger and bigger. Is it the heinousness and grievousness of your sins? Till you believe, they every moment grow more and more heinous, more provoking. They cry louder and louder to the Lord against you. You add to them more unbelief, which has in it a peculiar provocation above the rest.

If you be unworthy now, you will be much more unworthy hereafter. If it discourage you now, it will much more discourage you when it is greater; so that if you believe not now, it is like you may never believe. If you leap not over this discouragement, when it is but as a mole-hill in com-

* Qu. 'unworthy'?—ED. † On James i. 6; the next Sermon but one.—ED.

parison, how will you get over it when it is grown into a mountain? If you now suffer yourselves to be carried down with this stream, how will you get up it, when the waters of it are swelled higher and higher, and break in upon you with greater violence? It is most unreasonable to let unworthiness discourage you now from believing, unless you never intend to believe; for you will never be less unworthy.

If a man were to wade through a river, or die for it, he would enter it when it is lowest; for when he still sees it rising higher and higher, the longer he stays the more he may be afraid to venture. The water, which is but to the knees now, may be above his height in a little time. So here thy unworthiness is now at the lowest that ever it will be; thy life lies on it to believe on Christ. The longer thou stayest, the deeper, the larger will thy unworthiness grow. If thou beest not careless of thy life, venture now.

Ans. 8. Unbelief is the greatest unworthiness, the most provoking, that which seals thee up under all former unworthiness, binds it all upon thee, that which adds a new aggravation to all; not only incenses justice, but refuses mercy. It is the only excluding unworthiness.

Ans. 9. The Lord requires no other worthiness of thee but faith, nothing but a cordial acceptance of Christ as he is offered. He that hath this, the Lord will no more question him for his unworthiness, than the Lord's own goodness and faithfulness can be questioned.

Obj. 1. But I am not prepared for Christ; I am not sufficiently humbled, I have not had experience of the work of the spirit of bondage as others have. I never was so deeply afflicted with the apprehensions of God's wrath; nor have I had such terrors of conscience as are usual in others when the Lord is bringing them to Christ.

Ans. 8. It may be you lay more stress upon those terrors and legal humblings than is requisite. To prevent miscarriages, and remove mistakes herein, which seem to be the grounds of the objection (observe) that you may form right apprehensions of this matter, before which this scruple will fall.

(1.) Legal terrors are no parts of faith or conversion; they are neither essential nor integral parts. Those are essential parts which make up the essence of a thing, as soul and body are the essential parts of a man. Those are integral parts which make up the entireness of a thing, as the several members are integral parts of a man's body.

Those parts which give the essence to a thing begin with it, and continue with it while it is in being, but these terrors cease as soon as faith begins, and so they are no essential parts. A thing cannot be complete and entire without its integrals; the body, when it wants some members, is lame, or maimed, or defective; but faith may be entire and complete without these; it is not the more defective when these are gone and vanished; so they are not integrals. They are so far from being parts, as they are no degrees of faith; though some step to it, yet not the least degree of it. As the dryness of wood is no degree of heat or fire which kindles the wood, though it tend something to make it kindle more easily; so these, though they may something dispose a man towards faith, yet they are not any degree of faith. The least degree of true faith is saving, but these humblings may be in those who shall never be saved.

(2.) They are no causes of faith; no efficient causes to produce faith; nor subservient causes, by which alone the Lord does immediately produce it; nor moving causes, which oblige the Lord to work it.

They are not efficient causes which work faith, or have any virtue in themselves to effect it. The mere pulling off the gloves does not make clean the hands, there must be a farther act to do that, they must be washed. Those are but as the pulling off the gloves, something by way of preparation, but no causes that will do the work And as they are no causes of faith in themselves, so the Lord does not work faith by these only, nor by these as the next and proper means. These are wrought by the law, faith is wrought by the gospel; that is the means by which the Lord produces faith; not the law, nor any effect of the law. The Spirit of Christ begets faith, not as a spirit of bondage, but as a sanctifying Spirit. Unless this regenerating Spirit proceed to a farther work, those legal humblings will be vain and fruitless.

Nor are they moving causes, such as engage or induce the Lord to bestow faith. When these terrors are in the highest degree, the Lord remains free whether he will give faith or no, and we see his proceedings are answerable. Sometimes he bestows it, sometimes he denies; but if these laid any engagement upon him, he could never deny faith to any who are once under the spirit of bondage; for the Lord will answer all engagements.

(3.) These are no conditions of any promise. The Lord has not promised faith, or any grace, to these legal preparations; so that as these cannot engage him to give faith, so he has not engaged himself thereto. There needs no proof of this, because no such promise can be produced. But the ground hereof is clear; for those who have gone no farther than these legal humblings are yet in a state of nature, and these preparatory works are common to reprobates. Now the Lord promises no grace to nature, nor to any thing that can be found in a mere natural man; no such thing is ever made the condition of any promise: otherwise the Lord could not deny grace to reprobates, could not deny faith to vessels of wrath, without the forfeiture of his truth and faithfulness; for where the condition is found, to him the promise must be accomplished, the truth and faithfulness of God requires it. Nothing which can be found in castaways can be the condition of a gracious promise; but these terrors may be found in a high degree in reprobates and mere natural men, *ergo*, &c.

(4.) These are not necessary antecedents of faith, though they be usually antecedents of faith, yet not necessarily; though they ordinarily go before faith, yet not always. It is possible some may have faith without these, and so it is possible a man may be fit for Christ who never had them. There is no place for legal terrors in infancy; yet that some have been sanctified from the womb we have some instances in Scripture. And though it be denied that infants are capable of actual faith, yet few or none deny but that age is capable of the habit or principle of faith. So that the Lord may prepare some for Christ in another way than this of legal terrors, though this be the usual way; and therefore they are not necessary indispensable antecedents of faith, though they be the ordinary way to it.

Hence it follows that, as he who finds in himself undoubted effects and evidences of faith need not question the truth of his faith for want of legal humiliation, so he that finds in himself the clear evidences of a preparedness for Christ, need not be discouraged from coming to him for want of these legal terrors, because these do not always go before faith, at least in the same degree with it.

(5.) Though these legal humblings do ordinarily go before faith, yet there is a great variety both as to the measure and continuance. All have not alike as to the time they are under them, some have a quicker passage to Christ. All have them not in the like degree, in the height and depth of them; some have an easier passage to Christ than others. We find not that Zaccheus and Lydia were so deeply humbled, so much terrified, as Saul and the jailor. When good education prevents those gross enormities which are the occasions of those strong convulsions of conscience; or when the Lord begins to work in younger years, when sin is not so ripe nor so deeply riveted in the sinner by custom; or when wrath and mercy, misery and a redeemer, are both propounded together; there is many times some abatement of terror in these cases. And the Lord, who is a most free agent, and works how and in what manner he pleases, may make some abatement thereof in other cases, upon such reasons, and for such ends, as our shallowness cannot sound. That degree of humbling which is sufficient for some may not be enough for others. And that which is too little for one may be too much for another; his temper may not bear it, his case may not require it. That degree may fit one for Christ which will not so much as move another. And therefore you cannot upon any ground conclude that you are not prepared for Christ because you are not afflicted with such a degree of terror as you may meet with in some others; a threatening word, a light apprehension of wrath, may fright some out of their ways of sin, which others will not leave till they be fired out.

(6.) You must not judge of your preparedness for Christ by the depth of your humblings or the height of your terrors, but by the effects thereof. Judge of your fitness for Christ by those things wherein this fitness consists, that is a sure way, not by those things which are accidental to it and separable from it, as this or that degree of legal humiliation may be; to judge by these is the way to mistake. Inquire not how much or how long you have been under the spirit of bondage, but what is the issue of it, what is the end, and how much thereof is hereby attained. The end of those legal humblings is to fit you for Christ, they are but means used for this end. If the end be attained, the means are no farther necessary nor desirable. Whether more or less of those means have been applied, if you be prepared for Christ by that measure of humiliation you are under, be it more or be it less, no more is necessary or desirable, because the end of these means is attained. He is an unreasonable patient that will have more physic than is requisite for his health, a strange person that will have the chirurgeons to lance and scarify or cauterise him more than is necessary for the cure of his wound. If you be fit for Christ it is enough, how little soever your humblings have been.

Oh, but how shall this be known, whether I be fit for Christ? Why, it is best known by those things wherein this fitness consists. They are such as these; I will but name them.

(1.) He that is brought off from all dependence on himself and his own righteousness, so as to see and feel an absolute necessity of Christ.

(2.) He that is fallen out with every sin, so as to hate that which he has formerly most loved, and resolved to pursue every lust to the death.

(3.) He that hungers and thirsts after Christ, so as to be ready and willing to part with all for him.

(4.) He that is in love with holiness, purity of heart and life, so as he is heartily willing to comply with Christ in all his ways, even in those that are most strait and holy. He that, upon a faithful and impartial search, and observance of his heart, finds that he is truly and indeed brought thus far, whatever his humiliation have been, he is sufficiently prepared for Christ.

If this be thy case, thou hast no more ground (for want of legal humblings) to be discouraged from coming to Christ, and resting on him for pardon and life, than those who are already clasped in his everlasting arms.

Obj. Oh, but Christ does only heal the broken-hearted; he has comfort indeed, but it is only for the mourners. Now, alas! my heart is hard, it is a heart of stone; I find not that softness, that tenderness, those tears and meltings, which is requisite in those returners whom Christ will welcome.

Ans. 1. Observe, there is a threefold tenderness, a tenderness of heart and will, a passionate tenderness, and a tenderness in expressions.

Tenderness of *heart or will* is when the will is pliable, when it is facile and easy to yield to Christ. And so that is a hard heart which is stiff and untractable, which will not be persuaded, is not yielding and complying with the will of Christ. This the Scripture calls a hard heart; and it is so, whatever meltings or relentings there be in it upon occasion. There are some natural men who will find strange meltings and passionate motions within them at the hearing of some pathetical discourse on the sufferings of Christ, or the like affecting exercise, whose hearts are nevertheless as hard, in Scripture phrase, as the nether millstone; even as that wax, which you call hard, will melt if you apply it to a flame, but hard it is, and so we account it for all that. That is soft wax indeed which with a little warmth becomes ductile and pliable, so as you may mould it into any form, and is apt to receive any impression. And that is a soft heart which is pliable in the hand of Christ, which will be moulded as he would have it, which is not stiff against his word, but yields to any signification of his will.

The *passionate* tenderness consists in grief and sorrow, when these passions or affections are easily raised, excited, and drawn out by their proper objects and occasions, when the objects of them are sin, and the unkindness and dishonour to God that is in sin. The Scripture comprises this also under the notion of a soft and tender heart. The heart in Scripture is both will and affections.

The tenderness of *expressions* consists in tears and weeping, and this is properly a softness or tenderness of complexion.

Now, for the application of the several parts of this distinction to our purpose,

Ans. 2. This tenderness of expression in tears and weeping may be where there is no tenderness of heart in Scripture sense. This, as it is free, so it signifies rather a tender complexion of body than a tender constitution of the heart. This is not a property, but a common and separable accident of a soft heart. There may be tears, and that in abundance, and possibly in some consideration of sin too, where the heart is extremely hard. And, on the contrary, there may be a very tender heart, a heart of flesh, the blessing of the covenant, where there are no tears at all. It is in this case as it is with words in reference to prayer, there may be a prayer where there are no words, as in Hannah; and there may be words, yea, very high expressions, where there is no prayer; for the essence of a prayer consists in the desires and motions of the soul, the expressions are but the dress and outward garb of it. So here, there may be a soft heart where there are no tears, and there may be many tears where the heart is exceeding hard; for tenderness of heart consists principally in a pliableness to the will of Christ, seconded with some motion of the affections.

And as words and expressions in prayer, so tears may proceed from some other cause than tenderness of heart. Indeed, they depend much upon age, natural temper of the mind, or complexion of the body.

So that from want of this tenderness of expression you cannot duly conclude a hardness of heart either in yourselves or others. Indeed, if crosses, disappointments, loss of friends, and other sorrowful accidents in the world, can draw tears from you, and the consideration of sin, its unkindness, dishonour, heinousness will draw none, this alters the case; this signifies the want of them is from the constitution of a hard heart rather than a less tender complexion of body.

Otherwise you cannot from hence conclude your heart is hard, and so have no ground from hence to discourage you from coming to Christ and resting on him. If there were a just ground to discourage from believing, it might as well hinder those who have true faith from being true believers; for many, who are truly and eminently so, while they can find a heart bleeding for sin, yet want an eye that can weep for it; the renewed constitution of their souls help them to that, but the temper of their bodies will not afford this.

Ans. 3. The way to have clear evidence of a soft and tender heart, is to believe. This is the direct way, both to get present hardness removed, and to get a sure evidence that former hardness is removed. This is clear from what I have premised. Tenderness of heart, that which the Lord in Scripture most commends to us, consists principally in a pliableness with the will of Christ, an easiness to be persuaded by him, a facileness to yield to him, a softness that will be easily bended into a compliance with his good pleasure. Now this is the will of Christ, that thou wouldst come to him, believe in him, rest on him. This is his will, wilt thou comply? This he calls thee to, wilt thou answer his call? This he persuades thee to, art thou easy to be persuaded by him? This is thy present duty, that will afford thee the clearest evidences. We are apt to flatter ourselves with imaginary compliances in duties past or future. Oh, say the Jews, if the Messias would come, how would we receive him! how would we rejoice in him! but when he has come indeed, and they were put upon trial by a present duty, the deceit appeared. Instead of receiving him, they rejected him; instead of welcoming him with joy, they pursue and persecute him with a strong hatred. So in another case, they flatter themselves with a compliance, upon an imaginary supposal. Oh, say they, if we had lived in the days of our forefathers, we would never have treated the prophets as they did. And yet when Christ himself, the great prophet, was amongst them, and their present duty was to hear him, the deceit appeared, the hardness of their hearts was manifest. They treat him as unworthily as ever their forefathers did the former prophets. We have the same deceitful hearts, and are as ready to impose upon ourselves by the very like delusion. Oh, says one, if I should be assaulted with such a foul temptation, how far would I be from yielding to it! and yet the temptation that he is under at present, he yields to it. Oh, says another, if I were called to suffer, as martyrs formerly, I hope I should suffer cheerfully, and part with all; and yet his present duty he neglects; the sacrificing knife of a mortifying course must not touch his lust; he cannot suffer that, who fancies he would readily suffer all. Indeed, these imaginary compliances argue no tenderness of heart, but that which is merely imaginary; it is but a fancy, a delusion, there is no reality in it. But if thou wouldst not be deluded, here thou mayest have a just trial. How doest thou demean thyself towards thy present duty? If thy heart be tender indeed, it will not be stiff against it, it will yield to it.

Christ requires thee to abandon every sin, the lusts, carnal or worldly, which thou hast been so fast in league with; doest thou yield here? Does thy heart say, 'Lo, I come to do thy will, O God; thy law is in my heart; my soul has received the impressions of it, I desire nothing more in all the world than to be rid of sin.

Christ requires thee to receive him as thy Lord; does thy heart yield? Does thy soul answer, I'll have no Lord, no king but Jesus; his burden shall be light to me, his yoke shall be easy; Oh that he would bore mine ear, that I might be in his service for ever! Oh that he would free me from this slavery to sin and the world, which is so intolerable to me!

Christ requires thee to come and cast thyself on him; here is thy present duty. Wilt thou be persuaded to it? Yield now, and thou needest not doubt but thy heart is soft and tender. A persuadable heart is a soft heart; thou needest never any more make this a discouragement.

Ans. 4. As for that passionate tenderness, which consists in grief and sorrow for sin, never expect these to purpose, till thou believest. These ingenuous meltings, those passionate relentings, those streams of sorrow, which thou wantest and longest for, they are the fruits, not the forerunners, of faith. If thou expect them full and ripe before thou believest, thou expectest fruits of a tree before it be planted. That which pierces the heart, that which makes it a spring of sorrow, that which sends forth the streams of it in abundance, is the sight of Christ pierced, the sight of him by faith; it is the eye of faith beholding Christ pierced, and pierced for thee, that will so affect the heart, as to dissolve it into sorrow, and spring in it a bitter mourning, Zech. xii. 10. When the eye of faith sees Christ pierced, when it sees him lifted up in that highest expression of his love, when the heat of that love reaches the heart, when the shines of Christ's countenance, the beams of the Sun of righteousness, penetrate into the soul, then will it melt, then will it dissolve indeed, then will it flow out in streams of sorrow. Those meltings that are most kindly, that sorrow which is most ingenuous, is the proper issue of faith, that which follows it, not that which goes before it. When thou hast experience of the loving-kindness of Christ; when thou feelest his tender compassions to thee; when thou findest him as it were falling upon thy neck, and kissing thee; what, such love, such compassions, such kindness for me! for me, who have been so unkind, so unworthy! for me, who have been such a rebel, such a prodigal! oh, a heart of flint will melt now, and the rock will be dissolved into waters! This is the effect of faith; it is unreasonable to expect the effect till the cause is in being. The want of this should not discourage from believing; it is not to be expected before. But if thy heart desires it, the want, the desires of it, should quicken thee to make haste to Christ, make haste to believe; because this is the only way to obtain what thou desirest, to be possessed of this melting temper.

Obj. Oh, but I have slept out the day of my gracious visitation; I fear the time of mercy is expired. I have often resisted the Spirit, long neglected, yea, rejected the offers of Christ and mercy; and now I am afraid the decree is gone forth against me. Alas! I fear it is too late.

Ans. This is a tender point, I must proceed warily in it. The resolution may be useful to all, and therefore I shall insist a little on it. For answer, 1, I premise some things by way of concession; 2, add some things for satisfaction.

1. By way of concession. (1.) It is granted, there is a time wherein the Lord offers mercy; which being determined and come to its period, the Lord withdraws, the sinner is left to himself in a forlorn condition, to reap the woeful fruits of his own obstinacy.

This time expires, when the Lord, provoked by obstinate resistance and wilful refusals, gives over the sinner as hopeless and incurable; will use no more importunity, will strive no longer; leaves him to those lusts, and in that state which he has chosen; seals him up under spiritual judgments; gives him up to blindness of mind, hardness of heart, a spirit of slumber, a reprobate sense. Nothing more evident in Scripture than that there is such a time of grace, and such a period of it, Ezek. xxiv. 13. The Lord would have purged them, while he afforded means for this purpose. They resisting those means, rendering them ineffectual, this time ended. And this was the end of it, Thou shalt not be purged; and the Lord seals it, ver. 14. Mat. xxiii. 37, Christ would have gathered them. While he endeavoured this, it was their time of mercy; but they would not be gathered; this puts a period to that time. He leaves them, that is the issue of it, and their house is left unto them desolate, Luke xix. 42. They had light to discover the things which concerned their peace. All the while that shined, it was their day; but they neglected, shut their eyes, employed about other objects; so these things are hid from their eyes. There is their night, the sad period of that gracious day, Isa. lv. 6. There is a time when the Lord may be found, while he is near. That is the time of mercy. But the expression implies there is a time when he will not be found, when he is gone far out of sight, out of call. That is the time succeeding the former, a time of rejection. As sinners have their time of rejecting God, so he has his time of rejecting them, Prov. i. When the Lord calls, stretches out his hand, that is the time of mercy; but their continued refusals and neglects puts a period to that time, it ends sadly.

When this woeful period comes, the gospel, in itself a message of peace and love, has then a new commission of a sad tenor, Isa. vi. 10. When this period comes, then comes forth that dreadful decree, 'He that is unrighteous, let him be unrighteous still,' &c., Rev. xxii. 11.

(2.) This time of visitation is sometimes longer, sometimes shorter; it is continued to some more, to some less. The period comes sometimes later, sometimes more suddenly. And no particular man knows but his own share therein may be the shortest.

This time is in some places measured by years. Three years is allotted them who are represented by the fig-tree, Mat. xiii. 6, 7. With much importunity, one year longer is obtained. And about so many years was Christ gathering Jerusalem: the time of that their visitation was of betwixt three and four years' continuance. This time is elsewhere expressed by a day, as if it were confined in such a narrow compass: Heb. iii., 'To-day, if ye will hear his voice.' This is the day of salvation; and this, as other days, is sometimes shorter, sometimes longer. To some it is a longer day, like the days of summer; to others it proves a winter day, a day of short continuance.

To determine precisely of the continuance of this time, to say thus long it shall be, and no shorter, to fix its period, is a presumption for any son of man to undertake. The length and period of these times and seasons of grace, the Lord has reserved in his own power, they are amongst his secrets. He has cut off all occasions of presuming on his patience, leaving us at uncertainties. No man can make account of another hour, he is not sure of any further moment.

Only this seems clear in the negative: the time of grace to a particular man is not always as long as his life, how short soever his life be. The longest time of patience we find allotted to any, is that determined for the old world, Gen. vi. 3. These are those days of which the apostle Peter says, that the long-suffering of God waited on them, and that Christ, by his Spirit in his servant Noah, preached to them, 1 Pet. iii. 19, 20, which Spirit, in his ministry, did strive with them; so that this was the time of their visitation, and the continuance of it is an hundred and twenty years. Yet this was not the seventh part of the time to which their lives were ordinarily prolonged before the flood. An hundred and twenty years, compared with their lifetime, is not so long for them as ten years are now for us. I think we may conclude, though the time of grace be sometimes shorter, sometimes longer, yet it is seldom drawn out to the length of lifetime. Sin often puts a shorter period to it. Many men who live under the gospel, outlive their time of grace.

(3.) It were just with the Lord to put a period to the time of grace, upon the first refusal of any offer of grace. A wonderful thing if Christ and mercy be ever again offered, after it has been once refused; for as the apostle argues, 2 Pet. ii. 4, 'If God spared not the angels that sinned, but cast them down to hell,' why should man expect any favour or forbearance? The angels were glorious and powerful creatures; man is an impotent and contemptible worm in comparison. Those angels, for one sin, were destroyed; men loaden with multitudes of sins are spared. Those angels perished, for anything appears to us, without any mercy so much as once offered them; sinful men have Christ and mercy tendered, before justice seize on them. Now, if it were just with the Lord to destroy the angels, without any offer of grace made to them, may he not justly proceed against sinful men, after grace offered and rejected by them? Might he not justly proceed upon the first rejecting of it?

(4.) It must be granted that any refusal of Christ and mercy is exceeding dangerous. If we consider who Christ is, what pardon cost him, who the sinner is to whom these are offered, we may easily see that any slighting or refusal of these offers does highly provoke the Lord to take you at the first word. You make excuses. You cannot yet close with the terms of the gospel: you are too busy, you have no leisure. Well may the Lord say, Be it so; yet you shall have leisure enough to see your madness in eternal torments; you shall have leisure enough in that endless eternity. You use delays. You cannot yet enter into the strict and holy ways of Christ; you will have a little more ease, a little more pleasure, a little more gain by sin. Well may he say, Ye will not when ye may, ye shall not when ye would; ye shall never taste of the sweetness and happiness of my holy ways. Ye will not take Christ, and submit to him, on the terms he is offered. Well, it shall be so; ye shall never have Christ; 'ye shall die in your sins.' Ye will not come when I invite you. Well, 'not one of you shall taste of my supper.' It is Christ's threatening in so many words, Mat. xiv. 24. The apostle insinuates the danger in the form of that expression, Heb. ii. 3. Here is very great danger; here is occasion enough of fear, lest the Lord, being thus provoked, should 'swear in his wrath, Ye shall never enter into his rest.'

(5.) Some, in special manner, have great cause to fear that their day is past. I say not they have ground certainly to conclude it, but cause to fear it. Some signs of an expired day of grace are visible upon them, such as are probable signs, though not infallible. Such as these, to give you briefly some instances:

[1.] A long, wilful continuance in known sins, under a searching, convincing, and lively ministry. Take it as I deliver it, lest it be mistaken. When a man continues in sins, in known sins, continues long in them, continues in them wilfully and obstinately, and that is resolved to do it, under a ministry that shews him it, convinces him of it, threatens it, declares the danger and sinfulness, and brings this home to his heart and conscience, I say not this is a certain sign, but I say it is a dangerous sign, that the day of his visitation is expired. I say not this case is utterly desperate; but were I without assurance of heaven, and under doubts and fears of my eternal state, yet would I not be in that sinner's condition for ten thousand worlds, for such are scarce ever recovered.

[2.] When the means of grace are withdrawn upon contempt and refusals, when the candlestick is removed, the glory departed, the light of the gospel gone, then it is too plain the day is at an end. When you see the sun set and the light gone, you doubt not but the day is expired. When no gospel light is left, the things that concern a sinner's peace must needs be hid from his eyes. And this is it wherewith Christ shuts up Jerusalem's day.

[3.] When men withdraw from the means of grace, though the means be not withdrawn from them. A man may make it night in his chamber when it is day abroad, by shutting out that light which makes the day. Thus may a man bring a night upon himself in particular, though those in the same place enjoy a day of visitation, when, after other disobediences to the word, he adds this contempt, he will not so much as hear it; when he puts away the word from him, or puts himself from it. Thus the Jews' day ended. Though they might have had the word, they would not, Acts xiii. 46. That which was hereby brought to the Gentiles, departed from the Jews; that was light and salvation, ver. 47. Those that put themselves from the word, or put the word from them, put light and likewise salvation from them; and when they are gone, sure the day of grace is expired.

[4.] When the Spirit will strive no more with a sinner, then he is cast off. The means of grace are continued, and he attends on them; and has formerly, in the ministry of the word, found some motions of heart, some stirrings of affection, some strugglings of conscience; but now all is hushed and gone, the sense of his soul is locked up, as it were, in a deep slumber; a stupefying humour is seized upon every faculty, and the promises, the threatenings, the terror of the law, the sweetness of the gospel, fall on his heart with no more effect than if it were a senseless thing. This is a dangerous sign his time is past, When the Spirit will strive no more with a sinner, his day is at an end. The end of the old world's day is thus described, Gen. vi. 3.

2. Though all this must be granted, yet there remains enough to satisfy this scruple. We shall comprise it in these heads.

(1.) It is not usual with Christ to put an end to the time of grace when his gracious offers are first refused. Though he might justly do it upon the first provocation, yet such is his mercy, his patience, he will not be so provoked. He breaks not off the treaty with sinners when his terms are first rejected, but sends his ambassadors again and again to beseech, to importune, to persuade sinners to be reconciled, and to be at peace with him. The treaty, when sinners would break it off, is often resumed, and those gracious proposals renewed and also reinforced, 2 Chron. xxxvi. 15, on which you have a comment, Jer. xxv. 3, 4. The Lord from time to time diligently addressed himself to them by the prophets. No time was slipped; they rise early day by day, and that for divers years.

He uses not to depart, though he might justly, when the heart opens not to him at the first knock, but he stands knocking, Rev. iii. 20. He stands long, all the day long, Cant. v. 2. Though there is more provocation in the unkindness of his spouse than of strangers, yet this occasions not a sudden departure. He stays till his head be wet with the drops of the night. When they will not be gathered at first, he tries again, he tries often: Mat. xxiii., 'How often would I have gathered you?' &c. He withdraws not the golden sceptre, if sinners come not in, when it is first holden forth. He stretches it out all the day long, even to the stiff-necked, those that will not stoop to it, those that rebel and rise up against the sceptre of his Son. If the day should end at the first provocation, if this day should be thus shortened, no flesh would be saved. There are divers hours in this day; if they come not in at one, he tries another. He goes out at the third, the sixth, the ninth, the eleventh, all the hours into which their day was divided, Mat. xx. 3. He that, when he was first called, said he would not go, was not shut out because he went not at the first call, Mat. xxi. 28, 30. The Lord waits to be gracious; that imports a continued patience and expectance, 1 Pet. iii. 20. He strives, he gives not over at the first impulse. He comes seeking fruit for some years together, one year after another, Luke xiii. 6, 7. That seems great severity, Mark xi. 13. It was not a good, a seasonable year for figs; it afforded not many. This seems extraordinary rigid and severe, that he should be so quick with it as to curse and blast it at the first disappointment. But it appears so only as to the emblem, the fig-tree. As to Jerusalem, which it signifies, this was not the first disappointment. He had been with her again and again, and a third time, before he blasts her. He both comes and sends; and contents not himself to send once, how ill soever his messengers be treated, but sends a second, a third, a fourth time, as Mark xii. 1, 2, 4, 5, &c. He is not wont to take sinners at the first word; to offer no more, when they once refuse; to try no more, when they once resist. Alas! even the best, those that yield at length, yield not at first; they resist too long, too much. When Christ would lay his yoke on them, how easy soever it is, he finds them like an untamed heifer, a bullock unaccustomed to the yoke. So they demean themselves. So it was with Ephraim, when returning, Jer. xxxi. 18. His demeanour was no better than that of an untamed and unruly beast. So Ephraim complains, and so all the people of God, who observe the carriage of their heart towards God while he is reducing them. Before you make your resisting and refusals a discouragement, first see if you can meet with any who can truly say they never resisted or refused.

(2.) No man can certainly determine concerning himself or another that the time of grace is past, especially where the means of grace are continued and made use of. Some probabilities there may be, which I gave an account of in the premised concessions; but no peremptory certainty. Some cause there may be to fear it, but no ground absolutely to conclude it. Indeed, one exception there lies against this rule. When it is known that a person hath committed the sin against the Holy Ghost, it may be known that there is no mercy, no more time of mercy for him. If that be certain, it will be an infallible sign his day of grace is ended. And it may be sometimes known that this unpardonable sin is committed; for the apostle makes it a rule that we should not pray for him that has sinned unto death. Now if it could never be known when a man is guilty of this sin unto death, his rule would be utterly useless and unpracticable; he should lay down such a rule as none could ever practise or walk by. But to leave further inquiries into that, this may be sufficient for our present purpose, that the ground of the objection now before us, cannot be a ground to any one to conclude that he has committed the unpardonable sin. The ground of the scruple is refusing offers of mercy, resisting the Spirit. Now every one that resists the Holy Ghost, though he do it long and often, does not sin that sin against the Holy Ghost which shall not be pardoned. This is clear from Acts vii. 51. He tells the Jews they 'always resisted the Holy Ghost;' they had resisted, and resisted the Holy Ghost, and that striving with them in the most powerful ministry that ever the world enjoyed. Not only their fathers, in the ministry of the prophets, but in the ministry of Christ himself and of the apostles, wherein the Holy Ghost appeared in the clearest light and greatest power, in the glory, power, and convincing evidence of miracles. Here they had resisted the Holy Ghost; and that not once only, or seldom, or for a short time, but always. And yet these had not sinned against the Holy Ghost unpardonably; for Stephen, full of the Holy Ghost, prays for their pardon, ver. 60. Now if their sin had been that against the Holy Ghost, he would not have prayed for them, there is a rule which prohibits that, 1 John v. 16. Further, Saul was one of the resisters of the Holy Ghost, being one of his persecutors, ver. 58, and so one that he prayed for. And his prayer was heard for Saul; his conversion, of which you have an account presently after, is accounted a return of Stephen's prayer. So that though he did resist the Holy Ghost, yet sinned not unpardonably; otherwise Stephen would not have prayed for him, he could not have been pardoned, he would not have been converted. From hence also it appears that a man may resist the Holy Ghost much, long, often, so as to amount to an *always*, and yet his day of mercy may [not] be expired. And so it was with Saul, whom grace at last conquered, after such resistance. Though you have resisted the Holy Ghost, you cannot from hence be certain that you have sinned the unpardonable sin, you cannot hence be certain that the time of mercy is at an end. There is no certainty of it for all this.

(3.) There are strong probabilities, such as are next to certainties, for the sensible or gospel-sinner, that this day is not past. I shall give you some signs of it; some that will be probable grounds, some that may be certain grounds, that his time of mercy is not expired.

[1.] Fear that it is past is a probable sign it is not past; for Satan usually troubles those most with fears of this who have least cause to fear it, and leaves them most secure and fearless who have most cause to be fearful. This is the way whereby he promotes his great design upon sinners. His great interest is to make them sure to himself; to effect this, he strives to cut off all endeavours by representing them hopeless, so he tells them their day is past, it is to no purpose.

He would take off insensible sinners from endeavours by representing them needless; their state is safe, or else they have time enough, they need not fear, he will not have them disturbed with any such fears while they are in his custody, that being quiet, they may not so much as think of an escape. 'The strong man armed keeps the house,' &c., Luke xi. 21. They are asleep in sin, and while they are so, he is sure of them, so he is concerned to keep them from being awakened with any such fears. While they are thus lulled asleep, they dream that mercy, grace, heaven, and all is sure; they put away the evil day far from them when it is just upon them; 'They cry peace, peace, when sudden destruction is coming upon them;' they will not so much as apprehend, conceive of it, till they be in travail; they go on, bless themselves, say they shall have peace, Deut. xxix. 19. Such a security had seized on the old world when their day was expired, Luke xvii. 27. When the Lord had rejected the Jews, and so their day was gone, the effects hereof was a spirit of slumber, Rom. xi. 8. The word in the prophet, רדם, signifies to nod, Isa. xxix. 10, which is the consequent of a sleepy or lethargic humour, which leaves them senseless: 'Eyes they have, but see not; ears, but hear not.' They see no cause of fear, nor will they hear of any; without sense of danger, and so without fear. Such a spirit of slumber is a sign of an expired day. But when the soul is fearful it is wakeful, the spirit of slumber has not seized on it; that is a probable sign the time of mercy is not past. Your fears may give you hope in this case.

[2.] When there is a diligent attending upon the means of grace, it is a sign the day of grace is still continued. When the Lord gives the heart to be diligent in the use of his appointments, to be diligent in hearing him in the word, seeking him by prayer, and giving encouragements to his messengers, it is a sign the Lord is not yet gone, he has something further to do before he depart. We find not that the Lord utterly rejects a people till they some way or other reject him in his messengers, or in those means of grace wherein he offers himself. The Lord gives encouragement to those that diligently seek him; those that hear him, watching at his gates, and waiting at the posts of his doors; and so long as here is encouragement, the time of mercy is not past; when that is gone, all hopes are gone.

When the Lord sends forth his disciples, he orders, that when any received them, there they should stay, and their staying was a continuing, a prolonging of the day of grace and visitation; but if any would not receive them, *i. e.*, hearken to them, entertain them, encourage them, they were to shake off the dust of their feet, as a token that such were cast off by the Lord, Mat. x. 14. And we find Paul and Barnabas proceeding according to this rule, Acts xiii. 46, 51. When the Jews put away the word from them, they shook off the dust, to signify that the Lord had so shaken off that people, he had quite left them off, their time was past.

When the Lord is gone, a spirit of sloth and torpor seizes on the soul; he will not stir up himself to follow after God or wait on him, a spirit of contempt possesses him, he cares not for the means of grace. He hears now and then out of custom, but if some by-respects did not move him, he cares not much if he never heard at all. As this temper provokes God to put a period to the day of grace, so, when it is ended, this sloth and contempt increases. As it was before, in its beginnings and progress, a cause, and so it is now, in its height, a sign that the Lord has cast him off, his time is past and gone.

But when there is a heart to prize the means of grace, and to attend on them accordingly, it is a probable sign not only that the day of grace is continued, but that the Lord will continue it yet longer, if this be thy case.

[3.] When there are desires after the breathings and workings of the Spirit in the ordinances, this is a sign of more evidence and probability than the former. When the soul cannot be contented with this, that he enjoys the means of grace, and that he waits on them, unless he find himself wrought upon by them, unless he find some enlightenings, some motions of the heart, some stirrings of affection; cannot rest in the bare performance of holy duties unless he find some light and heat of the Spirit in them; is not satisfied that he prays unless he find that his heart moves therein more than his lips, nor that he hears the word unless his soul be affected with what he hears. If this be thy case, thou countest it a sad day, a sad duty (whatever other respect may commend it to thee), when no other impression is made on thy soul, thou hast no cause to fear thy day is past. The Lord never withdraws while his presence is desired. The Spirit never leaves that soul which is ready to make him welcome, while his workings and breathing are acceptable and desired. These desires argue he might be welcome if he would come in; his workings would be acceptable if he would vouchsafe it. The Lord is with you while you are with him; and so far as you truly desire his effectual presence, so far he counts you with him. The Lord does not judge of us by what we are, but what we would be.

[4.] When the Spirit is striving with the soul. When he not only desires the strivings of the Spirit, but feels them, this is not only a strong probability, but an evident certainty that his time is not past. When the Spirit looks into the mind, and lets in some light to discover the things that concern a sinner's peace; when Christ is knocking at the heart, and using importunity to get in; when he is awakening the conscience to a sense of sin and misery; when the Spirit is thus enlightening, convincing, persuading, humbling; when the word is brought home to the mind, heart, and conscience with these effects, it is evident the Spirit is not gone, for he is now at work. If this be thy case, thy day is so far from being ended, that it is now at the height. This is the accepted time, this is thy hour, take heed thou do not slip it. Satan makes the hour of thy visitation an hour of temptation; he would make thee let it slip by persuading thee it is past already; but as sure as he is a liar this is truth, it is now thy day; this is the accepted time, and will be a day of salvation if thou improve it, if thou yield to the Spirit's strivings, and resist no longer: 'My Spirit shall not always strive,' Gen. vi. 3, and then sets down how long the Spirit should strive. The length of our days is measured by the continuance of the Spirit's striving. Every hour that he strives is an hour of that day. It is not night till the Spirit will strive no longer. And therefore your day is not yet ended who feel the Spirit still striving.

[5.] When the soul is grieved for former refusal; when the heart bleeds to think of former resistance. This clearly signifies the day is not past. You may see this in Ephraim, Jer. xxxi. 18. Here is first observable his resistance: when the Lord took him in hand, would have laid his yoke upon him, brought him under his government, he demeaned himself as a bullock unaccustomed to the yoke; he was wanton, unruly, slung off and refused, withdrew his shoulder and resisted. Turn thou, else no turning. Then take notice how he resents this. When he came to himself he bewails it. This was it for which he bemoaned himself; of this he was ashamed, confounded; for this he smote upon his thigh, used all the actions of one moaning himself under pain and grief; such grief, shame, sorrow did the thoughts of his former resistings and refusals smite his heart with. If this be thy case, why then surely it is the time of mercy; for so Ephraim in this condition found it, ver. 20. Though he spake against him for his former froward refusals, and perverse resistings, yet when he saw Ephraim remember this, so as his soul was troubled for it, why the Lord does earnestly remember him, and his bowels are troubled for relenting Ephraim. I will surely see here. If Ephraim's case be thine, though thou have resisted as he did, yet if thou art troubled for it, as he was, the Lord assures thee of mercy; it is not only a time wherein he offers, but a time wherein he will vouchsafe it; he assures thee of it. It is so far from being past already, as it shall never be past; thou mayest be sure of it, if the Lord's word can make it sure.

[6.] When the Spirit has prevailed with the soul to refuse and resist no longer. When it does not only strive, but prevail with a sinner, so far as to be heartily willing to yield to Christ on his own terms. This is an undoubted sign that the time is not past, when the soul strives and wrestles with that principle of opposition and resistance that is in itself, &c. If this be thy case, thy day is so far from being ended, as it shall never end.

(4.) The readiest way to put this out of question is to believe, to cast thy soul on Christ. There is no danger for a sensible sinner to venture on this; there is all encouragement. Thy day is not so past, but if thou come in there is mercy for thee; if thou lay down thy weapons and submit, Christ will receive thee. He does not say, I have mercy, but it is only for those who have [not] refused and resented. This is contrary to the tenor of the gospel. The promises are not in any such strain. That whosoever believes, not that those only who have not resisted so long or so much, but that 'whosoever believes shall be saved;' 'He that comes, I will in no wise cast out,' upon no consideration, however he have resisted and refused. The apostle Paul is an encouraging instance. Who had more resisted and refused than he? Consider what resistance he made. It was a scornful resistance, Acts ix. 5. He kicked against Christ, he rejected his offers with scorn. It was a violent and bloody resistance; he resisted Christ unto blood and slaughter of his messengers; he embrued himself in the blood of Christ's members, Acts viii. 1, 3, ix. 1, 2. It was a continued resistance; he was one of those of whom Stephen complains, Acts vii. 51. Now, was his time of mercy expired for all this? No; he believed and found mercy, and he found mercy for this very purpose, that he might encourage thee, that he might be a pattern, an encouraging instance to all humbled and returning sinners, whatever their refusals or resistance have been. He tells you so expressly: 1 Tim. i. 16, 'For this cause,' &c. Christ holds him out as a standing instance of his great long-suffering, that every humbled and returning sinner, apt to be discouraged from believing by the sad consideration of his former rebellious and obstinate resistance, might in him clearly see that he is not so short and quick with sinners as to cut them off from mercy for some resistings, no, not for such resistings as Saul's were. They put not a period to his time of mercy, but upon believing he found mercy. If thou hadst resisted as he did, yet believe as he did, and thou shalt find like mercy. The Holy Ghost has recorded this example on purpose to encourage those that should believe hereafter.

Obj. 6. Another discouragement which keeps sensible sinners from believing, is a fear that they have sinned the unpardonable sin. There are two extremes of faith (as every grace and virtue has its extremes), presumption and despair. If Satan can drive the sinner into either, both being at the greatest distance from the middle, he keeps them far enough from faith. Now that his malicious attempts may be successful, he suits them to the condition of the sinner. Those that are secure he draws them to presumption, of which before. Those that are sensible and awakened, he would drive them to despair, and the most effectual engine to this purpose is that which is now before us, a suggestion that they have sinned against the Holy Ghost, and so there remains no more sacrifice for sin, Christ can profit them nothing, it is impossible they should be renewed either by repentance or faith.

This is a temptation whereby he too often perplexes awakened sinners; nay, this fiery dart he sometimes sticks in the consciences of believers too. Those that are not assaulted have no security but they may be. Therefore it will not be amiss to give some satisfaction to this scruple, such as may serve either for cure or prevention.

That which will be most satisfactory is a right understanding of the nature of this sin. The great advantage of that prince of darkness is, that he assaults the soul in the dark, and when he wants light to judge, puts that upon him for this sin, which indeed is no such thing. The texts wherein this sin is described will scatter this darkness. I shall not engage in a full discourse on this subject, but only open this sin by opening those texts, so far as may be sufficient for my present purpose, as briefly as may be consistent with perspicuity. There are many scriptures where this sin is mentioned, but I find but three where it is described: Mat. xii., Heb. vi. and x., with the other evangelists concurring. And from these scriptures we may collect this description of this sin. It is a blasphemous renouncing of Christ and his doctrine out of hatred, and against conviction by the Holy Ghost's light and testimony. We shall take it into parcels, that you may see distinctly how every part is contained in all and every of those alleged texts. (1.) It is a renouncing or denying of Christ. (2.) With blasphemy and reproaches. (3.) Out of hatred and malice. (4.) Against light and conviction. The two former are as the matter of it; the two latter the form which constitutes this sin in its peculiar being, and distinguisheth it from all other sins.

(1.) A renouncing or denying of Christ and his doctrine. You may see this in the scribes and Pharisees, Mat. xii. When Christ by a miracle had drawn the people to acknowledge that he was the Messias, ver. 23, nay, say the Pharisees, he is not the Messias for all this, this he does by the power of Satan; he is not the king of Israel, the king of the church, but he tampers with the prince of devils. He is not the prophet, but a conjuror, a deluder, and consequently he is not the great high priest that must be a sacrifice for sinners; for a sinner cannot be a sacrifice for sin. This more expressly elsewhere: 'We will not have this man to reign,' Luke xix., and so rejected him as king. No: 'but he deceives the people,' John vii. 12. So rejected him as prophet. And after crucifying him as a malefactor, shed his blood as the blood of a notorious sinner, and so utterly denied him to be the priest, even when they made him a sacrifice.

So answerably in Heb. vi. It is a falling away, a falling off from Christ, his ways and truths, a putting him to open shame; not only a putting Christ away, but a putting him away with shame and reproach; a crucifying him again, that is a renouncing of him with a witness.

So Heb. x. 29. A treading the Son of God under foot, a casting him down from being king, so as to trample on him; accounting the blood of the covenant an unholy thing, no better than common blood, the blood of a malefactor. So his priesthood is renounced; for it was that blood by which he was sanctified or consecrated to be a sacrifice, John xvii. 19.

Doing despite to the Spirit. So the prophetical office of Christ and the doctrine which he teaches is rejected; for it is the Spirit of grace and truth by which Christ executes his prophetical office.

Christ is renounced, both when there is a falling off from him, after he has been professed and acknowledged, so it is described in that Epistle, or when there is an opposing of him, when clearly and convincingly propounded, though he have not been openly professed. So it is described in the Gospel as the sin of the Pharisees. Here is some difference in the subjects, but the act is the same, a renouncing of Christ in both.

(2.) With blasphemies and reproaches. This sin is expressly called blasphemy, Mat. xii. 31 and 32, speaking a word, that is, a blasphemous word, such as is shameful and reproachful to him. The blaspheming of the Son is called blaspheming of the Holy Ghost, because it is against the Son as discovered and borne witness to by the Holy Ghost; against the person, offices, and doctrine of the Son, but against the light and testimony of the Holy Ghost. Their particular blasphemy is set down, ver. 24, where they do as bad as call Christ a conjuror, and the Holy Ghost, whereby he acted, an evil spirit, the prince of devils. Expressly, Mark iii. 22, 30. And this was their blasphemy, ver. 29; this sin is blaspheming too, as described Heb. vi. 6, a putting Christ to open shame, ascribing that openly to him which is shameful and reproachful. It is the same word which is used Mat. i. 19, *παραδειγματίζειν*, to make a shameful example of her. He was willing to put her away, but not so as to make her a public shame and reproach. But this sin is a putting Christ away, a rejecting him in a shameful and reproachful way, with blasphemies and opprobrious reflections and aspersions. So Heb. x. 29, *ἐνυβρίσας*; to use one injuriously and contumeliously, rendered *contumeliâ afficere*. When Christ, as held out by the light and testimony of the Spirit of grace, is shamefully abused, either in words or deeds, he and the Spirit are blasphemed; really blasphemed, by injurious affronts; verbally, by opprobrious and reproachful speeches. The word will bear either, so that in all the descriptions it is blasphemy.

(3.) Out of hatred and malice. This is the rise, the principle, from whence this sin proceeds; it is from hatred of Christ and his truth. It is not for want of care and watchfulness, as in sins of surprisal; nor from want of knowledge, as in sins of ignorance; nor from passion and fear, as in sins of infirmity; nor from boldness merely, as in some sins of presumption; but from hatred and malice. This was the rise of it in the Pharisees, this was at the bottom. That which appeared was horrible, they broke out into blasphemies; but Christ minds not that only, but what was within, Mat. xii. 24, 25. He takes an estimate of their sin, not by their words only, but by their thoughts, which were boiled up and set a-working by hatred and malice. And this he charges them with expressly elsewhere, John xv. 25; cited from Ps. xxxv. 19, where the word is חנם, used 1 Sam. xix. 5, hated him as Saul did David. This put them upon rejecting his government, Luke xix. 14, upon rejecting his doctrine, John iii. 19, John vii. 7. This put them upon seeking his life, and murdering him when they had found opportunity. It was not anger, for that acts rashly; but they consulted how they might do it, John xi. 53, acted deliberately, and so were wilful and malicious murderers.

Aristotle puts this difference betwixt anger and hatred, *ὁ μὲν γὰρ ἀντιπαθεῖν βούλεται ᾧ ὀργίζεται, ὁ δὲ μὴ εἶναι*. Anger would make him suffer who has occasioned it, but hatred would deprive him of his being. Nothing less would satisfy the hatred wherewith they were acted but a shameful and cruel death. And this hatred is expressed by the like acts, Heb. vi. 6; they crucify him again; not as to the physical action; that cannot be repeated,

Christ is now above their malice; but as to judicial interpretation. They disprove* not what the Jews did, they have the same malicious mind, they use him as far as may be like the Jews; if the same could be done, they would do it again. Their actings against him, his truth, his members, are equivalent, they will bear such an interpretation. What clearer expressions of hatred, than Heb. x. 29, to trample on him, to vilify his blood as the blood of a malefactor. If their tongues do not speak it, their actions do. All is of malice, they do despite to the Spirit of grace. Their actings are from spite and malice. It is clear, in all the descriptions, that there is in this sin a hatred against Christ.

But observe, that it is not necessary to this sin, that this hatred should be of truth as truth, or of Christ as Christ, *i.e.*, as a Redeemer, as a Saviour, as the Son of God, or the Messiah; for so he cannot be the object of hatred; but it is a hatred of the truth and of Christ, and of the Spirit witnessing of him, as these are contrary to their desires and expectations, to their lusts and interests, John iii. 19, vii. 7; Mat, xxi. 8; they feared Christ would deprive them of that power, honour, good opinion, which they then inherited amongst the people, &c.

(4.) All this must be against light and conviction. This is express, Heb. vi. 4–6; it is the falling away from Christ of those that have been enlightened; so Heb. x. 26, a sinning after the receipt of knowledge, a sinning wilfully, which cannot be but against knowledge.

There is some question of this concerning the Pharisees, started by some who would otherwise state this sin; but I see no reason for it, I see much in Scripture against it.

They knew that Christ wrought miracles, they acknowledge it, John xi. 47. It is strange if they were not convinced that these miracles were acts of a divine power, the finger of God. Can we think them more stupid than the Egyptian magicians? They saw and acknowledged the finger of God in Moses's miracles, Exod. viii. 19. Were they blinder than those instruments of Satan in the midst of Egyptian darkness? There was a convincing light went along with the miracles of Christ, which shewed their original, and convinced all the people who was the author of them: John xi. 47, 48, 'All will believe on him,' Mat. xii. 22, 23; John vii. 31; iii. 2. 'We,' *i.e.*, he, and those of his sect, the Pharisees, they knew it, were convinced of it; and when they spake otherwise, said they were of the devil, they had something within them that gainsaid them; they said it with some reluctancy of conscience.

They were convinced that Christ was the Messias; the light of the Holy Ghost, shining in his doctrine and miracles, discovered this unto them; though they were loath to see it, unwilling to believe it. Their rebellious will rising up against their judgment, did check and oppose this light, but it could not be avoided, nor quite suppressed. Christ tells them they knew him, John vii. 28. They knew he was the heir: Mat. xxi. 37, 38, 'This is the heir.' They knew who he was, and they perceived that Christ intended them in that parable, ver. 45, 46. All the three evangelists agree in it. This was that which completed this sin, so as it became unpardonable, Luke xxiii. 34. There were some of those actors against Christ that could not be forgiven, Luke xii. 10; for those Christ prays not; he would not pray for that which he knew could not be granted.

But there were some who might be forgiven, for such he prays; and who were those? Why, those who knew not what they did, acted not against

* Qu. 'disapprove'?—ED.

knowledge and conviction. So then, those who knew what they did, are they who could not be forgiven. Their sin, acted against knowledge and conscience, was the unpardonable sin. So Peter encouraging the Jews to repent, by proposing hopes of pardon, lays down this as the ground of the encouragement, Acts iii. 17–19, as your rulers, Herod and Pilate did, implying that if they acted against knowledge, if they had known him to be the Lord of life whom they crucified, there had been no hopes or encouragement for them.

Answerably, the apostle Paul shews how it came to pass that he found mercy, after he had so blasphemously and maliciously opposed Christ: 'I did it ignorantly,' 1 Tim. i. 13. There were all other ingredients of that unpardonable sin in Paul's sin, but this only, he acted not against knowledge and conscience; if he had not done it ignorantly, he had found no mercy, as the expression seems to insinuate.

This seems to be the reason why this sin directed against Christ is yet called the sin against the Holy Ghost. Light and conviction is the work of the Holy Ghost; his office and operation is to convey light, and thereby effect conviction. When Christ discovered convincingly by the light and testimony of the Holy Ghost is thus renounced, the Holy Ghost is blasphemed, which discovers and bears witness of him; his light and testimony is rejected and renounced. The Holy Ghost gave the Pharisees a double testimony of Christ. One,

[1.] Outward. Those miracles which he wrought were the work of the Spirit, ver. 28 (and elsewhere the receiving of miraculous gifts is called the receiving of the Holy Ghost), and they were wrought by the Spirit of God to testify of Christ, John v. 36; Mat. xii. 28.

[2.] Inward. And that is, when the Holy Ghost brings the light, which shines in the doctrine and miracles, home to the mind and conscience, with convincing evidence. When Christ appearing with this evidence is renounced, the Holy Ghost, whose evidence and testimony this is, is therein renounced, and so blasphemed.

And by this we may be led to conceive aright of that distinction, Luke xii. 10. Christ may be considered two ways, either as appearing in the weakness of human state, as merely the Son of man; or else as appearing in the light of the Holy Ghost, viz., in the light and evidence of his doctrine and miracles, whereby he is declared to be the Son of God with power. Blasphemy against the Son of God, in the former appearance, may be forgiven, but blasphemy against the Son, in the latter appearance, shall not be forgiven; because then it is the blasphemy against the Holy Ghost, which, attended with the fore-mentioned ingredients, is declared to be unpardonable.

Thus you see what this sin is. Not every blasphemy, nor every blasphemous renouncing of Christ; no, nor every blasphemous opposition of Christ out of hatred; but withal this is done against knowledge and conscience. It is not every sin against knowledge and conscience; nor every blasphemy against knowledge and conscience; nor every blasphemous renouncing of Christ against these; but when there is all this out of hatred and malice. You must not judge yourselves or others guilty of it, because of one or more ingredients; there must be a concurrence of all, both matter and form, the form especially, else there cannot be this sin.

And this being positively cleared, will afford some negatives which may be most satisfactory in this case. I shall instance in such as are most apt to be mistaken; such sins, which humbled souls or others may take to be the sin against the Holy Ghost, when indeed they are no such thing, fall short of it in something or other which is essential thereto.

1. It is not every forsaking of Christ. Then not only Judas, but the rest of the disciples had been guilty of this sin; for they forsook him, and that in his greatest extremity, when their love should most have shewed itself in cleaving to him, Mat. xxvi. 56, Mark xiv. 50. They all fled, and left him, to secure themselves. Only John must be excepted; we find him after in the high priest's hall. Hence is drawn an instance of Christ's faithfulness in making good his word, Mat. x., Luke ix. 23. John, who fled not from Christ to save his life, he saved it; he survived them all, lived to a great age, and died in his bed. All the rest, who fled to save their lives, lost them, and were plucked out of the world by violent death. But though they lost their lives, they did not lose their souls; they found pardon and favour, both to be saved themselves, and to be instruments for the saving of others. They were far from this sin, though one might think, by flying from Christ, they came near it.

2. It is not every resisting of the enlightening Spirit. A man may be guilty of sinning against the Holy Ghost, in such a high way as that of resistance, and yet not be guilty of *that* sin against the Holy Ghost. Many of those who did resist the Holy Ghost in the ministry of Christ, did yield afterwards to it in the ministry of the apostles, and so were converted and pardoned. I shewed you this before, from Acts vii. 51. Indeed, if all should sin unpardonably who resist the Spirit, who is there that would be pardoned? for who is there that has not resisted? Upon what account should the grace of the Spirit be called victorious, but that it meets with resistance? It is conquering grace, not because it is not resisted (that is no great conquest where there is no opposition), but because it prevails against resistance; not because it meets with no opposition, but because it masters all opposition.

3. It is not every persecuting of Christ, his truth, and members; no, not that which is out of spite and hatred. Such a persecutor was Paul, an eager persecutor, Philip. iii. 6, which zeal made it a piece of his religion. His zeal was as a burning flame, as wild-fire in the church; he wasted it, made havoc of it. His violence transported him beyond all bounds, Gal. i. 13. He did it out of hatred and malice, nothing would satisfy him but the blood and slaughter of Christ's saints, Acts xxii. 4, Acts ix. 1. An outrageous persecutor, pursued them with exceeding rage and fury, Acts xxvi. 11, his cruelty reached not only their bodies, but their souls. He 'compelled them to blaspheme,' and that was the high-way to destroy their souls. Now all this Christ takes as done against himself, Acts ix. 4, 5. All this fury and bloody rage is resented by Christ as let out upon himself, and yet he finds mercy.

4. It is not every blasphemy.

(1.) Not every blasphemy injected. There may be blasphemous suggestions cast into the mind, without any guilt of blasphemy, where they are not entertained and consented to, but rejected and cast out with indignation. In this case the soul is as it were ravished, and may be nothing the less chaste and pure, when it is a mere patient as to this force, and no consent yielded. Christ himself was assaulted by Satan with such suggestions. In the history of his temptation, you may observe Satan's drift is to fasten on him this doubt, that he was not the Son of God.

(2.) Not every blasphemy admitted. Blasphemous suggestions may be admitted so far by the saints of God, as to occasion some doubtings of a blasphemous tendency, *e.g.*, concerning the providence of God, the natures and offices of Christ, the truth and divinity of Scripture. What unworthy thoughts had the psalmist of the providence of God, Ps. lxxiii. for which he censures himself severely as a fool and a beast.

Some of the disciples, after his death, seem to question whether he was the Messias, the Redeemer of Israel, Luke xxiv. 21. They had believed this before, but now things being of another appearance, they call it into question, as the words imply. They had the word of God, the word of Christ, which is now scripture to us, that Christ after his sufferings should rise the third day, Mat. xviii. And yet when this was come to pass, and they had divers testimonies of it, they doubt of the truth of his word, so that he upbraids them, Luke xxiv. 25, 26.

(3.) Not every blasphemy expressed. Saul forced some blasphemous expressions from the saints that he persecuted, Acts xxvi. To secure themselves from his rage, they utter some reproachful speeches against Christ, his truths, or ways.

(4.) It is not that particular blasphemy, Mat. xii., in the matter and substance of it, if it be without that attendant, which formalised and aggravated it to that height in those Pharisees (though it has been of late otherwise determined). This to me is an evident reason of it. All the Jews, or others, who knew that Christ wrought these miracles, and yet did not receive or acknowledge him to be the Messias, I see not how they could avoid that blasphemy, at least in thought. For knowing that he wrought such miracles, and that they were wrought to testify that he was the Messias, either they thought that he did them by the Spirit and power of God, and then how could they choose but believe that he was the Christ, without running into as great a blasphemy, by thinking that the Spirit of God would give such a testimony to a lie? And it is evident many of them did not believe him then to be the Messias, being not converted till after his death. Or else they thought he did those miracles by some other spirit and power than that of God. No third thing can be imagined. And what other spirit and power could that be, but the same to which those Pharisees blasphemously ascribe it? Yet they might do that ignorantly, which those Pharisees did against conviction. And so, though they were guilty of blaspheming the Holy Ghost, yet not of that unpardonable blasphemy, though it was materially the same blasphemy, yet wanted that ingredient, which does formalise it into the unpardonable sin.

Yea, it seems probable to me, that Paul before his conversion was guilty of this particular blaspheming materially considered, as before expressed; that he ascribed those miracles to the working of Satan. Which may thus appear: he could not but know that Christ wrought miracles; this was generally known and acknowledged by those of his own sect, the Pharisees. It was not denied by the most malicious enemies that Christ had, John xi. 47. It is like Saul was an eye-witness of some of them, coming to the passover (as all such were bound to do), when Christ wrought many of his miracles, Mat. xxi. 14. At least he could not but know that the apostles wrought miracles; and they were done expressly to confirm this truth, that Jesus was the Messias. Either then he thought these miracles were done by the Spirit of God, and then he had been convinced that Jesus was the Christ; but this he says he was ignorant of while he was a persecutor. And since he thought them not done by the Spirit of God, what spirit could he think they were done by, but Beelzebub, that evil spirit? Now this was materially the very blasphemy of the Pharisees his associates.

And indeed he confesses he was a blasphemer, 1 Tim. i. 13, but adds, that which hindered his blasphemy from being that unpardonable blasphemy against the Holy Ghost, 'I did it ignorantly.' He did not know, he did not believe, that Jesus, whom he persecuted and blasphemed, was the Christ, acted and testified of by the Holy Ghost. If the rest of the Pharisees had done it ignorantly too, as he did, for anything I can see, their blasphemy had not risen up to the height of that sin which is declared to be unpardonable. So that, in fine, that particular blasphemy, Mat. xii., is not the unpardonable sin, but when it is against knowledge and conviction.

5. Every denying and renouncing of Christ, when it is against knowledge and conviction, is not the sin against the Holy Ghost. For Peter denied and renounced Christ, when he clearly knew, and was convinced that he was the Christ; when he fully believed it, and had openly professed and acknowledged it, Mat. xvi. 16. He denies him after admonition, denies him openly and scandalously, and this with cursing and swearing, against conscience, former resolutions, solemn engagements. A horrid sin indeed! Yet Peter repented, was pardoned. This was not the sin against the Holy Ghost. There was something of infirmity in it. He did it out of fear and passion, not wilfully, not presumptuously.

6. Every presumptuous sin is not the sin against the Holy Ghost. Though this be a sin of high provocation, and all persons, especially the people of God, are highly concerned to watch against it, as David, Ps. xix. 12. The Seventy render it, ἀπὸ ἀλλοτρίων, and vulgar, *ab alienis*, from strange sins. They are sins to which the people of God should be wholly strangers; and yet David himself was not altogether a stranger to it. There was too much presumption in those sins of adultery and murder. This latter especially was wilful, against knowledge and conscience, upon deliberation. He compassed not the death of Uriah, but by a series of plots and contrivances succeeding one another. And see how the prophet charges him, 2 Sam. xii. 9. In that he charges him with the despising the commandment of the Lord, he accuses him of sinning presumptuously. For this is the very phrase, by which the Holy Ghost expresses a presumptuous sin, Num. xv. 30, 31. And it is expressed by the same phrase, Heb. x. 28. A heinous sin indeed! There was no sacrifice for this sin under the law. If a man sinned ignorantly, an atonement might have been made for him by a sacrifice, so the Lord appointed. But if a man sinned presumptuously, no sacrifice was appointed, none could be accepted in lieu of his life, he was to die without mercy. This was a grievous sin indeed, yet not unpardonable; so David found it. But there is something more grievous in the sin against the Holy Ghost. For the apostle argues there from the less to the greater; from that as a less sin, to this as a greater, Heb. x. 28, 29. He that sins against the Holy Ghost (for he is describing that wickedness), shall be thought worthy of much sorer punishment, than he that, sinning presumptuously, despises Moses's law. And why worthy of much sorer punishment, but because it is a much more grievous sin? The sin against the Holy Ghost is not a sin of presumption only, but something more, something worse; something that has in it more provocation, and shall have sorer punishment.

Obj. 7. Faith is an application of the promise; the promise is conditional. And there are none have any ground to apply the promise, but they that have the condition, that is, it upon which the promise is suspended. Now, alas! I have not the condition, and what ground have I to apply the promise? I have no ground to believe. To apply the promise without ground, is not to believe, but to presume. It would be groundless presumption in me to offer it.

Ans. 1. Faith may be without the application of a promise. This cleared, the main foundation of this scruple falls. Now it is clear, both from the principal object and the first acts of faith.

The principal *object* of faith is *quid incomplexum*, it is Christ himself, not a proposition nor a promise; so that, if there be no promise which thou canst apply, yet is there an object for thy faith. Christ may be embraced, though not in a promise. It is true Christ must be discovered and offered, before he can be the object of faith; but so he may be in other parts of the word, not in the promise only. The whole gospel discovers and propounds Christ to sinners; the promises are but some parts of the gospel. The promise is not the only or the principal object of faith, but Christ himself.

And it is clear from the *acts* of faith too. The first acts of faith are acceptance of, or dependence on Christ, not the application of a promise. The application of a conditional promise is for assurance, and that is a consequent of faith, or faith in its growth and elevation, not in its first actings, Eph. i. The Spirit seals the promise to a soul by application, but that is after believing; some acts of faith go before it. The first act of believing is a hearty acceptance of Christ for a Lord and Saviour, or a soul's dependence on him for pardon and holiness. Indeed, these are both one; for to take Christ for a Lord and Saviour, which I call acceptance, and to commit myself to him, to be pardoned and governed by him, which is dependence, is the same thing.

You say you have no ground to apply the promise; well, but have you no ground to accept of Christ as he is offered, to apply yourselves to him for pardon and life, to commit your souls to him to be saved and ruled by him? have you no ground for this? Why, the command of God is a sufficient ground for this, he enjoins you to do it. The promise has a condition, you say, and the want of it hinders you from applying the promise. Ay, but what condition has the command to hinder you from obeying? Will not the Lord be obliged but upon condition? Is he not absolute Lord?

You say you may not apply the promise; but may you not give your consent that Christ shall be your Lord and husband, and rest on him accordingly? Why, this is it you are called to do; do but this heartily, and you believe on the Son, though you cannot apply the promise, John i. The receiving of Christ is the heart's consent to take him upon his own terms; and this is believing. Where this is there is faith, though there be no application of a promise.

Ans. 2. There are absolute promises, to which no condition is annexed; general offers of Christ, not restrained to special qualifications, Isa. xlviii. 9, Jer. xxxiii. 8, Micah vii. 18, Ezek. xxxvi. 26, Rev. xxi. 17. Now, though the want of the condition hinder a sensible sinner from applying conditional promises, yet why should want of the condition hinder him from applying those promises that have no conditions? I speak to those that are sensible and humbled; for secure and presumptuous sinners are too apt to catch at these, and thereby to harden and encourage themselves in their presumption, to their ruin; such have neither share nor lot in this encouragement. But for the humbled sinner, who is weary of sin, and would count it the greatest mercy to be rid of it, the way to these promises is set open to them. They were so delivered on purpose for their encouragement. To these I speak: Though ye cannot apply a conditional promise, yet can you not apply yourselves to Christ in an absolute promise? May you not apply Christ to yourselves in those free and general offers, wherein the Lord tenders him to you?

These are sufficient grounds of dependence, if not of assurance; sufficient encouragements to receive Christ, though not to apply him and rejoice in him as already received; sufficient to make him yours, if sons.* These offers will make him yours if you will close with them, though not prove him yours; that follows acceptance.

If a man should hold out his hand and offer you a jewel, you would think that a sufficient ground to take it, though he should not express by any special qualifications that he intended it for you in particular; nay, though he should speak never a word, yet being one who is not wont to delude any, his holding it out and offering it to you would be a sufficient encouragement to receive it. So it is here, the Lord holds out Christ to humbled sinners in the general offers of the gospel; and he is never wont to delude any, much less those that are returning to him. Is not his offer a sufficient ground for you to receive what he offers? If you cannot apply him upon promised conditions, yet may you not receive him offered freely? But 'whosoever will,' &c., close with that word, come and embrace Christ as he is offered; and in so doing you believe, though you cannot apply any other promise.

Ans. 3. The least degree of the condition in sincerity shews title to the promise. Perfection is required by the law, but it is not the condition of any promise of the gospel; perfection would be acceptable under the gospel, but sincerity is accepted. The gospel would have us strive after perfection, but it has pardon for imperfections; it has promises to the least degrees in truth, when accompanied with greatest imperfections, Mat. xii. 20. Though there be but in the soul a spark from heaven, more smoke than heat, almost smothered in corruptions and imperfections, yet this has the promise. Not to quench is to kindle, not to break is to strengthen; a μείωσις, where much more is intended than expressed, Mat. v. What less degree of righteousness or holiness than a sincere desire of it! Yet this has the promise of satisfaction and blessedness. And lest this should be thought a high degree of desire, it is expressed by willingness. It may be the sensible sinner concludes he wants the condition, because he has it not in such or such a degree, and then the discouragement is raised upon a mistake. The least degree shews thy right to the promise.

Ans. 4. He that has the condition of any one promise has title to all the promises; to all, except those which are made upon some special and singular account; for he that has the condition of any one promise is in Christ. And in Christ 'all the promises are yea and amen;' they shall all be accomplished to such a one faithfully and certainly. He that has the condition of any one promise is thereby admitted into the covenant of grace, the league with Christ. Now, the promises are so many several articles of the covenant, and he that is in league and covenant with Christ shall have the benefit of all the articles; he may upon that ground plead his right thereto.

The covenant is made up of so many promises, as a golden chain of so many links; one link draws with it all the whole chain. He that has hold of

* Qu. 'sinners'?—ED.

one, by virtue of that he has hold of all. Indeed, he that has the condition of any one promise, has the conditions of all the promises really; if not in his own apprehensions, in one degree or other, in principle or in act. For every condition of a promise evangelical is some gracious quality, or some act of such a quality. Now, as there is a concatenation of vices (as moralists), so there is a connection of graces (as divines). They are never found single, they are never divided; the soul that is possessed of one is possessed of all.

The sensible soul may be apt to conclude he has no qualification and no condition of any promise; it is because he has not such and such; but this is a great mistake, and he herein discourages himself from applying the promise without ground; for if he has any one, he has all and every one indeed, though not in his own apprehension; for they are never really divided.

Ans. 5. You may have the condition though you discern it not. It may be discernible in you though you do not see it, will not acknowledge it. Here is one difference between the humbled and secure sinner; the secure confident will conclude he has those qualifications which he never had; the humbled is apt to conclude he has them not when he is in possession of them. You cannot persuade those but they have that which they have not; you cannot persuade these that they have that which indeed they have. The least degree of the condition is not easily discernible; for that which is least is next to nothing, and it must be a quick eye that can discern that; and when it is come to be discernible by others, yet it is not easily discerned by himself; in that dejected state he is not apt to believe it; he has had such a sight and sense of his sinfulness and misery as hath brought himself quite out of conceit with himself, so he is more apt to suspect the worst than to believe anything that is good concerning himself; and, therefore, if the humbled soul would not mistake, he should not judge himself till he has duly examined, not pass sentence before a just trial.

And because he is more apt to mistake himself, he should consult with those who have more light to discover it, and will more impartially judge of it. Let me propound a question or two for trial: Hast thou not forsaken every sin? Is not thy heart resolved against every evil way? Doest not thou confess, bewail, and set thyself against every sin? Why, this is the condition of a promise, Prov. viii. 13. Wouldst thou not come to Christ if he would entertain thee? Wouldst thou not leave every by-path, how pleasant soever, wherein thou hast lost him? Doest not thou heartily consent to come to Christ upon those terms on which he calls thee? Why, this is a condition of a promise, John vi.

Ans. 6. Go to Christ for the condition. Believe, and you have the condition.

IV. It remains that I should shew by what means faith may be attained. Faith is the gift of God, but he gives it in his own way. Those that would come by it must walk in this way. If you would receive this gift, set yourselves in that way wherein he is wont to communicate it.

Faith is the work of God. But he works it not immediately, but in the use of appointed means. He can work it without means, but he will not do so ordinarily. It will be presumption to expect extraordinary acts, while the ordinary way is open.

The means prescribed cannot effect faith of themselves. They are no further effectual, than as instruments in the hand of him who is the principal cause. They can do nothing without him. But usually he does nothing in this business without them. It is his power that works faith; but in that way, and by those means, which he has prescribed. Though he has not absolutely tied and confined himself to them, yet he has tied and confined us. Though he is free, yet the means are necessary to us.

I shall but instance in two, viz., prayer, and hearing the word; and will endeavour to shew you that they are means appointed for this end; and withal how you may use them so as this end may be attained, laying down some particular directions for this purpose.

1. For *prayer*, that one way wherein the Lord will be sought, and wherein he may be found. That is one means which the Lord will have used for this end, Ezek. xxxvi. 26. Here is a promise of the first grace, under the notion of a new heart. He promises conversion and regeneration, of which faith is a principal part. But in what way will he accomplish this and those other promises? What means will he have used for this end? That he shews, ver. 37.

So Saul, after he was humbled and struck down in an extraordinary way, before his conversion was completed by the Lord concurring with the ministry of Ananias, before he was filled with the Holy Ghost, we find him seeking of God, Acts ix. 11. The Lord takes notice of this in Saul, and will have Ananias to take notice of it, to encourage him in his work. Here is the way wherein this chosen vessel was carried. And you see, both by precept and example, that it is your way; if ever you would meet with faith, walk in it. It concerns every sinner who is not careless of his soul, who has any regard of everlasting life, any fear of everlasting death, any care of his eternal state, who is not desperately regardless of all that is dearest to him, to be seeking God for faith. For upon this are the issues of life and death. You especially, to whom the Lord has shewed so much mercy, as to shew you your want of faith, your necessity of it, your misery without it, be diligent, be importunate with God in prayer, that he would give you faith. Whatever you do, pray; whatever you pray for, pray for faith especially. The life of your souls depends on it.

Pray diligently. Spend that time in prayer which you have been wont to mis-spend in idleness, in vanities, in unnecessary employments. You have thrown away too much time already; that which remains is short, you know not how short. Labour to redeem it. Redeem time from your vanities and recreations, from your worldly business, yea, from your meat and sleep, rather than want time to seek God for this. For faith is of far more concernment to you than the world, than your pleasures, yea, than your meat and sleep, than your bodies and lives; the everlasting life of soul and body depends on faith. The wrath of God is more dreadful than poverty and wants, yea, than death itself. And till you believe, the wrath of God abides on you. Oh then seek God for this, above all things seek him, seek him night and day, give him no rest, &c.

Pray importunately. Seek faith of God, as a condemned malefactor would beg a pardon. There is no pardon without faith. Seek this of God, as one that feels and sees a sword at his breast, sees death present before his eyes, would sue for his life. There is no life for you without faith. Fall down before God, and cry to him as for life, Oh give me faith, else I die! I may live without friends, or wealth, or honours, or pleasures; but I cannot live without faith. There is nothing but death for me in unbelief. Lord, whatever thou deny me, deny me not faith. I am lost, undone, I perish, I am a dead man, without faith. It had been better I had never been born, than to live in unbelief; the wrath of God abides on me, while I abide in this woeful state; and so it is like to abide on me for ever. I shall never see life, unless I believe; there is no hope for me till then. My case is miserable and desperate till I believe, and I can never believe unless thou give me faith. Lord, give me faith, or else I die. Get the sense of your misery without faith, and let this stir you up to be importunate. Content not yourselves to seek it in a careless, heartless, formal way; but seek it as that on which the life and happiness of your souls depends.

Obj. But what ground has he to pray, who is an unbeliever? His prayer is sin: 'The sacrifice of the wicked is an abomination to the Lord,' Prov. xv. What encouragement has he that his prayer may be heard, who cannot pray in faith? What has he to plead for himself, either for audience or acceptance, who has no promise to be heard, who has no interest in the intercession of Christ for acceptance? It seems either that prayer is not his duty, or else that he has no encouragement to perform it.

This is a difficulty which may be of very dangerous consequence, if it be not removed. There is that wrapt in it, which is apt to mislead some in their judgments, others in their practice, and that in a way very injurious and dishonourable to God, very dangerous and pernicious to the souls of men. And therefore it highly concerns us to remove this stumbling-block, and satisfy this scruple, which Satan may make such a great advantage of, both against God and men. That this may be done clearly and fully, I shall (1.) shew the ground of the objection is a mistake; (2.) prove that prayer is a necessary duty to unbelievers; (3.) shew that they have encouragement to pray; (4.) what pleas they may use for themselves in begging for faith. For the

(1.) The ground of the objection is this, that the prayer of an unbeliever is sin, that it is a sin for him to pray; and hence it is inferred, that he ought not to pray. That the mistake herein may appear, observe,

[1.] Though an unbeliever sin in praying, yet it is not a sin for him to pray. There is sin in the manner of his praying; but prayer, as to the act and substance of it, is his duty. He sins, not because he prays, that is required of him, but because he prays amiss, not in that manner that is required of him. There are abominations in the prayers of a wicked man, but for him to pray is not an abomination, it is the good and acceptable will of God, that which he commands. He commands him to pray, and he sins not in complying with the command, so far it is obedience; but he prays not as he ought to do, there is his sin. Now he should leave his sin, not his duty. He should pray better in another manner, that is all which can be inferred, not that he should not pray at all. For so he leaves not his sin, but his duty. A boy is learning to write; he scribbles at first untowardly, makes, it may be, more blots than letters. It is his fault that he blots, not that he writes, that is his duty; in this case you would have him leave blotting, not leave writing. So here, the act of prayer is a duty, but the manner of performing this act, therein is the fault; this should be corrected, but the act should not be omitted. Ay, but since an unbeliever cannot perform his duty in the manner that he ought, were it not as good he should not perform it at all? No, not so. For observe,

[2.] An undue performing is better than a total neglect. Better he should do what he can in a way of obedience than do nothing at all; better pray as he can, though he cannot pray as he ought, than not pray at all.

If your servant do what you command, you like it better (though he do it not in that manner, and for that end which you desire) than if he should refuse to obey you at all.

An unbeliever sins, whether he pray or pray not. Such a woeful necessity has sin brought him into, that he cannot but sin, whatever he does. But in this case the less evil must be chosen. Now when the Lord enjoins a duty, not to do it at all is a total disobedience; to do it in an undue manner is but a partial disobedience. Not to do the act is a wilful disobedience; to fail in the manner of doing it is an unavoidable disobedience. Now a total disobedience is far worse than that which is but partial; a wilful disobedience is far more provoking than an unavoidable failing. He may do the act if he will; if he do it not, he wilfully rebels: he cannot do it as he ought, his falling short therein is that which cannot be avoided. So it is far more excusable, far less sinful, to pray as he can, than not to pray at all. His best is bad enough; yet he must do his best, else he sins more, and shall suffer more.

[3.] If an unbeliever must not pray, because he sins in praying, then believers themselves must not pray for this reason too, because they also sin in praying. 'In many things we offend all,' James iii. 2. 'All their righteousness is as a menstruous rag,' Isa. lxiv. 6. The best of them, when they do their best, fall far short of praying in that manner as they ought; they sin in the manner themselves.

Oh, but they sin less herein than unbelievers.

I answer, If they may pray, though they sin in praying, because they sin less; by the same reason unbelievers may pray, because they sin less in praying than in omitting prayer, as before.

[4.] If an unbeliever may not pray, because he sins in praying, then by the same reason he must not do any thing at all, because he cannot do any thing in the world, but in doing of it he sins. He must not do any thing spiritual, or civil, yea, or natural; for he sins in all as much as in praying. He must not read, nor hear the word (though this be the plain duty of heathens and infidels), because not mixing the word with faith, he sins in that. He must not work, not do the necessary duties of his calling (if this were a sufficient reason) for he sins in that, Prov. xxi. 4. He must not eat; for that ensnares him in sin. His table is a snare. He must not speak; for therein he sins, Prov. xii. 18. He must not walk or converse with men, for even his way is an abomination, Prov. xv. 9.

Now if this be absurd, that an unbeliever must not hear, nor work, nor speak, nor eat, nor move, notwithstanding he sins in all these (as indeed there can scarce any greater absurdity fall into the imagination of a man), then it is absurd that an unbeliever must not pray, notwithstanding he sins in praying. If that woeful necessity of sinning in all these will not hinder any of them from being his duty, no more can it hinder prayer from being his duty. This may be sufficient to shew the vanity of the objection, the mistake of the ground upon which it is raised.

(2.) The necessity of it. Prayer is a necessary duty to wicked men and unbelievers; and that will appear many ways. But briefly:

[1.] The Lord's express commands directed to such, enjoining them to seek him and call upon him, Isa. lv. 6. It is taken by many to be an exhortation directed to the Gentiles not yet converted; and so prayer is a duty before conversion; but whether it be Gentiles or Jews for whom it is intended, it is for such as are wicked and unrighteous, as appears, ver. 7. Wicked and unrighteous men are enjoined to seek God, and call upon him, and those that are such in a high degree. The most abominable sinner in the world is called the man of sin, and that is the expression here; the 'unrighteous' is in the original the 'man of iniquity.' So Acts viii., Peter lays the injunction upon Simon Magus, when he knew him to be a graceless wretch, ver. 21, 23. He directs him to pray, ver. 22.

[2.] Neglect of prayer by unbelievers is threatened. The prophet's imprecation is the same in effect with a threatening, Jer. x. 25, and the same imprecation, Ps. lxxix. 6. The prophets would not have used such an imprecation against those that call upon God, but that their neglect of calling on his name makes them liable to his wrath and fury; and no neglect makes men liable to the wrath of God but the neglect of duty. Prayer then is a duty even to the heathen, the neglect of which provokes him to pour out his fury on them.

[3.] We have examples for it in Scripture, such as are unquestionable. The example of the prophets by divine instinct calling wicked men to this duty, Joel i. 14, all the inhabitants; and yet many of the inhabitants were extremely wicked, such as deserved to be cut off both from church and state, and such as the Lord is threatening to cut off by a destroying judgment, ver. 15. And yet all these must join in prayer, he leaves no scruple for joining in this duty with wicked men; yea, sucking children must join too, lest any think that little ones have nothing to do with prayer, Joel ii. 16.

[4.] The Lord charges the neglect of this duty upon wicked men as a heinous crime; as that which involves them, or shews them to be involved, in the greatest and most horrible guilt.

First. He charges it as an act of pride and contempt of God, Ps. x. 4. If prayer be not the duty of wicked men, then pride and contempt of God is no sin. The connection which the Holy Ghost makes between these does make this evident.

Secondly. It is charged as the casting off all fear of God, which is the height of profaneness, Job. xv. 4. If it be not a duty for all to pray, it is not a sin to cast off all fear of God.

Thirdly. It is charged as atheism, one of the characters by which the atheist is described, Ps. xiv. 1, 2. Those that do not seek God, say in their hearts there is no God. So ver. 4. Who are they that say in their hearts there is no God? Why, he describes them to be such as call not upon the Lord. This is a plain sign of speculative, a principal act of practical atheism. So Psalm x. It may be read, 'All his thoughts are, there is no God.' He that will not seek after God, does hereby shew that all his thoughts are, there is none. Those that would not have all men to pray, would have all men to be atheists. Atheism is not a sin, if calling on God be not their duty.

[5.] This will appear, if we consider what prayer is, in these particulars.

First. It is an act of respect and honour due to God from every man by the light of nature. It is not an act of positive and instituted worship, peculiar to the church and the true members thereof, as the seals of the covenant are; but it is an act of natural worship due from men, not as they are Christians, but as they are men; and so due from men always, and indispensably due. No sinfulness can disoblige any man from his duty; no, nor anything else but that which makes him cease to be a man; for that which is due by the law of nature is of eternal obligement; and we see the light of nature led the mariners in Jonah to this duty, though those heathens had no revealed light, no knowledge of Scripture.

Those that would not have wicked men to pray, would not have them give that honour and respect to God which is due by the light and dictate of nature.

Further. Prayer is an acknowledgment of your dependence upon God: Ps. lxxix. 6. 'That acknowledge thee not, by calling on thy name.' The plain import of prayer is to acknowledge that all we have we receive it from God, and that all we want we expect it from God alone. Now, if it were [not the duty of unbelievers to pray, it would not be their duty to acknowledge their dependence on the Lord; not to acknowledge that he is God, and that they are creatures; that in him they live and move, and have their being; that every good and perfect gift comes from the Father of lights; but that they might have these without him.

Finally. Prayer, if we consider it in its essence and nature, is a motion which the soul makes to God; it is the soul's desire of what it asks; it is but the turning God's commands into requests. Now, if it were not the duty of unbelievers to pray, it is not their duty to desire to please God, to know him, to obey him. To instance in that which is for our present purpose. If it be not the duty of unbelievers to pray for faith, it is not their duty to desire faith; for prayer is essentially a desire, &c. When the Lord has declared that without faith it is impossible to please him, it would not be their duty to desire to please him. When he has declared that faith gives glory to God, it would not be their duty to desire to glorify him. When he has declared this to be his commandment, that they believe, &c., it would not be their duty to desire to obey him, and to comply with his revealed will. When he has declared that he that believes not makes God a liar, it would not be their duty to desire not to give God the lie.

If it be a necessary duty for unbelievers to desire these things, it is their necessary duty to pray for them; for prayer essentially is nothing but the soul's desire.

(3.) I shall endeavour to shew what encouragement a man, yet without faith, may have to address himself to the Lord in prayer.

He has no such encouragement as the Lord offers to believers; but some encouragement he hath, especially a sensible sinner, one who is in the way to faith, though he be not yet arrived at it. I will give you an account of this in some particulars. And herein I shall not leave the good old way, though the path wherein I walk may seem solitary.

[1.] He may find some acceptance with God, some kind of acceptance; not a full acceptance, so as his person shall be accepted with his prayer; for the person cannot be accepted till he be in Christ, and he is not in Christ but by faith; and so the person of an unbeliever cannot be accepted.

Nor is it an absolute acceptance; for in that sense, 'without faith it is impossible to please God;' he cannot please him absolutely. But he may find in his prayer a comparative acceptance, and that both negatively;—the Lord is not so much displeased with his prayers, though there be sin in them, as with other sinful acts. He was not so much displeased with Ahab humbling himself, as with his other wickedness. A less degree of displeasure is something considerable; it may bear the name of acceptance by some warrant from Scripture; for as a less degree of love is called hatred, Luke xiv. 26, so a less degree of displeasedness may be called acceptance.

We may express it positively too. The Lord is more pleased with the prayers of such, than he is with not only their open sins, but than he is with other acts that have a show of goodness. For as acts of sin against the first table are more heinous, and do more provoke God, than acts of sin against the second, so, in proportion, acts of obedience to the precepts of the first table, such as prayer, being an act of worship immediately respecting God, are more pleasing to him than acts of justice or charity respecting men.

Such acts of worship, though in unbelievers, they are not spiritually good; yet there may be a moral goodness in them, which is pleasing and acceptable to God, so far forth that he likes the work, and approves it with that common allowance which he affords to all things done in compliance with his will, and bearing any stamp of his own goodness; though not so much as to accept the person, and receive it into any special favour. He has a common acceptance for common and moral goodness, and the more by how much the more it respects himself; and acts of worship, such as prayer, respect him more than others. When there is a moral and common affection and sincerity in prayer, Gen. xx. 6, as some yet in unbelief may have, though not a special and spiritual affection, the Lord likes it, and accepts it, so far as it is the work and effect of his own common grace. This our divines grant in their contests with the Arminians. (*Vid.* Pemble, p. 83.)

Now this is some encouragement to pray. You cannot do anything in unbelief more pleasing to God. You displease him more when you neglect prayer: he has a comparative liking of them, a common acceptance and approbation for them.

[2.] The Lord may hear such prayers; he may so far accept them as to hear them. Though he have not engaged himself by promise to do it, yet he has not tied up himself, so as he may not do it. Though an unbeliever have no promise, and so no certainty that his prayers shall succeed, yet he has some probability; there is some likelihood that they will not miscarry. He has a *may be* for it, and that is counted encouragement enough to act in other cases. Peter gives this encouragement even to Simon Magus to pray, Acts ix. 22. He determines it not against him, but leaves in suspense a question undecided for or against him; possibly thy sin may not be forgiven, but perhaps it may be forgiven, prayer may prevail for pardon. The men of Nineveh were hereby encouraged to pray, Jonah iii. 9. It is not certain he will, it is not certain he will not; he may, for anything we know. They had thus much, and no more encouragement, in Joel ii. 14.

The people of God sometimes find no more encouragement than such a *may be*, Amos v. 15. Caleb expresses no more, Jos. xiv. 12. You count this an encouragement enough to put you upon moral endeavours, and why not upon prayer? Though it be not certain that he will hear and answer, yet he may hear and answer; there is nothing certain to the contrary. Soldiers do continually venture their lives, and merchants do constantly venture their estates, when they have no surer ground to succeed. And is not this encouragement enough to engage in a necessary duty?

[3.] The Lord does many times answer the prayers of unbelievers. We have many examples hereof in Scripture. It is not only a *may be*, but we see it actually done. Ishmael is represented to us as a persecutor, and as one excluded from Abraham's spiritual seed, Gal. iv. 29, and yet the Lord heard his cry in the day of his extremity, Gen. xxi. 17. The mariners in Jonah are expressed to be heathens and idolaters, yet seeking God importunately that he would not let let them perish for Jonah's life, whom they cast into the sea, Jonah i. 14, and we have the return of their prayer in the next ver. 15, 'The sea ceased,' &c.; so the men of Nineveh, whose wickedness was gone up to heaven; yet crying unto the Lord, he was entreated, and answers them graciously, Jonah iii. 10. Yea, Ahab, the wickedest king that ever Israel had, though they had few or none but such as were wicked after the division, yet none like him, 1 Kings xxi. 25. Yet when he humbled himself, and sought God, he prevailed; and he sends him an answer of his prayer by the prophet, who had denounced the wrath of God against him, ver. 28, 29.

So that the Lord hears the prayers of such who have less ground to hope for any such thing than the sensible sinner. Here is that which may encourage all to pray, but here is more encouragement for such a one; he may fare better, when the worst fare so well.

[4.] The Lord has more respect to those prayers that are made for spiritual mercies than petitions put up for temporal blessings; such are more pleasing to him, more according to his will, and he manifests it by making readier returns thereto. He has expressed his liking and approbation of prayers, not so much in respect to the person praying as in respect to the things prayed for, and has answered them upon this account. There is a notable instance hereof in his acceptance of Solomon's petition, 1 Kings iii. 10–12. The Lord was well pleased with his prayer because of the thing that he prayed for, ver. 10; and because he asked an understanding heart, and not such things as nature is more apt to desire; upon this account the Lord grants his request, ver. 11, 12, and that with an overplus, ver. 13. Yet this seems to be but a moral accomplishment, an endowment that might fitly qualify him as a magistrate to discern between right and wrong, good and bad, to do judgment and justice.

And if the Lord be better pleased with petitions for moral accomplishments than with those for riches, or long life, and outward success, by consequence he may be better pleased with prayers for spiritual blessings than those for moral accomplishments; if he be so ready to hear prayers for moral virtues, he may be more ready to hear prayers for spiritual graces. Corrupt nature has less inclination to these, the Lord is more honoured by them, and is more pleased with them. What an encouragement is this for those that want faith, to pray for it; being the chief spiritual accomplishment, and that which is the root of the rest. What hopes are here, that such requests will be heard and granted. What encouragement that such a request will please the Lord, when that very thing is asked which is most pleasing to him.

[5.] If unbelievers should seek spiritual blessings of God, as far as natural men may do, the Lord would seldom or never reject their requests. I do not only say he would not ordinarily deny them, but he would seldom or never deny them. But this must be taken cautiously. It must be observed that few, or rather none, in the state of unbelief, do seek for spiritual blessings to the utmost of their ability, as far as they may do. It is likely that sensible sinners come nearest to this; but even they, when they stretch out their endeavours farthest, do fall short of what they might do; when they do most, they do not their utmost. And it must be farther observed, that if natural men should do their utmost, yet this would not oblige the Lord to confer grace on them. No prayers or endeavours of natural men whatsoever, not the utmost improvement of the power of nature herein, can lay any engagement upon God; but he remains free, when all is done, to bestow grace or deny it. This we hold firm against Pelagians of all sorts and sizes. But yet we say there cannot be an instance given of any one man in the world that ever sought God so far as a natural man may do for spiritual blessings, and was notwithstanding denied and rejected. Such an example cannot be produced, nor hath it yet fallen under any man's observation. There seems to be an instance to the contrary in Esau, but it is a mistake, Heb. xii. 14. For this was a repentance in his father, not a repentance in himself, that he sought so carefully and so passionately. The word *μετάνοια*, rendered repentance, signifies a change of the mind; and this was it which he sought of his father, to change his father's mind. Isaac, his father, had given the blessing to Jacob, his brother; he would have his father change his mind as to this particular, and give the blessing, not to his brother, but to him. This was the repentance that he sought; he would have Isaac repent of this, that he had given the blessing of the first-born to the younger brother, Gen. xxvii. Now as this consideration clears up the justice of God in his proceedings against sinners, since none perish but such as do not what in them lies, do not their utmost to be saved, so it gives a great encouragement to all, especially to sensible sinners, to stir up themselves to seek faith, seeing no instance can be given of any who sought it of God, so far as a natural man may do, that ever miscarried, or were rejected. It cannot be observed that any man ever sought it so far as his power would reach, and so far as he was hereto moved by the Spirit of God, and yet fell short of faith; it hath not been observed that such prayers did not succeed.

[6.] The Lord does more respect the prayers of those for whom he has designed faith, when they seek him for it, than the prayers of others. Their persons and prayers are not fully accepted till they actually believe, but their requests are more accepted than their prayers for other things, or the prayers of other men. And there is special reason for it; for the Lord has some love for them even before they believe; not that which is called *amor complacentiæ*, the love of complacency and delight, for so he affects none but those that actually believe, and are thereby brought into a state of union with Christ, and reconciliation to God; but he affects such with that love which is called *amor benevolentiæ*, a love of good will; he bears them a secret good will, though he do not yet express it. He has an inclination to do them good, it is his purpose to bestow faith and those spiritual blessings on them which they are praying for. Now their prayers concurring with his own purpose, and being agreeable both to his revealed and his secret will as to the matter of them, must needs be so far acceptable.

Besides, Christ has purchased faith and spiritual blessings for those to whom the Father has designed them. And the intercession of Christ is, as it were, a continual representation of those sufferings whereby he has purchased these blessings for them, that by virtue thereof, they may be communicated in their season. Therefore, when such pray for faith, they pray for that which he did not only purchase, but for which he is then interceding. Now such prayers as go along with the intercession of Christ, and are interested in it, must needs be so far acceptable and prevail. He that is seeking that of God, for which Christ himself is interceding, will surely be heard. As redemption, so Christ's intercession is not only for actual believers, but for those of his chosen who want faith, that they may be made believers. The prayers of such for faith will be heard and answered, not by their own virtue, but by virtue of the intercession of Christ.

But what encouragement is all this, though very great in itself, to a sensible sinner, since he knows not, nor can know, that God has designed faith for him, and consequently knows not that the Lord bears any good will to him, or that Christ has any respect to him in his intercession?

I answer, whether he know it or no, these things, though hidden and secret, will have their effect, and they will have such an influence on his prayers as will render them so far accepted as to prevail for answer.

And farther, though he know not this certainly, for there can be no certainty of it till he believe actually, yet he has some probabilities for it, some probable grounds on which to hope it. The Lord has brought the sensible sinner into the way that leads to faith, he has given him a heart to use the means whereby faith is attained, he has carried him on so far as few go but those that reach. And these are fair probabilities that the Lord has designed faith for him, that he has a good will to give it him, and that Christ is interceding for this purpose.

Such encouragement there is even for unbelievers to pray for faith, such encouragement the sensible sinner has to seek God for it. It is not only his duty to pray, there is not only a necessity for it, but he may do it with great hopes to succeed. He has special encouragement, not only to pray diligently, importunately, but to carry him on cheerfully in this duty. And though this last consideration speak peculiarly to the humbled sinner, yet the other particulars encourage every sinner to be much and often in seeking God for faith.

(4.) What pleas may the sensible sinner use in prayer? What has he to plead for himself when he is seeking faith of God?

A believer indeed has many and strong pleas. He may plead the promise, whereby the Lord has engaged himself to hear him. He may plead the covenant, wherein the truth and faithfulness of God is engaged. He may plead the mediation of Christ, his purchase and intercession. He may plead Christ's relation to him as his friend, his brother, as his head, his husband. Here is strength in these pleas, and such as afford strong support. But what has the sensible sinner to plead, who has no interest in the covenant or promise, who knows not that Christ has any love for him, or any relation to him? Why, even he has many things to plead, though they come short to these; such as may make him fervent, importunate, and affectionate; such as may encourage him thereto, and support his heart therein. And these are the proper ends of using pleas in prayer. Not to move God, or make any impression on him, for such motion would infer some change, some alteration in God, and that is inconsistent with his perfection, who is without variableness or shadow of changing. But the use and end of them is to make impression on our own hearts, to work upon our affections, to stir us up to more fervency and importunity, and to afford some support and encouragement, that our hearts may not be dead and formal, and our spirits may not sink and faint in our addresses to God. Now the sensible sinner has many things which he may make use of for this purpose. He may plead,

[1.] His misery. How miserable he is without faith. I spread before you the miseries [of] an unbeliever in the first use. The sensible sinner may spread this before God, as Hezekiah did Rabshakeh's letter in his prayer. This was the plea which the man in the gospel used for his son, Mat. xvii. 15, 'My son is miserably vexed.' He lays open his misery, ver. 16, and this plea prevailed, ver. 18. As he pleaded for his son, plead thou for thy soul, lay open its miseries before Christ. Lord, what misery is it to be excluded from life, to be dead while I live! Unless thou give me faith, I shall never see life. What misery is it to be under wrath! How great is my misery, who am under the wrath of the great God! How unavoidable my misery, who am under abiding wrath! What joy can I have in any enjoyment, when the wrath of God is mixed with all! What comfort can my life be to me, when the wrath of God hangs continually over me! Out of the depths cry unto God, out of the depths of that misery wherein unbelief has sunk thee. Lord, hear me! bring my soul out of this mire and clay, out of unbelief, the pit wherein there is no water, no comfort, no refreshment, no relief. Thou takest no pleasure of the miseries of wretched creatures. It is no delight to thee that I am miserable, but rather that I should live. Lord, give me faith, or else I shall never see life; give me faith, or else I shall be for ever miserable.

[2.] He may plead mercy. This was the publican's plea, Luke xviii. 13, and it prevailed, ver. 14. This is the proper plea for a sensible sinner, the suitableness, the largeness, the freeness of mercy. He may plead,

First, The *suitableness* of mercy. His misery, of which he is so sensible, renders mercy suitable to him. Misery is the proper object of mercy. Who is mercy for, if not for the miserable? Mercy would be lost, it would be an useless perfection, an attribute without use or exercise, if it did not let out itself to misery; for it has no other object, but those that are miserable.

Secondly, The *largeness* of mercy, Ps. cxlv. 9. His mercy is like the firmament spread over all this lower world; and every inferior creature partakes more or less of its influence, according to its exigence and capacity. True, may he say, I have made myself, by sin, the vilest of all creatures; I am become worse than the beasts that perish; as vile as a worm, as loathsome as a toad, by reason of the venomous corruption that is in my heart, and this woeful contrariety to the nature of a holy God. But there is mercy over all, even over such vile and loathsome creatures as these; there may be some over me, though wrath do now abide on me. Oh let that mercy, whose glory it is to stretch itself over all, reach my soul also! Oh that the blessed and powerful influence thereof would beget faith in my heart!

Thirdly, The *freeness* of mercy. That is its nature, its genius. It needs no motive, it expects no worth nor value in its object, to draw it out. It runs freely; no sin or unworthiness can stop the current of it. It is a great depth; though there be a mountain of sin, it can cover and overflow it; that can no more hinder the outflowings of mercy, than a rock can hinder the motions and flowings of the sea. Here is an encouraging plea for a sensible sinner. Lord, may he say, I have nothing to move thee to shew me mercy, nothing to engage thee to be gracious to me; nothing but what may engage thee against me, to shut me out from mercy. Oh but free mercy can move itself; it looks for no motive from without; there is enough to move it in its own bowels. If sin and unworthiness may exclude a sinner from faith and mercy, I may lie down in sorrow and despair for ever. Oh but it is the glory of mercy to run freely, to flow out upon those that are most unworthy. Such am I, O Lord, the unworthiest of any ever sought faith in thee, that ever found mercy with thee. But the more unworthy, the more will it be for the glory of thy mercy that I perish not; the more will the lustre and riches of thy grace appear, in giving me faith. Glorify thy mercy on such an object. Have mercy on me, O Lord, that I perish not.

[3.] He may plead his impotency, his own inability to believe, and the insufficiency of all things to help him to faith, unless the Lord help him.

This was the poor impotent man's plea, he that lay at the pool of Bethesda, John v. 6, 7, and it prevailed. Let this be thy plea. I have been sick of sin, nay, spiritually dead in unbelief many years; there is a fountain opened for sin and for uncleanness, a healing, sovereign virtue in that fountain, able to restore my soul to life and health. But, alas! I cannot move towards it of myself, and I have none to put me in. I have been a long time in this languishing condition, and I shall be so for ever, unless thou pity me. There is life for me in Christ, if I could but come to him, if I could but touch him; but such is my impotency, to such a low condition has sin brought my soul, that of myself I cannot come to Christ; I cannot move towards him, though I die for it. There is none come to him, unless the Father draw them. Lord, 'draw me, and I shall run after thee.' I would believe; 'Lord, help my unbelief.' Help, Lord; for vain is the help of man. There is no help for me in myself; there is no help for me in any creature. I am altogether helpless, I am utterly hopeless, unless the Lord help. Such is the violence of my distemper, such is the strength of my unbelief, as it is too hard for men or angels, it is too hard for all creatures, for all ordinances; nothing can overpower it but an infinite, an almighty power. Stretch out that almighty arm, and rescue my perishing soul from going down into destruction. This is a work beseeming the greatness of that power which worketh wonders, to which nothing is impossible, nothing difficult. Is anything too hard for God? Lord, shew thyself to be God; shew forth thy glory, by doing that for me which men and angels, which heaven and earth cannot do for me. They all say to me, while they see me perishing, If the Lord do not help thee, how shall we help? Oh I have destroyed myself, but in thee alone is my help. The more helpless my condition is, the more will it be for thy glory to help me. In vain is salvation hoped for from the mountains, in vain is faith expected from prayers, from ordinances, &c.; it is the Lord alone can help me to faith. Help, Lord, for vain is all other help.

[4.] He may plead the will of God. He commands sinners to believe; he threatens them in case they will not believe; he declares that he is highly dishonoured by unbelief. He appointed his gospel to be preached, and sends messengers to preach it, for this very end, that sinners might be brought to faith. He complains when his report is not believed, and he is glorified by believing. All this makes it evident that it is his will the sensible sinner should believe. Hence he may encourage himself to pray for faith. Lord, I have been too long disobedient to the heavenly call, I have too long resisted thy holy will; but now I would comply with the will of God, so far as I know it. I have no way to know it but by the word, and that speaks plainly, it is thy command I should believe. Why, Lord, let thy will be done in my heart; let this law of faith be written in my inward parts. If it were not thy will, I durst not ask it, I could not expect it; but since it is thy will, Lord, let it be done on earth, as it is [in] heaven. What may be done, if the will of God may not be done? What may I seek for, if not for this, that thy will may be done? What may be obtained, if this will not be obtained, that the will of God may be fulfilled? If I should ask of thee riches, or long life, or great things for myself, this might be thought rather my will than thine; but it is thy will that I should believe: 'Lord, not my will, but thine be done.' Give me a heart to believe, that I may obey thee, for thou hast commanded it. Give me a heart to believe, that I may please thee, for thou hast declared it to be thy good pleasure. Give me a heart to believe, that I may honour thee, for thou hast declared that gives glory to thee. He may plead this with great encouragement that his plea will prevail; for what petitions will succeed, if not those which are for things according to his will, those wherewith he is best pleased, and things which tend most for his glory? Though the person of a petitioner were distasteful to the prince, yet if his petition were for things that pleased him, and tended to the advancement of his honour and interest, and such as he had enjoined those that are least acceptable to him to sue for, in all probability they would be granted. So, though the person of the sensible sinner be not accepted in the sight of God, yet since, when he prays for faith, he petitions for that which is most acceptable to God, &c., there is great hopes they will succeed, there is much encouragement in such a plea.

[5.] He may plead the descent of faith, it is the gift of God: and the nature of this gift, it is a free gift. A gift, Philip. i. 29; a free gift, Eph. ii. 8. Not only salvation, but faith, the condition of salvation, the way to it, is χάρισμα, a free gift. Hence the sensible sinner may argue, Faith is a gift, therefore it may be asked, sued for; it is a free gift, and therefore it may be given to those that are unworthy; and then, why not to me? It is not to be bought or purchased, it is a gift; it is not to be merited or deserved, it is a free gift. The Lord expects no such thing as price or merit: the nature of the benefit will not admit it. Now, may I not seek that which the Lord is wont to give? May I not obtain that which is wont to be given freely? It is a gift that comes from the Father of lights, who gives liberally, and upbraids no man. The sinner may set this against all that sinfulness, unworthiness, unpreparedness, which Satan usually suggests to the humbled soul, to hinder him from praying, or to cut him off from hopes of succeeding.

[6.] He may plead the examples of those who have obtained faith, and that against the greatest unlikelihoods and improbabilities that may be. Who would have thought that she, whose heart was the seat of seven devils, should ever have been made a receptacle for faith and the Holy Spirit of promise? Who would have thought that those bloody wretches who crucified Christ should ever have found grace to believe, and entertain him in their hearts by faith? Yet so did some thousands of them, Acts ii. Who would have thought that Saul, who was such a persecutor, such a blasphemer, should ever have found mercy to become a believer? Yet he found mercy, and mercy to believe, and for this end that his example might be a standing plea for encouraging all that should believe after him to the end of the world, 1 Tim. i. 13, 15, 16.

[7.] He may plead his willingness to submit to any condition, the lowest, the meanest that can be, so he may but find this favour with the Lord. We find the prodigal making use of this, Luke xv. 18, 19. Lord, such a wretch as I have been, have little reason to expect that high relation of a son, that dear affection of a father, that is too much for one so unworthy. Only I would be thine, though in a lower relation; I would belong to thee; I would not be quite shut out from a father's house, though I can never look to be entertained as a child. Lord, do but entertain me, though in the lowest capacity, though in the meanest employment; let me be thy servant, so I may but have a place in the family; nay, let me be but the meanest of servants, a hired servant, no better used, no more respected. I will submit, I will be thankful, whatever my condition be, so I be not quite disowned. Lord, let me be thine, and it is enough, in what relation soever; and that I may be thine, give me a heart to believe; without faith I can have no interest in thee. This plea in the prodigal was prevailing for more than he had the confidence to plead for, ver. 21. 22. The father's affection breaks out in the midst of the plea, and cuts him off there, would not let him vilify himself farther. Instead of using of him as a hired servant, he commands his servants to wait on him as his son. Such a plea was that of the woman of Canaan, Mat. xv. 26, 27.

[8.] He may plead Christ's prayer. He, when he was on earth, prayed for those that did not then, that do not yet believe, John xvii. 20. He prays not only for those who did actually, but for those who yet had not faith, for those who yet were not in the way to faith, for those who yet had no being. Now the sensible sinner is in a more hopeful condition than some of those for whom Christ prays; for he is in the way to faith, and that is a strong probability that he is one for whom Christ put up this petition. And for what does he pray? see ver. 21. He prays that they may have union with the Father and himself. Now the bond of this union is faith. He prays then that those who did not yet believe may have faith in him, and so union with him. He prays that sensible sinners may have faith. Now, though the Lord hear not sinners, yet he always hears his Son. He was heard in that which he feared, he cannot be denied in that which he desired. Here is a strong plea indeed. Methinks it should be strong enough, not only to confirm faith in those that have it, but to work faith in those that want it. Methinks it should be effectual, not only to persuade the humbled sinner to pray, but to believe; not only to pray with some hopes, but to pray in faith.

[9.] He may plead the compassions of Christ to hardened and rejected sinners. For from hence he may argue there are more compassions for him, Luke xix, 41, 42. This was the city who shewed such obstinacy in rejecting Christ, that he gives her over as one whose condition was desperate, of whom he had not hopes; and yet even for such he has some pity, which breaks out into tears. Now if Christ have such compassions for those who so long and so obstinately opposed him, that he sees cause to cast them off as utterly incurable, has he not some compassion for the sensible sinner, whose soul is struck with remorse for his former disobedience to Christ, and whose heart is inclining to yield to him? If he be so passionately touched with their condition, who are so rebellious as to refuse all further treaty with Christ, has he not compassions for those who are in parley with him, and are about to submit to him? This is the state of a sensible sinner, and this is a hopeful plea which he may draw from Christ's tenderness. If he have such pity for obstinate enemies, he has some affections for those that incline to be his friends. If he lament the unbelief of those, he may be ready to further the work of faith in these.

[10.] He may plead the workings of the Spirit already begun, though they be but initial and preparatory. In the sensible sinner there is some illumination, some conviction, some humiliation, some sorrow, some hopes, some desires, some endeavours after more. These look like the beginnings, the foundation of a greater work. Some strongholds of Satan are demolished, the rubbish is removing, the materials are preparing, the outworks are begun. Are not these in order to that spiritual structure which is the Spirit's master-piece, the work of faith? Now the Spirit of God does not use to leave his work imperfect, unfinished, but upon some great provocation. The sensible sinner may plead this: Lord, thou hast let in some light into my mind and conscience, let it not end in darkness; let it be like that light which shines more and more unto a perfect day. The Spirit of conviction has awakened my soul, Oh let it not end in a spirit of slumber.

There are some sparks of thy own kindling, let them not be extinguished. All thy works are perfect, let not this be unlike the rest, but carry it on to perfection.

[11.] He may plead the respect which the Lord shews to irrational creatures. He hears their cries, will he shut out the cry of my perishing soul? He hears them crying for food, will he not hear me for that which unconceivably more concerns me, for that without which my soul will die for ever? Ps. civ. 21, 27, cxlvii. 9, 10, cxlv. 15, 16. Does the Lord take care for oxen? 1 Cor. ix. 9. Will he take care of lions and ravens, and will he not regard my perishing soul?

[12.] He may plead his necessity, his extreme need of faith: Mat. ix. 12, 'The whole need not a physician, but they that are sick.' O Lord, my soul is sick, sick unto death. Unbelief will be my death, it will be the eternal death of body and soul, unless the great physician undertake the cure. Will not he, who shewed so much compassion on diseased bodies, have some pity on a dying soul? 'Is there no balm in Gilead? Is there no physician there?' I die, I perish, there is no help for me in heaven or earth, unless Christ will cure me; none else can cure me of unbelief. Though others pass by, and have no regard to see me wallowing in my blood, yet will the good Samaritan so pass by? Has he no compassion for me? He came to seek that which was lost, Luke xix. 10. I am lost, not only as the rest of the world, but I feel myself lost, will he not seek me whom he came to find? He is found of those that seek him not, will he not be found of me who seek him? Will he not be found of me whom he came to seek? shall a lost soul find him?

2. The other means for the attaining of faith is *hearing the word*. This is a means of the Lord's appointing, and which he ordinarily uses for this end, John xvii. 20. He prays for some that were to believe afterwards, but were to believe through the word in the ministry of his servants. And all that the Holy Ghost mentions afterwards as believers were brought to believe by the ministry of the word. The Jews, Acts iv. 4; the Gentiles, Acts, xiii. 48; the Ephesians, Eph. i. 18; the Corinthians, Acts xviii. 8. And therefore the ministers of the gospel are called 'ministers by whom they believed,' 1 Cor. iii. 5. And the word preached is called 'the word of faith,' Rom. x. 8. He shews the necessity of this means by a gradation, verse 14, 15. There must be a mission, that there may be preachers; there must be preaching, that there may be hearing; there must be hearing, that there may be believing; and so he concludes his discourse, verse 17.

Those that will have faith without hearing would have it out of God's way, and are such ever like to find it? If the word be not preached it cannot be heard. The Lord may work it in an extraordinary way, but can it be expected the Lord should step out of his ordinary path to meet those who shew so much contempt of God and of their souls as they will not wait on him for faith in the way that he has appointed? Will God work miracles to save those who so much despise him and his great salvation? Nay, the Lord will have the ministry of the word more honoured in this respect than miracles. He has used miracles sometimes for to startle and humble sinners in order to faith, but has referred those persons at the same time to the ministry of the word for the working of faith. We find not that ever the Lord so much honoured miracles as to work faith by them without the word, though we find the Lord ordinarily so far honouring the ministry of the word as to work faith by it without miracles. Miracles are ceased many hundred years ago, yet the Lord has been working faith in all ages by the ministry of the word. And when miracles were in use, they were but used as subservient to the word, to prepare for faith, which the Lord would work by hearing the word. Saul was struck down and humbled in a miraculous way, but he was sent to hear Ananias, that he might be possessed with the Spirit of faith; he was not filled with the Holy Ghost till then, it descended on him in his ministry, Acts ix. 6. The jailor was humbled by a miraculous earthquake, Acts xvi. 27, 28, but the Lord would not work faith in him by that miracle, he reserved the honour of that work to the ministry of Paul and Silas, ver. 30, 31, 32, 34.

Hearing the word is the ordinary means to attain faith, and was the ordinary means when the Lord appeared in extraordinary and miraculous dispensations. If you would have faith, then,

(1.) Be diligent in hearing. Neglect no opportunities, especially none that are offered on that day which the Lord has set apart for this purpose. When men neglect these opportunities, it signifies too plainly that they yet have no faith. If it had been wrought in them by the word, the word would be more esteemed by them; they would not proclaim their contempt of it so openly by such gross neglects. It is strange, if men can so much despise that which has even been an instrument to save their lives, to deliver their souls from death; and as these neglects signify they yet have no faith, so hereby they run the hazard never to have it; for the word is not effectual without the Spirit, and the Spirit breathes not always. The Spirit blows where and when it listeth. What know you but the Spirit may vouchsafe a gale when you are wilfully absent? And when you have provoked him by neglecting such an opportunity, such an advantage for your soul, what know you but that the Spirit of God may never vouchsafe any more? You that would have faith, neglect no opportunity; the neglect of one may be the loss of your souls.

(2.) If you would have faith by hearing, give way to no prejudice against the word, nor him that delivers it. If the devil cannot keep men from hearing, his next attempt is to fill them with prejudice, that so they may get no more benefit by hearing than if they heard not. The apostle speaks of some whose consciences are seared with a hot iron. This prejudice was one of those hot irons wherewith he seared the minds and hearts of the Jews: so that the word, in the ministry of Christ himself, made so little impression on them; you find them frequently in the gospel expressing their prejudices against him, and this was it which made the gospel, in the ministry of the apostles, ineffectual to the Gentiles. The apostle was a babbler to the Greeks, and his preaching foolishness. Give not way to such prejudice against the word, if you would have it prove a word of faith.

I know a natural man cannot of himself pluck up the roots of this prejudice, it grows deep in the corruption of his heart; but yet the branches, the acts of it, are for the most part so unreasonable, as reason itself would cast them out if it were but exercised. To give you an instance or two:

He is not of our way and judgment, he complies not with our ancient customs and practices. This is the common rise of many men's prejudice against their ministers; but now, was not this the very rise of that prejudice which the Jews had against Christ and the apostles? They were not of their way and judgment, they decried their old customs and usages; is it reasonable to give way to that which was their ruin, and to entertain it upon the same account?

Oh, but he shews no learning, has no eloquence in his style, no ornament in his discourse. This is a common prejudice too, but very rarely objected by any, but such as cannot judge what is sound learning or true eloquence; a clear, masculine style, a spiritual, judicious discourse, signifies nothing to these persons, who have more of self-conceit than judgment. Some ridiculous quibbles, or affected jingles, is that which they count eloquence; some scraps of stories, and patches of Greek and Latin phrases, which school-boys may reach, and men of judgment count below them, is that which they call learning.

But if the objections were more judicious, yet would this prejudice be unreasonable; for must the face of divine truth be patched and painted before it can please you? must it be set off with the colours of fancy, and borrow some beauty-spots from human learning? can you not like it but in a wanton dress, nor embrace it but in the habit of a harlot? must the truth of God be adulterated to please you? or were not Christ and the apostles wise enough to know what habit did best become it? I question not but Paul, yea Christ himself, would have been counted a babbler by such profane and foolish wretches as these.

Oh, but he speaks out of spite, and his reproving my sins is edged with spleen. But is not this to take upon thee the prerogative of God? Dost thou presume herein to know the heart of him that speaks? This is not only to be unreasonable, but presumptuously wicked; to make thyself like God in knowing the heart, but to act like the devil, in forming an accusation that is without all ground.

Other prejudices, as unreasonable as these, I might pursue. But judge of the rest by these; and if ever you would have the word to beget faith, empty the heart of prejudice against it.

(8.) Take most heed to that word which most concerns you. Mind that most which is most suitable to the state of your souls. Now the truths that are most proper for a state of unbelief are such as these:—

First, Those which discover the sinfulness, the misery, and impotency of an unbeliever; his sin which brings this misery upon him, and his impotency that keeps him under it. Attend diligently to that word which discovers the sinfulness of a natural man's heart and life, which shews that his heart is a puddle of corruption, a spring of sin, a seed-plot of wickedness, a sink of uncleanness, a habitation of devils and impure lusts, a raging sea casting up mire and filth, which, though it may seem calm and quiet sometimes, yet ruffled a little with the wind of temptation, is restless, raging, and tempestuous, overflows all banks and bounds, which shews the sinfulness of his life, that it is a continued act of rebellion against him; that every thought, word, act, is an offence and dishonour to him; that his whole way is an abomination to the Lord; which shews the sinfulness of sin, which sets it out in its colours, which presents you with the aggravations of it, holds it out in its weight and pressure, which sets it forth in its dimensions, the height, and depth, and length, and breadth of his wickedness.

Attend to that word which discovers the misery of an unbeliever; that he is under the curses and threatenings of the law, under the sentence of condemnation, pursued by the justice of God, exposed to the wrath of the Most High, and every moment in danger of hell. Mind that word which expresses the weight of those curses and threatenings, the danger of that sentence, the severity of that justice, the terror of that wrath, the dreadfulness of those everlasting burnings.

Attend to that word which shews the impotency of an unbeliever; of himself he can do nothing to shake off this sinfulness, to escape those curses, to repeal that sentence, to satisfy that justice, to appease that wrath, or to avoid eternal torments; that while he continues in this state, all this sinfulness increases, this misery grows bigger and swells higher.

Secondly, Those truths which tend to conviction; mind those and apply them. When the word comes home to any of your consciences and tells you this is your case, if ever you desire faith, yield to such convictions, apply that word to yourselves, and say, I am the man that am thus sinful, whose heart and life has been such a provocation to God; I am the man who am thus miserable, the threatenings are directed against me, the sentence is passed against me; I am the man whom justice pursues, and on whom the wrath of God abides. When the word is applied in particular, and the soul convinced thus in particular of its own sinfulness and misery; Satan is dislodged out of one of his strongholds, and the sinner is in a fair way towards faith. To be convinced of unbelief is a good step to faith. Satan knows this, and therefore he opposes conviction with all his might, and raises in the soul all the prejudice against it that he can possibly; suggests to the sinner that this is the way to distract him and drive him to despair, whenas that malicious spirit knows it is the way of peace; but this way of peace he would not have the sinner know, lest he should lose him, and therefore he puts the soul upon resistance, would have him rise up against the convincing power of the word, and stave it off with all his art and might. When the word comes near the conscience, and the minister is fastening conviction on it, he cries out in the soul against him, as he did against Christ in the possessed man, 'Art thou come to torment me before my time? What have I to do with thee?' Whereas this is not the way to be tormented, but to avoid everlasting torments; this is not the way to wound you, but to make you sensible how you are wounded, that so ye may be more capable of cure, and may make haste to the physician who only can cure you.

And therefore, as you desire faith, as you love your souls, and would not gratify Satan in destroying them; yield to the conviction, yield to the convincing power of the word; resist not that Spirit whom Christ sends on purpose to convince you of sin, because you have not believed in him. When the Spirit has done this work effectually, when the soul is convinced of unbelief and of the miseries that attend it, when he applies these to himself, then he is under sail for faith and happiness.

Thirdly, Those truths that discover the rich grace and all-sufficient righteousness of the Lord Jesus. When the sinner is sensible of his wound, it will be seasonable to apply that word which leads him to the balm that is in Gilead, which discovers Christ lifted up for the healing of wounded sinners; when he sees himself miserable by unbelief, the word that discovers Jesus the author and finisher of faith will be in season; when the Spirit has convinced him of sin, the word should be applied to convince him of righteousness, that there is a righteousness sufficient to expiate his sin, sufficient to redeem him from misery.

He should mind that word that may moderate his fears, raise his hopes, quicken his desires, attract all his heart and affections to Christ.

Each part of the word, as it is in season, should be laid up in the mind and pondered there; diversions from the world or carnal company should be avoided; the loose vagaries which the mind is wont to take in hearing, and after, should be curbed; the word must be kept close to the heart by fixed thoughts till it works its effect.

And the soul should be lifted up in prayer to God for the concurrence and the co-operation of his Spirit.

OF LIVING BY FAITH.

Now the just shall live by faith.—HEB. X. 38.

THESE words are used four times, Hab. ii. 4, Rom. i. 17, Gal. iii. 11, and here. In the Epistles to the Romans and Galatians, they respect justification, Paul making use of them to prove that we are justified by faith. In Hab. ii. 4, and the text, they respect our conversation, and hold forth what should secure and support a righteous man in all dangers and necessities. It is plain in the prophet; for having, in chap. i., foretold the calamities which the Chaldeans should bring upon the Jews, in this verse he propounds faith as the security of just men in those miseries; he shall live by this, when others die by the sword; this shall keep him alive, hold his head above water, when that inundation of wrath shall break in upon Judea. And the apostle borrowing these words of Habakkuk (save that he follows the Seventy, and not the Hebrew text in the latter part), holds out this as the security of the Hebrews, in the midst of all trials, temptations, and persecutions, while they are in this world, till the Lord, who has promised to come, do come, and give them the end of their faith; he exhorts and encourages them to perseverance and constancy from verse 26, and propounds patience as a means necessary to this end, verse 36. And that they may be patient, tells them the exercise of it will not be tedious, nor fruitless, verse 37. The Lord will come suddenly, and reward their patience with a triumph in glory. And in the mean time they are well provided for, they have that which will keep them alive, will secure them in all necessities, against all dangers. 'The just shall live by faith.'

Obs. It is the privilege, or the duty, of the just to live by faith.

In the prosecution of it I shall observe this method: What? How? When?

I. What is it to live by faith?

Ans. This living by faith is not a single and transient act, but something habitual and permanent. And therefore its nature, as of other habits, will best appear in its acts and objects.

1. The acts of faith. The Scripture holds them forth under the notion of dependence and recumbency. And we may thus describe it: living by faith is constant dependence on God, as one without whom we cannot live. Three things concur to its constitution.

(1.) A sense and acknowledgment that we cannot live without God. This is presupposed. Our life depends on him; and it is our life to depend, life in its latitude; life and all that pertains to it; life and livelihood; life of body and soul; in its being and well-being; in its being and actings, and all that maintain it in both. God is that to the soul, which the soul is to the body, enlivens it and acts it; so Christ quickens and acts the soul. The body cannot live, or move, or act, or grow, it cannot hear, or see, or smell, or touch, without the soul. No more the soul without Christ. Christ is the life of the soul, and faith is the bond, the *copula* which unites the soul to Christ. And so by means of faith we live, faith uniting us with the principle of life. Both these are remarkably holden forth, Gal. ii. 20, 'I am crucified with Christ: nevertheless I live; yet not I, but Christ liveth in me: and the life that I live is by faith in the Son of God.' Even as we may say, the body lives; yet not the body, but the soul lives in it; and the life that it lives, is by means of its union with the soul. So in a spiritual sense, the soul lives; yet not the soul, but Christ lives in it; and the life that it lives, is by faith in Christ uniting Christ to it.

(2.) There is a relying on God for all these, for continuance of what we have, and supply of what we want; rolling ourselves, and the burden of our affairs, on God. This is the formal act of faith. And because it is above us, and few are acquainted with it, I will draw it down to your capacities, and offer it to your senses in a simile or two, which the words, whereby the Hebrews express it, afford us. The first is שען, to lean, to stay upon, to rely. It is used 2 Sam. i. 6, where it is said of Saul, 'he leaned upon his spear,' נשען על־חניתו, the same word: Pov. iii. 5, 'Lean not to thine own understanding,' *i. e.*, as some render it, 'trust not.' For these are used as synonymes: Isa. l., 'Let him trust in the name of the Lord, and stay himself upon his God;' ישען and יבטח are of the same force. For to trust God, is to stay ourselves on him. Even as one standing upon a high precipice, and perceiving himself ready to fall, takes hold of some bough, and stays himself by it, and hangs there, he is said to live by staying himself there, because it saves him from death, so we live by faith, because by this we stay ourselves on God, and so escape falling into hell, sin, and eternal death, though we stand continually on a precipice. We live by faith, because, were it not for faith, we should die; but for this stay, Satan would push us into hell, and our hearts into a gulf of sin, wherein we might sink and perish; but that faith, laying hold on Christ, leaning upon him, is held above water, and so lives by faith, as a drowning man lives by means of that which stays him from sinking.

The other word for faith is אמון which comes from אמן to nourish, and thence אמנה, a nurse. This affords another simile, which clears that other act, whereby we rely on God for all we want. As the infant depends and hangs upon the breast of the nurse, and so by depending and sucking is said to live, so we do live by such an act of faith. The Lord draws out and offers to our faith his promises, providences, ordinances, as so many breasts, on which faith hangs, and sucks out of them life, comfort, nourishment. As infants live by sucking, so the just live by believing, by faith.

(3.) Constancy, frequency. It is a continued thing; a life of faith, not one act of believing; a whole life of acts. Since we always stand upon the brink of sin and death, and have no security from falling, but God's maintaining, and our apprehending of him, we should continually depend and hang upon God, never let go our hold; for then we fall without recovery. If we live by faith, when we neglect faith, we die. Our whole life should be a continued act of dependence on God—when we eat, or drink, or sleep, or work, or pray, &c.; apply ourselves as often to God by faith, as the infant to the breast, without which it cannot live. We should exercise faith more frequently than we use bread; for we live more by it than by bread. 'Man lives not by bread, but by every word,' &c. If we believe, God can command other things to nourish in the want of bread. This for the act, the objects follow.

2. The object of faith is God in Christ, as made known in his attributes, offices, relations, promises, and providences. We may refer the objects and support of faith to these heads.

(1.) Divine attributes. Those are the pillows and grounds of faith, rocks of eternity, upon which faith may securely repose: 'Though the earth should be removed,' &c. 'The name of the Lord' (*i. e.*, his attributes) 'is a strong tower, the righteous fly into it,' and faith admits and there secures them. Hence this is faith's ordinary plea in Scripture. 'For thy name's sake,' *i. e.*, for the glory of those attributes whereby thou art known to us, as men are known by their names. These are frequently propounded and made use of as the objects and supports of faith.

[1.] Power. This is it on which the heroical faith of Abraham fixed: Rom. iv. 21, 'Being fully persuaded that what he had promised he was able to perform.'

[2.] Wisdom. This upheld Peter's faith, when Christ, so often questioning his love, might have made him doubt of it: 'Lord, thou knowest all things, thou knowest I love thee,' John xxi. 17. And David's faith acts upon the omnisciency and immensity of God, Ps. cxxxix.

[3.] Justice. This was David's plea: Ps. cxliii. 11, 'For thy righteousness' sake bring my soul out of trouble.' And Daniel's, ix. 16, 'O Lord, according to all thy righteousness, I beseech thee,' &c.

[4.] Faithfulness. This was the foundation on which Solomon raised that prayer, so full of faith, 1 Kings viii. 23, 'There is no God like unto thee, who keepest covenant and mercy with thy servants;' and Dan. ix. 4, Heb. x. 23.

[5.] Truth. David useth this, Ps. cxv. 1, 'For thy truth's sake;' and frequently, 'Do this according to thy word,' Ps. cxix. 154.

[6.] Mercy. Faith never finds more strong support, nor ever fixes with so much delight as here: Ps. cxix. 149, 'Hear my voice, according to thy loving-kindness;' Ps. cxxx. 7, 'Let Israel hope in the Lord: for with the Lord there is mercy;' Ps. lii. 8, 'I trust in the mercy of God for ever and ever.'

(2.) The offices of Christ. These are strong supports to faith as any, though less made use of: in special his

Priestly office. The apostle, Heb. iv. 14–16, urges them from this consideration to approach God with faith and confidence, to come boldly unto the throne of grace. Paul, Rom. iii. 24, makes Christ's satisfaction the object of our faith, 'whom God has set forth to be a propitiation through faith in his blood.' And this, joined with his intercession, raises his faith into a triumph, so as he makes a confident challenge to all opposers: Rom. viii. 33, 34, 'Who shall lay any thing to the charge,' &c.? 'Who is he that condemneth?'

Regal Office. Peter, persuading the Jews to believe, holds out Christ not only as a Saviour but a Prince: Acts v. 31, 'Him hath God exalted to be a Prince;' and Nathanael's faith pitches here, John i. 49, 50, 'Thou art the King of Israel.'

Prophetical Office. This was prophesied: Deut. xviii. 15, 'The Lord thy God will raise up unto thee a Prophet; unto him he shall hearken,' *i. e.*, believe; and cited twice in Acts iii. 21, and vii. 37, to persuade faith.

(3.) Mutual relations betwixt God and his people. These are the sweet food of faith, which, digested, nourish it into strength, and enable it to vigorous actings; and to this end we find them frequently used by the saints: Ps. cxix. 94, 'I am thine, save me;' and Jer. xiv. 9, 'Thou, O Lord, art in the midst of us, and we are called by thy name; leave [us] not.' And from particular relations: servant, Ps. cxliii. 12, 'Destroy all them that afflict my soul; for I am thy servant.' And Jer. iii. 14, the Lord, to encourage the faith of the backsliding Jews, clothes himself with the relation of a husband: 'Turn, O backsliding children, for I am married to you.' Father, Isa. lxiii. 15, *ad. fin.*, 'Doubtless thou art our Father;' where there are the strongest actings of faith upon divers relations.

(4.) Promises. These and faith are so usually joined, as though they were relatives. These are the breasts of consolation, out of which faith sucks. These are the wells of salvation, out of which faith draws joy, &c. These have been the supports of the saints' faith upon all occasions. Many instances will be needless. See it in Solomon, 1 Kings viii. 24–26, 'Who hast kept with thy servant David my father that thou promisedst him.' So Jacob, Gen. xxxii. 9, 12, 'Thou hast said, Return unto thy country, and to thy kindred, and I will deal well with thee,' &c.

(5.) Providences of God are objects and encouragements to faith. The consideration of what he has done for others, and for themselves, has supported the saints. These are the hands of God stretched out, on which faith takes hold. David, Ps. cxix. 132, 'Look upon me, and be merciful unto me, as thou art wont to do to those that love thy name.' And from his own experience, 1 Sam. xvii. 37, 'The Lord that delivered me out of the paw of the lion, and out of the paw of the bear, he will deliver me out the hand of this Philistine.' This was Paul's support when all forsook him in his greatest extremities, 2 Tim. iv. 17, 18. Some will not believe God, except, with Thomas, they may see and feel. Now herein God offers himself to be seen and felt, and leaves men without excuse if they continue in unbelief.

II. How do they, how must we, live by faith? Here I shall give particular directions how faith may act with most advantage upon its several objects formerly propounded, and shew what support and encouragement faith may find from them in all its actings.

1. Attributes of God. For the direction and encouragement of faith in acting upon them, observe eight particulars:

[1.] Study the attributes. Labour to know them distinctly, effectually. Though faith be not knowledge, yet it is not without it. Nay, the more we know, the more we believe: Ps. ix. 10, 'Those that know thy name will trust in thee;' thy name, *i. e.*, those excellencies whereby God is made known. Be much in thoughts of God, frequent, delightful, consistent, efficacious thoughts; such as bring a divine influence into the soul, and fill it with heat and light; leave deep impressions of God upon the heart, abstract him from all imperfection, and lift him above all perfections visible or imaginable, such thoughts as beget veneration; for high apprehensions beget great expectation, and this makes the actings of faith easy. Those who have known much have believed much; much in contemplation, strong in faith, as Abraham, Moses. Imitate David, who, studying the omniscience and immensity of God, Ps. cxxxix., cries out, ver. 17, 'How precious are thy thoughts unto me, O God,' &c. Then follows the actings of his faith, ver. 19, 'Surely thou wilt slay the wicked.' Let what you have seen of these divine beauties make you sick of love till you see more. Learn Moses's importunity to see God: 'Let me see thy glory,' Exod. xxxiii. 'Shew me thy glory: cause thy goodness to pass before me.' Display thy glorious excellencies; dart out some lightsome beam that may discover thee; unveil thyself: open my eyes, scatter clouds, remove interpositions. The more ye see, the more ye believe.

[2.] Assure thy interest in the attributes. Let thy knowledge be applicatory. Be not satisfied that thou seest God, till thou see him to be thine; what he is in himself, but what he is to thee. It was a great refreshment to Moses that he was admitted, from the top of Pisgah, to view the promised land; but how would he have rejoiced if the Lord had assured him that he should enjoy a share in it! It is a great encouragement to faith to view the excellencies of God in an abstracted sense; but the assurance of interest therein raises it to a triumph, to say with David, Ps. lxxiii. 26, 'God is my portion for ever;' and Ps. xvi. 5, 'The portion of mine inheritance.' For if the Lord be thy portion, then thou mayest conclude, Omnipotency is my portion, immensity, all-sufficiency, &c. Say not, If so, then I should be omnipotent, &c. There is a vast difference betwixt identity and interest, betwixt conveying of a title and transmutation of nature. A friend gives thee an invaluable treasure, and all the securities of it that thou canst desire; wilt thou deny it is thine because thou art not changed into its nature? The attributes are thine, as thy inheritance, as thy lands are thine; not because thou art changed into their nature, but because the title is conveyed to thee, it is given thee, and improved for thy benefit. If another manage it, who can do it with greater advantage to thee, than thou to thyself, it is no infringement of thy title. Even so the Lord has given thee himself, and interest in all his glorious attributes, that whatever is in him shall be thine, and for thee; but he improves these for thee, and does it with infinite more advantage than thou canst for thyself. It is true, he drives another interest, his own glory, but never separates it from thy happiness: these are accumulative, not privative. Whenever God advances his glory, he at the same time promotes thy interest: nor does this make thy title to God less than thy title to thy estate, for that is managed for God's glory too, else thou gainest nothing by it. It is true, we see not, we enjoy not, the total of these rich revenues which daily arise out of this glorious inheritance, but it is treasured up for us till we come at age in glory. Then the treasury shall be opened, and then we shall see that all the glorious outgoings of God, the appearance of his excellencies in this world, have been with special respect to enrich us, to enhappy us, when we never thought of it. Oh what support, what encouragement to faith, to be assured that all God's attributes are mine, thine; as much thine, as the portion thy father left thee as thine inheritance; as the drink in thy cup, or the meat on thy trencher! for so much is holden out in those expressions, Ps. xvi. 5, מנת־חלקי וכוסי, phrases taken from those shares which were assigned to every one in feasts, Gen. xliii. 34, 1 Sam. i. 4, &c., 'My lines are fallen in a pleasant place,' &c. With what confidence may faith take possession, and make use of them, at all essays, upon all occasions!

But some may say this is a high privilege, far above poor weaklings, and requires a high degree of grace to attain it. Not so; the lowest degree of faith gives thee interest in this, for the least act of faith puts thee into covenant with God; and the tenor of the covenant is, that God will be thy God. Faith begets assurance, and assurance begets faith; yet this is not a circle, because not *ad idem*. A weak faith will assure, but assurance begets a strong faith.

[3.] When thou art acting thy faith, so dispose and methodise the attributes of God as thou mayest thereby prove and make it evident to faith that God is both able and willing to do what thou wouldst believe. That God is willing and able are two *ansas*, two handles, on which both the hands of faith may take hold, and so act more strongly (as we do) than if it use but one. A man ready to drown, if he can lay hold upon anything with both hands to keep him from sinking, is more secure than if he can but stay himself by one. Faith is but weak when it fastens but upon one of these; the doubting of either will keep off faith from its stedfastness. Martha's faith was not stedfast, John xi., when she questioned whether Christ was able; and the leper's faith staggered when he doubted whether Christ was willing, Mat. viii. 2: 'If thou wilt thou canst.' The way to make it strong in its daily actings is to confirm it in both these, which we may do by making use of the attributes to prove it. That he is able, faith may be persuaded from his omnipotency, omnisciency, all-sufficiency; that he is willing, from his mercy, faithfulness, immutability; and some prove both these, as his infiniteness, immensity, eternity. Learn to draw arguments from these; and when these two premises are confirmed, faith will easily draw sweet and strong conclusions. Thus, the Lord is able to subdue my lusts, to make all grace abound, to tread Satan under my feet, and the Lord is willing, &c.; faith will easily conclude these shall be done. It is true the *minor* needs most confirmation; we are most subject to doubt of God's willingness; but the Lord has provided against this remarkably; for whereas there is but one attribute to prove God able directly, viz., his power, for the other do it by consequence, there are many titles that directly prove him willing, as mercy, goodness, bounty, grace, love, loving-kindness, compassion, bowels of compassion, patience, long-suffering. Get faith fixed upon this double basis, and it will stand firm.

[4.] Let faith fix on that attribute which is most suitable to thy condition. And here faith may meet with many encouragements: *first*, there is no condition thou canst possibly fall into but some attributes afford support; *secondly*, there is enough in that attribute to uphold thee, as much as thou standest in need of, as much as thou canst desire; *thirdly*, there is infinitely more; though thy condition were worse than it is, worse than ever any was, yet there is more than thou needest, more than thou canst desire, more than thou canst imagine, infinitely more. Some one attribute will answer all thy necessities; some most, some many. For, *first*, some of God's attributes encourage faith in every condition.

Omnipotency. When thou art surrounded with troubles and dangers, there is the power of God to rely on; so Jehoshaphat, 2 Chron. xx. Art thou called to difficult duties above thy strength, strong lusts to oppose, violent temptations to resist, weighty employments to undertake? Let faith support thee and itself on omnipotency, as Paul: 'I can do all things through Christ strengthening me.' Art thou called to grievous sufferings? Imitate the three children, act on God's power: 'Our God whom we trust is able to deliver us.' Dost thou want means for effecting what thou expectest, and so seest no possibility in reason or nature for obtaining it?

Act like Abraham; believe he is able, Rom. iv. 21, to perform without means, or against means. Art thou afraid to fall away? Stay thyself on God's power: 'We are kept by the power of God through faith.'

Omnisciency. Wantest thou direction, knowest not what to do, at thy wit's end? Eye omnisciency: 2 Chron. xx. 12, 'Neither know we what to do, but our eyes are upon thee.' The Lord knows how to deliver the righteous. When thou searchest thy soul, and art afraid a treacherous heart should deceive thee, trust omnisciency. He searches the heart, and can teach thee to search it. Art thou upbraided for hypocrisy, and borne down by Satan's suggestions, so as thou almost suspectest thy integrity? Let omniscience support thee here; he knows, he sees the least gracious motion. Fearest thou secret plots of Satan, crafty conveyances of wicked men, such as no eye can see or discover? Trust omnisciency.

Immensity. Art thou deserted by friends, or separated from them by imprisonment, banishment, infectious diseases? Let faith eye immensity; as Christ, 'Yet I am not alone,' &c. Fearest thou remote designs in other countries, nay, in the other world, in hell? Thou canst not be there to prevent; ay, but the Lord is everywhere.

All-sufficiency. Let faith set this against all thy wants. I want riches, but the Lord is all-sufficient; liberty, children, friends, credit, health, he is liberty, &c. I want grace, the means of grace, comfort; he is these. Dost thou fear death? The Lord is life. Dost thou fear casting off? The Lord is unchangeable. Nay, whatsoever thou fear, or want, or desire, there is one more that will give universal and full support.

Mercy. This will hold when all fail. It is the strength of all other supports, and that in all conditions. There is no condition so low but mercy can reach it, none so bad but mercy can better it, none so bitter but mercy can sweeten it, none so hopeless but mercy can succour it. It bears up faith, when nothing else can, under the guilt of sin and sense of wrath; in misery, that is the time when faith should eye mercy. Hence you may argue strength into faith. If one attribute answer many, yea, all, conditions, will not all answer one?

Secondly, There is enough in any one attribute to support thee as much as thou needest or desirest, let thy corruptions be never so strong, thy wants never so many.

Thirdly, There is more than enough, than thou needest or canst desire; more than is necessary for thy condition, for a worse than thine, for the worst that ever was. If thy dangers were greater than can be paralleled in former ages, if the impetuousness of all those lusts that have broke out since the creation were united in thine, yet there is more power in God than is needful for thy condition. If thou wert pinched with all the wants that all the indigent men in the world were ever pressed with, yet all-sufficiency can do more than supply. Suppose there were many more worlds, and in each ten thousand more sinful creatures than in this, and every one's sins ten thousand times more sinful than thine, yet mercy could do more than pardon. And faith may say, If mercy can pardon, more than pardon, so many more than mine, and so much more heinous, why may not mercy pardon mine?

[5.] There is no condition possible but some attribute encourages faith; so there is nothing in God that discourages faith in any condition, the most formidable condition. The most formidable attributes administer comfort and confidence to a believer, as purity, jealousy, justice. Oh, says a doubting soul, I am impure in heart, life, in my best services, and the

Lord is of purer eyes than to behold iniquity; what encouragement can I have to approach God in faith? Yes, enough; there is support in that which thou makest use of to deject thee. The Lord is pure, and loves purity; therefore may faith say, he will make me pure. He is jealous of sin, he hates it, punishes it; therefore faith concludes he will destroy my lusts, for they are the objects of his hatred, not my person; he will be a consuming fire to them, not to me. Faith may feel God embracing with one hand while the other is wounding his lusts.

Justice, both punitive and remunerative, encourage faith. That which is a rock of offence to crush unbelievers and grind them to powder, is a rock of repose and security to faith. The most terrible attribute is comfortable. Lord, I have sinned, deserved wrath; but my Surety hath done and suffered all that thy righteous law requires,—'he was wounded for my transgressions,' &c.,—and it is not consistent with justice to punish the same offences twice: 'Shall not the Lord of heaven and earth do justice?' Hence faith may conclude, justice itself cannot condemn, cannot lay anything to my charge, Rom. viii. 33, 34; nay, justice is my security that I shall not suffer, for that would be injustice. Punitive justice has now another object, thine enemies, sin, to subdue it, Satan, to trample him under foot, the wicked, &c.: 'It is a righteous thing with the Lord to render vengeance to those that trouble you,' 2 Thes. i. 6, 7.

[6.] Learn to draw arguments for confirmation of faith in acting upon attributes. These we may raise: *first*, from ourselves, laying this ground, that whatever engages God encourages faith; for it is easier to believe that one will act for us who is engaged, than one who has no inducement thereto. Now, to speak after the manner of men, yet not without Scripture warrant, the Lord seems to be engaged and induced to employ his attributes for us: 1, by our necessities, I am poor and needy; 2, our impotency, 'We have no strength against this great multitude,' as Jehoshaphat; 3, deficiency of other helps, 'Help, Lord, for vain is the help of man;' 4, danger, 'Save us, or else we perish;' 5, misery, 'I am brought low,' Ps. cxlii. 6; 'attend to my cry,' &c.

Secondly, From the attributes themselves separately considered. To instance in two that faith makes most use of, power and mercy. Power renders everything easy. This consideration much strengthens faith. For if we have a friend who can do for us a business of great importance with ease, without trouble or expense, with turning of a hand, or motion of a finger, or speaking a word, it is no hard matter to believe he will do it. Now thus it is. There is nothing that we stand in need of, but the Lord can do it as easily as we can move a finger, or speak a word. And can we doubt the Lord will not do it.

Then for mercy, this pleases him. 'He delights to shew mercy.' Now can we doubt the Lord will do that for us which he delights to do? Jer. ix. 24.

Thirdly, From attributes associated. We may doubt of creature power, because it is limited, but he is omnipotent. The creature may have strength, but want wisdom, and this may disable him, and weaken our confidence; but God is omniscient. A friend may have strength and wisdom too, but may be far from us; oh, but he is omnipresent. A man may have all these, but be prevented by death; but God is eternal. A man may have power, wisdom, propinquity, life, but not be willing; but God is merciful, gracious, compassionate, and joins other attributes to his mercy, the more to confirm faith. Mercy endures for ever; there is eternity.

Over all his works; there is immensity. Abundant in goodness, there is its infiniteness. His compassions fail not, there is unchangeableness.

Fourthly. From God's design in manifesting his attributes, viz., his glory. Here is a stronghold for faith. It is not only our interest, but the Lord's concernment, to employ his attributes for us; not our happiness only, but his own glory. Hence that argument so frequently used, 'For thy name sake.' It is no matter for us, Lord, though we perish; but what wilt thou do for thy great name? He will not lose his end, nor be crossed in his design. If faith may confirm itself in acting by one argument, how much strength will all add?

[7.] Compare the attributes with what men usually trust, and see how infinitely they transcend; how much more reason there is to rely on God's attributes than on riches, strength, princes. Riches are an uncertain, unsatisfying, insufficient, limited, deceitful nothing, Prov. xxiii. 5. God is an unchangeable, satisfying, all-sufficient, faithful, all things. Strength is a vain, depending weakness. God is perfect, independent, omnipotent. Princes are shaking, piercing, broken reeds, 2 Kings xviii. 20. God is the Rock of Ages. Is there not more encouragement to trust the Lord than to put confidence in princes? to trust in the living God, than in uncertain riches? to trust in the Lord of Hosts, than in chariots or horses? Ps. xx. 7. Shall men think it reason to trust in a spider's web, Job xviii. 14, to trust in a shadow, Isaiah xxx. 3, in vanity, Isaiah lix. 4, in a lie, Jer. xxix. 31, in nothing, Prov. xxiii. 5, and shall not we think it reasonable to trust in the Lord?

[8.] Learn from the attributes to answer all objections that may discourage faith, viz., I cannot believe, have used all means, &c.; God is able to work faith. But my own impotency is moral, sinful, contracted by sin; God is merciful. But I am unworthy; he is gracious. But I have turned grace into wantonness; he is patient. But I have abused patience, and what reason to expect he should longer forbear me? his love. But I have played the harlot; he is unchangeable. But he may cease to love me, as he did the angels, and yet be unchangeable; he is faithful, his faithfulness was not engaged to the angels. But I am unfaithful, and the unfaithfulness of one party disengages the other. But he is infinite; it is so, as you object, with men, but his thoughts are not as ours, nor his ways as our ways. But infiniteness discourages, if infinitely above; there is an infinite distance; how can, how dare my faith lay hold, approach? There is a Mediator, which brings me to the second.

2. The offices of Christ. To direct and encourage faith herein, take these rules.

(1.) Acquaint thyself with the offices of Christ, what they contain and hold forth to us, and for us. If faith be left in the dark, it will stagger, not know where to fix; may lay hold of a shadow, and rest upon a tottering basis; cannot be stedfast nor confident. Knowledge of Christ is put for faith in Christ. 'By his knowledge shall my righteous servant justify many,' Isaiah liii. 11. 'I know whom I have believed,' 2 Tim. i. 12. Find out what faith may lay hold on in every office, what are its supports in his

[1.] Kingly office. 1. As he is king, he is lawgiver; writes laws in our hearts. Gives not only laws to be obeyed, but hearts to obey; laws for obedience, and principles of obedience. 2. To subdue our enemies, Ps. ii. 6, 8, our lusts, the world, the powers of darkness. He will bruise them with a rod of iron. 'He leads captivity captive,' Eph. iv. 11, 12.

3. To rule us. The government is on his shoulders. He sets his throne in our hearts, and takes care that we live under his government in peace, plenty, safety; peace of conscience, plenty of grace, perseverance.

[2.] Prophetical. To declare his Father's will, the mysteries of salvation; to continue it as written and preached, and so to give pastors when he ascended, Eph. iv. 11; to make us understand it; to enlighten our minds; to send the Spirit of truth to clear up obscurities, resolve doubts, remove scruples, satisfy cases of conscience.

[3.] As priest. So he suffered, and intercedes. His sufferings are both satisfactory and meritorious. As satisfactory, he has redeemed us from the law's curse, God's wrath, death and hell. As meritorious, he has purchased all things, pardon, peace, grace, glory; and for this life all good things, a spiritual title to them, a sanctified use of them. He interceded on earth by fervent and affectionate prayers, with sighs and tears, Heb. vii. 5, John xvii.; and he now lives to make intercession, appearing before the Father, presenting his merits, and effectually applying them; silencing Satan's accusation, rendering our persons and prayers acceptable. Oh what work is here for faith! If the just had nothing else to live on, here is enough for the life of faith.

(2.) These offices are purely relative; wholly ours, for us, in reference to us; relative both *secundum esse et operari*, both in their constitution and execution. He was made king, priest, &c., for us, and does exercise these for us. They are essentially relative, depending on us, as one term of the relation upon another. As there cannot be a father without a child, so Christ had not been king without believers, who are kis kingdom, 1 Cor. xv. 24. There cannot be a priest without a sacrifice; nor a sacrifice, except some for whom to offer it. It is otherwise in the former object; God's attributes are absolute essentially, their relation to us is but accidental. Their being is not for us, but only their acting. God had been omnipotent, omniscient, merciful, &c., if no creatures had ever received a being. Therefore here is more support for faith than in the attributes. Where there is more interest, there may be more confidence. Faith may plead, Christ is my king, and was anointed, crowned, in reference to me. For this end he came to the kingdom, that he might govern me. He is my priest, consecrated for my sake, in reference to my guilt, my necessities, that he might satisfy for me. Christ is my prophet; for this end he was anointed, and received the Spirit without measure, Isaiah lxi. 1, that he might instruct me; *ergo*, I will be confident.

(3.) These being the offices of Christ, he is to perform them *ex officio*, as a duty. He, who was independent, and stood in no need of us, was pleased, for the encouragement of our faith, to come under the engagement of a duty. The Father's command is upon him, and therefore not only called a son, but a servant: Isaiah xlii. 1, 'Behold my servant, whom I have chosen.' It is [not] out of courtesy to us, but out of obedience to God, that he acts; Christ submits to it: Ps. xl. 5, 'Mine ear hast thou bored. Behold I come to do thy will.' A perpetual servant. Safely we may say there is as strong an engagement laid upon Christ, as upon any of us, to do our duty. This brings us to such a dilemma. Either we must believe, or else think Christ is impotent, negligent, or ignorant; for none else omit their office. Can he be impotent, unable, to whom all power is given in heaven and earth? Or ignorant, who is the wisdom of the Father? Or negligent, who was 'faithful to him that appointed him,' by the testimony of God? Heb. iii. 2. Nay, faith may draw arguments from the offices themselves to confute this blasphemous conceit, that Christ will not to the utmost execute his offices. If he should not, it must be for want of power, wisdom, or will. But the offices exclude these. As a king, he is able; as a prophet, he is wise: 'He that made the eye, shall he not see?' as a priest, he is willing, 'a merciful high priest.' So that you must either believe or blaspheme. Here is then as strong a plea as is imaginable: Lord, it is thine office to do this. It is true there was nothing that could oblige thee; but it pleased the Father so to appoint, and it pleased thee, dear Saviour, to submit, and undertake these offices. Such poor creatures as I may fail in our duties, and be unfaithful in our trust, but heaven and earth shall perish, the blessed angels shall turn devils, and glorified saints apostates, before my glorious Mediator fail his office; therefore I believe.

(4.) Christ, as he is Mediator, is both God and man, and executes his offices as Mediator. Here then faith hath all the encouragement that both heaven and earth can afford. He is God; for where he is called the Wonderful Counsellor, *i. e.*, our Prophet, and the Prince of Peace, that is, our King, there he is called the mighty God, the everlasting Father, Isa. ix. 6. And as our priest, so our God too; for his blood is called, Acts xx. 28, the blood of God. Therefore all the attributes of God are engaged for the performance of these offices. He is man too, 1 Tim. ii. 5, 'the man Christ Jesus;' and therefore all the affections of a man; not metaphorically, as they are ascribed to God, but properly: he loves, rejoices, delights, compassionates, as the sons of men. Nay, these affections are more tender in him than in any man; because his bodily constitution, upon which these motions depend, was more pure, and his temperament more exact. Nay, our faith in acting here has another great advantage, viz., Christ's experience. It is some encouragement for those who are pressed under afflictions and sufferings to consider him whom they depend on for relief, of a sweet affectionate nature; but are much more confident if they know that he has had experience of the like sufferings, and groaned under the same afflictions, knows what it is, &c. Now this support faith has from the consideration of Christ's manhood. He himself has been a sufferer, a man of sorrows, acquainted with the same griefs that afflicts us, Heb. ii. 16. He was made perfect through sufferings. He ran through the whole circle of afflictions. And why? See verse 17, 'That he might be a merciful and faithful High Priest:' and verse 18, 'For in that he himself suffered, being tempted, he is able to succour them that are tempted.' For this end he suffered, that he might learn to pity them, and be as ready as able to relieve them. And this the apostle holds forth as a ground of confident access, Heb. iv. 15, 16. Art thou poor, despised? He was set at nought. Art thou calumniated? so he. Deserted of friends, and hated of most? tempted by Satan, forsaken of God? So he, when he cried out to heaven, to earth. Let faith conclude, he does pity, he will succour.

(5.) Let faith begin first to act on the priestly office. This is the basis of the other. The high priest, a type of Christ, had a crown on his head, the ensign of royal dignity; and Urim and Thummim on his breast, emblems of the prophetical office, to denote that the kingly and priestly office are grounded on the sacerdotal. Begin then at the foundation. Persuade thyself that he is thy Priest, and it will be easy to believe him thy King and Prophet. If he have executed that, he will execute these. Believe that he suffered for thee, and thou mayest without difficulty believe that he will sanctify thee, illuminate thee; for faith has great advantage here. The worst is past, sufferings, the greatest employment is finished, the rest is small. That which is most difficult is overcome, the rest is easy. That which was painful and grievous is past, all that remains is delightful. That which was accompanied with shame and ignominy is past, that which is to be done is high and glorious. The conflict is over, that which remains is triumph and dividing the spoils. Here faith may act strongly. Has Christ suffered, done the greatest, the most painful, that which was ignominious? Will he not do the less, that which is delightful and glorious? Has he suffered? Will he not do? Has he conquered? Will he not divide the spoils? Was he wounded for my transgressions? Will he not wound them? Did he shed his blood? Will he not shed his love in my heart? Was he emptied of his glory, and filled with wrath? Will he not empty me of sin, and fill me with grace? Has he taken away the guilt of sin, which cost him so dear, so many prayers and tears, so many wounds and blood? and will he not take away the power of sin, which he can do with a word? 2. The other offices depend on this; grace, peace, light, glory, must be purchased before they can be bestowed. The purchase belongs to the priestly office, the communication to the other. Let faith first believe they were purchased, and it is easy to believe they will be bestowed, especially if it consider, 3, that the end why they were purchased was that they might be communicated. Here faith may act strongly. The end why Christ purchased knowledge and holiness was that he might impart them. Surely though poor, weak, improvident creatures fail of their ends, Christ will never so dishonour himself, never be so disappointed; especially in that which cost him so dear, in his master-piece, his greatest and most glorious design. Has he suffered so many things in vain, so much wrath, so much torture and soul-affliction, so much blood, &c., to sanctify me? Oh I shall be sanctified!

(6.) They are adequate to our conditions. This is necessary for the life of faith, that in every condition possible it have something to rely on. And in these we may find it. When lusts are strong, temptations violent, grace weak, God's ways unpleasant, let faith look on Christ as thy king; it is his office, it is his glory to succour thee; he triumphs when we conquer. Christ will act as a king, will be royal and magnificent: Luke xxii. 25, εὐεργέται, 'The kings of the Gentiles exercise lordship,' &c. He will give like a king, conquer like a king, like himself.

In sense of ignorance, want of the means of grace, want of the Spirit, danger of seducing, perplexity of mind, &c., look to Christ as your prophet; it is his office, his honour.

In sense of wrath, guilt of sin, let faith go to Christ's satisfaction. In the sense of its pollution derived on our persons and services, go to his intercession. It would be too tedious to direct how faith should act in every particular. We will instance in one less taken notice of, the prayer of Christ upon earth, the pattern of his intercession in heaven, John xvii., where he prays for union, freedom from evil, sanctification, joy, perseverance, glory, for all believers. Here what he prayed for. How he prayed, see Heb. v. 7, 'In the days of his flesh, he offered up prayers and supplications, with strong crying and tears.' Upon this faith may thus act, and as strongly as upon any ground in the world. The prayers of poor sinners that believe on Christ are always heard, much more the prayers of the Son of God. Their weak cries never return unanswered; how prevalent, then, are the strong cries of Jesus Christ! Their tears are so precious, as the

Lord puts them in his bottle; of how much more value are the tears of Christ! They never wrestle with sighs and groans but prevail with God; how much more prevalent with God are the sighs and groans of Christ. Those prayers, cries, and tears are not forgot, they are on eternal record in heaven; they were presently answered, he was heard in that which he feared, and the answers shall be returned to the end of the world, and shall fall, may faith say, into my bosom; for he prayed for me, wept for me, cried for me, and therefore was heard for me, for he was always heard, John xi. 22. Let faith go to God on this account, Christ has prayed that I might be sanctified, united, &c.

(7.) Consider how affectionately Christ executed these offices on earth, and it will be a strong ground to believe he will not neglect them in heaven. He looked upon this as his work, that for which he was sent, to which he was called, his calling and vocation, and went about it with all his soul, all his strength, strong desires: Luke xii. 50, 'I have a baptism to be baptized with; and how am I straitened till it be accomplished.' This baptism was his death and the grievous sufferings that attended it; he was to be drenched in a sea of wrath and sufferings, which, being the most intolerable that ever were suffered, might have been most formidable. But even death, which, when but ordinary, nature shuns as the most fearful evil, Christ desires it, and so passionately as can scarce be expressed. 'How am I straitened!' συνέχομαι, my soul is so big with desire, as there is not room for it in the body. How is my soul pained with desire to sacrifice my life, my blood, for my lost people! The intenseness of his desires appears in that sharp rebuke he gives Peter, when he persuaded him to save himself, not to expose his life: Mat xvi. 23, 'Get thee behind me, Satan; thou art an offence to me.' That temptation to save himself from death, which he so much desired, was as detestable, as offensive to him, as a suggestion of Satan, and he requites Peter with no better title for that unacceptable counsel, though immediately before he had pronounced him blessed, ver. 17. This appears in that he uses all means to bring men into a capacity of receiving benefit by his offices, invitations, commands, promises, threatenings, complaints, expostulations.

See with what delight: Ps. xl. 8, 'I delight to do thy will, O my God; yea, thy law is written in my heart.' The will of God in which he delighted, was (as appears by the coherence, and the quotation of this place, Heb. x. 5) that Christ should make his soul an offering for sin, as more acceptable to God than all other burnt-offerings and sin-offerings. This law was in his heart, בתוך מעי, in the midst of his bowels. He did as much delight in it as we do in following those inclinations which nature has implanted in our hearts, as we do in eating and drinking. So he expresses it, John iv. 33, 'My meat is to do the will of him that sent me, and to finish his work.' He was as willing to bleed and die for thee as thou art to eat when hungry. He delighted as much to be scourged, wounded, crucified, as thou delightest in meat when most delicious.

His sorrow you may see in his tears and pathetical complaints when men excluded themselves from the benefit of his offices: Luke xix. 41, 'He beheld the city, and wept over it.' There is his tears. And oh what a compassionate complaint was that, 'Oh that thou hadst known in this thy day!' &c.

For his joy, see Luke x. 21, 'In that hour Jesus rejoiced in spirit,' &c. For his zeal, it was so ardent, as the disciples apply that of the psalmist, Ps. lxix. 9, to Christ: John ii. 17, 'The zeal of thine house hath eaten me up,' *κατέφαγέ με*, אכלתני, *devoravit me*. The flame was so hot within, as it drank up the vital moisture. *Exhausit succum vitalem, et emaciavit me*.

Now, faith will say, if the Lord was so affectionate on earth, certainly he is the same in heaven, and will there execute his offices with as much delight, desire, and zeal. He changes not, whatever we do. Where is thy zeal, and thy strength, &c. Can the Lord neglect? No; we are his members, dearer to him than his natural body. Can he forget? No; though a mother may forget her sucking child, yet cannot he forget us. We are graven upon the palms of his hands. He remembers very well who they are for whom he was pierced.

(8.) The Father and the Spirit are engaged for the execution of these offices. The Father, he decreed it, so Christ is a 'Lamb slain from the foundation of the world.' He sent Christ: John xvii. 18, 'As thou hast sent me into the world.' He commands it: John x. 17, 18, speaking of laying down his life, he adds, 'This commandment have I received of my Father.' He approves it: when he entered upon his office, he had a wonderful approbation from heaven from the excellent glory, 'This is my beloved Son.' He therefore loves the Son: 'Therefore does my Father love me, because I lay down my life,' John x. 17. He swears the continuance of Christ in office: 'The Lord has sworn, and will not repent, Thou art a priest for ever,' Heb. vii. 21.

[1.] Faith here grows confident. If the Lord have decreed, and sent Christ for this end, and commanded him to execute his offices, if he do approve and love him for it, and has sworn he shall do it, shall sanctify, justify, enlighten, certainly he will do it, here is no room for doubting.

[2.] Faith appropriates. He decreed him for me, to sanctify me, &c., sent him to enlighten &c., me, commands him to subdue my lusts, &c., loves him because he does so much for me.

The Spirit is engaged too; for, 1, he furnished Christ for the execution, Isa. lxi. 1. And will the Spirit lose his labour, come short of his end? 2. He co-operates with Christ in the execution. Sanctification is the great work of the kingly office; he is the Spirit of holiness, Rom. i. 4, illumination of the prophetical office, he is the Spirit of truth and wisdom. And the issue of the priestly office is comfort from the sense of justification; and he is the Spirit of comfort, of adoption. Faith hath all the security that heaven can afford in acting on the offices of Christ.

3. Promises. How faith may act with most advantage upon promises, and get support and encouragement from them in its actings.

(1.) Consider the latitude of them. There are promises suitable to all estates. No condition wherein faith may not find support from promises. Soul, body, estate, relations, actions, there are promises for all; promises, I say, that are explicitly, in express terms, *quoad formam*.

But besides these, there are innumerable more that we take little notice of, which are promises implicitly, virtually, or by just consequence. And there is little in the Scripture out of which faith may not extract the comfort of a promise, titles, assertions, relations, prayers, commands, threatenings.

The *titles* of God are virtually promises. When he is called a sun, a shield, a strong tower, a hiding-place, a portion. The titles of Christ, light of the world, bread of life, the way, truth, and life; the titles of the Spirit, the Spirit of truth, of holiness, of glory, of grace, and supplication, the sealing, witnessing Spirit; faith may conclude as much out of these as out of promises. Is the Lord a sun? Then he will influence me, &c. Is Christ life? Then he will enliven me, &c.

Assertions. Many things delivered in Scripture as assertions may be applied promissorily. As, 'He that walketh uprightly, walketh surely;' *i. e.*, he shall walk surely: Gal. v. 22, 'The fruits of the Spirit are love, joy, peace, long-suffering, gentleness, goodness, faith, meekness, temperance.' Faith may conclude, therefore the Spirit in me will bring forth these fruits.

Relations of what the Lord has done for his people formerly are in effect promises, as is evident from Deut. viii. 3, 'He humbled thee, and suffered thee to hunger, and fed thee with manna; that he might make thee know that man liveth not by bread only,' &c. This here is a bare relation, but Christ seems to make use of it as a promise, Mat. iv. 4. From relations of what God has done for his people in times past, faith may conclude, the Lord will do the like for the future. If he delivered others who trusted in him formerly, he will deliver me if I trust in him now: Ps. xxii. 4, 5, 'Our fathers trusted in thee, and thou didst deliver them: they cried unto thee, and were delivered,' &c. He is the same God, the same engagements are on him. And from such we may not only conclude the same mercies, but others also proportionable to them, nay, exceeding them. David went against Goliah in the name of the Lord, and prevailed. If I go in like manner against my lusts, I shall prevail against them.

Prayers of God's ancient people are virtually promises to us. What prayers they made for the church and themselves, we may, *cæteris paribus*, apply as promises. We have a remarkable ground for this, 2 Chron. xx. 9, where Jehoshaphat makes use of Solomon's prayer mentioned, chap. vi. 28, as of a promise, and urges several of his petitions as though they had been promises. The reason is this, whatever the faithful pray for, it is granted, therefore their prayers are promises, and the answers to them performances.

Commandments of God are virtually promises, equivalent to them. Not only by proportion, as that command, Luke xvii. 4, Mat. xviii., to forgive our brother till seventy times seven, faith may conclude, the Lord will forgive much more. But directly as that, 'Thou shalt love the Lord,' &c., we may read it as a promise; for whatever the Lord command his people, he has engaged himself to give strength to obey. So that every command may be read by the eye of faith as a promise in this sense, I will enable thee to love me, &c. 'The just shall live by faith;' faith reads it, I will enable the just to live by faith; 'mortify your members;' 'let him deny himself.' The reason is, because the Lord writes his law in our hearts, Jer. xxxi. 33. And every law written there becomes gospel, every precept a promise; for to write laws in our hearts is to make our hearts answerable to the laws, *i. e.*, both willing and able to obey: 'We are not under the law,' for it is in us, 'but under grace.' If a man command a thing, and engage to enable the performance, his command is equivalent to a promise. He works all our works in us.

Nay, which is strangest, *threatenings* are by just consequence promises. The threatenings denounced against the wicked are promises to the godly. Where any sin is threatened, a promise to the opposite virtue is contained in that threatening. This by the rule of contraries. 'The wicked shall be turned into hell;' faith may conclude, the godly shall be carried into heaven. 'Cursed are those that do the work of the Lord negligently,' therefore blessed are those that do it faithfully. The antithesis we find in

Scripture betwixt these warrants faith: 'Say to the righteous, It shall go well with him; but woe to the wicked, it shall be ill with him,' Isa. iii. 10, 11; 'He that believes shall be saved,' &c., that is frequent. And when one member of the opposition is not expressed, faith may be bold to add it, as following by necessary consequence. Faith may extract as much comfort out of that terrible chapter, Deut. xxviii., as out of any. Here is food enough for faith to live on.

(2.) Collect the promises; treasure them up; methodise them aright; meditate on them. Many in one.

Gather them. They are the meat that you must live upon in this wilderness, angels' food. Be as careful to gather them as the Israelites to gather manna. Be often searching the mines. Suffer not these pearls of great price to lie neglected in the field. These must defray all the charges of your pilgrimage. The angels take much pains (so the word παρακύψαι implies) to pry into the gospel, much more should we; for these are the sweetest strains, the quintessence of the gospel, and we are more concerned than they. If the angels had had such promises as believers, none of them had fallen. In reading and hearing, take special notice of promises. Treasure them up. Let your memories be like the pot in the ark, always full of this spiritual manna. Otherwise you confine God's gracious working by way of promise to times and means, to reading and hearing, whereas we always stand in need of promises, but have not always opportunities to read and hear. A promise treasured up will afford comfort in our beds, in our callings, in a dungeon, banishment. Faith will starve or be unactive at such times if you have no treasure.

Dispose them so as you may have some ready for all occurences, emergencies, upon all occasions, that no accident, no employment may surprise you without a promise of support. To live by faith is to make every act of your life an act of faith; and how can that be except you have a promise suitable to every act, condition, and accordingly apply it? Pray, hear, eat, walk, work, all in the strength of a promise, for direction, protection, strength, success in all. This is the life of faith.

Meditate frequently and seriously on them. They are the sweetest lines that Christ writes to his spouse, will you not often peruse these? There is majesty in the commands, severity in the threatenings, but love is predominant in promises, nothing but sweetness, we should let them stay long on our palates. What concoction is to the natural life, that meditation is to this life of faith; no meat will nourish and preserve life except it be digested. They are sweeter than honey and the honey-comb; you get little sweetness except you squeeze it out by meditation. This clasps faith and the promises together, removes discouragements, suggests arguments. The comforts and acts of this believing life are much weakened and interrupted by neglect of meditation.

(3.) Accustom yourselves to a holy kind of discourse and reasoning. Faith does not abolish, but improve reason. Whatever is requisite to the constitution of a man may be useful to him as a Christian. The application of promises is nothing but sanctified reason exercised by faith. Argue from general promises to particulars, from specials to you as individual, from typicals to reals, from temporals to spirituals, from spirituals to temporals.

From generals to individuals. All things shall work for good, &c., therefore this loss, affliction, distemper, temptation. All the ways of God are mercy, therefore this way, though cross to my desires, interests, endeavours. Whatsoever ye ask, it shall be done; therefore this want shall be supplied, this lust subdued, this temptation conquered, this occurrence sanctified: 'It shall go well,' &c., Isa. iii., therefore now when it seems to be worst.

From specials to your own particulars. From those which seem appropriated to one person, if there be no peculiar reason for a restriction; for it is with these promises as with judicial laws, they are of universal extent if their reason be so. Hence the apostle applies that to the Hebrews which was made in special to Joshua: 'I will not leave thee,' Heb. xiii. 5. So may we those to Abraham: 'I am thy shield,' &c., Gen. xv. 1, 'I will bless those that bless thee,' &c., the same God, the like privilege. And that to Peter: 'I have prayed that thy faith fail not.' There is the same necessity, the like temptations, and as great weakness. And that of Paul: 'My grace shall be sufficient,' 2 Cor. xii. 9. The same engagements on God, such lusts in us, and less strength.

From typical promises to accomplishments in the antitype. There is ground for it, 1 Cor. x. 6, τύποι ἡμῶν ἐγενήθησαν. So Egypt was a type of our natural condition, Pharaoh of our spiritual enemies; the water out of the rock, and manna from heaven, of spiritual nourishment by Christ; the cloud and fire, of direction and protection, Canaan of heaven. The promises of these to them are promises of the antitype to us, and the accomplishment an encouragement to our faith, such as these: 'I will be honoured upon Pharaoh,' &c., Exod. xiv. 4; 'My presence shall go with thee,' Exod. xxxiii. 14; 'Ye shall eat the good things of the land,' Isa. i. 19.

From temporals to spirituals. From those to the body to those for the soul. Spiritual blessings are included in temporal promises. *Videntur temporalia proponi, quando speciale præmium occultè significatur.* Temporals are pledges of spirituals, hence Paul argues, 2 Tim. iv. 18, 'The Lord shall preserve thee from every evil work.' Christ useth the like argument to confirm faith: Mat. vi. 25, 'Is not the life more than meat, and the body than raiment?' And the apostle, 1 Cor. ix. 9, 'Does God take care for oxen?' &c. An argument *à minori ad majus* is strong with God. Will he give his beloved food for the outward man, and let the soul famish? Will he guard the body with angels, and let the soul be a prey to Satan? Will he maintain the outward man in health and strength, and suffer the soul to languish under spiritual distempers? Will he heal all bodily diseases, and not the soul's more grievous and dangerous ones? Will he take care for the body, and neglect the soul? do less for precious souls than vile bodies? Will special love afford but common mercies? Shall the body prosper, and not the soul, when he delights more in the soul's prosperity?

From spirituals to temporals. This is strong in all respects, *à majori ad minus.* Will he do the greater, and not the less? Will he give the kingdom of God, and not add the inconsiderable things of earth? Will he give the most precious things in heaven and earth, and not paper and thread to wrap them in? Will he afford the entertainment of a Father's house, and not a few husks? Will he deliver the soul from death, and not the feet from falling? Will he give special, eternal, and not common mercies? the upper springs, and not the lower? the fountain, and not a few drops? Faith may here be confident.

(4.) Confine not God in his performances to things, degrees, times, or persons. Let not faith so act, as to limit him in acting. This limiting of God occasions disappointments, and these discourage; and discouragements weaken faith, impair its strength and life. Expect not peremptorily, either the individuals which seem to be promised, or the degrees of them. The conclusions of faith in its arguings must not exceed the premises. *Conclusio sequitur deteriorem partem.* Conclude not peremptorily, but when the promise is peremptory. There are some things which God does not promise peremptorily, degrees of grace, arbitrary assistances, outward blessings, inward joy. In applying such promises, faith need not conclude absolutely, but either conditionally, I shall have this if it be good for me; or disjunctively, I shall have either this, or something better. It is an ordinary, but, I think, a great misapprehension, that we do not believe, but when we confidently expect the very things promised. I think it is more than God requires in applying any promises, but those which are necessary for our being; in those which concern our well-being, we do hereby limit the Holy One of Israel, where he hath not limited himself. This is not to believe, but to tempt God.

For times. In applying promises, we must not always expect a present accomplishment, but wait and depend. These are vital acts of faith, and to continue in the exercise of these, is to live by faith. Times and seasons are in God's hands, it is his prerogative to fit acts to seasons. We take notice of time, but he only knows opportunity, as what is good, so when it is so. When he seems slack, though time pass, yet he never lets slip an opportunity. How long did the faithful Jews expect the Messiah's coming, and Japhet's persuasion, yet both promised! How long have we expected the fall of Babylon, and erecting of David's tabernacle? The like for particular persons. Abraham had a son promised, he stayed long for performance. And so David for the kingdom; it was so long deferred, till his faith was near expiring; it was very weak, when he said, 'I shall one day fall by the hands of Saul.' The liveliness of faith is never more evident than in long expectations. 'He that believes makes not haste,' Isa. xxviii. 16. It is unbelief that hastes, Ps. xxxi. 22, cxvi. 11.

Confine not the accomplishment to persons. It is probable Isaac believed the promises made to him and his father should be accomplished in Esau, God performed them to Jacob. If the promise be performed to you or yours, to this child, if not to that; God is faithful, and faith is not in vain.

(5.) As to conditional promises, if you have the qualification in sincerity, let not the want of degrees discourage you from application. The lowest degree of grace entitles to the promise. It may be grace is not broke forth into a flame; it is acceptable to Christ when it does but smoke: 'He will not quench,' &c. It may be you are not grown to the tallness of a cedar, Christ delights in a reed, a bruised reed: 'He will not break the bruised reed.' He deals not with poor worms, as one that sells, but gives. Therefore he propounds conditions of so low a rate, as in contracts with men would scarce admit the notion of conditions; gives, if ask; satisfy, if desire; accept, if come; bestow, if receive. And in this respect the covenant of grace is in reality absolute, though, according to the form of proposal, it seems conditional.

God descends to as low conditions as are imaginable; and yet the least degree of the lowest condition gives interest in the promise. 'Blessed are the pure,' &c., he says not perfectly pure. Oh but I am impure in heart and life, how can I apply this promise? The Lord comes lower, 'Blessed are they that hunger and thirst.' To thirst after purity, is less than to be actually pure. Oh but thirst is a high degree of desire, I fear mine amounts not to so much. The Lord comes lower: 'If there be a willing mind, it is accepted,' 2 Cor. viii. 12. 'Whosoever will, let him take the water of life freely,' Rev. xxii. 17. Willingness, the lowest degree of desire, and desire, the lowest condition imaginable, entitles to the highest degree of blessedness.

But further; suppose you have but the qualification in so weak a degree as you do not discern it, yet should not this discourage from applying the promises. For observe it, believing is more acceptable to God, and gives clearer title to the promise than any condition annexed thereto. For this is the principal condition of the covenant, others are but accessories; this makes others acceptable, none can be accepted without it; by this the rest are attained, none are attainable without this. Therefore ye should believe, that ye may be qualified, not refuse because ye are not. If you bring faith to a promise, you bring that which most pleases God, and that which will bring the rest.

(6.) He that can lay just claim to one promise, has interest in all; he that can apply any one, has property in every one. This observation is necessary to advance the present design. For all the promises are requisite to maintain the life of faith; he that excludes himself from any, confines the influence of faith to some part of his life, which should be diffused through all. Yet this is ordinary with weak believers, to apply some, but restrain themselves from others, as pertaining only to saints of higher attainments and greater eminency. This is a mistake. He that applies one, should apply all; all the promises are his, as clearly as his inheritance; he that possesses one is heir of all. The first act of faith gives interest in Christ; and he that hath Christ, hath all; for in him all the promises are yea and amen, 2 Cor. i. 20. The least act of faith admits you into covenant; and the promises are but parcels of the covenant, he that has the whole has every part. If the Lord has given you possession of any one, though by the weakest act of faith, he has given you interest in all; and therefore let no discouragement hinder from applying any. 'He that overcomes shall inherit all things,' Rev. xxi. 7. All promises are included in this one. And who is he that overcomes? John tells us, 1 John v. 4, 'This is the victory, even our faith.' He, then, that believes has right to all promises, and shall inherit all; and therefore should confidently apply all.

(7.) The Lord's word is more valuable in his account, than all his works; he will suffer all the works of his hands to perish, rather than fail in the least degree to perform the most inconsiderable promise. Angels and men shall be destroyed, heaven and earth shall be annihilated, rather than one tittle of a promise shall fail of its full accomplishment: Luke xvi. 17, 'It is easier for heaven and earth to pass away, than one tittle of the law to fail;' and Mat. v., neither ἰῶτα, nor κεράια, nor the least letter, nor the least point. His glory is as much interested in the gospel, therefore he uses an expression comprehensive of both: Mat. xxiv. 35, 'My words shall not pass away.' The heavens shall vanish into darkness, and the earth sink into nothing, rather than the least letter of a promise shall not be fulfilled. Faith resting on a promise, has a surer foundation than the earth, and stronger pillars than the heavens; therefore let it repose there with confidence in every act, and live there secure in all occurrences.

8. Persuade thyself, that God had a particular respect to thee in every promise. This is the great objection, which does much prejudice faith in its life and actings. The Lord did not intend this for me; he might respect

others, those with whom he conversed familiarly, but not such a worm as I. This is an error which, though you think it arises only from a mean conceit of yourselves, yet indeed it proceeds from too low apprehensions of God, the impartialness of his love, and the infinite comprehensiveness of omniscience.

If the Lord should appear to you in a visible shape, as to Abraham, and make you a promise, as one friend to another, then you would not question his intention and respect. Why, consider you were as full in the eye of God when he engaged himself by promises, as Abraham was when he talked with him face to face. Nothing is past or future in respect of God's all-seeing eye. Things past to us will be present to him unto eternity. Things future from us were present to him to* all eternity. Nothing is hid or unobserved, Heb. iv. 13, τετραχηλισμένα. The faces of all things are naked and open, as one of our faces to another; even those things which are so small, as they seem unworthy to come under divine cognisance; every sparrow, every hair, much more his jewels, his peculiar treasure. All believers that were, are, or ever will be, were as fully and distinctly in God's eye, while he was purposing to engage himself by promise, as our fingers are to us, when our eyes are fixed most intensely upon our hands: 'I have graven thee upon the palms of my hands.' The Lord had as special and distinct a respect to every believer in each promise of the covenant, as a father has to each child in every legacy that he bequeaths by will, when he divides his estate among them, and sets out every child his portion. And therefore faith may with as much confidence make use of every promise, and live upon them, as any child may upon the portion left him by his father's will. This notion is well grounded; for God's covenant is not only called συνθήκη a compact, but διαθήκη, a will or testament, Mat. xxvi. 28, and so the Seventy-two ordinarily render בְּרִית. What a sweet encouragement is this to act and live by faith, to consider you were in the thoughts and eye of God promising, as a child in the eye of a father making his will; and that God gave you the promises to live upon, as a father gives a child an inheritance, a portion; and his eye as full upon you, as upon Abraham or David, when he made them promises face to face!

(9.) Consider, it is all one with God to do as to say, to perform as to promise; it is as easy, he is as willing, as able, to one as the other. There is no such distance betwixt God's saying and doing, as amongst men. His saying is doing: Ps. xxxiii. 9, 'He said, and it was done; he commanded, and it stood fast.' His τὸ λέγειν is κοσμοποιία: ver. 6, 'By the word of the Lord were the heavens made;' Heb. xi. 3, 'The worlds were framed by the word of the Lord.' There is omnipotency in his word, both of command and promise: therefore called, 'the word of his power,' Heb. i. 3. One word of his can do more in an instant, than the united powers of heaven and earth can do to eternity.

This consideration removes at once the chief discouragements that hinder the lively actings of faith; for what is it that weakens our confidence of the promises' performance, but because we look upon the accomplishment as uncertain or difficult, or future and afar off! Now from hence faith may conclude the performance is certain, easy, and present.

It is *certain*. The root of all certainty is God's will. He is willing to promise, for he has actually done it. He is as willing to perform, for it is all one with him to do as say.

It is *easy*. What more easy than a word! An act is not more difficult.

* Qu. 'from'?—ED.

And one word will give accomplishment to all the promises: no pains, trouble, cost, hazard. The covenant is our tree of life, the promises are its branches, laden with all precious fruits. The least word, the least breath, from God's mouth, will shake all the fruits into your bosoms. Will not he speak so little who has done so much, sent his Son to suffer so much, let his Spirit strive so much? There is but one word betwixt you and all the happiness contained in the great and precious promises. And is it not easy for faith to believe that it is easy for God to speak one word? This may be faith's plea, Only speak the word, and it shall be done. Nay, it is done, the accomplishment is *present*, the word is passed out of his lips. You have as much for the accomplishment of promises, as all things that now exist had for their creation, God's word. He does when he says; his saying is doing. Nothing remains on God's part to be done further. That which suspends your enjoyments is want of faith; do but believe, and all is said, all is done, to make you happy. You may as easily believe that he will perform, as that he has promised. It is easy to believe that he has promised: you question not that. There is as much reason to believe he will perform, for it is all one to him. Men promise great things, but cannot perform without trouble, expense, or hazard; therefore may we doubt of them. But there are no such things incident to God's performances; no more trouble or pains to perform a promise than to make it. He can perform all with less trouble than we can speak, do all he has said as easily as anything he does.

10. Believers have a just and unquestionable title to all things promised, besides that title which the promise conveys. They have right to them, and therefore have no reason to doubt but the gracious God will bestow them, especially when he has confirmed the former title by promise. All that is promised was bequeathed to believers by the eternal will of the Father, and purchased for them by the precious blood of Christ, and they are instated therein by many endearing and interesting relations. They have as much right thereto as an heir to his inheritance, or a wife to her jointure; for they are co-heirs with Christ, and married to him: 1 Cor. iii. 23, 'All is yours.' All. This is more than if he had said a kingdom, though this is much; nay, more than if he had said, all the kingdoms of the earth; nay, more than if heaven and earth were yours. What then is all? Why heaven and earth, and all in both. All in heaven that you are capable of, and all in earth that is desirable and good. Not only angels and men; not only riches, pleasures, glory; but the Father (that which is more than all), Christ, and the Spirit; all that they are, have, can do, so far as these are communicable, attributes, offices, functions. All these are your own, though you do not believe it. You have *jus ad rem*, right to these, upon other accounts besides the promise. Faith gives *jus in re*, actual possession. Here is great encouragement for believers to act faith in the promises, from this consideration. Will a child doubt that a pious and indulgent father will not give him his own, though he do not promise it? But if he engage himself by promise, he will be confident. Shall we be more confident of the justice of men, than the righteousness of God? He has made all your own, and will he be so unjust as to detain it? He has promised to give all that is yours, and will he add unfaithfulness to injustice, such injustice as is odious amongst men? Shall not the Lord of heaven and earth be righteous? Faith cannot doubt here. Either you must believe, or cast such horrid aspersions on God, as though he were as unjust or unfaithful as the worst of men.

The whole glorious essence of God is engaged for the performance of every promise. It is of as much concernment as the Deity. He would cease to be God if he should fail to perform any promise. This would undeify him. For he ceases to be God, when he ceases to be most perfect; for this is the proper and essential notion of God, to be *quid perfectissimum*. If there be absence of any perfection, or the presence of any imperfection, he would not be God. But non-performance argues both; this divests him of all perfection, and consequently makes him most imperfect.

Faithfulness. He is not faithful amongst men, who answers not his engagements; he fails his trusts who keeps not promise.

Truth. 'He that believes not, makes God a liar;' for how is he true who doth not what he says he will do?

Justice. That does *suum cuique tribuere*. The promise makes every thing promised our own, and it is injustice not to give it.

Goodness. He is bad amongst men, who is not as good as his word.

Holiness. His promise is as sacred as our vows to him. Violation of a vow is a profanation, so is non-performance of a promise. If he perform not, it is because either he will not, and then where is mercy? or cannot, and then how is he all-sufficient? If he cannot, it is either for want of wisdom, and then where is his omniscience? or ability, then how is he omnipotent? or opportunity, then how is he omnipresent? Nothing but absence in him can occasion the want of an opportunity. Either he never intended it, and then how is he upright? It is odious dissimulation, with men, to speak what they never intend. Or he did once intend it, but now does not; then how is he unchangeable? If he is not unchangeable, he is not eternal; for there is no succession, no variation in eternity. If not eternal, not infinite. If not all these, not God.

As sure as he is God, as sure as he has any perfection, he will perform his promises. He that doubts of performance, doubts of God's being by consequence. Unbelief is horrible atheism, it dethrones God. You may as well say there is no God, as say there shall be no performance. The glory of his being is concerned; that is infinitely more than our happiness. He loses nothing if he perform; all, if he do not.

His engagements are infinite. Every perfection engages, and every perfection is infinite; therefore the obligements are strong, and the performance sure, above the apprehension of men and angels.

We have all the confirmations and assurances, *ad extra*, that the most suspicious heart can desire.

God's *word*. That is more than the word of angels, more than all his works, as much as himself. He engages himself when he engages his word; he should deny himself if he should fail. Men may be men, though unfaithful, but God cannot be God: his being is concerned.

Writing. We have them under God's hand, have his hand to shew. He would not have us to depend upon uncertain revelations, here Satan might have deluded us, but inspired holy men of God to write what he dictated, has delivered it as his act and deed. His word of promise written, is more assuring than a voice from heaven would be, 2 Pet. i. 19.

Sealed. The sacraments are seals of the righteousness of faith, seals of the covenant wherein faith apprehends that righteousness. 'The covenant of promises.' 'The New Testament in my blood.' A double seal: without, the impressions are Christ's sufferings in blood; a seal within, the Spirit, Eph. i. 13; 2 Cor. i. 22.

Sureties. A surety equal with the principal. He who counts it no robbery to be equal with God; equal, both in faithfulness and sufficiency, as willing and as able; no robbery to be equal with God, a disparagement to be compared with men or angels; he who sees no stedfastness in saints or angels, sees nothing else in him: he has engaged with himself his Son and heir, and made him the mediator of this better covenant, Heb. viii. 6, and ix. 15; Heb. vii. 22, he who values his faithfulness more than his life.

Pledge. Of as much worth, and more than heaven and earth, the eternal Spirit: 2 Cor. i. 22, 'Who hath sealed us, and given us the earnest of the Spirit;' chap. v. 5, 6, 'Who hath given unto us the earnest of the Spirit. Therefore we are always confident,' &c.; Eph. i. 13, 14, 'In whom ye were sealed with the Holy Spirit of promise, which is the earnest of our inheritance.' God will forfeit his Spirit, rather than fail his promise.

Oath. He has confirmed it by an oath, Heb. vi. 17, 18; we have no more cause to fear the promise will not be performed than that God will be perjured.

Witnesses. Besides those in heaven who bear witness with the Father, the Word and Spirit; and those in earth, 1 John v. 8, the Spirit, the water, and the blood; 'Christ the faithful witness,' Rev. i. 5; and the 'Spirit which beareth witness with our spirits,' Rom. viii. 16; we have heaven and earth, men and angels, to witness. These things were not done in a corner. As the Lord calls heaven and earth to witness against the unfaithfulness of men, so may we call them to witness the faithfulness of God.

FAITH IN PRAYER.

But let him ask in faith.—JAMES I. 6.

THE apostle, in the former verses, after the preface, directs the Jews how they should bear afflictions, viz., with joy, ver. 2, 3; patience, ver. 4; wisdom, ver. 5.

'Servant.' 1, By universal subjection, and in respect of their state; not, 2, by particular employment in respect of their use, as Nebuchadnezzar, Cyrus.

'All joy.' Not in respect of the afflictions themselves, for they are grievous, and we are not required to be Stoics; but in respect of the issue, to prevent sin, purge corruption, increase holiness, glorify God, and try grace, ver. 3.

'Perfect work.' *Extensivè*, to all its objects, occasions. *Intensivè*, in all its acts.

'Lack wisdom.' To demean himself under afflictions so as to attain the former ends.

'It shall be given.' There is a promise, the object of faith, with an encouragement to act faith from God's gracious disposition. He gives, gives to many, to all men; gives much, liberally and freely too, he upbraids none; how much soever he gives, he never thinks much.

But the promise is conditional, and the condition is expressed: ver. 6, 'Let him ask in faith;' otherwise he asks in vain, ver. 7.

Obs. He that would have God to give what he asks, must ask in faith: Mark xi. 24, 'Whatsoever things ye desire, when ye pray, believe that ye receive them, and ye shall have them;' Mat. xxi. 22, 'Whatsoever ye shall ask in prayer, believing, ye shall receive.' A great privilege, but limited.

Quest. What is it to ask in faith?

Ans. To this some things are requisite as necessary conditions, though more remotely; some things as essential ingredients.

I. The necessary conditions respect the petitioner, asker, the thing asked, the manner of asking.

1. The asker must be in the faith, or rather faith in him; the petitioner must be a believer. How can he ask in faith, who has no faith? John xvi. 23; how can he ask in Christ's name who believes not in it? There

is no audience, no answer, for him that is not a believer: John ix. 31, 'God heareth not sinners.' Those that live in sin, live not by faith; or if you live not in it as to visible practice, yet if it live in you, have entertainment, love, approbation in the heart. When there is no faith there will be no audience: Ps. lxvi. 18, 'If I regard iniquity in my heart, the Lord will not hear me.' God will not hear that which displeases so as to answer it. But prayer without faith does not please him, it is impossible it should, for Heb. xi. 6, 'without faith it is impossible to please him: for he that cometh to God must believe that he is, and that he is a rewarder of them that diligently seek him.' God will not accept the service till the person be accepted, Heb. xi. 4; Abel obtained witness that he was righteous, and then God testified of his gifts. He obtained both by faith.

2. The thing asked for must be an object of faith; such things as you may upon good grounds believe that God will grant. There must be a belief, a persuasion, that the things desired are lawful according to his will: 1 John v. 14, 'And this is the assurance that we have in him, that if we ask anything according to his will, he heareth us.' No assurance he will hear, without assurance that what we ask is according to his will; now that is according to his will for which we have command or promise; for these, though not properly his will, yet are ordinarily so called, they are that will to which our practice must be conformable. His decreeing or secret will belongs not to us, it is not the rule of our practice in praying, hearing, &c., but that which is revealed by command or promise. Example, too, may direct and encourage this act of faith; but it must be the example of the godly, approved and ordinary. Extraordinary examples are no rule for us, as that of David, Ps. cix., praying against particular enemies; it is extraordinary, since he had (as it is supposed) extraordinary assistance to discern that his particular enemies were incorrigible; otherwise, though it may be lawful to pray against the public enemies of God, his ways, and people, or against the cause and practices of particular enemies, yet not against their persons. If there be no persuasion, or none upon these grounds, the prayer is not of faith, and so it is sin; for whatever is not of faith is sin, and sin can expect no comfortable return from God. He that cannot behold it will not hear it, or hear it so as to reward it but with punishment. A fervent prayer for a thing unlawful is a crying sin.

3. The manner of asking must be faithful. As it must be *in fide* as to the person, and *de fide* as to the object, so *fideliter* as to the manner. As he must be *bonus* that asks, and *bonum* that is asked, so must he ask this *benè*, in three particulars.

(1.) With fervency. He does not ask in faith that asks not fervently: James v. 16, 'The effectual fervent prayer of a righteous man availeth much.' And what prayer that is, see ver. 15, 'the prayer of faith.' It must be δέησις ἐνεργουμένη, it must be an inwrought prayer, proceeding from the powerful working of the Spirit in the heart. Now what the workings of the Spirit are in the heart as to prayer the apostle tells, Rom. viii. 26, 'sighs that cannot be uttered.' Such prayers as shew the parties to be ἐνεργουμένοι in a good sense, *i. e.*, possessed with the Holy Spirit, and acted by it. Prayers must be strivings: Rom. v. 30, 'Strive together with me in your prayers.' He that will prevail must wrestle, as Jacob; give the Lord no rest, as Isaiah lxii. 7. Cold, heartless prayers argue want of faith, and will want success; teach God to deny. If there be only lip labour, draw near with the lips only, God will withdraw. If we pray as if we prayed not, God will hear as though he heard not, take little notice except to correct. Strong cries only reach and pierce heaven; such were Christ's.

(2.) With submission. We must not limit God. To limit the Holy One of Israel is to tempt him, and that is a notorious effect of unbelief, Heb. iii. 9, 12, and xi. 18. We must not limit God as to time, place, persons, things, degrees.

Time. Be willing to stay God's time. He that believes, makes not haste. It was an unbelieving prince that said, 'Why should I wait on the Lord any longer?' And Hab. ii. 3, 4, 'The vision is for an appointed time; though it tarry, wait for it,' &c.

Place. Jacob would not have prayed in faith for provision, if he would not have had it in Egypt.

Persons. Noah would not in faith have asked blessings for Ham, if he had limited God as to the person. We must leave the Lord to his own way of free dispensation.

Things. Lawful things are temporal or spiritual; and these necessary for being, as grace, and the means of grace; or well-being, as joy, assurance, enlargements.

Temporal blessings must be desired with such conditions as they are promised, and besides, with reference to God's good pleasure, and caution of their expediency for us; if it seem good to thee, if they be good for us. Spiritual blessings for well-being, though they may be desired with more importunity, as being of more worth, and more expressly promised, yet with the like references. But spirituals necessary to salvation may be desired absolutely, without reserves, conditions, exceptions, because they are so promised, and we are so commanded.

Degrees. We must not limit God to degrees of grace, or plenty or plausibleness of the means, but refer it to infinite wisdom to bestow what degrees he knows will make us most serviceable, and what kind of means soever he will please to make effectual for attaining those degrees.

(3.) With right intentions. It is not *bene*, except *ad bonum:* James iv. 3, 'Ye ask, and receive not, because ye ask amiss.' We must pray to glorify God, make us serviceable to him, capable of communion with him. We must not desire grace to excel others, or, as Simon Magus, the Spirit, to be admired, praised. We must not desire gifts, to advance our credit, get applause; riches, to satisfy lusts, to live at ease, &c. This is to ask amiss; and he that asks amiss, must miss of an answer.

These are the necessary conditions of this duty. I call them but conditions, because, though we cannot pray in faith without them, yet we may have these, and yet not pray in faith.

II. The essential ingredients of this duty are the actings of faith in prayer, which are one or other of these four. He whose faith puts forth any one of these acts prays in faith.

1. Particular application. Believing the promise whereby God has engaged himself to give what he asks; so to ask in faith is to pray with confidence the Lord will grant the petition, because he has promised; to pray with David, 'Do good to thy servant,' &c., and to rest assured he will do it, because it is his word, his promise, 1 Kings viii. 24–26.

2. Fiducial recumbence. Casting himself upon God, without the mediation of a promise, and relying, depending on him for the grant of what he asks, when faith in prayer supports itself upon God immediately; which act of faith has place either when there is no particular promise of the

thing asked, or faith is so weak as it cannot make use of it by way of application. There are other supports of faith besides a promise, and other acts of faith besides applying a promise, which the soul putting forth in prayer may be said to ask in faith, and this act of dependence is one in special. Faith can read an answer of prayer in the name of God, and stay itself there, when a promise appears not, or, through faith's weakness, cannot support it, Isaiah l. 10, 11.

3. A general persuasion that the prayer shall be heard. I call it general, to distinguish it from that particular persuasion that the thing asked shall be presently granted, or granted at all, which is not simply necessary to this duty. The prayer may be heard, though the thing desired be not presently bestowed, or not bestowed at all. And so a man may pray in faith, though he be not confident that what he prays for shall be given him, much more that it shall not be presently given. Zachariah prayed in faith, and it is like he prayed when he was young, yet a child, though that which he asked, was not given him till he was old, Luke i. 13. Noah prayed that God would persuade Japhet to dwell in the tents of Shem, and he prayed in faith; yet this was not granted till many hundred years after. Christ prayed in faith that the cup might pass from him, the bitterness of death; yet he had not a particular persuasion that this should be granted; for this persuasion had been false, for it was not granted; yet was his prayer heard, Heb. v. 7. Paul prayed in faith that he might be free from that messenger of Satan; that mercy was not granted; yet was his prayer heard and graciously answered: 2 Cor. xii. 9, 'My grace is sufficient.' A prayer may be heard, though the mercy desired be not granted; therefore it is not necessary to this duty that a man should have a special persuasion to receive what he asks. He prays in faith, who is persuaded in general that his prayer shall be heard, referring the answer to the wisdom and goodness of God, to be returned when and in what kind he pleases. He that believes God will hear his prayer, though he be not confident that he will grant this particular desired, yet prays in faith.

4. A special confidence that the very same thing which is asked shall be given. This is the highest and rarest act of faith; and if the mercy desired be temporal, it is extraordinary, not raised in the heart but by special instinct; yet may it now and then be vouchsafed to some who are admitted to sweeter familiarity and nearer communion with God, Ps. xxvii.

Use. Take notice of the misery of unbelievers. They that cannot pray in faith must not expect to have their prayers heard. All men have not faith, though most presume. They cannot give an account how or when it was wrought, cannot shew their faith by their works. Such, though they make many prayers, God will not hear. If this be your case, what will ye do for support in distress, for supply of wants, for removal of fears and dangers? It is the great, the sweet privilege of believers, whatever they ask in Christ's name it shall be given. It is the misery of unbelievers, whatever they ask it shall be denied, or given in wrath. 'Call upon me,' says the Lord to believers, 'in the day of trouble, and I will hear you.' Unbelievers must read the contrary: 'Though ye call, I will not hear,' &c. To believers Christ says, 'Ask, and it shall be given; seek, and ye shall find; knock, and it shall be opened unto you:' but to them, Though ye ask, I will not give, &c. Christ says to them, as to the Jews, 'Ye shall seek me, but shall not find me, and whither I go ye shall not come;' and if they must not come to Christ, whither then? Christ will neither hear them in life, nor at death, nor after death. Those that live in unbelief may read their doom, ver. 7; those that die in it, Christ will send them to the gods they have served. He will say, Ye would not come to me, believe in me, that ye might have life; therefore ye shall die in your sins, die now, die for ever. And after death, if you come with the foolish virgins, and knock at the bridegroom's chamber, Christ will profess, 'I know you not,' and command a sad and everlasting departure.

Obj. The Ninevites prayed, and were heard, Jonah iii. 7, 8, 10. Ahab prays, and is heard, 1 Kings xxi. 27, 29; yet both unbelievers, Ahab notoriously, ver. 25, 26.

Ans. 1. As a prayer may be heard, yet the thing prayed for not granted, so the thing desired may be granted, and yet the prayer not heard: so it is with unbelievers; for, to speak strictly and properly, a prayer is not heard, but when both person and prayer is accepted. None are accepted but in Christ, and none are in Christ but by faith; therefore unbelievers, both person and prayer, are not accepted, and consequently their prayer not heard; though what they pray for be granted, it is not out of respect to the prayer.

Ans. 2. The Lord gives nothing but temporal things upon the prayers of unbelievers. The Ninevites obtained but a temporal deliverance, no more does Ahab; not a removal of the judgment threatened, but a delay of the execution; not forgiveness, but forbearance. In the next generation, as some observe, Nineveh was quite destroyed; and the evil threatened to Ahab's family surprised it in his son's days, and the severest part of it is executed upon himself, chap. xxii. 24. Unbelievers do not unfeignedly desire spiritual mercies, grace, regeneration, holiness; none desire these but those that in some degree have them, 'found of them that seek him not.' And will the Lord hear a prayer not accompanied with unfeigned desires?

Ans. 3. He gives not temporals in mercy, when unbelievers pray for them. Israel desires a king, he gives them one in wrath: they desire flesh, he sends quails, but sends his wrath upon them; that pleasant meat had bitter sauce, Ps. cvi. 15, Num. vi. 11, 33, Ps. lxxviii. 29–31. He gives them outward blessings, but curses them. Unbelievers, as such, have nothing in mercy, because neither rise nor issue merciful; not the rise, they proceed not from love; nor the issue, they make them not better. That is cursed which brings not a soul-blessing with it. Then only prayer is heard properly when mercy is the return of it.

Obj. If the Lord will not hear, why should we pray?

Ans. 1. We are obliged to obedience, though we be not assured of any reward. Subjection to God is necessary, being founded in our natures, as his creatures, and such creatures. Reward is arbitrary, as being grounded merely on his will, which moves freely. Though God do not hear, we are bound to pray, for he has commanded.

Ans. 2. Though unbelievers sin in praying, and therefore God will not hear them, yet they sin worse in not praying at all. It is a more heinous sin not to pray, than not to pray in faith. A total omission is a greater abomination than an undue performance. It is much worse to fail in the substance than in the manner only.

Ans. 3. It is more dangerous not to pray at all, than to pray amiss. The danger is proportionable to the heinousness of the sin. He may deny mercy to those that pray amiss, but he will pour wrath on those that pray not at all, Jer. x. 25.

Use. Exhortation to practise this duty. Whatever ye do, ask; whenever ye ask, ask in faith. Nothing more necessary than prayer; no qualification of prayer more necessary than faith. Of all duties and privileges, none more advantageous and comfortable than prayer; but it is faithful prayer: for without faith there is neither advantage by it, nor comfort in it. To pray, and not in faith, is to profane the ordinance, to take God's name in vain, and to pray in vain. Pray as much, as often as you will, if not in faith, you lose your labour. The apostle is peremptory: ver. 7, 'Let not that man think he shall receive any thing of the Lord.'

Now to prevent this wavering, this doubting, so dishonourable and offensive to God; so prejudicial, dangerous, uncomfortable to you: let me prescribe some directions, the observance of which will establish the heart, and encourage faith, in your approaches to God.

Direct. 1. Get assurance of your interest in the covenant; that Christ has loved you, and washed you from your sins in his blood; that he has given you his Spirit; that you are reconciled and in favour. If you be sure you are his favourites, you may be sure to have his ear. As acceptance of persons goes before acceptance of services, so assurance of that is the ground of confidence in this: 1 John v. 13–15, 'These things have I written, that ye may know that ye have eternal life, and that ye may believe on the name of the Son of God. And this is the confidence that we have in him, that, if we ask any thing according to his will, he heareth us. And if we know that he hear us, whatsoever we ask, we know that we have the petitions that we desired of him.' First, assurance that ye have eternal life, and then confidence that he will hear. If ye know that ye have right to eternal life by faith, the first fruits of it, then ye may be sure he will hear and grant; not hear in vain, but make sweet returns to the petitions he hears, ver. 15.: John xv. 7, 'If ye abide in me, and my words abide in you, ye shall ask what ye will, and it shall be done unto you.' First assure your union, and then doubt not of your audience. Union goes before audience, so assurance of one goes before assurance of the other.

Faith in its infancy may put forth some weaker acts of recumbency and dependence upon God for answer of prayer; but till it be grown up to assurance, it cannot be confident that he will hear or answer.

Direct. 2. Consider, the Lord is engaged to hear prayer. If the Lord be engaged, strong engagements lie upon him to hear. Faith may conclude he will hear, for he will not, he cannot, be false to his engagement; but he is engaged strongly, by his titles, attributes, &c.

(1.) His titles: Ps. lxv. 2, 'O thou that hearest prayer!' This is one of his titles of honour, he is a God that hears prayer; and it is as truly ascribed to him as mercy or justice. He hears all prayer, 'therefore unto thee shall all flesh come.' He never rejects any that deserves the name of a prayer, how weak, how unworthy soever the petitioner be. All flesh! and will he (may faith say) reject mine only? Rom. x. 12, 'He is rich unto all that call upon him;' Ps. lxxxvi. 5, 'Thou art plenteous in mercy to all that call upon thee;' Heb. xi. 6, 'A rewarder of them that diligently seek him.' This must be believed as certainly as we believe that God is. As sure as God is the true God, so sure is it that none who sought him diligently departed from him without a reward. He rewards all seekers, for *indefinita in materia necessaria æquipollet universali*. And if all, why not me? You may as well doubt that he is God as doubt that he will not reward, not hear prayer; so James i. 5, 'If any man lack wisdom, let him ask of God, that giveth to all men liberally, and upbraideth not, and it shall be given him.'

(2.) His attributes. To instance in his power and goodness; from hence faith may infer that he is both willing and able to hear, and from hence confidently conclude that he shall be heard. These are strong supports of faith, like the pillars of Solomon's temple: *Boaz*, 'In him is strength,' *i. e.*, he is able; and *Jachim*, 'He will establish,' *i. e.*, he is willing, 2 Chron. iii. 17. When you pray, consider he is,

[1.] Able to hear and give what you ask. It is gross atheism to doubt of this, to question omnipotency. If able to do all things, then sure what you pray for. Omnipotency has no bounds, no *nil ultra* to it, no limit to this but his will: Ps. cxxxv. 6, 'Whatsoever the Lord pleased, that did he in heaven and earth.' Consider he can do,

First, Abundantly, Eph. iii. 20. He can do more than we ask. We can think more than we have any reason or necessity to ask; he can do more than we can think, abundantly more, exceeding abundantly. He has done more at the requests of his people than we can ask, and he can do more than he has done: create more worlds; Heb. vii. 25, 'Save to the uttermost.'

Secondly, Easily. He can do the greatest thing you ask more easily than you can do the least thing you think. That which all the united strength of men and angels, the whole creation, cannot do at all, or not without great labour and travail, he can do as easily as you can move a finger or turn an eye; he can do that with a word, with a look, which all the creatures in heaven and earth cannot do with their whole strength; Mat. viii. 8, he can work a miracle with a word, how easily then can he do all that you need ask! And if it be so easy for him to grant, why should faith doubt?

Thirdly, Safely. Without any loss or damage to himself, without any diminution of that infinite store that is in himself. Whatever he gives he has never the less, for he bestows favours as the sun communicates light; the sun loseth nothing by shining, the more it shines the more illustrious; the more he bestows, the more glorious. All that you can desire is not so much to God as a drop is to the whole ocean. The sea would lose something, though an inconsiderable loss, by the subtraction of a drop; but God, whatever he gives, loses nothing, because what he bestows are things without him.

[2.] He is willing. Faith seldom questions God's power; that which hinders its actings is doubts whether he is willing. But there is more reason to question this, for he is as willing as he is able. His goodness is infinite, and so nothing less than his greatness. Nay, he is as willing (if not more willing) to hear as you are to pray, as willing to grant as you to petition, as willing you should have what you desire as you are to have it; nay, more; which appears from,

First, His secret will. He was willing, resolved, determined to hear, before you were willing to ask. He decreed it from eternity; he was willing before you had a will, a being. Nay, he was not only willing before, but he was the cause why you are willing. You must not think that your prayers move God to be willing; his will is the same for ever, not subject to the least motion or alteration. Prayers are rather a sign than a cause that God is willing. He is not made willing because we pray, but because he is willing he stirs up our hearts to pray: Ps. x. 17, 'Lord, thou hast heard the desire of the humble: thou wilt prepare their heart, thou wilt cause thine ear to hear.' He is first desirous to do us good, and then makes us desire it, and pray for it, that we may have them in his own way,—

a clear evidence he is more desirous than we, because he makes us, so our desires spring from this.

Secondly, His revealed will. He that prescribes the only course whereby prayer may get audience without fail, and commands us to follow that course, is more willing prayer shall be heard than those that are negligent in observing that only fallible way. But so it is, the Lord has commanded and prescribed such a course, which punctually followed, prayer can never return without the answer desired. But the best of men are more or less negligent in observing this prescript; therefore he is more willing our prayers should be heard than we ourselves.

Now, since the Lord is willing, and so willing, to hear, why should we not believe that he will hear? What strong encouragement is here to pray in faith! There is as much reason to believe that God will hear as there is to believe that you are willing to be heard. You may as well doubt that you are unwilling to be heard, as that God is unwilling to hear.

Thirdly, Christ's intercession. A great encouragement to faith, and so it is propounded by the apostle: Heb. iv. 14, 16, 'Seeing that we have a great high priest, that is passed into the heavens, Jesus the Son of God, let us hold fast our profession;' 'Let us come boldly unto the throne of grace, that we may obtain mercy,' &c.; *μετὰ παῤῥησίας*, a confident freedom to speak all your mind and heart. And speak it with assurance of prevailing: Heb. x. 19, 22, 'Having boldness to enter into the holiest by the blood of Jesus; let us draw near with a true heart, in full assurance of faith:' *ἐν πληροφορίᾳ πίστεως*. Why? Having a high priest whose office is to intercede. In him, as such, we may have access with boldness and confidence, Eph. iii. 12; *τὴν παῤῥησίαν*, &c., *ἐν πεποιθήσει*. This affords many things to embolden faith, and make it confident in its access by prayer.

First, He appears for us, Heb. ix. 24; he entered into heaven for this purpose; and for this end he sits on the right hand of the Majesty in the heavens, Heb. viii. 1. How confident might you present a petition, if assured that one who not only has the greatest power, but all power, in the court where you prefer it, would appear for you! Christ has all power in heaven and earth; in that court where your petition is to be presented, he appears for you who thinks it no robbery to be equal with God, he who can do whatever he will in the whole world. And can you doubt but that your petitions will prevail, when Christ owns you and stands up in your behalf?

Secondly, He presents us, our persons, unto God; presents us as acquitted from guilt, adorned with his righteousness, united to himself; in so near relations, as if we be rejected he must be rejected. He presents us as free from whatsoever might exasperate justice, provoke wrath, or render us in our addresses in the leastwise unacceptable, Zech. iii. 4. No filthy garments, nothing in our persons, so presented, can prejudice our petitions. This was typified by the high priest carrying the names of all the tribes on his breast into the holy of holies. He presents us to his Father as the travail of his soul; as though he should say, 'Behold I, and the children whom thou hast given me.' He presents us as those that are as dear to him as his spouse, does as it were take us by the hand and lead us to his Father and our Father, Eph. iii. 12; *προσαγωγὴν* seems to intimate such a similar posture. And Paul's expression, as some think, does imply as much: Philip. iii. 12, 'I follow after, if that I may apprehend that for which I am apprehended of Christ Jesus.' He presents us as those that are as near to him as his own members. And in reference to that intimate union we are said, Eph. ii. 6, to 'sit with him in heavenly places.' He presents us in such a lovely, endearing posture, as we need not doubt of acceptance, though himself should not pray for us: John xvi. 27, the Father himself loveth you, because he hath loved me. And when we are thus presented, what reason to doubt but that the Lord will hold forth the golden sceptre?

Thirdly, He offers our prayers. This was the high priest's office, Heb. v. 1, and viii. 3. And he was a type of Christ therein. The Lord receives our petitions from his hand, Rev. viii. 4. He, as it were, takes us in one hand, and our petitions in the other, and in this engaging posture delivers them; and can you fear the Lord will reject a petition delivered by the hand of Christ?

Fourthly, He sanctifies our prayers, and separates whatever is offensive from them. The Levitical priests were his type in this, who were to bear the iniquity of the holy things, Exod. xxviii. 36, 38. When the Lord looks upon Christ he takes notice of nothing but holiness in the prayers presented by him; he reads nothing in them as offered by Christ, but holiness to the Lord, Christ expunges the rest. Christ is always ready at hand to present them: 'He ever lives,' &c. He intercedes as Paul for Onesimus: 'I beseech thee for my sons,' Philem. 9. And if there be anything blame-worthy, put that on mine account, ver. 18, 19. He stands up as our advocate, to prevent the prejudice that sin might bring to our prayers, 1 John ii. 1. He not only petitions, but pleads. It is just and equal that the Lord should not take notice of sin in our prayers, so as to reject them, because he has fully satisfied even for every failing. If anything should make faith doubt of the success of prayer, it is their sinfulness; but Christ prevents that, for he has so fully satisfied for that, as the Lord will not, cannot take notice of it, so as to be angry with prayers. It is through the virtue of Christ's intercession that our prayers are not dead works, that they are freed from that guilt that would make them deadly. For this end he entered into the holy place with blood, Heb. ix. 12, sprinkling unclean prayers, that they may be sanctified and pure, 13, 14. And when they are thus purged, they are services acceptable to God, 1 Peter ii. 5. It is Christ's work to purge, and this his end, Mal. iii. 3, 4. He shall sit as a refiner and purifier of silver, and he shall purify the sons of Levi, &c. Now, is there any room for faith to doubt here? Will not the Lord accept of that which is rendered acceptable by Christ? Can he be displeased with that which through Christ is pleasant to him? Will he reject a peace-offering? Mal. i. 11. Christ's intercession leaves no exception. Will he deny a prayer against which he has no exception? Faith must either be confident here, or entertain blasphemous thoughts of God.

Fifthly, He answers all accusations that can be framed against our prayers. And indeed he having undertaken to remove all just ground of accusation, whatever is that way suggested reflects upon the sufficiency of his undertaking; and therefore it nearly concerns him to vindicate them, since if any exceptions can be taken to our prayers, for the utter rejecting of them, his own merit and satisfaction is equally liable thereto. Hence it is that he takes up Satan with such indignation for accusing Joshua: Zech. iii. 1, 2, 'The Lord rebuke thee, Satan,' &c. And hence it is that Paul's confidence rises up into a triumph: Rom. viii. 33, 'Who can lay anything to the charge of God's elect?' &c. And if our prayers can be charged with nothing to hinder the Lord from answering, why should we doubt but he will answer them? Will the Lord reject that against which there is no exception? Can we imagine the Lord will be of such a disposition, as none but the perversest of men are guilty of, to except against that which is freed from exception? Or will the Lord hearken to Satan rather than his own Son? Such reason is there for confidence here, that we must either believe, or entertain most horrid thoughts of God.

Sixthly, He mingles his own prayers and intercession with our requests. He joins with us, and as it were petitions that our petitions may be received. He adds the virtue of his merits to our prayers, and this, as incense, does sweeten and make them acceptable; so that these and all other services are like those contributions of the saints which Paul mentions, Philip. iv. 18, an odour of a sweet smell, or like Noah's offering, Gen. viii. 21, from which the Lord smelled a sweet savour.

This was typified by the legal service. While the people under the law were praying without, the priest offered incense within, Luke i. 8–10; answerably, while we are praying, Christ offers incense to sweeten them, and make them ascend as a delightful odour before God, Rev. viii. 3, 4.

Seventhly, That Christ does not only present us and our petitions unto the Father, but does as it were prefer a petition himself to the Lord, that he would answer our prayers, so that if the Lord deny us he must deny him too; and can we doubt Christ will be denied? We are as sure to be heard as Christ himself, and the Father always hears him, John xi. 42, xii. 28. No surer ground of confidence in the world than Christ's prayer for us.

It is true indeed, the Scripture, in describing Christ's intercession, uses some expressions which must not be taken properly; for if so understood, according to the letter, they import something inconsistent with Christ's glorious state, and his equality with the Father. But yet we have ground enough to say and believe that Christ prays for us, for Christ himself professes it, John xvii. He did pray, and he promises he will pray, John xvi. 26, John xiv. 16. And the Father expects and requires it, Ps. ii. 8, even after his exaltation.

There are four acts of Christ which amount to as much as prayers for us, are more than equivalent thereto, and afford more encouragement to faith than if he should now pray for us after the manner of men. I do the more willingly insist on this particular, because Christ's praying for us, and the success of our prayers, is such a confirmation of faith as leaves no room for doubting.

(1.) His requests on earth, which are properly and formally a prayer, and such a prayer as, though made on earth, is no less effectual than if it were now made in heaven, for he is always heard, then as well as now, John xi. 42. This prayer is delivered to us, John xvii. Wherein observe for whom, ver. 20, not only for his disciples, but for all that shall believe to the end of the world. For what? For all things that we stand in need of while we are on earth, nay, to all eternity. It is so comprehensive as there is nothing we can desire of God but may be reduced to some of his petitions; so that whatever we need desire was granted to Christ praying for us, before we actually pray for it. Therefore in respect our petitions are as good as granted before they be performed,* Christ has prevented us in desiring all things of his Father for us that we can desire for ourselves. Therefore when we go to pray, faith may be encouraged to

* Qu. 'preferred'?—ED.

consider that Christ prayed for us, and was heard as to those very particulars which we are to pray for.

(2.) The cry of his blood; that is metaphorically, yet really a prayer. It is a pleading, a speaking blood: 'It speaks better things,' &c., Heb. xii. 24. It is as effectual to procure the bestowing of those things which are purchased by it as innocent blood is to procure vengeance for those that spill it. Christ's blood is an importunate, a prevailing advocate, it is never non-suited; its plea is justice; it is just the Lord should hear our prayers, since this was one end for which the blood of Christ was shed; it is just our request should be granted, since his blood was the price of this privilege; the Lord should be unjust, and undervalue the blood of his Son, if he should not give that which he shed his blood to purchase. You must either believe upon this consideration, or blaspheme. It is the blood of the covenant, Heb. x. 29, by which the blessings of the covenant were purchased and are confirmed. Now that is one article of the covenant, that whatever we ask in Christ's name shall be given; and his blood cries for the performance of this, and justice itself hears it. It is but a righteous, a just thing in reference to Christ, though pure mercy to us, that all our prayers should be heard.

(3.) The will of his divine nature; this is transcendently a prayer. A prayer I call it, because his prayer on earth runs in the same tenor: John xvii. 24, 'Father, I will,' &c. It is the will of Christ, as he is God, that all our prayers should be heard, else he would not so often promise it. A prayer transcendently, because though it differ from ours in form, yet it far, yea infinitely, transcends them in efficacy. His bare will, as he is God, is more effectual for the comfortable returns of our petitions than if as man, and as he was upon earth, he should prostrate himself, and with strong cries and tears importune the Lord to answer us; for his divine will is all one with his Father's will, they differ not; therefore if the Father should deny him, he should deny himself. Here is encouragement indeed; we may as well imagine he will deny himself as doubt he will deny us.

(4.) The desires of his human nature. This is effectuallly a prayer, it has all that is essential to a prayer. The voice and outward posture are but accidents. It is a mental, though not a vocal prayer; has as much of a prayer in it as any angel or soul can make, 1 Sam. i. 13. This was his desire on earth, and this is his desire in heaven, that all our prayers may be answered. His affection to us was not impaired by his removal, but rather improved, and he that was heard in that which he feared will be heard in that which he desires. Now let faith put all these together, and it will be easy to read the necessity of an answer. Let it observe the premises, and it may well conclude the Lord will answer. If the Lord will hear his Son, if he will not deny himself, if he cannot be unrighteous, if he cannot be changeable, then he will hear us.

4. The Spirit's office. He is a Spirit of supplication, Zech. xii. 10. It is his function to intercede for us, to pray in us, *i. e.*, to make our prayers. He, as it were, writes our petitions in the heart, we offer them; he indites a good matter, we express it. That prayer which we are to believe will be accepted, is the work of the Holy Ghost; it is his voice, motion, operation, and so his prayer. Therefore when we pray he is said to pray, and our groans are called his, and our design and intent in prayer his meaning, φρόνημα τοῦ πνεύματος, Rom. viii. 26, 27, συναντιλαμβάνεται; he joins with us in prayer, and supports us under infirmities with his own

strength, *ὑπερεντυγχάνει ὑπὲρ ἡμῶν.* That prayer is the work of the Spirit, appears in many particulars.

(1.) He stirs us up to pray. He prepares and disposes, incites and inclines the heart to make requests; removes that backwardness, averseness, indisposedness, that is in us naturally unto this spiritual service: Ps. x. 17, 'Thou wilt prepare their heart.' He prepares it by his Spirit. *Interpellat,* says Augustine, *quia interpellare nos facit.* He intercedes for us, because he makes us to intercede. He stirs us up to do it, *nos ad preces instigat,* excites us, provokes us to pray. *Nemo sponte præmeditari vel unam syllabam potest,* no man of his own accord can premeditate one syllable, says Calvin, *nisi arcano spiritus sui instinctu nos Deus pulsat,* but that God by the secret instinct of his Spirit does knock up the heart to it; he puts the heart into a praying frame, and sometimes excites us so powerfully, as we cannot withhold from pouring out our souls before him. As it was with the prophet in another case,—Jer. xx. 9, 'His word was in mine heart as a burning fire,' &c.,—so, as to prayer, the workings of the Spirit are sometimes so powerful in the heart, so fill the soul, that it cannot contain, but must vent itself, and pour out its requests. Thus with David: Ps. xxxix. 2, 3, 'I was dumb with silence; I held my peace, even from good; and my sorrow was stirred. My heart was hot within me; while I was musing, the fire burned: then spake I with my tongue.' Those that have the spirit of prayer, do find this by experience, especially when the Lord intends, and is about to shew them some special favour, or do some great thing for them, he stirs them up answerably to seek it; so that often, if they observe it, they may discover the return of their prayers in the temper and workings of their hearts to it. The Spirit's preparing the heart to pray, signifies the Lord will cause his ear to hear.

(2.) He presents matter, teaches what we shall pray for. This is plain in the apostle's expression, Rom. viii. We know not what is proper and expedient for us, what is seasonable, what is best for us, or when it will be so. We of ourselves would be ready to ask that which is impertinent, or unseasonable, or hurtful to us; we would have ease, and liberty, and plenty, and deliverance out of troubles, or freedom from sufferings; we would have joy and assurance, yea, triumphs and raptures; we would have these or the like presently, and in full measure, at such a time, or in such a degree as might be prejudicial to our souls; and so we would seek them if we were left to ourselves, if the Spirit did not better direct us, and lead us to what is most necessary, and proper, and advantageous. And this *κατὰ Θεὸν ἐντυγχάνει,* he helps us to pray according to the will of God, for such things as are according to his will. *Ut bene possit mens orare,* says Ambrose,* *præcedit Spiritus, et deducit eam in viam rectam;* that the soul may pray well, the Spirit goes before it, and guides it into the right way, that we may not seek what is carnal, nor things that are either too small or too great for us. A good physician knows what diet is most proper, and when it will be most for the advantage of health. The opportuneness of meat sometimes restores the health, which, if it be taken unseasonably, endangers the patient; therefore, says he, because we know not what to pray for, and how we ought to seek it, *postulat pro nobis Spiritus,* the Spirit intercedes for us, viz., by directing us what to ask.

(3.) He helps his people to expressions; and therefore that manner of praying seems best, which gives most liberty to the Spirit in its workings, and leaves us under his influence and assistance, not only as to the inward,

* Ambr. l. iv., Epist. 28.

but also as to the outward manner of praying, letting the Spirit clothe his own matter in his own dress, and taking words from him as well as things, when he is pleased to afford them. I do not say that all the expressions used by his people in prayer are from the Spirit, nor that he always helps them to expressions immediately. Whether they have them by the use of such means as he has appointed and concurs with, or whether they have them by immediate suggestion, either way they are from the assistance of the Spirit; and that he is ready to assist them some way, even as to words, seems signified by the apostle's expression, Rom viii. which I have opened before, and shall now further insist on. The word is ὑπερεντυγχάνει; ἐντυγχάνειν κατά τινα, is to act as an accuser, a κατήγορος; ὑπερεντυγχάνειν ὑπέρ τινος, is to act as an advocate, a συνήγορος. And so the Holy Ghost is frequently in the New Testament called an Advocate. Παράκλητος, as the Spirit is called by our Lord Jesus, is an Advocate, one called in for the assistance of a client. And very fitly may παράκλητος be rendered an advocate, this comprehending the other notions, whereby it is expressed, particularly that of a comforter, by which it is translated. For an advocate is the comfort and encouragement of his client, advises him, pleads for him, moves for him, draws up his petitions or motions, dictating the form or words. And so παράκλησις in other authors is sometimes used for a prayer or petition, and παρακαλεῖν is to petition or invocate. Now the Holy Ghost is an advocate for his people, both with men and with God. And by observing how he performs this office for them with men, we may probably collect how he performs it for them with God. He acts as an advocate for them with men, by telling them what they shall say when they are brought before men's tribunal, Mat. x. 20, Mark xiii. 11, Luke xii. 11, 12, and xxi. 14, 15; answerably he acts as their advocate with God by dictating or suggesting to them what they shall say in prayer, when they come to the throne of grace. And so the best interpreters that I meet with explain the expression. *Veluti verba et suspiria nobis intus dictat*,* he doth as it were inwardly dictate to us words and sighs; he assists us by his holy inspiration both with powerful and effectual words and sighs; he telleth us as it were within what we shall say, prompteth as it were our lesson to us.†

(4.) He stirs up affections in prayer suitable to the subject thereof, joy or sorrow, and love and delight, with earnest desires, called στεναγμοὶ; fills the heart with affections and motions, as manifest themselves by sighs and groans, and cannot otherwise be expressed, therefore called ἀλαλητοί; so full of affectionate workings as it cannot find vent by words.

A pretender to the Spirit has more in his expressions than is in his heart; but one effectually assisted by the Spirit, has more in his heart than he can express; the words of those over-reach, but the expressions of these fall short of what they feel within. The Spirit helps his people to the sense of their spiritual state, makes them sensible of their spiritual wants, their inward distempers, their soul-grievances; makes them apprehensive of the importance, the necessity, the excellency of what they are to seek, and hence spring love to them, desires after them, zeal and fervour in seeking them. Hence those affectionate workings in their hearts, which are too big to be let out by words, which are signified by sighs and groans, such as cannot otherwise be uttered.

(5.) He acts graces in prayer; helps the weakness and infirmity of spiritual habits and principles, and draws them out into vigorous exercise. He helps the soul to approach with confidence, and yet with reverence;

* Beza. † Eng. Annot.

with filial fear, and yet with an emboldened faith; with zeal and importunity, and yet with humble submission; with lively hope, and yet with self-denial. As it is the Spirit of supplication, so it is the Spirit of grace, not only works grace in the heart, but sets it a-work, and brings it into exercise, as in other acts and duties, so especially in that of supplication.

(6.) He removes, or helps the soul against distempers which are ready to seize on the soul in prayer, distractions, straitness of heart, indifferency, formality, lukewarmness, hypocrisy, weariness, pride, self-confidence. Now since thus much of prayer is to be ascribed to the Spirit, since he gives both matter and form, expression and affection, the act and motion to the act, since he teaches both when, and what, and how we should pray, affords assistance answerable, well may believers' prayers be counted the work, &c., of the Spirit. And this consideration affords great encouragement to faith. If prayer were our own work only, we might fear it would be rejected, for all our righteousness is as filthy rags; but the work of the Spirit must needs be acceptable, yea, accepted. If we ourselves only spoke, the Lord might shut his ear and refuse to hear sinners. But prayer is the voice of the Spirit: he speaks in us and by us, Mat. x. 20; and the Lord will certainly listen to that voice. Prayer is the motion of the Spirit, and whatever motion he makes in the court of heaven, it can never be rejected. If we prayed of ourselves only, the Lord might refuse to send any comfortable returns; but since the Spirit intercedes for us, the Lord cannot deny him, else he should deny himself. *Nobis gemendi et interpellandi imponit affectum.** The Spirit intercedes as effectually, though not in the same manner, as Christ. Christ intercedes by office, the Spirit by operation. Christ appears in person for us, and pleads our cause himself; the Spirit inspires and assists us to plead for ourselves. Not only through Christ, but by the Spirit we have access, Eph. ii. 18. And will the Lord exclude those who have access by the Spirit? The Spirit 'strengthens us with might in the inner man,' Eph. iii. 16, and the strength of the Spirit will prevail, as Jacob. Come armed with this strength, and you may come boldly, Heb. x. 15, 19.

5. Consider his providence. That affords many encouragements to faith.

(1.) He hears those that cannot pray, answers that which cannot be called a prayer. He hears irrational creatures, brutes, listens to their cries, though they want both matter and form of praying. He rewards their very looks, answers their expectations, fulfils their desires, though they do not, nor cannot be properly said, either to look up to him, or wait on him, or desire of him. Ps. civ. 21, 'The young lions roar after their prey, and seek their meat of God;' ver. 27, 'These wait all upon thee, that thou mayest give them their meat in due season: thou openest thine hand;' ver. 28, 'They are filled with good;' Ps. cxlvii. 9, 'He giveth to the beast his food, to the young ravens that cry;' Ps. cxlv. 15, 16, 'The eyes of all wait upon thee, and thou givest them meat in due season: thou openest thine hand, and satisfiest the desire of every living thing.' They do but open their eyes, and God opens his hand. They do but intimate a natural desire by crying and looking, and God satisfies.

Now may faith say, as 1 Cor. ix. 9, 'Doth God take care for oxen? or saith he it altogether for our sakes? For our sakes no doubt, that he that prayeth should pray in faith,' &c. Will the Lord hear lions and ravens, and will he not hear me? Will he satisfy their natural, and not my spiritual desires? Will he regard when their eyes are lift up, and not the lifting

* August.

up of my heart? Am not I much better than they? It is Christ's own argument to strengthen faith, Mat. vi. 26. Shall he not much more hear me? ver. 30. He that will doubt here, deserves the brand of ὀλιγόπιστος, may well pass for one that has little faith. It is very weak, if this will not support it.

(2.) He grants some things to men that they pray not for; much more will he grant when they pray: Isa. lxv. 1, 'I am found of them that sought me not;' ver. 24, 'Before they call, I will answer.' Some things, nay, the greatest, are granted to those that pray not. No prayer had any influence in election, and our prayers did contribute nothing to the glorious work of redemption. These fountains of all our mercies were digged without the help of any; the greatest, the sweetest streams of love that issue hence run freely, before our prayers can draw them out. Regeneration, justification, pardon, adoption, reconciliation, are bestowed on those who cannot, who will not pray for them. For we cannot unfeignedly desire these, before they are given; and will we pray for that which we do not desire? And how many other mercies, which we thought not of before we enjoyed them! Much precious fruit falls into our laps, before we by prayer shake the tree. It may be they were the issue of some other's prayers, but not of ours. Now if the water of life do flow in such streams upon us when we pray not, how pleasantly will they flow when they are drawn by the attractive power of prayer! If the Lord is found when we seek not, open when we knock not, answer when we call not, how much more will he open and answer when we knock and call! If the greatest be vouchsafed before we have hearts to pray, how confident may we be that prayer will obtain the less!

(3.) He makes some kind of returns to the prayers of unbelievers. He heard the voice of Ishmael, Gen. xxi. 17, 18, &c., a persecutor; of Ahab, the most abominable of all the twenty kings of Israel. Now if they be heard in any sense, who hate God and are hated of him, they whose prayers are as the howlings of dogs, an abomination, to whom God is no way engaged, who have none to intercede, none to help their infirmities, no promise, how much more those who are his servants, and have interest in the intercession of Christ?

6. Consider the nature and dignity of prayer, which affords divers arguments to confirm faith.

(1.) It is God's ordinance, instituted and enjoined for this end. He commands us to pray, that we may be heard; and therefore ordinarily, where you meet with a command, you find a promise: 'Call upon me in the day of trouble, and I will answer;' 'Ask, and ye shall have,' Mat. viii. 7, 8. When he commands prayer, he promises audience. It was his intention in this institution. Therefore if the Lord should not hear, his ordinance would be in vain, the Lord should lose his end. And is it not more easy to believe the Lord will hear it, than to believe he will come short of his end?

(2.) He in Scripture adorns it with, and ascribes to it, many transcendent privileges, such as, considered, may fortify the most languishing faith. There is a strength in prayer which has power with God: Hos. xii. 3, 4, 'By his strength he had power with God: yea, he had power over the angel, and prevailed; he wept, and made supplication unto him.' That strength was weeping and supplication. With this he wrestled, Gen. xxxii. 24. He had power, i.e., was a prince, a princely deportment. Poor dust and ashes, in a praying posture, are in the state of princes, honourable and powerful, in such a state as the Lord will not resist; therefore it must prevail. The Lord may seem to wrestle, as though he would give a repulse to the assaults of prayer, but this is but to exercise the strength of this princely champion; he honours it so much, as in the issue he always suffers it to prevail. No wonder if it be powerful, for it lays hold on God's strength. So some apply that, Isa. xxvii. 5, 'Let him lay hold of my strength, that he may make peace with me, and he shall make peace.' The Lord, for our encouragement, condescends to express the power of grace in such terms, as though it laid some restraint upon his infinite self: Exod. xxxii. 10, 'Let me alone.' He seems so unwilling to deny prayer, as though he were unable to act anything against it. That is a transcendent expression, Isa. xlv. 11, 'Thus saith the Lord, the Holy One of Israel, and his Maker, Ask me of things to come concerning my sons; and the work of my hands, command ye me.' A wonderful indulgence! An astonishing condescension! As though asking were commanding. It is blasphemy to imagine that the creature should command the sovereign Majesty of heaven; yet thus much we may safely infer, prayer shall as surely prevail, as though it could command; it shall prevail as much with God, though infinitely above us, as we can do with those who are under our command.

(3.) Prayer is the Lord's delight, the most pleasing service we can ordinarily tender; therefore he does not only most frequently command it, but importunately sue for it. Let me hear thy voice, says Christ to his spouse, Cant. ii. 14, for thy voice is sweet. It is sweet as incense, Ps. cxli. 2; Prov. xv. 8, his delight; ascends as the odour of a sweet smell; no sacrifice more acceptable. One sincere prayer pleases him better than hundreds of rams, or thousands of rivers of oil. Therefore, after he had declared how little he needs or regards sacrifices and burnt-offerings, he tells what would better please him: Ps. l. 14, 15, 'Offer unto God thanksgiving; and pay thy vows to the Most High: and call upon him in the day of trouble; I will deliver thee, and thou shalt glorify me.' The reason is, it most glorifies him; it acknowledges and gives a clear testimony to most of his glorious perfections, power, wisdom, bounty, goodness, immensity, all-sufficiency, providence. Now that which most glorifies him does most please, for his glory is the end of all his administrations. Now, will the Lord reject that which pleases him? will he not listen to that wherein his soul delights? will he not make gracious returns to that which is the most acceptable service?

(4.) He threatens men for not answering prayer: Prov. xxi. 13, 'Whoso stoppeth his ears at the cry of the poor, he shall cry himself, but shall not be heard.' Now, will he do that himself for which he threatens us? Mat. xviii. 28. He will deal severely with those who will not hearken to the importunity of such as seek to them in their want and distress.

7. The things prayed for may afford arguments for faith. Either they are of great consequence or of small consequence. If small, then faith may argue, Will the Lord stand with me for small things? will he deny inferior mercies? will he who has granted greater things deny less? will not infinite love vouchsafe small favours? will he who has given me Christ deny any thing, any small thing? will not he who has delivered your souls from death deliver your feet from falling? If of great consequence, faith may argue, Though it be great, yet the Lord has granted greater to me, to others. Is anything greater than Christ? any of more importance than pardon of sin? is any more precious than the blood of Christ? I can ask nothing so great but the Lord has already granted greater; or, suppose it

be the greatest thing that ever was granted to or desired by you, the greater it is the more encouragement to ask it, the more hopes God will grant it. It becomes the great God to grant great things, 'To him alone who does great wonders,' Ps. cxxxvi. 4. When you ask great things, you ask such as becomes God to give, 'whose mercy is great above the heavens,' Ps. lvii. 10. Nothing under heaven can be too great for him to give. The greater things he bestows, the greater glory redounds to his name. Great and wondrous works speak the glorious honour of his majesty, Ps. cxlv. 5. Great personages shew their magnificence by great presents; it is their delight, their honour. God shews his infinite greatness by doing such things, bestowing such favours, as are above the creature's power. Jehohsaphat argues, 2 Chron. xx. 6, 'Art thou not God in heaven? and rulest not thou over all the kingdoms of the heathens? and in thine hand is there not power and might, so that not none is able to withstand thee?' But suppose the greatness of what you desire does discourage, consider it is great only in your apprehension. Nothing is great to God. See how he is described, Isa. xl. 15, 17, 22. What greater than this vast fabric of heaven and earth? How did the Lord make this only with a word? Let there be, and it was so, Ps. xxxiii. 6. It is true the Lord speaks not, but this manner of expression tells us the effecting of the greatest things is no more to him than the speaking of a word is to us, 2 Chron. xiv. 11, so 1 Sam. xiv. 6. It is all one with God to save by few or many; to do that which seems great to us, as that which seems small.

8. Consider the promises. The Lord has promised he will hear. If ye doubt he will hear, ye doubt he is not faithful. Consider how many, how universal, how engaging.

(1.) The *multitude*. No duty, no act, to which the Lord has made so many promises as to prayer. Now, why should the Lord multiply his promises, but that he will never fail to answer, but that he would have us to be confident we shall never fail?

(2.) *Universality*. He has promised again and again to hear whoever prays, and grant whatever is prayed for. Whoever prays, whatever they pray for, they shall be answered, it shall be granted. *Whosoever:* Joel ii. 32, 'Whosoever shall call on the name of the Lord shall be delivered;' repeated Acts ii. 21; 'plenteous in mercy to all that call upon him,' Ps. lxxxvi. 5; 'nigh to all,' Ps. cxlv. 16; 'rich unto all,' Rom. x. 12. *Whatsoever:* 'All things whatsoever ye shall ask in prayer, believing, ye shall receive,' Mat. xxi. 22; John xvi. 23, 'Ye shall ask me nothing; whatsoever ye shall ask the Father in my name, he will give it you;' 1 John iii. 22, 'Whatsoever we ask, we receive of him;' John xv. 7, 'Ask what you will, and it shall be done unto you.'

(3.) The *obligement*. It is more engaging to him than an oath, he more values it than we our lives. It is more valuable to him than heaven and earth; he will suffer these to perish rather than a jot of his word shall fail: 'Heaven and earth shall pass away, but my word shall not pass away.' The Lord would lose more by failing to answer than you by failing of an answer. That is engaged for your security, which is more precious to God than anything you ask: his word, truth, faithfulness, his seal, his oath, the blood of his Son, all these are engaged in a promise.

9. Consider your relation to God. He is your Father; Christ teaches us to begin with this. This is a strong support to faith, and Christ makes this use of it, to encourage us to pray, and pray in faith: Mat. vii. 7, 8, 'Ask, and it shall be given you; seek, and ye shall find; knock, and it

shall be opened to you,' &c. There is the promise. The argument whereby he would persuade us to believe the promise in praying, see ver. 9–11. The Lord is ready to give to them that ask, as the most indulgent father to the best beloved child; nay, more ready, much more ready: 'How much more shall your Father which is in heaven give good things to them that ask him!' ver. 11. He is much more ready to give the greatest favours, than earthly parents to give the least. That which is *good things* in Matthew, is the *Spirit* in Luke xi. 13. And what greater gift than the Spirit? There are many things may hinder earthly parents, poverty, or covetousness, but nothing to hinder God, he has infinite treasures and a large heart; he can give whatever we ask, 'The earth is the Lord's,' &c.; and he is more willing, as much more as heaven is above earth.

10. He gets glory by hearing prayer. We do not only glorify him by praying, as I shewed before, but he glorifies himself by answering prayer, Ps. l. The Lord gets by giving, gets that which is of more account with him than what he gives. It is his interest to grant as well as ours to receive. If the Lord should reject our prayers, he would reject his own honour.

11. Consider the success of others, how effectual the prayers of God's ancient people have been; this affords great encouragement.

(1.) You never find any prayer wholly denied. In all the Scripture, not one example of a faithful prayer without a gracious return. 'He never said to the house of Jacob, Seek my face in vain.' Those instances which seem to contradict this do confirm it. David prayed for the life of his child and prevailed not, but his prayer was answered in that the Lord gave him another child, honourably born, and rarely endowed. Moses prays that he might take possession of Canaan, he was not heard as to that particular, but the Lord gratifies his prayer with a miracle, shews him what he desired in a miraculous way, commits the conduct of the Israelites to a dear relation of his, his servant Joshua, and, instead of the earthly, translates him into the heavenly Canaan, where Moses will acknowledge it was the sweetest return of prayer he ever had experience of. Though on earth he complained the Lord would not hear him, yet there he does praise the Lord for so answering his prayer. And if the Lord did never deny prayer, will he begin now?

(2.) He usually gave more than was prayed for: Ps. xxi. 4, 'He asked life of thee, and thou gavest it him, even length of days for ever and ever.' So to Solomon, 1 Kings iii. 9–13. Abraham prays for one, God gives many, by Hagar, Gen. xvii., Sarah, Keturah, Gen. xxv. David desired one thing, Ps. xxvii.; he gives that, and withal a kingdom, dominion, glory. Jacob seems to desire nothing but for safety and necessity, bread and raiment, and to return in peace; but the Lord adds plenty to safety, brings him back with great substance and a numerous issue: Gen. xxviii. 20, 'If God will be with me, and will keep me in this way that I go, and will give me bread to eat, and raiment to put on.' There is his vow, his desire. See his return, chap. xxxii. 10, 'I went over this Jordan with this staff, and now I am become two bands.' And if the Lord will give more than is prayed for, sure, may faith say, he will give as much. The Lord is not less bountiful now than in former times; his ear is not straitened nor his hand shortened, his ear is as open to hear, and his hand as open to reward.

(3.) Prayer procured greater things in former times than any you have now occasion to ask. It wrought miracles, and that may be ascribed to it which the apostle attributes to faith, Heb. xi. 33–35; faith in prayer, faithful prayer. This, as handled by Elias, was the key of heaven, which he thereby opened when and how he pleased, James v. 17, 18. Prayer preserved Daniel in the midst of devouring lions; the opening of his mouth did shut theirs. This brought Jonah out of the midst of the sea, out of the belly of a whale, safe on shore. This revoked the sentence of death passed on Hezekiah, caused the sun to go backward, and brought an angel from heaven to destroy Sennacherib's host. This ruined an army of ten hundred thousand, and made them fly and fall before Asa, 2 Chron. xiv. 12. It drew out the Lord's hand, destroys Jehoshaphat's enemies by their own hands, arms them against themselves, and ruins them without his help, chap. xx. This brings light into a dungeon, an angel from heaven into a prison, breaks off chains, and opens iron gates, Acts xii. 5–7, &c. Did it work miracles in former times, and will it not procure ordinary mercies now? Is it less effectual? Does the Lord less regard it, or love us?

(4.) He heard his ancient people not only for themselves, but for others; for those whom he would not hear praying for themselves; for unbelievers, for the most abominable of sinners; and that not only for one, or few, but for whole cities, whole nations; Abraham for Abimelech, a heathen, a prince in whose territories there was no fear of God. The Lord tells him this, Gen. xx. 7, and he was as good as his word, ver. 17. How often did he hear Moses for a whole nation in high rebellion against God! Even in the height of his fury he appeased him. Nay, he hears Abraham for five cities, the most abominable that were to be found on the earth, Gen. xviii. 23–33. He makes six motions for the Sodomites, and the Lord rejects not one. He condescends, even to astonishment. We may think it had been wonderful if the Lord had but yielded to the first, to save five whole cities destined to destruction, if there had been in them but fifty righteous persons; but so prevalent is prayer, as the Lord yields to save five cities for ten men, verse 32. Now if the Lord will hear his people for others, will he not hear me for myself? If he would hear them for heathens, rebels, idolaters, Sodomites, will he not hear me in covenant with him, justified by him, obedient to him, approved of him?

Obj. But does not the church complain: Ps. lxxx. 4, 'O Lord God of hosts, how long wilt thou be angry against the prayer of thy people?' Lam. iii. 8, 'When I cry and shout, he shutteth out my prayer.'

Ans. This may be misapprehension; think the Lord angry when he is not; or when not at their prayers, but at their sins. Zion complains, 'The Lord had forsaken,' &c., but the Lord convinces her it was a mistake, Isaiah xlix. 14–16. They thought the Lord denies because he delayed; think him angry, because he did not answer presently; whereas delay itself is sometimes a gracious answer, a sign of love rather than anger. To bestow mercies when petitioners are unfit for them, is to answer prayer in anger; to defer till then is love. Their eyes may be so fixed on the particular desired, as to take no notice of whatever other is returned.

12. Consider your own experiences, how many times God has answered your prayers formerly; that will be a great encouragement to trust him for time to come. Those that have tried God, are inexcusable if they will not trust him. His word is a sufficient ground for faith in prayer; but experience, withal, should exclude all doubting. This should both encourage to pray and believe. David made this use of it: Ps. cxvi. 2, 'Because he hath inclined his ear unto me, therefore will I call upon him as long as I live.' Those who know what it is to enjoy communion with God in prayer,

and make conscience to pray frequently and fervently, must needs have many experiences of sweet returns. It may be you have been afflicted in conscience, and by crying to God, found comfort, as David, Psalm cxvi.; or in doubts and perplexities, 'I cried to God, he resolved me;' or in wants and necessities, and 'he supplied me;' or in fear and dangers, and 'he delivered me;' or in trouble and affliction, and 'he supported and relieved me,' and sanctified it to me; or under temptation, buffeted by Satan, and 'his grace was sufficient for me;' or assaulted with some strong lusts, and 'he subdued them, and strengthened me;' or very desirous of some blessing, and 'he bestowed it on me.' Now faith should argue from these experiences, The Lord has heard me formerly, and why should I doubt but he will hear me now? He is the same God still, and prayer is as prevalent, as acceptable. My person and services were unworthy then, and this did not hinder, therefore it will not now, Ps. vi. 9. Paul's faith grows confident from former experiences: 2 Tim. iv. 17, 'The Lord stood with me, and strengthened me,' &c. There is his experience. See what inference his faith makes, verse 18, 'The Lord shall deliver me from every evil work,' &c. So David, 1 Sam. xvii. 34–37. In like manner we should conclude, because the Lord has heard me so frequently, so freely, so graciously, notwithstanding all my failings, weaknesses, unworthiness, therefore I will believe he will hear me still, he will answer me for time to come.

13. Limit not yourselves, nor the Lord, to the particular desired. You may pray in faith, though you be not confident that the very thing desired shall be granted; for if you apprehend that this is the only way to pray in faith, you will neglect other ways. And since this particular confidence is but required sometimes, you will but pray sometimes in faith, whereas this is always required. To prevent this, consider there are divers acts which faith may put forth in prayer, any of which, in its season, will make the duty a prayer of faith.

(1.) Sometimes determinately; or, if the word be not too bold, peremptorily. Faith may so act when you pray, being in covenant, for things absolutely necessary for God's glory and your salvation, those things which have a necessary connection with these. So you may ask in faith so much of temporal or spiritual blessings, as without which you cannot honour God, or be serviceable in your callings, and be confident of receiving them.

Or, when the Lord promises peremptorily and absolutely, faith is to keep proportion with the promise. If he promise absolutely, we may believe absolutely that we shall receive: so Heb. xiii. 5, 'I will never leave thee, nor forsake thee.' He promises peremptorily; so we desire he would not forsake us, and believe we shall be heard in this determinately: so John xiii. 1, he says absolutely, 'Having loved his own, he loved them to the end.' So we may pray he would love us with an everlasting love, and believe that he will hear us in this particular: so Rom. vi. 14, 'Sin shall not have dominion over you.'

Or when he promises conditionally, but has made you partakers of the condition; for then it is equivalent to an absolute promise: so Mark xvi. 16, 'He that believeth and is baptized, shall be saved.' If he have given faith, you may pray for salvation, and believe that he will hear, *i.e.*, he will save: Prov. xxviii. 13, 'He that confesseth and forsaketh his sins, shall have mercy.' If he have enabled you to confess and forsake your sins, in judgment, affection, and practice, you may pray for and expect to find mercy. So Mat. v., if you mourn, you may pray for comfort, and believe you shall receive it.

(2.) Sometimes indefinitely. That is, when you believe your prayer shall be heard, though faith define not, *i.e.*, pitch not upon any particular way, how, or when, or in what kind. He may be sometimes said to pray in faith who believes his person and prayer shall be accepted, though faith expect not a particular answer. This has place when the promise is indefinite, when a mercy is promised under a general notion, without defining the way, time, manner, kind, when, and how, or in what it shall prove a mercy to me: so Rom. viii. 28, 'All things work together for good to them that love God, to them who are the called according to his purpose.' If you pray that such an occurrence or dispensation may work for good, and believe that it shall in general, though you be not confident that it shall do it in such a manner, time, way, degree, yet you may pray in faith: so Isaiah iii. 10, 'Say to the righteous that it shall be well with him.' If you pray it may go well in every condition, and believe it shall, and you shall receive a suitable answer: so Joel ii. 32, 'Whosoever shall call on the name of the Lord, shall be delivered.' Though ye believe not ye shall be delivered at such a time, in such a manner, by such means; yet if in general ye be confident of deliverance, ye shall have it.

(3.) Sometimes disjunctively. Believe not precisely that you shall receive this you pray for; but either this, or some other; something as good or better in reference to God's glory and your happiness; this is sufficient when you are not certain whether that you pray for be best for you; I say not, whether it seem, but whether it be. In this case, it is not required you should believe determinately that you shall receive what you pray for, but disjunctively, either this, or some other. In such a condition was Paul: Philip. i. 23, 24, 'I am in a strait betwixt two, having a desire to depart, and to be with Christ; which is far better: nevertheless to abide in the flesh is more needful for you.' When you are in such a strait you may pray for what you apprehend to be best, but not believe you shall be heard in that precisely; but either in that, or some other thing better or equivalent; so in praying for riches, posterity, deliverance, and indeed all things that are in their own nature, or to you, indifferent; you may desire riches, &c., but it is not necessary you should be confident that God will make you rich; but either do this or something as good.

(4.) Sometimes conditionally. We are to pray for nothing but what is commanded or promised; and the things we are to pray for are held forth in the word with two sorts of conditions, some annexed to the promise, some to the thing promised. Spiritual blessings are conditional, because sometimes conditions are annexed to the promises, whereby God engages himself to give them. Now when he has already wrought the conditions, we may pray in faith for them absolutely, as before. When the conditions are not wrought, then we should for the conditions themselves, not for the blessings conditionally: as Mat. v. 6, that we may hunger and thirst after righteousness; and Rev. ii. 10, that we may be faithful unto death. Temporal blessings are conditional, because conditions are annexed to the things themselves, and they are such as these: if it seem good, if it be thy will, if it be for thy glory, if it be for my soul's good. Temporal favours are to be asked in faith, but faith must act conditionally. The like is to be observed about the removal of afflictions, and vouchsafing of spiritual favours that tend to our well-being: faith in asking these must be acted, but acted conditionally, and with submission. An example we have in

David, a man strong in faith and much in prayer: 2 Sam. xv. 25, 26, 'If I shall find favour in the eyes of the Lord, he will bring me again, and shew me both it and his habitation. But if he thus say, I have no delight in thee; behold, here I am, let him do to me as seemeth good unto him.' And in Christ himself, his faith acted conditionally: Mat. xxvi. 39, 'If it be possible, let this cup pass from me: nevertheless, not as I will, but as thou wilt.'

14. Labour to remove those discouragements which hinder the exercise of faith in prayer, or weaken it in its actings.

(1.) Great discouragement is, jealousy that the Lord has not heard you formerly. If you entertain such conceits that God has denied, rejected your petitions formerly, you may be apt to fear he will, or may do so for time to come. Such fears and jealousies are as worms at the root, or as a palsy in the hand of faith, deprives it of strength and stedfastness; they are as storms, which unsettle, shock faith, and make it waver as a wave of the sea, ver. 7. This must be removed, as inconsistent with that confidence which the Lord expects in all that approach to him. To remove it, consider, the Lord may answer your prayers when you take no notice of it. He has many ways to answer our petitions, whenas we ordinarily take notice but of one; and if the return come not that way, we conclude there is none, and thereby both wrong the Lord and ourselves. We may think he does not hear, we are not answered, when he both hears and answers us. Take notice how many ways God may answer your prayer, and you will see much more reason to conclude that he granted all, though you did not observe how, than that he ever denied any.

[1.] Prayer is answered when it is accepted, though there be no other effect of it visible. Prayer is not in vain, if the person be accepted, and the service approved. Do you think it is nothing to please God, to do that wherein his soul delights, to offer that which ascends to him as the odour of a sweet smell? Is it nothing to obey God, to honour him, to give a testimony to his glorious perfections? Is it nothing, to be admitted to such sweet intimate communion with God in such a familiar way, to speak to him as a man to his friend, as a child to his father? Suppose you should reap no other benefit by prayer, is not here as much as will amount to an answer? If you will not measure the return of your prayers by lower inferior advantages, these are the most blessed returns. It should be more desirable in your account to please him, than to be happy yourselves. His glory should be more valuable than your salvation, or all the means that tend to it. And such society with him should be esteemed the first-fruits of heaven. Yet these are the privileges of every accepted prayer; and therefore, if it be accepted, though it obtain nothing more, it is abundantly answered.

[2.] He sometimes makes prayer an answer to itself, answers when you are praying: Isa. lxv. 24, 'While they are yet speaking, I will hear;' not only hears, but answers, answers the prayer by enabling us to pray, Dan. ix. 20, 21. While Daniel was speaking in prayer, an angel was sent in answer to his desires. You will judge this is a sweet return. But how much more is it for the Holy Ghost to be sent into the heart, and thereby to have powerful assistance, comfortable enlargements, heavenly affections, and vigorous exercise of graces; to have the soul winged with holy affections, to fly into the bosom of Christ; to have heaven as it were opened, and the veil withdrawn, that the light of God's countenance may break out and shine upon the soul! These are the greatest, the sweetest of spiritual blessings, and infinitely transcend all outward enjoyments, Ps. iv. 6–8. Well then may they be accounted most blessed answers.

[3.] He sometimes answers prayers by discovering the defects of prayer, convincing his people of those failings which might make them fail of being answered; discovers the defects of prayers, and the sinfulness of them, formality, lukewarmness, unbelief, carelessness, sloth, irreverence, hypocrisy, self-seeking, or what else may render their prayer offensive. If prayer obtain this, to have such sins, and the evil of them discovered, it is a great advantage, a great mercy; and if it obtain so much, sure it is not unanswered.

[4.] It is a gracious answer sometimes to be denied. You account it a good answer to a petition when you have that which is better than the things desired; but when you desire that which is not good, the denial is better than the grant. The denial is a mercy, the grant would be a judgment. So it was with David: he was importunate for the life of his child; but was it not better for him that the Lord granted not its life, since it would have been a living monument of his ignominy, wherein every beholder might have read both his shame and heinous sin? The Lord is merciful oftentimes in denying outward blessings, worldly enjoyments, to his children; denies them plenty of temporals, lest it should bring leanness into their souls; denies them health, that their souls may prosper; denies comfort in dearest relations, by making them cross and uncomfortable, lest they should steal away the heart from himself. These denials are great mercies, and therefore sweet returns of prayer.

[5.] He sometimes answers, by bestowing only some degree of the thing desired, not the whole. The Lord answers Moses's prayer, by giving him a view of Canaan, not the full possession. Those who pray for increase of grace are answered, when the Lord draws out the heart in stronger desires after it. Desires after grace are a degree of grace. If the messenger of Satan, against which Paul prays, were some corruption, his prayer was answered, not totally, so as to be freed from assaults, but in some degree, so as to have power sufficient to resist. The prayers of God's people for the destruction of antichrist are answered in some degree, in that the impostures of that man of sin are discovered, and so many nations fallen off; many hate her, though make her not desolate.

[6.] He may hear the prayer, though he do not answer it presently. Delay is no denial: prayer is sure to be heard, though the Lord sometimes seems slow in granting what is prayed for. Delay is sometimes a mercy. He never defers, when it is seasonable to grant: 2 Pet. iii. 9, 'The Lord is not slack, as some men count slackness;' *i. e.*, as though he had altered his purpose, forgot his promise, or careless to accomplish either. He deferred in mercy, in long-suffering. He is not slack, though he may seem so to us, ver. 8. The promise was of the day of judgment, the coming of Christ, which is the prayer of the church, Rev. xx. 20. Quickly, because as soon as ever it is seasonable, he will come instantly, not defer one moment. As soon as it will be a mercy: Luke xviii. 17, 'Shall not God avenge his elect, though he bear long with them? I tell you that he will avenge them speedily.' Stay long, and yet speedily. He stays that we may exercise faith in prayer, Heb. x. 35, &c. Christ prayed for his enemies, and was answered after his resurrection. Stephen prayed for his persecutors, and answered after his death in Saul's conversion. How long did God's ancient people pray for the coming of the Messiah, and the primitive Christians for good magistrates, all the faithful for the ruin of antichrist, and the primitive martyrs for vengeance against their persecutors? Rev. vi. 10. Prayers are seed, though they as it were lie under ground; talents laid up in heaven for improvement. One talent in prayer will be improved to ten in its return. Though the answer be as a cloud in your days, it may cover the heavens for your posterity, and rain showers of blessings. The last times will be times of greatest mercies, because the times of so many prayers, many answers are reserved for them. There is therefore no reason to conclude you are denied, because not presently answered.

[7.] He may grant the mercy desired, though not to the person for whom it is desired. He may answer your prayers by bestowing that on another which you desire for yourselves. So Moses was answered; he desired himself might conduct the Israelites into Canaan; the Lord appoints a dear relation of his, Joshua his servant, to be their conductor, and provides better for Moses; or he may bestow that upon yourselves which you desire for others; so he answered David, Ps. xxxv. 13; his prayer returned into his own bosom. The Lord will not suffer prayer to be in vain for hypocrites, for such were these, ver. 11, 12; or by bestowing it upon one as dear to thee as he that is prayed for. Abraham desired the promise might be accomplished in Ishmael, the Lord fulfils it to Isaac. Isaac intended and desired the blessing might fall upon Esau, the Lord bestows it on Jacob; and what David desires for his first child by Bathsheba, he grants to the second, to Solomon; the apostles desired the benefits of the Messiah might principally be the portion of the Jews, the Lord vouchsafes them to the Gentiles. There is no reason to conclude he denies, because he answers not as to the individual.

[8.] He answers by granting something else in lieu of what is desired, though he bestow not the same thing. He answers if he grant something as good, something better: Jer. xlv. 5, 'Seekest thou great things for thyself? seek them not: for, behold, I will bring evil upon all flesh, saith the Lord; but thy life will I give unto thee for a prey.' It was better for Baruch to have his life where he went, than to enjoy a plentiful estate where he would have no security of his life. God seldom or never denies the particular desired, but he gives something as good or better, in one or all these four respects.

1st, In kind. When we pray for temporals, he gives spirituals. The apostles desired Christ would rule as a temporal king; he uses them as his instruments to erect a spiritual kingdom. They desire outward preferment, to sit at his right hand or left in worldly pomp; he assures them of spiritual and eternal glory, they should sit upon twelve thrones.

2d, In reference to the rule of goodness, his own will; which being *summè bona*, that which is agreeable must needs be best. That is ἄριστον, which is Τῷ Θεῷ ἄρεστον. That is best for us which pleases him best. If he make not a return according to our wills, yet always according to his will; and that being the rule of goodness, that which is conformable to it is best for us.

3d, In reference to the great end of all we pray for, God's glory. If he give not the very thing desired, yet he will give something that will tend more to his glory; and that which most conduces to it is best; not only in respect of God, but us, for our chief happiness consists in his glory; the more we honour him the more is our happiness, and that is best, sure, which makes us most happy. That is a sweet answer to prayer, when he gives that which is better than what we desire.

4th, In reference to the particular end of your desire. If he give not the mercy desired, yet something that will as much advance the end for which you desire it. And if you have your end for which, what you aimed at, you have your desires, for the means is not otherwise desirable. As if you desire a blessing that you may live contentedly; if he bestow not that, but another mercy that will afford as much or more contentment. You desire an alteration of your condition, that you may live more contentedly; if the Lord do not alter your condition, but change your heart, so as to make it contented with your present state, though he do not raise your condition in respect of riches, credit, as high as your desires, yet if he bring down your heart and desires to your condition, so as to be therewith fully satisfied and contented, he gives that which is as good or better than what you desire, and so returns a sweet answer to your prayers. Or if your desires pitch upon some particular means to subdue a lust, though he grant not, yet if he offer another, which is as or more effectual to subdue that lust, he grants what is as good or better. Or if you desire the removal of some affliction, that you might with more liberty and cheerfulness serve the Lord, though he remove it not, yet if he enable you under that affliction to serve him with as much cheerfulness and enlargement of heart, he grants your request, and answers your prayers.

2. Discouragement is sense of unworthiness. A humble soul will be apt to say, How can I believe the Lord will hear me who am so vile, not only in respect of the common condition of mankind, being but dust and ashes, a worm, less, worse, but also being more than ordinary sinful, having often profaned this ordinance, and abused former comfortable returns; and in respect of my condition in the world, being so mean and contemptible, as I cannot be confident of access to men of any extraordinary note in the world; how much less can I be confident of acceptance or audience with the great and holy God?

To remove this, consider,

(1.) The Lord never heard any that either were really worthy, or did account themselves so. All that ever had access to, and audience with God, have been really, and in their own esteem, unworthy. The Lord requires not that his people should bring any worth with them to commend their prayers to him. The want of personal worth did never hinder the Lord from answering prayer. Therefore no reason to be discouraged for want of that which is neither necessary nor ever was present. No flesh is justified in his sight.

(2.) The more unworthy, and withal the more sensible of it, the more hopes of answer and acceptance. This is so far from being any just impediment to faith, as it should rather encourage it; for Scripture and experience tell us it is both the Lord's gracious disposition and practice to do most for them who are, or seem to themselves to be, most unworthy: 'He fills the hungry,' Luke i. 53, 48, but 'casts down the mighty,' ver. 52. He pronounces them blessed who are poor, Mat. v.; calls not many wise and noble, 1 Cor. i. 26–28; seeks that which is lost, Luke vi. 19, 20; saves sinners, the chief of them, 1 Tim. i. 15; invites beggars, sends out his servants to fetch them, Luke xiv. 21, 23; those who have no money, no worth, worth nothing, Isa. lv.; pities those whom no eye pities, Ezek. xvi. 6; condescends lowest to those who are lowest. He takes pleasure in it, he gets honour by it. Hereby is the freeness, the riches of grace made more conspicuous, infinite mercy appears more merciful.

Consider but the different demeanour and success of the Pharisee and publican as to this duty, and it will put it past doubt. Consider what self-confidence and conceitedness in the one, what humility and sense of unworthiness in the other: Luke xviii. 10 to the 15th, 'This man went away justified, rather than the other.' Justified, *i. e.*, pardoned, accepted, answered. *Rather*, *i. e.*, exclusively; he was justified, and *not* the other. The reason is observable: ver. 14, 'For every one that exalteth himself shall be abased; and he that humbleth himself shall be exalted.' Sense of unworthiness should rather strengthen than discourage.

(3.) Prayer and praying in faith is not only a privilege, but a duty; and is any one unworthy to do his duty? If it was only a privilege, unworthiness might be some plea to keep off sinners from meddling with prayer or acting faith, but since it is a duty, you cannot with any reason, cannot without absurdity make use of it to discourage you. What, are you unworthy to obey God, to do what he commands, to do as he requires? The very conceit of this is absurd; men would laugh at such a plea; God will be far from accepting it. Would you take it well from your servant, if he should neglect to do what you command under pretence that he is unworthy to obey you? Yes, you would count it a jeer, you will think him idle, and foolish too in finding no better excuse for his idleness. The case is alike in reference to God; we are unworthy to receive, but not to obey. There is no show of reason why this should be a discouragement.

(4.) Though you be unworthy to be heard, yet Christ is worthy; it is he that undertakes to present your petition, and procure an answer. Believers, when they are found praying, they are found as Paul, Philip. iii. 9, 'not having their own righteousness, but that which is through the faith of Christ, that which is of God by faith.' Faith makes Christ yours, and so his righteousness yours. It unites to Christ as to your head: *Caput et membra sunt quasi una mystica persona.* When the Lord looks on you he finds you having Christ's righteousness, and that is enough to make both persons and prayers righteous, to cover all unworthiness in either that might hinder acceptance. Though Christ communicates not his merits, so as we can deserve anything, yet he communicates the efficacy and benefits of interest in his merits, so as if they be not ours they are for us; he deserves, he is worthy that we should be heard.

3. Discouragement is weakness of prayers. A humble soul will be apt to say, I am not only unworthy, but my prayers are weak; much unlike to the prayers of God's people formerly, accompanied with many infirmities, deadness of heart, straitness of spirit, formality, distractions.

To remove this, consider,

(1.) You may mistake, and think your prayers weak, when they are strong. The strength of prayer consists not in anything outward, not in expressions either by word or tears, not in outward gestures or enlargements. It is a hidden, an inward strength. Those may be sometimes the signs, but never the sinews. Men may judge of its strength by multitude, vehemency, or patheticalness of expression; but 'the Lord seeth not as man seeth; man looketh on the outward appearance, but the Lord looketh on the heart,' 1 Sam. xvi. 7. Man's judgment differs far from his; man may judge that weak which he judges strong. The strength of prayer lies in the heart, in the motion of the affections, and the exercise of graces; and above all affections, in zeal; above all graces, in faith. Faith and fervency is the strength of prayer; faith principally, and fervency but as it springs from faith. All affectionateness without this is not prevalent, not powerful. Cut out of faith, and you cut out of the strength of prayer; for though it be the most prevalent exercise on earth, and has power both with God and men, yet without faith, it is like Samson deprived of his locks, Judges xvi. 17. The great champion of Israel, his strength went from him, and he became weak, and like another man. So prayer when without faith it becomes weak, and like those bodily exercises which profit not. You should not be discouraged from believing, because your prayers are weak, but rather he hereby persuaded to exercise faith that your prayers may be strong.

(2.) Examine whether those weaknesses be voluntary or involuntary, whether through unavoidable infirmity, or carelessness, sloth, and negligence. If they be voluntary, prayer is weak, and you willing and content it should be so; if slothful, and will not stir up yourselves to lay hold on God; want strength, because you will not exercise it, will not summon up spiritual forces of affection and graces to follow after God, then I confess your condition is sad, and full of sin and discouragements. So long as you continue thus slothful, the word affords little encouragement. You must pray, if you would be heard, not pray as though you prayed not. You must cry, if you would be answered; offer up strong cries. You must follow hard after God, if you would find him; lay hold on him, and stir up all your strength to do it, if you would enjoy him. But if these weaknesses be involuntary, *i.e.*, if you bewail, mourn for them; if they be your burden and affliction; if you long, thirst, breathe after more strength; if you earnestly endeavour to shake off these distempers, and be diligent in the use of all appointed means to gather more strength to your prayers; this mourning, longing, endeavouring are signs the Lord will not take notice of your infirmities, will not charge your weaknesses upon you, nor impute them to you; they shall not hinder the Lord from hearing and answering, nor should not hinder you from believing. In these cases, the Lord accepts the will for the deed, 2 Cor. viii. 12, answers and rewards weak prayers as though they were strong. He stands not so much upon the quantity of your strength, but that he will accept the sincerity of your endeavours. He will look upon you and reward you, not according to what you are, but would be. He that has but a little strength, and puts it all out in prayer, shall more prevail than he that prays with much strength comparatively, if he do not pray with all. This is plain from Christ's testimony of the widow, Luke xxi. 3. Her two mites was more than twenty talents cast in by one that had an hundred. The Lord is so gracious, he will accept of a little from those who cannot do much, better than of much from them who can do more. He despises not the day of small things, takes special notice of a little strength in Philadelphia, Rev. iii. 8. There is no reason, therefore, to be discouraged from weaknesses, if not voluntary.

(3.) If you be weak, labour to pray in faith, that you may be strong. This should rather be a motive, than a discouragement. Would you think him reasonable who, being weak, would neglect or refuse nourishment, because he is weak? He should rather receive it, and has more need to do it, that he may be strong. So here. To act faith in prayer, is the best way to get ability and strength to pray powerfully. Faith draws together both domestic and auxiliary forces, stirs up the strength of the soul, and withal engages the strength of Christ; and they that wrestle with that strength shall surely prevail. The efficacy of the head is divided into the body, by means of the union betwixt head and members. Now it is faith that unites to Christ; he who has all power in heaven and earth dwells in our hearts by faith, it makes his strength ours. The ancients, through faith, 'out of weakness were made strong,' Heb. xi. 34; not only strong in battle, to prevail against the armies of the aliens, but strong in prayer, to prevail with God. If you would be strong in prayer, you must pray in faith, that your weaknesses may be hereby scattered, infirmities put to flight. These should not drive you from your confidence, but engage you to be confident, since this is the only way to grow strong.

4. Discouragement. My prayers are not only weak, but sinful. The weakness is too voluntary; slothful, and too willing to be so, loth to stir up myself; lukewarm, and shake it not off; pray as though grace were asleep, and my soul in a slumber.

Ans. I must suppose that, though there be much sinfulness and weakness in your prayers, yet there is something gracious, else there can be nothing spoken that will afford the least encouragement; though much corruption, yet something spiritual; though much of the flesh, yet some workings of the Spirit; some actings of grace, though in a low degree; some desires after God that are sincere, though weak; some motions toward Christ, though slow and feeble; some apprehensions of the Lord, though distracted and hindered with other impertinencies; some heat, so much as argues the soul alive to God, though in a slumber; though much of sin, yet something of holiness. This supposed, take what I have to say in this case in two propositions.

(1.) So far as your prayers are sinful, you can expect no answer; God will not reward, cannot approve the sinfulness of prayer.

[1.] Sinful prayers, as sinful, are all one in God's account as other sinful acts. And the wages of these are death; no other reward can be expected for these but this; expect rather he should punish than answer. It is true these or other sins are pardoned, through the satisfaction of Christ, to those that repent and believe. You must repent for the sins of those prayers, and pray that the Lord would pardon them, and then believe he will pardon; and this is all faith is to expect in this case. Christ never purchased anything, nor did the Lord ever promise anything, to prayers as they are sinful. You cannot expect God should answer or reward them as such; it is infinite mercy that he will pardon them. Gracious acts, as such, will be rewarded; but as sinful, it is well if they be pardoned.

[2.] Though the Lord pardon, yet he may, and usually does, correct his people for them. They will not be rewarded; all that Christ procured for them is pardon, nor such a pardon as will exempt them from smarting sufferings. He does visit sinful prayers with stripes. Though he pardon, yet he may chastise severely, Ps. xcix. 8. It is madness, a hellish imposture, to think God is as well pleased with us acting sinfully, as graciously. He rewards this, he will not pardon that without satisfaction of infinite value; nor so, but he will manifest his displeasure by afflicting.

[3.] Though these afflictions tend to good, yet the way is grievous. They tend to good to believers, as it is promised, Rom. viii. It is good for them that are afflicted. So it is good for one in a lethargy to be cupped, for one whose wounds are gangrened to be cut, lanced, cauterised. These are good in these cases, but grievous in themselves. Were it not better to be in health, to want wounds, than to need such cures, to be in such a condition, when nothing will be so good as that which is so grievous? It is madness to think it is not better to shake off sloth, than to pray so as we can expect no answer, so as we must pray for pardon of prayers and bring afflictions. Prayers as sinful must not be answered, may be pardoned, will be chastised for the good of believers, but in a way that is grievous, and in itself no way desirable. You see what we must expect from prayers as sinful.

(2.) So far as the prayer is gracious, there is encouragement. For,

[1.] The Lord will accept, and in some way or other answer, a prayer in any degree gracious, though there be much corruption or weakness in it. That prayer where grace is acted, though weakly, and in which the Spirit assists, though less powerfully, is more or less acceptable. For, 1, grace is the work, the gift of God, *Deus coronat dona sua.* He accepts, rewards his own gift, wherever it is. And the work of the Spirit is well pleasing to him, though its attendants be offensive; he can discern and separate wheat from chaff, gold from dross. 2. He will not quench the smoking flax. Heavenly, spiritual heat is pleasing to him, though it flame not, though nothing but smoke be visible. He takes notice of a little strength in Philadelphia, Rev. iii. 7, 8, and promises much to that little. 3. If the mixtures of corruption and weakness be bewailed and repented of, they are pardoned. If the righteousness of Christ be applied by faith, this will be a satisfaction for those offences; and if the Lord be satisfied, what can hinder him from answering? Offences not imputed, are in effect no offences; and the Lord, satisfied, will be as gracious as though he had not been offended.

[2.] When there is much of corruption and little of grace in a prayer, though the Lord may answer, yet ordinarily, if not always, the answer is not so full, speedy, comfortable, satisfying, nor perceivable. Though the Lord pardons the sins and failings of weak prayers, yet he may, and often does, afflict for them; and part of the affliction may consist in the quality of the answer. The Lord often proportions his answer to our prayers; slothful prayers have slow answers, &c. Experience bears witness to this, and David observed it, Ps. xviii. He tells us the Lord answered him: ver. 6, 'He heard my voice, my cry came before him.' He tells us how he answered him: ver. 20, 'The Lord rewarded me according to my righteousness; according to the cleanness of my hands hath he recompensed me.' Though he answer not *propter*, yet *secundum preces*: though not *for* the holiness, fervency, affectionateness of our prayers, yet *according to* the holiness, &c., of them. Though they be not causes why he answers, either meriting, as papists, or moving, as ignorants conceive, yet they may be qualifications to fit us for, or presages or signs of, gracious answers. They may qualify, *aliud est de causa agere*, &c., *aliud de quantitate*, as Gregory. Though they do not procure, yet they may prepare, dispose, and fit, the soul for receipt of an answer. When the Lord will open his hand to bestow a bountiful answer, he enlarges the heart to seek it, and withal to receive it: see it in Dan. ix. A dead, lukewarm heart would not prize spiritual mercies, could not make good use of temporal blessings. When the Lord will give an answer of a better nature, he puts the heart into a better temper. They are signs of a gracious answer. Bernard says of works, they are *futuræ responsionis præsagia*, comfortable signs of a comfortable answer; *occultæ predestinationis judicia*, arguments that the Lord intends, and is resolved to deal bountifully. When the heart is shut, it is a sign the Lord intends to shut his hand, Mat. vii. 2. According to the measure of our prayers, the degrees of grace and affection exercised in them, God measures out his blessings in answer to them. So it is ordinarily. He that sows sparingly must reap accordingly. He that prays but little, and prays not well, has no reason to expect large or gracious returns.

[3.] Since the Lord is so gracious as to accept, and in some degree or other answer weak and sinful prayers, and to own that which proceeds from grace and his Spirit in them, though accompanied with such corruptions as might provoke him to reject them, and punish you for them, hence you have encouragement to believe the Lord will answer them, and to expect the returns thereof; and you will have good warrant to do this, if you do that first which he requires. If you exercise repentance, *i. e.*, bewail the sins and weakness of your prayers, abhor yourself for giving so much way thereto, and resolve to endeavour, with all your strength, in the use of all appointed means, to avoid them for time to come; if you exercise faith, *i. e.*, rest upon Christ for pardon of those provocations, apply those promises which offer pardon, and lay hold on that righteousness of Christ whereby he has satisfied the Lord for those offences; this done, you may, nay, you ought, to believe that the Lord will not only answer your prayers for time to come, but to expect returns of prayers past.

3. *Use*. For examination. Try whether we pray in faith. It is a work of great importance; for if ye pray not in faith at all, it is a sign ye have no faith; and then ye are under the law, cut off from Christ, exposed to the curse, liable to eternal wrath. What is hell but abiding wrath? If ye have faith, but act it not in prayer, you deprive yourselves of the benefit of this ordinance, ver. 7; prayer is the conduit-pipe appointed by God to convey all the blessings of the upper and lower springs to the children of men; but if the passage be obstructed, it will be useless, of no advantage to you. Want of faith is a dangerous obstruction; this will hinder the passage of all mercy; not a drop of the water of life will be conveyed by prayer without faith. Therefore there is great reason to examine; and to help you, take some characters.

(1.) Backwardness to pray is a sign you pray not in faith. He that believes he shall have whatever he asks, freely, without upbraiding, will be ready and forward to ask upon all occasions. If you did believe, you would omit no opportunity to address yourselves to God this way; you would not neglect it in your families, in secret, in public: those who omit it, undervalue it, make no great account of it, spend whole days without it, count it a burden, say, What a weariness is it! take no pleasure, no delight, come to it as a task, cannot be said to pray in faith.

(2.) Carelessness in praying. Prayer is a blessed engine, which, being carefully managed by faith, will procure all mercies that you need, for time or eternity; never made use of it in vain; if you did believe this, you would not be so negligent in prayer, but would stir up yourselves and diligently improve all your might in prayer. Those who pray only with their lips, draw near only with their mouths, make it only an exercise of the body, and suffer their hearts and thoughts to wander without control, pray as if they prayed not, do not pray in faith; if you prayed in faith, you would observe the condition of such a prayer, one of which is fervency. Where lukewarmness, indifferency, formality, distractions are tolerated, faith is not exercised.

(3.) Perplexity and solicitousness after prayer. This was a sign Hannah prayed in faith, 1 Sam. i., because, though she spake out of the abundance of her complaint and grief; yet, after, her countenance was no more sad. Faith is expressed by casting our burden upon the Lord; he that groans and is oppressed under a burden, when it is laid on another is at ease; he that acts faith in prayer casts his burden upon God; therefore, after such a prayer, the oppressed soul will be at ease, 'return to its rest;' no heart-dividing cares molest it: 'Be careful for nothing.'

(4.) Is the promise your encouragement in prayer? Does this draw you to pray? does this quicken you in praying? does this encourage to expect a return after prayer? do you plead the word? do you urge the promise? Then it is faith. Thus the people of God have done in their prayers of faith; so Moses, Num. xiv. 17, 18; and Solomon, 1 Kings viii. 23–26; Neh. i. 8; so David, Ps. cxix. 25, 28, 58, 65, 76, 116. Do you plead the word of promise, Though I be unworthy to be heard, yet the Lord is worthy to be honoured; and it is not for thy honour to neglect thy word; though I can do nothing to engage thee, yet thou hast engaged thyself, and the Lord will be true to his engagements; though nothing be due to me but wrath, yet the Lord hath made this mercy due to me by his promise, therefore I will expect it; the Lord will not detain what himself has made due; though I forget my promises and resolutions for God, yet the Lord will not forget his covenant; it is his attribute, 'a God keeping covenant;' and though the Lord may deny me, yet he will not deny himself? Does the faithfulness and righteousness of God encourage you to ask and to expect an answer? Do you plead these, as David frequently, 'Deliver me in thy righteousness,' Ps. cxix. 40; Ps. cxliii. 1; though my unrighteousnesses do testify against me, yet the Lord is righteous from everlasting to everlasting; and is it not a righteous thing with the Lord to do what he has said? Though I am unfaithful, and have dealt falsely in the covenant, yet my unfaithfulness cannot make the faithfulness of God of no effect. The Lord has promised, and faithful is he who has promised, who also will do it; thus to conclude, thus to act upon the promises, and upon the righteousness and faithfulness of God engaged in the promise, is the work of faith; and the prayer where such actings are found, is of faith; where the promise raises the heart to hope, and hope quickens it to more frequency, more fervency in prayer.

(5.) Can you submit to the Lord's time for an answer, believing that your prayer shall either be answered now or hereafter, when it is best for you? This is enough to denominate your prayers. Faith is a submissive grace; it will not prescribe to the Lord, nor limit the Holy One; it will acknowledge him to be both *κύριος τοῦ δοῦναι καὶ τοῦ πότε δοῦναι*, as Chrysostom, both Lord of what he gives, and of the time when he will give it; sometimes the Lord answers presently, Gen. xxiv. 12–15, Dan. ix.; sometimes 'the vision is for an appointed time,' Hab. ii. 3; and then, 'though it tarry, we must wait for it;' so do those who live (who pray) by faith, ver. 4. It is uncertain to us when the appointed time is, whether now or hereafter: 'It is not for us to know the times and the seasons,' Acts i. 7; so Christ told his disciples when they were a little too peremptory as to a present answer: 'Wilt thou at this time?' &c., 'It is not for you to know,' &c., and withal commands them to wait, ver. 4. Faith will be content to act upon what God has revealed; it is unbelief that pries into God's secrets: faith will be content with God's time; it is unbelief would confine the Lord to our time: 'He that believes makes not haste;' he will stay God's leisure, refer himself for the time to him who knows what time is best; it is unbelief that is so hasty, must have it now, or not at all, as that wretch, 2 Kings vi. 33. It is sufficient, ordinarily, to constitute a prayer of faith, to believe the Lord will answer, either in our time or his, either now or hereafter; either at present, or when it will be more seasonable, more a mercy; and to rest satisfied with this; if faith act thus in prayer, you pray in faith.

(6.) Are you persuaded the Lord will give either what you desire, or what is better? Do you rest in this, that you shall have what you ask, either in kind or in an equivalency; that the Lord will satisfy your desires, either as to the letter of your petition, or as to the intention of it? Do you acquiesce in this, that the Lord will answer you, either according to your will, or according to his will; that he will give either what you think best or what he thinks best? Do you believe you shall be heard, either *ad voluntatem*, or *ad salutem?* as Augustine; that he will give either what you desire, or what is better than the thing you desire? if so, you pray in faith.

It is a great mistake to think you pray not in faith, unless you believe the very particular shall be granted which you ask. Faith acts in a greater latitude, hath a larger sphere, it reaches as far as that providence which orders the returns of prayer; faith acts for an answer, according as the Lord is wont to make answers. Now this is clear in Scripture and experience, that the Lord doth answer, not only by giving the thing desired, but by vouchsafing something else, as much, or more desirable: Acts i., 'Wilt thou restore the kingdom?' &c., ver. 6; this was it they desired, a temporal kingdom. He gratifies them not in this, yet grants that which was much better: ver. 8, 'Ye shall receive power, after that the Holy Ghost is come upon you: and ye shall be witnesses unto me,' &c.; and as faith is not confined in such narrow bounds, so it will not confine the Lord to them, it will not limit the Holy One of Israel. To limit the Lord is to tempt him; and to tempt God is an act of unbelief, that unbelief whereby the Israelites provoked God in the wilderness, Ps. lxxviii. 41; this is censured under the notion of unbelief, ver. 22; it was from their unbelief that they limited God. They were not contented with manna, though angels' food, that which the Lord thought best for them; they must have flesh too; they must have flesh or nothing, ver. 18; their lusting was a peremptory desire, an issue of unbelief. We may judge of the nature of this desire by the quality of the answer; if it had been a desire of faith, it had been answered in mercy; but the Lord answers them in wrath, ver. 29-31. *Ad voluntatem auditi sunt Israelitæ.* He gave them their own desire; since they would not be satisfied, unless they had that very thing which they desired, they had it indeed, but they had the wrath of God with it. The Lord does not answer the desires of faith in this manner; they are of another strain; they will be satisfied either with what is desired, or with what the Lord counts better. It is unbelief that must have that which is desired, or nothing; faith is not so peremptory. When we pray for things not absolutely necessary, or not comparatively necessary, *i. e.*, not so necessary, but something else may be more necessary, we may pray in faith, though we believe not that the particular we desire shall be granted; it is sufficient in these cases, if we believe the Lord will either vouchsafe that, or something else which he knows to be more convenient: and therefore if your faith act accordingly in prayer, it may be called a prayer of faith.

(7.) Can you suspend your hopes of an answer upon a condition, upon such conditions as have warrant and approbation in Scripture? Faith acted conditionally is enough, in some cases, to constitute a prayer of faith. Abraham prayed in faith, yet his prayer runs in a conditional strain, Gen. xviii. 29, 30, 32; so Solomon, 1 Kings viii, 35, 44, 47; so Christ himself, Luke xxii. 42. The apostle mentions a conditional confidence, 1 John v. 14. The confidence is, that he will hear when we ask; the condition is, if we ask according to his will; or, which comes to the same issue, if we ask what is good for us, all things considered, for what is good for us is according to his will.

In case, then, you are uncertain what is according to his will, if he have not absolutely manifested, by command, promise, or other equivalent that what you desire is that which he wills, either in substance or circumstance, or in case you are uncertain whether that you pray for be absolutely good for you, or so good, but something else may be better, in these cases, when you believe that what you pray for shall be granted, if it be according to his will, or if it be best for you, you pray in faith; no more is required.

Augustine gives this rule for regulating our prayers as to temporals, and it holds in spirituals, when there is that uncertainty now spoken of: *Quando petitis temporalia, petite cum modo*, ask them with restriction, *i. e.*, conditionally, *illi committite, ut si profit, det; si scit obesse, non det*, refer it to him to give if it be good, to deny if it be hurtful, *quid autem obest, quid prosit, novit medicus, non ægrotus;* submit will and wisdom to him.

Before we conclude, it is requisite to resolve some cases.

1. Since it is necessary that those who would receive must pray in faith, *i. e.*, must be confident and assured that their prayers shall be answered, what can they expect who want assurance, who (as to their own apprehensions) have not the grounds of this confidence? How can they be confident of this privilege, who are full of fears and doubts that they are not in that state on which this privilege is entailed? How can they pray in faith, who fear they have not faith? How can they believe their prayers will be accepted, who see no ground to believe that their persons are accepted? This is the case of those who, being in or newly past the pangs of the new birth, have the seeds of faith, but not the evidence. Faith is in its infancy, not grown up to that maturity as to know itself. Such walk in darkness, and see no light; have no light to discover that God is their Father, that the promise is their portion, that Christ intercedes for them, or that the Spirit intercedes in them. What support can these have in reference to the success of their prayers? This may be the case also of such who have had assurance, but have now lost it; who are in that sad condition as they have occasion to invert the apostle's expression, that they were sometimes light in the Lord, but now they are darkness; their former evidence is blotted, former light clouded, the Spirit of God suspending his assuring and evidencing testimony, either for trial or upon some provocation. The question here will be, What encouragement and support such may have as to the issue of their prayers? can such pray in faith? or can they pray so as their prayers shall be granted?

Ans. A faith of dependence may constitute a prayer of faith, where assurance is wanting; and therefore those who, through the weakness of faith, or through the withdrawings of God in time of desertion, are destitute of assurance, may yet pray in faith, if so be they exercise this faith of dependence. To open this a little, a faith of dependence, as but a *may be*, God *may* answer; a faith of assurance has a *will be*, says, God *will* answer. That says, Probably the Lord will hear; this says, Certainly the Lord will hear. Jonathan went out against the Philistines in the strength of that faith we express by depending or relying upon God, and it rose no higher than thus, 'It may be,' 1 Sam. xiv. 6. Now, faith thus acted in prayer makes it a prayer of faith. But to resolve this case more fully and clearly, I shall endeavour four things.

(1.) To shew that this relying on God for answer is sufficient to make a prayer of faith, that this faith of dependence is enough in some cases. And thus I proceed. It is this faith which justfies a sinner. The person being justified is accepted; the person being accepted, the prayer is accepted, and so will be answered. A sinner is not justified by assurance, but by an act of dependence or relying on Christ; for he is justified by the first act of faith, when he first believes. But assurance is after the first act of believing, Eph. i. 13. The Spirit's sealing, which causes assurance, is after believing; upon which he is justified, person and prayers accepted. A faith of dependence, without assurance, is sufficient to render the prayer acceptable and capable of an answer. And therefore this relying, acted in prayer, makes it a prayer of faith. Besides, this faith is sometimes all that is required, and all that is expressed, in those prayers which have been graciously answered, Joel ii. 12–14. The prophet directs them how to address themselves to the Lord. Faith is necessary in all such addresses, yet all the faith whereby they made this address is in those words, 'Who knoweth?' &c., which amounts to no more than this faith of dependence. It is no more than this, It may be the Lord will return and repent, &c., Jonah iii. 9. That faith, in the strength of which they were to send up those mighty cries, goes no farther than a *may be, Who can tell?* &c.; yet this prayer prevailed, ver. 10. So that it is clear from hence, that a faith of dependence, acted in prayer, will prevail with God for an answer, and make it a prayer of faith.

(2.) I will shew the objects upon which this faith is acted, and by which it is supported, and how it is to be exercised on them in the cases propounded. The objects to which I will be confined at this time are three.

[1.] The name of God. The Lord directs those that are in darkness to this object, Isa. l. 10; and there is enough in this name to encourage and support the weakest, and to silence all his fears and doubts as to the success of his prayers. See it declared, Exod. xxxiv. 6, 7. Here is firm footing for that faith which is so weak and small as it cannot be discerned by him that hath it. It is said of Abraham, that he 'staggered not through unbelief,' Rom. iv. 20; and the reason is, because he had firm footing for both feet. He that stands but upon one leg may easily stagger; he that is persuaded that God is able, but not willing, or willing, but not able, his faith stands but upon one leg. But Abraham was persuaded of both: the promise, that persuaded him God was willing; his power, that persuaded him he was able; both expressed, ver. 21. Therefore his faith having ground for both feet, stood sure and stedfast; it staggered not. Now the name of God affords as good ground for faith; there is that in it which may persuade a doubting soul that God is both able and willing. 'The Lord, the Lord God;' *Heb.*, 'Jehovah, Jehovah El.' The strong God; he that has his being of himself, and gives a being to things that are not. This shews he is able, able to give a being to all you want or desire, though they are to be brought out of nothing; able to make thee pray, and able to make all desirable returns to thy prayers, nay, 'above what you can ask or think.' And that he is willing, the rest of his name shews, 'merciful, gracious,' &c. He is merciful, and misery is a proper plea for mercy, and am I not miserable? He is gracious, and grace expects no motive from without; free grace will move itself; nor will it be stopped by any hindrance within me. Unworthiness cannot hinder, for then it is most grace when it rests in the most unworthy; and am not I such? Long continuance in sin cannot hinder, if broken off by repentance, for he is long-suffering; no, nor the abounding sinfulness of sin, for he is abundant in goodness; no, nor the infinite multitude and variety of sins, for he forgives iniquity, transgression, and sin; nor the huge number of petitioners, he keeps mercy for thousands. And though the doubting soul cannot in prayer plead his truth (another letter of his name) in reference to the covenant, as not knowing his interest in the covenant, yet he may plead it in reference to the declaration of his name; as sure as God is true, so sure he is merciful and gracious, &c.

[2.] The free offers of Christ. The Scripture abounds with them; I will but instance in one: John vi. 37, 'All that the Father giveth me shall come to me; and him that cometh to me, I will in no wise cast out.' That which faith principally eyes in Christ for the success of prayer, is his intercession, his office as advocate. Now, though a doubting soul dare not rely upon Christ as one that *is* his advocate, yet may it rely on him as one that *offers* to be its advocate. He professes that he will in no wise refuse any that will retain him. Christ, may the soul say, prayed for his enemies, for those that were murdering him, and may he not then intercede for me? It is true I have been an enemy, but oh how do I hate myself for that enmity! I have now laid down arms, and now, though I can do little for him, yet I resolve never more to oppose him, though I perish. And since he was so gracious, as to pray for his murderers, who knows but he may intercede for me? And further, Christ prayed not only for those who did actually believe, but for those who should afterwards believe, John xvii. 20. He prayed for those who then had no faith when he prayed. And is not this thy case, poor doubting or deserted soul? Is not this the worst thou canst make of it? Canst thou say anything worse of thyself than this, I do not believe, I have no faith? Well, then, seek to Christ, rely on him, as one that prayed, as one that intercedes for unbelievers; and hereby thou wilt shew thou hast faith, and thy prayers will be answered, as the Lord useth to answer prayers of faith.

[3.] The general promise; such as are not restrained to those qualifications and conditions, which the dark soul apprehends to be out of its reach; such as that, Heb. xi. 6, 'He is a rewarder of them that diligently seek him;' Joel ii. 32, 'Whosoever shall call on the name of the Lord, shall be delivered.' The doubting soul may thus reason. There was nothing in man could move the Lord to make these promises, and there is nothing in man can hinder him from performing them when and where he pleases. And who knows but he may perform them to me? It is true I have neglected Christ formerly, oh but now I resolve to seek him indeed. And though I be not certain that he will be found of me, yet I will seek him early, seek him first, before all others, seek him principally, above all others; who knows but I may at last find him? He has been found of those that sought him formerly; he has been found of those that sought him not; and will he not be found of me that seek him?

(3.) The acts of this faith, in which it is exercised, and by which it may be discerned.

[1.] A renouncing of all supports and refuges, but Christ. See it in returning Ephraim: Hosea xiv. 3, 'We will no more rely on Assyria, nor trust in our armies of horse.' So the soul will no more rely on his own wisdom and righteousness, on his own works and performances. When he comes to pray, he will not ground his confidence on what he doth, or what he is, or what he is not, as the Pharisee; he perceives these to be but a refuge of lies. And though he become hereby destitute and helpless, and has not thus much to comfort him, that God is his Father, yet here is his support in this orphan state, 'In thee the fatherless find mercy.'

[2.] Submission. A depending soul will be content with anything, if the Lord will but own him, if Christ will but smile, entertain him. This is visible in the returning prodigal, Luke xv. 18, 19. To my father; there is faith. Though thou hast dealt with me as a Father, yet I am unworthy to be called a son, unworthy to be entertained and employed as a son. Lord, let me be anything, so as I may have a being in thy house; let me but come under thy roof, and I will be content though I have no other usage, respect, reward; the meanest office in thy house is too good, only let me not be shut out of doors.

The woman of Canaan, though she followed Christ with such strength of faith and importunity of prayer, as he admires her, yet so submissive, she will be content with crumbs, anything that has relation to children, though not the relation itself, yea, though it be but the crumbs that fall from the table, Mat. xv. 22. So 2 Sam. xv. 25.

[3.] Acceptation. He will yield to any terms, so as the Lord will but grant his chief desires. Tell him, if he will have Christ, and follow him, he must forsake all; he embraces the motion, he says, This is a faithful saying, and worthy of all acceptation. He says with Mephibosheth, Nay, let him take all, if my Lord will return to my soul in peace. Tell him, if he will inherit the land of promise, he must come out of Egypt, he is content, he will not leave a hoof behind. All his lusts shall go, if Christ will but come, small and great, secret and open, pleasant and profitable; his Zoars, his little ones, shall be turned into ashes; his Herodias, his pleasant beloved sins shall be divorced. The best and fattest of the cattle, his profitable and gainful sins, shall be put to the sword, with the rest of the children of Amalek; his secret idols, those that are hid in the stuff, shall not only be buried, but, as Moses with the calf, ground to powder. Tell him, if he will be joined to Christ, he must forget his kindred and father's house, his former old acquaintance and conversation; he is satisfied, so as the King will delight in his beauty, so as Christ will but take pleasure in him. Tell him, if he will have Christ as an intercessor, he must submit to him as a king; Oh, says he, if the golden sceptre may be but holden forth, I will submit to it for ever. Tell him, if he will have the Spirit of Christ, he must have him as a Spirit of grace, as well as a Spirit of supplication: he yields with cheerfulness; he looks upon holiness as garments of wrought gold, that which will both enrich and beautify him; the sanctifying work of the Spirit is acceptable to him, as well as the sealing work. Tell him, he that will name the name of the Lord with acceptance, must depart from iniquity: he answers presently, 'What have I any more to do with idols?' This accepting Christ, and the Spirit of Christ, upon gospel terms, is called faith, John i. 12.

[4.] Appropriation. Coming unto Christ, stretching out his soul to lay hold on him, opening his heart to embrace him, flying upon the wing of desire to draw near him. Thus faith is expressed by 'drawing near,' Heb. x. 22. Though he cannot draw near with full assurance of faith, yet with a full sail of affection. By 'embracing the promise,' Heb. xi. 13; though he cannot embrace the promise, as having received it for his present portion, yet he embraces it as seen afar off. By laying hold, Heb. vi. 18; though he cannot lay hold of Christ as his treasure and possession, yet on the hope set before him. By 'coming to Christ,' John vi. 35; I am unworthy to come near him, yet he is worthy to be obeyed, and he commands me to come. Though I be not sure he will entertain me, yet there is no way but ruin if I come not. He invites me, and who knows but he may receive me? I have none else to come to, the world I have renounced, and to come to it is to run upon the sword of an enemy; my lusts I have forsaken, and to return to them is to run back into ruin. There is none but Christ, none but Christ, my soul can come to for refuge. And lo he calls me, why, 'Behold I come unto thee, for thou art the Lord.'

[5.] Resolution. Being come, he resolves to continue there. If he die, he will die at his feet. If he perish, he will perish with Christ in his arms. If justice seizes on him, it shall slay him at the horns of the altar. Nothing shall fright him from his hold. Come death, come hell, I will not let thee go. Nay, the more he is afraid, the faster he clings. 'What time I am afraid, I will trust in thee.' 'Though he kill me' (as he may justly), 'yet will I trust in him,' yet will I hold him fast; and those that find me dead, shall find my heart, my hands fastened upon Christ. And as nothing shall fright, so nothing shall persuade him to leave his hold. He answers all, as Ruth did Naomi: Ruth i. 16, 17, 'Whither thou goest, I will go,' &c.

[6.] Expectation. Being thus resolved to cleave to Christ, he expects something from him. Though his hopes be weak, his hold is strong. There is a hope before him, though he apprehend it not in him, which he lays hold of. Although he cannot come to the throne of grace with that full assurance of hope which the apostle mentions, though he arrive not there with full sail, yet he has a sweet breeze of probability, enough to keep him in motion, and hold his head above water, and this may support him in the mean time: Ps. ix. 18, 'The expectation of the poor shall not perish for ever.' Though it may stick upon the flats, and dash now and then against the rock, yet it shall not perish; or though it may seem to perish for a time, yet it shall not perish for ever.

(4.) The special encouragements which this faith may have, in reference to the success of prayer.

[1.] This relying upon God, engages him to answer, and the Lord will not fail his engagements. If one rely upon a great person for a favour, and have encouragement from him so to do, it will not stand with his credit and honour to disappoint him; much less will the Lord fail those whom he has encouraged to depend on him. He is tender of his honour. If such a soul come to him, and tell him, Thou hast invited me to fly to thee for refuge; I have none else to defend me, I have renounced all other dependencies; if thou fail me, I perish; he that thus flies to the Lord for refuge, shall find in due time strong consolation. Christ will not deliver those up to justice, who fly to him for sanctuary.

[2.] Christ highly commends this faith of dependence, seems to admire it, and to be extraordinarily taken with it: Mat. viii. 8, 'Speak the word only, and my servant shall be healed.' Here is no more expressed than a faith of dependence; if there be any assurance, it is but a half assurance, that which respected the power of Christ, not his willingness, no intimation of that. So Mat. xv., of the woman of Canaan. Christ beats her off there from all assurance; that which she asked was not proper for her: 'It is not meet to cast the children's bread to dogs.' Nor was he sent for this purpose. He leaves her no ground for assurance, yet by this faith of dependence she clings to him, pleads with him, urges him so far till he yields, till she prevails, and she prevails as far as she will. See here the power of this faith put forth in prayer, it can prevail with Christ for the obtaining of all we desire.

[3.] The obedience of one that has but a faith of dependence in seeking

God is in some respect more excellent than theirs who have assurance. For a child that has his father's smile and love to be affectionate and obsequious is no great matter; but for one whom his father does not own, who knows not that he shall have any share in the inheritance, [to] be obedient and affectionate, this is excellent and rarely ingenuous; so for one that is assured of the love of God, that walks in the light of his countenance, and knows heaven is his portion, to be much in seeking God, and waiting on him, is not so much, but for him who sees nothing but frowns in the face of God, and has no assurance of any reward for his attendance on him, to be much in prayer, eager in following him, diligent in waiting on him, this is obedience of a rare ingenuous temper, and cannot but be highly acceptable in the sight of God. For one to say as the martyr, Though I know not that Christ loves me, yet will I die, be burned for him. Will not the Lord value such an affection? will he not reward such? will he not make sweet returns to such prayers?

[4.] He that has this faith of dependence has really interest in all the privileges that attend assurance, though not in his own apprehension. This faith justifies the person, and the person being justified, the prayer is accepted. This gives an interest in the covenant, and he that is in covenant has right to all promises. This gives interest in Christ, and he that has that has interest in his intercession, his Father's love, his Spirit's assistance; and what more is required to make prayer successful? If prayer be accepted, it will be answered, though he apprehends it not, if the Lord be engaged by promise, if Christ intercede, if the Spirit assist.

2. Case. There is a confidence to be found in unregenerate men in their addresses to God. We see too many are confident as to their state that they shall be saved, and they may be as confident as to their duties that they shall be accepted, as to their prayers that they shall be heard when they pray for salvation. As nothing is more dangerous, so nothing more common than such presumptions. And they are so high and strong, as it is one of the most difficult works of gospel ministers to demolish and level these confidences, to beat sinners out of them. This is one of Satan's strongholds, wherein he secures natural men against the assaults of law and gospel tending to reduce them, and bring them to surrender and yield themselves to Christ upon gospel terms. Such confidence we see in the Pharisee, Luke xviii. And the prophet declares against it in the degenerate and profane Israelites, Amos iii. 9–11. Here the question will be, how the confidence of faith may be known and distinguished from this presumptuous confidence, how a true believer may discern that his confidence in approaching to God is not the presumption of hypocrites, and how presumptuous sinners may be convinced that their carnal boldness is not the confidence of faith? that so the prayers of faith may be distinguished from the prayers of presumption and carnal confidence.

Ans. The confidence of faith in prayer differs from this presumptuous confidence in its rise, grounds, attendants, and effects.

(1.) In its *rise*. The carnal man arrives at this confidence he knows not how. If we should say to it, as the master of the feast to him that wanted the wedding garment, 'How camest thou hither?' he can give no satisfying answer, he can give no rational account how he came by it, he has had it ever since he can remember, ever since he was accustomed to pray. He attained it with ease, it cost him nothing; it sprang up in him as a mushroom, on a sudden, without his care or industry. Whereas the confidence of faith is not in an ordinary way so soon, nor so easily, nor so insensibly attained. Believers can many times remember their carnal confidence was cast down by the spirit of bondage, and that their spiritual confidence was not raised but with difficulty, and by degrees; it was a work of time and labour, like the casting down of mountains and the filling of valleys. The work of law and gospel too were little enough to effect it. After the convictions of sin and wrath, their own vileness and unworthiness had made a valley in their spirits, had undermined their mountain of presumption which stood so fast, and had laid them low and vile in their own apprehensions, it was a work of difficulty to raise their souls to this confidence. They found fearfulness and confidence struggle in their souls, as the twins in Rebecca's womb, Gen. xxv. 22; a strife as betwixt Pharez and Zara, Gen. xxxviii., which would get out first; doubtings and fearfulness putting out the hand before this confidence could break forth, and the soul in the mean time, as it were, in travail.

(2.) In the *grounds*. Presumption has either no ground at all, or else it is raised upon nothing but the sand; in some it springs from their natural temper, they can be bold and confident with men, and they will be so with God; he may complain of them as of those, Ps. l. 21, 'Thou thoughtest I was altogether such a one as thyself.' Their apprehensions of God differ little from those they have of men, and so they make as bold with him as they do with their familiars. They sometimes ground it upon their prayers, especially if they be long and often in this duty, they think they oblige God thereby, and conclude something is due to them from God upon this account, and accordingly they expect it. Hence it is that when the returns do not answer their expectations, they are ready to expostulate with God, as though he did them wrong, like those, Isa. lviii. 2, 3. Sometimes they raise it upon the same foundation with the Pharisee, Luke xviii. They are not so bad as some, and they do more good than others, and therefore are confident they shall fare well at God's hands. But now the confidence of faith is to be found in those who are most bashful and modest as to their natural constitutions, when once they are renewed and fortified by the power of grace. Christ and the promise is the ground of this confidence. They rest not in their prayers, nor any part of their own righteousness; they know that all their shreds put together will make no more than a menstruous cloth, a garment both ragged and loathsomely bespotted. This is occasion of shame and blushing, they can have no confidence to be seen in such a woful habit. They count all their prayers, abstinences from sin, and actual righteousness but loss, look on them all as lost, and have no confidence to be found anywhere, in anything, but in Christ, Phil. iii. But what the grounds of it are I have given a large account before.

(3.) In the *attendants*. Confidence of faith is accompanied with,

[1.] Reverence; a filial and a holy fear of God. The apostle, who so often exhorts the faithful Hebrews to draw near with boldness, with confidence, with full assurance of faith, brings it attendant with it: Heb. xii. 28, 'Being confident we shall receive,' &c. Let us hold fast this confidence, and thereby we shall be enabled to serve God with reverence. Hope (often put for faith and confidence) is joined with fear: Ps. cxlvii. 11, Ps. v. 7, 'In the multitude of thy mercy, there is confidence,' &c. A believer is sensible of his own vileness, and apprehensive of the majesty and holiness of God, low thoughts of himself, and high thoughts of God. These thoughts impress upon the soul an awful respect of God, fill it with reverence, and an ingenuous dread lest any action or word should pass him in this duty not beseeming such a majesty, that might be in the least offensive or dishonourable to him, as we see a child is then most afraid to offend his father when he is nearest him. The presumptuous have a good conceit of themselves, but low thoughts of God. The Pharisee was an emblem of such. In his prayer, he is more in praising himself than praising God. Or if upon any occasion their thoughts of God be raised, yet so slight and powerless, as they leave little or no impression upon the heart. The higher they rise in these speculations, the weaker is their influence; as the stars, we see, they are so high they give little light. Their apprehensions leave no awe or dread of God upon their hearts : Or if there be any impressions of fear, yet it is a fear of smarting and suffering from him rather than of displeasing or dishonouring him; as slaves, that would not dread the displeasure or disparagement of their master, but that they are afraid of stripes and blows.

[2.] Resignation of his will and wisdom to the will and wisdom of God. He will be content with God's time, his way, his measure, his will, as to the answer of his prayers, and all the circumstances thereof. But presumptuous confidence must have what he desires, or nothing; when he expects it, or not at all; in that way and degree he looks for it, or else it is not worth the having. It is a proud stiffness of spirit, his will must be the rule to measure his receipts, his wisdom must be judge what is best; these must not veil nor lower to the will and wisdom of God. He is like a sturdy beggar, that must have what he asks, or else you must look for ill language from him. If the Lord will not punctually gratify his desires, he has hard thoughts of him, murmurs and repines against him, as you see in the Israelites all along under their conduct by Moses. True confidence is like the ground of it, Christ; a tender plant will bow and bend to the will and at the pleasure of God, but counterfeit confidence is like a sturdy oak, or a dry stick, that will break rather than bend.

(4.) In the *effects*. Confidence begets,

[1.] Fervency. We see by experience, where there are hopes of attaining, they will quicken up to eagerness in pursuing. A due confidence of receiving will make a believer vehement and fervent in asking. The apostle makes a prayer of faith to be a fervent prayer; James v., that which is a prayer of faith, ver. 15, is described to be a fervent prayer, ver. 16. And Elias, who is given as an instance of one praying in faith, and his prayer is there expressed by this character of fervency, verse 17, προσευχῇ προσηύξατο; according to the letter it is, 'he prayed in his prayer,'—a form of speech, it is usual with the Hebrews, to express vehemency; he prayed vehemently. True confidents *pray* their prayers, others do but *say* their prayers.

If a man desire a thing above him, and have hopes that he may reach it, he will stretch out himself to do it. This hope, this confidence of attaining what we desire of God, will make our prayers to be a stretching out of our souls to God, according to the import of that expression, Acts xii. 5, προσευχὴ ἐκτενής, an extended prayer was made, a prayer wherein the soul was extended and stretched out to God.

That prayer which springs from this confidence is a soul-labour, the travail of the soul; the heart is in labour while it is in prayer. But that of the presumptuous is but lip-labour, a labour of the outward man, a bodily exercise; the heart and affections are cold, dead, without lively motion. Or if there be any heat, life, fervency, in them, it is but at some times, and for some things. There may be some eagerness at some times, as when they are under some strong convictions, in some imminent danger, or under some sharp affliction; 'in their affliction they will seek me early.' Then diligently, at other times carelessly.

Or they may be eager for some things, for temporal blessings, for outward deliverance. They may howl upon their beds for corn and wine, but not for holiness, not for power against endeared lusts; they pray for these, like Augustine before his conversion, as if they were afraid to be heard. Or they may be affectionate in some parts of prayer. There may be some heat and importunity in petition when their necessities of outward things are pressing, Isa. xxvi. 16. They poured out a prayer; their hearts, as though they were dissolved by the ardency of desires for deliverance, ran out in their petitions. Oh but what melting was there in their confessing and bewailing sin! what heat and affectionateness in their praises of God! No; when such are to offer a sacrifice of praise, there is no fire on the altar, no heat nor ardour of affection; no fire from heaven, at least nothing but strange fire, such as their own interests and concernments kindle.

⁂ This Sermon appears to be unfinished.—ED.

OF DYING IN FAITH.

These all died in faith.—Heb. XI. 13.

The apostle having in the former chapter exhorted them to persevere in the faith, in this he explains the nature of it. 1. Describing it by some properties, ver. 1. 2. Confirming the description by examples of the faithful in general, ver. 2, particularly of Abel, ver. 4, Enoch, ver. 5, 6, Noah, ver. 7, Abraham, ver. 8, 9, 10, Sarah, ver. 11, 12, and gives an account of their faith in four particulars, ver. 13. 1. The continuance of their faith: died; as lived by it, so died in it. 2. The object of it, the promises. 3. The acts of it: (1.) see; (2.) persuaded; (3.) embraced. 4. The effect of it, an acknowledgment they were strangers. From the first,

Obs. The elders died in the faith.

1. In the profession of the faith. They held fast the truths of God to the death. They denied not, they made not shipwreck of faith; they suffered not Satan or his instruments to cheat them of it; exchanged it not for fancies, delusions; did not apostatise, fall from it, as was prophesied of many in the last times; made not their opinions subservient to carnal interests; did not tack about, not carried about with every wind. Judgments firmly anchored in truth could ride out foul weather, bear up against storms.

2. In the state of faith. As they lived, so they died believers. Having begun in the Spirit, they did not end in the flesh. They kept faithfully the Spirit's παρακαταθήκη. They lost not the habit of faith; suffered it not to decay, languish; but strengthened it, bore on towards perfection; that when their outward man decayed, faith increased, and was strongest in the greatest weakness, in death.

3. In the expression of faith. The genuine expression of faith in God is faithfulness to God; and they were faithful unto the death. Though sometimes in the place of dragons, yet did not deal falsely in the covenant; endeavoured to perform the conditions of it, to walk before God in uprightness. Deal faithfully in the covenant, when do what is promised, answer engagements, as intent upon repentance and new obedience.

4. In the exercise of faith. Though the other be true, this seems most proper. As they acted faith in their life, so in their death. Their life

was the life of faith, as Paul, Gal. ii. 20. Faith had an influence into every act of their life. *Natural* acts, Sarah conceived by faith, and was delivered, Heb. xi.; *civil* acts, Abraham sojourned, ver. 9; *spiritual* acts, Abel sacrificed by faith, ver. 4; *ordinary* acts, Abraham's travel, ver. 8; *extraordinary*, Noah's building an ark, ver. 7. What they did, they did by faith, *i.e.*, depending upon Christ for strength, believing the promise for assistance and success. And from the considerations of God's nature, attributes, providence, and their experiences of his goodness and faithfulness, did whatever they were commanded, went wherever they were called, expected whatever was promised. Thus they lived, and thus they died in faith, with confidence that God would perform what he had promised, even after their death, to them or theirs. Those that were begun to be performed in their lives, should be perfectly accomplished in or after their death; and those that were not at all performed before, should be fully accomplished after. God had promised to Abraham the land of Canaan, and heaven which that typified, and the Messias the purchaser of it. Abraham died in faith, that is, went out of the world confident that he should be admitted into heaven, ver. 10, and that his posterity should inherit the land of Canaan, and that the Messias should proceed from his loins. He saw the day of Christ, and that sight, strengthened by faith, made the day of death a day of joy, a gladsome day. Died in faith, *i.e.*, in expectation of the performance of promises.

Use. Let us endeavour to imitate the ancient worthies; so to live by faith, as we may die in it. There can be no scruple of endeavouring an imitation here, since their example is commended to us by God, verse 2. Paul exhorts, Philip. iv. 8, 'Whatsoever things are of good report,' &c. He that dies in the faith dies honourably, comfortably, happily.

1. Honourably. He honours God, and God honours him. A strong faith does honour God at any time, Rom. iv. 20, sure then in death, since faith has then the most discouragements. How the Lord honours faith, we need go no further for instance than this chapter, where the apostle, by special instinct from God, makes honourable mention of faith and the faithful, and leaves an eternal monument thereof to all posterity. Thus shall it be done to the men who honour God, whom God will honour; their memory shall be blessed, and all generations shall call them so. When they are dead, and turned to ashes, rather than they shall want a testimony, the Lord will give one from heaven, a sufficient vindication against all the slander of the world. And who will put dishonour upon these whom the Lord will honour?

2. Comfortably. Faith and joy are mutual causes. Where strong faith, there is strong consolation in life or death. When faith ebbs, joy ebbs; a spring-tide of faith brings a strong stream of joy. Where there is πληροφορία πίστεως, full assurance of faith, then the soul is carried with full sail into the bosom of Christ. A weak faith does but creep into heaven, strong faith gives an abundant entrance.

3. Happily. 'He that continues faithful to the end, shall be saved.' It is he who must hear that ravishing welcome from the mouth of God, 'Well done, good and faithful servant,' and must receive a glorious crown from the hand of Christ; 'Be thou faithful unto death,' &c. Faith enters with triumph into heaven, it conquers all opposition; 'This is your victory whereby ye overcome the world, even your faith.' It conquers Satan; the shield of faith quenches his darts, conquers sin, conquers death, *jam deventum est ad triarios;* it disarms him, and then enters heaven with a

triumph, 'O death, where is thy sting?' Given victory through Christ. What we have through him, we have by faith in him.

Directions. 1. That you may live and die in the faith of Christ, in the faith once delivered to the saints, *i.e.*, in the truths of Christ; that you may be constant and immoveable, not tossed to and fro, not carried away with the error of the wicked, the prevailing delusions of the times; that you may not be carried down the stream of error, the waters which the dragon vomits, Rev. xii. 15; take this golden rule: 'Receive the truth in the love of it,' 2 Thes. ii. 10. If you would continue in the truth, and have the Lord establish you in it, love the truth for itself, and love it above all inferior respects whatsoever. He that loves, espouses the truth only for some sinister advantages, out of custom, for applause, to avoid censure, &c., when these cease, will divorce the truth, and embrace any error that will comport with these respects. This is the great reason of the unfaithfulness of these times; why do many relinquish, disclaim those truths, which they formerly held, maintained, professed? Why, they did not love the truth for itself, but for some base respects; they never were in love with the beauty of truth, but only its garb, its dowry; and therefore when error comes in a garb more pleasing to carnal minds, with a dowry more advantageous to their base hearts, these wantons will entertain the truth no longer, but embrace error, a strumpet in room thereof. He that loves truth only for applause will embrace error when it is more plausible. He that loves carnal pleasures more than truth, will be ready to entertain those errors that will grant a toleration. He that receives the truth only, or principally, because it is generally received, will change his opinion when the times change. Nay, if a man's carnal heart were not apt to fall out with truth, yet the Lord is so much in love with it as he will not suffer those to be blessed with it, who will not love it for itself, who prostitute it to base respects. He gives such up to strong delusions, &c.

2. That you may live and die in the state of faith, get into that happy state. Get faith rooted and grounded in your hearts, and then you are sure: 'Kept by the power of God through faith unto salvation.' You can neither live nor die without faith. While ye live without faith you are under the sentence of condemnation, and if ye die without faith, death will lead you to execution. Be not deceived, think not that to be faith which is not; think not you have faith, because you believe the word of God is truth, and what it reveals concerning God, and Christ, and holiness, and happiness, is true. This is faith indeed, but such a faith as the devils have; such a faith will be no advantage either in life or death; it will distinguish thee from an infidel, but not from an unbeliever. That faith which is saving, which receives testimony from God, &c., is such a faith as will make you willing to embrace Christ both as prince and Saviour; willing to obey him, as to be saved by him; to be sanctified as well as justified; that worketh by love, purifieth the heart, brings forth the fruits of the Spirit. This is the faith by which ye must live, in which ye must die, if ye will die happily, comfortably, &c. That you may attain this faith, be diligent in attending upon the word. This direction is the apostle's, Rom. x. 14, 17. It is the word that both begets faith, and nourishes it. Those that neglect the word (it is evident to me) care not how they live, nor how they die.

3. That you may live and die in the expression of faith; *i.e.*, that you may not deal unfaithfully in the covenant; consider how horribly wretched such unfaithfulness is. Those that use to deal unfaithfully with men, lie,

or forswear, to get some advantage, there may be some temptation to this; but he that deals unfaithfully with God, deals unfaithfully with God to undo, to ruin himself. There is no advantage in the world to be got hereby, to tempt a man to it; the sin is desperately wicked and inexcusable. He that deals unfaithfully in the covenant does God a high displeasure, that he may damn himself. What do ye, when you neglect faith, repentance, &c.? what tempts you to it? what advantage expect ye?

4. That ye may die in the exercise of faith, (1.) learn to live in the exercise of it. The more faith is acted, the easier it will be to exercise. Those who are strangers to the life of faith while they live, will find it a strange work to act it when they die. If you exercise it not now, it will in an ordinary way be impossible to act it then. The way to die in faith is to live by it. Learn now to live in a continual dependence upon God, to trust him with all you have, for all you want, to rely on him for supply of wants, assistance in duties, success of endeavours, strength to resist temptations, subdue lusts, bear afflictions, a blessing on your enjoyments. Walk always leaning upon God; so the word שען imports; depend on him, as the child upon the mother's breast; by the attractive power of faith, draw out of his all-sufficiency whatever you want. The life that you live, let it be by faith, &c., and then your death will be like these worthies'; and this may be writ upon your monument, at least it will be writ in heaven, 'These all died in the faith.'

(2.) Treasure up the promises in your hearts, in your memories. No such treasure as this. You will find riches a vain thing in that hour, they cannot deliver from death; but faith acted on the promises will both support in it, and deliver from it. These you will find the best cordials, sweeter than manna, the bread of life. That soul can never faint that feeds on them. Faith supports the soul when death assails, and these support faith; they are the staff of bread; if faith feed on them, they will nourish it into strength, such strength as will break through the terrors and pangs of death in a triumph. Let not the promises lie neglected, as though of no use. Choose out those that are most pertinent, those that will support in the conflict, and raise your expectation of approaching glory.

(3.) Clear up your evidences for heaven. While your title is dark, faith will be weak. How can ye be confident of the eternal blessings of the covenant, while ye have no assurance that you are in covenant? How can ye with confidence go out to meet the bridegroom, when ye know not whether ye have oil in your lamps? Oh then give all diligence to make your calling and election sure. Till that be sure, faith will scarce find any firm footing, and so stagger and waver. Examine yourselves whether in the faith; give no rest to yourselves till ye know ye have interest in him, who through death has destroyed him that had the power of death, Heb. ii. 14, 15. You can never be confident ye shall depart in peace, till ye be assured that Christ is your salvation.

When you have cleared this evidence, endeavour to keep it clear. Sin blots it, guilt is a blur in the evidence. If you avoid not these in your lives, you will scarce read your evidence at death, and then faith may be nonplussed and to seek, when most [you] need it. Endeavour to keep a good conscience always, in all things, towards God and man, that so you may have the testimony of God and of your conscience on your deathbeds: as 2 Cor. i. 12, 'That in simplicity and godly sincerity you have had your conversation.' Oh, such a testimony will be a great encouragement to faith, when all outward encouragements fail.

(4.) Lay up experiences. The remembrance of experiments of God's mercy and faithfulness in your lives will be a sweet support to faith in death. God's people have made good use of experiences to this purpose; David, Paul, 2 Tim. iv. 18. Faith from such promises* will draw sweet conclusions. The Lord has delivered me from the dominion of sin, and the cruelty of Satan, therefore he will deliver me from the power of death. The Lord has given me the first fruits of heaven while I lived, he will give me a full harvest of glory after death.

* Qu. 'premises'?—ED.

OF LIVING AS STRANGERS.

And confessed that they were strangers.—Heb. XI. 13.

You have here an account of the life and death of those faithful servants of God, the patriarchs. Of their death, 'These all died,' &c.; of their life, 'Strangers and pilgrims.' That they thus died, we have God's testimony, 'These all,' &c. That they thus lived, we have their own confession; they were strangers all their life, they were faithful to the death, and are thus recorded as examples to the people of God in all ages, that they may thus live, thus die.

Obs. Those that would die in the faith, should live as strangers and pilgrims.

For explication I shall shew, 1. What it is to die in the faith; 2. What to live as strangers.

For the first, it is to die as those ancient people of God did: 1. In the profession; 2. In the state; 3. In the expression; 4. In the exercise of faith, of which before.

For the second, I shall first shew the *ὀτὶ*, secondly, the *πῶς*.

The people of God in all ages thus lived. Jacob professeth it to Pharaoh, both of himself and his fathers, Gen. xlvii. 9. The Lord himself, in the following age, styles all the Israelites thus, Lev. xxv. 23. But they were not settled in Canaan, and that might be the reason. No. After it was given them as their inheritance, when they had possession of it, and had continued in possession some hundred years, in David's time, yet does he profess this of himself and all his fathers, Ps. xxxix. 12. But it may be David spake this when he was under persecution and in banishment, when he was hunted as a partridge, &c. No; it was when he was established upon the throne of Judah and Israel, when he had conquered all opposers abroad and at home, as it is evident, 1 Chron. xxix. 15. Nor was this the condition of God's people under the law only; no other is their state under the gospel. The apostle writes to them under this notion, 1 Pet. ii. 11. That it is so is evident; but in what respects are they so?

Ans. They are strangers and pilgrims:

1. In respect of their station, the place of their abode. While they are in the world, they are in a strange country; while they are present in the world, they are far from home. The world is a strange country, and their habitations in it, how much soever their own in civil respects, are but as

inns in that journey homeward. The land of promise was but to Abraham a strange country; his dwelling there was but a sojourning, so far was he from thinking himself at home, ver. 9.

The world is a strange country to the people of God, and the men of the world are men of a strange language, strange customs, strange laws, far differing from that of their own country. A strange language, the language of Ashdod. To hear God's name profaned, his people reproached, holiness vilified, miscalled; to hear unclean, unsavoury, revengeful language; to hear men wholly taken up with discourse of the earth, and earthly things, oh this is, or should be, strange language to the people of God; there is no such word ever heard in their own country. While in the world, they are amongst a people of a strange tongue, strange customs and laws too, such as were never enacted, nor had place in their own country. To neglect the worship of God in public, in their families, to make provision for the flesh, &c., to lay up treasure on earth, to neglect God, their souls, eternity, these and such like are customs of the world; and they think it strange (so common is it) that God's people will not run with them, 1 Pet. iv. 4, not swear, be drunk. A people of strange doctrines, Heb. xiii. 9; strange vanities, Jer. viii. 19; of a strange God too, 2 Cor. iv. 4. He is their lawgiver; the course of this world is according to his laws, Eph. ii. 2. The laws of their own country have no place here: the law of faith, love, self-denial, loving enemies, &c. Such a country is the world to the people of God, a strange country; and in this respect they are strangers.

2. In respect of their design, their motion, it is still homewards. This strange country likes them not, nor they it; they are travelling towards another, that which is, that which they account, their home, that better country, that heavenly country, that city prepared for them, that city whose builder and maker is God. Thus these faithful worthies, ver. 14, they that say, *i. e.*, that confess, &c., do plainly declare, ver. 16. That heavenly country is the place of the Lord's abode; and because he is their God, this is their country, their home. This they look for, ver. 10, this they seek, ver. 14, this they desire, ver. 16; their expectations, their affections, their endeavours are for heaven, when they are like themselves. While they are present in the world, they are absent from home. So their life here is in motion; they are in a journey; they are travelling homewards, and that is to heaven. This is their journey's end, the end of their pilgrimage; and till they come there, till they be at home in heaven, they are strangers.

3. In respect of their enjoyments. They are but accommodated here like strangers. Much would be a burden, a hindrance to them in their journey; they have more in hopes than hand. These worthies died, not having received the promises, *i. e.*, all the good things promised: no, their richest enjoyments are at home; no matter for state and superfluities in a journey. They are not known in those strange places where they pass, no matter how they seem to strangers. Though they be princes, sons of God, heirs of a crown, their Father sees it best, safest for them, to travel in a disguise. No matter what strangers take them for, 1 John iii. 2, what they now enjoy are but like the accommodations of an inn, enough for travellers. Their treasure, their crown, their glory is at home, their Father's house; till they come there they are strangers.

4. In respect of their usage. They are not known in the world, and so are often coarsely used. In this strange country they meet with few friends, but many injuries. See how the world used those of whom it was not worthy, ver. 36–38. Here is strangers indeed, and strangely us ed. No wonder if

a stranger be jeered and derided; his habit, his manners, his language, is not conformed to the place where he is. Their habit, language, practices, must be after their own country fashion, such as become heaven: now this being contrary to the world, meets with opposition, scorn, reproaches, hatred. This was the portion of Christ, of his disciples, of his people in all ages; and this is the reason they are not of the world, they are strangers, John xvii. 14. If they have something that commands outward respect, it may be they will find some; but the hearts of worldly men are against them, John xv. 18, 19.

5. In respect of their continuance. Their abode on earth is but short. A stranger, a traveller stays not long in one place. Upon this account does David call himself and the people of God strangers, 1 Chron. xxix. 15. They dwell but as Abraham in tabernacles, ver. 9, in tents, moveable dwellings, quickly, easily removed; no dwelling that has a foundation that is lasting, durable, till at home, ver. 10. Continuance on earth but a shadow, but a passage.

6. In respect of their relations. Their dearest relations are in another country. Their Father, their Husband, their Elder Brother, their dearest Friend, their Comforter, and the far greatest part of their brethren and fellow-members, are all in heaven. He that lives at a distance from his relations may well pass for a stranger.

Use 1. Reproof of those who profess themselves to be the people of God, and yet live not like his people; live on earth, as though earth was their home, and mind heaven as little as they mind a strange country; suffer their thoughts, affections, endeavours, to be so taken up with the earth, and the things of it, as though the world were all the home they expect; instead of being strangers to the world, are strangers to the thoughts of, to the employments of, to the endeavours for heaven; rise up early, &c., to lay up treasure on earth, and lap up their hearts and souls with it. No wonder if these people be unwilling to die, since they must part from the world as one parts from his own country to go into banishment. They that thus live in the world cannot expect to die in the faith. Whose image and superscription do they bear?

Use 2. Exhortation to the people of God. You are strangers and pilgrims, oh endeavour to live as strangers. You expect to die in the faith, oh live then as you may so die.

(1.) Be not familiar with the world. Let the pleasures, the carnal interests of it, be strange things to you, 1 Pet. ii. 12. 'Be not conformed to the world,' Rom. xii. 2. If you count heaven your home, your country, disparage not heaven so much as to prefer the customs, the fashions, the practices, the language of the world, before those of your own country. To be ashamed to hold forth a heavenly conversation before the world, is to be ashamed of your own country, of heaven. Let your lives testify that you are citizens of heaven, that you are strangers.

(2.) Be patient under sufferings, under the affronts, reproaches, hard usages you meet with from the world. It is the portion of strangers. If ye were known, ye might expect better usage; but here you are strangers, you must put up wrongs and injuries. What folly for one in a strange country to seek to right himself? Expect no vindication till in your own country.

(3.) Be content with what things you enjoy. Though it seem small or poor, it is enough for a stranger. More would be a burden to you, and travellers should avoid burdens, if they long to be at home. The things of the world are cumbersome; they may make your journey tedious, and keep you longer from your desired home. Be content for a while; it is but a while, and you will be at home, and then you will find better entertainment, and more plenty.

(4.) Set not your hearts upon any thing here below. Remember, while you are on earth, you are but in an inn. What folly would it be for a traveller, who has far* home, to fall in love with, and fix himself in his inn? Such folly, or worse, would it be for you to fix on the world. Mind the things here below as *in transitu;* use them as though ye used them not.

(5.) Make haste home. Make no longer stay than needs must in this strange country. Make straight steps to your feet; disburden yourselves of worldly cares, projects, fleshly lusts, that weight that does so easily beset you. What you have to do here, do it with all your might, that you may be fit for home. Despatch, make haste; remember whither you are going, and to whom. Your Father expects you; the Bridegroom thinks long till you come, he that will delight in you for ever. You are but now contracted; the marriage will not be solemnized till you come home; and there he stands ready to entertain you, to embrace you in the arms of everlasting love. Hear how sweetly he invites you: Cant. ii. 10, 'Rise up, my love, my fair one, and come away.' Oh turn not aside into by-paths of sin and vanity. Look not back, close with sweet exhortation, Heb. xii. 1, 2. Oh let the sight, the thoughts of Jesus, quicken your pace. And while you are absent in the body, let your hearts be at home, your hearts in heaven, where are your treasure, your joys, your crown, your glory, your inheritance, your husband. Oh, is not here allurement enough? This is the way to be at home while you are from home.

(6.) Be not too fearful of death. It is a sleep now; Christ's death did change the property of it? and will a pilgrim, a weary traveller, be afraid of sleep? When you are come to the gates of death, there is but one step then betwixt you and home, and that is death. Methinks we should pass this cheerfully, the next step your foot will be in heaven. How does it cheer the weary traveller, to think this is the last day's journey; to-morrow, to-morrow I shall be at my own home, with all my dear relations. There I shall have ease and rest, and many welcomes. Suppose this last be the worst, the most stormy day of all my journey, to-morrow will make full amends for it.

Now such a day is the day of death, the last day of a wearisome pilgrimage, and that which brings the stranger to his long home, into the bosom of God, into the embraces of Christ, unto all those joys and engagements that his own country afford, such as eye has not seen, nor ear heard, &c. This is partly the way to live as strangers, to live so as ye may die in the faith; and those that die in the faith die in the Lord, and those are blessed.

* Qu. 'a fair'?—ED.

THE EXCELLENT KNOWLEDGE OF CHRIST.

Yea doubtless, and I count all things but loss for the excellency of the knowledge of Christ Jesus my Lord: for whom I have suffered the loss of all things, and do count them but dung, that I may win Christ.—PHILIP. III. 8.

HERE are the sweet strains of a gospel spirit, letting out itself in expressing a dear love to, a high esteem of Christ, and him alone; advancing Christ above all, giving him the throne, and making all competitors his footstool.

The occasion of them we may find in the former verses, wherein I cannot let pass some sweet and raised expressions without giving you a taste, glancing at them by the way, that you may understand them, and the coherence of these with them. Some teachers there were amongst them who drove on a pernicious design to corrupt the doctrine of the gospel and dishonour Christ, by joining with him the works and observances of the law, in point of justification and salvation. To prevent the mischief of this unworthy medley, he gives them saving advice, which we may take up in four parcels.

1. To rest joyfully in Christ alone, to embrace him with delight, and rest satisfied in his righteousness, the all-sufficiency of his undertaking and performance for pardon and glory, ver. 1; and lest they should nauseate this doctrine as too often repeated and inculcated, he tells them 'to write the same things, to him was not grievous,' because most sweet and delightful, most necessary and profitable; 'to them safe.' They were in danger to be removed from him that called them unto the grace of Christ, unto another gospel. The repetition of this was necessary to prevent the danger; it was safe, *i.e.*, saving; no doctrine saving but that which advances Christ alone, and preserves his glory entire in those points.

2. To beware of false teachers, those that adulterated the gospel, and made a medley of righteousness by works and faith, and bring in their ceremonial or moral observances to share with Christ, as partial grounds at least of their confidence and rejoicing. And he sets on this advice with sharp terms, as being tender of the glory of Christ, bitter and vehement against his co-rivals. He rebukes them ἀποτόμως, cuttingly, sharply, *vide* ver. 2. He calls them 'dogs,' those that did rend and tear the simplicity of gospel doctrine, and divide the glory of man's salvation betwixt faith and works; such as did bark out reproaches against the apostles and their

doctrine delivered in its native purity and simplicity. It will be useful to observe here the different temper and carriage of this divine apostle in different cases. When things were indifferent, and less necessary and doubtful, farther from the heart of gospel truth and the great mystery of Christ, then who more mild, who more indulgent? who more complying in things indifferent? He became all things, &c. In things doubtful, of less moment, he calls for meekness, forbearance, peace, love; he breathes nothing else but the mild spirit of his gracious Lord, Rom. xiv. 1. But when opinions were broached that intrenched upon the glory of Christ, and tended to subvert souls, and pervert the gospel, why then the apostle is another man, a Boanerges; he seems to speak fire and thunder, *mera tonitrua*. No terms are bad enough, too bad for such seducers. Though they were cried up and applauded as the only pastors and shepherds, he calls them 'dogs.' They thought themselves the only patrons of good works, he calls them 'evil workers.' They would be thought the only legitimate children, he calls them 'concision;' to shew his dislike of their abusing and idolising circumcision, he gives it a by-name. So Hezekiah calls the brazen serpent (at first set up by God's appointment), when it was abused and idolised, Nehushtan, in contempt of that which was advanced to the dishonour of God, a piece of brass; or concision, cutting off. This advancing of circumcision into Christ's place tended to cut them off from Christ, from the church of Christ. It did not only occasion division amongst the members, but did tend to cut them off from the head; a ruining, destructive evil. Let us be followers of the apostle, as he followed Christ; learn when to be mild, and when to be zealous. (See Luther on Gal.)

3. He opposes to these seducers the examples of the apostles and faithful, to encourage them to cleave to that doctrine which advanced Christ alone, and renounced all things coming in competition with him, ver. 3. As though he had said, Ye shall lose nothing by closing with this doctrine, and following us herein; whatever they pretend, we are the circumcision, we only are truly circumcised in the account of God. You reject not God's institution, he himself has laid it aside; you lose no privilege by it, we have that which these rites intended and held forth. We have it in Christ more perfectly, more excellently. They have the shadow, we have the substance. They have the outward rite, we have the spiritual benefit intended by it; we have it in a transcendent manner, in its growth and height. They, by sticking to the ceremony, keep themselves in nonage; we are heirs, and enjoy the substance of these ceremonies. We are circumcised in heart; Christ has cut off the foreskin of our hearts, the guilt and power of sin.

'Worship God in spirit;' we understand the spiritual sense of all rites, types, ceremonies. Christ is the truth and substance of them; in him we have all. We worship him, accordingly, in spirit and truth, and so by Christ's verdict are the only true worshippers, John iv. 14. We place not worship in carnal observances, as they do. 'Bodily exercise profits nothing;' it is the heart and spirit that God requires, and this we give him. Follow their example. No worship without the spirit.

'And rejoice in Christ;' καυχώμενοι, we glory in him. Let them glory in their carnal rites, ceremonial observances, legal righteousness, outward privileges, we will rejoice in Christ alone; nay, glory, exult, triumph in him. Joy in its strength is exultation, which is a kind of vaulting or leaping of the soul, yea, a leaping out of itself to its object. Their souls leaped for joy at the contemplation of the infinite fulness, all-sufficiency, glorious and transcendent excellency, of Christ. A man boasts when he is full of that which he thinks excellent. They counted it not only their happiness, but their glory, to have Christ, and Christ alone. They, with undauntedness and full contentment, set Christ against all that the false teachers could pretend to, all that could be offered in competition with Christ. He was the only ground of their joy and confidence. In him they exulted, triumphed, gloried, though they parted with all, lost all for him. See here Christians' temper.

'No confidence in flesh;' carnal rites, ceremonies, privileges, performances; of which after. These were not ground of joy, satisfaction, confidence; they relied not upon these for pardon, acceptance; expected not mercy nor salvation for these. Christ only, he alone was the ground of their confidence, rejoicing, exulting.

4. He enforces his advice by his own example. If there were any reason to glory, or be confident in carnal prerogatives, outward performances, he had as much reason to do it as any of them all, ver. 4. He could boast of as many privileges, as much self-righteousness, as they that could most, which he shews in many severals, ver. 5. 1. 'Circumcised;' the seal of the covenant, and thereby he was outwardly in covenant with God; a great honour, and that which entitled him to many privileges. 2. 'Stock of Israel;' of that nation which the Lord set apart for himself when he rejected all the nations of the earth besides. One of the 'Israelites,' to whom, Rom. ix. 4, 5, belonged the adoption, &c. 3. 'Of the tribe:' as he was one of the most honoured people, so one of the most noble tribe, that of Benjamin; born, not of a bondmaid, but the patriarch's beloved Rachel; a tribe honoured with the first of Israel's kings, in reference to whom, it was like, himself was called Saul. He might have gloried in his nobility, born of a tribe, a family, which was not strangers to the blood-royal. 4. 'A Hebrew:' one of that honoured people, and noble tribe, in the most honourable way; not by affinity, but by pure descent both by father and mother. A proselyte's offspring might be a Hebrew, but not a 'Hebrew of the Hebrews,' as he was. 5. 'A Pharisee:' one of the strictest and most honoured sects amongst them; those were counted eminently religious, both negatively and positively, &c. 6. Ver. 6, 'zeal:' as one of the most religious sect, so was he most zealous in that way of religion; not profane, careless, indifferent, but zealous and active, according to his judgment and conscience. 7. 'Righteous:' not eager only in persecuting those whom he counted enemies of righteousness, but righteous himself, in point of outward conformity to the law and institutions of God; so observant thereof, as he was ἄμωμος, in the eye of men, and in his own account, 'blameless,' without spot; his conversation not stained with any gross sins; an exact man in his life and deportment, living answerable to his knowledge and judgment.

All these grounds of confidence the apostle had before he was converted, and if he would have been as vain-glorious as the false teachers, if he would have been injurious to Christ and his soul, might have rested here, and gloried therein as well as they; but far was he from this temper. He adds, ver. 7, those things fore-mentioned which formerly he counted gain; thought to gain pardon, acceptance, salvation by them; now, since he knew Christ, he was of another judgment; now he counts them loss. He saw he had lost his soul, been a lost man for ever, if he had rested on these for salvation, if he had made these the grounds of his confidence;

and therefore Christ being made known to him as the only way to gain pardon, acceptance, life, he renounced his former privileges, his former legal righteousness. He would not lean upon these broken reeds, which might have let his soul fall into hell. He would have no more confidence in the flesh, but in Christ only, by whom he expected to gain that which in vain he expected from these.

Now, because this might seem a wonder and hard to be believed, that the apostle should renounce, cast away that which others counted their gain, treasure, ornament, their glory and confidence, that which they thought highly commended them, and made them acceptable in the sight of God, and glorious in the eyes of men; to procure the easier belief, to express further the height of his resolution herein, and the fixedness of his heart in what he had done, he affirms it again, and that with an asseveration, together with divers heightened expressions, ver. 8, 'Yea, doubtless,' &c. He did not only count them loss, but he had actually renounced them. It was not only his judgment, but his practice. He did not only count them loss, but dung, filth, excrements, when compared with Christ. He did not only thus account, thus renounce these things fore-mentioned, but all things, even those things that he had done and suffered for Christ, since he knew Christ. Not that he repented of what he had done or suffered, nor that he thought these would not be graciously rewarded, but in point of confidence, in point of justification. If he had brought these before God's tribunal to be accepted, pardoned, justified, saved for them, he had been lost, they would have proved the loss of his soul. God would no more accept of these as satisfaction for sin, or meritorious of eternal life, than he would accept of dung. And therefore in these respects he did that which the Lord would have done, he counted them loss and dung. He smelt a savour of death in those things which had been his confidence before for acceptance and life.

And further, he adds the cause of this strange effect, 'The excellency of the knowledge,' &c. It was the discovery of Christ that wrought his heart to this temper. It was his view of a sinner's transcendent advantage by Christ, that made him account all these loss. It was the wonderful excellency of the knowledge of Christ, that made all these things seem as dung. When we are in the dark, we are glad of candle-light, and glow-worms will make a fair show in our eyes; but when the sun is risen and shines in his full strength, then candle-light seems needless or offensive, and the worms that glittered in the dark, make no better show than other vermin. So when men are in the state of nature and darkness, then their church privileges and carnal prerogatives, then their outward performances and self-righteousness, make a fine show in their eyes. They are apt to glory in them, and rely on them, as that by which they may gain the favour of God and eternal life. Ay, but when Christ appears, when the Sun of righteousness arises in the heart and discovers his excellency, his all-sufficiency, then a man's own sparks vanish; then all his formerly beloved and rich esteemed ornaments are cast off; then all he has, and all he has done, privileges and outward services, are loss and dung. None but Christ, none but Christ, for pardon, acceptance, life. This is the excellent effect of this excellent knowledge.

We may explain the other expressions hereafter. Now (that we spend not all the time in exposition), take from the cause this

Obs. The knowledge of Christ is an excellent knowledge. There is a transcendent excellency in the knowledge of Christ.

Now to proceed most for edification in handling this truth, we will shew,

1. What knowledge of Christ is that which is so excellent. It is not every knowledge, nor every knowledge of Christ that is so. The devils, the reprobates, have, living under the gospel, some apprehensions of Christ, and so have the elect before conversion, which yet is not this excellent knowledge. That which is transcendent, is such as the apostle was, such for nature, though not for degrees. The Scripture abounds with characters of this knowledge, and it were easy to be large in describing it. But I shall confine myself to such as the apostle's discourse in these verses offers to us; and three we have in the text. That knowledge of Christ which is excellent, is,

(1.) Extensive; apprehends him in all those notions and respects wherein the gospel principally discovers him. Three words in this verse which the apostle uses, do comprise all or most of the rest, 'Christ,' 'Jesus,' 'Lord;' not only as Christ, but as Jesus; not only as Jesus, but as Lord. Apprehend what he is,

1st, In his nature and offices; these are included in the word Christ, *i.e.*, the Messias, him whom the Lord anointed to be Mediator. Know him as God, as man, and what necessity sinners had of such a mediator; and so in his offices, apprehend what he is, as king, as prophet, as priest; what excellent and rich advantages flow from each of these into the state and souls of believers. What was the inducement which brought him under such engagements for sinners? The dimensions of his love. Eph. iii. 18, 19, 'To know what is the height, length,' &c., we can, though we have no measure will fully reach the dimensions.

2d, In the intention and execution of his offices, that in the word Jesus, a Saviour, how he exercises these offices to bring about man's salvation. What saving acts belong to each office, and how to apply yourselves to every one of them for salvation.

3d, In the consequents of his offices, that is, dominion in Christ, subjection in us. We have both in the name Lord, Rom. xiv. 9. Many will take notice of Christ as a Saviour, but not as Lord; but this is to take a view of Christ in an eclipse, to apprehend Christ without his crown. This is not to know Christ in all his discovered excellencies, and so is not the excellent knowledge of Christ.

(2.) Appropriating; so the apostle, 'Christ Jesus my Lord.' The marrow of the gospel, as Luther observes, is in these pronouns, *meum*, *nostrum*. He bids us read these with great emphasis. *Tolle meum et tolle Deum*, says another, take away propriety, and you take away God, take away Christ. To apprehend him yours upon good grounds, is the excellency of this knowledge. Christ is notionally known by the evil angels; they know he is a Saviour, a King, a Priest; but they apprehend him not with application as their Saviour, their Head, as a Priest and Mediator for them. But this excellent knowledge apprehends him, and propriety in him; *my* Lord, *my* Jesus, *my* Advocate, who intercedes for *me; my* King, who has writ his laws in my heart; *my* Prophet, who has turned my darkness into light, shining in my dark heart; *my* Sacrifice, who has loved me and washed me, &c.; *my* Head, who quickens and conveys holy quickening influences into me, ἐμὸς ἔρως.

(3.) Effectual. Has a powerful efficacy both upon heart and life, both upon judgment, affection, and practice. We see it in the apostle; this excellent knowledge of Christ raised his esteem of him, possessed him with contempt of all things else, kindled his affections, ardent desires after him, intense delight in him, made him both active and passive for Christ: 'for whom I have suffered the loss of all things.' Where this excellent knowledge is, there Christ is exalted as the chiefest of ten thousand, as the highest excellency, as the richest advantage, as the sweetest enjoyment, as the only matchless beauty, as the most glorious object. Christ outshines all in his judgment, where this excellent knowledge shines. The greatest glory in the world is but as a glow-worm, compared with the sun in its noonday brightness; the choicest excellency seems base when Christ appears; the chiefest gain in the world is loss, when Christ is gained; the richest treasure is dung, when Christ's riches are displayed; the most esteemed accomplishment is vile, when the preciousness of Christ appears; all things put together which natural men, which the most judicious of them, do value and most prize, put in the balance with Christ, are then but vanity, and then apprehended to be lighter than vanity. Whatever the heart was set upon before, it leaves them, it shakes them off, and turns to Christ, and cleaves to him with unspeakable complacency and contentment. Did he before admire riches, or pomp and greatness, or honour and authority, or natural parts, a strong memory, or a good judgment, or a nimble wit, or a reaching head, acquired accomplishments or moral honesty? Ay, but when Christ appears, he has the pre-eminence. He says to the best of these, when they would take his heart and judgment, Friend, sit lower; a worthier than thou must have this place. He that is higher than the heavens must have the highest place in my esteem, the chiefest room in my heart. If you will sit at Christ's feet, and minister to him, then welcome; but the throne is for Christ Jesus my Lord. It has a powerful efficacy upon the affections, to kindle desire, and raise joy in Christ, as the object transcendently desirable and delightful. He covets no gain so much now, but to gain Christ. He sees no righteousness now available, but the righteousness of Christ; he pants and gasps after this righteousness, as that only that can shroud him from revenging justice, and stand betwixt him and that righteous God which is otherwise a consuming fire to sinners. His chiefest desire on earth is to be found in Christ. He cares more indifferently in what state as to the world, in what condition soever the Lord find him, so he be found in Christ; cares not though he be found in prison, found covered with reproaches, found environed with afflictions, found naked as to his own righteousness, privileges, enjoyments, personal excellencies, so he may be found in Christ. This was the apostle's temper, &c. Christ is his glory, and the crown of his rejoicing; he exults, triumphs, glories in Christ, though he lose all for him. Even as a poor beggar discovering a rich mine or some vast treasures, is ready to leap for joy that he has found that which will make him rich for ever; he casts away his former rags, he despises his former poor and wooden furniture, for he has discovered that which will enrich him and make his condition plentiful; so the soul to whom the Lord has made this rich, this excellent discovery of Christ, he has found a mine more precious than gold, and larger than all the face of the earth; he casts off the menstruous rags of his own righteousness; his former accomplishments are now but as a beggar's furniture; his heart is full of joy; he says, Rejoice, O my soul; he says, Rejoice with me, O my friends, for I have found the pearl of great price; I have discovered the unsearchable riches of Christ, that which will make me rich and happy for ever: 'My lines are fallen,' &c.; 'Return to thy rest, O my soul.' So the apostle: 'We are the circumcision, and that rejoice in Christ Jesus.' And it has an influence upon his practice. If he have not, as the apostle,

Eph. iv. 20, 'suffered the loss of all,' he is ready to do it when Christ calls for it. Whatever he cannot enjoy with Christ, he casts from him with indignation, casts to the moles. He renounces the profits of sin, abandons the pleasures of sin, lays aside the honour of his own righteousness, parts, gifts, performances, so far as would obscure the glory of Christ; is ready to lose all, that he may gain Christ, to part with everything, that Christ may be all in all.

(4.) Fiducial. It brings the soul to rest upon Christ and his righteousness alone, for pardon, acceptance, salvation, and to cast away all those rotten props, good nature, well meaning, harmless life, honest carriage, just dealing, church privileges, natural accomplishments, religious performances, upon which he relied, and made the grounds of his confidence before. Who more confident than Paul before he knew Christ? His being numbered amongst the people of God, his strictness in an outward way of religion, his zeal in the way of his conscience, his blameless conversation, were the things for which he thought himself sure of heaven. Here was his confidence; but when Christ was made known, to rest in these he saw was to trust in the arm of flesh, to lean upon a broken reed; and therefore, when the joyful discovery of Christ was made to his soul, he had no more confidence in the flesh, then he would not own his righteousness of the law as a ground of confidence: 'Not having,' &c. The soul that has this excellent discovery of Christ, will make nothing but Christ his confidence; despair in himself, how good soever he be, what good soever he has done, and only rely on Christ his righteousness.

(5.) Useful. He that has it studies to improve Christ, to make use of him for those glorious and blessed purposes for which he knows Christ is given, such as the apostle expresses, ver. 9, 10: to find the blessed advantages of his righteousness for pardon, acceptance, and right to glory, and that upon all occasions of doubting, all contracting of new guilt. 'Power of his resurrection:' lifting him up, not only out of the state of sin, but also above all pressures, incumbrances of life and the world, to seek those things that are above, and enjoy him who is exalted for, &c., and to be raised of him, and brought to him who is the earnest of our resurrection, the first-fruits of the dead. 'Fellowship of his sufferings,' in union and participation. To find by comfortable experience that Christ suffered in his stead, and to receive what he purchased by his blood, merited by his sufferings; and to find a compassionate presence and support from Christ in all sufferings for him, knowing, Heb. viii. 18, 19.* 'Conformable to his death:' to find the power of Christ's death killing sin, crucifying his heart unto the world and the world unto him, that so he may be crucified with Christ, but so die and suffer as he may reign with him. This is the notion, these the properties of that knowledge of Christ which is excellent.

2. Why is the knowledge of Christ excellent? in what respects? upon what account?

(1.) Because it is that knowledge which the most excellent creatures on earth, yea, the most excellent in heaven, did ardently desire, laboriously seek after, and which obtained, they rejoice and glory in. The most excellent on earth are the saints, Ps. xvi., and amongst them, the most excellent were the patriarchs, the kings, the prophets, the apostles; and all these counted the knowledge of Christ their joy, their chief desire. So Abraham, John viii. 56, he saw but the discoveries of Christ afar off, and he rejoiced; he saw but the dawnings of that day wherein Christ's knowledge should

* So in the text; evidently a misprint.—ED.

shine in its strength and glory, and his heart was glad; a glimpse of this excellent vision, at many hundred years' distance, filled him with joy and gladness. Moses preferred the reproach of Christ before all the treasures of a flourishing kingdom, Heb. xi. 26; and if sufferings for Christ were so precious in his esteem, what then was the knowledge of Christ's sufferings for sinners? This was the great inquiry of the prophets, this was it after which they searched diligently, 1 Pet. i. 10, 11. They inquired, they searched, and searched again (it is twice repeated), and searched diligently; they searched for this as for hidden treasures. Oh how excellent was it in their account! Nay, both prophets and kings were ambitious of this as their greatest glory, Luke x. 23, 24. Nay, the Lord Jesus himself rejoiced that the Lord would vouchsafe this excellent discovery to the unworthy sons of men, ver. 21, ἠγαλλιάσατο, his spirit leaped within him for joy, that this excellent knowledge should be vouchsafed to sinners. Sure there was something transcendent, something exceeding excellent, in that which would occasion the Spirit of Christ to leap for joy within him, when he was in the condition of a man of sorrows. For the apostles, it is most visible in Paul, who was, while in darkness, a deadly enemy to Christ and the knowledge of him; but the appearance of Christ to him wrought a wonderful alteration. He was afterwards privileged above the rest, rapt up into the third heaven, and saw there visions of glory such as transported him, such as were past expression; but whatever glory he saw, he saw nothing that more affected his heart than the sight of Christ, than the excellent knowledge of his Lord Jesus. The excellency of this took up his heart, engrossed his affections, 1 Cor. ii. 1, 2. He sought not excellency of speech or wisdom; his eye was so taken with the splendour of Christ's knowledge, as nothing else seemed excellent to him. Some might expect, if of the like temper with divers in these times, that an apostle coming from the third heaven should have brought with him some new glorious discoveries, some lofty seraphical notions, above the pitch of the other apostles' doctrine. But what brought he? Why, that which he preached. And what was that? He tells us in 1 Cor. i. 23; and that not with wisdom of words, but in such a way as the wise men of the world counted it foolishness, ver. 17, 18. But was it thus indeed as vain men imagined? No; the preaching of Christ was the wisdom, the power of God, ver. 24; glorious and excellent, if anything in God be so. A constellation of glorious excellencies appears in discoveries of Christ. Christ crucified, preached in plainness and simplicity, if the Spirit of God be a competent judge, is the most excellent, the most glorious discovery that ever was, that ever will be made to the sons of men on earth. And if this glory be hid, as it seems to be to those who expect something more new, rare, costly, nauseate the plain preaching of Christ, 2 Cor. iv. 3, 4. . . .

Nor is this only the joy and desire of the most excellent on earth, but also of the most excellent creatures in heaven. The angels, though they enjoy the blessed vision of God, and are eternally happy in it, yet one sight more they earnestly desire, and that is of Christ the Mediator, as manifested in the gospel, 1 Peter i. 12. They stoop down, they stretch out themselves to pry into the things preached in the gospel, to know the mystery of Christ there manifested; and this was prefigured by the posture of the cherubims upon the ark, Exod. xxxvii. 9. Now, Christ was typified by the mercy-seat, and the name itself is ascribed to him, Rom. iii. 25; whom God has set forth to be ἱλαστήριον, a propitiatory. Now, towards Christ was the face of the cherubims; they looked earnestly, they pried into the glorious mystery of God reconciled to man through the blood of Christ; their faces were towards it, their eyes continually on it; so wonderful, so excellent is it in their account, as they think it not below them to learn more of this by the discoveries made to the church, Eph. iii. 10. The Lord makes known the mystery of Christ to the church in the preaching of the gospel, and even the principalities and powers learn more of this mystery by the preaching of the gospel to the church. And how they rejoice in this knowledge, you may see by their deportment at the first appearance of Christ in the world, Luke ii. 13. Sure that must be an excellent knowledge which the cherubims of glory, the principalities and powers in heavenly places, do so earnestly desire, do so greatly rejoice in, when they are less concerned in it than men in many respects.

(2.) In knowing Christ we know the glorious excellencies of God, John xiv. 7. The Father and Christ are so like, as he that knows the one knows the other also, sees the Son, sees the Father. This is so apparent, as Christ seems to wonder that Philip, who had seen him, should speak as though he had not seen the Father, ver. 8, 9. He is known in the knowing of Christ, and seen in the seeing of Christ. Hence he is called 'the image,' Col. i. 15,—that which represents, and in a lively manner holds forth to us, the infinite perfections of God; therefore styled, Heb. i. 3, 'the character,'*—not a shadow of him, not a dead, superficial representation of him, such as pictures and portraitures are, but a living, express, subsisting, perfect representation. The similitude seems to be borrowed from a signet's impression, which represents all the sculptures and lineaments of the seal. But no similitude can reach this mystery; only this we learn by this expression, that as Christ is perfectly distinct from, so is he a full and perfect resemblance of the Father, of the same nature and essence with him, so that there is no perfection in the Father but the same is substantially in the Son, so that in knowing Christ we apprehend (as weakness will suffer) the excellencies of God; hence the glory of God is said to shine in the face of Christ, 2 Cor. iv. 6, so that those who know Christ, thereby see the glory of God in the face of Christ. That knowledge, that light which discovers Christ, discovers the glorious excellencies of God, the brightness whereof appears in the face of Christ. Nor is this only true of Christ as he is the Son of God, of the same nature with the Father, but also as he is Mediator. In the great work of redemption, the Lord caused his glory to pass before the sons of men. Never was there such a full, such a clear, discovery of God's glorious perfections, as was made to the world in Christ. In him we may see infinite power, wisdom, justice, mercy, holiness; glorious truth, faithfulness, unchangeableness; the glory of love, of free grace, of goodness; he even caused all his goodness to pass visibly before us in Christ, so that he who knows Christ knows all these glorious excellencies; *ergo*, &c.

(3.) It makes those that have it excellent, 2 Cor. iii.; having preferred the gospel ministry before the legal ministrations, as far more exceeding glorious, he prefers also our state under the gospel before theirs under the law. They knew but little and darkly, the veil was before them; but we may know more, and more clearly, for the veil is taken away in Christ, ver. 16. So that now, as verse 18, in the gospel, as in a glass, we may with unveiled faces behold the glory of Christ; and so behold it, as it will work a glorious change in the beholders. As Moses by conversing with God seemed to be changed into the same image, from the glory of God

* That is, χαρακτης, translated 'express image.'—ED.

with whom he conversed there passed some glory upon him, which shined in his face; so that, as verse 7, they could not stedfastly behold, &c. Even so by knowing Christ, and beholding the glory of God shining in his face, the soul is as it were changed into the same image, from glory to glory; *i. e.*, from his glory there passes a glory upon the soul, as there did upon his face; but this is done by the Spirit of the Lord, the Spirit of holiness working in the soul those gracious qualities which are the beginnings of glory here, and the most glorious accomplishment of which created nature is capable, holiness being a conformity to, a resemblance of, the image of Christ, who is the Lord of glory. So that you see there is an excellent transforming virtue in this knowledge, it leaves a glorious tincture upon the soul, it assimilates the soul to Christ, in part here, and perfectly hereafter, 1 John iii. 2. The seeing of Christ will make those that see him like unto him. Set a glass full in the sun, and you will see in it something like the glory of the sun, a bright, shining splendour, dazzling the eye of the beholder. Such a glory appeared with Moses when he had been with God; such a glory (though not visible) shines in every soul that is much with Christ, often viewing him, fixing his eye on him; and if the grossness, the incapacity of the subject did not hinder, they would be and seem more glorious; but hereafter this shall be removed, and then not only the soul but the body shall be like unto Christ, in Christ in glory, Philip. iii. 21. Even as the moon, conceived to be a gross, dark body in itself as the earth is, yet when it is full against the sun (in opposition) we see in it some resemblance of the sun's glory; the lustre of the sun darted on it makes it seem a lightsome, glorious body like itself; even so will the enjoyment, the sight of Christ, glorify those that truly know him. So excellent is this knowledge, as it will make those that have it excel in glory.

There are four steps and degrees by which the Lord raises fallen man, now more vile and base than the beasts that perish, to the height of glory and excellency; and they are all ascribed in Scripture to this knowledge of Christ.

[1.] The removal of that which makes him vile, that which is his greatest debasement and deformity, that which renders him not only contemptible, but odious and loathsome, and that is the pollution, the filth of sin, wherewith the soul fallen from God is besmeared; it covers him as a garment, and it is a garment of filthiness, a covering of excrements, Zech. iii. 3. Man is sunk into the mire and clay, into the puddle of corruption, and there he sticks, no escaping for him by anything in the power of nature; that which works his escape is this knowledge of Christ, 2 Peter ii. 20.

[2.] Partaking of the divine nature; one of the highest expressions in Scripture. Not of the essence and nature of God, but of holiness, the nearest resemblance of God that is to be found in anything created. It is the image of God, Col. iii. 10. The image of God stamped upon the soul of man in his creation, was by the fall broken and shattered, quite defaced. Now how is it renewed? He tells us, 'in knowledge.' Holiness is the image of God, as being a resemblance of him who is 'the Holy One,' &c., and so called the divine nature; and by this knowledge of Christ we come to partake of this: 2 Peter i. 3, 4, 'All things that pertain,' &c., are given, but how? 'Through the knowledge of Christ.' Now what things are these that are thus given? He instances in two most considerable: verse 4, 'exceeding great,' &c., and 'the divine nature.'

[3.] Investing us with the righteousness of Christ; a privilege so high and glorious, as man or angel could never have expected it, never believed it, if the same mercy that vouchsafed it had not clearly revealed it; an excellency, in comparison of which the apostle counts all other excellencies as dung; in the apprehending of which consists the excellency of this knowledge which he so highly advances, as appears, ver. 9. How we come to be invested with it, the prophet shews, Isa. liii. 11. We are justified by his righteousness; but how justified? By his knowledge. It is this fiducial knowledge that leads a man out of himself, and all confidence in the flesh, to rely only upon Christ, by which he is made partaker of Christ's righteousness.

[4.] Eternal glory. And then man is at the height, he can rise no higher; and hither he is raised by this knowledge of Christ, John xvii. 3. The knowledge of Christ is the light of life, the dawning of approaching glory. When Christ is first known, the day of glory breaks, and the more it increases, it shines more and more unto the perfect day, unto perfect glory.

Oh how excellent is this knowledge, that raises a man to such a height of glory, that invests him with so many excellencies!

3. Christ himself is most excellent, *ergo*, &c. We may conclude of the act by the object; the knowledge of the most excellent object is the most excellent knowledge, such is Christ's.

(1.) There is nothing in him but what is excellent. There is a mixture in all created beings; where there is something excellent, there is also something deficient. Search out the best accomplished creature on earth, and something or other will be found distasteful in it. The heavens, though they seem the most excellent of all things visible, and their excellency seems to be their lucidness and purity, yet in the Lord's sight even they are not pure, Job xv. 15. Nay, the angels, though the most excellent of all invisibles, and their chief excellency be wisdom,—'wise as an angel,'—yet the Lord charges them with folly, Job iv. 18. Those glorious creatures are conscious of something not fit to be seen by the eye of God; they cover their feet, Isa. vi. 2. Ay, but Christ he is altogether lovely; whatever is in him is excellent, nothing in him deficient, distasteful, imperfect; 'fairer than the children of men,' 'higher than the heavens;' so far transcends the angels, as they adore him, Heb. i. 6, as infinitely below him; nothing in Christ but what is worthy of all love, all delight, all admiration, everlasting praises of saints and angels.

(2.) All excellencies that are in the creatures are eminently to be found in Christ. Take a survey of heaven and earth, and whatever you see that is truly excellent in any, in all things therein, look up to Christ, and you may see it transcendently in him. Whatever is truly amiable, desirable, delightful, or admirable, whatever takes thy heart, if it be worthy of thy heart, look upon Christ, and there it shines in its full brightness. Every excellency that is scattered here and there in the creatures, are altogether in Christ; all the several lines of perfection and transcendent loveliness do all meet and centre in him.

(3.) All these excellencies are in him in a more excellent manner: perfectly, without any shadow of imperfection; infinitely, without any bounds or limits; unchangeably and eternally, they ebb not, they wane not, they are always there in the full, they alter not, they decay not. He is infinitely all excellencies, without variableness or shadow of changing. The angels kept not their first habitation, the heavens shall wax old as a garment, the glory of man is as the flower of the grass, but Christ is yesterday, and to-day, and the same for ever, for ever altogether excellent.

(4.) Not only all that are in the creatures, but innumerable more excellencies than are in all the creatures together, are in Christ alone. Not only the creatures' fulness, but the fulness of the Godhead dwells in him, bodily, *i. e.*, substantially, personally. Besides all that he has communicated to heaven or earth, there are unspeakably more excellencies in him than eye ever saw, or ear heard, or can enter into the heart of man to conceive, Col. ii. 9.

Oh how excellent must that knowledge be, whose object is so transcendently excellent!

Use I. *Reproof*, to those that despise, neglect the knowledge of Christ. If it be excellent in itself, and so in the account of God, so by the testimony of the Holy Ghost, so in the esteem of all that are excellent, then they deserve rebuke who despise it. But is there any Christian who despises the knowledge of Christ? Oh that most that bear that name were not guilty thereof, and worthy of this rebuke! Who they are, you may know by these two characters.

1. Those who are not diligent to get and increase this knowledge. Nothing excellent is attained without diligence, τὰ καλὰ χαλει,* knowledge especially. Those that think it not worth their diligence, despise it. If you thought it precious, you would search after it; if it were a treasure in your esteem, you would dig for it; you would carefully, constantly search the Scripture, for that is the mine where this treasure is to be found, that is the field where it is hid,—hid, not that it should not be found, but that it should be sought after. What a sad thing is it, that those who profess themselves Christians, should spend whole days, nay, whole weeks, without looking into, without reading, without searching the Scripture. The Lord has writ to us (as he complains), not only the great things of the law, but the excellent mysteries of Christ, the great things of the gospel, and these count them a vain thing. Do ye not count it a vain thing, when ye care not for looking into it? Say not ye are too busy. What, are ye too busy to know Christ? are ye too busy to be saved? or is there any possibility of being saved without this excellent knowledge of Christ? Say not you want time; alas! it is want of heart, not want of time; want of affection to it, not want of time for it, that keeps men from knowledge. That time which you merely mis-spend in idleness, or needless pastimes, or satisfying your unclean, intemperate, or worldly lusts, would be sufficient to get this knowledge. If ye counted it excellent, ye would redeem time for it. Say not, What needs so much knowledge, so much diligence? Those that think it excellent will never think they can have too much knowledge, or that it cost them too much diligence, Prov. ii. 2–4. No getting knowledge without crying to God for it, seeking diligently after it. Those that have not thus sought it do yet want it, and those that are not diligent to get it despise it.

2. Those that strive not to communicate this knowledge to others, to their relations, brethren, children, family. That which ye count excellent, ye will not withhold from dear relations. You would catechise, instruct your children and servants, you would be often instilling the principles of the knowledge of Christ into them; you would not let any one be ignorant that has relation to you, or abides with you. This was Abraham's commendation, and will be to all generations, Gen. xviii. 19. He would not only make them know the way, but command them to keep it. Those that would be found faithful must follow him; whatever Satan or a corrupt

* Probably the author wrote τα καλα χαλ. ε—ι, meaning τα καλα χαλεπα εστι.—ED.

heart may tell thee, none shall come into Abraham's bosom but those that walk in his steps. Those parents that instruct not their children, they are like the cruel ostrich, Job xxxix. 14–17, you bring them forth, but you leave them carelessly, to be a prey to Satan and every vile lust; you let their souls perish, and by this you shew that you are hardened; this is to use them as though they were not yours; this is the most woeful, the most unnatural neglect, not to care what becomes of their souls, to leave them to perish for ever; better they had never been born, than live without the knowledge of Christ. You would think her an unnatural wretch, that having brought a child into the world, would let it starve for want of nourishment. Why, those are more unnatural, more cruel, that bring not their children to the knowledge of Christ. 'My people perish for lack of knowledge,' says the Lord. Your children perish for want of knowledge, and you neglect to help. Oh consider, if they perish, at whose hands must their blood be required? Will it not be a sad thing, that children should appear against their parents at the tribunal of Christ! Oh these are they who gave me life, but they let my soul perish! Woe is me that ever they brought me into this world! through their neglect must I be tormented in that flame for ever! That ignorance in which they suffered me to live has brought me into this outer darkness! You that have the charge of families must give an account of them; not only for their profaneness, which you may restrain, but for that ignorance which you might remove. Oh bring not the guilt of their eternal ruin upon your souls! Oh that the Lord would give you hearts to resolve upon more care of the souls of your family, &c., to instruct them at home in a way of catechising, and to bring them hither to be instructed! And here I shall endeavour it by explaining the principles of the knowledge of Christ, in the most easy and familiar way. Oh that you would concur herein, and let it appear that the knowledge of Christ is excellent in your esteem! This is one of the greatest ornaments, this is one of the best provisions you can make for your children, to bring them to the excellent knowledge of Christ. But ignorance of Christ, in yourselves or them, is a pernicious evil.

(1.) This is to despise Christ, to contemn God, to contemn him in the most full expression of his love. The Lord, in revealing Christ to the world, made out the richest manifestation of his glory that ever he vouchsafed to the children of men; therefore to neglect the knowledge of Christ is to contemn God in the riches of his glory. What greater contempt of Christ than not to take notice of him?

(2.) This is a brutish sin. A man without knowledge is scarce a man; let him be what he will for other accomplishments, how comely, how rich, how noble, how powerful soever, if he want the knowledge of Christ, he is like a beast. It is not I, but the Holy Ghost that so terms him, Ps. xlix. 20. He that is in the world's account a man of honour, is in God's account, without this, little better than a beast. He deserves no more the name of a Christian that wants the knowledge of Christ, than an ape deserves to be called a man; he may have some resemblance of a Christian, as an ape has of a man, but without this he wants the soul, the life of a Christian.

(3.) It is a mother-sin, the root of all destructive evils. The two main cursed branches that spring from the root of bitterness, are unbelief and profaneness. No faith without knowledge, whatever the blind papists imagine, who are concerned to shun the light, lest their apostasy should be discovered. 'Those that know thy name,' &c. Ps. ix. 10.

These are so inseparable, as the Holy Ghost puts the one for the other, Isa. liii. 11. All your confidence without this is but presumption, no justifying faith, for that gives honour to God, and is of a saving virtue and efficacy to the soul; but confidence without knowledge is dishonourable to God, destructive to the soul. No benefit by Christ's death, no partaking of his righteousness, without faith, and no faith without knowledge. Ignorant persons are apt to say, Christ died for me, and then what needs so much to do? Ay, but those that will live without the knowledge of Christ shall find that Christ died for none but those that know him; as for others, he never knew them, so far was he from dying for them.

It is the mother of profaneness. Why does drunkenness, uncleanness, so abound? Why, some have not the knowledge of Christ, they love darkness rather than light, and therefore their deeds are evil. If the Sun of righteousness did shine in their hearts, these works of darkness would never appear in their lives. Men have not yet learned Christ as the truth is in Jesus, for, Eph. iv. 21, 22, every knowledge will not be effectual to restrain sin. We see that the air is not by the light of the moon preserved from stinks and unwholesomeness; it is the light of the sun does this. Whatever knowledge you have, if your lives be corrupt, you want the excellent knowledge of Christ. These vermin appear not where Christ shines. The grace of God, manifested in Christ, when it appears effectually unto men, it teaches them to deny ungodliness, &c. Where this ungodliness, this worldliness is, where there is not sobriety, godliness, there Christ has not yet appeared to purpose. You are yet in darkness, if these works of darkness be yet in request; nor is there any escaping out of these snares of the devil, but by the knowledge of Christ.

(4.) It is most contrary to Christ: he is light, and this is darkness; he is wisdom, this is folly. What communion has light with darkness? You have nothing to do with Christ while you know him not, nor will he have any thing to do with you. These are they to whom Christ will say hereafter, Depart from me, I know you not.

Contrary to the design of Christ. His sovereign end is his glory; therefore did he create the world, and manifest himself to his creatures, that he might be glorified. Now he can no other way be glorified by the creatures but by their acknowledging him to be glorious, and how can they acknowledge him who do not know him?

Contrary to his interest. He can have no soul-worship without this, no fear, no love, no desire. All these presuppose knowledge; *non feruntur in incognitum*. If there were none in the world but such as know not Christ, he would have no service in the world. This renders men unserviceable to Christ, to others unfruitful, such as cumber but the ground; it calls for the axe to the root, it brings forth nothing but briers and thorns.

(5.) It lays you under many dreadful threatenings. It is the occasion of the Lord's controversy with a people, Hosea iv. 1. A dreadful thing to have God contend against you; the issue of this controversy was the utter ruin of that people, ver. 6. A fearful thing to fall into the hands of the living God. Do ye? Are ye stronger? Oh, ye will say, he is merciful; ignorance is not such a sin, but mercy will pass by it; he that made us will save us; he will not damn his creatures for a little ignorance (thus will some be ready to say): but see how punctually, yet how dreadfully, the Lord answers, as though he intended to meet with this objection, Isa. xxvii. 11. How contrary are God's thoughts to yours herein; that which they make their reason why they hope to escape, he alleges as the reason why they shall not escape; no mercy, no favour, no, not to those that he made and formed: that does not so much engage him for you as ignorance engages him against you. I add no more but that, 2 Thes. i. 7–9, than which I know not if there be any more terrible expressions in all the book of God.

(6.) Ignorance in this land is altogether inexcusable. Invincible ignorance does excuse in part, but all ignorance of those who have the use of reason, and enjoy the gospel, is wilful. If ye know not Christ, since there is light enough vouchsafed to discover him, it is because you will not know him. This is it which will render the condition of many amongst us more intolerable in the day of judgment than that of Sodom and Gomorrah. Light is come, and men shut their eyes. If this land had been a place of darkness, where Christ had never appeared in his gospel, if it had been a shadow of death, where the light of life never shined, then the Lord's controversy with us had not been so great, then we might have had some plea to mitigate his indignation; but when he has made this land a valley of visions, when no nation under heaven has more means of knowledge, and yet gross ignorance continues amongst us, we are laid open to wrath without the least excuse to shroud us from it: 'If I had not come to you,' &c., John xv. 22. Oh, sad condition, that we who have the word in our tongue, the gospel preached in season and out of season, and so many excellent discoveries for the opening and applying it, should make no other use of all this, but to leave us inexcusable! So will all that know not Christ be; they will not have a word to plead for their ignorance at the tribunal of Christ, because they might have known him, but that they were unwilling to know him, wilfully neglected it.

Use II. *Exhortation.* 1. To those that want it, Be exhorted to get it; 2. To those that have some degrees of it, Be exhorted to grow in it: Prov. iv. 5–7, 'It is excellent;' and this should be a sufficient motive to put you upon endeavours to attain it. Excellency is a powerful attractive to every spirit that is not debased, degenerated, and sunk below itself into the earth; why here is a transcendent excellency, this knowledge far exceeds all natural, all moral accomplishments whatsoever. The apostle, who was able to judge of things that are excellent, counted his highest privileges, his rarest endowments, dung in comparison of it. And as it is excellent in itself, so will it make you excellent in the esteem of God; but without it, whatever ye have besides, ye are vile persons. Oh, but how shall we get this excellent knowledge? What means shall we use to attain it?

Ans. 1. Be convinced of your want of the knowledge of Christ, be sensible of it, be humbled for it, bewail it in the presence of God. He that thinks he knows Christ sufficiently, when indeed he has not attained to this excellent knowledge, his case is desperate, his blindness is next to incurable, Prov. xxvi. 12. Far more hopes of one that knows not, and bewails his want of knowledge, than of him that thinks himself wise enough.

Ans. 2. Begin at the foundation, lay a good ground-work in the principles of the knowledge of Christ, otherwise you will but build in the air. This is the apostles' method, the first nourishment they tendered was milk, afterwards strong meat; he would not carry the Hebrews further till he had fully established them in the principles of the doctrine of Christ, Heb. vi. 1. This is one main reason of the woeful apostasies in our times; many professors never laid a good foundation, never were well grounded in these principles of Christ; because they are ordinarily taught in catechisms, and learnt by children, they think this below them, trouble not themselves with them, and so these prime fundamental truths being never fastened and rooted by sound understanding in their judgments, they are easily plucked from them; and the foundation being gone, no wonder if all the rest easily follow. It is an easy matter indeed to say the words of a catechism, and to get some slight apprehension of these truths, but to have a clear and well-grounded knowledge of them is an excellency not below the highest professor on earth, indeed that which many never attain to. This you must endeavour if you would know Christ to purpose.

Ans. 3. Let the word of God be familiar to you. What is to be known of Christ is here to be learned, Col. iii. 16. Be much in reading the Scripture, it is Christ's advice to the Jews, John v. 39, ἐρευνᾶτε, search daily, search diligently, search as for a treasure, as for the pearl of great price, here it is to be found. Those that are strangers to the Scripture will be strangers to Christ. You may as well see without light as know Christ without the knowledge of the Scripture. Follow the Lord's advice to Israel, see how strictly, how punctually he enjoins this, Deut. vi. 6–9.

Be much in hearing the word. Christ is wrapped up in the Scripture, here the covering is unfolded and exposed to open view, here he is set as crucified, &c. It is the Lord's ordinance, instituted for this end, to bring sinners to the knowledge of Christ, to open their eyes that they may see him, to unveil Christ that ye may behold him with open face. Whenever you read or hear, be sure to meditate; you must not think the Lord will work knowledge by a miracle, this is the means by which he makes it effectual, the knowledge of Christ will never be rooted in your souls without meditation.

Ans. 4. Make use of those who are already acquainted with Christ, 'Forsake not the assembling,' &c., Heb. x. 25, Pro. xiii. 20 and xv. 7. Turn your vain worldly discourse into inquiries after Christ. When you meet with anything dark, see whether the Lord has discovered it to others; when anything doubtful, seek resolution; let not the fear to bewray your weakness hinder you from propounding the doubts and difficulties you meet with.

Ans. 5. Be much in seeking God; beseech him to open your eyes, to remove the veil, to discover Christ more clearly; both advice and promise, James i. 5.

2. To those that have attained some degree of this excellent knowledge: Content not yourselves with present attainments, let this light shine more and more unto the perfect day; follow the apostle's advice, 2 Peter iii. 18, grow in knowledge of the excellency of his person, the fulness of his satisfaction, the worth of his graces, the mystery of his will in the gospel, the sweetness of vision and communion with him, the dimensions of his love, the riches of his righteousness.

For direction:

(1.) Make all your other knowledge subservient to this. Learn the heavenly art of making use of all other knowledge, so as to discover more of Christ, to make him better known. The knowledge of the world; when you discover anything vile, mean, worthless, useless, hence you may infer there is no such thing in Christ; so the world may be a foil to set off Christ, to represent him to your minds as purely, perfectly, transcendently excellent, as the darkness of a dungeon sets off the sun.

When you see anything lovely, desirable, in the world, see Christ in it, this came from him, all lower excellencies dropped from this fountain; thence you may conclude there is infinitely more of this value in him. What are these sparks, these weak glimmerings, to the Sun of righteousness.

The knowledge of sin; the more you see of its guilt, and pollution, and damnableness, the more you may discover of your necessity of Christ; of the wonders of his love, who would become sin for us, who would bear our sins, &c., who would be wounded, of the value of his blood, of his righteousness, which could expiate and remove such horrid evil, and bring heaven out of such a hell.

Make such use of the knowledge of yourselves, of the creatures, of the Scripture, even those parts thereof that seem more remote from Christ; they all point at him, and will lead you to discover more of them, if you be wise to observe, and careful to follow their direction. I, says the apostle, 1 Cor. ii. 2, Paul had much other knowledge, he was brought up at the feet of Gamaliel; he had improved it by his studies, his travels, his experience, but as he valued it not in comparison, so he cared not for it but in a subserviency to the knowledge of Christ crucified. As the light of grace shall end in that of glory, so the light of nature shall end in that of grace, that light which will discover more of Christ. Other things should serve and be made use of as vantage-ground to help us to a better prospect of Christ. Every advance in other knowledge should be to us as Zaccheus getting up into the tree that he might see Jesus passing by. Other light should serve us as a candle to find the jewel, the pearl of great price, and view it better; it should be as the opening of the window, or the withdrawing of the curtain to let in the sun, to let in more of this excellent knowledge.

(2.) Get nearer him, and keep near him; the nearer to him, the more full, and clear, and satisfying view you may have of him. Oh, live not at a distance from Christ, be not satisfied with such a temper of heart, such a performance of holy duties, such a manner of conversation as theirs who are far off from him! You will have but a dim sight of Christ at so great distance. Take heed of what may estrange you, take heed of neglects, unkindnesses; beware of sin, it is iniquity that separates, Isa. lix. 2; take heed especially of sins against light and love, there is more of offence in these, more of provocation, and so they will occasion greater estrangement, further withdrawings; and the more remote you are from Christ, the more you will be out of sight of him; your sight will not be so clear, nor full, nor refreshing. Beware of sins against light; if you abuse it, if you disobey it, if you follow not the conduct of it, if you turn aside into by-paths when the light shews you the right way, if you stand still, or draw back when it is going before you, if you detain it in unrighteousness, so to use the light you have is the way to be left in darkness. If a friend hold you a torch, and you turn aside or demean yourself as if it were an offence to you, that might move him to knock it out, or leave you without it.

Beware of sinning against love. You may well think Christ will less bear this than other miscarriages. This will provoke him to depart, as the spouse found, Cant. v. 6, and when he removes, the light is gone, and you will be at a loss for the sight of Christ. Christ, like the sun, is seen and discovered by his own light; but such miscarriages will raise clouds, or cause an eclipse, and you may see no more of Christ than of the sun in a dark gloomy winter day; nay, these may raise a dismal storm, wherein you may see neither sun nor stars for many days.

(3.) Fix your minds, the eye of your souls, upon him; let your souls be to Christ in the like posture as the cherubims were to his type the mercy-seat: 'Towards the mercy-seat was the faces of the cherubims,' Exod. xxxvii. 9. Let the face of your souls be still towards Christ, your eye often on him, as the angels, Mat. xviii. 10; that is not only their duty, but their happiness; and count it yours, for it is so. Such a vision of God does establish them in their blessed and glorious state, such a beholding of Christ will enhappy you with more of this excellent knowledge of him. Let the thoughts of Christ be pleasing to you, let him be your meditation, and let your meditation of him be sweet, Ps. civ. 34; that will be the way to have your eye fixed. We stay not in the sight of that which does not please us, a short view will be enough or too much; but a short view of Christ, a glance by some transient, fleeting thought, will not be enough to get much knowledge, to make any considerable discovery of him. The mind should stay on him, and view him well; and that it may stay there, it must be pleased with the sight, else it will be on and off, as soon off as on. Let no sight be so taking, so delightful, as a sight of Christ; then your minds will not be backward to dwell on him, as it dwells on that which it would study, and study thoroughly. Labour so to study Christ, that is the way to know him more fully, more thoroughly.

Study the excellencies of his person, the infinite advantage of his offices. What riches of wisdom and knowledge are held forth to you in his prophetical office, even all the treasures of wisdom and knowledge, Col. ii. 3; what riches of power and glory are offered you in his kingly office; what safety and protection in all dangers; what power and assistance in all services; what supplies and sufficiency in all wants; what encouragements and supports in all trials and sufferings; what victories and triumphs, after all conflicts with the world, with the powers of darkness, with the strength of corruption; what assurance this regal, this glorious office affords us, that in all these we shall be more than conquerors!

What riches of grace and compassion, of pardon and forgiveness, in his priestly office; what riches of holiness and glory he has purchased by his suffering, and is prevailing for by his intercession; what we gain by his sufferings, what we are redeemed from by his death, what we may expect from his appearing for us at the right hand of God, and ever living there to intercede for us!

View Christ all over, as those that would see something of all the dimensions of his love, which appear in all his offices, in the undertaking, in the performance of them: 'The height,' &c. Let your minds stay here, as those that have a mind to know what you can of that which passes knowledge; study Christ, as those who have the minds and souls of men principally for this end, that they might be employed upon Christ; you should dig for this as for hidden treasure. The mind is digging while it is studying; the more you study, the further you dig, and the further you dig, the more you will discover of this infinitely large and precious mine, the unsearchable riches of Christ.

(4.) Seek not the knowledge of Christ merely to know, that may be the end of a vainly curious mind; but seek to know him, that you may enjoy him more, that you may improve him better, that you may gain more heavenly and spiritual advantage by him, Mat. xiii. 45, 46. A merchant that travels into other countries, his end is not to view the places, and the rarities of them; that he minds but upon the by; but his design is to meet with commodities, whereby he may get the advantage to raise an estate.

Such should your design be, a labouring to get more acquaintance with Christ, not merely to see and know more than others,—that may be done for ostentation, or out of curiosity,—but to discover that which may make your souls rich unto God; that you may discern that in him which may make you willing to sell all to possess and enjoy him, to suffer the loss of all things to gain Christ. Press to get near him, as the woman in the Gospel, that you may find a healing, a sovereign virtue coming from him; labour to get into the light which discovers him, that you may be under his influences, those healing, quickening, strengthening, comforting influences upon which the strength, life, comfort, and activeness of your souls depends; that you may derive from him more spiritual life, sense, strength, refreshment, motion, and activeness; that you may partake more of his riches, taste more of his sweetness; that you may adore, admire him more, and be more in his praises; that you may be engaged and enabled to honour him more, and serve him better, to do and suffer more for him; so to discover him, as to know the power of his resurrection, &c., Philip. iii. 10, so as to be excited and enabled to follow after, ver. 12, 13.

(5.) Content not yourselves with light without heat. Let every spark of knowledge beget some spiritual and heavenly heat, let it kindle you into more zeal for him, more ardent desires after him, more flames of love to him, more fervour of spirit in seeking, in following him. If the light whereby you discover anything of Christ be not accompanied with spiritual heat, it will prove but a fruitless blaze, which will soon go out, and end in smoke, come to nothing or worse. Satisfy yourselves with no knowledge of Christ, but such as makes you in love with him, Cant. i. 3. The apprehensions they had of Christ gave them a taste, a delicious relish of him, such as made them in love with him, sick of love. Let it raise you to such a heat of resolution as it did Peter, Mat. xxvi. 35. Let it excite in you such desires as in David, Ps. lxiii., raise you to such a value of Christ as the spouse had, Cant. v. 5, 6, 10, 16. If it beget not heat of affection, it will not be like the light of the rising sun, which shines more and more, &c., but like a flash of lightning, which appears and vanishes in a moment, and often does more hurt than good.

(6.) Live up to the knowledge you have; that is the way to attain more. Let the light that shines in your minds shine in your lives. Imprison not the truth; so you do when it is in your understandings, but confined there so as the influence of it does not reach your conversations. This will provoke the Lord to leave you in darkness, it was the effect of this crime in the heathen; this was the cause of that darkness and those delusions amongst the papists, 2 Thes. ii. The pleasure they had in unrighteousness prevailed against the belief and knowledge of Christ and his truths, and rendered it impractical; so that though they knew his ways, they would not walk therein; though they knew the will of Christ, they would not do it, therefore he gave them up to be blinded by Satan. If you so abuse the discoveries of Christ, they will be rarely, sparingly vouchsafed; the Lord will not entrust you with more, but rather take from you what you have. But on the contrary, there is a promise to improve knowledge, John vii. 17. If according to your knowledge ye do more for Christ, ye shall know more of him. If you follow the light, the light will follow you, you will have it in more abundance; but if you walk not answerable to your knowledge, if you contradict it in the temper of your hearts, or course of your lives, you take the course not to have it augmented, but to have less of it, or none at all. If a friend hold a light to you, and you will not follow it, that will not move him to add to it, or make it brighter, but rather to put it out. If the light whereby Christ discovers himself to you be not used for those purposes for which it is vouchsafed; if it do not lead you effectually to a fuller compliance with him, to an exacter conformity to him, to higher degrees of holiness, self-denial, mortification, contempt of the world; this is the way not to have the light increased, but rather extinguished.

(7.) Let humility keep pace with knowledge, and be of an equal and proportionable growth. If knowledge puff you up, take heed the light be not puffed out. Pride would be the attendant of knowledge, but it never thrives nor comes to good where this is not checked. It is such a weed as sucks away the life and sweetness of knowledge; it is not only an enemy to it in its own nature and quality, sucking away the moisture that should make it grow, but it provokes the Lord to blast it. He resists the proud, beats down that in which they exalt themselves, but gives grace to the humble, inspires both mind and heart with more grace, gives both more holiness and more knowledge.

(8.) Make use of Christ's prophetical office. As he is a prophet, he is engaged to give the light of the knowledge of himself. He came under the obligation of this office for this end, that he might instruct his people by his word and Spirit, and lead them up to clear and effectual apprehensions of himself. Let this encourage you to labour for it, to seek him for it, to trust him for it. Endeavours succeed through prayer, and prayer prevails through faith.

II. *Doct.* Those that have attained the excellent knowledge of Christ will not think much to lose all things that they may gain Christ.

Explication. What by gaining Christ? What by all things? What by losing or suffering the loss of these all things?

First, To gain Christ is to get interest in him, and participation of him.

1. He gains Christ who gets interest in him, right to him, union with him; he who is joined to Christ, as members to the head, married to Christ in an everlasting covenant; he that has interest in his person, his offices, his righteousness, his sufferings, his intercession, his administrations, and that which is the spring of all this, his love; he that is interested in the affection, the love of Christ, the acts and expressions of it,—he has gained Christ.

2. He that partakes of Christ, the benefits of his purchase, all those spiritual and eternal blessings wherewith those that have interest in him are blessed; he that gets the graces and advantages of his mediatorship, of his offices, righteousness, sufferings, resurrection, &c., so as to have communion with him in all these, and a communication of all that he has procured, and bestows upon all that are his, he has gained Christ. To gain pardon of sin, right to eternal life, reconciliation with God, holiness in its life, power, exercise, increase, perseverance, the exceeding great and precious promises, high and glorious privileges, sweet and honourable relations which the gospel tenders, all things that are good in this life, the presence of Christ in every state, employment, the assistance of Christ in every service, acceptance through Christ of every endeavour, the joys and comforts of the Spirit, the foretastes of heaven, and a full assurance of actual possession; to partake of Christ in these respects is to gain him. This is that for which he, and all that know Christ with him, are ready to lose all. And if the worth and value of Christ, and these invaluable

advantages by him, be duly weighed, it will seem no wonder that those who know him think not much to suffer the loss of all to gain him.

But what are these 'all things?' The apostle gives us an account of them in this chapter, and elsewhere in his Epistles. By 'all' things we may understand his privileges, his accomplishments, his enjoyments, his righteousness too; much more all and every sin.

1. His *privileges*. He was born of a noble tribe and family, was one of the blessed seed, the seed of Abraham, had that blessedness sealed to him by circumcision, and so was outwardly in covenant with God, and numbered amongst his people. This he once counted a gainful, an advantageous privilege; but after he had attained the knowledge of Christ, he saw that without Christ this would not at all avail him, ver. 7.

2. His *accomplishments*. He was a man of great natural parts, and he had raised, improved them by art and learning: he sat at the feet, *i.e.*, was the scholar of Gamaliel, a great rabbi, a master in Israel. He might have advanced his esteem amongst men by excellency of words and wisdom, but he wholly denied himself, and waived these, when there was danger thereby of obscuring the glory of Christ. He was content to lose the reputation of them, 1 Cor. ii. 1, 4. The like mind is in those who have attained not to make ostentation of their gifts.

3. His *enjoyments*. His credit, ease, plenty, friends, liberty, safety, he was willing to lose all for Christ's sake; he was content to be accounted as the filth and offscouring of the world, 1 Cor. iv. 13. His ease; in labours more abundant, in journeyings often, in weariness and painfulness, in watchings, 2 Cor. xi. 23, 27. The plenty and advantages of a good estate, ver. 27, hunger and thirst, in fastings often, in cold and nakedness, choosed rather to serve Christ in such necessities, than to enjoy a plentiful estate without him. His friends, these became his enemies for Christ's sake; hence he was in perils by his own countrymen. Instead of favours he received stripes, and that often, ver. 24. His liberty; in prison more frequent, bonds and afflictions, Acts xx. His safety; run the hazard of his life often for Christ, ver. 25, 26. Those that are savingly acquainted with Christ are like-minded; rather lose anything than part with Christ.

4. His *righteousness* too. His exactness in outward observation of the law, his zeal in the way of his conscience and judgment, all his outward performances, how specious or plausible soever, he was willing to lose, to renounce these, in point of confidence. He knew, after he knew Christ, if he had relied upon these for pardon, acceptance, salvation, it had been to the loss of his soul. So in this consideration he suffered the loss of them; he was willing to renounce, to disclaim them as grounds of his confidence.

5. As for his *lusts*, all and every of those sins that he was formerly addicted to, he counts it no loss to part with them; they scarce come into this account. It was a thing without question not only with him, but even the false teachers, that he who would not part with every known sin could not gain Christ, could have no interest in him, no advantage by him.

Thus you see the effect of this excellent knowledge of Christ in the apostle. Whatever was sinful, he utterly rejected it; those things that were indifferent, he had either actually suffered the loss of them for Christ, or it was the purpose and resolution of his soul so to do, whenever the interest of Christ should require it. And the things necessary, he renounced them as to any confidence in them, for those purposes for which they were not sufficient. They were loss, of no value to him in this respect. But to open this more clearly, which is the

Third thing to be explained, viz., What is meant by losing all these things? To prevent mistakes in a matter of so great concernment, that no tender conscience, who has resigned itself up wholly unto Christ, may be perplexed or troubled at this truth, which, barely proposed, seems a hard saying. That none may misunderstand it, observe, that we may be said to lose all things to gain Christ in five respects.

(1.) In respect of utter rejection. Thus, in reference to sin, every one that will gain Christ must, every one that savingly knows Christ will, readily lose and freely part with every known sin. Till this be utterly rejected, Christ is never gained. There is not one word in Scripture that gives the least hope to any sinner of gaining Christ that will continue in any known sin. You utterly lose Christ, and all the benefits which sinners can expect from Christ, if ye will not part with every lust. No matter how gainful, how advantageous soever it seem, you will, you must lose Christ for it, if you will not lose it for Christ.

(2.) In respect of submissive deprivation. This in reference to outward enjoyments. Every one that knows Christ, as the apostle did, will quietly submit, and be content to be deprived of his ease, credit, honours, estate, safety, friends, liberty, and life too, whenever Christ calls for them, whenever Christ requires this of him. But when does Christ call for these? Why, then he requires us to part with these, when these, or any of these, cannot be enjoyed without sin. When the case is thus, that either Christ must be denied, dishonoured, or otherwise offended, or else you must part with these enjoyments, he that will rather offend Christ than submit to part with them, shews that he does not effectually know Christ: Luke xiv. 26, 27, 'He that hates not,' *i.e.*, 'He that loves not me more than these,' as he explains it Mat. x. 37.

(3.) In respect of disposition and purpose of heart. He that savingly knows Christ, even while he does enjoy outward comforts, does heartily purpose and resolve to quit them whenever he shall be called to it, and in this regard may be said to lose them, because it is in his heart to do it whenever occasion is offered. The enjoyment of outward comforts, and the enjoyment of Christ, are not inconsistent; many times both may be enjoyed together. Christ does not always require every one that has interest in him actually to part with their earthly enjoyments, but he always requires a heart fully resolved to quit them, in case they cannot be enjoyed without the dishonour or displeasure of his Lord. The apostle, in his lowest condition, had always some or other outward enjoyment, at least his life; how, then, is he said to have suffered the loss of all things? Why, because it was the resolution of his soul so to do, whenever the interest of Christ called for it; and thus is every soul resolved that savingly knows Christ.

(4.) In respect of judgment and estimation; this in reference to all. So invaluable is Christ in his account, as all his enjoyments, accomplishments, privileges, performances, seem loss compared with him. They make a fair show in the dark before Christ is known, but when he appears and shines in the heart, these disappear, vanish into nothing. In respect of those ends for which Christ is given, those benefits which are gained by Christ, he makes no more account of these than a man does of that which he is sure he shall lose by. When these come in competition with Christ (as the false teachers set them), they will really prove the soul's loss, and so he accounts them. If a man should have offered to his choice a heap of dung or an inestimably rich jewel, if one should come and advise him to choose the dung rather than the jewel, Oh no, would he say, you offer me loss, the jewel is more worth than a world of dung. Thus was it with the apostle, all these were dung in his account; Christ was the pearl of great price; to have chosen them before Christ, was to have chosen loss before gain, and made a woeful bargain. Thus it is with each soul that, &c.

(5.) In respect of confidence and affection. He relies not upon his parts, privileges, righteousness, for pardon, acceptance, or salvation. He has no more confidence in these, he makes them no more the grounds of his rejoicing, as attainable hereby, than if he had them not at all, than if he had quite lost them. He knows, if he should rest upon these, expect to get pardon by them, or for them, he should lose by it, it would prove the loss of pardon and salvation to his soul. He has lost them as to any confidence in them, as to any rejoicing therein, as though hereby he might be saved; so the apostle, verse 3. And so every one that knows Christ, he will have no more confidence to gain the favour of God, and life by these, than in that which if he depend on he is sure to lose by.

Thus you see in what respects they think not much to suffer the loss of all.

Reason 1. Because they know that they will lose more by any one of these things retained, not quitted, in the foresaid respects, than they can gain by them altogether. They know this is the way to lose Christ, to lose heaven, to lose their souls for ever. Any one known sin allowed and lived in, is enough to lose heaven, Gal. iii. 10, and v. 21. Good reason not to think much to part with sin, &c.

Any privilege not quitted in respect of confidence, when we expect salvation by and for it, cuts off from Christ, Gal. v. 2.

Any enjoyment not parted with, when the honour of Christ calls for it, excludes the enjoyer from any benefit by Christ, Mat. x. 37–39. Nay, your own righteousness, your observance of the law of God, performance of the duties the Lord requires, if it be not quitted as to any confidence of obtaining pardon and life by and for it, makes Christ of none effect to you; you lose Christ by it, Gal. v. 4, if you look upon it as that for which God will pardon you, as that by which ye may be justified, &c. Great reason to suffer the loss of all for gaining Christ, since the retaining of any one would be the loss of Christ.

Reason 2. They know that all these things cannot be available to gain any saving benefit, and therefore good reason to quit them, that they may gain Christ, by whom only the benefits that accompany salvation are to be gained. If any of these can be imagined as available to attain saving blessings, it must be either covenant privileges or religious performances; the rest are in an utter incapacity for such a purpose, but both these are renounced as altogether unprofitable for this end, Gal. vi. 15, for righteousness, see Gal. iii. 10, 11. If not justified, then not partakers of any saving benefit for salvation, and all the blessings that accompany salvation do depend upon justification.

Use I. By this you may know whether you have attained this excellent knowledge of Christ. Those that know him effectually will count all things but dung in comparison of him, cannot but be willing to suffer the loss of all for him. They have suffered the loss of all that is inconsistent with the enjoyment of Christ, they have renounced their sin, and all confidence in their own righteousness, in any privileges or performances, which those that are not indeed acquainted with him rest on as a sufficient support for pardon and life. They rely not on anything else for happiness or peace with God, and they are willing to suffer the loss of all, which they may lawfully enjoy otherwise, when it will be inconsistent with the enjoyment of Christ. They will count it no loss to part with their most endeared enjoyments in this world, when the keeping of them would part them and Christ, Mat. xiii. 85. Christ is this pearl of great price, a pearl of inestimable, of incomprehensible, of infinite value. He that has found him, that has effectually discovered him, and apprehends truly of what worth and value he is, he will sell all, part with all, as a man would part with all the farthings he has for an inexhaustible mine of gold; or as a beggar would part with his rags and poor function, that he may have the possession of a crown, and enjoy the riches and glory of a kingdom.

Use II. *Exhortation*. Shew that you know Christ, by being willing to suffer the loss of all for him. Make use of the knowledge of Christ to dispose you to this great but difficult duty, to be ready and resolute to lose all for Christ, whenever he calls you to it. If you know Christ indeed, there is enough to induce you to it, even in those instances which may seem most intolerable and hardest to be digested. Let me shew this in one or two particulars.

1. As to your outward enjoyments and earthly possessions. To tell you, you must be ready to part with these, may seem an hard saying; it is so to those who are well accommodated in the world; it was so to him in the Gospel, who presumed that all the other commands of God he had observed, he fell off at this; when he was tried here, he left Christ, went away sorrowful, Mat. xix. But the apostle Paul had actually done it (as in the text), and so had the rest of the apostles, Mat. xix. 27. And none are or can be the disciples of Christ indeed, none are Christians really, but such as are resolved on it beforehand, and actually do it when they are tried, when the honour and interest of Christ requires it, Luke xiv. 33. And those that know Christ effectually will see no reason to stick at it; for he has assured us, that to suffer the loss of all for him is no loss at all, how great and intolerable soever the loss is in appearance, yet really it is the greatest gain, the richest advantage. We cannot possibly make a richer, a more gainful improvement of what we have in the world, than by losing it all for Christ. How great a paradox soever this seem, Christ has assured us of it, and if we do not believe him, we do not know him, Mat. xix. 29. You think it a good improvement of what you have, if you could gain twenty or fifty in the hundred, but what is this to gain an hundred-fold! You would think it a rich return of an adventure to double it or treble it; what is it then to double it more than forty times over? What merchant is there that would not venture all he has, nay, that would not throw his goods into the sea, upon assurance (as good assurance as he can desire), that for every pound he so loses he shall certainly gain an hundred? Why, Christ himself assures you of no less advantage by any thing you lose for him, and can you desire better assurance? or can you expect greater advantage? If you think not this advantage enough, if you desire more, he assures you of more, in the next world everlasting life; an hundred-fold here in this present time, and besides that, everlasting life hereafter, Mark x. 29, 30. Now eternal life in the kingdom of glory is not only an hundred-fold more, but ten thousand times more, ten millions more, unspeakably, unconceivably more, beyond all computation than all you can lose for Christ. And will you think much to lose a pound upon assurance

to gain many millions? You shall gain no less by suffering the loss of all for Christ, than if by the loss of a farthing you should gain ten millions; the advantage will be greater, vastly greater, beyond all proportion.

Yea, but what assurance is there of this? It is a gainful adventure indeed; beyond all in the world, if it were sufficiently insured. Why, you have the best assurance of it that the whole earth, yea, or heaven itself can give. Christ himself is engaged for it, he who is the mighty God, the faithful and true Witness, who has all power in heaven and earth to make it good; and heaven and earth shall perish, rather than one *iota* of his word shall fail and not be fulfilled. You shall sooner see the heavens fall, and the whole earth sink, than see the least failure as to the performance of his word.

And this being so, certainly if Christ were known, if he were believed, if there were faith concerning this thing, to suffer the loss of all for Christ would be so far from being counted an intolerable loss, that it would be esteemed the richest and most advantageous bargain that we can possibly make for ourselves in this world. It would be so far from being feared and avoided upon unworthy terms, that it would be welcomed and embraced as that which is richly desirable.

2. Our personal righteousness, the best of it, holiness of heart and life, this must be quitted in some respect, and only in some respect. To speak or think of suffering the loss of all absolutely, is intolerable. A personal righteousness is in its own place transcendently excellent, and absolutely necessary; without it we cannot be qualified for glory, we cannot be serviceable on earth, we can never come to heaven; without it we cannot honour Christ here, nor shall ever see his face hereafter, Heb. xii. In these respects we must not think of suffering the loss of it, we must not lose it for a world, we lose heaven and our souls if we suffer it.

But in point of justification we must quit it, *i.e.*, we must not rely on our personal righteousness as a justifying righteousness. To quit it thus far will be no loss, for it is no loss to quit anything so far as it is not useful, how excellent soever it be otherwise. Now our personal righteousness is not useful to justify us before God against the accusation of the law of works; to quit it here, to lose it thus, is to lose nothing but a false conceit, a conceit that it is what it is not, and can do for us what it can never do.

No person on earth ever had in himself a justifying righteousness. It is true if our first parents had continued in their primitive state, without sin, their righteousness would have justified them; but since their fall, sin entering into the world, and spreading over it, no man ever had in himself a justifying righteousness but the man Christ Jesus; no other personal righteousness besides can answer the demands of the law in a full, perfect, spotless conformity to it; none can satisfy for the transgressions of it, none can give a title to eternal life. This I call a justifying righteousness. The best personal righteousness of the most eminent saint on earth is no such thing, it can no more justify him than dung can feed him; how excellent soever it be for other purposes, it is not sufficient, it is not useful, for this, here it leaves us at a loss. On this account the apostle did suffer the loss of his own righteousness; if he was to appear before God, to be justified or condemned, he would be found not having his own righteousness, he durst not rely on that. Elsewhere, 1 Cor. iv. 4, and others, Ps. cxliii. 2, they decline the consideration of their own righteousness in this case, as knowing upon that account they could not be justified, the sinful effects of it would rather expose them to condemnation.

But if we rely not on our own righteousness for justification, what righteousness is there to rely on? We shall be at a loss for a justifying righteousness. So the papists, so the Socinians and their followers, determine. But the apostle was otherwise minded, he knew where to find a righteousness fully sufficient for this purpose: 'Not having his own righteousness;' if he might be found in Christ, even in him who is 'the Lord our righteousness,' in him who is 'made of God wisdom and righteousness,' &c., who is 'the end of the law for righteousness,' 'who was made sin for us, that we,' &c. This is a righteousness far transcending any personal righteousness that sinners are capable of; yea, and that righteousness too which would have justified our first parents if they had not sinned, as being the righteousness of God, the righteousness of faith, an everlasting righteousness. It is a better, a more excellent, righteousness than that in the state of innocency would have been, if it had been perfected in respect of the subject, it being 'the righteousness of God,' so called verse 9, and not of man only. 2. In respect of the facility of obtaining, it is attainable by faith, and so described, ver. 9. Faith interests those in it who can neither personally satisfy for past disobedience, nor perfectly observe the law for the time to come. 3. In respect of its perpetuity, it is everlasting: Dan. ix. 24, 'Righteousness of eternity' (*Heb.*). Adam's righteousness, if it had continued a thousand years, might have been lost by sin; but this righteousness makes an end of sin, and so makes a justified state endless. Those that believe this effectually, need not think much to suffer the loss of all, that they may win Christ and be interested in his righteousness, so they may be found in him, not having, &c.

JUSTIFICATION BY THE RIGHTEOUSNESS OF CHRIST.

And be found in him, not having mine own righteousness, which is of the law, but that which is through the faith of Christ, the righteousness which is of God by faith.—PHILIP. III. 9.

YOU have heard, verse 8, of the wonderful effect of Christ's excellent knowledge: 'For whom I have suffered.'

Here you have the end why he was willing to lose all, 'to be found in him.' The apostle cared not though he were found without all other things, so that he might be found in Christ. Hence

Obs. Those that have Christ desire above all things to be found in him; are willing to do, endure, to want, to renounce anything, all things; care not in what condition they be found, how low, poor, despised, afflicted, so they may be found in Christ.

Nothing needs explanation but this phrase, what it is to be found in Christ.

Now, this includes three things:

First, Spiritual intimacy in respect of union. A sinner cannot be found in Christ till he be in him. Union is necessarily presupposed, such an union as the Holy Ghost expresses by that of head and members, Eph. i. 22, 23; by that of root and branches. Hence Christ is frequently called a root, Isa. xi. 10, Rev. xxii. 16; by that of vine and branches, John xv. 1. As the branches are in the vine, and thereby receive juice, strength, growth, fruitfulness, so is a believer in Christ; and the union is so intimate, there is such an oneness betwixt them, as both have one name; so much are they in him as they are him, are called Christ, 1 Cor. xii. 12. Now, this it is which is to be desired above all, to be in Christ, united to him, to be looked upon as one of his members, as implanted into him.

Secondly, Judicial account in respect of representation. Christ is a public person as Adam was, represents those that are his as Adam did, and what he doth or suffers in their stead the Lord accepts it as if they had done or suffered it. This acceptance I call judicial account, and this I take to be the principal import of the expression. Then are we said to be found in Christ, when the Lord accounts, accepts what Christ performed for his elect in way of satisfaction, as if they had performed it. Mind this notion well; for the greatest, the sweetest mystery of the gospel cannot be understood without it.

Christ is by the Father's appointment the sponsor of his people; he doth *vicariam presentiam agere*, they whom he represents are looked upon as present in him, and what he acts doth pass as though they did act it.

In this sense did the apostle desire to be found in him, that Christ might be looked upon as his sponsor, and what he performed might be looked on as undertaken in his stead, on his behalf, and so set upon his account. The Scripture offers us this notion in divers expressions, in special, to instance in no more, when Christ is called a surety, a sacrifice, Heb. vii. 22; when the surety pays the debt, the bankrupt is discharged, as though himself had paid it. Every sinner since the fall is under a double obligation:

He owes the Lord both perfect obedience, and, through his default, the penalty due for disobedience.

Justice will not suffer any man to enter heaven till this debt be paid; nay, in default of payment, the Lord in justice is engaged to cast every sinner into hell, there to pay the utmost farthing.

Man has utterly disabled himself from paying either the one or the other; he can neither obey perfectly, nor satisfy for the least disobedience, and hereupon every son of Adam becomes guilty before God, and liable to eternal wrath, without the least hopes of recovery from and by himself; no more hopes of payment nor of freedom from the penalty than that a beggar should pay an hundred thousand talents.

This is the forlorn condition of every sinner by nature.

But now the Lord, out of infinite love to his elect, accepts of Christ, freely offering himself to be their surety, and to pay that for them which they were never able to pay themselves; and this he did by performing perfect obedience, which was the principal debt, and suffering death and the wrath of God, which was the penalty. Now this surety's payment being accepted for those that believe, they are discharged as though themselves had paid it. And this is it the apostle desires, that he might be found in Christ as his surety, that the Lord would look upon him in Christ satisfying in his stead, and would discharge him upon Christ the surety's payment. To be thus discharged for Christ is to be found in him.

So Christ was a sacrifice, Heb. ix. 26, Eph. v. 2, Isa. liii.

Now the sacrifice was offered in the stead of him that brought it; there was *actio vicaria*, the death of the sacrifice was instead of the death of him that brought it, so that it passed as though the sinner had suffered in the sacrifice.

Thus, those for whom Christ offered himself are looked upon as though they had suffered in him, and in this sense should we desire to be found in Christ as in our sacrifice, as in our surety.

Thirdly, Real efficacy in respect of participation: when by virtue of his being in Christ a believer is secured from what he fears, and hath that procured for him which he most wants; when he hath in Christ acceptance to life, and by Christ is delivered from the curse and threatening of the law; when he obtains the blessings, as Jacob by being in his elder brother's garments, and escapes vengeance, as the malefactor by being in the city of refuge; these were typical, and very significantly shew us what it is to be found in Christ.

To be found in him is to be covered with his righteousness, held forth in the notion of a garment, Isa. lxi. 10, Rev. xix. 8. Every sinner is full of uncleanness and deformity, the pure eye of God cannot behold him without loathing, nor will he admit any unclean thing into his presence. If he seek a covering of his own righteousness, it helps not, it is but as a menstruous rag, it adds to his uncleanness rather than hides it.

How then shall a wretched sinner stand in the sight of an holy God? Why, the Lord hath made provision; when the sinner returns as the prodigal, the Father bids bring out the best robe, he covers, he adorns him with this; he takes order with a returning sinner, as with Joshua, Zech. iii. 3, 4. A believer puts on Christ, Gal. iii. 27, Rom. xiii. 14, Rev. xii. 1. This is his robe, his garment, and when he is found in it, then he is found in Christ; his person, his services are accepted, the way to heaven is opened for him, the Father delights in him, and blesses him with spiritual, eternal blessings. So that to be found in Christ is to be found in his righteousness, and that the apostle explains himself, 'Not having,' &c.

Then for security from evil: to be found in Christ is as the malefactor to be found in the city of refuge. The man that had slain his neighbour casually was to fly to the city of refuge; if the pursuer overtook him before he was in the city, he had liberty to slay him without mercy; if he found him in the city of refuge, he was not to touch him. Thus here, every sinner out of Christ is liable to the stroke of revenging justice, but when he is found in Christ he is secure, justice then will not touch him. To be found in Christ is to be found as in the city of refuge.

Use. Exhortation. Oh that hereby you would make it evident that you have Christ, by desiring above all things to be found in him! Oh that the same mind might appear in you that was in the apostle, that you might desire it above all, and so desire it as to count all things dung!

And indeed, whether you so account them or no, so they will prove. All your privileges, outward performances, earthly enjoyments, they will no more avail you than dung, they will render you no more acceptable to God than excrements, unless you be found in Christ.

That I may a little enforce this exhortation, consider,—

Except you be found in Christ you are lost; your persons, services, happiness, and hopes of it, all are lost, unless you be found in him.

1. Your *persons:* it is as impossible that any person in the world should escape the wrath of God, out of Christ, as it was impossible any man in the old world should escape drowning, when the flood came and found him not in the ark; some of those perishing creatures might scramble up into some mountain or tree and preserve themselves a little while the waters are low, but they were all swept away ere long who were not found in the ark. So here, there is a deluge of wrath coming upon the world of unbelievers and obstinate sinners, and though some may think to escape by flying to outward duties, and relying upon their privileges and enjoyments, yet those are but a refuge of lies, there is no escaping for any but those that are found in Christ, the deluge of wrath will sweep away every sinner sooner or later that is not found in Christ.

2. Your *services* too are all lost: whatever you do in a way of religion, or in a way of charity, except you be found in Christ doing of it, it is lost, it will never be accepted. Do what you will, it is impossible to please God if he find you not in Christ, in whom only his people are made acceptable: 'Without faith it is impossible to please God,' Heb. xi. 6. Why? Because it is faith that brings a man into Christ, that faith which purifies the heart and life, that faith which runs to Christ out of deep seas of sin and wrath, that faith that will take Christ upon his own terms.

3. Your *happiness*, and *hopes* of it, are lost too: 'There is no name under heaven,' &c. The Lord blesses his people with spiritual blessings in heavenly places; but how? In Christ only, Eph. i. There is no enjoyment of happiness, there is no hopes of it, but for those that are found in Christ: 'Christ in you the hope of glory,' Col. i. Without Christ, without hope in the world. Those who anchor not within the veil, will see their souls and hopes wrecked together. In what condition soever you be found, if found without Christ, you are miserable. Though you be found in health, in plenty, in prosperity; nay, though you be found in a throne, if you be not found in Christ, there is no hopes of happiness, they give no rest.

But what course shall we take to be found in Christ?

1. If ye will be found in Christ, you must not be found in your sins. You must not be found in love with any sin, you must not allow yourselves in the practice of any; you must hate it, you must depart from it, else there is no coming at Christ, no being found in him; these are utterly inconsistent, as light and darkness; you cannot be found in both at once. 'What fellowship,' &c., 2 Cor. vi. Joshua's filthy garments must first be taken from him, before he could be clothed with change of raiment. Lot could not possibly be in Zoar until he left Sodom. The manslayer, if he would stay in the place of guilt, where he had shed blood, could never be found in the city of refuge. It is as impossible you should be found in heaven while you are in hell, as that you should be found in Christ while you continue in sin. If any sin be so endeared to you by pleasure, advantage, custom, or interest, that you will not leave it, you thereby abandon Christ, and can never expect to be found in him, or near him, unless only at his left hand. They do but delude themselves, if there be any truth in Christ, who hope to be found in Christ, and yet will be found in the love and ways of sin. It is a disparagement to Christ, for any to name him who will not depart from iniquity; and can such hope to be found in him? 1 John i. 6.

2. You must have no confidence in your own righteousness. The apostle joins these both in his doctrine and practice, ver. 9. If you would be found in Christ, you must lay aside all conceits of any sufficiency in your own righteousness to justify or save you; those that lead you to this draw you from Christ. It was such conceits that kept off the Pharisees from Christ, and made it less feasible for them to be found in Christ than the publicans; and against this is that parable directed, Luke xviii. 9. This cut off the Jews from Christ and his righteousness: Rom. x. 34, 'In the Lord have we righteousness, in the Lord shall all the seed of Israel be justified,' Isa. xlv. 24, 25. But this self-confidence will make men say, 'We are lords,' Jer. ii. 31. This makes Christ of none effect, discharges them from being found in him, or finding any advantage by him, Gal. v. 4. An expectation to be justified by conformity to, or observation of the law, tends to disannul and abolish Christ; such are fallen from the doctrine of grace, which doctrine teaches that we are justified freely by another righteousness, Rom. iii. This renders the death of Christ a vain and needless thing, Gal. ii. 21. Christ was obedient unto death, that we might have righteousness in him to justify us. If we can have such a righteousness by our observance of the law, he died in vain and to no purpose, we might be as well without him.

3. Put on Christ. He that will be found in him, must put him on, Rom. xiii. 14. Desire the Lord to plant faith in your souls, for by this

only is Christ put on. This is coming to him as to a city of refuge, John vi.

4. Walk in Christ, 1 John ii. 6. Those only will be found in Christ who walk in the steps and ways of Christ; those ways of holiness, humility, self-denial, meekness, contempt of the world, activeness for God, wherein he walked, Eph. ii. 10; for those are neither the causes nor conditions of justification, either as begun or continued, yet they are the inseparable companions or effects of that faith by which we are justified at first, and by which our justification is continued.

'Not having my own righteousness,' &c. You have heard (1.) Of the dignity of the knowledge of Christ; (2.) Of the efficacy of it, it made him suffer the loss of all things; (3.) The end why he suffered, that he might win Christ, be found in him; (4.) The way how he would be found in Christ: [1.] Negatively, 'not having,' &c.; [2.] Positively, 'But the righteousness of the faith of Christ.'

The negative expression is that which I shall now insist on; and that I may clearly ground a particular observation, explain,

First, What he means by righteousness. It is a conformity to the rule of righteousness, such a conformity as is found in man since the fall; and that either inward, in respect of the temper and motions of the soul; or outward, in respect of the actions of his life, religious or moral. He concludes all acts in his soul, or conversation, that had a show of righteousness, which seemed to answer the law of God.

Secondly, Hence he calls it that 'righteousness which is of the law,' because the law is the rule of righteousness; and any motion or act is more or less righteous, as it comes nearer to the law, or less answers.

Thirdly, 'His own righteousness.' His own in opposition to that other righteousness, which he calls the 'righteousness of faith,' 'of Christ,' 'of God;' for though this was his too, as it is every believer's, yet not in the same way. That which he calls his own; for this was his by personal performance, but that of Christ was not his personally; but in respect of God's gracious acceptation, imputing it to him, accepting the performance of a surety for him, as though it had been his personally.

Fourthly, 'Not having;' that is, not having confidence in it, not relying upon it, as that for which the Lord will pardon, accept, save me. The gospel hath revealed another ground to rely upon for this, and had discovered the insufficiency of his own righteousness for this purpose; and therefore he renounced this in point of confidence, not otherwise. You must not think the apostle accounted a personal righteousness or observance of the law unnecessary, he endeavoured it in himself, he urged it upon others, to bring their hearts and lives to an accord with the law, the will of God; and pressed holiness, which is nothing but a conformity to the law, as that 'without which no man shall see God.'

Thus far he retained his own righteousness as excellent in its own place; but he renounced it in point of confidence when it took the place of Christ's righteousness; when it was urged as that which could justify, make acceptable in God's sight, and give him a title to heaven. These are the privileges and offers* of the righteousness of faith; and therefore in this respect he disclaims his own legal, personal righteousness. Hence the

Third Obs. Those that would be found in Christ must renounce their own righteousness: they who have attained the excellent knowledge of

* Qu. 'offices'?—ED.

Christ will not rely upon it, rest in it, or make it the ground of their confidence.

The apostle in this respect counts it loss, calls it dung; and those that have truly learned Christ will be like-minded. Though personal righteousness, observance of the law, be necessary and useful in other respects, yet in point of confidence it must be renounced, it must in no case be relied on; it is commendable and advantageous in its own place, when made use of for those ends, and in that way which God requires; but if it be relied on, it may prove dangerous, pernicious; it will be found a broken reed, deceive the soul that puts confidence in it.

The reason is, because personal righteousness of any man since the fall is defective, and comes far short of that righteousness which should be the ground of our confidence.

That only may be relied on, 1, which fully answers the rule of righteousness; 2, which can give title to life; 3, which can make satisfaction for sin; 4, which can render us acceptable in God's eye; 5, which will justify us in the sight of God: such a righteousness it must be. But now no man hath such a righteousness of his own as will do any one of these, and therefore it must in no case be relied on. To shew particularly, no man's personal righteousness, take it at the best since the fall,—

1. Doth answer the rule of righteousness; for the law of God, which is the rule, requires perfect obedience, perfect both in respect of habit and act, both in respect of parts and degrees: but the best righteousness of any fallen man is imperfect; imperfect both these ways, therefore can scarce so be called righteousness; it is but a sinful and unrighteous righteousness; it is crooked, and comes not up to the rule; it is defective, unanswerable to the purity of the law: and hence the church acknowledges her righteousness is but as a menstruous cloth, Isa. lxiv. 6.

Four reasons:

Reason 1. *Omnis justitia humana injustitia esse convincitur*. All man's righteousness is detected to be unrighteousness, if it be strictly examined, James iii. 2. There are many sinful flaws in all, in the best, in the most righteous. The apostle includes himself, 'We offend in many;' whereas, if we did but offend in one point, that would be enough to deface our righteousness, to make it another thing than the law requires; to denominate us guilty rather than righteous, James ii. 10. He that transgresses but in one point, would by the sentence of the law be found guilty of all, rather than righteous, Job xv. 15.

Reason 2. Obedience, if it be sincere and universal, it may evidence a title, but it can give none: 2 Tim. i. 9, 'He saves us,' *i. e.*, gives a title to salvation; but how? 'Not according to our own works,' our own righteousness; 'but according to his grace in Christ.' If we had it, were entitled to it by our own righteousness, we had it not by grace; these are still opposed as inconsistent. If we had it in ourselves, we had it not in Christ.

Reason 3. It cannot satisfy divine justice, it can be no compensation to his laws and honour, violated by sin; it can be no vindication of his holiness and justice. There is that in our best righteousness which exposes us to more severity, and makes us further obnoxious to justice; that which may provoke him, instead of appeasing or satisfying.

Reason 4. There is that in it that may procure loathing, rather than acceptance, Hab. i. 13. There is a mixture of evil in our own righteousness, the Lord cannot behold it; but he will see iniquity in it, which his pure eye cannot look on with acceptance, Dan. ix. 18. Daniel, and the people of God who prayed with him, ventured not to present their supplications for their own righteousness; they durst not presume to expect their prayers would be accepted for their righteousness, but for his great mercies. Those great mercies for which they presented their supplications, that they might be accepted, include Christ, through whose mediation and righteousness a way is opened for those mercies; and without which no sinners under the law, or under the gospel, would be capable thereof. It is not in ourselves, not in our own righteousness, but in Christ, that any are accepted, Eph. i. 6.

Reason 5. As touching the righteousness of the law, he was blameless, unspotted. But this was before conversion, no wonder if he did not expect to be thereby justified. Ay, but after conversion too, when what he had and did was from grace, he had no confidence in his own righteousness, that it would justify him, how exact, how eminent soever it was, Acts xxiii. 1. His righteousness was universal, in all good conscience; it was sincere, it was before God that he thus lived; it was continued, uninterrupted; he had thus lived to that very day. But did he rely on this to justify? No, 1 Cor. iv. 4. He was not conscious to himself that he had been unfaithful or unsincere in anything, yet would he make no account that thereby he should be justified. Here is an evangelical righteousness, an unspotted, a sincere, an universal, a constant righteousness, an apostolical righteousness, of an extraordinary quality and degree, both as to the habits and acts of it, such as transcended that of the other apostles: 'He laboured more abundantly than they all, suffered more abundantly than they all;' yet was he not hereby justified. Now if such a righteousness could not justify, what personal righteousness can be found in the world that may be counted a justifying righteousness? Well might he lay it down as a general rule, Gal iii. 11, and ii. 16.

It will be yet more evident, that our own righteousness cannot justify us, by two or three particulars.

(1.) Our own righteousness answers not the demands of the gospel, no more than those of the law, and so falls short of every rule of righteousness, and therefore cannot justify us with respect to any. The gospel calls for perfection as well as the law, it abates no degree of holiness which the law required, it allows us not to love God less, to fear, trust, serve him less than the law would have us. It is true, the gospel has pardon for imperfections, which the law had not; but we are as much obliged to perfection under the gospel, as under the law, and cannot be justified by that which falls short of what we are obliged to.

(2.) Our own righteousness cannot justify itself, much less can it justify us. It needs another righteousness to justify it, being many ways faulty; otherwise it is, and will be under the condemning sentence of the law, Ps. cxxx. 3. If there be iniquities in our righteousness, it cannot stand in judgment, it cannot be justified, it needs another righteousness, by virtue of which it may have pardon.

(3.) It cannot justify us in our own consciences, much less can it justify us before God. There is no man's conscience, if it be not senseless, but will see something to be condemned in his own righteousness. Now God is greater than our consciences, he sees more therein that is worthy of condemnation, 1 John iii. 21.

2. It cannot entitle any man to life, nor give right to happiness; this is evident from the former. The first charter man had for eternal life runs

upon these terms, 'Do this and live;' that is, perform perfect obedience, and thou shalt have eternal life. It is only perfect righteousness, obedience, that gives a man title to heaven; whereas, that which is defective (as the best is since the fall) leaves a man under the curse, Gal. iii. 10. There must be a better provision than man's personal righteousness, before he can be free from the curse, so far is he from procuring eternal happiness.

3. It cannot satisfy the justice of God, it cannot make a recompense for the least sin. Nay, suppose it was perfect, it is most imperfect: perfect obedience cannot satisfy for the least disobedience. 'O my God, incline thine ear, and hear; open thine eyes, and behold our desolations, and the city which is called by thy name: for we do not present our supplications before thee for our righteousness, but for thy great mercies,' Dan. ix. 18.

If a man could perform perfect obedience without sin, yet this being his duty, and that which he owes, this would not satisfy for any former sin; for the payment of one debt is no satisfaction for another.

4. It cannot render him acceptable in God's eye. The Lord will accept no man till satisfaction be tendered; this agrees not with his justice, and no man's personal righteousness can satisfy justice, as appears by the former. No man since the fall is or can be accepted upon his own account, and men's personal righteousness being stained with sin, is so far from rendering the performance acceptable, as the performance itself cannot be accepted without the mediation of a better righteousness than that of the law, of which here, Eph. i.

5. It cannot justify the performance before God's tribunal. The apostle clears this by his own example: if any man might expect to be justified by his own righteousness, he much more; for 'as touching the righteousness of the law he was blameless;' he lived in all good conscience towards God, &c. He was not conscious to himself of any gross misdemeanour or neglect: 'I know nothing,' &c., 1 Cor. iv. 4. He lays it down as a general rule, Gal. iii. 11, and chap. ii. 16.

Use; of exhortation. If you desire the comfort and happiness to be found in Christ, take heed of relying upon your own righteousness. There are two ways whereby Satan leads the greatest part of the world to destruction. The one is, the open way of profaneness and ungodliness; the other is, the retired way of self-confidence. If that great enemy of souls cannot prevail with men to run with other* excess of riot, when he sees some through religious education, or common workings of the Spirit, to have escaped the gross pollutions of the world, he attempts their ruin another way, by possessing them with a conceit of the sufficiency of their own righteousness, tempting them to neglect Christ by resting in themselves. And though this way be fairer than the other, yet ordinarily it proves more dangerous, because those that are entered into it are not so easily convinced of it, and brought out of it; publicans and sinners are more easily brought to Christ than Pharisees. The word to which the apostle compares self-righteousness tells us thus much. He calls it σκυβάλα, which is rendered to you dung; but some critics observe, the word signifies such costive excrements as the power of physic doth hardly purge out of the body.

It must be an extraordinary power that will work a man that is civilized, and hath the form of godliness, to deny himself, and renounce his self-righteousness; and yet nothing doth more cross the great and glorious designs of God in the gospel, nothing is more dishonourable to Christ, and more affronts him; nothing more dangerous to the soul of sinners, than to

* Qu. 'others to'?—ED.

rely upon their own righteousness for pardon and salvation. And therefore, if you would not be found fighters against God in his most gracious contrivement of man's happiness; if you would not be contemners of Christ and the grace of the gospel; if you would not be found accessory to the destruction of your own souls, take heed of depending upon your own righteousness, take heed of making anything the ground of your confidence but Christ and his righteousness. And that you may the better escape this snare of the devil, let me discover those several dresses wherein Satan presents this self-righteousness, that he may the more easily entangle the more in a soul-deceiving confidence therein; and few that know Christ will find but they either have been, or are upon the borders of it, if not further in some of these by-paths.

1. Some rely much upon a natural righteousness, that which we call good nature; if others persuade them, or they can persuade themselves that they are of good dispositions, mild, candid, gentle, ingenuous, kind and peaceable temper, they rest here, and are apt to conclude, the Lord will not be so severe as to cast so good nature (though there be nothing more than nature in them) into hell.

2. Some rely upon a positive righteousness, and observance of some rites and circumstances in religion. They are baptized, and accounted members of the church, and partake of ordinances, and come under church order, submit to this or that form of ecclesiastical government, and adhere strictly to some outward observances prescribed by God, or perhaps received by tradition from their superiors or forefathers. Here they ground their hopes of heaven. This was part of the Pharisees' righteousness, and that in which their false teachers grounded their confidence, which the apostle here opposes, and overthrows elsewhere, when he tells us, 'The kingdom of God comes not by observation,' &c., Luke xvii. 29; Rom. xiv. 17. And Christ raises it: 'Except your righteousness,' &c., Mat. v. 20.

3. Others rely upon a moral righteousness, because they have some care to observe the duties of the second table, because they are just, sober, temperate, liberal, love their neighbours, do no man wrong, give every one his own; hence conclude they are sure of heaven. Whereas if this were a sufficient ground of confidence, we might conclude many heathens in heaven, such as never knew Christ, nor heard of the gospel. If such righteousness be sufficient, then Christ died in vain, as the apostle concludes to like purpose, Gal. ii. 21.

4. Others rely upon a religious righteousness, their outward performances of some religious duties. Because they pray, and hear the word, and read the Scriptures, receive the sacraments, converse with those that are religious, and in some sort observe the Sabbath, upon this are confident that they shall die the death of the righteous, and it shall be well with them in the latter end. But even this support the apostle rejected as rotten; though he was one of the most religious sort among the Jews, and blameless as to his outward performance of religious duties, yet he durst not be found with this rightoousness alone; he disclaims all confidence in it.

5. Others rely upon a negative righteousness. Because they are not so unrighteous, not such idolaters, atheists, not such apostates or heretics, not such swearers or Sabbath-breakers; because they are not drunkards nor adulterers, not murderers or oppressors, not covetous, proud, or ambitious, therefore it shall go well with them. This was the Pharisees', as in the parable; but it was far from justifying them, Luke xviii. 11, 14.

6. Others rely upon a comparative righteousness, their being or thinking

themselves to be more righteous than others, because they do more in a way of religion, of justice, of charity, than others who have like engagements; whatever their principles be from which, or the ends for which they do it, conclude for this they shall be saved. This is like that of the labourers sent into the vineyard early in the morning. They expostulate about their wages, as though they had deserved some extraordinary reward in having borne the burthen and heat of the day, Mat. xx. 12. There is a sad intimation, that though these were called, yet they were not chosen, ver. 16, Mat. vii. 22.

7. Others rely upon a passive righteousness. Because they have suffered for the truth, being jeered, reproached, persecuted for some way of religion, therefore they are confident that for these sufferings they shall be saved and pardoned. But the apostle here sheweth the vanity of this confidence, for who had suffered more than he, who had suffered the loss of all things for Christ? He makes not his sufferings, but Christ, the ground of his confidence; he durst not be found, not in his sufferings for Christ, except he might withal be found in Christ: that he desired above all. Nor would he rest in anything but in Christ: 'Not having his own righteousness;' he counts it loss so far as it was unuseful and insufficient, he counts it dung so far as it invades Christ's prerogative, so far as it would usurp the place and office of his righteousness; it was no better than dung when it would supplant and dishonour the righteousness of God.

(1.) Man being made a rational creature, and so made capable of moral government and obedience, he was necessarily subject unto God as supreme governor, who, that he might rule him according to his nature and capacity, gave him a law by which he was to be ordered in all things, and according to which he was to be judged. To enforce this law, he added a penalty in case of transgression, the import of which is this, that if he rebelled, he should be miserable here and hereafter, Gen. ii. 17. To enjoin man not to eat of the tree of knowledge, to obey him herein and in all other particulars, he was obliged by the law of nature; and the penalty is death, which is elsewhere called the curse, Deut. xxvii. 26, Gal. iii. 10.

(2.) Man transgressed this law. Our first parents disobeyed God, and we in them, Rom. v. 12. Hereby the image of God, wherewith he was created in holiness and righteousness, was lost, and the nature of mankind universally corrupted, and all so inclined unto sin, that they sin actually as soon as they are capable of acting, and continue to sin while they are in the state of nature, and all are concluded under sin, Rom. iii. 9, 10, &c. 'All are become guilty before God,' ver. 19. 'All have sinned.' This the apostle premises before he delivers the doctrine of justification, ver. 23. Thus it was with all the world after the flood, and so it was with the old world before, Gen. vi. 5. All are sinners from the womb and from the conception, Ps. li.

(3.) Sin being entered into the world, the Lord was concerned not to let it go unpunished. It is enough for our purpose, which is out of question, that it was the Lord's will and determination to punish all sin. But there seems to be a sufficient proof, that it was not from the mere pleasure of his will that he should be punished, but there was a necessity for it, from the nature and perfections of God, and from his relation to man as his governor, and from the law enacted as the rule of his government. The Lord is obliged, not only by his truth and unchangeableness, but by his wisdom, holiness, and justice, to punish sin.

His *truth* engages him to it. He threatens it in his law, and if he will rule according to law, it must be inflicted. His truth is obliged for the executing of the threatening, and to make good what he had declared to be his resolution.

His *unchangeableness* makes it necessary. He did determine from eternity to punish it. The event shews that it was eternal purpose, and the counsel of the Lord must stand: he is not as man.

His *wisdom* makes it necessary. The end and designs of his law and government would be lost, his law would appear to be powerless and insignificant, his government would be rendered contemptible, the authority of the one, and the honour of the other defaced, if sin is not punished.

The *holiness* of God requires it. Sin is contrary to him; he hates it. If he will shew himself to be what he is, 'an holy God, of purer eyes than to behold evil, and who cannot look on iniquity,' Hab. i. 13, it is necessary to shew his hatred of it by punishing it: Josh. xxiv. 19, 'he will not forgive,' that is, he will punish, because he is holy, where, as in other places, the necessity of punishing is grounded upon his holiness.

If the Lord be necessarily an holy God, it will be necessary to hate sin; for hatred of sin is essential to holiness, and cannot be conceived or apprehended without it. Now to hate sin is *velle punire*, necessarily includes a will to punish it. It is essential to holiness to be displeased with sin. Now as the love of God is our chief reward, so God's displeasure is the chief punishment of it. If then it be not necessary that he punish sin, there will be no necessity that he be displeased at sin. It will be arbitrary to the holy God to be pleased with sin, if it be arbitrary not to punish it. We might conceive that he may as well be pleased with sin as displeased with it, which is intolerable to say or imagine.

Finally, His *justice* obliges him to punish it; for suffering is indispensably due to sin, and the sinner justly deserves it, and justice requires that everything, every one, should have his due, that every disobedience receives a just recompence of reward, Heb. ii. 21, Rom. i. 32, 2 Thes i. It is righteous with God to give to every one according to his work.

An earthly governor cannot without injustice decline to punish the violation of righteous laws, unless in case he can otherwise secure the end of government. The ends of the divine government are his honour, the authority of his laws, and the good of his subjects. His honour and majesty must be vindicated, the authority of his laws (wherein the interest of the world is so much concerned) must be asserted; and sin, seeing it entrenches upon all, unless it be punished, how can they be vindicated or asserted?

And there is more necessity that a compensation be made to the laws and honour of the supreme Governor of the world, by how much his person and majesty is higher, and the dishonour greater, his laws more advantageous to the world. Here the necessity of a vindication by punishment rises higher, and appears to be greater in all respects.

It is true a private person or a magistrate, as to his own particular concern, may in some cases remit injuries, without any prosecution, he may do it as the offended party; but as a governor he cannot justly do it when the interest of government is concerned [in] it, and the public would suffer thereby. Now in reference to God, it is plain the universe would suffer if these rights of his sovereignty and honour were not vindicated, the assertion thereof tending so much to the good of the whole.

And the Socinians confess that it is repugnant to justice for a private person to relinquish his right in case of some injuries, and the injury they instance in, viz., notorious defamation, is not more intolerable to man than sin is to God. And therefore to think it is not necessary for the great God to vindicate his rights by severity against sin is altogether unreasonable.

In short, the honour of the divine perfections cannot be secured or vindicated unless sin be punished; therefore it is highly necessary that sin should not escape without punishment.

(4.) Since there is such necessity that sin be punished, and the Lord so highly concerned to inflict the penalty due to sin, either the sinners themselves must bear the penalty, or some other for them; if the sinners themselves must bear the punishment, no flesh could be saved, all mankind must be eternally miserable, for it is the penalty expressed by death and curse.

If some other bear the penalty for them, it must be such a person, and in such a way, that will be as satisfactory to justice, and as full a *salvo* to the divine perfections concerned in his law and government, as if the sinners themselves suffered it.

The design of the law must be secured, and the ends of divine government attained, and the justice, holiness, truth, and wisdom of God vindicated and manifested, as much as if the penalty was inflicted upon the transgressors themselves.

(5.) It was Christ that undertook this, and the way wherein he effected it was by suffering in our stead.

This is it which we are concerned to maintain; Christ suffered in our stead; for if he did not, the punishment due to sin is not inflicted (since his bearing the punishment due to our sin, and his suffering in our stead is all one), neither we nor any for us undergo it.

Thus sin, as to all that are saved, will go unpunished every way, and so the ends of government are neglected by the infinite wise and righteous Governor of the world, and the glory of his wisdom, truth, justice, and holiness are by himself exposed and left to suffer without any *salvo*. If we be saved in a way that will not secure the honour of the divine perfections, salvation will be effected in a way not consistent with the honour of God. But no salvation can be expected on these terms, and therefore either none will be saved by Christ, or else it is upon the account of his bearing the penalty of the law in their stead.

But by Christ's suffering in our stead all is secured, justice is satisfied for them, sin hath its deserts, that which is due to it, and which justice requires should be inflicted for it; his holiness is demonstrated, for what clearer evidence, that he is of purer eyes than to behold it, that he perfectly hates it, than by punishing it in his own Son, when he appeared but in the room of sinners. His truth is manifested, when the Lord of life must die, rather than what the law denounced shall not be executed; his wisdom is no way impeached, the ends of government fully attained, the law vindicated from contempt, the authority of the great lawgiver upheld, and the children of men deterred from sin, when the Son of God must suffer for it.

I need not here give an account of that abundant evidence we have in Scripture that Christ should suffer in our stead, only this in short: the several notions whereby his death is represented to us in Scripture, make it plain that he suffered and died not only for our good, but in our stead.

His death is held forth as a *punishment*, as a *ransom*, and as a *sacrifice*.

His death was a *punishment:* 'He was wounded for our transgressions;' he died for our sins; that is, he suffered what our sins deserved, that we might not suffer; and this is the very thing that we mean by his suffering in our stead.

His death was our *ransom*, Mat. xx. 28. He paid that in our behalf which justice required of him, and this is to pay it in our stead.

His death was a *sacrifice:* he died that we might escape that death which was the penalty of the law transgressed by us. As the life of the sacrifice went for the life of the sinner for whom it was offered; this is to die in our stead, as the sacrifice died instead of the offender.

(6.) Christ's sufferings were accepted for us, and accepted as suffered in our stead. None who believe he suffered will question but his sufferings were accepted; nor will any deny that they were accepted as suffered in our stead, but those who against all evidence of Scripture deny that he suffered in our stead. (1.) The ground of his death and suffering; (2.) The end and design of them; (3.) Their full sufficiency for their end; (4.) The dignity and quality of the person suffering; everything, in a manner, which occurs therein tends to make this unquestionable among all Christians.

It was the will of the Father, expressed in the form of a covenant between Father and Son, that the Son taking our nature should thus suffer, Ps. xl. 6–8, Heb. x. 5. The Father promises that these sufferings should be accepted, Isa. liii. 10, 11. The Son, upon assurance of the Father's acceptance, submits to the sufferings.

He suffered all that in justice was required, that way might be made for our acquitment.

His sufferings were a full demonstration of his truth, wisdom, holiness, justice, yea, of his mercy too; the Lord was hereby every way transcendently glorified, and that which thus glorifies him must needs be highly acceptable.

He that suffered was not only man, but God, of the same essence, power, and will with the Father. His sufferings and blood was the sufferings and blood of him who is God, and therefore of infinite value, and so most worthy of all acceptance, such as could not in justice but be accepted. The Lord was herewith fully satisfied, and that which fully satisfied him was unquestionably accepted.

(7.) Since Christ's sufferings were accepted for us, it is undeniable that they are imputed to us (this is the conclusion which necessarily and unavoidably follows from the premises); for such acceptance of them for us, and imputation of them unto us, is the same thing. To impute Christ's sufferings to us, is nothing else but to accept them for us, as suffered in our stead. Hence, [1.] let me give some account why I express imputation by acceptance; [2.] to shew that they are the same thing, and nothing else meant by the one than by the other.

[1.] What others means here by imputation I express in these terms, accepting thereof as done in our stead, for us; but they are clear and proper (and help to state this point more advantageously), and to distinguish this from other sorts of imputation. Imputation in general is to account a thing to belong to us. This general is specified and differenced by three severals, all here comprised, viz., the state of the thing imputed, the ground of the imputation, and the quality of what is imputed.

First, As to the state of the thing imputed, they are either ours, or not ours, personally. That is denoted in the words 'for us.' He endured it for us, not we for ourselves; and so the imputation of Christ's sufferings is accounting of that to belong to us which is not personally ours.

Hereby it is distinguished from the imputation of things which are personally ours. Phinehas's act was imputed to him for righteousness; it was his own act personally, Ps. cvi. 31; and so Rom. iv. 4.

Secondly, As to the ground of the imputation, that is here Christ's suffering in our stead; that is the ground why his sufferings are accounted to belong to us. So the imputing of his sufferings is the accounting that to belong to us which he suffered in our stead. Thereby it is distinguished from those imputations which are injurious or groundless, from such also as have other or different grounds from these.

Thirdly, As to the quality of what is imputed; it is either good for us, or evil. The sufferings of Christ are good for us; that is denoted in the word *accepted*, and serves to distinguish of* the imputation of that which is evil. The imputation of that which is good is called the accepting of it for us, as the imputation of that which is evil is called the laying it to our charge, 2 Tim. iv. 16; so that I express the imputing of Christ's sufferings to us by the accepting thereof for us, to distinguish it from the imputation of that which is evil. To impute that which is evil to us, is to charge it on us; to impute that which is good to us, is to accept it for us.

Thus, as the imputation of evil to us is distinctly expressed by laying it to our charge, so the imputation of that which is good is distinctly and properly expressed by accepting it for us. Both the charging of the evil, and the accepting of the good, is the accounting it to belong to us, which is the common notion of imputation.

[2.] Hereby the other thing propounded is manifest, viz., that to impute Christ's sufferings to us, and accept them for us, is the same thing. But let us clear it a little more. Take imputation in its full extent, and it is the accounting of a thing to belong to us, and dealing with us accordingly. These two things it includes, and it is all we mean by it. Now a thing may be accounted to belong upon several grounds; that particularly belongs to us which is done or suffered in our stead, which is the case before us. And in this case, to accept for us what is suffered in our stead, is to impute it to us; for to accept it as suffered in our stead, is to judge it to belong to us, and to deal with us answerably in respect to the advantages thereof; and this is all that imputation imports.

Thus, when a friend pays a ransom for a captive, if it be accepted for the captive, it is imputed to him; for to accept it for him, is to account it to belong to him, being paid in his stead, and to deal with him accordingly, by discharging him.

Thus, when a propitiatory sacrifice was offered for the sinner, the accepting of it for him was the imputing of it to him; for, being accepted in his stead, it was accounted to belong to him, and he had the advantage of it for atonement, Lev. i. 4. He laid his hand upon the head of it, to signify that it was to suffer in his stead, and it made atonement for him; so that, being accepted, it was accounted to belong to him, and he fared according; atonement was made by it; where it is plain in those sacrifices accepting and imputing are all one, and so they are expressed by Lev. vii. 18, where not to accept is explained by not to impute; and there is sufficient warrant by accepting to understand imputing in other places where it is applied to sacrifices, Ps. xx. 3, Isaiah lvi. 7.

* Qu. 'it from'?—ED.

Hereby it is clear, that to accept Christ's sufferings for us, as suffered in our stead, and to impute them unto us, is the very same thing; so that those who grant his sufferings are thus accepted for us, can in nowise deny that they are imputed to us, unless they will be so absurd as both to grant and deny one and the same thing; so ridiculous as to grant it in one expression, and deny it in the other, which doth express the very same thing. There are no small advantages I may expect from thus stating the question.

(8.) Hereby it appears that none can deny the imputation of Christ's death and sufferings but those who deny his satisfaction (and so subvert the foundation of the gospel); for since the imputation of his sufferings to us, and accepting of them for us, are one and the same thing, if they be not imputed to us, they are not accepted for us, as suffered in our stead. If they be not accepted for us, as suffered in our stead, he did not suffer in our stead; and if he did not suffer in our stead, he did not make satisfaction, for by satisfaction nothing is to be meant but the suffering the penalty of the law in our stead; so that this draws deep, and tends directly to undermine the foundation of Christianity. I would they who make bold to deny the imputation of Christ's sufferings, would shew us, things thus stated, how it is possible to secure his satisfaction. I am confident that Socinus himself, if he had not denied the satisfaction of Christ, would never have denied the imputation of it to us, as before explained; for even a Mahomedan hath so much respect for Christ, as not to deny but what he undertook in our stead was accepted of God as accomplished in our stead.

Let me say farther, that as the case is stated, we may force any who grant the satisfaction of Christ, to acknowledge the imputation of it, even those who oppose it so passionately, and are possessed with the greatest prejudices against it, if they can but procure leave of their prejudice and passion to use a little reason when they are masters of much; if they do but discern the true notion of the things in question, when it is clear and obvious; nay, if they but understand themselves and the matters they contest about, while some of them are ready to charge the clearest, the greatest lights of the protestant world with ignorance or inadvertency.

That Christ satisfied for us they grant; no protestant, no papist, no Christian, none but Socinians question it. Well, if he satisfied for us, he suffered in our stead; if he suffered in our stead, his sufferings were accepted as suffered in our stead; if they were accepted for us, they are imputed to us, for we mean nothing else in the world by imputation but this acceptance.

This they grant, and cannot but grant, and must yield the very thing we contend for, while they will have the world believe that they deny it, and write bitter discourses against it, as though they were in such a transport as not to understand what they do or say.

That I do not misrepresent them will be hereby evident; ask dissenting protestants, such who have forsaken the doctrine of the Church of England, and of all reformed churches in this point, whether the righteousness of Christ be imputed to us? No, by no means, will they say; and some of them have the discretion to smut it with black invectives, as a dangerous doctrine, of I know not what pernicious consequence; well, but ask them again, Did Christ suffer in our stead? Was what he suffered accepted as suffered in our stead? This they will readily grant, as being maintained by the whole Christian world against the Socinians. The papists themselves will not have the face to deny it, how much, how satirically soever they write against the imputation of Christ's righteousness; now where is the reason and ingenuity of those men, papists and others, when they presume so much upon the strength and the clearness of their reason? They grant the sufferings of Christ in our stead accepted for us, yet deny they are imputed to us, when the accepting of them for, and imputing of them to us, are the very same thing; they both grant and deny one and the same thing, only expressing it in differing terms; and these terms differing only in the sound, when in truth they are of one and the same import.

This is not to deal like men of reason; it is no more reasonable than to grant that this is a living creature, but to deny it to be an animal; or to grant they have received twenty English shillings, but to deny they have received one pound sterling. The Socinians are more impious, and bid more defiance to the gospel, in denying the imputation of Christ's satisfaction, because they deny he made any satisfaction; but those are more repugnant to reason, who grant that he made satisfaction, but deny that it is imputed.

If they will use their reason, they must either fall into the detestable error of Socinus, and deny both, or submit to the doctrine of the gospel, and acknowledge both; both must stand or fall together; and both must be denied, or both must be acknowledged.

(9.) Hereby it appears that there is abundant evidence in Scripture for the imputation of Christ's suffering for us; there is as much ground to confirm and establish us in the belief of it, as there is for the most, the greatest points of the Christian faith; for truths that depend upon mere revelation, have more ground in Scripture. Those testimonies which are usually alleged and insisted on as direct proof thereof, are but a very small part of its confirmation; they are but, as it were, some few drops, in comparison of a full stream of Scripture, wherewith it is enforced: all those multiplications of divine testimonies, which prove the satisfaction of Christ, against the Socinian, are full evidences of the imputation thereof.

For the satisfaction of Christ being proved, none can or will deny the Lord's acceptance of it; and so the imputation of it being the same thing with that acceptance, will be thereby out of question.

So that all those sorts of scripture, almost innumerable, which signified that he suffered in our stead, are just proofs that his sufferings are imputed to us; all those texts which declare, he died for us; was delivered for our offences; that the Lord laid our sins on him; that he bare our iniquities; was wounded for our transgressions; was made sin; made a curse for us; that he gave himself, his life, a ransom for us; that he redeemed; bought us with a price; obtained redemption; that he was a propitiation, made atonement or reconciliation; made his soul an offering; gave himself a sacrifice; offered himself without spot, &c. These, and all of the same import, more than can be soon or easily reckoned up, do declare that he suffered in our stead, and so are sufficient proofs that his sufferings are imputed; for it being proved that he suffered in our stead, that his sufferings are imputed, *i. e.*, accepted for us, must and will be granted without other proof.

For it cannot be denied that Christ's sufferings are imputed to us, if they be accepted for us, because they are both one. It cannot be denied that his sufferings are accepted as suffered in our stead, if they were suffered in our stead. For none will have the face to question the acceptance of Christ's sufferings as they were suffered.

Therefore it being proved that Christ suffered in our stead, all is proved that can be denied; that which evidences Christ to have suffered in our room makes all evident which needs any proof in this question.

Now a great part of the Bible makes it evident that he suffered in our stead, and no less than all this evidence there is for the imputation of his sufferings, since it is carried by the same evidence beyond all reasonable denial, and needs no other testimonies to clear it.

(10.) Hereby the vanity of what is objected against this imputation of Christ's sufferings will be manifest; to instance in two or three which are counted considerable.

[1.] It is objected, that the Scripture doth nowhere express the imputation of Christ's righteousness to us; it is not said anywhere in Scripture, that the death or sufferings of Christ are imputed to us.

Be it so, that these very words are not found in any place in Scripture, yet the thing we mean thereby is found in hundreds of places, wherever we find that Christ died or suffered for us. Wherever we find any expressions signifying that he suffered in our stead, which any but the Socinian can see in all parts of Scripture, there the acceptance, or which is all one, the imputing of his sufferings, is held forth.

For his sufferings and the acceptance thereof do so clearly and necessarily involve one another, that one of them cannot be apprehended or believed without the other; we cannot believe that he suffered, without believing that his sufferings were accepted, and so without believing that they are imputed, since they are the same thing.

Let me only add this, it is dangerous reasoning from the want of some words to the want of the thing; such reasonings may overturn our faith, and leaves us no gospel. If we must not believe the imputation of Christ's sufferings, because those words are not in Scripture (I mean in any one place together, for that they are not in several is not pretended), we must not believe the satisfaction of Christ, nor the merits of Christ, no, nor the incarnation of Christ, because those words are not in Scripture.

[2.] It is objected, that there is no evidence of this in the Evangelists, that Christ nowhere delivered this doctrine concerning the imputation of his righteousness or satisfaction, neither in his sermons nor private discourses with his disciples; that since Christ is faithful in the discharge of his prophetical office, this point would never have been omitted, if it had been necessary to be believed.

Ans. The premises discover this to be a great mistake; for Christ so delivered this doctrine in his sermons and discourses, as to leave nothing therein questionable. There is abundant evidence in the evangelists of all that need any proof in this matter. For as it is stated, nothing can be questioned, but whether Christ suffered in our stead. If this be not denied, all that we assert is and must be granted. Now there is full evidence for this from Christ's own words, in all the evangelists; and so clear, that none can avoid it, but those who, with the Socinians, shut their eyes. Let me point at some few: Mat. xx. 28, 'Gave his life a ransom.' The same words in the evangelist, Mark x. 48. And so Mat. xxvi. 28, 'This is my blood,' &c. That also, Mark xiv. 24, and Luke xxii. 19, 'This is my body,' &c.; the 20th verse, 'blood shed for' &c. So in the other evangelists, John i. 29, 'the Lamb of God;' John xv. 13, 'laid down life for friends;' John x. 11, 'life for sheep.'

Now if we will understand these phrases, either according to the common usage of Scripture, or the common sense of mankind as to such expressions, the meaning of them must be, that Christ died and suffered in our stead. And this being proved by Christ's own words, recorded by the evangelists, all is sufficiently thereby proved that we intend. Nothing more concerning the imputation of his sufferings need any proof, because there is nothing of it that is or can be denied.

[8.] It is objected, that if Christ's sufferings be imputed to us, then we must be reputed to have suffered what he suffered, and then we must be accounted to have satisfied justice ourselves, and consequently to be our own saviours and redeemers.

Ans. From imputation in the sense fore-explained, it cannot with any reason be inferred that we suffered personally, but only that Christ suffered in our stead. And from thence it cannot be inferred that we ourselves made satisfaction, but only that Christ in our stead satisfied divine justice. And so in short the foundation of this fallacy being removed, the rest of the consequences fall.

Thus much for the imputation of Christ's death and sufferings, commonly called his passive righteousness; the truth whereof I hope is rendered so plain and firm, that it cannot (as I said) be denied by any, but such as will deny Christ to be a Saviour and Redeemer in the style and sense of Scripture.

I proceed to the imputation of his active obedience, or, as it is called, his active righteousness. This, I confess, seems not of so great importance as the former, nor the denial of it of so dangerous consequences; for there are some who are zealous assertors of Christ's satisfaction, and walk with a right foot in other truths of the gospel, who take occasion to dissent here, and to declare it publicly; yet, because I apprehend it to be a truth of some moment to the honour of Christ and comfort of believers, and this discovered in the gospel, and in the text particularly, and asserted by the community of protestant divines, from whom I would not be tempted to straggle, and wish others would not upon slender grounds, especially in our present circumstances, wherein papists make so great an advantage of stragglers, and make it the matter of no little triumph, when they see any part of the common protestant doctrine deserted by its professors. Therefore I shall endeavour to make this also evident in the same method as I did the former, and hope to do it so as to satisfy dissenters; such, I mean, as dissent for want of evidence, or out of some sense that this truth is or may be abused; not those who oppose it out of ill design, or affectation of singularity, for in such there may be something too hard for light otherwise convincing.

First, Christ performed perfect obedience for us. He was born of a woman, and made under the law, for the same purpose, and on the same account, as the apostle signifies, Gal. iv. 4. He was born of a woman for us, and not for himself, and so he was made under the law, substituted* to it for us, and not for himself.

The Socinians will not deny, but that his obedience was for us, that is, for our good, only they will not have it meritorious for us. As they will have no satisfaction in his sufferings, so no merit in his obedience.

But herein they are opposed by all sorts of Christians, both protestants and papists. The papists, who arrogate a meritorious excellency to their own obedience, how defective soever, cannot deny it to the perfect obedience of Christ. As for protestants, to instance only in such whose concurrence may be less expected, those who will not have Christ to have performed obedience in our stead, yet maintain his obedience was meritorious for us,

* Qu. 'submitted' or 'subjected'?—ED.

both his obedience to the moral law, and to the law of Moses, to the special law of mediation. He perfectly fulfilled all that was required of him in the covenant of redemption, and so deserved what is promised in that covenant, the sum of which we have, Isa. liii. And he perfectly fulfilled all that was required of man in the covenant of works (as to the substance thereof, and the duties common to all), and so deserved for us what was promised in that covenant, viz., to live.

Thus his obedience was meritorious, *jure pacti*, in respect of that covenant, whose conditions he exactly performed; but this is not all, it is but merit in a large sense, such as some divines will have Adam's obedience capable of, if it continued perfect.

Christ's obedience performed for us was meritorious not only thus, but also *jure operis*, in respect of the value of the performance, the divine nature deriving an infinite value upon what the human nature performed in our behalf; so that on this account it deserved, and was truly worth the life and blessedness procured by it for us; they do acknowledge that it is infinitely meritorious.

Yea, those of our divines who are most reserved in asserting what is due to the active obedience of Christ, do grant that his obedience, in respect of the condescension of it, was meritorious. Now there was active obedience in condescending; it was his Father's will that he should condescend, he complied with his will, so that there was condescending in every act, and thus there was merit in every act of his obedience.

Indeed, I should be sorry to find any protestant divines denying the merit of Christ's active obedience, for thereby his whole undertaking will be divested of its meritorious excellency. If there be no merit in his obedience, there will be none in his sufferings; for penal sufferings, as such, do not merit, as is confessed on all hands, they are not meritorious but as there is obedience in them. And therefore if his obedience be not meritorious, there will be no merit in his sufferings, and consequently none in his whole undertaking.

And his satisfaction will fall with his merit, for that only is satisfactory which is meritorious; so that, when there is no merit, there is no satisfaction.

This then we may take for granted, as being generally acknowledged, that Christ fulfilled the law, performed perfect obedience on our behalf, so that it was meritorious for us.

Secondly, Christ performed perfect obedience in our stead, not only for us, for our good, but *vice nostrûm*, in our place or stead.

This, as to what I intend, is of more consequence than the former, and will clear the whole business before us, if we can but clear it. If we can gain this one point, we shall go near to carry all that we desire; and, if I mistake not, it may be easily done. Indeed, there are divers who stick at this, those who acknowledge that Christ's obedience was for us, and that it was meritorious for us, will scarce grant that it was performed in our stead; but if they take notice what we mean thereby, they will not, they cannot stick at it.

A duty is said to be done in another's stead, when that is performed for for him which he was obliged to do himself.

As when one pays a debt for another which he himself was bound to pay, it is truly said to be paid in his stead.

Or when one is obliged to do some work, but is some way or other disabled for it, another undertaking to do it for him, doth it in his stead. So

Christ fulfilling the law for us, which we were obliged to have done ourselves, he truly and properly did it in our stead.

This seems clear, past all denial; no more is required that it be done in our stead, but that what we were bound to do ourselves be done for us. That it was done for us, all grant; and that we ourselves were obliged to do it, none can deny.

Nor can it be denied that he performed it for us but for that end for which we should have performed it, that is, that we might have life; so that he did for us what we should have done, not accidentally, but out of design; for it is acknowledged that his end and design in performing perfect obedience was to merit life for us, that is, purchase for us a title to heaven.

All that I find objected against Christ's obeying in our stead is only this: if he performed obedience in our stead, we shall be thereby exempted from obedience ourselves, as his sufferings in our stead did free us from sufferings.

But this which is alleged to enforce the objection serves to dissolve it. By Christ's suffering in our stead we are freed from suffering anything for that end for which he suffered, that is, for satisfying of divine justice; so by Christ's obeying in our stead we are freed from obedience, for that end for which he performed obedience in our place, that is, that we might have title to life. For these ends for which he suffered and obeyed, it is not required of us either to obey or to suffer, for he alone satisfied justice by the one, and he alone purchased title to life by the other.

For other ends we suffer afflictions and death, not to satisfy divine justice; and so for other ends we are as much obliged to obedience as if he had not obeyed for us, but not to purchase a title to life, not for that end.

In short, I cannot see how those who will have Christ's active obedience to be satisfactory or meritorious for us, can reasonably deny that it was performed in our stead, since they must grant all that is requisite thereto; for no more is necessary that it be done in our stead, but that what we are obliged to do be done for us. That it was done for us they assert; that we ourselves were obliged to do it, they cannot deny.

Thirdly, What Christ performed in observance of the law, is accepted in all points as he did it. What he performed was accepted; what he performed on our behalf is accepted in our behalf; what he performed in our stead is accepted as done in our stead.

This is clear and unquestionable, no Christian will deny anything of it. Those that make Christ to be what he is, that believe he is the beloved Son of God, in whom he is well pleased, which was declared by a voice from heaven, Mat. iii. 7, that the Father is transcendently pleased, fully satisfied both with Christ's undertaking and the accomplishment of it; that believe the divine dignity and excellency of his person, and the infinite virtue of his performance; that it was the Father's will and pleasure that Christ should do this, and do it exactly in all points as he did, Heb. x. 7; that the will and design of Christ in this was one and the very same with the will and design of the Father, John v. 30 and iv. 34; that it was a covenant and agreement between them that this should be thus done, and thus done should be accepted; that it was the pleasure of the Lord which was in Christ's hands, and that he had promised it should prosper and succeed, and be effectually accepted, Isa. liii. 10, 11;—those that believe these severals, or any of them, cannot in the least doubt but his obedience was accepted for those persons, and in that capacity in which it was performed; will not question but if it was performed on our behalf, and in our stead, it is so accepted. A Socinian, I had almost said a Mahomedan, will not deny the acceptance of what Christ performed, so far as they admit his performance. There needs no more proof in the case, if so much as is premised be needful of a thing past denial.

Thus far we have gone upon clear and undeniable grounds; there remains but one thing more, and that must pass as clear as the rest with all men of reason, and be as far from being denied, and that is the conclusion.

Fourthly, Hence it follows, that the active obedience of Christ is imputed to us. This cannot be gainsaid, the former being granted. If Christ performed such obedience on our behalf, and that be accepted for us, then it must be imputed to us; for to be imputed to us is nothing else but to be accepted for us, as performed on our behalf and in our stead. Those who cannot deny that he performed this obedience in our stead, and that it was accepted for us, must grant that it was imputed to us, unless they will be so unreasonable as when they admit the premises to deny the conclusion.

I mean nothing by imputation but what is included in that acceptance which themselves grant. When a surety's payment is accepted on behalf of the debtor, it is imputed to him. If Paul had paid what was owing to Philemon, or satisfied for the injuries done him by his servant Onesimus, Philemon's acceptance of that payment or satisfaction on behalf of Onesimus would have been the imputation of it to him; for imputation here is nothing else but the accepting of what another doth for us, instead of that we should have done ourselves. I shewed this before by instances in such things whereby the satisfaction of Christ is held forth in Scripture, and gave you a plain text, where imputing and accepting are terms of the same import.

Nor need I give any further account than I have done why I express imputation by acceptance, a term not so usual on this subject, only this,

Imputation in general is an accounting of that which is not personally ours to belong to us as if it were ours, or the setting it on our account; and thus either that which is evil, or that which is good, may be accounted to belong to us. When that which is evil, and* done by us, is set on our account, the imputing of it is expressed by charging it on us; so our sins are said to be charged on Christ, imputed to him: Isa. liii., 'The Lord laid on him,' &c; laid them to his charge, imputed them to him. And this was the ground why our sins were set on his account, laid to his charge; it was because he became our surety, and undertook to suffer in our stead the punishment due to sinners; the Lord accepting of this substitution, is said to be made sin for us, 2 Cor. v. 21, to impute our sins to him. He accounted our sin to belong to him, though he was not guilty of any sin personally.

As in the other case, when that which is good, and performed by another, is accounted to belong to us, the imputing of it is expressed by accepting of it for us; and so his obedience is accepted for us, that is, imputed to us. And the ground why it is set on our account is, because he performed it in our stead and on our behalf.

Now, they who cannot deny but Christ's obedience was accepted for us, must grant the thing we mean by imputation; and who can give any rational account why they should decline the word? Those who see the definition belongs to it, why should they deny it the name? Why should

* Qu. 'not'?—ED.

not he who is a rational creature be called and pass in their account for a man? And further, those who cannot but allow the grounds of this imputation, viz., Christ's performing in our stead, I cannot see how they can reject that which clearly and necessarily results from it. For anything I can perceive, this doctrine, as stated here, cannot be opposed without offering some violence to one's reason. If I much mistake not, neither protestants nor papists can deny the principle upon which I proceed; and so there is hopes, that if the principles were sedately and impartially considered, there might be no longer a controversy among Christians.

Fifthly, Let me clear what I have insisted on from an exception which it seems liable to; and there is but one that I can discern, after I have looked carefully every way to discover what weakness there may be in it, or what inconvenience may follow from it; and it is this, If imputing of Christ's righteousness to us be the same thing with accepting it for us, then it must be imputed as soon as it is accepted, and it was accepted as soon as it was performed. It will hence follow, that we are justified at the death of Christ, and so we shall be justified before we believe, yea, before we have a being; whereas the Scripture speaks of no justification but only of believers, and will have none to be justified but by faith, in no wise without or before faith.

This is the charge which the principle I insist on is subject to in appearance; but it is only in appearance, and may soon and easily be discharged.

It is true and evident in Scripture, that none are actually justified before or without faith; and whatsoever is inconsistent with this doctrine of the gospel cannot be maintained. But that principle which I insist on doth not at all clash with this evident truth; and this will be apparent, if you take notice, that the acceptance of Christ's obedience, active or passive, may be considered in two different notions. It is accepted as from him, and it is accepted as for us; it was accepted as from Christ, as soon as it was performed, but it was not accepted for us till we believe.

It was accepted absolutely as performed by Christ as soon as it was finished, as being the full performance of all that any law, or covenant, or justice did require of him, and being fully worth all that he designed to obtain hereby; but it is not accepted with relation to particular persons, for application to them, and to instate them actually in the privileges and advantages of it, till the terms agreed on in the covenant of redemption be fulfilled; that is, till they believe. I will endeavour to make it clear by this comparison: as if one undertakes to pay the debt of another, upon terms required of him who contracted the debt, when the surety pays the full sum that is owing, it is accepted as to him, but it is not accepted as to the debtor; he hath not an acquittance, a discharge, till he performs the terms agreed on; so here Christ undertakes to pay what we owe to the law, but it is required that we believe on him; that is the terms agreed on.

As soon as Christ had performed all that was due, it was accepted as to him, no more was required on his part; but it is not accepted as to us, so as we should be actually acquitted, and receive the benefit of it, till we believe, and so comply with the terms agreed on.

Now it is acceptance as to us that I call imputation, and then Christ's righteousness is not imputed but to those that believe; and so there can be no occasion to infer from hence, that any are or can be justified before or without faith.

Sixthly, Hereby it appears evidently that the righteousness of Christ is imputed to us, and not only the effects of it. There are many that say, the righteousness of Christ itself is not imputed to us, but only as to the effects of it.

The Arminians acknowledge that the righteousness of Christ may be said to be imputed to us, because he thereby merited that our faith or obedience should be accepted for our justification, as if it were, though it be not, a perfect righteousness.

The papists grant that Christ's righteousness may be said to be imputed to us, because thereby he purchased, as other benefits, so inherent holiness, which with them is our justifying righteousness.

The Jesuits, Vasquez, Bellarmine, and others, expressly own the imputation of Christ's merits or righteousness in this sense.

So others among us grant that Christ's righteousness may be said to be imputed to us in this sense, and no other; but because he thereby purchased pardon of sin, and title to life, in which, they say, consists that righteousness which justifies us, they will have us justified not by a righteousness which Christ performed for us, but by a righteousness which by his performance he purchased for us.

Not by his own righteousness, but by that which is the effect of his own.

All these admit not of any imputation of Christ's righteousness in itself, but only in its effects and benefits.

But it is plain, by what is premised, that the obedience of Christ itself is imputed; for to be imputed to us is nothing else but to be accepted for us, as performed in our stead. But the obedience of Christ was performed in our stead, and is accepted for us, therefore his obedience itself is imputed to us.

Indeed, either the righteousness of Christ is imputed to us or nothing; for the effects of it, viz., pardon of sin, and title to life, &c., are not imputed to us, because it cannot be said with any tolerable sense, that right to life, or pardon of sin, were performed in our stead, or accepted for us as so performed.

Besides, that which is imputed to us is not personally or subjectively ours; but the effects of Christ's righteousness, our faith, our inherent holiness, pardon of sin, title to life, are ours subjectively and personally; we are the subjects of them, as we are not of that which is only imputed to us; and to say these effects of it are only imputed to us, is to deny all imputation of it.

But I have hopes that the premises being impartially and duly considered, as they should be by the lovers of truth, none that are unquestionably Christians (for whether the Socinians be so is a question), will scruple to grant that Christ's obedience is itself imputed, since it cannot be denied but that it was performed in our stead, and accepted for us, as it was performed in the sense explained; and no more but this is intended when we say Christ's righteousness is itself imputed to us.

Seventhly, It remains that I should answer some objections that are made against the imputation of Christ's obedience. I shall take notice of two or three that are counted most considerable.

Obj. 1. If Christ fulfilled the law for us as our surety, and so we be judged to have kept the law perfectly by him, then we must be accounted never to have sinned, and so Christ's death will be needless, and many other consequences must follow.

Ans. The main consequent here, upon which all the rest are founded, is the same. If we be judged to have perfectly kept the law by Christ as our surety, then we must be reputed not to have sinned. The inference is to be denied, because plainly the Lord may account us to have kept the law by our surety, he fulfilling it in our stead, and yet judge that we have transgressed it as to ourselves. He may judge that we are righteous on Christ's account, and yet that we are transgressors on our own accounts.

As on the contrary, he made him sin for us, that is, imputed our sin to Christ, when he himself never transgressed the law.

Their inference would hold, viz., that we had never sinned if the law had been fulfilled by us personally; but it holds not at all, since it is only fulfilled for us by another. All that can be inferred is only this, not that we have not sinned as to ourselves, but that we sinned not in our surety.

They may as reasonably conclude, that because the bankrupt hath discharged the bonds, and paid all by his surety, therefore he must be reputed not to have been in debt, as that we must be esteemed never to have broke the law ourselves, because Christ discharged what the law required of us in our stead.

Obj. 2. Christ's death and suffering freed us from all punishment, both pain and loss, and so from the loss of heaven, and consequently procured for us a title to heaven; and therefore there is no need of his active obedience, that we may have a title, and so no need of the performance or imputation of it for this end.

Ans. Those who argue thus, do hold that his active obedience was meritorious, did deserve heaven for us, and so procured a title to it, will not have any to conclude from hence, that his death and sufferings were needless for that purpose; what they will answer to it, will answer your own argument. If they say that both his obedience and sufferings procured our title to heaven, we may say so too, both are needful; and so the objection falls, and whatever account be made of it appears to be frivolous.

Indeed, we should not separate what the Lord hath not disjoined; the obedience and sufferings of Christ are not disjoined in themselves, in their virtue, or in their effects.

Not in *themselves:* he suffered in all his obedience, and obeyed in all his sufferings, Phil. ii. 8. There was obedience in all his sufferings, because he suffered in compliance with his Father's will, and there were sufferings in all his obedience, because his acts of obedience were acts of humiliation and abasement, all performed by the Son of God in the form of a servant.

Nor in their *virtue:* his obedience was both meritorious and satisfactory, and his sufferings were both satisfactory and meritorious. His obedience was not only meritorious, but also satisfactory; if not as obedience, yet as it was penal.

And his sufferings were not only satisfactory, but also meritorious; if not as they were great, yet as they were obediential.

Nor in their *effects:* his sufferings could not have satisfied justice without his perfect obedience.

Because sufferings simply considered without obedience find no acceptance with God, his perfect obedience could not have procured for us a title to life; for we have no title to life by obedience, unless freed from condemnation by his sufferings.

Obj. 3. If Christ fulfilled and obeyed the law in our stead, so that his obedience be imputed to us, then we are not ourselves to obey or keep the law; the necessity of personal holiness is hereby taken away; it will be no more needful for us than it is to suffer personally what Christ suffered in our stead.

Ans. I said enough before to satisfy this; we are neither bound to obey and fulfil the law on that account for which Christ fulfilled it in our stead, as we are not liable to suffer on that account for which Christ suffered in our stead, &c.

But because this consequence is importunately forced on us, however we disclaim it, I know not why, unless some be resolved to render this truth odious, right or wrong, let me add,

That we are for a necessity of obedience and personal holiness indispensably in the highest degree, and for all its acts of necessity which they pretend to, who charge us with making it unnecessary; nor is there anything in this doctrine to hinder us from holding it to be so necessary as to our judgment, or from shewing it in our daily practice.

There are but two sorts of necessity which can be ascribed to things of this nature; and we maintain both, and that in a full and fair consistence with this truth. There is a *necessitas precepti*, the necessity of it as a duty indispensably required; and *necessitas medii*, the necessity of it as the means or way to salvation, without which it cannot be attained.

1. It is necessary as a duty; obedience, holiness of heart and life, is required by the law of God; the law of nature requires it of all, no less of those for whom Christ's obedience was performed, and is actually accepted, than of others.

It is enjoined by a law, whose obligation arises from our very nature and being, and is founded in the relation between God and man, as he is governor of intelligent creatures, and they subject to him, so long as they are such creatures, and he their ruler and superior; that is, so long as they are men, and he is God, they cannot but owe him absolute obedience in all things. Nothing can free us from this obligation, unless God and man cease to be what they are in themselves, and what they are as thus related to one another. To deny perfect obedience to be due from man is to deny him to be man, and to deny it to be due to God is to deny him to be God.

As it is impossible that we should be freed from this obligation, so it cannot be imagined that Christ should either dissolve or weaken it.

He came not to dissolve the law, but to fulfil it; his undertaking and performance was so far from taking off the obligation to obedience, that it strengthens, and adds more powerful enforcements to it, even all the constraints of his great love, that wonderful love which he expressed in dying and suffering so much for us. They are more justly charged with this who would charge it upon others; those of them I mean who will have the law requiring perfect obedience to be abrogated, and the obligation of it dissolved.

2. It is necessary as a means: holiness of heart and life is necessary as the way that leads to life, as the way wherein we must walk if we would arrive at it, Eph. ii. 10. Acts of holiness are the end why we receive new life, and are made new creatures; and this is the way wherein all must walk that will be saved by grace. There is no attaining of happiness, or arriving at the enjoyment or sight of God without holiness, Heb. xii. 14; no happiness without seeing the Lord; no seeing the Lord without holiness, without following it. We make holiness with the Scripture necessary as the way to life; ay, but you make it, they say, not necessary to procure a title to life; that is true; the Scripture doth it not, and we dare not do it. To

make it not needful for that end is only to make it not necessary to supplant Christ and invade his prerogative. It is he, and he alone, that procures for us a title to life; this is all the necessity we deny, viz., the necessity of it to dethrone Christ and pluck the crown from his head, to usurp his purchase, honour, and office.

We leave them to do this who will shew themselves traitors to Christ, pretending a necessity of obedience and subjection to him.

Eighthly, Others rely upon an actual righteousness, some acts of righteousness, some good works, some deeds of charity. This is the foundation upon which many build their hopes of pardon and salvation in the dark darkness of popery; and notwithstanding the light of the gospel, many yet discover not the sandiness of it; though the Lord in the gospel doth confound this Babel and the builders of it, yet how many think to secure themselves thereby in opposition to what the apostle professes, Titus iii. 4–6.

Ninthly, Others rely upon an internal righteousness, such as they fancy in their good meanings, intention, inclination; though their conscience tells them they do little or nothing for God, yet since they have the confidence to think they mean well, have a good mind to do something, are of a willing mind, though they want the deed, and when they sin, find some kind of remorse and inward sorrow for it, for this they conclude God will pardon and save them.

All these several rooms, and many more, hath Satan contrived in men's own righteousness, and persuades sinners that they may be secure therein, and rely safely thereon.

Whereas, indeed, whatever refuge men fancy in their own righteousness, it will prove a refuge of lies, it will deceive and betray those that fly thereto.

1. They are but imaginary sanctuaries, they are none of God's appointing; there is nothing in them to hinder revenging justice from proceeding against the sinner in a way of wrath and vengeance.

These are altars of your own erecting, though you fly to the horns thereof; nothing hinders, but the wrath of God may seize you there and proceed to execution, these can afford you no more security than the horns of that altar did to Joab, 1 Kings ii. 28. If you stay here, the Lord will say to justice, as Solomon did to Benaiah, 'Fall upon him, and slay him there.'

The apostle, though he had more reason to think himself safe in his own righteousness than others can have, yet he durst not be found there; the 'not having,' &c. He flies to another refuge, runs to Christ, desires to be found in him; ay, there is none but Christ, none but Christ, no other refuge, no other sanctuary, no other altar that can secure a sinner from the wrath and justice of God, but Christ and his righteousness; though the hills and mountains should fall upon you and cover you, yet could they not hide you from the wrath of him.

How high soever your righteousness be in your own opinion, the flood of God's indignation will overwhelm it, and your souls with it, if you get not into this ark.

To neglect Christ and his righteousness, and to rely upon your own, is to forsake the fountain of living waters, that fountain which is open for sin and uncleanness, that which can only cleanse you from the guilt and pollution of sin, and to dig broken cisterns, such is your own righteousness; take it in what notion you will, it will hold no water, there is no virtue in it to cleanse you from the least evil; your souls will perish if you stay here, rely on it.

If you will not trust in the righteousness of Christ only, and stay yourselves upon him, but rely on your own righteousness, as the prophet saith: Isa. l. 11, 'You kindle a fire, and compass yourselves about with sparks: you walk in the light of your own fire, and in the sparks that ye have kindled.' But what will be the issue? 'This shall,' &c. To lie down in darkness, for all your own sparks, in that darkness where there is eternal sorrow, where there is weeping, and, &c.

2. This is to oppose the glorious design of God in the gospel. His design there is to advance the riches of his grace and mercy; and how doth he advance it, but by pardoning and saving those who find nothing in themselves why they should be pardoned and saved. If I should write all those places which declares this to be the Lord's intention, I should quote a great part of the New Testament; let two places suffice, Titus iii. 5, Eph. ii. 8, 9.

Now this being God's design, and he thus promoting it, those that rely upon their own righteousness, upon anything in themselves, for pardon and salvation, they cross the design of God, the most glorious design that ever he promoted in the world, they are herein found fighters against God, and fighters against their own souls too; for hereby you put yourselves out of that way wherein the Lord will only save and justify sinners.

3. This frustrates the death of Christ, it speaks the sufferings and bloodshed of Christ to be in vain. So the apostle, Gal. ii. 21. If a man by a personal observance of the law may have a righteousness, by which or for which he may be justified and saved, then Christ's death was to no purpose, he might have saved his pains and labour, the expense of his blood was needless. For why? Christ lived and died, obeyed even unto the death, that guilty sinners might have a righteousness for which the Lord might pardon and save them.

But if sinners could attain such a righteousness by their personal obedience, as would entitle them to pardon and life, then Christ's undertaking is to no purpose. He obeyed and suffered to effect that which might as well have been effected without him. And therefore, in vain did he assume our nature, in vain took on him the form of a servant, in vain was he made under the law, in vain did he suffer the wrath of God, in vain did he shed his blood; it was to as little purpose as water spilt upon the ground.

Why, man might by his personal obedience obtain that righteousness which was the end or issue of Christ's undertaking, and wherefore then was all this waste?

This is the language of your self-confidence. Dependence on your own righteousness, it makes Christ's undertaking to be in vain, and to no purpose.

Thus you see how trusting to your own, &c., is highly dishonourable to God, exceeding injurious to Christ, and evidently destructive to your souls. And what more powerful motive to dissuade you from it?

But because this is a secret evil, is not easily discerned, hath such sly streams, such retired conveyances, as those that are guilty of it do many times think themselves innocent, let us in some few particulars shew wherein by an observing eye it may be discovered; and shew such streams of it as those may in part be guilty of, who for the main make Christ their chief confidence.

They bewray some confidence in their own righteousness.

(1.) Who look not up to Christ for strength to do the work of righteousness; who go about the duties they are called to, as though they were sufficient of themselves to do them, and think they can pray, hear, meditate, restrain sin, do acts of justice and charity, in a spiritual manner, without a special assistance from Christ to perform them, without hearty actual application of themselves to Christ for that assistance; whose hearts mutter some such things as those proud confidents speak out, of whom the Lord complains, Jer. ii. 31; who depend not on Christ as him who only works all their works, who only can enable them to work them; as on him without whom they can do nothing; who in the sense of their own weakness to that which is spiritual, cannot speak from their hearts what the apostle professes, 2 Cor. iii. 5. Where there is not this continual dependence on Christ, there is some self-dependence, some relying on righteousness, a sufficiency in yourselves.

(2.) Who are not sensible of the worthlessness of their own righteousness; who look not upon their best acts, inward or outward, as a menstruous cloth.

Who are apt to think there is something in their services, especially if plausibly and affectionately done, that may commend them to God, without any other mediator. If they pray with enlargement, or relieve those that are in need cheerfully, hear the word so as to be affected with it, &c., and think they shall be accepted for the work so done, which makes the work done, or the manner of doing it, the ground why they hope for acceptance, the heart least minds Christ in duties (as they think) well performed. Here is a visible appearance of confidence in your own righteousness.

When apt to think the spiritualness or affectionateness of any performance could make amends for the other defects of it, as though upon this account the Lord would not take notice of other sinful infirmities in them. Those that observe their hearts, &c.

The church was of another mind, Isa. lxiv. 6. And the apostle, 1 Cor. iv. 4, Ps. cxliii. 2.

(3.) Those that think they oblige God by an act or work of righteousness; imagine anything they do can make anything due to them from the hand of God; *ex. gr.*, think because they have prayed so fervently, so affectionately, therefore God is bound to hear them; because they have acted in this or that business so sincerely, so conscientiously, therefore God is bound to reward them. This argues too much presumption upon, too much confidence in, their own righteousness.

It is true, the Lord rewards the sincere obedience of his people, but his rewards are of grace, not of debt, freely bestowed, not due to them upon the account of what they do, Rom. iv. 4.

It is true also, he hath promised, but this makes him not a debtor to us, but to his own faithfulness. (Of this more in the next.) *Gratis promisit, gratis reddit.** *Promissio divina in sacris Scripturis non sonat in aliquem obligationem, sed insinuat meram dispositionem liberalitatis divinæ.*† Luke xvii. 10, we have done no more than we owe, and what can be due to us for paying our debts? *Deus sine dubio præstabit quod promisit propter veritatem, non propter obligationem; quod si non præstet, mendax est, non injurius.*

(4.) Those that pacify their consciences with what they do in a way of righteousness, without looking for further ground of peace and pardon. To clear it by an instance, the man is afflicted in conscience for sin, he goes

* Ferus. † Durand.

and mourns for it, and prays for pardon; if he hereupon speaks peace to himself, as though for thus doing he shall be pardoned, he relies on his own righteousness. It is not for anything we can do, but for what Christ hath done and suffered, that sin is forgiven.

It is true, the sincere acts of faith and repentance, they are signs of pardon, but they are not the ground or causes for which the Lord grants pardon; even faith and repentance itself, in respect of their sinful imperfections, stand in need of pardoning mercy.

Thus you see the several appearances of self-confidence. Take notice of them, bewail them, get further out of yourselves, and your own righteousness, with the apostle, that you may be found in Christ, 'not having, &c.'

'But that which is through the faith,' &c. The way how the apostle desired to be found in Christ is expressed:

First, Negatively: 'Not having,' &c., of which formerly.

Secondly, Positively: 'That which is through the faith,' &c. Explained in the following words: 'The righteousness which is of God by faith;' and this is it we shall now speak of. But before we proceed to fix upon the observation which these words afford, it will be necessary to inquire, what righteousness this is which the apostle desired to have? Why it is set forth in such terms in this verse?

For the first, Whose righteousness is it?

He knew he must have some righteousness, else the Lord would never justify or save him, Exod. xxxiv. 7, Prov. xvii. 15.

He had renounced his own righteousness as insufficient for this end; he terms it 'flesh,' ver. 3, a word that ordinarily sounds ill in Scripture language; at the best he could with no more security rely upon it for pardon and life, than the 'arm of flesh,' which the Scripture terms 'a broken reed,' rather pierces than supports, rather hurts than helps a guilty soul, if relied on for this end. He counts it 'loss,' ver. 7. He made account that confidence in this would be the loss of his soul, of his salvation; he should come short of pardon and life if he trusted on his own righteousness; for he counts it 'dung,' ver. 8, of no more value for procuring of pardon, acceptance, salvation, than dung is for procuring, purchasing of what we count most valuable. Thus, and in such significant, such vilifying expressions doth he renounce his own righteousness.

What righteousness then would the apostle have?

Why, the righteousness of Christ; there is no other imaginable; so the words, 'That righteousness which is through the faith of Christ,' bear the same sense as if they ran thus: 'That righteousness of Christ which is through faith.' Many other scriptures confirm this: Jer. xxiii. 6, 'The Lord, whose righteousness is ours;' 1 Cor. i. 30, how is he made unto us righteousness, but because his righteousness is made over to us, is made ours? Rom. v. 18, 'the free gift of righteousness,' &c., ver. 19.

Now the righteousness of Christ is sometimes by the apostle called 'the righteousness of faith,' Rom. ix. 30, chap. x. 6, chap. iv. 13; and sometimes 'the righteousness of God,' Rom. x. 3, chap. i. 17, chap. iii. 21, 22. And because both these expressions are used in this verse, we must give some account of them, that they may be rightly understood before we go further.

The righteousness of Christ is called the righteousness of faith,

First, Not because faith is this righteousness, but because it is made ours by faith. The reason is not because faith is this righteousness, as some novelists fancy; we need go no further than the words to prove this. It was the righteousness of another, not his own, that the apostle desired to have, but his faith was his own, inherent in him, acted by him, Hab. ii.; *fide sua.*

Again, That righteousness which is through faith is not faith itself, but this righteousness is through faith.

Secondly, But because through faith applying, apprehending, receiving it, it is accepted for, imputed to believers, and so becomes theirs.

It is called the righteousness of God, not because it is that righteousness which is *in* God, but because it is the righteousness which is *from* God. When it is said God's righteousness, you must not understand by it that righteousness which is essentially in God, for that is not communicable, we cannot have it, it can no way be made ours: neither by inherence, for this being God's essence, hereby the creature would become God; nor by imputation, for this cannot be performed for us; and what is imputed must be performed.

But it is called the righteousness of God, because it is of his appointing and bestowing. It is his appointment, it is his gift, he appointed Christ to perform it for us, he accepts of his performance in our stead, and so imputes it to those that believe. Thus it is his gift of righteousness.

Luther, the great vindicator of Christ's righteousness, and free justification by it, from Romish corruptions, before his conversion did very much stumble at this expression, 'the righteousness of God.' The phrase which is the spring-head of all gospel comforts, when rightly understood, did terrify and affright the soul, while the scales of popish blindness were upon his eyes. Such mistakes may befall others, and that may be a sufficient apology for a larger exposition, but let this suffice.

This righteousness was appointed, is imputed, bestowed by God, and therefore called 'the righteousness of God.'

It is received, applied, made ours by faith, and therefore called 'the righteousness of faith.'

It is inherent in Christ, and was performed by him, and therefore called 'the righteousness of Christ.'

And now a clear way is made to the observation which I intend to insist on, which I shall deliver, and in it the mind of the apostle, and the sweetest mystery of the gospel, in these words:

Obs. Those that know Christ will desire above all things to have the righteousness of Christ; they will count all things loss that they may gain Christ's righteousness; those that will be found in Christ must have his righteousness.

Hence three points must be opened:

1. What is this righteousness of Christ?

2. How we may have it, how it becomes ours?

3. What is the use, what are the advantages of it, what makes it so desirable? and then come to the application.

This doctrine of Christ's righteousness made ours being the principal doctrine of the gospel, and that which Luther called *articulus stantis et cadentis ecclesiæ*, the article which being maintained, the church of Christ stands; being overthrown, the church falls, Satan, the great enemy of the church and gospel, hath set himself by all means to oppose it; he hath raised assaults against it on all sides, some denying it, some obscuring it, some perverting it, some through woeful ignorance and carelessness neglecting it. It is assaulted both on the right hand and on the left, both by seeming friends and open enemies of the gospel.

Therefore it highly concerns all that profess the gospel, all that will walk with a right foot in this principal and most comfortable part thereof, to be fully established in this present truth. And to this end I shall be longer in opening the particulars premised than usual, and yet shall endeavour to make the doctrinal part as practical and useful as may be.

1. First question, What is the righteousness of Christ which we must have?

Ans. 1. It is not his righteousness as God, not his essential righteousness; for that cannot be made man's, but man thereby will be made God.

Ans. 2. It is not his habitual righteousness; that is, those habits of holiness and righteousness wherewith the soul, the human nature of Christ, was endued by the Holy Ghost, by whose secret operation he was conceived.

The reason which sways me (though some be otherwise minded) is this, that righteousness of Christ which is made ours must be performed by Christ for us. But the habitual righteousness of Christ was not his performance for us, but the Holy Ghost's performance in him.

Ans. 3. But it is Christ's actual righteousness; that is, his actual fulfilling the law of God, his perfect obedience thereby.

For righteousness is a conformity to the rule prescribed; this rule is the law of God. This law hath two parts, the precept prescribing duty, the penalty or threatening in case of disobedience.

Now Christ was conformable to the law in both respects, both in doing what was commanded, which is called active righteousness, and his suffering what was threatened for our disobedience, which is called passive righteousness, though less properly.

Hence the effects of a perfect righteousness are sometimes ascribed to his active obedience, Rom. v. 19.

Sometimes to his blood and sufferings; 'By whom redemption,' &c., and Rom. iii. 25. Hence he is said to be 'the end of the law,' Rom. x. 3.

So, then, the righteousness of Christ is his fulfilling the law, by doing and suffering what it required for us. Thus the righteousness which we should have, &c.

2. Second question, How come we to have this righteousness? How can that which is Christ's become ours? In what respects may it be so said, &c.? It concerns believers to be inquisitive about this, because herein depends their title to the richest treasure that ever the Lord vouchsafed to the sons of men.

Ans. 1. In respect of substitution, Christ performed this righteousness in their stead; he performed for believers what they should have performed themselves, and this is properly to do a thing as a substitute, in the stead of another. Christ hath done and suffered for them what they themselves should have done and suffered. He did *succedere in eorum locum*,—he did it in their place.

When Christ is said to die for, to give himself for, &c., his people, the words *ὑπὲρ* and *ἀντὶ* rendered *for them*, the other doth always denote such a substitution, or a doing in their place; *qui utriusque partis vicem apud alterum agit.* Hence those titles given to Christ in Scripture, which speak him a common person, a mediator, one who supplies the place of either part to other. Christ supplies the place of man to God, and the place of God to man, that he might reconcile one to the other.

Now what he doth in the place of sustaining the persons of believers, that passes as though they had done it, as though it was their own performance.

Now when the surety pays a debt instead of the debtor, it stands in law as though it was the debtor's payment. So here, Christ fulfilling the law instead of believers, stands as though they had fulfilled, as though the performance was theirs. Hence that expression Rom. viii. 4: that fulfilling it in our stead, the righteousness of the law is hereby fulfilled in them.

Ans. 2. In respect of acceptation, when what Christ performed for believers is accepted of God as performed for them. If it were not accepted for them, the performance of it in their stead would not be sufficient to make it effectually theirs, but God's acceptation concurring, the righteousness of Christ becomes as much a believer's as that which is done by another can be. Acceptation is that which the Scripture, and our divines, according to Scripture phrase, calls imputation.

There is indeed, through the heat of contention, a great dust raised about this word, so as an ordinary Christian can scarce clearly see what it is, though it be of great consequence to apprehend it clearly.

I shall give you an account of it in these few and plain words, obvious to the meanest capacity.

Then doth God impute the righteousness of Christ to a believer, when he accepts of what Christ performed for him, as though he had performed it (not as having performed, but as though he had), as we say; then the creditor imputes the payment of a debt to the debtor, when he accepts of what the surety paid for him, as though the debtor himself paid it.

Answerably Christ is called the Surety, Heb. vii. 22. Our sins are called debts, sinners are the debtors, the law is the creditor: then doth the Lord impute the righteousness or satisfaction of Christ to a sinner, when he accepts of what Christ performed for the sinner in a way of satisfaction, as though the sinner himself had performed it.

And by the light of this familiar simile a mean capacity may see a clear answer to the greatest objections brought against Christ's righteousness imputed. To instance,

(1.) If Christ's righteousness be ours, imputed to us, then we are saviours, we are mediators, as having a Saviour's, a Mediator's righteousness; and so Bellarmine.

But hence it appears he may as well argue the debtor is the surety, because his surety's payment is accepted for him.

(2.) If Christ's righteousness be ours, then we are as righteous as Christ; so Bellarmine.

Ans. He might as well argue, the bankrupt is as rich as his surety, because his surety pays his debts.

(3.) If Christ's fulfilling of the law be ours, then we need not fulfil it; no need of our repentance or obedience; so some among us.

Ans. It is true, we need not fulfil it for those ends for which Christ fulfilled it, viz., to satisfy justice, to purchase heaven, &c.

But in other respects it doth no more follow that we should not endeavour after repentance and obedience, because of Christ's fulfilling the law for us, than it follows from the surety's paying, the debtor needs express no thankfulness to the surety, nor sorrow for unnecessary contracting that debt, or diligence in his calling for the future. You see here the unreasonableness of what can be objected against this doctrine. Indeed, taking imputation in the sense fore-expressed, and none that acknowledge Christ's satisfaction, can with any colour of reason deny the imputation of his righteousness. However, the Scripture is clear. Rom. iv. 6, This righteousness can be no other than the righteousness of Christ, as aforesaid. As Adam's first disobedience is ours, to make us sinners, so is Christ's obedience ours (if believers) to make us righteous; but his first disobedience was ours only by imputation, and no otherwise doth it make us sinners; so Christ's obedience is ours by imputation, 2 Cor. v. 21. Christ's righteousness is ours, as our sin was his; but our sin was his only by imputation, *ergo* his righteousness is ours by imputation, or that which is all one, by acceptation. That is the second way.

Ans. 3. In respect of participation. The benefits and blessed advantages of it, as if it were ours; so we have it equivalent, as much benefit by it as though it were ours never so much: That leads me to the

3. Third query, Of what use is the righteousness of Christ? What are the advantages of it, that it should be so desirable? What gain we by it, that we should lose all for it? Why come out of all, to be found in it?

Ans. I shall be the larger in shewing the usefulness, the blessed advantages of this righteousness, that Christ and his righteousness may not be so much neglected, as he is too much, not only by the men of the world, but even by such as have interest in him.

That you may learn to esteem, highly prize and value this righteousness of Christ, see it desirable above all things, and apprehend the necessity of it, not only at first conversion, but every moment of our lives; not only in respect of these great concernments of soul, pardon, acceptance, and salvation, wherein the need of it is obvious, but also in every occurrence, every enjoyment, every undertaking.

Now this usefulness, necessity, advantageousness of Christ's righteousness, will be evident in many respects. We will reduce them to ten heads.

First, In respect of sin. By the righteousness of Christ, believers have the pardon of sin, and power against it: pardon of sin, continuance of pardon, sense of pardon; pardon by this righteousness performed, continuance of it by this righteousness presented, sense of it by this righteousness applied.

A sinner, whose conscience the Lord hath in mercy touched, awakened (as for secure sinners, they little regard Christ or his righteousness, or pardon by it), will be apt to say, Can, will the Lord pardon my sins,—mine, that are so many, so grievous, by which the Lord hath been so highly provoked, so exceedingly dishonoured? Against so much light, such means, such mercies, sins of such a deep die, so heavily aggravated, that cry so loud for vengeance? Can the Lord, or will he, pardon such sins, such a sinner?

Why, no; till he hath received a ransom, till his law and his justice be satisfied, the truth and justice of God will not permit him to pardon any sin; but when through the righteousness of Christ his law and justice is satisfied, then it is no more for the Lord to pardon them (though all the sins of all the elect from the beginning of the world were thine), than it is for a creditor to cease his suit against a debtor, when his surety hath fully discharged the debt. Christ's righteousness is the price of pardon, that which purchased it: Eph. i. 7, 'In whom we have redemption,' &c. Redemption is freedom procured by a price paid, remission of sins is freedom from guilt, and the price by which it was procured is the blood of Christ, his righteousness, his passive obedience; this is the fountain where alone guilty souls can be cleansed, though sins be red as scarlet,

Isa. i. 18; it is but 'wash and be clean,' ver. 16; 1 John i. 7, Rev. ii. 5. The righteousness of Christ is expressed by his blood, because that is the cost.

Oh, but though there be pardon through the righteousness of Christ, yet I have sinned since pardon, since conversion. All the love of the Father, of the Son, hath not restrained me from sinning against the sweet expressions of pardoning love, sometimes by apparent evils, dishonouring Christ and my profession itself, continually provoking him by sinful infirmities. The Lord may justly revoke his pardon, he may be weary of forgiving one who multiplies provocations; he may say, I will spare, I will forgive no more. Will the Lord continue to pardon one who doth little else every moment but offend him?

What can support a soul under such sad reasonings? Why, only the righteousness of Christ; this being continually presented by Christ, is the occasion of continued pardon: 1 John ii. 1, Heb. vii. 25, 'Always making intercession.' Now what is his intercession, but the presenting of his righteousness, his will and desire that all his people may be pardoned and saved by virtue of his righteousness? So Rom. viii. 33, 34. Pardon is everlasting, because the virtue of his righteousness is everlasting, Dan. ix. 24. Whenever sin appears, there appears to cover it Christ's righteousness.

Oh, but saith the awakened sinner, though the Lord be so gracious as to pardon, and Christ's righteousness effectual to procure it, yet I want the sense of it; my conscience is still wounding, accusing me, the sting of it continues with pain and anguish in my soul. It is this blood sprinkled, that is, applied to the conscience, that speaks better things, Heb. xii. 24, which speaks peace. By this the heart is sprinkled from an evil conscience, Heb. x. 22, that is, from a guilty, accusing, terrifying conscience.

Oh, but though the Lord hath pardoned me, and given my soul the comfortable sense thereof, yet what will this avail me if I should still continue to provoke and dishonour him, if my lusts still prevail against me? Though the guilt be removed, yet the power and dominion of sin still continues. And, 'O wretched man,' &c., Rom. vii. 24, 25.

Why, there is no deliverance but by virtue of this righteousness, Rom. vi. 14. Under the grace of the gospel, the foundation of which grace is Christ's righteousness.

God had never let out any gracious expressions to the sons of men after sin, had it not been through the interposal of Christ's righteousness: 'In all, we are more than conquerors;' but how? 'through him;' and what we are through him we are through his righteousness.

Secondly, In respect of your persons. Look upon any person as destitute of Christ's righteousness, and he is loathsome, accursed, abhorred, and woefully enslaved, and no redress for any of those miseries but by Christ's righteousness: no such loathsome deformity as sin. Hence in Scripture every soul, by reason of its natural sinfulness and corruption, is as loathsome in the eye of God as a toad or serpent is in our eyes; and how shall such loathsomeness become lovely? How shall such odious creatures be rendered acceptable? Only in Christ, that is, by virtue of his righteousness, Eph. i. 6, 7.

How shall such an unclean, polluted soul, become clean? Only by washing in the fountain of Christ's righteousness, Rev. vii. 14. Every person out of Christ is under the curse, all the curses written in the book of the law are bent against him, Gal. iii. Not only thy sin, but thy person is cursed: 'Cursed is every one.' Nothing in heaven or earth can remove this curse, but only Christ's righteousness, Gal. iii. 13. How was he made a curse, but by being obedient, even to a cursed death.

God is an enemy to every person destitute of Christ's righteousness; he hates him, his wrath is kindled against him, his indignation burns like fire against such a sinner, and will seize on him, and consume him to eternity, if nothing interpose between this wrath and a guilty soul; and nothing can effectually interpose but the righteousness of Christ, nothing can quench this fire but his blood. This enmity between the Lord and a sinner is only abolished by Christ's righteousness, Eph. ii. 15, 16. The Lord would never be reconciled to a sinner but by the mediation of this righteousness; no peace for sinners but by virtue of Christ's undertaking, Col. i. 20–22.

Every person without this is a woeful slave to Satan, a slave to the vilest thing in the world, to his own lust; no redemption from this slavery but by a ransom; no ransom will be accepted but only Christ's righteousness, 1 Peter i. 18, 19.

No way to bring such vile persons into a capacity of being the sons of God, except the Son of God would become a servant, and be made under the law, to fulfil the righteousness of it; and so he did effect it, Gal. iv. 4, 5.

Thus you see the necessity and usefulness of Christ's righteousness as to our persons; without it no acceptance, no redemption, no reconciliation, no adoption.

Thirdly, In respect of graces and qualifications. The very being, the implanting of grace in the soul, is from the righteousness of Christ. No spark of holiness had ever been found, had ever been kindled in the heart of lost man, had it not been procured by this righteousness, Heb. x. 5. Other sacrifices God would not, therefore Christ took a body, that he might become a sacrifice; this was the will of God, ver. 9, and this was Christ's will too: 'By which will,' ver. 10. So Heb. xiii. 12, we owe the very being of sanctification to Christ's righteousness in his blood. We may conclude of the rest of what the apostle speaks of faith, 2 Peter. i. 1. Why so precious, but because the price of it was the invaluable righteousness of Christ; and 'like precious,' because the same price for all, Eph. i. 3. What we have in Christ we have by virtue of his righteousness.

Ay, but when the soul is sanctified, and the principle of spiritual life implanted in it, what need then of Christ's righteousness? Yes, even then in many respects. The gracious heart, sensible of its spiritual condition, apprehensive of the weakness and defects of grace received, will mourn under them, even as worldlings mourn under outward wants and afflictions. Now the spring-head of redress in this case is Christ's righteousness; we owe not only the being, but the means of grace to his righteousness, 2 Peter i. 1. Through God, by the mediation of Christ; as no otherwise doth God multiply any blessings on us.

But to what purpose is grace, or the means of it, if it be not exercised? And no acceptation of it, but by the virtue of this righteousness; for the actings of grace depend upon the influence and operation of Christ's Spirit; and the sending forth of the Spirit was the purchase of Christ's righteousness.

Nay, further, though grace, holiness, be the most excellent accomplishment, yet it is of itself a frail thing, and too weak for the opposition it meets with, if it were not supported with an almighty power; and how is this procured but by the righteousness of Christ? How is this continued, but by his continual presenting of that righteousness in his intercession? This made the apostle confident of his perseverance, Rom. vi. 14, 15, 17.

Thus you see the usefulness of Christ's righteousness in respect of grace, for its being, increase, exercise, perseverance.

Fourthly, In respect of our obedience and services, and that many ways.

1. That we have any power or will to tender any service or obedience unto God, it is from Christ's righteousness; therefore you find obedience and sprinkling of the blood of Jesus joined by the apostle, 1 Peter i. 2. What the apostle saith of prayer, Rom. viii. 26, is true of all other duties. We are so far from being able to perform any duty spiritually, that we do not so much as know how to do it; it is the Spirit that helps our infirmities, and the assistance of the Spirit is the effect of Christ's righteousness, Gal. iii. 14.

2. There are many failings and infirmities, such as are sinful, and cannot appear in the pure eye of God, in our best services. In every act of obedience we offend in many respects, in manner, measure, intention, and other circumstances: 'In many things we offend all.' Now what shall expiate these offences? Why, nothing is effectual but Christ's righteousness. This seems to be typified in the method of the legal service; the daily sacrifice, which was a sacrifice of expiation (to take away guilt), was offered before any of their other oblations. In vain had the rest been offered had not the Lord provided a propitiatory sacrifice, which by virtue of Christ, the Lamb without spot, thereby typified, did expiate the guilt of their other offerings. There is enough in our best sacrifices to condemn us, if the blood of Christ doth not cleanse, if his righteousness do not expiate them.

3. As they cannot be expiated, so they cannot be accepted but through the righteousness of Christ; if our services be not mixed with the incense, they will never ascend to God as the savour of a sweet smell.

Nothing can be well pleasing unto him but through the mediation of Christ, Heb. xiii. 20, 21. Though we do the will of God, and do it impartially in every good work, and do it sincerely, be perfect in doing it, yet will not this be well pleasing in his sight but through Christ, that is, by virtue of his mediation and righteousness.

4. Our services can have no success, no reward, but through and for the righteouness of Christ: 1 Cor. xv., 'End in the Lord;' that is, in respect of the Lord Christ; 'through whom,' he saith, ver. 57, 'we have the victory.' Were it not in respect of him and his righteousness, all our labour would be without success, without reward; though we abounded in the work of the Lord, yet would it be in vain, but that through Christ's righteousness he vouchsafes both blessed success and gracious reward.

Fifthly, In respect of the covenant of grace. The Lord hath not, will not shew himself merciful and gracious to the sons of men, but in a way of covenant.

All the favours and special blessings he vouchsafes to his people, are conveyed this way. That therefore to which the covenant owes its being, is that to which we owe all the blessings of this life, and that which is to come; and this is the righteousness of Christ, for the foundation of, admission into, the confirmation and perpetuity of this covenant is from Christ's righteousness.

1. It is the foundation of the covenant of grace. The Lord had never more made any covenant with fallen man, had it not been through the

mediation of Christ's righteousness. And here Christ is called 'the mediator of the covenant,' Heb. xii. 24. The Lord having in the first covenant promised life eternal to man and his posterity, upon condition of obedience, man breaking this covenant, and dealing unfaithfully with God, exposed himself and his to eternal death, which was the penalty thereof; and eternal death we all had suffered, nor could the Lord in justice admit of any new covenant, without satisfaction given for man's first treachery and disobedience; till then the truth and justice of God would not suffer him to have anything to do with man in a way of mercy, such as the covenant offers.

Man thus lying under the curse and sentence of eternal death, as utterly unable to make satisfaction for the dishonour he had done God, in breaking covenant made with him upon such advantageous terms, oh, Christ here interposes and offers, if lost man might be again received into favour, and have terms of mercy and reconciliation offered in another covenant, he would undertake and satisfy offended justice for man's disobedience and treachery, for the unfaithfulness of all that believe. That he may not die eternally (saith Christ), I am willing in him to die for him; and for his obedience, the condition of life eternal, since he can never perform it, I will perform it for him; let my life go for his, and my obedience satisfy for his disobedience, I engage myself to do and suffer what justice and the law requires of him, so that he may be admitted to mercy in a covenant of grace.

Hereupon the Lord, through the mediation of Christ and his righteousness, condescends to make a new covenant. The covenant of grace and salvation, it was made through this mediation of Christ. He is called often the Mediator of the covenant, Heb. viii. 6, and ix. 15.

So that of the apostle may be taken, Gal. iii. 20.

Man was before his sin as one with God, joined in league, in covenant with him, no need then of a mediator. But sin set them at variance, raised dissension between them, and they could never be reconciled but by the interposal of a mediator. Christ was this mediator, who by his righteousness satisfied the offended God, brought God and man again together, and joined them in a league and covenant. So that you see the righteousness of Christ is the foundation of the covenant of grace, Christ hereby is all in all in the new covenant. Hence he is called the covenant, Isa. xlii. 6, and xlix. 8.

2. Admission into covenant is by virtue of Christ's righteousness, Isa. liii. 10. Christ in performing this righteousness was 'a man of sorrows,' and his sorrows were *dolores parturientis*, the sorrows of one in travail, verse 11. The issue of his travail was the children of the covenant. We have the expression, Acts iii. 25, 'children of promise,' Rom. viii. 9, Gal. iv. 28.

Now, how comes it to pass that Christ had such a seed, such a numerous issue, that so many became children of the covenant? The prophet tells, 'When thou shalt make,' &c. If he had not made his soul an offering for sin, that is, performed this righteousness, he had never seen this seed, none of the sons of men had been admitted into covenant. If thou and I be in the covenant of grace, if we be impaled in the bonds of grace and saving mercy, and so separated from the lost world, who are 'strangers from the covenant of promise, having no hope, and without God,' &c., Eph. ii. 12, it is for the righteousness of Christ, it is because he made his soul an offering for sin.

3. The confirmation of the covenant is from Christ's righteousness. By

this it is ratified, made sure, therefore Christ is called the surety, Heb. vii. 22. He made it sure on both hands.

On God's part, because by fulfilling righteousness he removes whatever might hinder the Lord from performing the gracious contents of the covenant to believers.

On man's part, hereby procuring whatever the Lord requires on their part in this covenant of grace.

And because it is confirmed by his righteousness, therefore it is called the covenant, the testament in his blood; for it was the custom to make, dedicate, confirm covenants by blood, the blood of sacrifices; see Gen. xv. Hereon, Heb. ix. 18, the covenant of grace under the first administration was dedicated with blood; the ceremony you may see in Exod. xxiv. 6, 8. Moses took half of the blood, and put it in basons, which was so reserved to be sprinkled upon the people. By this blood was signified the blood of Christ, by the virtue whereof the covenant of grace is established between God and his people; and the dividing of this blood (half being sprinkled upon the altar, which did represent God, and half upon the people), signified that the performance of the covenant by both parties, God's favour and grace to his people, and the people's faith and obedience to God, were to be ascribed to the blood, that is, to the righteousness of Christ.

Whence also it is called the testament, Διαθήκη, Heb. vii. 8, 9.

A will or testament is not in force till the death of the testator; it is that which makes it firm and inviolable. So the apostle, Heb. ix. 16, 17. It is the death of Christ (in which his righteousness was completed) which so confirms the covenant as no men nor devils can alter or disannul it, Gal. iii. 15. How was it confirmed? He tells us, verse 17, 'of God in Christ,' and how in Christ but as other testaments are, by his death. This it is which makes it firm and sure, the righteousness of Christ. If thou hast sure covenant, strong consolation in this covenant, it comes from Christ's righteousness, who makes it strong and sure.

4. The perpetuity of the covenant. It is not only made firm and sure for some time, but for ever, by Christ's righteousness. Hence it is called 'the covenant of salt,' 2 Chron xiii. 5. The reason is this, there is a virtue in salt to preserve things from corruption; so that by a covenant of salt is meant a stable, firm, and incorruptible covenant, a covenant of an everlasting continuance. And why it is so, the apostle's expression shews, Heb. xiii. 20, 'an everlasting covenant;' because the blood of Christ, his righteousness, is of everlasting virtue.

Here is the greatest comfort, the strong consolation of God's covenanted people, the covenant between them and God (the great charter of all their peace, hopes, present enjoyments, and future happiness) can never be broken, never violated; all the blessings of it are to continue, not only like Joseph's blessing, 'to the utmost bounds of the everlasting hills,' Gen. xlix. 26, but while the Rock of ages, the Rock of eternity continues, Isa. liv. 10. And why? Verse 14, 'In righteousness shalt thou be established.' It is founded upon that righteousness which is far more durable than the mountains.

It is this that bears up the people of God in all fears and assaults from hell and the world; when they are afflicted and tossed with tempests, here is their anchor both firm and sure, when it enters within the veil, when it fastens on Christ and his righteousness: 'Though the earth be removed, and the mountains, &c., yet the covenant of peace shall not be removed.'

It is true, Satan is a mortal enemy to this union between God and man in a way of covenant. It torments that envious, malicious spirit, to see man, made far lower than himself at first, now advanced to this glorious privilege of being in league, when himself is cast out. He set himself to break the first covenant, and then prevailed, as the lost sons of men found by woeful experience. That covenant had no such sure foundation, it was quickly broken. And now he employs all his craft, all his stratagems to disannul the covenant of grace. And why don't the gates of hell prevail against it? Why, it is founded upon a rock, upon Christ, upon his righteousness.

Besides, such is the weakness, the sinfulness, the unfaithfulness, the unstedfastness of the best that are now in covenant with God, such are their provocations, as the Lord might justly break with them, even with them that are most observant of covenant terms.

Nay, if there were nothing to continue the best of us in covenant but the observance of what the Lord therein requires of us, there would certainly be a breach; the holy and wise God must needs cast us out. What is it then that keeps the Lord and his people together, notwithstanding his justice and holiness, notwithstanding their backsliding and unfaithfulness? Why, it is Christ's righteousness only, this is the foundation of it which can never be shaken; take away this, and the covenant of grace, with all the hopes and happiness of believers, fall to the ground. But this continuing, by virtue of it the Lord is satisfied, reconciled, when he is angry, and ready to break with us; by virtue of this our revolting hearts are again turned unto the Lord, and our treacherous declinings pardoned; otherwise there would be no peace, no league, no covenant between the Lord and such creatures, no, not the least moment.

Doth not this affect your hearts (ye that believe), that the Lord will be your God to everlasting? that those great blessings you have by virtue of the covenant, are everlasting blessings, everlasting forgiveness, Jer. xxxi. 33; and everlasting joy, Isa. xxxv. 10; everlasting salvation, Isa. xlv. 17; everlasting life, John iii. 16; everlasting love, Job xxxi. 3; and everlasting kindness, Isa. liv. 8.

Doth not your hearts leap within you, when the Lord helps you to think on this in secret? Why, then, look to the rock from whence these everlasting blessings are digged, whereon this everlasting covenant is founded: look to the righteousness of Christ. And if this everlasting happiness be dear to you, oh let this endear Christ and his righteousness to you! For therefore are the covenant and its blessings eternal and everlasting, because Christ's redemption is eternal, Heb. ix. 12; because his righteousness is everlasting, Dan. ix.

Sixthly, In respect of the promises: 1. Through Christ's righteousness they are made. 2. By it believers have interest in them. 3. For it they are performed to them.

1. Upon account of Christ's righteousness were all the promises made. The Lord, after the violation of the first covenant, had never made one promise to the sons of men, had it not been through the mediation of Christ's righteousness; all these 'exceeding great and precious promises' (the riches, the treasures of the saints on earth), they were made upon this account, given through Christ, 2 Pet. i. 2–4. To instance in two of the greatest promises, wherein the Scripture is express, the promise of spiritual life, the promise of the Spirit, and the promise of eternal life. For the first, Gal. iii. 13, 14, 'the promise of the Spirit'; that is, of all the graces and comforts, all the light, life, and strength, all the assistances and in-

fluences of the Spirit; this promise, which is the all of the believer in this world, is given and received through Christ. And how through him? The 13th verse shews, viz., by his being made a curse for us, his subjection to the law, and fulfilling the righteousness thereof.

Here is all that concerns spiritual life promised through Christ, and so it is all for eternal life, Heb. ix. 15. It is received by means of death, which being the consummation and completement of Christ's righteousness, is ordinarily put for the whole. Therefore if thou hast ever been refreshed with the sweetness of a gospel promise, as those that are in covenant have one time or other found sweeter refreshment in a promise than in any outward comforts, and while their souls are in good temper, do feed on them with great delight.

If thou hast ever tasted how gracious the Lord is in a gospel promise, then let Christ and his righteousness be dear unto thee; for this is the spring, the fountain from whence all these streams of comfort flow, which are the great refreshment of believers on this side heaven.

2. By Christ's righteousness believers have interest in the promises, both those that are absolute and conditional. Nothing promised becomes due, nor is the Lord engaged to perform any promise, but by the mediation of Christ's righteousness.

This is evident in absolute promises, such as that of the first grace, Ezek. xi. 19, 20, chap. xxxvi. 25, 26. Now before this promise be performed, who can challenge interest in it? There is no qualification expressed to a promise, to one more than another. To whom then is it due? Why, only to those who are given to Christ, and for whom he hath given himself; only to those for whom he hath satisfied the law and justice, by fulfilling the righteousness required of him. To such only are these promises due; and hereby it is apparent it is Christ's righteousness which makes them due.

It is clear also in conditional promises; and let it be the more carefully observed, because herein is an ordinary mistake, not only of vulgar Christians, but of those who have their senses exercised to discern between truth and error. It is taken for granted, that the mercy promised is due, and the Lord engaged to perform the promise, when the condition or qualification annexed to the promise is in sincerity performed. *Ex. gr.*, Since God hath promised to save those that believe, and pardon those that repent, it is concluded, when a man believes, salvation is due to him; when he repents, the Lord is engaged to pardon him, without looking further than those conditions, to that without which no mercy promised can be due, nor any promise engaging. It is true, he that truly believes shall be saved, and he that truly repents shall be pardoned; but these mercies are not due merely upon our believing and repenting, but upon another account.

I clear it thus: there are many sinful defects and imperfections in the faith and repentance of the best, and there is a curse due to every sin, even to every wilful imperfection, Gal. iii. The wilful defects of these qualifications are under a threatening. Now, both a blessing and a curse cannot be at once due to the same person, the Lord cannot be under two contrary engagements, both of a promise and a threatening, to the same person, at the same time. Therefore, though a man repent and believe, yet the mercies promised cannot be due to him, unless the curse due to the sinful imperfections of his faith and repentance be removed. Now it is Christ's righteousness alone that removes the curse, that takes off the threatening; and therefore it is his righteousness (not our qualifications, faith, repentance, holiness, obedience, considered in themselves merely), that gives us right to the mercies promised; without this, even all those gracious qualifications would leave us under the curse; so far are they from making the promise due, or engaging the Lord to bestow it.

This deserves further enlargement, but I leave it to your own thoughts; the clear apprehension of it would clearly discover to you the freeness of grace in the promises, the worthlessness of man's best righteousness, and exceedingly endear the righteousness of Christ to us. There is no interest, no right to the promise, but through Christ's righteousness.

3. It is for Christ's righteousness that any promise is performed: 2 Cor. i. 20, 'In him,' in him as mediator, and so by virtue of his righteousness, 'are yea,' &c. *Yea* always; not sometimes *yea* and sometimes *nay*, but always *yea*: there is constancy; *and amen:* there is faithfulness. In him, through his mediation, the Lord will constantly and faithfully perform his promises to all believers.

Indeed, if a wicked man, a worldling, &c., comes and inquires at these oracles, if he ask, as she of Jehu, 'Is it peace?' shall I have peace with God? will he pardon me? will he save me? the answer to him will be negative, not *yea* but *nay;* no peace, no pardon, &c. And why so? Because he that lives in sin is out of Christ, hath no interest in his righteousness; 'but every one that nameth the name of Christ departs from iniquity,' 2 Tim. ii. 19.

But let a believer come, one who hath given up himself to Christ in a way of faith and gospel obedience; let him inquire, Shall I have peace, grace, life, glory? the answer will be then affirmative, the promise to him is *yea;* and it is so constantly, 'it is yea and amen,' the Lord will be faithful in performing promise. The righteousness of Christ engages the truth and faithfulness of God to the performance of every tittle: 'Heaven and earth shall pass away, before,' &c.

If thou hast had experience of the accomplishment of promises, thou owest this to Christ's righteousness; if thou expectest the performance of any promise, thou must depend upon Christ and his righteousness for it.

That the promises are given, that we have interest in them, that they are performed to us, all must be ascribed to Christ's righteousness.

Seventhly, In respect of the law; and that in reference to all its parts, the precept, the threatening, the promise.

1. In regard of the *precept.* This requires perfect obedience, and that universally, in all things, of all persons, at all times.

It requires perfection both inward and outward, both perfect holiness of heart and perfect acts of lives, and that both for parts and degrees; a perfect observance of every precept, and that in the highest degree. It is not a good intention or meaning, or a sincere resolution, nor a conscionable endeavour, nor a bewailing of imperfections and failings, that will satisfy the demands of God's righteous law. That calls for absolute perfection, and that from all persons, both regenerate and unregenerate, both of those that are in the covenant of grace, and those that are under the covenant of works, and this always, from the moment of man's creation to eternity. This is essential to him while he is a reasonable creature, to be perfectly subject to God as creator; and being essential to him while he is a reasonable creature, he cannot be freed by any dispensation from his obligation to perfect obedience.

Well then, when the Lord comes to demand what is due to him, when he calls for such obedience as we owe him, alas! what can we answer him?

He requires that every act of our hearts and lives should be perfectly holy; and there is not one act since we had a being that comes near what he requires, though at first we had power to do it. We owe him an hundred thousand talents, and we cannot bring him the value of one farthing upon the account of perfection. Where then shall the best of us appear? what shall we plead? or how shall we satisfy his righteous demands? Why, if Christ's perfect obedience be not accepted, if his righteousness doth not here satisfy for us, we are utterly cast, we are eternally lost, as will appear further in the second.

2. In regard of the *threatening:* 'In the day thou sinnest, thou shalt die.' Death is the wages of every sin, death temporal and eternal. The law entails the curse of God upon every sinner, and exposes him to the everlasting wrath of the almighty and eternal God, Gal. iii. 10. Secure sinners, though under the heaviest part of this curse, weigh it no more than the wind.

But one who is under the spirit of bondage, as all must be more or less before they receive the spirit of adoption, will hear those words as thunder and lightning from the presence of an incensed God; they will smite his soul with trembling and affrightment. Alas! is the curse and his eternal wrath due to every sin? Oh then, how woeful is my condition! What wrath is due to me, who am guilty of more sins than I have lived hours, moments in the world! Oh how shall my soul bear the burthen of that wrath that is heavier than the hills and mountains, and will sink me into the lower hell! Oh how shall I abide with devouring fire! how shall I dwell with everlasting burnings!

Why, there is no remedy, saith the word, nothing but curse, and wrath, and hell for thee, for any sinner, except the Lord's justice be satisfied; and there is nothing will satisfy him but a righteousness of infinite value, nothing but the righteousness of Christ. Get interest in this. Christ's righteousness must be fully imputed to thee, or else wrath and hell must be thy portion for ever. This method the Lord ordinarily uses to awaken secure sinners, to bring them unto Christ; therefore the law is called the schoolmaster, Gal. iii. 24; and happy that apprehension of wrath that is thus effectual.

Here is the usefulness of Christ's righteousness. No sinner in the world ever was, or ever shall be, freed from the wrath of God and curse of the law, but by the virtue of this righteousness.

3. In regard of the *promise* of the law, 'Do this and live,' that is, perform perfect obedience, and thou shalt have eternal life. This perfect obedience was the way to life under the law, and if the gospel shew not another righteousness, it is the way still.

Now Christ, when he was interpreting the law, tells us, 'One jot or tittle shall in nowise pass from the law till all be fulfilled.' So that unless perfect obedience be fulfilled, it seems there is no life to be had under the gospel, Mat. v. 17. Nay, the apostle, when he is proving justification by faith only, which seems quite to repeal the law in this point, Rom. iii. 28, answers this very objection: ver. 31, 'Do we then make void the law through faith? God forbid,' saith he; 'yea, we establish the law.' So that it seems the way to heaven by perfect obedience, which the law prescribed, is not contradicted by the gospel, but established. No eternal life now without perfect obedience. But you will say, Alas! if it be so, then no flesh shall be saved, for perfect obedience in man's fallen estate is impossible. See here then the necessity of Christ's righteousness. It is indeed impossible for man, though a believer, but not impossible for his surety, Christ; so the apostle tells us, Rom. viii. 3, 4, 'What the law could not do,' &c. The law could not bring any to life, because of man's inability to satisfy its demands. Christ was able to do it, and he did it, performed all that the law requires, 'in the likeness of sinful flesh, that the righteousness of the law,' ver. 4, that we, being unable to fulfil it ourselves, might have it fulfilled in us. So that the gospel doth not contradict the law, but favourably expounds it. Whereas it might be taken thus, Do this in person, and live, the gospel expounds it thus favourably, Do this (if not by thyself, yet) by thy Surety, and thou shalt live. So that the doctrine of the gospel is not contrary, but subservient to the law.

The righteousness of Christ turns the law into gospel to a believer, and of a doctrine full of dread and terror, renders it the most acceptable message that ever was brought to the world. The law, which stands as the angel with a flaming sword, to bar all flesh out of paradise, when the righteousness of Christ is applied, it becomes an angel to carry every believer into Abraham's bosom; Christ's righteousness added, it loses its name, and we call it gospel. The way in both seems to be the same for substance; perfect obedience is requisite in both. They differ in the circumstances of the person performing this obedience. In the law it was to be personal, in the gospel his surety's performance is sufficient.

However, if there be any terror, dread in the law, Christ's righteousness removes it; if any grace, comfort in the gospel, Christ's righteousness is the rise of it. Take away Christ's righteousness, and the gospel can give no life; take it away, and the law speaks nothing but death; no life, no hope of life without it, either in law or gospel.

Eighthly, In respect of the ordinances. The enjoyment of them, the sanctifying of them, the presence of God in them, and the efficacy of them, are for and from the righteousness of Christ.

1. The *enjoyment* of ordinances: they are the gift of Christ, the purchase of his righteousness, 2 Pet. i. 3. All things that pertain to godliness are given through the knowledge of Christ; that is, through faith in him, faith that lays hold on his righteousness, particularly the seals of the covenant; they are the signs of the New Testament in his blood; the ministry of the word, the great ordinance for the begetting and increasing of godliness. This is the purchase, the gift of Christ, Eph. iv. 8, 11. These are the gifts of his triumph, and what he gave in his exaltation he purchased by his humiliation. The apostle ascribes both his office and ability to execute it unto Christ, Rom. i. 5.

2. The *sanctifying* of the ordinances is from Christ's righteousness, by virtue of his blood. So polluted are we by sin, and such is the defilement of sin within us, that everything we touch, or meddle with, or make use of (even the holy institutions of God not excepted) are unclean unto us, except the blood of Jesus makes them clean to us, and makes us clean in the use of them. To signify this, the Lord prescribed in the law that 'almost all things should be purged by blood,' Heb. ix. 22. 'Both the book and the people, both the tabernacle and all the vessels of the ministry, were sprinkled with blood,' ver. 19, 21; sprinkled with blood, that they might be purged, whereby was typified the virtue of Christ's blood to sanctify not only our persons, but also the ordinances we make use of.

And therefore, when we go to the ordinances, we should be apprehensive of a necessity of Christ's righteousness in the use of them; look up to the blood of sprinkling for its sanctifying virtue to remove that defilement, whereby we pollute the ordinances, whereby they become unholy, unhallowed, unclean to us; else nothing is pure, nothing sanctified to our use.

3. The *presence* of God in the ordinances is only vouchsafed through his righteousness. The presence of God, which is the life and comfort of them, cannot be enjoyed but in and through Christ, the mediation of his righteousness. A sinner cannot draw near to God, nor will the Lord draw near to him, till he be found in Christ's righteousness. He is a consuming fire to a sinner out of Christ, he beholds him afar off, he cannot endure to come near him, not in the use of his own ordinances, where he draws nearest to his people, nor can a sinner draw near to God. Those that are out of Christ have no interest in his righteousness; they are far off when they seem to draw near unto God; there is no access to him but in the blood of Jesus, Eph. ii. 13. While without Christ, they were not only without God in the world, but without God in his ordinances; they were always strangers, God took no notice of them, but now in Christ Jesus, &c., through him only they have access, Eph. ii. 18, 19. The Lord will converse with them as a man with his friend, his familiar, he will use them as children, as friends, they are then the household of God. But it is in Christ's mediation, of his righteousness; he saith to us, as Joseph to his brethren, Gen. xliii. 5, 'Ye shall not see my face, except your brother be with you;' no seeing God's face, except Benjamin, except Christ, the Son of his right hand, the Son of his love, be with us, and we in him. If ever thou hast seen the face of God in his ordinances, if he ever have vouchsafed himself, if ever he hath unveiled himself and caused his glory to pass before thee, if ever thou hast seen light in his countenance, that light which is better, sweeter than life, it must be ascribed to his righteousness; if ever thou expectest the comfortable, enhappying manifestations of God to thy soul, thou must depend on Christ and his righteousness for it.

4. The *efficacy* of the ordinances is from Christ's righteousness; all the spiritual use and strength, all the peace and comfort, all the growth and fruitfulness, all the light and heavenly refreshments, all the blessings and blessed advantages found in any or all the ordinances, flow from this fountain, that are effectual for the perfecting of the saints, for the edifying of the body of Christ, &c. It is the gift of Christ, Eph. iv. 12, 13.

No blessing can be expected from God, except we come as Jacob, in the garment of our Elder Brother, except we be found in Christ's righteousness; if the Lord hath made the word effectual to turn thee from darkness to light, to convince, enlighten, comfort, quicken, strengthen, encourage thee, &c.; if he hath made thee joyful in the house of prayer, satisfied thy soul with marrow and fatness, made the Sabbath thy delight, a day of refreshment from his presence; if in the use of ordinances thy secure conscience hath been awakened, blind eyes opened, hard heart melted, cold affections inflamed, thy soul raised to a spiritual and heavenly temper.

Ninthly, In respect of outward enjoyments. By Christ's righteousness believers have a spiritual right to a comfortable use of spiritual advantages by, and sincere improvement of, these temporal enjoyments.

1. A spiritual right to them. Another kind of right than unbelievers have; those that are strangers to Christ may have a civil right to what they lawfully obtain and enjoy, and such a right as is grounded on the laws of men; and so far as the Lord approves of these laws, so far they have them by divine approbation, and he approves of laws tending to the good of mankind. A civil right they have; but no spiritual, evangelical right,

for that is grounded upon the covenant of grace, which hath its being from Christ's righteousness.

Now believers, who have interest in the righteousness of Christ, have hereby a spiritual right to temporal blessings; they have them *jure promissionis:* 'Godliness hath the promise,' 1 Tim. i. 8; it hath the promise, and all the promises are in Christ *yea. Jure donationis:* 2 Pet. i. 3; 1 Tim. vi. 17; 'Through the knowledge of Christ,' ver. 2. *Jure emptionis:* Christ hath purchased these for them, his righteousness was the price, 2 Cor. viii. 9; though it be true of spiritual riches, yet the context leads us here to include outward enjoyments; and the same warrant we have to understand Philip. iv. 19.

Christ is the heir of all things, and none can come to this spiritual right but by being found in him; and those who are found in him hold their enjoyments *in capite*, their right is derived from their head, Christ. Hence, 1 Cor. iii. 22, 23, 'If you be in Christ,' he yours (for the interest is mutual), then 'all is yours,' by the best, the noblest, the surest title under heaven.

Besides, wicked men, by their treason and rebellion against the Lord and his Christ, have forfeited all they enjoy, and deserve to be deprived of all temporal enjoyments; the Lord may most justly (though men cannot) take his forfeiture.

You will say, the best have forfeited all and deserve to enjoy nothing. It is true, but observe a vast difference herein, even believers have forfeited, but the ground of the forfeiture is removed; their sin is pardoned, and satisfaction made by the righteousness of Christ, which is a just stop to the seizure; so that it is a righteous thing with the Lord to continue them in the enjoyment of all things good for them. Why? They have forfeited, but Christ hath satisfied; they have lost all, but Christ's righteousness hath purchased all good things for them, Rom. viii. 32. How shall he not for him give us all things, who gave himself for us, that all things might be freely given us.

2. Comfortable enjoyment. Strangers to Christ have the use of these things, but cannot be properly said to have the enjoyment; they seem to be masters of them, but indeed they are servants to them; possessors as to outward use, but slaves as to their inward affections; they serve them while they seem to dispose of them; they do not *dominari*, but *servire;* have not the command of, but are enslaved.

Nor is their use truly comfortable; they may fancy comfort, but their comfort is but a fancy; it flows from another fountain than can be digged in earth; true, solid comfort is the portion of those only who have the righteousness of Christ for their portion.

These may look upon every temporal enjoyment as a token of everlasting love, as a pledge and earnest of eternal glory; and both these, because they may receive them as the purchase of the blood (of the righteousness) of Christ; ay, here is the well-spring of comfort, the fountain of that comfort which is better than life. Oh what comfort is it to taste the sweetness of Christ's love in every enjoyment! when we can say, 'Christ loved me, and gave himself for me,' that I might enjoy these blessings! Oh how will this raise the value of every common mercy! Christ's righteousness which was performed, the highest expression of his love, purchased this for me!

Upon this account is that of the psalmist true, Ps. xxxvii. 15; he that hath but food and raiment, hath in this respect more than he that hath the Turkish empire, or the gold of the Indies; he hath more ground of comfort in his little than they in all.

Alas, what comfort can they take in any enjoyment if they are but apprehensive of their condition; the fatter their pastures are, the fatter will they be fed for slaughter.

What pleasure will a malefactor take in the things that continue his life till the day of execution?

He that is not in Christ is condemned already; for anything thou knowest, this day shall thy soul, thy life, be taken from thee; and then whose shall these things be? what comfort in them?

No comfortable enjoyment of the chiefest outward comforts, without interest in Christ's righteousness.

3. Spiritual advantage. Strangers to Christ seldom use these things lawfully, much less spiritually; and where there is no spiritual use of them, there can be no spiritual advantage by them; if the Lord hath made a distinction between thee and others in the use and improving of these things that are common, so that thou canst reap spiritual advantage from temporal enjoyments, even this must be ascribed to Christ's righteousness.

If they are as cords to draw thy heart up to God and tie thee to him; if they endear Christ to thy soul, and engage thee more to love him; if these drops make thee thirst after the fountain, where there is more sweetness, in much more abundance; if they raise thy esteem of heavenly enjoyments as more valuable; if they provoke thy zeal for his honour, who gives thee experience of the riches of his bounty; if they strengthen thy faith to expect greater things from him, who will not let thee want the less; if they engage thee to lay them out, to improve them as a good steward, for the honour, for the service of him who entrusts thee with them; if they encourage thee to serve him with cheerfulness and gladness of heart in abundance of all good things; if the Lord bless them to thee so as thy soul prospers the more for this outward prosperity;—if thou gettest these or other spiritual advantages by them, without which they are not blessings, even this thou owest to Christ's righteousnsss; for when temporal enjoyments are thus spiritually improved, their property is altered; they are in effect spiritual blessings, and such wherewith we are only blessed in Christ, Eph. i.

4. Secure improvement. If you improve them so as to avoid the snares which Satan conveys into every outward comfort. Since sin entered into the world, all the things of the world are full of snares; whatever we use, whatever we see, nay, what we do but imagine, though we neither see nor enjoy it, is apt to ensnare us.

There are snares in our beds, snares on our tables, snares in company, snares in solitariness, snares in riches, credit, pleasures; everything apt to entangle us in sin, pride, security, licentiousness, neglect of God, our souls, eternity, &c.

Those that are strangers to Christ lie miserably entangled in these snares; so they live, die, perish. Hence these outward things prove not blessings but curses to them, as the Lord threatens, Mal. ii. 2.

Now if any of you escape these snares, if you have been delivered out of them, if you do not perish in them, this must be ascribed to Christ's righteousness, Gal. i. 4. Why is it evil? because it is so full of sin, so full of snares. How are we delivered from it? by Christ's giving himself for our sins; that is, by Christ's performing this righteousness for us. The Lamb's company, Rev. xiv., are said to be redeemed from the earth, ver. 3, that is, the defilements of the earth, ver. 4; to redeem is to deliver by payment of a ransom; so are we delivered, and the ransom is the blood of the Lamb, the righteousness of Christ.

Tenthly, In respect of afflictions and death, upon divers accounts:

1. Those afflictions which befall believers are not punishments, it is to be ascribed to the righteousness of Christ. A sweet privilege, &c. That is a punishment which is inflicted for the satisfaction of justice. A father corrects his child, not to satisfy the law, which is the intent of a judge. Under this dreadful notion must those that are excluded from Christ's righteousness receive their sufferings, they are inflicted by a Judge for satisfaction of offended justice; and because they can never fully satisfy, they must ever suffer, sometimes here, always hereafter; but he that is found in Christ's righteousness, shall never be found under the stroke of punishment. Whatever he suffers there is no revenge in it, no intention thereby to seek satisfaction; the sting of affliction is gone, the bitterness of death is past, Christ's righteousness hath disarmed, hath sweetened, the sharpest sufferings; the Lord requires no satisfaction of them, and therefore he inflicts no punishment on them. And why? Because the righteousness of Christ hath fully satisfied offended justice on their behalf, and it is not agreeable to justice to demand satisfaction twice; and when the Surety hath fully satisfied for the offence, he will not require satisfaction also of the offender, Isa. liii. 5.

The sufferings of believers are not to wound, but to heal them; when this Head hath been wounded even to satisfaction, he will not wound the members also. On that account their afflictions are the chastisements of a father, not the revenges of a judge; to reclaim the offender, not to satisfy for the offence. Christ's righteousness hath done that in abundance, nothing now can be laid to their charge; no ground of punishment, since all their sins have been punished in Christ, ver. 6.

A believer may say upon another account as Christ did, John xviii. 11, It is but a cup, and it is a Father's cup; how bitter soever it seems, it was love that mingled it; and it is given me, it is a gift, a pledge of love, the gift of a friend, of a father; not the wounds of a judge, of an enemy. It is not a deadly potion, as given to a malefactor who is sentenced to death, and must die to satisfy law and justice. Christ took this cup out of my hand, and drank it up all in my stead, even the dregs of it; though the bitterness of punishment, of penal, cursed death, was in it, he left not a drop of this nature for me to drink.

That which is reserved for me is a draught of physic, a medicinal potion; how bitter, how distasteful soever it seems, the design of it is health and life. From Christ's righteousness it is that the most afflicted condition of a believer is more happy, more desirable than the most prosperous estate of the ungodly; affliction is with the people of God to be chosen rather than the pleasures of sin. The bitterest things that befall Christ's people are more desirous* than the sweetest enjoyments of sinners, the very pleasures of sin. Oh the wonderful virtue of Christ's righteousness! were it not for this, every suffering would be a foretaste of hell, and the first-fruits of eternal sufferings, a spark of those everlastings burnings. The sufferings of finite unbelievers on earth, and the sufferings of the damned in hell, differ but in degrees; they agree in common nature of punishments, both for satisfaction of revenging justice. If thou beest not in the same condition, if thy sufferings are not the beginnings of hell on earth, it is because of Christ's righteousness.

* Qu. 'desirable'?—ED.

2. Hence it is also that the sufferings of believers are mitigated; the Lord inflicts nothing but in that proportion which he knows is best for them, Isa. xxvii. 7, 8.

If Christ's righteousness be thine, no reason to fear the bitterness of sufferings, he will not put one drop into thy cup, but what is necessary for thy soul's health; no other end but this, or what may be assigned to this.

No reason to fear his hand will lie too heavy on thee; thou shalt not feel one stroke, one scourge more than what will tend to cure thee.

No reason to fear the king of terrors, the dreadfulness of the last enemy; thou shalt not endure one pang more in thy last agony but what will tend to thy good. Why so?

It is hard to believe this, faith hath need of some ground to support it. Why, here is the reason: if the Lord should inflict more than what is good for thee, it would savour of revenge; but Christ's righteousness hath left no place for revenge, revenging justice did satisfy itself fully upon Christ, while he performed this righteousness; if this be thine, it hath left nothing for thee but mercy and love; this shall be the portion of thy cup, even when it seems most bitter; that deadly mixture and wrath he drank himself.

3. The blessed fruits of afflictions are from Christ's righteousness. If this be thine, thou shalt want nothing but what thy soul would be a loser if it did not want it, thou shalt suffer nothing but it would be far worse for thee if thou didst not suffer it.

Wonderful things are spoken in Scripture of the happy issue of sanctified afflictions. It is a riddle indeed to flesh and blood, such as Samson's to the Philistines: 'Out of the strong comes forth sweetness;' and honey is found in the carcass of devouring afflictions. You will never expound this but by consideration of the righteousness of Christ, of whom Samson was a type. It is this that sweetens the water of Marah; like Elisha's salt, so heals them as there remains no more death nor barrenness in them, 2 Kings ii. 21. If thou hast had David's experience, and canst say ——. And if by this thy iniquity hath been purged, thy heart estranged from the world, learned to love the appearance of Christ, if hereby thou art made partaker of his holiness, if they have brought forth in thee the peaceable fruits of righteousness, even these are the fruits of Christ's righteousness, who having answered all other ends of such sad dispensations by his own sufferings, hath left no other end why his people should suffer, but that their souls might thereby prosper; no other end but this, or what may be reduced to this. You may see other effects of suffering in others: Rev. xvi. 9, 11, 'Men were scorched with great heat, and blasphemed the name of God: and they repented not to give him glory.' Who were these? They were the enemies of Christ; though they seemed to profess him, had no share in his righteousness, and so had no better issue of their sufferings.

4. Strength to bear afflictions. Support under sufferings is from Christ's righteousness: Philip. iv. 13, 'I can do all things through Christ which strengthens me;' this doing includes both acting and suffering, as appears, ver. 12. Strength to bear up in every condition is through Christ, and we have nothing through Christ but by virtue of his righteousness. That believers can suffer with patient submission, with contentedness, comfort, and courage, as becomes the dependents of Christ, it is from his righteousness.

Not only strength to suffer, but to conquer in suffering, is from Christ, as Rom. viii. 37. 'In all these things,' see what they are, ver. 35. When they seemed to be killed, they conquered, and triumph when they are led as sheep to the slaughter, ver. 36. Hell, and death, the king of terrors, and the thrones of darkness, the devouring lion Satan, and the raging world of persecutors, are under the feet of believers, while they seem to be oppressed by them; they do more than conquer when they seem to be captives. And how comes this to pass? He tells us: 'Through him,' &c.; and therefore through that which was the highest expression of his love, the fulfilling this righteousness for us, this is it which raises a believer even in his lowest condition above the height of a triumph, makes him more than conqueror.

Thus I have at large shewed you the usefulness of Christ's righteousness upon a manifold account, so that you can scarce meet with or think of anything in this world or the other but may endear the righteousness of Christ to you, provoke you highly to esteem and demonstrate the necessity of it.

The *uses* are,

First, Of confutation and reproof. If it be so, as hath been declared, here is a just reproof of those who profess they know Christ, yet neglect, oppose, deny his righteousness. It is strange that any who enjoy the gospel should be herein guilty, but this shews the woeful depravation of man's mind since the fall. Such is the corruption of it, as rather than it will yield to the revealed truths (when they cross the interests of men, and their pre-engaged apprehensions), men will deprive themselves of the richest treasure which ever the Lord discovered to the world.

We have too many instances in this case:

1. Those who deny the end of this righteousness, deny the satisfaction of Christ, as doth Socinus and his wretched followers; hereby in effect denying the righteousness itself, and rendering it of no value; for if it be not satisfactory, it is not meritorious. Sure nothing can be procured of mercy until satisfaction be tendered to offended justice; and if neither merit nor satisfy for us, of what use is it? of what value? why should the apostle so highly esteem it as to suffer the loss? &c. Surely these men are not led by the same Spirit which guided the apostle, who so much disparage that which he so highly prized.

2. Who deny the sufficiency of it. So the papists, who, as though Christ was not sufficient to satisfy justice and procure eternal life, join their own fond merits and satisfaction with that of Christ's righteousness; as though man's own righteousness could be either satisfactory or meritorious, which are the prerogatives and sovereign virtues of Christ's righteousness alone.

Far was the apostle from apprehending any such worth in his own righteousness (and sure he was not behind any of the papists), when he styles it flesh, and loss, and dung; when he disclaims it expressly, is afraid to be found in it, in any, save the righteousness of Christ.

3. To deny the participation of it, deny that it is imputed to us; as do the Arminians, with both the former. What this imputation is, I have shewed before; and thence it may appear how unreasonably they deny it to be imputed to believers, who grant it is accepted for them; since imputation is nothing but the acceptation of it declared and pronounced in the gospel.

I would fain know how that which is neither in us nor performed by us can be ours otherwise than by imputation. Either they must grant it is imputed, or deny that we can have it. If so, what made the apostle disclaim all, suffer the loss of all, that he might have that which is impossible he should have?

4. Those who deny the righteousness of Christ in effect, though they confess it in words, live so unacquainted with it as though they did not acknowledge it; are such strangers to the use and improvement of this righteousness, as if there were no such things.

Many there are who disclaim popery in words, and yet are too like papists in undervaluing the righteousness of Christ; many who rely not on it alone for pardon, acceptance, and life, who set up their posts by God's post, and join their own righteousness with the righteousness of Christ, if they leave any place at all for this. Their good meaning, honest dealing, religious duties, or works of charity, must share with Christ in the honour of procuring for them pardon and life. Here they rest.

And this is too common, and the grounds of it seem to be pride and ignorance; the motive, corruptions* of our minds and hearts. Such pride there is in every man by nature, as he will have something of his own to commend him to God; he will not be beholden to another for his salvation. He is loath to think himself so vile as that he hath nothing, or can do nothing, that may help him to pardon and life.

That self-denial, self-abhorrence which the gospel requires, is quite contrary to nature; and if there be nothing but nature in thee, thou wilt never attain them.

This pride is it which keeps multitudes (who yet think themselves humble enough) out of that way of life which is revealed in Christ. This is it which is the great enemy of the honour of Christ in his righteousness, and so deeply is it rooted in man's nature, as nothing but an almighty power can pluck it up. Those weapons must be mighty through God that cast down these high imaginations.

Another ground is ignorance. Men are not well acquainted either with Christ or themselves, for† if they know, yet do not effectually lay it to heart; they consider not what perfection and exactness the law of God doth indispensably require of them; they consider not into what misery every act of disobedience sinks their souls; they consider not how impossible it is, by anything they have or can do, to free themselves from this misery; they consider not that Christ's righteousness is only sufficient to do it. And thus they go on in the dark, neglecting Christ and their souls, till he sends his Spirit with power and evidence, to convince them of sin, of wrath due to sin, of misery by reason of wrath, of their absolute necessity of Christ to free them from this wrath. Till you have lively apprehensions of these things, Christ's righteousness will be of little value; and so it is with a great part of those who daily profess the gospel, which is a lamentation, and will be for a lamentation.

Secondly, The second direction is, Be apprehensive of its necessity. In other cases, we need no other motive to raise our desires of a thing, than the apprehension that it is absolutely necessary for us. The righteousness of Christ is of absolute necessity, and that in the weightiest concernments; it is absolutely necessary for thy life, for thy soul, for thy salvation. And that appears briefly in three particulars.

1. Nothing but this can answer the law of God. This requires perfect obedience of all that will have life, perfect righteousness under pain of death. Now no man in the world can perform such obedience, can produce such a

* Qu. 'native corruptions'?—ED. † Qu. 'or'?—ED.

righteousness. It is only to be found in the man Christ Jesus. Either thou must be found having this righteousness of Christ, or else there is no life for thee; else there is nothing but death for thee, and that as sure as God is true and unchangeable.

2. Nothing but this can satisfy the justice of God. It must be a righteousness of infinite value that satisfies justice, for sin is against an infinite majesty, and therefore the injury is infinite; the satisfaction must be answerable to the injury, and therefore it must be infinite. But no righteousness, no satisfaction is of infinite value, but only that of Christ. Therefore thou must be found having Christ's righteousness, or else justice will press thee to death, justice will cast thee into hell, justice will there exact the utmost farthing, justice will have satisfaction on either, from the offender or his Surety. If thou hast not interest in Christ's satisfaction, to tender it unto justice, justice will require of thee in person; and because thou canst never fully satisfy, thou must ever suffer.

3. Nothing but this can justify a sinner. There can be no justification without a perfect righteousness, for where there is imperfection there is some guilt, and the righteousness of God will never justify a guilty person, Exod. xxiii. 7, Prov. xvii. 15.

Now where must this perfect justifying righteousness be had? Thou hast no such of thine own, Isa. lxiv., nor can any men or angels afford it thee. The angels have no more than will justify themselves, and fallen man hath not so much, Job xv. 14.

Either thou must have this righteousness of Christ, or else thou canst never be justified, and without justification no salvation: Rom. viii. 30, 'Whom he justifies, them also,' and them only, 'he glorifies.'

If, then, salvation be necessary for thee, then thou must count the righteousness of Christ necessary; and if that be to be desired above all things, which is absolutely necessary to salvation, then is Christ's righteousness to be desired above all things.

Thirdly, The third direction is, Labour to get an interest in it. We are apt to esteem those things which are our own, and this esteem will make us desirous to continue in possession of them. So that the way to raise our esteem and quicken our desire after this righteousness of Christ, is to get interest in it. Make this your business and your great design, to get an interest in it; and mind this as the one thing necessary, 'Seek first the kingdom of God, and this righteousness of him,' Mat. vi. 'Seek it first,' that is, primarily, before all, and principally, above all. It is a preposterous course to seek the things of the world first and most, and this after, with less care, less affections. This is the way to lose both, both heaven and earth, both the glorious things above, and the comforts of all enjoyments below. Make sure of this, and all is sure: 'All these shall be added.'

Now the way to obtain this righteousness we may find out in this phrase by which it is here expressed, 'The righteousness of God through faith.'

First, It is the righteousness of Christ; and therefore, if we would obtain it, we must renounce our own righteousness, for these two are opposed by the apostle in point of confidence. If we rely upon our own righteousness, we disclaim the righteousness of Christ; and if we rely on Christ's righteousness, we must disclaim our own. If these two could be joined, the apostle would not divide them; but he professes, 'he would be found in Christ, not having,' &c., 'that he might have that which is,' &c.

Be convinced, then, of the insufficiency of your own righteousness. It cannot satisfy justice, it comes far short of what is required, it cannot make amends for the least sin, it cannot entitle you to heaven, it cannot justify you in the sight of God: 'By the deeds of the law,' &c., Gal. ii. 16. Since it is thus insufficient, rely not on it for what it cannot perform, depend not on it for pardon, acceptation, or life; think not your praying and being sorry for sin, or works of charity, is that for which the Lord will pardon or save you, Tit. iii. 5. The like of justification, adoption, acceptance.

Be convinced no righteousness that you have, no works of righteousness that you do, will make any satisfaction for sin, or procure you any title to glory.

If you place your confidence herein, you cut yourself off from Christ and his righteousness, Gal. v. 4. Your own must be renounced, or else there is no hope of the righteousness by faith; renounced, I say, not in respect of performance, but in respect of confidence. The works of righteousness must not be omitted, neglected; this was not the apostle's practice nor intention; he saw the necessity of these in himself, he urged them upon others; they are commendable, yea, necessary in their own place, for those ends, and in that way which the Lord requires; to testify your submission to God, to express your thankfulness for gospel mercies, to honour him, adorn your profession, evidence your sincerity; for this and such like ends there is an excellency in them, a necessity of them.

But in respect of confidence you must renounce them; perform them you must, but when you have performed them, you must repose no more confidence in them than if you had performed nothing at all. 'When we have done all, say,' &c., Mat. xvii. 10. Your own righteousness is good in its own place, but when you rely on it you misplace it; and a good thing out of its own place may prove a dangerous evil. What more necessary and useful than fire when it is confined to the chimney? Put it in the thatch, you know it will prove a dangerous, destructive evil. So here, righteousness confided in is a good thing out of its place, and so it may prove pernicious; it will exclude you an interest in, and benefit by Christ's righteousness; and therefore, in point of confidence, you must renounce it, if ever you would partake of Christ's righteousness.

The ground hereof is signally expressed by the church, Isa. lxiv. 6. Not righteousness, this or that act, but righteousnesses; not some, but all put together; let no rags, a rag will not cover you, it is not a garment; stretch it as you will it cannot so hide your nakedness but some of it will appear; your own righteousness cannot cover your guilt or pollution from the eye of God, it is a rag, there are many rents and holes in it, many defects and sinful imperfections in all, even the best. It is a rag, that which you have cause rather to be ashamed of than glory in, that which can neither secure you from extremity of heat or cold. It cannot secure you from the wrath and justice of God, it leaves you exposed thereto, it is not therefore to be trusted to.

Nay, filthy rags, not only defective, but polluted, and filthily polluted; if the Lord observe it there is no standing in his sight; it needs another covering to hide its filthiness from the pure eye of God, and nothing can so cover it but Christ's righteousness; it must be cast off in point of confidence before we can put on Christ. Those that will be found in it cannot be found in Christ: it is the Lord's method to strip a sinner of his own rags before he put on him the best robe, Zech. iii. 3-5. The apostle observed this method: 'Not having,' &c. The way to Christ's righteousness is renouncing your own. If you would rejoice in Christ Jesus, in the participation of his righteousness, you must have no confidence in the flesh.

Secondly, It is this righteousness which is of God. He ordained it, he appointed Christ to perform it; he accepted it performed, and imputes it, gives it believers; it is his gift, Rom. v. 15–19; and therefore if you would have it, you must ask it of God. Go, then, take to you words, desire it of him in all humble importunity. To beg for this as for life, pray as Rachel for children, Gen. xxx. 1. Give me Christ, give me his righteousness, or else I die: I die spiritually, I die eternally; nothing less can satisfy revenging justice, every hour ready to destroy; can appease that curse that burns like fire against me; can deliver me from wrath to come; can preserve me from going down into the pit. Oh give me this, or else I die, I perish eternally! Heaven and earth cannot save me without it; my soul is lost, my condition is desperate; I am undone for ever, if the Lord deny me this. Oh, this calls for your strongest cries! Life or death, and that of soul and body, and that to eternity, depends on it. Beg for it, as you would beg for life; say, nothing but this can procure me pardon of sin, can render myself or my services acceptable in his sight, can give me the least grounded hopes of heaven. If my hopes were only in this life, I am of all men most miserable. Why? Without Christ's righteousness I am without hope; this life cannot be comfortable, and there is no hopes at all of eternal life. If thou deniest this, I am of all men most miserable; I may be happy without worldly enjoyments, but all things in the world cannot make me happy without this. And therefore, however thou disposest of me in the world, whatsoever thou deniest me, Lord, deny me not this. I can be happy without riches and abundance, as was Job and Lazarus; happy though reviled and reproached, so was Christ, so was his disciples; happy and comfortable in prison, so was Paul and Silas. Oh, but I cannot be happy without this; all the riches, places, honours on earth, will leave me miserable, if I be left without this; so I should be rich and increased so with goods as to stand in need of nothing, yet if I want this, I shall be wretched, and miserable, and poor, and blind, and naked. If I had all things else that heart can desire on earth, yet what would all this avail me without Christ's righteousness! What profit in riches, while I have them with the wrath of God! What comforts in honour, while I am a son of perdition, a child of wrath! What sweetness in pleasure, while I am hastening to everlasting torments! Oh, miserable comforts, miserable enjoyments are these, whilst Christ's righteousness is not my portion!

Lord, however thou dealest with me in outward things, whatsoever thou takest from me, whatsoever thou deniest me, oh, deny me not Christ, deny me not interest in his righteousness! Thus follow the Lord with strong cries, lie at the Lord's feet, cast thyself at this throne of grace, resolve to give the Lord no rest till he gives thee Christ and his righteousness.

Thirdly, It is a righteousness through faith. The righteousness *by* faith here, and elsewhere a righteousness *of* faith, and that because it is made ours by faith. It is the righteousness of God, because his gift; the righteousness of faith, because faith is, as it were, the hand by which we receive this gift. Hence believing and receiving are all one in Scripture, John i. 12. If you would have Christ's righteousness, you must have faith. But here mistake not that for faith which is not faith, an ordinary but dangerous mistake, when Satan persuades men they have Christ's righteousness, though they have it not, by persuading them they have justifying faith, when they have no such thing.

Think not you have faith because you believe the word of God, and what he there reveals is true. This is not justifying faith; this is no more than devils may have. Think not it is an easy thing to believe; those that think so know not what faith is. A man, whilst in the state of nature, can no more believe of himself, and receive Christ's righteousness, than a dead man can stretch out his hand to receive meat, for natural men are dead in trespasses and sins.

Those that say they have faith ever since they can remember, know not how they came by it, may suspect they never had it at all. It is an almighty power that works faith in a sinner, and there is a wonderful change wrought in the heart when faith is there planted, a change answerable to the greatness of that power that works, answerable [to] such a power as raised Christ from the dead, for such a power is requisite to work faith, Eph. i. 19, 20.

Observe the way, the method, which the Lord ordinarily uses in working that faith which receives this righteousness.

He convinces the soul of sin, sets his sins in order before him in its sinfulness, heinousness, aggravations, and desert; of the wrath of God due to him for sin, and his misery by reason hereof, so as his conscience is affected, his soul burthened therewith; he discovers Christ, his excellency, all-sufficiency, and the absolute necessity of him. He had heard of this before, but now sees them; his present apprehensions of these things differ as much from his former, as those of a quick-sighted man differs from his who is blind.

He hereupon quickens his desires after Christ, begets in him hungering and thirsting after his righteousness, such as a famished man after meat.

He persuades the heart to accept of Christ upon his own terms, makes it willing, resolute to abandon every known sin, how dear soever, and to walk in every way of holiness, how strict and precise soever he hath judged it formerly, how much soever it be hated or derided by the world.

And in the deep sense of his misery and lost condition, by reason of sin and wrath, and the insufficiency of all things to deliver him, but Christ only, he inclines the soul to cast itself upon Christ for pardon and life, and to rest upon him as the only refuge from wrath and misery; the soul lays hold, rests upon Christ, even as a drowning man lays hold on a plank and stays himself thereupon from sinking; this is that faith which receives Christ's righteousness, and this you must believe if you would partake of it.

Fourthly, Be diligent to improve this righteousness of Christ. We little value or desire those things whose use and virtue we know not, and the virtue of a thing is not fully known till it be improved and made use of. Labour to improve the righteousness of Christ, and then the sweet and blessed advantages of it will be known effectually; for hereby you will know them experimentally, and an experimental knowledge hereof is the most effectual means to raise your apprehensions of it, and draw out your desires after it.

For further directions I intended to shew how Christ's righteousness may be improved for the encouragement, increase, and exercise of every grace, of love and zeal, of humility and self-denial, of hatred of sin and contempt of the world, with many more. I intended also to shew how you may improve it in every duty, enjoyment, occurrence, and undertaking;

but if you forget not what I have formerly delivered in many particulars concerning the usefulness and advantage of Christ's righteousness; if you conscientiously make use thereof accordingly, there will be no need of further directions herein; and lest I should seem to stay too long upon this subject, thither I must refer you.

I shall now only insist upon one particular, or rather two in one, but that which will be instead of many; and this is to shew you how we may improve it in praying and believing, for the strengthening of faith and your encouragement to pray in faith.

These two are as it were the life, breath, of a quickened soul; that which it lives upon is Christ and his righteousness, Gal. ii. 20; he that can pray and believe needs want nothing, this will fetch him rich supplies in abundance; the treasury is Christ's righteousness.

He needs fear nothing, this will scatter all occasions of fear, Christ's righteousness will be his security.

He is a Christian indeed that is much in prayer and strong in faith; these two must be joined, for faith is best experienced in prayer, and prayer is most effectual when in faith, James i. 5, 6.

These are the two great attractive faculties of the new creature, they draw into the soul all that virtue of Christ's righteousness which is communicable; these are the ways, the means to make the utmost improvement of the righteousness of Jesus.

And which is here most considerable, nothing affords more encouragement to improve this righteousness by faith and prayer than this righteousness itself.

As the best way to improve this righteousness is by praying and believing, so the greatest encouragement to faith, to prayer, is from this righteousness; this strengthens the hands of faith, this suggests arguments to make the soul earnest, affected, importunate in prayer; this answers all objections, removes all discouragements that might dishearten the soul from praying, or hinder the acting of faith in prayer.

Let me shew this more particularly, that you may see the way herein to improve Christ's righteousness.

(1.) A humble soul, sensible of his spiritual condition, and the weakness of his best services, will be apt to discourage himself with such thoughts as these. Alas! my prayers are weak, if I could pray with such fervency, such enlargements, such affections, such importunity as other servants of God have done formerly, and some I see are wont to do now, then I might be encouraged to pray, and to expect an answer of my prayers; but my prayers are so weak, faint, imperfect, as there is little hope they should be regarded, little hope they should prevail.

Ay, but consider, though thy prayers be weak, yet the plea of Christ's righteousness is strong, this hath a voice which the Lord hears, though we take no notice of it; *nunquam tacet*, &c.

It speaks better things than the blood of Abel, Heb. xii. 24. The weakest prayer, enforced with the righteousness of Christ, is more effectual, more prevailing than that which seems strongest, if Christ's righteousness be neglected; if Christ should now, as in the days of his flesh, send up for thee strong cries, with tears and sighs, thou wouldst not doubt, whatever thy weakness be, but he would prevail for thee; why, the righteousness of Christ presented to the Lord now in heaven, doth as effectually speak for thee (if a believer), as if he did now pray for thee with sighs and tears. There is a more powerful plea in the blood of Christ than there could be in his tears: and that is as fresh in the Lord's remembrance, as if it were now, as if it were every hour shed for thee; it ever pleads, and therefore he is said for ever to make intercession; and canst thou doubt that this plea ever joined with, always enforcing thy prayers, will not prevail? Oh what encouragement is here to faith in prayer from Christ's righteousness!

(2.) Secondly, Oh but my former sins are great, my provocations many, and when I come to pray, nay, would believe the Lord will hearken, then I fear my sins may come into remembrance, may meet my prayers at the throne of grace, and this dashes my hopes, sinks me into distrust and doubtings. My sins cry louder than my prayers, and what hope then my prayers should prevail? The Lord's ear is not straitened. Methinks I see my sins spreading themselves as a thick cloud about the throne of grace, so as my prayers cannot come near.

Ay, but to remove this, consider there is a virtue in the righteousness of Christ to scatter thy sins as a thick cloud. Let faith carry with it the righteousness of Christ to the throne of grace, and thou wilt see thy sins vanish as a mist before the sun, and this is applied by and to a believer, and presented by Christ in his behalf, his sins shall never more be had in remembrance; nay, he will cast them into the bottom of the sea. So that thou mayest say of them as it is said of Pharaoh and the Egyptians, 'Those that ye now see, ye shall see them no more.' Christ's righteousness will be continually presented on purpose to nonsuit sin and Satan. When this is applied, though sin appear in judgment and plead against the believer, yet it will certainly be cast, Rom. viii. 3. Christ, by virtue of his righteousness, is the most powerful advocate, he always hath the judge's ears and heart, and that cause will always be found righteous that Christ's righteousness is engaged in; it is impossible it should miscarry.

To bring this with faith to the throne of grace, and then whatever sins yours have been, you may plead there with confidence to prevail; hence triumphant challenge of the apostle, who otherwise was as sensible of his sins as any, Rom. viii. 33; your sins may outcry your prayers, but they cannot outcry the blood, the righteousness of Christ.

(3.) Thirdly, Oh but I am unworthy, how can I expect the Lord should take notice of such a worm? there seems no more reason the great God should regard my prayers than that he should regard the crawling of a worm, or take notice of the regardless motion of dust or ashes; I am less, I am worse than these, sin hath made me more unworthy.

Ay, but though thou beest unworthy, yet Christ is worthy; though there be no worth in thee, yet there is worth enough in Christ's righteousness; though thou and thy services be found too light, lighter than vanity, yet put Christ's righteousness in the balance, together with thee and thy prayers, and then they will be current, acceptable, without question.

If thou be found in Christ, then look not on what thou art simply in thyself, but what thou art in him; now he hath made thy lust his, and his righteousness thine, no matter then for thy unworthiness since he is worthy; say, Most unworthy am I, O Lord, but worthy is Christ; and so the angels and saints cry with a loud voice, Rev. v. 12.

Now, as he is worthy to receive all this for himself, so he is worthy to obtain, to receive all good things for his people; if thou beest found in him, having his righteousness, his merits, his worthiness will be as available for thee though thou beest most unworthy; thou shalt as easily obtain what thou prayest for as though thou wast worthy to receive it; though thou art the vilest of slaves by reason of sin, yet believing this, by this righteousness art made a king and a priest to offer up spiritual sacrifices, &c.

(4.) Fourthly, But I fear the Lord is not willing to grant what I pray for. Ordinarily there seems to be no doubt of the Lord's power, but that which most weakens faith and discourages the heart in praying is fear, or doubting that the Lord is not willing. Here is the greatest discouragement a believer meets with, Gal. iv. 5.

But the righteousness of Christ removes this, hence thou mayest persuade thyself the Lord is most willing, most ready to grant what thou desirest; for if thou be found in Christ, and if thou ask what is good, what is necessary for thee, the righteousness of Christ hath purchased this for thee; now, will the Lord be unwilling to put thee in possession of what Christ hath purchased for thee? You cannot imagine him unwilling here, except you will think him unjust, unrighteous.

Besides, the relation wherein Christ's righteousness instates thee may persuade this; hereby thou standest in that relation to God as a child to his father, Gal. iii. 26. Now, will a father so gracious, so indulgent, be unwilling to afford his child what is good, what is necessary for him, when he asks it affectionately, begs it with all importunity? It is Christ's own argument, Mat. vii. 9–11.

(5.) Fifthly, Oh, but it is a great request I put up; if it were a small matter, I should with more confidence look to have it granted, but in this case, here is more ground for doubting.

For answer, no more ground at all; the righteousness of Christ satisfies this on a double account.

[1.] If the Lord hath given thee Christ and his righteousness, he hath given thee the greatest mercy that can be given or received; if he hath given thee the greater, mayest thou not with confidence ask the less? He that thought not Christ himself too much for thee, will he stand with thee for a small matter? The greatest is small compared with Christ, Rom. viii.

[2.] Is this great thing of more value than Christ's righteousness? No such instance can be given. Why, then, it was bought for thee by Christ's righteousness, this was the price of it; and if it be purchased for thee, can the greatness of it hinder the Lord from giving it to thee?

(6.) Sixthly, Oh, but there are many provocations even in my prayers, much deadness of heart, much unaffectedness, much indifferency and lukewarmness, much self-seeking, and many distractions, much backwardness to it, dulness in it, weariness of it, &c., and many other provoking evils. Those that observe the temper of their hearts in spiritual duties, and take an account of their ways and walking with God, will find cause to bewail the sinfulness of their best prayers; and Satan, he takes an occasion hereby to assault their faith, and discourage from expecting any gracious returns to such offensive petitions. How can this offering (will he suggest) ascend up as a savour of a sweet smell unto heaven, when there is so much corruption in them?

But for answer: If these sinful imperfections be bewailed, and the blood of Christ applied by faith for pardon, then they are pardoned; and what sins are pardoned can no more hinder the answer of prayer (if good) than if they were not committed.

The prayers of believers appear not in the sight of God simply as they come from them, they are presented by Christ; their petitions are, as it were, offered by his hand, and his righteousness presented with them; if the sin appears, the satisfaction is at hand too, and how then can the appearance of sin be prejudicial? See this comfortably set fort in Rom. viii. 3, 4.

It was the priest's office to offer incense, and this angel that here offers is the High Priest of heaven, the Lord Jesus; he offers the prayers of the saints, they ascend before God out of the angel's hand, and needs must they be accepted from his hand, whatever they be in themselves.

Nay, further, he offers them with much incense, or, as it is in the Greek, he adds much incense to them; that is, he adds his meritorious and satisfactory righteousness, for incense was a type of his mediation. The prayers that ascend up with this incense must needs be the savour of a sweet smell, must needs find gracious acceptance and sweet returns.

Thus you see how this righteousness may be improved to strengthen faith, and remove all discouragements in praying, to answer all objections that may occasion any doubt of gracious returns. And by this one instance you may judge how advantageous it would be to the rest. Oh that the comfort and precious advantages which arise from the improvement of this righteousness might be effectual to raise your thoughts of it, and quicken your desires after it, so as ye might be willing to suffer the loss of all things, &c.

MEN BY NATURE UNWILLING TO COME TO CHRIST.

Ye will not come unto me, that ye might have life.—JOHN V. 40.

THE Lord Jesus having miraculously cured an impotent man on the Sabbath day, the unbelieving Jews are so far from believing in him, that they blaspheme, persecute, and reproach him as a profaner of the Sabbath, ver. 16. Christ hereupon makes an apology for himself, and proves by unanswerable arguments, that his act was no violation of the Sabbath, to the 31st verse. But the Jews, full of malice and unbelief, were apt to object, that the weight of his own arguments lay upon his own testimony, and a man's testimony of himself in his own cause is not counted valid or credible, ver. 31. But though this objection have only place amongst men (whose testimony of themselves is not satisfactory and convincing), and cannot be made use of to weaken the testimony of Christ, who was more than man, no less God than man, yet he so far yields as to waive his own testimony; and for confirmation of what he had delivered, produces variety of testimonies against which there could be no just, nay, no plausible exception; and he alleges,

1. The testimony of John, ver. 33, which you see, John i. 7, and this he makes use of, not out of any necessity in respect of himself (who being God, and truth itself, needed not the witness of man to testify of him), but out of respect to them, with whom John's testimony was more valid than his own of himself; for John was a burning and shining light, he came both with evidence and power, such as was not altogether ineffectual upon these hardened Jews, ver. 35.

2. The testimony of miracles, this was a real witness. If they could not hear, they might see a testimony, the miraculous power of Christ testifying the truth of his doctrine, and so confirming that he was God, and sent of God. This was the testimony which the Jews required as that wherein they would rest satisfied: 'What sign shewest thou?' ver. 36.

3. The testimony of the Father: ver. 37, 'The Father which hath sent me, hath borne witness of me;' not only by wonders on earth, but by a voice from heaven, Mat. iii. 16, 17. But if ye will not acknowledge that ye have heard his voice, no more than ye have seen his shape, yet there is a further witness that ye cannot, dare not deny; and that is,

4. The testimony of the Scripture, ver. 39. Moses and the prophets, even all that have been from the beginning of the world, they testify that I am the Messias. Now as to the rest, so to this he subjoins an application, and that by way of complaint, ver. 40. Though the Scriptures testify that life is to be had only in the Messias, and though they testify that I am the Messias, in whom only life is to be found, 'yet ye will not come to me,' &c.

Wherein three things are observable: 1. Men's misery out of Christ; they are off from him, dead without him, unwilling to come to him. 2. Men's happiness in Christ; they that find him find life, the sentence of life as to justification, the principles of life spiritual as to sanctification, the comforts of life temporal as to their present enjoyments, the joys of life eternal as to their future condition. 3. Christ's resentment of man's condition; he complains of it, it grieves, it troubles him; he vents his grief to a sad complaint, 'Ye will not come to me.'

Each part affords some fruitful observations, and from man's misery we may collect two very useful doctrines:

I. *Doct.* Men by nature are far from Christ.

II. *Doct.* Men without Christ are unwilling to come unto him.

I. For the first, men by nature are far from Christ. This is clearly implied. What need of coming to him, but that they are at a distance from him? All, every man by nature is so, the Lord speaks this of the Jews, and the apostle witnesses the same of the Gentiles: Acts ii. 39, 'The promise is to you and to your children, and to all that are afar off;' the like, Eph. ii. 13, 17. The Jews were nearer in respect of some privileges and enjoyments, but far off in respect of spiritual saving improvement of them. The prodigal is an emblem, a lively representation of both, both Jew and Gentile. We departed from our father's house in Adam, and till the Lord convert us, we, as he, dwell in a far country, at a great distance from Christ, far from him in respect of knowledge, union, participation, converse.

1. In respect of *knowledge*. Far from knowing Christ savingly, effectually, experimentally; far from apprehending such excellency in him as to count all things dross and dung in comparison of him; such necessity of him as to part with sin, self, the world, and all for him; such all-sufficiency in him, as to be content with him in the want, in the loss of all; far from clear knowledge of Christ, as a poor prisoner, locked and bolted in a dark dungeon is far from seeing the light of the day, or as a man stark blind is far from seeing the light of the sun; so, and far more than so, is a natural man from seeing Christ; shut up in darkness, under the power of Satan, having the eyes of his mind blinded by the God of this world, that he cannot see the light of the knowledge of the glory of God in the face of Christ.

2. In respect of *union*. He is far from being united with Christ, from being one with him; wedded to sin, glued to the world, and unwilling to be separated, and so far from Christ, because there can be no contract betwixt Christ and the soul till there be a divorce betwixt the soul and sin, the soul and the world. No league with Christ till the covenant with hell and death, with sin and the world, be broken. Far from faith, which is the bond of this union, shut up under unbelief, and a gravestone laid upon the soul, which nothing can roll away but an almighty power; far from marriage-union with Christ, even as a child yet unborn is far from

the hopes and comforts of a conjugal life and union; so far are men from Christ, who are yet in the state of nature, not regenerated, not born again.

3. In respect of *participation*. As far from union with the person of Christ, so far from partaking of the benefits of Christ; far from pardon, being yet under the sentence of condemnation; from adoption, being yet servants of sin, and slaves to Satan; from reconciliation, being enemies to Christ in their minds through wicked works; from sanctification, the old man keeping still possession with a strong hand, and the interest of the flesh and the world prevailing in the soul; from heaven, there is a great gulf betwixt him and heaven, a gulf deep and large, no passage possible by the act or power of nature. Far from enjoying any of the benefits of Christ's purchase, as he that is in the Indies, without ship or boat, is far from enjoying any comforts or accommodations here with us.

4. In respect of *converse*. A stranger to Christ, far from communion with him; a stranger to his thoughts, Christ is not his meditation; his heart is not with him, his affections not on him, his inclinations not towards him, his desires not after him, his delight not in him, his designs not for him; he lives not to Christ, acts not for him, walks not with him; Christ is in heaven, and his heart is on the world. As far as heaven is from earth, so far is a natural man from Christ.

Use. See here the misery of every man by nature, far from Christ, and consequently near to hell and Satan; and since man is always in motion, the longer he continues out of Christ, the further he wanders from him. While you are in the state of nature, till ye be converted, till ye be regenerated and born again, till ye be translated out of that state wherein ye were born, wherein ye have lived, this is your condition, ye are far from Christ. Oh sad state, if ye were sensible of it! There is something of hell in this condition, far from Christ! It is heaven to be with Christ, it is his presence that makes heaven glorious, it is his presence enjoyed that makes heaven happy; but to be far from Christ, is to be in hell upon earth; to be far from Christ, is to be in the suburbs of hell; when Christ is farthest off, then is hell opened. What is hell, but the state farthest from Christ? And now if this be your state, if ye be far off from Christ, why there is but a step between you and hell.

Oh the misery of this condition! If natural men were not possessed with a spirit of slumber, if they were but sensible how miserable this condition is, they would scarce sleep, or eat, or count anything comfortable, while they are in it.

While far from Christ, you are far from comfort, happiness, hopes of either; you are far from the dearest friend, the sweetest relation you can desire in the world; far from being rich, however you are provided in the world, for Christ is the only treasure; far from comforts, however ye solace yourselves in things below; all your springs of comfort are in Christ. Dig where you will, bitterness will spring up, no pure comforts; while far from this fountain, far from happiness. Christ is the foundation of all happiness. Ye may delude yourselves with fancies, but you will find it really true, till ye be near to Christ, you are far from happiness, ay, and far from hopes of happiness; without Christ, without hope; far from Christ, far from hope: Christ, where he is, is the hope of glory, Col. i. Ye are far from heaven, far from glory, far from hopes of glory, while ye are far from Christ.

Oh then, never rest in this condition, make haste out of the state of nature, never be at quiet, till ye be converted, born again; till ye feel the power of Christ's Spirit drawing your souls off from sin and the world, till then ye are far from Christ.

II. *Doct.* Sinners are unwilling to come to Christ. It is evident in the words, Christ complains of it, and he never complains without cause. If this were not so, Christ should wrong them, his complaint would be groundless.

Nothing more true than this, and yet nothing less believed. Indeed, every one will acknowledge this in general, but come to particulars, and inquire, Art thou willing? &c. And you shall scarce find one man that bears the name of a Christian, but he will confidently tell you, he is not only willing to come, but is already with him; even as it was with the Jews, so it is now with most Christians. Those of the people whom the apostle calls Jews outwardly, if one had told them they were unwilling to come to their Messias, they would have looked upon it as a groundless slander, as a most intolerable reproach. What, not we who make it our daily prayer, who live in continual expectation of him, who desire nothing more than to see him in the world? What more false than that we should not be willing to come? And yet nothing was more true; for when Christ the Messias was really in the world, they were so far from coming to him, as they would not receive him when he came to them: 'He came to his own, and they received him not.' So it is with those amongst us who are Christians outwardly. What, are not we willing to come to Christ, who call upon his name, and are called by his name, and expect salvation only by him? This seems a most uncharitable, groundless charge; and yet there are but few (of all that many that profess Christ) that do, or will really come to him; and they are apt to be most confident who are farthest off. They are his own, those who bear his name, to whom Christ comes, and yet they will not receive him: it is the generality of those who are called Christians of whom Christ may complain, 'Ye will not come to me.' They will not come to Christ for spiritual life, they will not come to him at all for the life of holiness and sanctification; and though they seem willing to come to him for pardon and heaven, for judicial and eternal life, yet they are unwilling to come to him even for these in his own way; and as good sit still as not come in Christ's way. He that will walk in his own way towards Christ, he goes from him, not to him. Nothing more clear in Scripture and experience than this, else what needs so many invitations, so much importunity, Isa. lv. 1, Rev. xxii. What needs he cry aloud unto them, Prov. i. 20, but that they are unwilling to hear? What need he send so many messengers? What need so many entreaties and persuasive arguments, 2 Cor. v. 20, but that unwillingness is not easily removed? What needs he come himself to call them? Mat. xviii. 11. Why does he wait so long, and stand without knocking, Rev. iii., if there need be no *if*, but that men are unwilling? What need so many commands to come, so many threatenings if they do not, Luke xiv. 24, so many expostulations for not coming? What need he take the rod, and whip them home to himself, but that they are loath to come, fair means will not prevail? Why does he weep and sigh at the obstinacy of sinners? Luke xix. 41, 42. To conclude: What needs an almighty power to draw sinners unto him? Are not they unwilling that must be drawn to it?

You see, it is as clear in the Scripture as the sun, that it is so. Let us inquire why it is so, and who they are that are unwilling, that every one may know what to judge of himself in this particular; and both these we shall shew with one labour.

1. Many think they are already come to Christ, when indeed they are far from him. They conceive they are come far enough, and therefore are unwilling to come farther, so they sit down short of Christ, and are not willing to come to him. What is the language of men's hearts but this, We profess Christ, are baptized in his name, hope to be saved by him, submit to his ordinances, hear his word, call on his name, and who then can say that we are not come to Christ? And whereas, alas, many go farther than thus, and yet live and die without Christ, and so far from him as he knows them not; and so he professeth to the foolish virgins, and to those, Mat. vii. Did not Judas, did not Simon Magus do all this, and more than this? which yet is all that most can allege to prove they are come to Christ.

Do you come to Christ as a Saviour to deliver you from the wrath to come? It is well; but if ye go no further, ye go but half the way to Christ. If you will come home to Christ indeed, you must go to him, not only as a Saviour, but as a Lord; not only to receive pardon from him, but to be ruled by him; not only to be saved, but to be sanctified; not only for happiness, but for holiness too, for Christ is both or neither; and if ye come for one and not for the other, indeed you come not at all; you do but delude yourselves with thoughts that you are already come; Christ will have as much cause to complain of you as of the Jews, 'Ye will not.'

2. Many do not fully apprehend their necessity of Christ. And if they think it unnecessary, no wonder if they be unwilling. But what ignorant wretches are they, you will say, who think it not necessary? Oh that the greatest number of those that profess Christ were not such! A little search into the thoughts and ways of men, will discover that there are multitudes who did never thoroughly apprehend what necessity there is of Christ.

Are there not such, who when they sin, think it enough to be sorry for it, to ask God forgiveness, or to be more careful for the future? Do not some think they make amends for sinning by doing some good work, or falling upon some religious duty after it? Is not this ordinary, even amongst the better sort of ordinary Christians? (for some miscreants there are who run on in sin without any remorse at all). Now what necessity of Christ do they apprehend, who can thus satisfy their consciences? Do such duly apprehend, that the least of those many millions of sins which they are guilty of, deserves eternal torments? that the justice of God is engaged to inflict those torments for every sin, though it be but a vain thought or idle word? that justice can never be disengaged from thus punishing such sin, till it be fully satisfied? that nothing can satisfy justice for the least, but that which is of infinite value? that none in heaven or earth can offer this to justice, but only Jesus Christ? If these were truly apprehended, which are the sure truths of the gospel, you would be far from thinking to make amends for the least sin, though you should fast, and pray, and weep for it to all eternity.

There is none but Christ, none but Christ, can satisfy for the least sinful motion that ever was in thy heart. Oh, if men believed Christ thus necessary, they would not only go, but run, but fly to him. You would not work, nor sleep, nor eat in quiet, till you were sure that Christ had satisfied for your sins. Sure when men sin, and are not disquieted; or, if they be, yet can quiet their consciences with anything in the world but the application of the blood of Christ, they see not their necessity of Christ, they are not yet come to him.

Further, are there not such who believe they shall be saved because they mean well, and do no man wrong, and give to every one their own, and now and then serve God in some religious duties? They think God is more merciful than to damn such harmless, well-meaning people. Why, but if you can come thus to heaven, what need is there of Christ? Sure you never were convinced of your necessity of Christ, and then it is evident enough you are not yet come to him.

Besides, are there not many who see no need of regeneration, of an universal change in their whole souls? who, if they can restrain their lusts, see no need to endeavour the subduing them? think their natures sufficiently sanctified, if the corruption of them break not forth in gross sins; think the outward performance of religious duties sufficient; see no need of so much zeal, faith, fervency, delight, and spiritualness, and aims at God in the performing them; think it enough if their conversation be honest and civil, though it be not spiritual or heavenly? If these be not the thoughts of most, let your consciences, let your former or present experiences judge. And if it be thus, what need is there of Christ for regeneration or mortification, for exercise of grace or holiness of life? Alas! it is plain here are no due apprehensions how necessary Christ is in all these respects, but here are clear evidences that such never yet came to Christ, no, nor ever yet were willing to come; for since they think it unnecessary, they cannot but be unwilling. Christ has yet cause to complain of such, 'Ye will not come to me.'

They that are come to Christ indeed, have been led to him by the sense of their necessity of him. When sin has wounded the conscience, they fly to him as the wounded, dying man in the wilderness to the brazen serpent; they make haste to him, as the fainting hart hastes to the waters, panting after them.

They know a change in their lives without a change in their hearts, will but leave them as painted sepulchres in God's eye, and none can change their hearts but Christ; therefore they come to him for sanctification. They know it is to little purpose to restrain sin, except it be subdued; and Christ being only able to subdue their lusts, they come to him for strength. They know outward performances are but the carcase of religious duties: the soul of them is the exercise of grace in them; therefore they come to Christ for quickening grace. They know a civil conversation is not enough to adorn the gospel: there is need of Christ to make them spiritual and heavenly; therefore they come to him for it. They know when they have done their best, and put forth their souls to the utmost in holy services, yet they are but unprofitable servants: there is enough in their exactest performances to damn them, and kindle God's displeasure against them; therefore when all is done, they run to Christ for acceptance. Those who never saw these things necessary, nor their necessity of Christ for those ends, were never yet willing to come to Christ.

3. Many are too busy to come to Christ, they have not leisure for such a journey; some busy in following their sports and pastimes; some eager in pursuing their unlawful pleasures; some wholly taken up with the cares of earth, have their hands, and hearts, and heads, so full of the world, as there is little or no room to think of coming, that must be laid aside till more leisure. If Christ call, they bid him have patience, or come another time, when sickness, or old age, or death approaches; then it may be

they will think of it, at present they must be excused, they cannot come.

You have the temper of these men plainly represented in that parable, Luke xiv. The Lord sends to invite many to the marriage-feast, but they all with one consent make excuse. One is too busy about his farm, he must be excused; another is taken up with his marriage, he cannot come; another is employed about his oxen, he must be excused. Thus it is with most to whom the Lord sends the gospel, they are too busy to be saved, too full of employment to mind Christ or their souls.

Though Christ invite them again and again, though he lift up his voice and cry aloud to them in the ministry of the word, yet such a noise does the world make in their ears, they do not hear Christ; he speaks to stocks and stones, no more are they moved by his invitations. Or if there be any resemblance in them of living creatures, the deaf adder is their emblem. which stops his ears though the charmer charm never so wisely.

Though Christ weep, as we read he did in the Gospel, to see such wretched unkindness unto him, and such strange cruelty to their own souls, yet they regard not; their eyes are so fixed upon other things, that though Christ be held forth to them as a man of sorrows, yet they mind him not, they hid their faces from him.

Though Christ knock at the door of their hearts, and stand there knocking from Sabbath to Sabbath, by his word and Spirit, yet they are so taken up with entertaining the world and their lusts, as they have no leisure to mind him; knock he may, and stand knocking till his head be wet with the dew, and his locks with the drops of the night, yet they will not open. Or if his importunity make them listen, yet usually he gets no other answer, no other return than this, We are not now at leisure, trouble us not now; come another time and we may hear thee. Oh brethren, is not this the language of those delays wherewith ye put off Christ from time to time? Oh take heed lest he who now complains, but ye will not hear, be provoked to turn his complaint into that dreadful threatening, Because ye will not come to me for life, ye shall die in your sins. And that leads me to the

4. Many will not part with that which keeps them at a distance from Christ. They will not part with sin to come to Christ, and there is no coming to him without turning from that; these two are the opposite terms of this motion, &c. Now this is the condition of most that hear the gospel, they have one sin, if not more, which they cannot endure to part with. If Christ and my sin may be joined together, says the sinner, then with all my heart I will accept of Christ's invitation, I will come to him; but if there be no coming to Christ without parting from my sin, oh this is a hard task, a hard saying, I know not how to live without my sin; and thus he leaves Christ.

This is the fatal rock upon which millions of sinners have shipwrecked their souls, and lost eternal life and Christ together. They are wedded to sin, and will live separated from Christ rather than be divorced from their lusts, for there is no enjoying of these together. It is as possible to reconcile light and darkness, or join heaven and hell together, as to join sin and Christ together in one soul; the ways of sin, and the way to Christ, are as far distant as heaven and earth. You may as well expect to have your bodies both in heaven and earth at once, as to have your souls act sin and come to Christ together; no serving of these two masters. Now, because there is no coming to Christ without turning from sin, and most have no mind to part with sin, hence Christ has cause to complain of so many, 'Ye will not come unto me.'

5. Many are possessed with prejudice against Christ, as represented in the gospel, and offered in the ministry of it; and this prejudice renders them unwilling to come to him. This was that rock of offence at which the Jews stumbled, and so fell short of Christ; they expected another kind of Messias than Christ appeared to be when he offered himself to them; they looked for a Messias in the garb of a temporal monarch, to reign amongst them in worldly glory, and to subdue all nations to them by the force of secular power, and to make their country the head of the world's empire. This appears in that petition of the mother of Zebedee's children. Nay, the disciples themselves were possessed with this conceit, as is manifest by their question, Acts i. 6, 'Wilt thou at this time restore the kingdom to Israel?' Now, Christ not answering their expectation, but appearing in the form of a servant, disclaiming all secular jurisdiction, and professing that his kingdom was not of this world, that he came not to rule, but to minister, not to reign, but to suffer, hereupon the carnal Jews were filled with prejudice against him, rejected him, hid their faces from him, and would not come to him as the Messias.

Thus it is now with the carnal professors of the gospel; because Christ answers not their expectation (though not the same, yet altogether as groundless as that of the Jews), therefore they entertain prejudice against Christ as represented in the gospel, and so they will not entertain Christ; they are unwilling to come to him; they expect a Saviour that should let them live quietly in their sins, and be indulgent to them in their sinful, voluptuous, licentious courses, and yet should bring them to heaven when they can live in sin no longer. But now, when the gospel represents Christ as one who requires strictness and holiness in all his followers, who calls for mortification and estrangement from the world in all that come to him, who tells them they must suffer any evil rather than sin, and take up the cross if they will have him for their Christ; when the gospel offers a crucified Christ, one whom nothing will please but that holiness, purity, strictness, which the world scorns and derides; one whom tribulation, persecution, reproaches, will attend in all his followers; hearing this, presently they are offended, prejudice seizes on their souls; This is not the Christ, say they in their hearts, that we expected; this is a Christ of some preciser men's setting up; we will not come to him for life. The Lord, who is the searcher of hearts, knows and sees such secret motions as these in the hearts of most who bear the name of Christ, but will not own him, close with him, as the gospel offers him, but separate Christ from holiness, from sufferings, from which he is not separable. Thus you see why so many will not come to Christ, and who they are.

Use 1; of information. See here the wretchedness of man's nature, take notice of it, and let it be particularly applied. Every man, Jew and Gentile, pagan or Christian, is by nature unwilling to come to Christ; and oh what wretchedness is this! Ye are all by nature far from Christ, far from happiness and life; we are all, till converted and regenerated, in the jaws of death, in the gulf of miseries; all spiritually dead, and the sentence of eternal death passed upon us. The Lord has awarded this heavy sentence not only in the law, but in the gospel, John iii. 18, 36.

And as we are thus miserable, so are we unable utterly to free ourselves from it. Nay, all the powers in heaven and earth cannot revoke this sentence, cannot draw us out of this misery; none in heaven or earth but

Christ; and yet, though our life and death be in the hands of Christ, though our eternal happiness or misery depend upon our coming or not coming to Christ, yet we had rather die and perish than come to him for happiness; rather die in our sins, than come to him for life.

Christ has now, or has had formerly, cause to complain of every one, Thou wilt not come to me, &c. And if Christ have such cause to complain of us, what reason have we to complain of ourselves. Oh the wretchedness of this my nature! oh the desperate depravedness of this heart, that has been, nay, that is, may most say, so unwilling to come. Oh what woeful, what hellish perverseness lodges in this soul, that will use so many excuses, put him off with so many delays, nay, give him plain refusals, when he invites thee, beseeches thee, urges thee with all importunity to come to him for life! I cannot part with my sin, says one, and there is no coming to him without parting from it. I cannot endure that holiness, that strictness (nor none of my companions), says another. I shall be jeered, derided, forsaken, and Christ will not endure me without it. I am well enough as I am, says another; I thank God I am no drunkard, adulterer, extortioner, &c., and what need I go farther? I have time little enough to provide for myself and family, says another; I cannot spare time for prayer, self-examination, mortifying duties, as Christ requires. I may come hereafter, says another; at what time soever I repent and turn to him, he will receive me, and there is time enough before I die. Thus men put off Christ with such pleas and excuses as the devil and their corrupt hearts suggest. And what need is there of any other argument to prove that our natures are desperately wicked above all expression! Such an averseness is in them unto Christ, as you will rather die than come to him. Nor fear of death, nor desire of life itself, can make men wiling to come to Christ. Christ himself could not prevail with many sinners to make them willing, though he preached divers years together, and made this the chief scope of his sermons, and spoke so to this purpose as never man spake, yet all that he could say or do was not effectual with the greatest part of those that heard him. Hence he concludes his sermons sometimes with complaints, sometimes with tears, Luke xiii. 34, Mat. xxiii. 37. So few did he prevail with, as he expostulates in the Prophet as though they were none at all, Isaiah liii. 1, applied to this purpose, John xii. 37, 38, and elsewhere, Isaiah lxv. 2, and xlix. 4. Such obstinacy did Christ meet with against himself, and such will his messengers meet with. This is a lamentation, and will be a lamentation, and oh that every one would lament the wretchedness of his own nature! and then the servants of God would have less cause to weep in secret that Christ's message is so fruitless. We abhor toads and serpents, and such creatures, who seem to be made for the mischief and ruin of others; how much more should we loathe our poisonous mischievous natures, which, by their obstinacy against Christ, shew we are worse than these, as tending not only to the mischief of others, but are obstinately bent to ruin themselves. We abhor the devil for making it his work to devour souls, but are not our natures, till renewed, worse devils to ourselves, being more unwilling to come to Christ for life than Satan is desirous to push us on in the ways of death? May ye not find a toad, a serpent, a devil, or that which is as bad in this respect, in your own bosoms? Oh, bewail the rebellion of your natures against Christ, be ashamed to say or think that you have good natures. And if there were nothing but this, it is sufficient to confound this conceit, and to make you ashamed and confounded for it.

You are by nature unwilling to come to Christ, had rather die than come to Christ for life.

Use 2. Examination. Since sinners, for* the greatest part of men are unwilling, it concerns every one of you to try whether ye be in the number of those who are not willing; that is a most undoubted truth, if that be such which truth itself speaks, and yet who is there that believes it as to himself? It is not easy to determine whether it be more difficult to persuade men to be willing, or to persuade men that they are unwilling to come to Christ. All will easily assent to this in general, sinners are unwilling, but come to particulars, and ask, Art thou unwilling? and most will deny it, and with detestation; I was willing to come to Christ ever since I heard of him; he is unworthy to live, unworthy to be counted a Christian, that will not come to Christ; thus will every one be ready to answer. And as this is an evidence that these confidents never yet came, so it is one great impediment that hinders them from coming. The way to remove this dangerous obstruction in your way to Christ is to be convinced of your unwillingness, and the way to get this conviction is to put yourselves upon serious trial whether ye be willing or no; and this is the intention of this present application, to direct you how to know this.

If ye be willing to come to Christ, you are already come, for there is nothing stands betwixt Christ and a sinner but this unwillingness; as soon as you are willing, you are with him.

Now, whether ye be come to Christ, ye may upon serious trial know by these particulars. Those that come to Christ,

1. Are sorry that they were so long ere they came to him; they know when they were without Christ in the world, they remember when Christ strove with them in his word, by his Spirit, and they resisted, as others do; but now, being by his almighty power drawn to him, they know by experience what they lost by living without him, they are sensible how they provoked and dishonoured Christ by slighting his invitings, neglecting his entreaties, resisting his motions; this is their grief, their sorrow; so it was with the prodigal when he was come home to his father, the first thing that bewrays itself is grief, remorse, for departing from, neglecting to return to him: 'I have sinned,' &c. Their unkindness pierces them, that they kept Christ so long out, that they suffered him so long to stand knocking at their hearts, striving by his Spirit, beseeching them in his word, yet they excluded him, closed their hearts against him. Oh, says the soul, what a wretched rebel was I, who, when Christ stretched out his hands all the day, I refused; when he called, entreated, I would not answer; when he drew me, I resisted! Oh, what love, what indulgence, what kindness was this! and what wretched unkindness was mine! This melts the soul into sorrow. Oh, how happy might I have been long ago if I had yielded to his motions! What a wretch was I, to choose rather to feed on husks than to be entertained with the pleasures of a father's house, than to feed on those delights which communion with Christ affords. If this be your temper, it is a good evidence you are come; but those who say they never were unwilling to come to Christ, they came to him ever since they can remember, have reason to suspect they are not yet come.

2. They are acquainted with the way to Christ. Those that have walked in that way do know it by experience, they have clear, distinct discoveries of the multitude and heinousness of their sins, have been apprehensive of the wrath of God due to them for their sins, have been sensible of their

* Qu. 'far'?—ED.

misery by reason of sin and wrath, even as a man sinking under a burden is sensible of the weight thereof; have been hereupon convinced of an absolute necessity of Christ, even as the man pursued for slaughter under the law saw his need of the city of refuge, so as he must die if he did not without delay get into it; felt their hearts drawn out in ardent desires after Christ, so as their souls could say of Christ as she of children, Give us Christ, or else we die; and upon this have been drawn to consent to take Christ upon his own terms, to part with all the Lord requires, submit to all he enjoins, undergo all that he will inflict, so as he might enjoy Christ; cares not what he want, so as he may have him; cares not what he lose, so he may gain him. This is the way whereby the Lord brings sinners to Christ. If ye know this way by experience, you are come to Christ indeed; but if strangers to it, you are not come.

3. They have a high esteem of him. While the soul is afar off, as all are by nature, he sees little of Christ, and enjoys less, and his esteem of Christ is answerable; he is apt to ask, 'What is thy beloved?' sees no such beauty nor comeliness in him but that other things may have his affections, tastes no such sweetness in him, but that the pleasures of sin are as delightful; and no wonder, for he is at a great distance, and so cannot see and taste that which is afar off; but when he is come to Christ, he sees such beauty and excellency in him as darkens all outward excellencies, makes them seem dross compared with Christ; so did Paul when he was found in him, Phil. iii., σκύβαλα, those things which he formerly admired were now not counted worthy to have place in thoughts or affections; he cast them out, as more fit for dogs than for that heart which had entertained Christ.

Now the soul wonders at his former blindness, that he could see so little of excellency in Christ, when there is (as now he sees) so infinitely much, now he tastes that the Lord is gracious. He had heard of him before but by the hearing of the ear, and his apprehensions were suitable, such as a blind man has of the sun when he hears a discourse in commendation of that which he never saw; but now his eye sees him, and his eye affects his heart, and his heart is filled with admiration of him, as the chiefest of ten thousand, as fairer than the children of men; worthy of all his love, if his heart could be all turned into love; worthy of his highest thoughts, if his thoughts could be raised to the pitch of the angels; worthy of all his praises, if his lips could speak nothing but praises to all eternity. Who is like to thee, O Lord, glorious in holiness, in beauty, in all transcendent excellencies! wonderful in love, in sweetness, and all delights! Thus does he esteem Christ, who is come to him. Those who are so taken with vain delights, sinful pleasures, as they can forego the sweetness of communion with Christ, or know not what this is, who dare usually sin away Christ's favour for worldly advantage, shew they esteem him not, are not come to him.

4. They are in a new condition. He that comes to him, comes, as it were, into a new world; 'old things are passed away, all things are made new.' He finds such a change, as a man who has lived many years in darkness finds when he is brought into the light; so it is expressed, Col. i. 13. He has new thoughts and new affections, new companions and new employments, a new heart and a new life. 'If any man be in Christ, he is a new creature;' can say as Augustine, *Ego non sum ego*, I am not the man I was. If no such inward and outward change, you are not yet come to Christ.

5. They walk with Christ. That is the end of their coming; formerly

they had fellowship with the unfruitful works of darkness, now their fellowship is with the Father and with the Son; formerly, they had their conversations in the world, now their conversation is in heaven, now they know what it is, as Enoch, to walk with God; communion with Christ is no mystery, experience has made them acquainted with it, their mind is with Christ, he is their meditation, their thoughts are of him, they prevent the night-watches, and when they awake, they are continually with him; their hearts are on Christ, he is their love, delight, desire; the bent of their wills is towards him, and so carried with strong inclination, they live to him, act for him, aim at him, depend on him. If it be not thus with you in some degree, you are not come to Christ.

6. They are at a greater distance from sin and the world. For this motion is betwixt these terms, it is a passage from sin and the world to Christ; as when they lived in sin they were at a distance from Christ, so when they are come to Christ they are at a greater distance from sin; as when they were wedded to the world they were separated from Christ, so now when they are married to Christ, they are divorced from the world, they are estranged from it when acquainted with him; crucified to them when alive unto Christ.

7. They have renounced their own righteousness. So Paul, Philip. iii. 9, 'And be found in him, not having mine own righteousness, which is of the law, but that which is through the faith of Christ, the righteousness which is of God by faith.'

Use 3; of exhortation. Then it is the duty of all that the Lord has persuaded to come, to endeavour to persuade others, to strive against this unwillingness in their several places and relations. You that are entrusted with children, &c., have the charge of servants, you that have any dear friend or relation, who you suspect are yet far from Christ, oh use all means, motives, to persuade them to come to Christ, strive against it in yourselves, and in all with whom you converse; this is a common duty, but the special charge of it lies upon ministers; it is their office, they are sent and authorised by Christ for this purpose, 2 Cor. v. 19, 20. Now that I may discharge this trust, let me propound some motives and inducements, which, through the concurrence of God, may be effectual to make you willing, and these drawn from—1, necessity; 2, advantage; 3, equity; 4, danger.

1. Consider what necessity there is. You cannot look upon anything, but, if duly weighed, will convince you of this necessity. Look upon heaven or hell, upon this world or the world to come, upon present enjoyments or future hopes, upon mercy or justice, upon the word of God or his works, look upon what you will, you may see an absolute necessity to make haste to Christ; look upon heaven that is shut up against you; upon hell that is set open to swallow you, till you come to him who has the key of David, &c.; look upon this world, there is nothing will afford you comfort; upon the world to come, there is nothing but endless torment; here nothing but a world of vexatious vanities, hereafter nothing but a world of eternal miseries, till you come to Christ, who is a world of comforts here, a world of blissful enjoyments hereafter; look upon present enjoyments, they are all cursed; upon future hopes, and they are all blasted, till you come to Christ, by whom the sinner's curse is slain, and his hopes revived; look upon mercy, that cannot save you; upon justice, that is engaged to destroy you, till you come to Christ, in whom mercy is magnified, justice satisfied; look upon the word, that does nothing but threaten you; upon his works,

they are nothing but the executions of God's threatenings upon you, till you come to Christ, who makes all the word of God as sweet expressions of love, as a promise, and all the works of God acts of mercy. But more fully thus, till you come to Christ.

(1.) You are under the power of Satan. You are his children, his members, his vassals. The interest of Christ and Satan divide the whole world: there is the world of sinners, and Satan is the god of this world; there is the world of believers, and Christ is the king of this world. Till ye come to Christ, ye belong to Satan really, however in word ye may disclaim him; he that is not with Christ is against him, joins with his mortal enemy, fights under Satan's colours against Christ and his interest, even when he thinks he does Christ service; so Paul before his conversion.

Till ye come to Christ, you are under the power of darkness, you are one of the kingdom of Satan; he rules you, works in you, tyrannises over you. You are in more grievous bondage to him, than the Israelites under Pharaoh, for it is soul-slavery, a bondage that you are not sensible of, that you will not believe, though the Lord in Scripture aver it over and over. Hence this coming to Christ is described by a turning from Satan, Acts xxvi. 18. If sinners perceived their slavery, they might seek to escape; Satan, to make sure work, deals with you as the Philistines did with Samson, he puts out your eyes. Thus woeful is your slavery; your souls are enslaved, and slaves you are to the worst of tyrants, to Satan, till ye come to Christ. Oh is there not necessity to haste out of this condition! Had you rather serve Satan in cruel bondage, than come to Christ for liberty? rather sit in darkness, in the confines of hell, under that hellish taskmaster, than come to Christ for redemption, and be partaker of the glorious liberty of the sons of God?

(2.) You are under the guilt of sin. You have done nothing but sinned since ye came into the world; every of your thoughts, words, deeds, have been sins against God. And of all these numberless millions of sins, not one of them is pardoned, nor ever will be pardoned, till ye come to Christ; there is as much guilt lies upon every of your souls, as is sufficient to sink a soul into hell, and not the weight of one dram that can be removed, till ye come to Christ. Oh you cannot long bear up under such a burden; there is but a cobweb life betwixt you and sinking. If you make not haste to Christ to lay the burden on him, it will certainly press you down into the lower hell. All your sins are in continual remembrance with God: they are set in the light of his countenance, they are in his eye as writ with a pen of iron and the point of a diamond; this handwriting will never be cancelled, these sins will never be blotted out of his remembrance, except you come to Christ; all the dishonour, injuries, affronts you have offered the Lord, will be continually in his eye, till ye come to Christ to interpose. Oh what need is there to make haste! As you have lived, so ye will die in your sins.

(3.) You are under the wrath of God. He is your enemy: the Lord of hosts is his name; his anger is kindled against you. He is angry with the wicked every day; his indignation burns like fire; he loathes your persons, he abhors your services; all you do adds but more fuel to that flame which will scorch you here, but will burn to the bottom of hell, except ye come to Christ to quench it; it is he only that has slain this enmity, it is he only that has brought you righteousness. Oh fly out of this condition, as you would fly from everlasting burnings! Make haste to Zoar; look not back till ye come to the mountains, lest you perish by fire from heaven, lest the wrath of God consume you; your sins have kindled it; it burns so as none can quench it but Christ only. Oh look upon this warning as that message from heaven to Lot's family! Your natural condition is a Sodom; if you slight this warning, as Lot's sons-in-law, Gen. xix. 14, you will certainly, like them, be consumed in the iniquity of that state. God has prepared Christ, a Zoar for the safety of his chosen ones; and now hear the Lord speaking by me, as he spake to Lot, ver. 17, Escape, poor sinner, for thy life; look not behind thee, neither stay thou in this condition; escape to the mountain, fly to Christ, lest thou be consumed.

(4.) You are under the curse, Gal. iii. 10, Deut. xxix. 19. All the curses of the law are levelled against you, all the threatenings of the Lord fall heavy on you, till ye come to Christ; there is not one word in all the book of God that speaks the least comfort to a sinner out of Christ; you cannot strike the least spark of hope out of any expression in the word of God, till you come to Christ; whatever curses and threatenings you meet with, they are yours; whatever comforts or promises you meet with, you have no more to do with them than with your neighbour's inheritance. The word is the last will and testament of God in Christ, wherein he has left every man his portion, his legacy. Now look this will over, from the first line to the last, and you will find nothing bequeathed to you in this condition but a curse. Oh sad legacy! Esau lift up his voice and wept, yea, and cried with a great and exceeding bitter cry, because his father did not leave him a blessing equal with his brother Jacob, Gen. xxvii. 34, 38. But how would Esau have cried, have wept, if his father had left him nothing but a curse! Why, this is all the inheritance of those who will not come to Christ; they have no other portion by this will but the Lord's curse. If you will have any better portion, you must come to Christ for it; if ye will inherit the blessing, if ye will be heirs of the promise, ye must be adopted in Christ; till then, the curse, the threatening is your inheritance. Oh make haste out of this cursed condition, fly to Christ, who has borne the curse, and purchased title to the promise, for all that come to him!

(5.) The justice of God is engaged to destroy you. As sure as God is just, all that come not to Christ must perish. Observe it, the mercy of God, infinite mercy, cannot save you, except you will come to Christ, for the justice of God must be satisfied before any sinner, any offender can find mercy; and none can satisfy justice but Christ, and he satisfies for none but those that come to him. God will never be so merciful as to violate his justice. Now, God would be untrue, unfaithful, unjust if he should spare, if he should save, any sinner that comes not to Christ. If you think God will be merciful to you (unless ye come to Christ, and upon his own terms, so as to forsake sin, renounce your own righteousness, and give up yourselves to holiness), you make an idol of God, and conceive not of him as he is, but represent him to be a God according to your own fancy and likeness, an image of your own forming, not the true God. God will cease to be God if he save a sinner that continues in sin, and will not come to Christ. Justice stands betwixt heaven and every sinner, there is no entering there till justice be satisfied; if you come not to Christ who tenders it, the Lord will require satisfaction at your hands, and you must pay it in hell to the utmost farthing. This is your condition, mercy cannot save you, justice will seize on you, except ye come to Christ; and is there not need to make haste? But though a man without Christ (may some say) be thus miserable in respect of his spiritual and eternal state, yet there is some comfort for him in respect of his temporal estate, he has many outward enjoyments wherein he may solace himself. No; even in these, which are his only support, he is miserable. For,

(6.) His outward enjoyments and accommodations in the world are uncomfortable, unsanctified, accursed. Nothing is sanctified to an unbeliever, Tit. i. 15; and if not sanctified, then not blessed; and if not blessed, then accursed, and so they are in all they enjoy, Deut. xxviii. 15, 16, &c. Outward things are indifferent in themselves, but are to be judged blessings or curses by their rise and issue. If they proceed from the love of God, and tend to the spiritual good of the enjoyers, they become blessings, otherwise they prove curses. And so they are to those that will not come to Christ; the Lord gives them in anger, and when they are lost, he takes them away in his wrath; and when they are continued, they are continual snares, harden them in wickedness; they abuse them as provisions of lust, use them as occasions of sin, and so aggravate their condemnation; and hereby treasuring more wrath against the day of wrath, instead of laying up a good foundation for the time to come; and so bear an impression of wrath with them all along, in their beginning, increase, continuance, departure. Thus it will be with you and all your enjoyments till ye come to enjoy Christ. But if their condition without Christ be so sad and lamentable, how is it (may some say) that they live in so much mirth and jollity? Who more pleasant usually than sinners without Christ? It may seem strange indeed, yea, an astonishment, especially for those that live under the gospel; but consider one instance, and the wonder will cease. Have you never seen distracted men in Bedlam or elsewhere? They laugh, and sing, and dance, as though no men were so happy as themselves, no condition so pleasing and comfortable as theirs. And why are they so merry in such a sad state? Alas! they know not what their condition is, they are beside themselves, and are not sensible what they are or do. Thus it is with sinners out of Christ, they are just like the prodigal, of whom it is said, when he thought of returning to his father, 'he came to himself,' Luke xv. 17; implying that before he was willing to return, he was beside himself. And so is every sinner, while he is unwilling to return to Christ he is beside himself. No wonder if he be so full of mirth when his condition is so sad and lamentable. Alas! he is a distracted soul, he has lost his senses, all spiritual sense; he knows not, he is not sensible, what he does, nor what his soul's condition is, and this is the height of a sinner's misery without Christ; though he be miserable beyond apprehension, yet he is not in the least apprehensive how miserable he is. And this shews what necessity you have to come to Christ, even such need as a distracted man has of an expert physician. Till ye come to Christ, ye are, in a spiritual sense, beside yourselves. And if these considerations draw you not to Christ, it will be an evident symptom of this madness. Till you come to Christ, you are under the power of Satan, the guilt of sin, the wrath of God, the curse of the law; justice is engaged to destroy you, and so engaged as mercy cannot save you; nor can any outward enjoyment afford you the least true comfort. Oh, then, if ye be not quite without sense of your miserable condition, make haste to Christ, resolve to close with him upon his own terms; give no rest to your souls till ye come to Christ and find rest in him.

2. The advantage. As the necessity should force you, so the sweet and precious advantages you will gain hereby should allure you to come to Christ. As soon as you are with him, all the fore-mentioned miseries will instantly vanish.

Come to Christ, and he will free you from the power of Satan, he will knock off those fetters wherewith Satan has loaded your souls; he will judge the prince of this world who does now tyrannise over you, tumble him down from his throne, and make him your footstool. Ye shall be no longer slaves of Satan, but the sons and daughters of the Most High; this shall be your honour, your liberty: 'If the Son make you free, you shall be free indeed,' John viii. 36.

Come to Christ, and he will free you from the guilt of sin, he will tell your souls, himself has borne your iniquities on his body upon the tree; those sins that come now in remembrance before God shall be remembered no more; they are now before God's face, but then they shall be cast behind his back; they are now open to his view, but then they shall be covered. Come to him, he has loved you, he will wash you from your sins in his blood; come to him, his name is 'Jesus, he will save his people from their sins.'

Come to Christ, and he will make your peace with God, he will slay that enmity which is betwixt the Lord and your souls, he will quench that wrath which threatens to consume you; though he seem now to be all in a flame against you, yet then will he say, 'Anger is not in me;' that cloud of displeasure will be scattered, and the light of his pleasing countenance will shine on your souls.

Come to Christ, and there shall be no more curse; all the threatenings shall be turned into promises; then you may look upon threatenings without dread or terror; Christ has satisfied them, you may draw the sweetness of a promise out of them. Then you are in covenant with God, in the covenant of grace; and all the promises are so many articles of that covenant which the blood of Christ has sealed to be yours.

Come to Christ, and then justice itself will be your friend; that which stood before as a cherubim at the way of paradise, with a flaming sword to keep you out of heaven, will then be your security, and conduct you thither. He that comes to Christ has as much security for his happiness from the justice as from the mercy of God; Christ has engaged both for all that come to him, 2 Thes. i. 6, 7.

Come to Christ, and then all your outward enjoyments will be comforts, blessings indeed, sweetened by the love of Christ, sanctified by the blood of Christ, ordered by the wisdom and power of Christ, to make your lives truly comfortable and serviceable here, and happy and glorious hereafter. Death will be no more in the pot, nor fly in the box of ointment, when you are in Christ. When Moses had cast the tree which the Lord shewed him into the waters of Marah, the bitter waters immediately were made sweet, Exod. xv. 25. When Christ mixes himself with your enjoyments, their bitterness is past, they then become sweet and comfortable indeed. Nay, your very crosses and afflictions shall then be sweeter than the sweetest enjoyments of sinners without Christ. 'All things,' Rom. viii.; these shall work for your good, spiritual, eternal, whereas their prosperity shall tend to their ruin; you shall have cause to rejoice and be exceeding glad when men persecute you, &c., whereas they shall have cause to mourn and lament, even when their corn, wine, and oil increase. These are some of those sweet advantages that you reap by being willing to come to Christ. And oh that the Lord would persuade you to be willing, that you would go hence with resolutions never more to give Christ occasion to complain, 'Ye will not come to me,' &c.

Particularly, the advantages you will gain by coming to Christ I will reduce to three heads: union to, communion with, participation of Christ. Come to Christ, and you shall be

(1.) *United* to him, one with him. This is Christ's aim in inviting you, this he desires, this he prays for, John xvii. 20, 21. He invites you, not to your prejudice or disparagement, but to make you happy and glorious; and whereby can you become more happy and glorious, than by being one with him who is the King of glory, the spring of happiness? What greater glory can a poor worm aspire to, than to become a member of Christ, to be a member of that glorious head which is advanced in heavenly places, far above all principality, &c., Eph. i. 20, 21. And what greater happiness than flows from this union! When you are come to Christ, you are as near, as dear to him, as any members of your bodies are to yourselves, Eph. v. 29, 30. Then not only your souls, but your bodies, are members of him, 1 Cor. vi. 15.

And though this union be mystical (not gross, carnal, you must not so conceive of it), yet will it interest you in as much love and tenderness from Christ as though it were corporal. Christ has given a real demonstration of it; he loved his mystical body, the members of it, more than his own natural body, more than any, nay, more than all the parts and members of it; for he gave his natural body, and exposed it in all parts, to wounds, and tortures, and death, rather than his spiritual members should suffer their deserts. Now when we give one thing for another, that for which we give it is more loved and valued than that which we give for it. Even so Christ shewed, by giving himself for his people, that he more loved, more valued them than he did his own body. This will be the sweet issue of your coming to Christ, you will hereby become one of his members, he will be no less tender over you than of his own body. Of what part is any man more tender than his eye? Come to Christ, and the Lord will count you as dear to him as his eye, as the tenderest part of it, 'the apple of his eye,' Zech ii. 8.

Come to Christ, and you shall be admitted to such union with him, such a relation to him, as will not only engage his tenderness and love, but his joy and delight. You are now the bond-slaves of sin and Satan, but come to him, and he will espouse you to himself, 2 Cor. xi. 2. You are now in league with hell and death, but come to him, and he will join you to himself in an everlasting covenant, a marriage-covenant, that shall never be broken, nor you ever divorced. Now you are loathsome in his eye, by reason of the pollution of sin, but then shall the King, the King of glory, greatly desire your beauty, Ps. xlv. 11. Even when ye see cause to loathe and abhor yourselves, yet then shall ye be the joy and delight of Christ: 'As the Bridegroom rejoiceth,' &c., Isa. lxii. 5. Now you are forsaken and cast off, but then you shall be the Lord's *Hephzibah*, his *Beulah*, his spouse, his delight, ver. 4. Now you are viler in his account than the vilest creatures, than the beasts that perish; then you shall be as a crown of glory, a royal diadem, ver. 3; and though ye be now blind and lame in a spiritual sense, poor, deformed, miserable, and naked, enough to discourage any apprehensive soul from expecting such wonderful love, such glorious privileges, such a high relation, yet is there no just cause of discouragement, if ye be but willing to come to him. He looks not you should bring with you a portion, or beauty, or parts, or relations: all that Christ requires is but your consent; consent but to come, and the match is made, your Redeemer will be your husband, Isa. liv. 5. The love of the most affectionate husband in the world will be nothing, compared with the love of Christ to those who are willing to come to him. Hence Christ's love is made the pattern of conjugal love, Eph. v. 25. The copy here, when best drawn, comes far short of the original; the love of the conjugal relation is but a shadow of Christ's love, ver. 32. Thus shall it be done to the man who will come to Christ. And is there nothing of all this that will make you willing to come to him?

(2.) *Communion* with Christ. That communion which, when perfectly enjoyed, is the height of happiness in heaven; and as vouchsafed here, is the beginnings of heaven on earth; a privilege to have it with angels; such communion as is betwixt head and members, such as is betwixt dear and intimate friends. No such distance, estrangement between Christ and you as formerly, but a blessed intercourse, a sweet intimacy, a holy familiarity. He will walk with you, you converse with him; he will confer with you, you may speak to him, Eph. iii. 12. He will visit you, and you may have some access to him; he will feast you, and you may entertain him, Rev. iii. 20.

Oh what an high privilege is this! Are you not willing to come to Christ upon such terms? He will admit you to speak to him, as a man to his friend. You may empty all your grievances into his bosom, who is merciful and gracious; you may ask counsel of him in all straits, who is the 'wonderful Counsellor;' you may desire supply of all wants of him, who has all power in heaven and earth to supply, and is as willing as you can desire, John xv. 17. Oh what is it to have Christ dwelling in you, walking with you, communing with you, speaking to your hearts, leading you as it were by the hand in all your ways, bearing you in his arms when you are weak, guiding you by his eye when you are to seek, lifting you above difficulties which you cannot else overcome, standing by you when all forsake you, supporting you in all pressures, comforting you in all tribulations, arming you against assaults; in a word, to have an all-sufficient Saviour to be all in all to you, in a way of sweet communion, and this for ever, John vi. 37. This, even such communion does Christ offer you, if you be but willing to come to him.

(3.) *Participation* of him. Come, and you shall partake of all that Christ can communicate, and man can receive. Satan and sin will promise much to stay you from him, but though they promise more than ever they perform, yet they cannot promise so much as Christ will really give. Upon condition you will come, you shall have all that Christ can give you, and what cannot he give, who is Lord of heaven and earth, and has the disposing of all in both! You shall have all that heart can desire, Job vi., provided you desire nothing but what is good for you, nothing but what is truly desirable; you shall have all. All what? you will say. Why, all that Christ is, all that he has; all that he has done, and is doing, and all that he has suffered: all these, so far as they are communicable, and you capable; all this, if you will but come for it.

All that he is. Is he God? He will be your God, and this is infinitely more than if I should tell you, that all the kingdoms of the earth shall be yours. Is he man? Then you shall know that he was made man for your sakes, that he stooped so low as to become man, that he might raise you to the enjoyment of God. Is he Mediator, God and man in one person? Then you shall find that he is your Mediator, for your sakes to take up the differences betwixt God and your souls; he was both, that God and you might be at one. Is he a king? Then you shall know that for this end he came to the kingdom, that you might be advanced, and he might be the ruin of your enemies. Is he a prophet? Then you shall find him to be your prophet, to let you know the mind of God, and teach you the way to life. Is he a priest? Then it will appear it is for your sake, that he might be a sacrifice for your sins. In these respects principally the Scriptures declare to us what Christ is, and in all these he will be yours, if you be willing. If this be not enough, here is more than all this: come to Christ, and you shall have

All that he has. Christ, I told you, will marry those that come to him, and this shall be the dowry, all that he has, which is communicable to the creatures; all those riches which the apostles calls unsearchable, Eph. iii. 8. That which is his shall be yours, he will withhold nothing that you are capable to receive; his righteousness is yours, Rom. v. 18. Christ's own robe shall cover you, Isa. lxi. 10. Then you need not be afraid or ashamed to stand in the sight of God, this robe will hide all your deformities; whereas they that want it will call to the mountains to fall on them, and the hills to cover them, rather than appear before him who sits on the throne. His holiness, the ornament of his human nature, and the resemblance of his divine excellency, John i. 16, hence called the divine nature, 2 Peter i.; his peace yours, John xiv. 27; the peace of Christ shall be yours, and that is the peace of God, Philip. iv. 7; his joy, John xv. 11 and xvii. 13, their joy is the joy of the Lord; his glory, John xvii. 22, the glory wherewith Christ as man shall be glorious in heaven, those that come to him shall partake of hereafter; his kingdom, those who upon Christ's invitements will come to him on earth, shall hear that sweet invitation of Christ hereafter, Mat. xxv. 34, 'Come, ye blessed of my Father, inherit the kingdom prepared for you,' &c.; the same kingdom where Christ reigns shall be your inheritance hereafter, Luke xxii. 29, 30; his throne, Rev. ii. 21; those that come at Christ's invitation shall not only be admitted to his table, but to his throne; not only sit, but reign with him, 2 Tim. ii. 12; the poorest sinner that will come to Christ shall be crowned with royal majesty, and reign gloriously with Christ for ever and ever;—all these are yours if you will come to Christ. And is there no power in all these to make you willing?

Nay, further, more than all this,

All that he has done is done in your stead, or in your behalf, or for your advantage; all that he did on earth, and all that he is doing in heaven, it is all for those, and only for those, that come unto him.

His observance of the law yours. You will then find, that 'he was made under the law, that the righteousness of the law might be fulfilled in you,' Rom. viii. 34. That shall be as available to entitle you to eternal life, offered in that first covenant, 'Do this and live,' as if you had perfectly done it in person.

His miracles yours, *i. e.*, for you to ascertain the truth of that doctrine, of those promises, which are your evidences for all the happiness you can expect here or hereafter.

His prayers yours. They shall be as effectual for you as if he had prayed for you by name, or as if he were now on earth to pray for you, John xvii. 20. And oh how precious, how invaluable is interest in those prayers!

His resurrection yours. Those that come to Christ are risen with Christ, Col. iii. 1. Then you shall know that he rose from the dead, that you might be raised out of the grave of sin, to sit with him in heavenly places, Eph. ii. 5, 6.

His ascension yours. Then you shall find he ascended to prepare for your entertainment in heaven, to make ready those mansions of glory where you shall mutually enjoy one another to all eternity, John xiv. 2, 3.

His intercession yours. As he lived on earth to act for you, so he ever lives in heaven to make intercession, Heb. vii. 25. No plea shall be admitted against them, he stands to rebuke any that will attempt it, Zech. iii. 1, 2. No service of theirs rejected in heaven, he offers them with his own hand; and lest sins and failings should appear, he interposes his merit, righteousness, satisfaction; this is that incense mentioned, Rev. viii. 3, which turns all their imperfect offerings into the smell of a sweet odour. Oh what comfort is here for those that are come! What encouragement for those that are not come to resolve upon it! Nay, more,

His present administrations. Not only all he did on earth before his ascension, and all he does in heaven since he left the earth, but all he does on earth when he is in heaven; all his dispensations are with respect of them, and for singular advantage to them, though they take no notice of it, though it seem so much of another tendency as they can scarce believe it, Rom. viii. 28. 'All things,' none excepted; 'called,' those that answer his call, come when he calls. Nay, further, not only all that he did on earth, all that he does in heaven and earth, but

All that he suffered shall be yours, as much for your advantage as if you had suffered them in person. Did he endure poverty? It was that you might have the riches of glory, 2 Cor. viii. 9. Did he live in the form of a servant? It was that you might obtain the adoption of sons. Was he forsaken? It was that you might be eternally owned. Was he slandered and condemned? It was that you might be absolved and justified before God's tribunal. Did he weep? It was that you might rejoice. Did sorrow oppress his heart? It was that everlasting joy might be upon your heads. Was his soul burdened with wrath? It was that you might be freed from that burden. Was he wounded? It was that your languishing souls might be healed. Was he made sin? It was for you, that you might be made the righteousness of God. Did he bear the curse? It was that you might inherit the blessing. Was he scourged? It was that you might be embraced in the arms of everlasting love. Was he crucified? It was that you might be crowned. Did he bleed and die? It was that you might live and reign for ever and ever.

Come to Christ, and you shall know this so assuredly as if an angel from heaven were sent to tell it to you. But if you will live in sin, if all this move you not to part with all to come to Christ, you shall have neither share nor lot in anything that pertains to Christ; if, when Christ has made known to you these great things of the gospel, and when he has offered you his unsearchable riches, you continue obstinate in your evil ways, and confident of your good estate, while strangers and enemies to him in your minds through evil works, why, then, these glorious discoveries are as a vain thing to you, it is a sign the Father has not given you to Christ, for 'all that the Father hath given him will come to him;' it is a sign the offers of sin are more prevalent with you than the offers of Christ, and that 'the god of this world hath blinded your minds,' &c., 2 Cor. iv. 4; but if hereby you resolve to deny yourselves, renounce your sins and come to Christ, then all these glorious riches of Christ shall be your portion. Conclude with Deut. xxx. 19, here is set before you a curse and a blessing, sin and Christ; set before you life and death, sin with death, if ye continue in sin, ye shall die; Christ and life, if ye come to Christ, ye shall live. Oh then, come to Christ, and ye shall have life! choose him, and your souls shall live!

3. The equity of it. If there were neither necessity nor advantage, yet

since it is most equal to do this which Christ requires of you, even this should be a prevailing motive. The equity appears in these particulars,

(1.) Ye lose nothing by coming to Christ. If ye were invited to your loss you might then refuse, there would be some excuse to make your delays and refusals more plausible, but ye can be no losers; gain you may much, infinitely much, but ye can lose nothing; all you get by this journey will be clear gains. But shall we not lose our sins? Must we not part with our dear, gainful, delightful lusts? True, you must part with these; but if you did duly apprehend what sin is, and believe what the Lord in Scripture speaks of, you would never count it a loss to part with any sin whatsoever. Sin is your misery, the spring of all that you count miserable; Satan and the world could never injure you were it not for and by sin, it is sin that is the foundation and complement of your misery. Now, is it any loss to part with misery? Does Christ offer you loss when he would have you come to him upon condition you will part with your misery?

Sin is your fetters, your dungeon; hence the state of sin is set forth in Scripture as a state of darkness and bondage, these are the chains wherein Satan keeps you captive. Now, will a poor captive think he loses anything by leaving his prison and shaking off his fetters? No more can you lose by parting with sin to come to Christ.

Sin is your sickness, your soul's consumption: hence the prophet expresses the sinfulness of Judah in these terms, Isa. i. 5, 'The whole head is sick;' hence freedom from sin is promised under the notion of healing, Hosea xiv. 4, implying sin is the soul's disease. Now, is it any loss to part with a disease? You lose no more by parting with sin than a languishing consumed man loses by parting with his sickness; and will you refuse to come to Christ rather than part with this?

Sin is the wound, the plague of your souls. The more sins the more plague-sores; for sin is that which is called 'the plague of the heart,' 1 Kings viii. 36. By reason of this, the prophet says, there was no soundness in his people, nothing but wounds, &c., Isa. i. 6. Now, is it any loss to part with the plague? is it any loss to be cured of a mortal wound? This is all that Christ would have you lose, and will you refuse him rather than part with it?

Sin is your ugliness, your deformity, that which makes your souls loathsome, Prov. xiii. 5. Why loathsome, but because wicked? Every creature is lovely in God's eye, but this whom sin has polluted and putrified; it is sin that is your loathsomeness. Now would any woman that stands upon her preferment think it a loss to part with a loathsome deformity? This is your case: Christ would have you come, that he may espouse you; he requires no other terms than that you would be willing to part with your deformity; and will you lose Christ, rather than part with your loathsomeness?

Sin is your poison; so it is called, Deut. xxxii. 33; James iii. 8, 'Full of deadly poison;' what is that but full of sin? If the tongue, much more the heart, for that is the spring of sin; being full of sin, it is full of deadly poison. This then is your condition: there is a deadly poison working in your bowels, working in your heart; it will certainly be your death if you do not void it; and this is all you lose by coming to Christ, only part with your poison, be willing to vomit up that which will otherwise ruin you. And will you love your poison more than Christ?

Sin is your frenzy and madness. The prodigal, till he was coming to his father, came not to himself. This is all Christ would have you part with. Will any but a madman be unwilling to be rid of his madness? It may be you slight these things now, and have quite other apprehensions of sin; but you will find it no better, you will apprehend it to be much worse than I have represented it; much worse, either here, or when it will be too late, if you persist. I beseech you, consider the day is coming, when you must stand before Christ's tribunal, to give an account of this very thing, why you would not part with sin, why you would not come to Christ. Will you then say, you thought better of sin than now you find it? But Christ will tell you, you heard what sin was from his mouth, from his messengers; you heard it was your sickness, your plague, your poison, your deformity, and yet you would lose me rather than part with it, you would prefer your plague and poison before me, offering you life and glory. Oh how glorious will the justice of Christ be in sending such sinners to hell, who will not have one word to plead more for themselves why they should not perish! How justly may he say to them, 'Depart from me,' who will not hear for all he can do or say, who will not here come to him, who will not part with the plague to come to him, who prefer their fetters and frenzy, their diseases and deformity, before Christ!

If Christ required you to cut off your members, there might be some plea, but it is only to part with your wounds; if he should bid you pluck out your hearts, &c., but he would only have you part with the plague of your hearts; if he should bid you abstain from meat for ever, then you might have something to plead; nay, but he would only have you abstain from poison: and then judge you, are not Christ's ways equal? Does he require you to come upon any unreasonable terms? Oh no. Even those that must perish for their refusals, as all must that will persist refusing, will be forced to confess that it was the most equal thing in the world that Christ desired, when he bade them leave their sins to come to him.

(2.) He waits till you come. The great God stoops so low as to wait upon sinners, Isa. xxx. 18; he waits as one ardently desiring the motion, the return of sinners to himself, and shall he wait in vain? He stands willing to entertain you. If there was any fear not to be admitted, there might be some plea for not coming; but he never rejects a returning sinner, he never did, he never will withdraw from them, or shut them out from himself, provided they come when he invites them. There is a time, indeed, when sinners shall not be admitted, but that is hereafter; when sinners have worn out his patience, and rejected his offers and entreaties, till there be no remedy; but 'now is the accepted time,' the time when you may be accepted: 'To-day, if ye will hear his voice,' and come to him, you shall undoubtedly enter into his rest. He that now resolves to come needs not doubt of entertainment, John vi. 37; no matter what you have been, or what you are, how sinful, how unworthy, resolve but to come, this shall not hinder; he never did, he never will, cast out a returning sinner; he will not do it in anywise, upon any terms and considerations whatsoever: If you come when he calls, he will in nowise cast you out.

And so he waits for your coming, waits industriously, waits patiently. He waits so as he uses all means to draw you to him. He speaks to you by his providence, he woos you by his word, he sends his messengers to invite, to entreat, to beseech you to come, he puts words in their mouths by which he would have them woo you, he suggests arguments to their minds by which he would have them persuade you, he assists them by his Spirit to manage these persuasions, to enforce these arguments, so as they may prevail, or leave you inexcusable; he sends these to you, when he neglects others; he sends them early and late, he sends them, and sends by them to you, rising up betimes, because he has compassion on you, 2 Chron. xxxvi. 15; he bears with the disrespects you put upon his messengers, though they reflect upon himself; and though you refuse to hear, and be weary of hearing, yet is not the Lord weary of waiting, not weary of entreating; and when others or yourselves would put away the word, and break off this treaty for reconciliation, yet the Lord maugres all provocations, continues it. Oh the wonderful indulgence of Christ!

Nay, he comes himself, he leaves not himself without witness as to the vouchsafement of his presence; your consciences can tell, you are convinced, though not persuaded; he 'stands at the door and knocks;' he stretches out his hands to you, you see him held forth by the gospel in a posture ready to receive you, and when you take no notice, he calls, he lifts up his voice and cries to you; he calls to you over and over, Come, come, come unto me, Mat. xi., &c.; and thus he waits with patience, he waits whole days, all the day long; he stands day and night till his head be wet with the dew; nay, he waits whole years, 'These three years have I come, expecting fruit,' &c., 'Forty years long have I been grieved with this generation,' &c.; and when all this will not do, he breaks forth into sad complaints, and laments their wretched disregard of himself, and woeful cruelty to their own souls: 'Oh that thou hadst known,' &c., 'O Jerusalem,' Ps. lxxxi. 13; 'Oh that my people had hearkened unto me!'

But then, if any sinner listen unto him, and be willing to come, why this is his joy, his delight; in this Christ rejoices, and heaven rejoices with him, Luke xv. 7–10: Christ does, as it were, say to the angels, as he to his friends and neighbours, ver. 6, 'Rejoice with me;' this poor sinner was given me by the Father, he was mine by eternal purpose, but he had lost both himself and me, and now, after much seeking, I have found him, he is returning to me: 'Rejoice with me,' &c.

Oh if you will come to Christ, you will make Christ glad, you will make heaven rejoice! All this is clearly exemplified in the next parable of the prodigal: 'When the prodigal was yet a great way off, his father met him.' The son *comes* but towards his father, but the father *runs* towards an unworthy child; the son is ashamed of himself, his father had compassion on him; he stands accusing himself, his father falls on his neck and kisses him; he confesses his offence, his father never once mentions it; he expects to fare like a servant, but is entertained as the most beloved son; the father provides him a robe, a ring, a feast, and entertains him with great joy: 'For this my son,' says he, ver. 24, 'was lost, and is found,' &c. See here, poor sinners, how you shall be entertained if you will return to Christ, even as the father entertained his prodigal son; he will run and meet you, he will have compassion on you, he will never upbraid you, he will fall, as it were, upon your neck and embrace you; he will think nothing too good, too fine, too costly for you; he will rejoice, and call others to rejoice with him for you. The Lord thinks it meet to rejoice and be glad: ver. 32, 'This my son was dead, but he is come to me for life: he was lost, but I have found him.' Oh how equal, how more than equal, is it to come to Christ, since he is so ready to meet you, since he will so joyfully entertain you.

4. The danger. And this is exceeding great, whether you consider the sin or the punishment; not to come to Christ is a most grievous sin, and will be most grievously punished; a heinous sin. For not to come

Is murder; and which is more, soul-murder; and which is more, wilful murder of your souls. You know the cry of murder is louder than the cry of other sins, it is a loud crying sin; but soul-murder is more grievous, and cries louder for vengeance than that of the body, inasmuch as the soul is more precious and permanent than the body; but wilful murder is this sin in its highest exaltation of guilt and heinousness. Now you wilfully murder your souls if you will not come to Christ; for why does he invite you? he bids you come for life. Now if you will not come, you will not have life, you are resolved to die in your sins; you wilfully put away the life of your souls, and so murder them.

Nor does it hinder that sinners are already dead in a spiritual sense: for to prevent life, is murder in the sight of God, as well as to take away life; those that wilfully procure abortions are as guilty of murder as those that cut the throats of their children. And this is the case, by refusing to come to Christ, you prevent the life of your souls; and this is as much murder as if one should deprive his soul of spiritual life after she is quickened. Here is an Italian cruelty indeed, to murder a soul, yea, and wilfully too. What means has Christ used to make you willing to come for life, and ye would not! what arguments have his messengers used to persuade you to come for life, and ye will not! what remains then, but if you perish, the blood of your souls will be upon your own heads? None else can be accused, of none else can your blood be required, Ezek. xxxiii. 8, 9; if you come to Christ, you may have life, but you will not; you may escape death, but you will not. If so, are you not then the death of your own souls? do you not wilfully murder them? Oh tremble at the apprehension of such a crime! and you that are afraid to shed the blood of others, imbrue not your hands in the blood of your own souls; as you would avoid the guilt of self, of soul murder, come to Christ, that you may have life.

Dangerous, in respect of the severity of Christ's proceedings against this sin.

(1.) If you will not come to Christ, he will come against you, either in a severer way to reclaim you, or utterly to destroy you. This he threatens to Ephesus in case she returned not from a partial backsliding, Rev. ii. 5; if you will not come when Christ calls, he will make you smart for it; so he warns Laodicea, Rev. iii. 19; if he love you, he will whip you to himself rather than quite lose you; if the word prevail not, Christ will take the rod; if you will not hear, he will make you feel what it is to neglect him. Wise parents that are afflicted with rebellious children, if no other means will reclaim them, will rather send them to the house of correction than suffer them to come to the gallows; be sure of it, if the word move you not, Christ will sharply correct you, rather than let you perish, except you be castaways.

Manasseh was an obstinate sinner, he little regarded what the Lord spoke to him by his messengers, while he was in prosperity; but the Lord took another course with him, he gave him into the hands of the Assyrians, who bound him with fetters, and led him captive, and then he bethought himself of returning to the Lord, 2 Chron. xxxiii.

The prodigal was resolute in his evil ways till he was almost starved, but want brought him first to himself, and then to his father. The Lord can take a course to starve you out of all the strongholds of sin, that hold out against Christ, and detain you from him; and if he take any pleasure in you, this course he will take, if the word prevail not. When Joab would not come to Absalom, he fired his corn-field, and that brought him. Look to it, if the Father hath given you unto Christ, he will not lose you; if fair means will not prevail, he will take another course; if your hearts be so much on any enjoyment, as it hinders you from Christ, he will find a way to take it from you; therefore if you would enjoy what he has vouchsafed you, come to Christ, that is the way to secure it; better you should not have anything left you in the world, than that anything in the world should keep you from Christ. As Christ has cords of love, so he has a rod of iron; if you break his cords, he will take his rod; such a rod, as if mercy manage it, it will bruise you, but if justice wield it, it will dash you in pieces; though you belong to him, he may bruise you. David's fall cost him broken bones; but if you are not his, the weight of it will grind you to powder; had you not better come to Christ at a word, than force him to take his rod, put him upon a severer course?

(2.) If you will not come to him, he will depart from you, and you know not how soon. Christ may wait long, but he will not wait ever; his patience will have a period, and thou knowest not how suddenly as to thy self. If thou now refuse, may be Christ will depart this instant; and when he is once gone, then woe to thee for ever, Hos. ix. 12. Thou mayest hear his word, but it shall never profit thee; though it be spoke to thy ear, he will never speak to thy heart; then though thou call, yet will he not answer thee; though thou cry unto him, yet he will not regard thee, no more than thou wouldst formerly regard him; nay, he will 'laugh at thy destruction, and mock when thy fear cometh,' Prov. i. This will your sad estate be when Christ is gone, and it is your refusals that provoke him to depart. When Jerusalem would not come to him, would not be gathered by him, what follows? Mat. xxiii. 37, immediately to their *would not* he returns, 'Behold your house is left unto you desolate,' ver. 38. Why desolate? Not only because of those desolating judgments that were to follow, but because of Christ's departure, which was their forerunner; so he adds, ver. 39, 'Desolate, because ye shall not see me there.' Ay, that place is desolate where Christ walks not, where he is not seen and enjoyed, whatever other company frequents it. And how many places that enjoy the gospel are left desolate in this respect? Their refusals have occasioned Christ's departure. The gospel does not convince, convert, persuade, it prevails not. Why? The people have sinned away Christ's presence. And then, though the gospel be sent, yet it is sent in wrath; for such a time we read of, when it is sent, not to heal and convert, but to harden and make blind, Hosea vi. 9, 10. This is the issue of refusing to come when Christ calls, and oh woeful is their condition to whom the only ordinary means of life is turned into the savour of death.

These are the sad effects of Christ's departure, and it will not be long ere he depart if ye still refuse him; though he be long-suffering, he is not ever-suffering. The spouse herself delayed but a little to admit Christ, and presently he was gone, Cant. v. 2, 3, 6. Make haste then before it be too late; now you enjoy the light, come to Christ while you see the way, walk in the light while ye have the light; when Christ is gone, darkness comes, and he that walks in darkness knoweth not whither he goeth. Now Christ stands and knocks, make haste and open to him; ere long he will not stand, he will not knock any more; now he seeks to you, if you will come, he will be found of you; if you put him off, you may seek him, but never find him more: 'Now is the accepted time, now is the day of salvation;' but ere long this time, this day will be no more; now he invites, entreats, beseeches you to come. Oh that you would answer with the church, 'Behold, we come unto thee, for thou art the Lord our God!'

Now he speaks, 'To-day, then, if you will hear his voice, harden not your hearts, lest he swear in his wrath you shall never enter into his rest.'

(3.) If you will not come to Christ now, you shall not come to him hereafter. This was the sad issue of the Jews' refusal, John vii. 33, 34. Thus will it fare with all refusers; Christ will say to them, I sought you, and you would not be found of me, therefore now, though you seek me, you shall not find me; I came to you in my word and ordinances, by my messengers, by my Spirit, but you would not entertain me; sin and the world was more welcome than myself, therefore I will be gone, I will leave you; and whither I go, you shall not, you cannot come: I go to my Father, my abode will be henceforth in heaven, but you are joined to the world and your lusts; enjoy what you have chosen, me ye shall not enjoy, where I am, ye shall not come. Oh sad doom! Whither will wretched sinners go, since they must not come where Christ is! Now ye please yourselves with sin and outward enjoyments, but sin shall then be your torment, and all your delightful enjoyments shall then be consumed before your eyes; no joys, no hopes of any then, but in Christ (that which you will not believe now, your eyes shall then see); but when these are gone, Christ will be gone too, and whither he goes, ye shall not come. O forlorn sinner, 'thine own wickedness then shall correct thee, and thy backslidings shall reprove thee: then thou shalt know and see, that it is an evil thing and bitter, that thou hast forsaken the Lord thy God,' Jer. ii. 19. Forsaken of all comforts in the world, and forsaken of Christ too! Oh woeful condition! This is it that your refusals lead to. If ye will not come to him, he will be gone; and whither he goes ye shall not come; if ye will not have Christ now, ye shall not have heaven then; if you say, We will not have this man (so holy, so strict, so severe against sin, so jealous of our compliance with the world) to rule over you now, why, you shall not rule, you shall not reign with him then. His kingdom will not be open for all comers, only for those that come to him here. Those that will not come now, must then go. Go whither? Why, go from Christ. Oh dreadful word! Go from Christ! There is hell in this word; yea, and then obstinate sinners will find it so. Christ now says, 'Come,' that is the voice of his love, of his gospel; ay, but if ye now refuse, Christ will change his note, ye shall hear other words from him; he that now says 'Come,' will then say, 'Go,' get ye hence, 'Depart from me, ye cursed;' you would none of me, my ways were too straight, too holy, too solitary; my yoke was uneasy, my burden too heavy in your account; well, now I have nothing to do with you, depart from me into everlasting burnings; get ye hence from me to the devil and his angels; to him ye came, to him ye shall go; from me ye departed, and now ye shall depart from me for ever; since you would not believe, now you shall feel what it is to prefer sin and the world before me. Go to the gods that ye have served, feed on the fruit of those lusts that ye have loved; get ye to him whose suggestions you would rather obey than my invitements, this is the doom of all that will not come, Mat. xxv. 41.

(4.) If ye will not come to Christ, ye shall not have life. This is the sense of the words, no life but in Christ, no partaking of life but by coming to Christ; if ye will not come to him for life, ye shall die in your sins, die spiritually, die eternally. No life at all, nothing but death, without Christ, without coming to Christ; if you will not come to Christ, why then bid adieu to Christ and life together, for they can never be parted; if ye will not come, ye shall die; if ye will come, ye shall live.

Obs. Those that come to Christ shall have life. It is clearly implied, the scripture is in nothing more express than this, 1 John v. 12, as Christ professes that he is life in himself, John xiv. 16, so is he life to his people, to those that come to him, Col. iii. 4. But how come they to have life by Christ, but by believing? John xi. 25, and believing is coming, John vi. 35.

But what life is this?

All that the Scripture compriseth in this word life, all that is opposite to that death which Adam brought into the world, Rom. v. For as the first Adam was the original of death in its full extent, so is Christ, the second Adam, of life in its utmost latitude; of life spiritual, eternal, yea, and of natural too; if not in its being, yet in its well-being. For though the two former be principally intended, yet must not the other be excluded, since it is a safe and received rule to understand Scripture in the largest sense, where there is no reason to restrain it. But the Jews were alive naturally when Christ thus spoke to them; what need was there to come for that which they had already? may some say. It is true, they had natural life in its being, but not in its well-being; they, and all, must come to Christ for that, or want it. Natural life without Christ is as good as no life; *non est vita vivere, sed valere;* it is the welfare of life that is life indeed, and this men get by coming to Christ, another kind of life natural than natural men partake of, in respect of the tenure, blessing, comfort, usefulness, tendency of this life, without which better not live than have this natural life.

1. Those that come to Christ shall have another kind of temporal life.

(1.) In respect of its *tenure.* Until sinners come to Christ, they hold their life only upon common providence, that is their title; but believers they hold their lives by virtue of the covenant of grace, and that is the most sweet and blessed tenure in the world, 1 Tim. iv. 8. They have the promise of life, the Lord gives them a title by covenant; now covenant-mercies are the chief, if not the only mercies. Sinners out of Christ live as a condemned malefactor under a reprieve; sentence of death is passed, only the judge's patience suspends the execution. Such is the condition of a sinner's life; he is only suffered to live, he owes his life to the Lord's patience, he lives but by permission; ay, but he that is in Christ has his life by gift, a gift of love and free grace, not common patience, but special mercy gives him life, 1 Cor. iii. 22, and life among the rest. Until Christ be yours, even this temporal life is not yours upon covenant terms, not yours by virtue of special mercy and distinguishing love. Before your lives can thus be yours, Christ must be yours, you must come to him, or else want life while ye have it, want it upon those blessed and gracious terms.

(2.) In respect of the *blessing* of life. Life is not a blessing special but by Christ. Sinners out of Christ, as they are cursed when they die, so, while they live, the curse cleaves to their life, as the leprosy to Gehazi. It leaves not their natural life till they leave their natural condition, and come to Christ. Your temporal life is an accursed life till ye come to Christ; so it is from the womb to the grave, Deut. xxviii. 18. As soon as life is received, the curse is conceived, and expires not till the sinner comes to Christ, who became a curse, that those who come to him might be delivered from it. Life is a blessing in itself, but sin turns this blessing into a curse; and till sin be taken away, the curse continues, and guilt is not removed till the soul move to Christ; then, and not till then, does life become a blessing, when the sinner comes to Christ.

(3.) In respect of the *comfort* of life. Natural life can never be truly comfortable while the sinner lives out of Christ. He has the possession of life, but not the comfort of life, till Christ make it comfortable: Ps. lxxxvii. 7, 'All my springs are in thee.' Christ is the only spring of comfort in the world. Sin, at its first entrance into the world, made all other springs dry, and ever since, all the earth, and every part of it where Christ is not enjoyed, is a dry and thirsty wilderness, where there is no water, no drop of comfort. It is true sinners think their lives comfortable, but their comforts are but fancies, at least unhallowed comforts, such as will be bitterness in the end. If their coming to Christ prevent not, even their chiefest delights will end in the greatest bitterness. They will see (what now they are far from believing) that their mirth is but like the mirth of madmen. If they knew their condition, their joys would be turned into sorrow and astonishment. The Lord is in Christ the Father of mercies, and the God of all comfort. As all comforts are in him, so not a drop of comfort comes from him but through Christ; and none is conveyed through Christ to any but such as come to him. The fountain is sealed to all other sinners, 2 Cor. i. 3; there is not the least ground of comfort in your lives while ye live without Christ. The comfort of life, which is indeed the life of our lives, is only from Christ, only for those that come to him.

(4.) In respect of the *usefulness* of life. Of what else* is the life of a sinner living without Christ? Serviceabler, indeed, it is to make provision for the flesh to fulfil the lusts thereof, serviceabler it is to Satan to increase his subjects, and strengthen his kingdom; but how is it serviceable to God? how useful for promoting those great ends for which it is vouchsafed? In these respects it is of no use, renders the sinner a vessel in which the Lord takes no pleasure, as being unfit for his master's use. Indeed the Lord serves himself of sinners, and overrules their lives, so as to force honour to himself out of them, but otherwise of their own accord they are unserviceable and useless.

A sinner's life without Christ is a talent hid in a napkin; the Lord of it gets no advantage by it; it serves to bring the sinner under the doom of an unprofitable servant. Of what other use is it? Your lives without Christ are as lamps without oil; if ye make not haste to Christ to light them, you will fare as the foolish virgins; the bridegroom may pass by, and shut you out of the marriage-chamber, shut you out of heaven for ever.

The usefulness of your lives depend upon your coming to Christ; then only will they become serviceable, 'vessels unto honour, sanctified, and meet for the master's use, and prepared unto every good work,' 2 Tim. ii. 21. What Paul says of Onesimus, Philem. 11,—'Which in time past' (viz., before he came to Christ) 'was to thee unprofitable, but now profitable to thee and me,'—may be said of the life of every sinner before he comes to Christ. He is unprofitable to Christ, to his church, to his family, to his relations; not spiritually useful to any, no, nor to himself; a burden of the earth, one that cumbers the ground; barren himself, and keeps others barren; is fruitful in no respect, except in the unfruitful works of darkness; but when he comes to Christ, then serviceable to the Lord, to his people, &c. Oh, what is an useless life worth! Why, it is not worth the having, the desiring. If you would have your lives worth either, come to Christ; that is the way to make them useful; the usefulness of them depends on this.

* Qu. 'use'?—ED.

(5.) In respect of the *tendency* of life. Natural life in a sinner without Christ tends to death; it is always as Jordan, running towards the Dead Sea. The tendency of it is to lock up the sinner faster in the grave of spiritual death, to roll more stones to the mouth of that woeful sepulchre, that he may be more sure of eternal death. The tendency of this life is deadly. Ay, but when he comes to Christ, his life tends to spiritual life and peace, to glory and happiness, to the glorifying of God, and being glorified with him. Christ turns the current.

Thus you see that natural life, in all respects wherein it is truly desirable, depends upon coming to Christ. Till then, this life is little better than death; and the sinner, while he lives without Christ, is, as the apostle speaks of our living in pleasure, 1 Tim. v. 6, 'dead while he lives.' And so was the prodigal, till he came to his father; he was frolic, merry, active, lively enough in his own ways; but when he was not himself, his father, who could better judge of his state, took him for a dead, a lost man: 'This my son,' says he, 'was dead,' &c. And herein, as otherwise, he was an emblem of a sinner out of Christ; how merry, jovial, lively soever he be in the ways of sin, he is as a dead man in the Lord's account. Natural life does then become truly life when a sinner comes to Christ, and those that come shall find it so in the premised respects.

Thus in these respects temporal life is from Christ. Now,

2. Spiritual life is from him in all respects. Those that come to him, and only those, shall have spiritual life from him, both a life of righteousness and holiness.

(1.) A life of *righteousness*. That is it which the apostle calls, Rom. v. 18, 'Justification of life comes upon all men.' Not all and every man, but all that come to him, all that are his. As condemnation came upon all that were Adam's, death came by Adam's sin, justification to life by Christ's righteousness; *that* to all that were in Adam, *this* to all that are in Christ, all men being in Adam, and death threatened in case he should sin; 'In the day thou eatest thereof thou shalt surely die,' Gen. ii. 17. He sinning, the sentence of death passed upon him, and all his posterity in him; so that all men by nature are dead men in law, they are condemned already, John iii. 18. Now the sentence of God's condemning man to death being most just and righteous, it is irrevocable, and so death unavoidable. Christ then, seeing God's justice could not be salved nor satisfied without death, was willing to suffer the death threatened, and this he suffered for those, and only those, that come to him. Wherefore a sinner coming to Christ, when he finds in the law the sentence of death awarded against him, it is true, may he say, the sentence is most righteous; death is due to my sin, but Christ has suffered that death; he died in my stead, and God looked upon him dying for my sin as though I myself had died for it; and death being suffered, the law is satisfied, and I am absolved; I am in Christ, come to him, and there is no condemnation to such, Rom. viii. The Lord himself has justified me, as having suffered in Christ what justice required, and therefore now nothing can be laid to my charge, according to ver. 33, 34. Can any charge me that by law I am condemned to death? No, 'it is God that justifies me.' He absolves me, 'who is he then that condemneth?' But how can this stand with the truth and justice of God, who has peremptorily passed the sentence of death against thee, and said, 'In the day thou sinnest thou shalt surely die'? Why, very well, for Christ has died in my stead; so he adds, 'It is Christ that died.' Thus by Christ's sufferings and righteousness comes the justification of life to those who come to Christ. Hence the favour of God, Ps. xxx. 5, lxiii. 3.

(2.) A life of *holiness*. This is life in Scripture phrase. Hence, when a sinner is translated out of the state of nature into the state of grace, he is said to pass from death to life, 1 John iii. When he first receives the principles of holiness, he is said to be born again, John iii., and the progress in holiness is called a new life: Rom. vi. 4, 'newness of life,' after the Hebrew phrase, who put the abstract for the concrete, newness for new, &c. This life is from Christ, and those that come to him have it from him in these respects:

[1.] Principles of this life. The seeds, the habit of grace, every perfect gift, comes from above, as all light comes from the sun; but how do these gifts come from him? By, or in whom are they conveyed? The apostle tells us, Eph. i., in Christ. When the soul, coming to Christ, has union with him, it is united to the fountain of life. Christ is that to the soul which the soul is to the body; accordingly it is expressed, Gal. ii. 20, 'Nevertheless I live; yet not I, but Christ liveth in me.' Even as we may say, the body of a man lives, yet not the body, but the soul lives in it, by virtue of its union with the soul; so a believer lives, yet not he, but Christ lives in him; and the life that he lives is by virtue of his union with Christ, by faith uniting him with the Son of God. No life of grace, no seeds, no principles of it, without coming to Christ, without union with him; those that come to him shall be united with him, shall be replenished with these principles.

[2.] The increase of this life. This is from Christ, John x. 10. Justification and glory are not capable of addition or diminution, cannot be said to decay or abound; it must be meant of the life of holiness. As Christ lays the foundation, so he carries on the building; both the being and increase is from him; even as animal spirits (upon which the life, and motion, and sense, the vital acts of the body, depend) are conveyed in abundance by the several parts through the whole body, from the head, so from the head Christ (it is the apostle's similitude, which he uses more than once, Eph. iv. 15, 16). All that tends to the growth of Christ's body is conveyed from the head to the several parts and members, compacted together for the better conveyance of this lively influence to the whole. And this is by and 'according to the effectual working of Christ in every part,' according to its capacity, and hence arises the increase thereof, which he expresses by the same resemblance, Col. ii. 19. From Christ the head, all his members, mutually united amongst themselves, and unto him, as it were by joints and ligaments, have nourishment ministered, so as they increase with the increase of God, *i. e.*, with an exceeding great increase; according to the property of the Hebrew tongue, much followed in the New Testament, who, when they would express the exceeding greatness of a thing, they add the name of God unto it: Ps. lxxx. 11, goodly cedars, ארזי אל, the cedars of God; so Ps. xxxvi. 7. Righteousness, as the great mountains, כהררי אל; so Cant. viii. 6. So here, the spiritual nourishment which he conveys to those who come to him, are one with him, tends to make their increase, their growth in grace, an exceeding great increase; to him we must go if we would grow in grace, if we would have this life in more abundance. If we would not be guilty of the backslidings, barrenness, non-proficiency, for which the Lord has a controversy with the professors of our times, we must come to Christ for it; it is he that causeth all grace to abound, it is of his fulness that his people receive grace for grace.

[3.] The acts of this life. The exercise of holiness, as the habit is from him, so is the act; it is he that worketh in us both to will and to do; both the inward motion, to will, and the outward expression, to do, is from him. If a man have never so much strength, yet if he sleep, he acts not, till he be stirred up; if a man have never so much grace, if he be not acted, excited by Christ, if he have not a special assistance from Christ's Spirit, he cannot, he will not exercise it. We see many sanctified, as having the principles of holiness implanted in them, yet few acts, little exercise of it in their conversation; why? They neglect Christ, rest on what is received, depend not on him for special assistance to act them, and draw grace into exercise. Independency in acting is God's prerogative: Philip. iv. 13, 'I can do all things through Christ which strengtheneth me.' He wanted not habitual, but actual strength, without which we can do nothing, with which a weaker Christian can outdo a stronger: 2 Cor. iii. 5, 'Not that we are sufficient of ourselves to think anything as of ourselves; but our sufficiency is of God.' What sufficiency was wanting? Why, Christ's special help, to move, act, determine holy principles; without which, not sufficient for a good thought; if we would have the lively, vigorous actings of grace, we must come to Christ; if we would not have the principles of life received to lie unactive in the soul, as though they were dead, we must come to Christ for this life; he has it for those who come.

[4.] The continuance of this life. Though ye have received it, and that in abundance, and exercise it accordingly, yet without Christ, grace itself would die and expire; it is he that keepeth our soul in life, Ps. lxvi. 9. The continuance of this life depends upon Christ's intercession and acting for us; he tells Peter, Luke xxii. 32, 'I have prayed for thee, that thy faith fail not.' And every one that comes to him is included in this prayer: John xvii. 15, 'I pray not that thou shouldst take them out of the world, but deliver them from the evil;' from those evils that are destructive to life, and threaten the death of the soul. In order hereto, he strengthens them to resist those assaults, those blows, which would else prove mortal; he enables them to oppose corruption within, and Satan and the world without, so that they are in all these 'more than conquerors.' But how? 'Through him that has loved us,' Rom. viii. 37. He keeps them in his hand, else they might be plucked from him, life itself plucked from them, John x. 26. Spiritual life in all these respects is from Christ, and those that come to him may have it of him.

3. Eternal life is from Christ. Those that come to him shall have eternal life, in respect of title, hopes, and earnest here, and possession hereafter.

(1.) *Title* to eternal life. Adam in his integrity, and we in him, had a right to eternal life, the promise of God was our patent, but sinning, and failing in the condition, he, and we in him, utterly lost all title to eternal life; nor can any son of Adam, out of Christ, lay any claim to it. But the Lord Jesus Christ has bought a new title for those that come to him. It cost him dear indeed, the price was his blood, but all that come to him shall have it freely; he bought it for this end, and therefore heaven is called a purchased possession, Eph. i. 14. The patent is renewed, another title is acquired. But for whom? Those only that come to him; none else have right to it: Rev. xxii. 14, 'Blessed are they that do his commandments, that they may have right to the tree of life.' What commandments are those upon which this right is suspended? Why, the first and chief commandment is, that we come to him, and if there be any other, it depends upon this; when this is done, Christ gives a sinner right to the tree of life.

(2.) *Hope* of eternal life. A lively hope, an assuring hope, a well-grounded hope, such a hope as makes it so sure as though we were in possession. Hence believers are said to be already saved, Eph. ii. 8, Titus iii. 4. But salvation is yet to come; how are we then said to be already saved? The apostle tells us: Rom. viii. 24, 'By hope.' But whence comes this hope? See 1 Tim. i. 1, Col. i. 27. Christ is the foundation of this hope, and to them only who come to him, 1 Peter ii. 4, 6. Those alone shall not be confounded. Those who hope for heaven, and yet are so much in love with sin as they will not come to Christ, and yet will hope for heaven, shall find their hopes delusions, and thereupon, as men who beyond all expectation meet with great disappointments, shall be confounded, their hopes shall make them ashamed. That hope which makes not ashamed, is the hope of those who have fled to Christ for refuge, to lay hold on him, the hope set before them, Heb. vi. 18, 19. This is the anchor of the returning soul; it will secure him in all storms, for it is both sure and stedfast, it is firmly and deeply fixed, and that in a sound bottom too: it entereth into that within the veil, the bottom where it is fixed is heaven, figured by the holy of holies, which was separated from the body of the temple by the great curtain or veil. He anchors in heaven who comes to Christ, who is entered there as his forerunner; he may safely ride out all storms, and is sure to arrive where his forerunner is landed, even in heaven.

(3.) *Earnest*, the first fruits of eternal life. Those that come to Christ shall have the beginnings of heaven here on earth, the first fruits of eternal life even in this life, some clusters of Canaan's grapes in the wilderness. Heaven is a place of joy, here they shall have joy unspeakable; a state of enjoyment, here they shall enjoy the presence and favour of God, fellowship with the Father, a state of glory; here some buddings of glory, that which makes them all glorious within, that for which they are said to be changed from glory to glory; a state of vision, here they shall see with open face the glory of God, though but in a glass, here they shall have a Pisgah sight of heaven at least.

(4.) The *possession* of life eternal, John vi. 40. They are so sure to possess it, as though they were in present possession. The expression is answerable, ver. 47, 1 John v. 10, 11.

Use 1. Information. Take notice of the misery of those who will not come to Christ. Those only that come to him have life; those, therefore, that come not to him are without life.

Without the blessings and comforts of natural life. The life you live without Christ is but such as the life of condemned malefactors; it is an uncomfortable, an unuseful, an accursed life, such as tends to death.

Without spiritual life in all respects. Justice has passed the sentence of death upon every such sinner, and it will never be repealed without satisfaction, which being of infinite value, none can tender but Christ, and he tenders it for none but those that come to him; till then, every such sinner is בן מות, a son of death: 1 Sam. xx. 31, rendered, 'He shall surely die;' or, as the Hellenists phrase it, John xvii. 12, ὁ υἱὸς τῆς ἀπωλείας, a lost, a dead man; so he is in law already condemned, John iii. 19. Light Christ revealed in the gospel, and men love darkness, sin, the work of darkness, their natural sinful state, which is the state of darkness, and this is condemnation. For this cause sinners are under the sentence of condemnation; and if God be just, as just he is essentially, no less than merciful, the sentence now passed will be executed on all that come not to Christ. This was the issue of the first sin: Rom. v. 18, 'Judgment came upon all;' so that every son of Adam, as soon as he lives, has judgment of condemnation to death, and so he continues a condemned person under the sentence of death, till he come to Christ, and then only is he absolved, Rom. viii. 1. Till then, as justice has sentenced him, so wrath attends him, he can have no sense of the favour of God, which is better than life, and so his condition is in this respect worse than death.

Use 2. Examination. By this ye may know whether ye be come to Christ or no. It concerns thee as much as thy life to know this, and yet few regard. Most take it for granted, when they have no ground for it, and therefore I have delivered many things formerly tending to conviction, that none may deceive themselves in a matter of such consequence; but because Satan and men's corrupt hearts are great enemies to this conviction, and it is the hardest thing we meet with to convince any of those who profess Christ that they are not come to Christ, let us make use of this truth for a further discovery. Would ye know whether ye be come to Christ or no? Why, by this you may know it: if ye be come to Christ ye have life, spiritual life. But how shall this be known? Why, by such resemblances betwixt natural and spiritual life as the Scripture holds forth; as where there is natural life there is breath, motion, sense, so where there is spiritual life there is spiritual breathings, motions, sensibleness.

1. Where there is life there is *breath*. Death is expressed by want of breath: Ps. civ. 29, 'Thou takest away their breath, they die;' and life is expressed by breath, as that which is inseparable from it, Ezek. xxxvii. 5, 6, 8, 10. Where there is spiritual life there is breathings after God; so Lam. iii. 56. The quickened soul breathes after God, the sense of his favour, communion with him; breathes after Christ's righteousness, the power of his death, the virtue of his resurrection; after growth in grace, and increase of holiness, victory over sin; after the enjoyment of God, Christ in his ordinances, nothing else will satisfy; so David, Ps. xlii. 1, 2, Ps. xxvii. 4, Ps. lxiii. 1, 2. Think not we go too high in making David's example our rule; our gospel enjoyments require more, though few answer them. Where spiritual life is, there will be in some degree such breathings after Christ, such ardent desires, in some degree, more or less, according to the degrees of spiritual life: where no such breath, no life; that soul is not yet quickened, not yet come to Christ.

2. Where there is life there is *motion*. These are joined: 'In him we live and move;' they are inseparable both in grace and nature. When the soul is quickened, it moves towards God, the bent and inclination of the heart is after Christ, the affections are carried out to him, the conversation is an acting for him, it has another centre, and moves to other terms, from sin and the world, to Christ and heaven, Col. ii. 1. It moves spiritually. A natural man may move in God's ways, but he moves not spiritually; he may pray, read, hear, meditate, but not spiritually, not out of love to Christ, but out of custom, self-love, enforcements of conscience; not to honour Christ, not with any desires to enjoy him, but for by-ends, sinister respects; not affectionately, but in a heartless, careless, unaffected manner. If the work be done, he is satisfied, whatever the temper of his heart was in doing of it; whether God get glory by it, or he enjoy Christ in

it, he regards not; so the duty be performed, it is enough. Such motion there may be without spiritual life, but it is spiritual motion which is the pulse by which ye may know this spiritual life. Where no heavenly inclinations, no holy tendencies towards Christ, with desires to enjoy and honour him, there is no spiritual life, such as are* not yet come to Christ.

3. Where there is life there is *sense*.

The quickened soul *sees* a transcendent excellency in Christ, as to contemn, part with all for him; sees a loathsome deformity in sin, sees a wonderful beauty in holiness, sees a woeful misery in a natural condition, and sees so as his soul is affected with it. Where these objects are not spiritually seen, affectionately discerned, there is no spiritual life.

Hears. The heart hears. That which comes but to the ears of others, when the gospel makes known the mysteries of regeneration, of Christ's righteousness imputed, of self-denial, of mortification, hears them as things which he finds, and has experience of in his own heart. When Christ commands to leave sin, to mortify lusts, be crucified to the world, decline his own carnal humours, interests, inclinations, he hears so as to obey, to resolve and endeavour it.

Feels a weight, a burden in sin, feels the wounds it has made in his soul; he wonders he should be so much past feeling before, as not to be sensible of that load of sin which was pressing his soul down towards the pit. His conscience smarts by those sins which the world count not worthy the name of sin. Those that are past feeling are without life.

Tastes the sweetness of Christ, 1 Pet. ii. Christ is sweeter to him than any of the pleasures of sin. Formerly he heard of Christ's sweetness, and had such apprehensions of it as he had of the Israelites' manna, which he never saw nor tasted; he thought of Christ's sweetness before, but now he has tasted his sweetness.

He tastes sweetness in the promises. They are sweeter to him than the honey and the honey-comb, he feeds on them as on manna, he lets them lie long on his soul, in his thoughts, as sweet things on our palates; they are his dainties, his refreshment in the night-season, he has meat to feed on which the world knows not of.

He tastes sweetness in spiritual enjoyments. Enjoyment of Christ in his ordinances, this is to his soul as marrow and fatness; as David promises himself, if he should again see the power and glory of God in the sanctuary: 'Then my soul shall,' &c., Ps. lxiii. 5. If you never tasted this, never had experience of so much pleasure in word, or prayer, or meditating on Christ or promises, but you have taken more delight in worldly pleasures; never tasted such sweetness therein, but that you can live comfortably without them, if outward comforts be but continued, then it is evident you are yet without spiritual life, not yet come to Christ.

* Qu. 'such are'?—ED.

THE LORD THE OWNER OF ALL THINGS.

AN INDUCEMENT FROM EARTHLY-MINDEDNESS.

For all . . . is thine.—1 CHRON. XXIX. 11.

THESE words are part of David's praise and solemn thanksgiving to God. In which we may observe, 1, the occasion or ground; 2, the form and mode of it.

1. The occasion of it is this, as laid down in the former verses: David, in a general assembly of his people, declaring his design to prepare for the building of a temple for the solemn worship of God, moves them to contribute towards it, and encourages them by his own example. They comply with him herein, and contribute 'willingly,' cheerfully, of their own accord, without further importunity; ver. 6, 'sincerely,' not out of ostentation, not to gratify their king, but to honour God in promoting his interest and service; ver. 9, 'liberally,' in great proportion; for reckoning a talent of silver at £375, and a talent of gold at £4500, what they offered amounted to above twenty-six millions of pounds sterling (besides the ten thousand drams of gold, the other metals, and precious stones, ver. 7), which, with what David himself gave out of his private treasury, being above sixteen millions more, ver. 4, makes a very vast sum. For this he and the people rejoice. Pleasure is τελείας ἐνεργείας ἐπιγινόμενον τέλος, the result of an excellent act, ver. 9, and David lets forth this joy in public praises, ver. 10. He blesses and praises God, not because they had so much, but because they had hearts to lay out so much for God and his worship. It is more occasion of joy and praise to expend much for God and for his service than to have much to expend. To have much may be a curse and a snare, and matter of greater condemnation; but to have a heart to employ it for God is a happiness indeed, a far more blessed thing than to keep it, or to gain it, or any way to receive it, Acts xx. 25. And this is a truth so evident to reason (though a paradox to worldlings), that the heathen did acknowledge it. Isidore tells us it was the maxim of some amongst the Persians.

2. The form or mode of his praising God we have in this verse. It is an ascribing all excellencies to him. Whence we may learn wherein the true praising or blessing of God consists; it lies in acknowledging that to be God's which is his. We can give him nothing, for all is his; we can add nothing to him or his glories by blessing him, he is far above all such

praises and blessings; he wants nothing that is excellent, he is all-sufficient of himself, and infinite in all his perfections, and was so from, and will be so to, everlasting. All that men and angels can do is to acknowledge him to be what he is, and to have what he hath. And to do this is to praise or bless him. Thus, when our Lord Jesus is teaching his disciples how to pray, and how to praise the Most High, this is the mode of praising him, Mat. vi. 13, 'Thine is,' &c. And after the same manner does David here praise him.

'Thine is the greatness.' Thou art immensely, infinitely great, and all other greatness besides is from thee, it is thine.

'The power.' Thy power is almighty, and the power of all others is derived from thee, and depends altogether upon thee, it is thine.

'The glory.' Thou art all-glorious, and all other glory is but the shadow of it.

'The victory.' Thou conquerest all that oppose thee, and givest victory to all that vanquish, the victory is thine.

'The majesty,' or 'authority' as some render it. Thou hast all authority in heaven and earth, and all that have authority have it from thee; what is not exercised for thee is no authority, and what is duly exercised is thine.

'The kingdom.' Whoever rules in any realm, the kingdom is thine; O Lord, they do but rule by commission from thee, and as substitutes under thee; thou art supreme governor of them all, thou art exalted as head above all, and, in a word, all is thine, all that is in the heaven and in the earth is thine.

All dominion is here ascribed to God, whether it signify rule, or whether it signify propriety; God is both the ruler of all, and likewise the owner of all. I have insisted on the former at large in some late discourses, and the latter I have chosen for my present subject. Take it in this observation, clearly held forth in the words of the text,

Obs. The Lord is the owner of all things.

Whatever is in being is either in heaven or on earth, and all this is the Lord's; he has the best title to it, he is the true proprietor and owner of it.

This is a truth of great moment and consequence, yet little, or not at all (so far as I have observed) insisted on in pulpits, and but sparingly touched in writings; but since it is of much importance, and exceeding useful to stay a little on, it may not be amiss.

In the prosecuting hereof, I shall endeavour to shew, I. What evidence there is in Scripture for the Lord's title to all things. II. What kind of title it is for which he is called the owner of all. III. What the ground and foundation of it is, upon what account he challenges it and will have it acknowledged. And then, IV. What useful application may be made of it, how much and excellent fruit it will bear if it be duly improved.

I. For the first, the Scripture abounds with evidence for this purpose, asserting the Lord's title to all things, even such as we count ours, whether ours in *common* with others, or such as we think to be *properly* ours.

1. Of the former sort; the world in general is said to be his own, Ps. l. 12, the fulness, the furniture of it, whatever fills it or adorns it, whatever does replenish or beautify it: 'The world, and all that it contains, is mine.' More particularly the principal and integral parts of this great fabric, with appurtenances. Heaven is his, Ps. lxxxix. 11, and whatsoever has the name of heaven, Deut. x. 14. The heaven of heavens; *i. e.*, the highest heavens, these are the throne of the Most High; and the heavens,

i. e., both the ether, the place of stars and planets, and the air, called heaven, Gen. i. 20, &c., this is called his chamber, Ps. civ. 3, the beams of his upper rooms in the watery clouds; and these clouds are his chariot, and the winds (which are but air in motion) are the wheels of his chariot. All, from the highest to the lowest, are his own.

The sea also is his, Ps. xcv. 5, and so are the rivers; and he resents it as an intolerable arrogance in Pharaoh, king of Egypt, that he would lay claim to the river Nilus as his own, Ezek. xxix. 9. The earth likewise, Ex. xix. 5, not one, or many regions of the earth, but all, and all the parts of it, high and low, even to the centre, Ps. xcv. 4, and all the furniture of the whole, and every part of it, Ps. xxiv. 1, whatsoever in the least takes up any part of the earth, whatsoever is in it, Deut. x. 14. He lays claim to whatever is under the whole heaven as his own, Job xli. 11.

Finally, no more need be, if any more may be added, under this head. Time is his, and every season and moment of it, Ps. lxxiv. 16, 17. We are ready to say, We have time enough for this or that; but if we presume that it is ours, and at our disposing, it must be such time as falls neither under night nor day, nor any season of the year; for every moment of this is the Lord's, and so wholly at his disposal.

2. But there may be more question of things under the other head, such as we count properly ours. Yet here we may be deceived in the title, and mistake the true owner. There is as much evidence that the Lord is the true proprietor and right owner even of these. We may be proprietors in respect of men, so far as none of them may be able to produce any good title, or lay any just claim to what we have, nor can of right deprive us of it; but we are no proprietors in reference to God. He is the owner of us, and all we have, and not ourselves, as will be manifest by an induction of particulars collected from the Scriptures.

(1.) Lands; that which is left one as his inheritance, or that which he purchaseth, or which he is otherwise legally instated in; this he counts unquestionably his own: and so it may be, as to any title that man can set up against it: Ps. xlix. 11, they impose their names upon their lands, signifying thereby that they are the undoubted owners of them; and others agree with them herein, and say, This is such a man's land, and that is such a man's. But the Lord puts in another claim, which will carry it: 'The land,' says he, 'is mine,' Lev. xxv. 23. This is spoken not of the land as it was then only, but as it would be when the Lord had given it them, as much as he gives anything, when they had conquered it, and the law of nations, *κρατοῦμεν ἐκ* τῶν κρατούντων εἶναι φασί*, when it was divided amongst them, and each one had possession of his share; when it was as much theirs as anything could be among men, yet then says the Lord, 'The land is mine.' You cannot dispose of it as you will, but as the chief landlord, the true proprietor will allow you.

And the same may be said of houses as of lands; we are no more the owners of the one than of the other in reference to the Lord of all. The Lord shewed how much they are his own in giving not only the lands, but the houses and cities of the Canaanites to the children of Israel. And when the Israelites built a house, they used to dedicate it, Deut. xx. 5; and the solemnity of the dedication was feasting and thanksgiving, and by this means they acknowledged the Lord's interest in their habitation. The 30th Psalm is such a thanksgiving at the dedication of David's house, as the title of it tells us. So when the walls of Jerusalem were built, they

* Qu. '*κρατούμενα*'?—ED.

were solemnly dedicated, Neh. xii. 27. And because they were wont to be dedicated by other nations, hence the civil law determines, that the gates and walls of cities, *nullius in bonis sunt*, are no man's property, *ædificio* * *cadit solo*.

(2.) The fruits of the land, whatever it yields, is as much the Lord's as the land itself. Though among us he that does but farm some ground, and pretends to no other title, yet the fruits of it, and what through his industry it produceth, he counts his own; yet whoever let it, or take it, whatever care, or pains, or culture is spent upon it, the Lord is the owner of all that it yields, Hosea ii. 9. She calls all her own, ver. 5; but the Lord shews her who was the true owner, and will make her understand effectually whose it was by disposing of it as he pleases. He that has the present disposal, has the propriety. So it is made an aggravation of the people's idolatry, that what was the Lord's of right they offered to idols, Ezek. xvi. 18, 19.

Cattle also, wherewith the land is stocked, and wherein, in ancient times, their riches did principally consist, Job i. 3, are as much his. Whoever have the possession, the Lord is the owner, Ps. l. 10, 11. Hence it was ordained under the law, that the children of Israel should offer the first-born of their cattle, and the first-fruits of their trees and lands, unto God, Exod. xxxiv. 19, 20. This was the tenure by which they held of him all they had; by this part they acknowledged him to be Lord of all, and that he was the proprietor, though they had the use of all. Thus what was not fit to be offered, was to be redeemed; and if they did not redeem it, though it were but an ass, no man had any right in it so much as to use it, Exod. xiii. 13. God's propriety in such things is evident by one instance, Mat. xxi. 2.

(3.) Money and clothes also are as much his, though they be on our backs, or in our coffers, as that which is most our own; yet the Lord is more the owner thereof than the possessor, Haggai ii. 8. This David acknowledges in this chapter. All the silver, and gold, and precious stones, and other metals which they offered so willingly for the building of the temple, it was all the Lord's, even before they offered it, ver. 14, 16. And thus the act of the Israelites is best justified, when they spoiled the Egyptians, and restored not the jewels of silver, and gold, and raiment which they had borrowed, Exod. xii. 35, 36. To detain that which is not ours, without the owner's consent, is theft; but here the Israelites had the consent of the chief Owner; they had his special warrant for it, who was the Lord of all the Egyptians had, and had right to dispose of it to whom he pleased. If the Lord had not been more the owner of the Egyptians' raiment and jewels, then they themselves, the Israelities could not be excused.

(4.) There is something counted more ours than any of the former, viz., our children; the parents' relation to them is such as cannot be extinguished, nor transferred to any other; they have such interest in them, and such power to dispose of them, as amongst the Israelites they might, in some cases, sell them, as when they could not otherwise pay their debts, or were not able to sustain them, Exod. xxi. 7. And amongst the Romans they had power of life and death over their children: *καὶ πιπράσκειν τοὺς παῖδας τοῖς γονεῦσιν ἐπέτρεψαν καὶ φονεύειν ἀτιμωρήτως*. The ancient laws of the Romans, says Simplicius,† allowed parents both to sell their children

* Qu. '*ædificium?*' That is, the building goes with the ground on which it is erected.—ED.

† Ad Epicteti Enchiridium.

and to put them to death without being questioned for it. Yet for all this parents are not so much the owners of their children as God is, who is the owner of all, Ezek. xvi. 20, 21. The ground of parents' interest in their children, and why they are judged so much their owners, is because they give them life and being; but this reason will shew the Lord more the owner of them, for he contributes more to the life and being of children than the parents do, and without him they could do nothing towards it. It is in him that all the children of men live, move, &c., Acts xvii. 25, 28. And we find when he calls them 'my sons,' then the ground of it is added, 'the work of my hands,' Isa. xlv. 11.

(5.) We are thought to have much propriety in our children, but much more in ourselves, and yet the Lord has more propriety in our persons than we ourselves; so much more, that we are said in Scripture not to be our own in comparison, 1 Cor. vi. 19. His title and interest in us is so great, that all which we conceive we have in ourselves is swallowed up by it. We are not our own. Whose are we then? who has more right to us? Why, his we are who made us, Ps. c. 3. He hath made us, and (as it may be as well read) his we are. We are his people, his servants. A bond-servant was no way *sui juris*, could no way dispose of his own person, it was part of his master's goods; *peculium domini*, he might sell it, or do what he would with it, *in servum omnia licent*. Our persons are no more our own than such servants were. We are more the Lord's than they were their master's.

(6.) It need not now seem strange to tell you that the Lord is the owner of our bodies, that he has so much propriety therein as they are more his than ours. The apostle tells us as much: 1 Cor. vi. 20, 'Glorify God in your bodies, which are his.' Our bodies, and every member thereof, are his; for if the whole be so, no part is exempted. And therefore they spake proud things, and presumptuously usurped the propriety of God, who said, 'Our lips are our own,' Ps. xii. 3, 4; as though their lips had not been his who is Lord and Owner of all, but they had been lords thereof, and might have used them as they list. This provoked God to shew what right he had to dispose of such lips and tongues, by cutting them off.

(7.) But what shall we say of our souls? Our bodies indeed may be so in our power, and at the disposal of others, that we cannot count them, nor use them as our own; they may be imprisoned or enslaved, yea, or sold. That has been ordinary heretofore, to make sale of the bodies of men as well as anything else; but the soul would remain free in such a condition, and is not in danger of any such bondage, confinement, or alienation, nor anything else that can hinder it from being called or used as our own. Is it not so, are not our souls our own? The Lord answers this himself, Ezek. xviii. 4; and the apostle says both the body and the spirit or soul is the Lord's, and not our own, 1 Cor. vi. 19, 20; consequently all the powers of the soul are his, and all the abilities of those faculties, in what degree soever they are found or exercised in the soul of man, for he that is the owner of the principal has right to the accessories.*

So you see it is most clear in Scripture that God is the owner of all, and every thing and person.

II. Now, since all just propriety and right has some good ground and foundation, let us inquire in the next place what is the ground and foun-

* Caius. Si in alienis scribat, licet aureis vel argenteis litteris, ejus est scriptura cujus est charta.—*Instit.*, lib. ii. tit. 1, sect. 6.

dation of the Lord's title to and propriety in all things, and so discover the reason why he is the owner of all; and this will shew the justness of his claim, and the necessity and reasonableness of acknowledging it, and yielding to it. Now, the ground of God's propriety in all things is his creating of all, and (which is equivalent to creation) his upholding them. Redemption is a ground of peculiar interest in the redeemed; but it is not pertinent here to insist upon that, because the question is of an universal propriety, not in some, but in all, and the foundation of this general title to all is creation. Accordingly, you may observe in many of the scriptures before quoted, as also in others, where the Lord's propriety is asserted, this, as the ground of it, is annexed: Ps. lxxxix. 11, 12, the heavens, the earth, the whole world, and all therein is thine. Why so? 'Thou hast founded them.' And so are all the regions and quarters of the world, northern and southern, western and eastern; for Tabor was on the west, and Hermon on the east; all are thine, for thou hast created them. So sea and land, Ps. xcv. 5. As all things measured by time, so time itself, the measure of all, Ps. lxxiv. 16, 17. 'Thou hast made the light,' *i.e.*, the moon for the night, and the sun for the day. He lays claim to all the climes of the earth, and all the seasons of the year, on this account; he made them. So children are his, being the work of his hands, Isa. xlv. 11; and our persons his own, because he made us, Ps. c. 3. He still produceth.* He that gave all their being is clearly the owner of all; he has all right in the work of his hands, to dispose of it as he will. This will be more evident and unquestionable, if we take notice of these particulars.

1. He made all for himself. He was not employed by any to make it for another, for in that case the maker is sometimes not the owner; but the Lord did employ himself in that great work, and for himself did he undertake and finish it, Prov. xvi. 4, Col. i. 15, 16. The first-born, the heir of all, because all created, not only by, but for him, Rev. iv. 11. Not for the pleasure of another, as the Israelites wrought for Pharaoh.

2. He made all things of nothing, either without any matter at all, or without any but what himself had before made of nothing. A potter when he makes an earthen vessel, if the clay be not his own which he makes it of, he is not the full owner of the vessel, though he formed it: the form is his, the matter is another's; but since the Lord made all of nothing, or of such matter as himself had made, all is wholly his, matter and form, all entirely. *Caius; Ex alienis tabulis navim fecit, navis ejus erit de cujus ligno.*†

3. He made all without the help or concurrence of any other. There was none that assisted him, or did in the least co-operate with him in the work of creation. He created all, οὐδενος ἐπιδεόμενος, as Athanasius. He needed none, he used not any help foreign, Isa. xliv. 24. Those that assist and concur with another in the making of a thing, may claim a share in it; but here lies no such claim in this case, where the Lord alone did all, alone made all. All is his only.

4. He upholds all things in the same manner as he created, continues the being of all things in the same way as he gave it. He does it of himself, without other support, without any assistant. All would fall into nothing in a moment, if he did not every moment bear them up. So that all things upon this account have still their being from him every moment, and their well-being too, and all the means which conduce to it; and there-

* Ps. civ. 30. He still produceth. All things within the course of nature receive being, so they are his works, ver. 31.

† Tom. i. page 188.

fore all are his own, Col. i. 16, 17, Heb. i. 2, 3. His Son is the heir, *i. e.*, the owner of all things, not only because he made the worlds, but also because he, as one God with the Father, upholds all things. He that thus created all, thus maintaineth all, must needs be the owner of all. There cannot be a more full and clear title to propriety in all or any things, than the Lord's so creating, and so upholding of all and every thing. Why the Lord is owner of all hereby we see.

Now for the ὅτι that he is so, may be thus made evident. Propriety is a right of possessing, disposing, and using the thing or person owned. And such a right the Lord has in reference to all things and persons, and shews he has it by acting accordingly.

1. He has a right to possess all, and is actually in possession of all. The 'possessor of heaven and earth,' *i. e.*, of the whole world, is his title and attribute, Gen. xiv. 19, 22. Ps. cxxxix. 14, he 'fills heaven and earth;' he is actually everywhere and in everything, as the maker and preserver of it; and so, as the owner, he has taken possession of all, and keeps it, and will do, while it is capable of possession. And sure he would not take and keep possession of anything but what is his own; he has undoubted right and title to all he possesses.

2. He has right to dispose of all as he will, and does actually dispose of any things and persons as he thinks good. He disposes of the things in this world when, and to whom, in what manner, and upon what terms, and for what time he pleases. He has *jus præsenter disponendi*, the right of present disposal, which is properly dominion or property.* He gives possession and ejects, puts in and throws out, lifts up and casts down, whom and when he will, Isa. xl. 22–24, 1 Sam. ii. 6–8. Why does he thus dispose of all? Why, because all is his own. The pillars, *i. e.* (say many), the poles of the earth, the whole earth from one pole to the other, is all his own. Dan. ii. 21, he gives kingdoms as we give farthings; he disposes of them to beggars, and throws the loftiest princes out of their thrones upon the dunghill, Isa. xliii. 3, and xlv. 12, 14. You see he disposes of persons and things, kingdoms and countries, houses, and lands, and cities, of money and merchandise, and all. He would not do this, but that he has right to do it; and how could he have right to do it, if all were not his own? And he has right to dispose of persons as he pleases, not only as to their outward condition in all circumstances, but as to their eternal state. So much propriety has he in soul and body, that he can make both everlastingly happy or miserable as he will, Rom. ix. 18–20. Can any reasonably except against God for dealing with man as he pleases, since he is his own creature, of his own forming? He shews how much right the Lord has herein, by one that has less, ver. 21. He that disposes of all things and persons as he pleases, shews thereby they are his own. If they were not his, what right could there be to do it?

3. He has right to use all as he will, to make what use of persons or things he pleases. Accordingly, he can make the land barren or fruitful, he can improve the ground or consume it, he can hold up kingdoms, cities, houses, families, or let them fall. Who can tie him to keep the world, or any part of it, in repair? He can sow it with man and beast, or he can sow it with salt or with fire, and has right to do it. He can turn a place like the garden of God into a vale of Sodom, or let Sharon run into a desert. He shews what right he has, Jer. i. 10; he has right to use all as he will. He can employ what persons he pleases for the highest or the meanest

* Dominium est jus, sive facultas habendi, regendi, utendi rebus vel personis.

uses. He can make use of Hazael, as a man or as a dog, 2 Kings viii. 13: as a man when he was a subject, and as a dog when he was a king; and could use the great Nebuchadnezzar as a king or as a beast. He binds all others to such use of what they have, as he thinks fit;* and they have no right to use anything otherwise. They are obliged to employ whatever they possess, and all the improvement of it, for his use, for his interest and honour. And if they do not thus employ it, they forfeit it, and he has right to take the forfeiture, though he always does not. And how could he of right do this to all the world, if all were not his own?

Thus much may serve to shew both that the Lord is owner of all, and why he is so.

III. Let us now further endeavour to be satisfied concerning the nature and quality of this propriety, that so we may understand in what sort and way, in what capacity or degree, the Lord is the owner of all. Take an account of this in some particulars.

1. He is the primary and original owner of all. His title and propriety is underived. Whatever right any other has, it descends from him; but his right is not derived from any other. He had it not from any former owner, for he was the first; he had it not by inheritance, for he has no predecessor, nor does he succeed any; nor had he it by contract, for in that very instant wherein he created anything, it was upon that account then his, before any moment wherein we can conceive any contract to have been possible. That which he gave for all things that are his, was their very being; and from his giving this, his right to them did result immediately, before and without any act of theirs, and so without any contract or bargain, which includes mutual acts.

Nor had he it by gift, Rom. xi. 35. The question here is a peremptory denial. No creature can pretend that he gives God anything, any right which he had not before. It is true the holy angels and sanctified men do give up themselves unto God; but this does not make them his first, but is an acknowledgment that they were so before. As soon as they were creatures they were his, even before they did act either as good or intelligent creatures; and when they resign up themselves unto him, they do not hereby give him a title to them, but effectually recognise it. They were his before, whether they would or no; but now they are his voluntarily, and hereby acknowledge it. They now oblige themselves to regard him as their owner, and he now owns them in a more peculiar manner. But he was before the owner of them, as he is of all things, by a primary and original right.

2. He is the absolute owner of all, without any condition or limitation. His right and propriety is not in any way limited, nor in the least conditional. He holds not anything *sub certa lege*, upon certain terms and conditions. For who could give law to God, or prescribe him terms, or tie him to conditions, or any way bound or limit him who was Lord of all, before any were in a capacity to deal thus with one another. Some, in what they possess, are limited as to the time, they may hold it so long, but no longer; some as to disposing, they may not alienate it at all, or not convey it but to such and such; and some as to the use, it must not run to ruin or out of heart, and some proportion of the profits must be paid out of it. But the Lord is not under any such restraint, as to all, or anything. None can limit him but himself. He makes his own terms, and has no other

* ἔξεστιν ὅπως ἂν θέλοι χρῆσθαι

bounds but his own will. He holds all as long as he will, disposes of all as he pleases, uses all as he thinks fit, and none can say unto him, What doest thou? They that are, or count themselves most absolute in their possessions or kingdoms, in respect of God, have but a limited and conditional tenure. And if they transgress their bounds, and observe not the conditions they are under, they do it at their peril, and he will call them to account for it, they must answer for it before the great God of heaven and earth. But he is accountable to none, being under no tie nor obligation from any in the world, Dan. iv. 34, 35. The work of his hands could not tie him to terms, more than the clay can bind the potter; nor would he limit himself to the prejudice of his own right. His title to all remains such as becomes him, the greatest, highest, and most excellent, and therefore every way most absolute.

3. He is the principal owner. All others that have right to anything, have it under him, and in subordination to him, and are tied to acknowledge it by doing him service for whatever they have.

No creature has such a dominion or propriety, as the feudal laws call *allodium*, an independent and sovereign right, so as to be *nemini leudes*, under none, and to owe no service or acknowledgment for what he hath; though some owe it not to men, yet all owe it unto God. For he is Lord paramount, and all hold of him and under him, not only their estates, but their beings; and so are obliged to him, more than he that had *feudum ligium*, who upon that account *contra omnes fidelitatem domino debet*, was bound to be faithful to his lord against all men, the emperor not excepted. Amongst us, some hold what they possess of their landlords, some of manors, some of the king. But lord, and king, and all, hold of God, and owe him service and fealty as his liege vassals; they have all from him, and can duly dispose of nothing but by him, nor use anything but for him, Rom. xi. 36.

4. He is total-owner of all. He has a full title to all, and the right is wholly in him; he has no copartner nor associates therein. When David gave the possession mentioned, 2 Sam. xix. 29, between Ziba and Mephibosheth, they had a joint interest therein, as Jehoshaphat and Ahaziah would have had in the navy and adventure, if they had joined their ships, according to the proposal, 1 Kings xxii. 49. But none has a joint interest with God. He has a plenary title to the whole world, not a half, or a divided right. As none could have such a title to the land of Egypt and the people thereof, as Pharaoh had, Gen. xlvii. 20, but he that was king of Egypt; if he had had a partner therein, he would have had a share in the royalty; so here, it is the royalty of God to be the owner of all things. This is not separable from him, nor communicable to any, but he that is God. If any should share in his title, they would share in his lordship; but he is Lord alone, Isa. xliii. 10, and xlv. 5, 6. Besides, the foundation of this propriety, as I shewed before, is God's creating of all things. Now, none can have a share in the right, but such as have a share in the ground of it. But God alone createth all things, and none beside him can create anything; and therefore, none can pretend to partake in the title with him. He had no partners in making all of nothing, or of sustaining all so made; and therefore he has no partner in the title to all. The propriety is wholly in him, he is the total owner of all.

5. He is the perpetual owner of all. His interest and right to all is never transferred, never diminished, never lost or extinct. However things are disposed of in the world, he still remains proprietor, and will do so for

ever, and he alone. In respect of God, there are no such owners as the civil law calls *perpetuarios*. For though one man may convey to another estates of inheritance to him and his heirs for ever, and thereby cuts off himself from all right, to deprive the other of his possession, yet the Lord always retains a right to dispossess whom, and when he pleases, being ever the full and absolute owner. This right abides in him for ever, for none can deprive him of it. What is said of one particular, holds true as to his propriety, in all, John x. 29. He must be greater and more powerful than the Almighty, that can wrest his right from him. There is no way of parting with it, unless he himself will voluntarily quit it. But neither will he divest himself of it, for it is one of the glories of his crown, that all should hold of him as the chief Lord and absolute Proprietor. And this honour will he not give, this glory will he not part with, to any other. It is annexed inseparably to his kingdom, and so must last no less than that which is everlasting, Dan. vii. 14. It can no way cease, unless the ground of it should fail. *Dominium non amittitur, nisi amisso eo in quo fundatur*,* property is not lost, unless the foundation of it fail. But that is here impossible, unless the Lord should cease to be what he is, the maker and preserver of all things, for therein his propriety is founded. And whereas it may be said, The Lord gives away many things, and that in one way of alienation, the propriety passes by gift to him that receives, he becomes the owner, I answer, So it is amongst men in full donations. But the Lord gives nothing so as to divest himself of the propriety he has therein. He gives us the use of things, an use limited as he thinks fit, and an answerable possession of them; but he never gives away his interest and propriety in what he bestows on any. And so you may observe in Scripture, that after he has given things, yet they are said to be his own still. He has given the earth unto men, Ps. cxv. 16, yet not so given it, but that it is his own still, Ps. xxiv. 11, 1 Cor. x. 26, 28. So he gave the land of Canaan to the Israelites, and gave it for an inheritance, Deut. iv. 21, yet did he not give away the propriety, it continued his own still. 'The land is mine,' Lev. xxv. 23. So Hosea ii. 8, 9, he gave, and yet still they were his own, and Ezek. xvi. 18, 19. So he gives us our souls, Eccles. xii. 7. The Father of spirits gives the spirit, the soul, but so as it is his still, Ezek. xviii. 4. He gives to the children of men some use and possession of things, but he does not give his interest and right in them. He is as much the owner of them as before he gave them, and so perpetually.

6. He is transcendently the owner of all. He has the greatest right to them, a super-eminent propriety and interest in them, far exceeding all that any other can challenge. He has more right to all than we have to any thing, and is more the owner of all than we are of that which is counted most our own. The nature and being of all things are his, he being the maker and upholder of them; but the use of things only is ours, and therein also we are subjected to him, and are to be ordered by him, having no right to use any thing, but as he appoints us, or gives us leave, no otherwise than according to the rules of our tenure prescribed by him. But he in this is ordered and regulated by none, but has right to, and may use all or any thing as he pleases. We count that which we pay for more our own than that we borrow, and an estate of inheritance more ours than that which we have but as tenants, and our children more our own than other possessions, and our persons more our own than children are; and our souls more our own than any thing. Yet the Lord is more the owner of

* Gerson.

all things than we are the owners of our souls; for propriety in things is more or less as the right and power to possess, dispose of them, or use them, is more or less; for herein dominion or propriety consists. Now we cannot hold, or retain, or possess our souls as long as we will: Eccles. viii. 8. No man has dominion over his spirit or soul, to keep it in his body while he pleases. Death comes (when the Lord will send it), and takes away the soul, whether we will or no, we have no right to keep it a moment longer; but the Lord has right to keep, or hold, or retain any thing as long as he pleases. And so, in this respect, all or any thing is more his own than our souls are.

Further, We have no right or power to dispose of our souls in what state we will, either a state of grace here, or of glory hereafter; but the Lord, who worketh or disposeth of them and all things, according to the counsel of his will, Eph. i. 11, has right to dispose of all things, in any state, as to their being or well-being, as to their happiness or misery, as he will. And so, in this respect also, all things are more his own than our souls are ours.

Finally, we have no right to use our souls, or any faculties thereof, as we will, but only according to the laws and rules he has given us; but the Lord has right to use all, or any thing, as he will himself; and so, in all respects, he is more the owner of all things than we are of our souls. He has more propriety in any, in all things, than we or any else have, even in that which is counted most our own.

7. He is the sole owner of all things. He is the only proprietor in the sense expressed in the former particulars; yea, none else but he is strictly and properly the true owner, not only of all, but of any thing. And that you may be satisfied herein, and assent to it as a truth, which at first sight may seem new and strange, and upon a bare proposal may meet with some contradiction, let me give some reason for it; for I would not impose any thing upon you of this nature, liable to exception, upon my bare assertion.

(1.) If the whole right be in him, none can have a part of it; but he is the full owner of all, and the right to all is wholly in him, as I made it evident in the fourth head.

(2.) If he have right to take all, or any thing away when he will, and to dispose of it to whom, and when, and how he pleases, and to tie and oblige the possessors to what uses they shall employ all they have, so as they have no right to employ it any otherwise, then is he the sole proprietor, and the right and title is only in him; for this power is a clear and undeniable evidence of it, as appears by the nature and essence of propriety, and the severals wherein it consists, of which I have given an account before. He that has right to do what he will with all, and every thing, and none else but he, is the sole owner of all, and every thing; but such is the Lord's dominion over all, such a right hath he as to all and every thing. Therefore, &c.

(3.) If the persons of the possessors be not their own, then nothing else is. He that is not the owner of himself, is owner of nothing; ὁ δεσπότης τοῦ ἡγεμονικοῦ, πῶς οὐχ ἕξει τό ὑποϐεϐηκός; he that is the lord and owner of the principal, cannot but be the owner of the accessories; but so is he who is Lord of all, the owner of all persons, and so the owner of all that belongs to them, and not they themselves. So a bond-servant, being part of his master's goods, *domini in bonis*, since himself was not his own, he was owner of nothing; all that he had was his master's. Thus, a Hebrew having sold himself, or being sold by others, to be a servant, so that his person was become his master's possession, all that he had in that capacity was his master's, even his wife and children, Exod. xxi. 4. When he himself was free (as he might be by law in the seventh year), yet, by the same law of God, his wife and children were to continue with his master as his own goods. And so we need not wonder, that in the Roman empire, by the common laws of it, if a servant had an inheritance or a legacy left, it was his master's, he being not his own man, could not be the owner of it. So Ulpian, *Si hæredes instituti sunt, et hæreditates nobis adquirunt, et legatia ad nos pertinet.* If our servants be made heirs, the inheritance is ours, and the legacy left them belongs to us. So Caius,* *Quicquid iis a quâlibet personâ donatum, vel venditum fuerit, &c., id dominis sine aliquâ dubitatione conquiritur.* Whatever by any person is given to (servants) or sold to them, that without all doubt is their master's; so that in all law and reason, if our persons be not our own, nothing that we possess is ours, but his who is lord and owner of our persons. But I shewed before, that our, and all persons are his, and therefore he is the sole owner of all.

Obj. But are we owners of nothing (may some say)? Both Scripture, and law, and common sense, make and speak many things to be ours.

Ans. I shall shew you how these things are ours, and how they are not, both to prevent mistakes, and also thereby to declare more fully and evidently how the Lord is owner of all things, and how he is the sole owner of all. Take it in these particulars:

(1.) We are not true proprietors of any thing in respect of God, though otherwise what we possess may be called ours. To clear this, and leave no room for misunderstanding, observe, that things in our possession may be considered either in respect to the right lord and true owner, or in respect to others. In reference to God, who is the right Lord and true Proprietor of all things, we are not properly owners of anything. But in reference to others, such things as the providence of God in a just way gives us the possession and use of may well be called ours, because no others can challenge them, or lay any just claim to them. This will be clearer by some parallel instances.

That which we borrow may be considered with respect either to the lender, or to others. In reference to the lender, we have no propriety in that which is borrowed; for, as the Civilians say,† *in commodato res non ita datur, ut fiat accipientis.* A thing lent, is not so given as to become his who borrows it. 'Alas, master, it was but borrowed!' 2 Kings vi. 5. The lender is still the owner, though it be in another's possession.

But in reference to others, that which we borrow is so far ours, as another may not take it from us, nor hinder us from the use of it. So in what a tenant possesses, in reference to the landlord, he is no owner, for he has the possession and use only, not the propriety. So it is a rule in the feudal laws,‡ *Possessio per beneficium ad eum pertinet, proprietas ad alium spectat,* possession belongs to the tenant, propriety to the lord. But in reference to others, it is and may be called his land, his own farm, because no other has anything to do with it; he may challenge it as belonging to him, and if any take it from him, they do him wrong, and he may maintain a right against them.

In like manner, in reference to God, we are no more owners of what we have, than a borrower is in reference to the lender, or a tenant is in respect of his landlord; but in respect of others, they are and may be called

* Institut. Tit. 19, sect. 19, vid. 18, 20, 21. † Jura Gothofred. ‡ Lib. ii. tit. 8.

ours, because others have no interest therein, cannot justly deprive us of them, have no right to disturb us in our possession, or hinder us in the use, or from the profits thereof. In these respects we are *quasi domini*, as it were owners, but not *verè domini*, not true owners, as Civilians distinguish* between *verum dominium*, and *quasi dominium*, true propriety, and that which is but as it were such. The Lord alone is truly proprietor, we are but the improvers of his possessions; so some understand those expressions in Scripture, where the servants of God are called strangers, or sojourners; and in two places there seems good ground for such a sense in the context: one is in this chapter, where, having in many expressions ascribed all to God as the owner of all, and he only, he adds, ver. 15, *Non proprietarii sed tui coloni*, say divers of great note, we are not proprietors, but thy husbandmen; so Levit. xxv. 23, ye shall reap the fruits of it, but the land is mine; ye are עמדי, ye are my labourers, or husbandmen, *coloni*, it is rendered. Now, husbandmen in the Roman empire, such as were *ἐναπόγραφοι*, enrolled, had nothing of their own, but all they had was their master's, as appears by that of the emperor Anastasius, *in Cod.*,† τὰ τούτων πεκούλια τοῖς δεσπόταις ἀνήκει, their proper goods belong to their lords. Answerably the Lord says here to the Israelites, 'The land is mine,' not yours; and David, in the other place, acknowledges, 'All is thine own;' so that we are not what landlords are accounted in reference to their tenants; nay, we scarce are so much as tenants in respect of the Lord of all. For,

(2.) We have not a full tenant's right to what we count ours. Those who are thought to be most the lords of their lands, are not so much as tenants in respect of God.

[1.] For a tenant is sole possessor, though he be no proprietor. He that lets him a farm, keeps it not in his own hands, but gives whom he lets it to investiture,‡ or, as we call it, livery or seisin, gives him possession, and so parts with that to the tenant, though he give him no propriety.

But we are not sole possessors in respect of God; for though he give us possession of what we have, yet he gives it not away from himself; he puts nothing out of his own hands, but continues always in possession of heaven and earth, and all things, as much as if there were none else in possession, Gen. xiv. 19; he has *jus retinendi*, and *insistendi rei* (as possession is defined), a right to hold and abide upon everything, everywhere; he never divests himself of this right, as others do to their tenants; yea, he always actually exercises this right, keeping all in his hands, and remaining in and upon his possessions, and every part thereof, every moment (as none else can do), Jer. xxiii. 24.

[2.] A tenant hath usually some time in what he holds; some have it for life, some for years; and if less, yet for some time certain; and those that have no lease are not turned out without some warning; but we have no time certain in anything that we possess. The Lord may turn us out when he will; he may take it from us, or us from it, whenever he pleases; nor is he obliged to give us a moment's warning, Mat. xxiv. 42, 44, 50. Our tenure is no better than that of the most ancient feudatories,§ whose possessions *domini quando vellent auferre*, their lords might take away at their pleasure; or theirs of old in England, who were called tenants at will, but were really bondmen,‖ who had nothing of their own (person or estate),

* Feud. Lib. ii. Tit. 8, ibid.—*Gothofred.* † Lib. xi. Tit. 47, lin. 18.
‡ Investire est in possessionem mittere.—*Gothofred.* § Feud., Lib i. Tit. 1.
‖ Villainage tenure.

and no time in what they improved for another, but were wholly in the power and at the will of their lord for all. It is not so good as that of those feudal tenants,* who, after a year, their lord turned out of possession, *quacunque hora vult*, at any hour when he list; they had a year certain, but we have not an hour nor a moment. We have warning, indeed, not to let us know what time we may be certain of, but to give us notice, that we are not certain of any time at all, nor of the least parcel of it, Mat. xxv. 13. Whenever he comes, he turns us out of all our earthly possessions; and we know not but he may come the next day, the next hour; he comes whenever he will, Mark xiii. 35, and ordinarily when we least expect it, Luke xxi. 34, 35.

[3.] A tenant, observing conditions and paying his rent, hath the rest of the profits for himself and his own use.† *Proprietas rei penes dantem remanet, usus fructus vero rei ad accipientem transit*, is the rule in law betwixt lord and tenant; though he have not the propriety, yet he has the use and profit for himself; so when Pharaoh had got all the land of the Egyptians into his own hands, he lets it out to them upon these terms, that paying a fifth part to him, the rest of the profits should be their own, for the use of them and theirs, Gen. xlvii. 20, 23, 24.

But all that we have must be employed for the use and interest of our Lord; not for ourselves, but for him. Accordingly, the Lord represents himself to us by a householder, who, having planted a vineyard, lets it out to husbandmen, but sends his servants to receive the fruits of it for him and his use, Mat. xxi. 33, 34; all the fruits of our lands, trading, labour, studies, belong to him; and he expects they should be wholly employed for him one way or other; and we have no right to spend them upon ourselves, or relations, or others, any otherwise than may be for his service and interest. We have nothing simply for our own use (as tenants are supposed to have), but all we are bound to use for him; all the profits and advantages of what we have should be ordered so, as to advance his honour, and serve his pleasure, and promote his interest, or else they are abused, and usurped against all right, and contrary to the terms and conditions upon which we hold all we have; but if we are neither true proprietors, nor have so much as the right of tenants, how are things said to be ours? I answer positive:

(3.) We have them as stewards, entrusted by their master with his treasure, or goods, to dispose thereof to such persons, and for such uses, as he appoints. Thus we are frequently in Scripture represented as stewards, particularly Luke xii. 42. A steward has his master's stores committed to his trust; he has them in his custody, and so far they are in his possession; he has power to dispose thereof according to his trust, and so he is said to be the ruler over the household, *i. e.*, the disposer of things belonging to the family, ver. 44. And accordingly he makes use of, and employs what is in his hands: he provides and brings forth necessaries for the family, gives them their meat, &c. And so Abraham's steward is בן משק, one who runs to and fro to provide what is requisite; or as others, *filius eductionis*, who brings forth necessaries out of the stores, Gen. xv. 2; but all according to his master's order and appointment, Mat. xx. 8, Gen. xliv. 1. And no other has any right to take from him what is in his custody and possession, or to dispose thereof as he may, or to hinder him from so using or employing it. And so far, that which he, and no other, has right to possess and dispose and use, may be well said to be his; but

* Use of the Law, Lib. i. Tit. 11, page 37. † Lib. ii. Tit. 23.

it is not his to keep, or use as he list, as the steward in the parable found, Luke xvi. 1, and xi. 45, 46.

And even thus are things ours. The Lord has entrusted them in our hands, to dispose of them as he appoints, and use them as he has given us order, and no otherwise; because we have right to such a possession, disposal, and use of them, a right which no other can claim to the things in our trust; upon this account they are and may be called ours.

Or as an artificer's tools, which he entrusts in the custody of his servant, so as he may dispose them most conveniently for his work, and use them for his service; another has no right to take them from him, or to use them without his leave. So far they may be said to be the servant's tools.

We are the Lord's servants, and a servant is, as Aulus says, *τοῦ δεσπότου ὄργανον*, his master's tool. So are we, so are all our members and faculties, our Lord's instruments; but he gives us them to be employed in his work, and used for his service, and none can justly hinder us from so employing them. So far they are ours; and other things which we possess proportionably, ours in trust, but the Lord's in true propriety.

So much for the explication and proof of this point, in which I have stayed the longer, that our judgments might be more clearly and firmly settled in this truth, too little understood, or too little regarded, as we may suspect, since the genuine consequences of it in practice are so much neglected. That which is dubious or obscure being cleared, we may proceed more currently with the practical improvement of it, to which I now pass.

Use 1. Of information, in many particulars of great concernment.

1. Herein we may discern the greatness of that Lord whom we serve, and whose we are. The whole world, and its fulness, all that is in it, both persons and things, are his own, wholly and absolutely his. The heaven is his throne, the earth is his footstool; hell is his prison, the devils are his executioners; the angels are his ministers, as much his servants as those who are bought and sold; they do nothing but his will, and have nothing but at his allowance; they cast their crowns at his feet, as having them and all from him, and holding them and all at his pleasure. The greatest monarchs in the world, and those that are called *terrarum domini*, lords of the earth, are his vassals; they hold what they have of him, by a tenure of as much subjection as that which was anciently known here by the name of villainage. They have nothing of their own; all they possess is his. They have it but to improve for him and his service, and they are turned out of possession at the will of the supreme Lord; and though they may seem to have much in their hands, yet the greatest empire, that of Ahasuerus, consisting of one hundred and twenty-seven provinces, or that of Alexander greater than the Persian, or that of the Romans much larger than the Grecian was, is but as a mole-hill, or the small possession of an ant, yea, much less, compared with the dominions of the great Lord of all. The whole earth is but as a needle's point to the visible heavens, and how much less these are than the heaven of heavens we cannot tell. But this we know, that these and all are his own, and more at his disposal, than any clod of earth is at ours. In brief, all that are in the heavens, or on the earth, or under the earth, are his, his creatures. Whoever they are, whatsoever they have above mere nothing, they have it all from him, and so hold it as that they and all are still his own. Oh what reason have we to adore and admire him, to ascribe all to him, and to him alone! Thine

is the greatness, and the majesty, and the kingdom, and the dominion. 'Great is the Lord, and greatly to be praised, and his greatness is unsearchable,' Ps. cxlv. 3; 'Great is the Lord,' &c. He is exalted far above all. What high thoughts should we have of him! How should we revere him! How should all the earth tremble before him! 'For the Lord most high is terrible; he is a great king over all the earth,' Ps. xlvii. 2, over all the heavens, over all the world. Let us strive for suitable apprehensions of him, and praise him according to his excellent greatness.

2. This may inform us that the Lord hath right to deal with us, or any creature, as he will. However he use us, he can do us no wrong. This is manifest, in that we are his own. This is enough to answer whatever may be objected against his disposing of us or anything at his pleasure. Shall I not do with my own as I will? Mat. xx. 10, 15. If our diminutive, limited, dependent interest gave us right to do what we will with what we call our own, we think it our due to exercise it as we please upon the inferior creatures, what right and power has he, who is Lord of all, to use us or anything as he will, when he is so fully, so absolutely, so transcendently the owner of us and all things? It is true, and should be observed and remembered, that in reference to rational creatures, the Lord has restrained the exercise of his plenary right by his laws and promises; he has declared hereby, that though he has undoubted right to use us any way as he will, yet he will not use us but so and so, according to the import of those laws and promises. Yet though he will not exercise all that right and power over us, as he is our ruler, yet otherwise, as he is our owner, it fully belongs to him. And thus, if we consider him as a lord and proprietor antecedently to his determination of forbearing such exercises of his right, so he might use us however we would; nor could whatever he did be any wrong to us. No usage of us whatsoever, no, not that which seems most grievous to nature, or most harsh at first sight unto reason, could possibly be unjust in him or an injury to us; for justice or righteousness ἐν τῷ ἀφεκτικῷ καὶ ἀβλαβεῖ κεῖται, consists in abstaining from what is not our own; or, as others commonly place it, in giving *suum cuique*, every one his own; so that which is unjust or a wrong to us, must be a withholding or taking from us that which is our own. Therefore nothing that he can take or withhold from us can possibly be injurious to us, because in respect of him nothing is our own; he is the true owner of us, and all we have or can have.

Yea, if we were innocent, and without sin, yet the Lord, as our proprietor, might deny or take from us anything whatsoever, our estates, lives, being, or well-being, righteously, and without doing us the least wrong; for what injury could it be to take that from us which is his own and not ours?

If he should take from us what estate we have, as he did from Job, and as is generally conceived, without respect to his sin, he would not thereby wrong us, he takes but his own.

If he should take away life, or give others a special command to do it, as he did to Abraham in reference to his son Isaac, Gen. xxii., the taking away his life in that case had been no murder in Abraham, no wrong to Isaac, because the Lord and owner of his life gave order for it, who had right to call for his own, and take it in what way he pleased.

If he should take away our being, and quite annihilate us, he would but take his own, and that which we wholly owe to him. Thus, as our Lord and proprietor, he has right to do, but only that he has declared he will not do it. If we have so much power over the being of other creatures, as to destroy them, so as they are never restored again, though they be not reduced to nothing; if we may kill them for our use, food, or physic; if we may burn wood and other things, turn them to ashes for our service, and yet do them no wrong, what right and power hath he over our being who is full and absolute Lord and owner thereof!

If he should take away our well-being, if he should inflict pain on us in any degree or for any continuance, so as to deprive us of a comfortable, a well-being, this would be to take his own, and that which he owes us not; this he might take, considered as our proprietor, and without respect to his promise; that indeed declares that he will not so use us, but otherwise, setting that aside, he hath right to do it, and might inflict what pain he would, and continue it as long as he pleased, as a mere affliction, without respect to sin, though not as a punishment. If freedom from pain, any degree of it, be not due to us, then it would be no wrong to inflict it on us in any degree, and if freedom from it for a moment is not our due, then it would be no injury to inflict it for any continuance; for it is no wrong to deny us that which is not due to us, and that is not due to us which we cannot challenge as our own. And what can we count our own, if being, well-being, and all, be wholly and absolutely his, who is Lord and owner of all? In that which is not due to us, we can have no right; and in that where we have no right, we can have no wrong; and so the Lord, as owner of us and all things, may deal with us, or any, as he will, without doing us any wrong. *Rationabiliter autem negatur, quod nulla ratione debetur.**

3. Let this inference be minded and believed according to the reason you see for it. It clears up the absolute dominion of God, and those difficulties which concern it, very much to my own satisfaction, and it may do such service to others. It is no curiosity nor useless speculation, but tends much to illustrate the freeness of grace, and to manifest the righteousness of God's decrees with the execution of them, and by the help thereof we may vindicate it from the reasonings of such as would impeach it.

But so much for the general inference. The truth before us will give us more special information concerning the Lord's righteousness in some particulars, which our partial reason may be apt to call in question. As,

(1.) That the Lord has right to pass by some when he chooses others; to leave some to misery, while he sets apart others for life and happiness. Unless the sovereign Lord of all have less right and power to dispose of that which is more his own, than common reason acknowledges men to have for the disposal of that which is less their own, he may righteously, and without any show of injury to others, do what he will with his own, and so may choose some of the sons of men to be the objects of his special favour, and refuse others, without any injury to those that are rejected; for, in this case, both the persons whose state he will have to differ, and the things which make the difference, are more incomparably his own than anything we have power to dispose of is ours. The persons are his own, they are the work of his hands entirely, they are his creatures; whatever they are, or have beyond nothing, is wholly his. And may not he of right dispose of that which is so much his own, into what state he will? And then the things are his too; life and happiness are his gift, Eph. ii. They are more his than anything which we have right to give to whom we will. And has not the Lord right to give what is his own to whom he pleases, and to bestow his bounty on what objects he thinks fit, and to single out

* Aquinas Disp. de Prædest., Art. 2.

some from amongst others to partake of it? Till the common notions of equity and righteousness be razed out of the souls of men, methinks this should be counted most equal and righteous. The Lord asserts his own right to dispose his mercy to whom he will, Exod. xxxiii. 19. This the apostle applies to the present case, and by the light and evidence of it disperses the objection of unrighteousness, as a mist is scattered by the sun going forth in its strength, Rom. ix. 13–15. If it be not righteous with the Lord to shew his mercy, or refuse it to whom he will, he has not the right (which men have) to do with his own what he will. Those who dispute against this, leave not the Lord so much right over his own as the potter hath over his clay or his vessel, as the apostle's argument proceeds, ver. 20, 21. Both persons and things here concerned are his own, more the Lord's than either the clay or the vessel is the potter's. If he have not as much power and right to dispose of us for happiness or misery, for honour or dishonour, as the potter has to dispose of his clay or vessel, then he will have less right when the ground of it is more.

And whereas it is said that the Lord, dealing thus differently with persons otherwise equal, makes him chargeable with respect or acception of persons, which he both disclaims himself, Acts x. 34, 35, Rom. ii. 11, and forbids and condemns in others, Lev. xv. 16, it will appear by the truth we insist on, that this objection (how much soever some great pretenders to reason would make of it) is altogether impertinent; for acception, or respect of persons, which is culpable, has place only in judicial acts (or those of like nature), where justice must be done according to the merits of the cause, without respect to the quality, relations, accomplishments of the person concerned. He that is swayed by such personal respects, to pass sentence otherwise than the cause itself in justice requires, is an accepter of persons in a criminal sense. But in acts of bounty it has no place, where one is not deciding what is right and just betwixt others, but where he is disposing of his own; he may dispose of his own, and express his bounty to whom he pleases, and not be liable to any charge of unrighteous respect to persons.* And this is the case here: the Lord proceeds not in these acts as a judge, distributing to every one what is due in law, but as a lord and proprietor, disposing of what is his own to whom and how he pleases. And there is not herein any shadow of respecting persons, since he is not moved thus to deal with us by any external respect whatsoever.

(2.) That the Lord has right to vouchsafe his gospel unto some, and not to others. It is his own, and if he have right to dispose of his own as he will, he may vouchsafe it or deny it to whom he pleases. He has used this right in all ages, apparently under the law, Ps. cxlvii., and afterwards also, Mat. xi. 25. In the apostles' times, the gospel did go through all the world; but that world was little more than the Roman empire, for anything appears in Scripture, and that empire is called the world, Luke ii. 1. Take the world in its full latitude, and there are many parts of it in which no footsteps of the gospel could be discerned in latter ages. This some cannot digest, that the ordinary means of salvation should be denied to any. But the Lord does them no wrong that want it; it is no injury to withhold that from any which is no way due to them. And how does it appear that the gospel was due to any that want it. By what right can they challenge that of the Lord which is his own and at his free disposal?

* Nulla est acceptio personarum quia sic alius honoratur, et alius debito non fraudatur.—*Augustin.* in Tom. 825.

(3.) That the Lord has right to deny his grace to some when he gives it to others. It is his own, he may give it or deny it to whom he will. He has declared it to be his right, by communicating or withholding it as he pleased, Deut. xxix. 2–4, Mat. xxii. 14. 'Many are called' (he says not all any way), 'but few are' called effectually; few have grace to answer the call, 1 Cor. i. 26, 27. Yet the Lord wrongs none to whom he imparts it not. If it were a debt indeed, this might be alleged, but it is grace, Rom. iv. 4. It is his own, and comes not to any but by free gift, and so with right and liberty to bestow or deny it to whom he pleases. He owes it no way to any, unless he have promised it;* and where has he promised it to all, or to any that never have it?

(4.) This shews us evidently the freeness of the love of God, to all that are the objects of it, men or angels, and of all the acts and expressions of it. If the Lord could not love most freely, he would love nothing at all besides himself. For hereby it appears, that all else is most worthless; not only utterly uncapable of deserving love, but far from any way of obliging his affection, or moving him to vouchsafe any expression of it.

1. We are most worthless creatures; we are worth nothing at all; we have not anything of our own, not anything that is good or fit to be loved that we can call our own, James i. 17; whatever we have that is any way good, it comes from him; it is his gift, and he gives it not so, but that it is his own still. If we were stripped of all that is not our own, we should have nothing at all left, that could be the object of any love, or capable of any expression of love; we should not have so much left as our mere being, for even that is not our own; we should be no better than just nothing.

If a prince should take a beggar from off the dunghill, and set his affections on her, the freeness of his love, to such a wretched object, would be a wonder; and yet the beggar would have more of her own in respect of him, in such a condition, than we in our best estate have in respect of God. Her person would not be his till she gave her consent; but our persons, parts, accomplishments, all are not our own, but his, whether we yield to it or no. Oh then, how wonderfully free is the love of God! how admirable is it, that he could think of loving such as are worse than nothing! What we have of our own, we may take an account of, in the description of Laodicea, Rev. iii. 17. Who can love wretchedness, and misery, and poverty, and blindness, and nakedness? Why, we have nothing better of our own; and if the Lord loves us not for our own, he loves us freely. If the Lord could not have loved most freely, we had never been the objects of his love; for we had nothing at all of our own, but what might rather stop and non-plus love, than any way encourage it. Oh with what sense and affection, with what admiration, should we look upon such declarations of his love! Hosea xii.

2. How far are we from deserving his love! How ridiculously unreasonable are those conceits of our deserts in reference to the love of God, or any expression thereof! There are three conditions necessary to make anything in us deserving; and this truth discovers them, and every of them, to be utterly impossible, and so the fancy of merit to be an absurd chimera.

[1.] If we deserve anything, it must be by virtue of that which is our own. But we have nothing of our own; all that we have and are is his

* Neque cuiquam obnoxius est, nisi quatenus se per promissiones suas obligavit. —*Arminius.*

that loves us, and therefore lets us have whatever we have. Can one deserve anything of another by letting him have what is his own? He that lends may deserve something of us, but not he that only restores what he borrowed; he is so far from meriting hereby, that he would be no better than a thief if he did it not. The Lord lends us what we have, he deserves of us for trusting us; but can we deserve anything by letting him have his own when he calls for it? Prov. xxii. 7. Whatever we do, whatever we bestow for God, we give him but his own, 1 Chron. xxix. 14, 16. We deserve nothing of him, unless it be the reputation of not being cheats and thieves; no more love or expression of it than this.

[2.] If we deserve anything, it must be by virtue of that which we owe not. Now, since we have nothing of our own, but all is the Lord's, and from him, we owe him all we have, and all we can do, it is a due debt; and no man merits by paying his debts. Not to be grossly dishonest, is far from being meritorious.

[3.] If we deserve anything, it must be by virtue of that which is of some advantage to another; but what advantage has the Lord by us? Job xxxv. 7 and 22, and Job xli. 11. Who has prevented him? Who has given him anything which he had not first received of him? He prevents all; for all is his, before any be in a capacity to give to him. And if we should give him what is his (as, alas! we do not) he is but as he was; it was his before, he is no better for it, we do but give him his own; and upon this account, when we have done all, we are but unprofitable servants, Luke xvii. 10. We deserve not so much as thanks; and that which merits not so much, deserves nothing, ver. 9. We are but such servants as a master has no advantage by. He gets but barely his own by us, seldom so much. When he that was by his Lord entrusted with a talent restored it to him, and said, 'Lo, there thou hast that is thine,' he suffers as an unprofitable servant, Mat. xxv. 25, 30. And if we make any improvement of what he entrusts us with, even that is his also, and for him we have it, Philip. ii. 13.

So that if the Lord express any love to us, we do not any way in the least deserve it, and so he loves freely.

And this is not only true of the children of men in the state of degeneracy and imperfection, but even of the angels in the height of their blessed and perfect condition. All they do for him cannot deserve his love; they give him but his own; they do but what they owe him, and he is no better for it. Whether he loves angels or men, he loves freely.

[4.] We cannot oblige him to love us, or to express it. Yet one may be obliged to that which is not deserved of him; that which is deserved is due in justice; but we may be obliged as to equity and ingenuity, and so we are engaged to return love for love; but thus we never do, we never can oblige him to love us, for his love is before ours, 1 John iv. 10, 19. Even our love to him is from him; this is his as all things else, he works it in us. As he puts his fear, so his love, into our hearts, else it would never be there, Deut. xxx. 6.

We cannot any way oblige the Lord to love us. It is his promise that obliges him to express love to us; and our love, and whatever else we can think may oblige him, is that which is promised, and so is his gift, and given after he has obliged himself; and so no possibility of our obliging him beforehand, since all that might be thought to do it is the issue and effect of his own love.

He loves us freely, we can no way oblige him to do it.

[5.] We can no way move him to love us, or to express it. We have not anything of our own to attract his affection. We have nothing of our own that is lovely, nothing that is delightful, nothing desirable. Whatever of this nature is in us, it is his, not ours. We have no estate (and that moves some to love) but what he is the owner of; no sweetness of temper, but what he helps us to; no good quality, but what he plants in us; no beauty, but what is lent us by him. And who will love a person that has no loveliness of her own, no beauty at all, but what is borrowed? We may discern how far we are from having anything that may move the Lord to love us, by looking ourselves in the glass of that description, whereby he represents Jerusalem; we may see our unlovely state therein, Ezek. xvi. 6, instead of rare, fine complexion, and lovely features, all covered with blood and pollution; so far from being amiable, as we were ghastly and loathsome, more fit to be cast out with abhorrence than to be embraced; not only too bad to be loved, but to be pitied; not only without beauty and ornament, but without life; no more in us to move love, than in a dead carcase. Such were we, such the state of our souls; and could the sovereign Lord of the world set his love on such objects as we, having nothing in the world that we can properly call our own, but sin, the most hateful, the most ugly, and loathsome deformity in the eye of God? Oh how free is that love, that would pitch on such objects as we, who had nothing in us fit for love, nothing of our own that could deserve it, nothing that could oblige it, nothing that could any way move or attract it, nothing of our own, but what might sooner have provoked hatred and loathing.

Oh if the Lord had not loved most freely, if his love could not have moved itself, we had never met with it, nor any expression of it. We see hereby the Lord loved us (as he shews mercy), because he would love; we see that wonderful freeness of it exemplified again in us, as it was in Israel, Deut vii. 7, 8.

[6.] This shews us the great evil of sin, how exceeding heinous, how extremely dangerous it is; what reason there is both to hate it, and fear it, and bewail it, and be ashamed of it; how much we are concerned, both to avoid and mortify it.

First, It is the worst that we can possibly do against the greatest benefactor; we cannot act or contrive anything worse against him who deserves the very best, infinitely the best of us. And so it is the most horrid ingratitude that a creature can be capable of; *si ingratum dixeris, omnia dixeris*, when you call a person ungrateful, you brand him in one word with all that is odious. Oh but there is no ingratitude to men that has anything in it of a like hateful and abhorred import, as ungratefulness to God in sinning against him. It is ungratefulness not to return good for good; one kindness for another; what is it then to return evil for good? It is ungratitude to return the least evil for a small courtesy, for any one good turn; what is it then to return the greatest evil for all that is good? This, in reference to men, would be counted, not only inhuman, but devilish. A devil cannot be more odiously disingenuous than to render the worst he can for the best, and to do him the greatest mischief who has done him most good. Yet this, how odious and horrid soever it seem, we do, and are guilty of in reference to God, when we sin against him; for sin is the worst thing of all in the account of God; it is all the evil we can do him, and we do it against him from whom we have all the good we are possessed of; for he is the owner of all, we have nothing at all of our own; all we have, all we are, we had it from him. Our very being, our well-being, all that belongs to, or makes up, or sustains either of them, is from him; and so when we sin against him, we do the very worst against him, from whom we have all the good we have. And what can be more odious and disingenuous in the worst of creatures, of devils, than this! Oh think of this when you are tempted to sin, when you would excite a greater hatred of it in your hearts, when you would engage yourselves more resolutely for the mortifying of it. It is ingratitude hateful to our natures, odious and abhorred by a temper that is anything ingenuous. It is ungratefulness in the highest degree, and of the most hateful and intolerable strain, not tolerable in the account of any, who have not exchanged humanity for devilism; it is a return of the worst evil for all good.

Secondly, Hereby it appears that sin is an abusing of the good things of God against himself. It is a turning of the goods you are entrusted with against him that entrusts you; as it were, the converting of the instruments which he lends you for your advantage, to do execution upon him who lends them. There is no sin which you act any way, but it is by the help of some instruments or enjoyments which you have from God, which he is the true owner of. You have nothing of your own, he is the owner of all, and so when you sin you employ that which is his own against him. When you think evil, when you conceive it, when you incline to it, or resolve on it, or affect it, your minds, wills, or affections are the instruments of this evil. Now your souls, and all their faculties, belong to God; he challenges them as his own, and so you make use of his own against him; they are his; so are your tongues, when you speak evil; so are your other members, when they act sin; so are your estates, when they minister to pride, or covetousness, or sensuality, &c. You make use of these to help you to sin; and these are not yours, but his who is the owner of all, and so you employ that which is God's against himself. What a horrid and intolerable provocation is there in this dealing with God! And what would it be accounted if you should deal thus with one another? It is as if a wretch should take the clothes and jewels of his wife to adorn his harlot; she would be ready to say, when she saw her rival tricked up with her ornaments, Can flesh and blood endure this? Oh but the Lord endures more, and has worse usage at our hands. We bestow more upon sin, and that which is more his, when it is a rival, more odious to him than any can be to us.

It is a great evil not to employ for the Lord what we have from him, as appears by the dreadful doom passed on the slothful servant, Mat. xxv. 30; his crime was, not the using his talent against his lord, but only not using it for him. It would be a horrid thing to employ anything against God, if it were not his own; to be found striking at God with any weapon, from whomsoever we had it. What is it then to turn his own weapons, which he has furnished us with for our security and advantage, against himself; to make use of that which is his own, to do him the greatest injury; not only not to employ it for him (which he may reasonably expect, since we have it upon these terms), but to employ it against him! Sure this is most intolerable. As if one should give you wood for firing to warm you, and you should make use of it to set his house on fire, from whom you have it.

By this the Lord sets forth the sinfulness of Jerusalem's sin; this made it not only abominable, but did aggravate it into an abomination in the abstract. That what was his she employed against him, laid it out on idols, made use of what was his own to serve her idolatry, Ezek. xvi. 17–23.

She employed what was the Lord's against him; this made her actings so exceeding abominable. And this we do in every sin against God. When he is the owner of all, we still make use of something or other which is his to help us to provoke and dishonour him.

Thirdly, This shews us (and thereby the extreme danger of sin directly appears) that we cannot make the Lord satisfaction for the injury we do him by sin. We have no way to satisfy his justice, so as to obtain freedom from what it is most just to inflict on us for sin. We can make him no satisfaction but what is our own, and what we do not owe him, and is not his, and due to him, though we had not offended him.

If we have injured a great person in his honour, it will be no satisfaction to give him some of his goods, or to pay him what was his due if we had not injured him.

How then can we satisfy the Lord, since we can part with nothing but what is his own, nor do anything but what was due to him on another account than the injury we have done him?

If you perform most perfect obedience for time to come, as sinless as that of any saint in heaven, yet this would be no satisfaction for any former sin; for such obedience is due to him if you had not sinned; you owe it him, because you are his own, his creatures; and so being no more than is due on that account, it cannot discharge that which is due on another. The paying of one debt is no satisfaction for another.

If you should offer all your estates, yea, or all the treasure in the world for satisfaction; if you should 'come before him with thousands of rams, or ten thousand rivers of oil; if you would give your first-born for your transgression, or the fruit of your body for the sin of your souls,' Micah iv. 7; if you should offer him your lives, your well-being, or your very being itself, this would be no satisfaction for any of your sins; for all this is his own already, and you tender as good as nothing for his satisfaction, when you can give no more but what was his own before.

Oh consider this when you sin; you do the great God such an injury as neither you, nor all the men on earth, nor all the creatures in the world, no, nor all the angels in heaven, can make satisfaction for. The dreadful penalty of sin will be inflicted, if the Lord be not otherwise satisfied. And you having nothing of your own, nothing but what is his, who is owner of all, can give no more towards a satisfaction, which will procure a discharge, than that which comes to nothing.

Use 2. For exhortation. This truth leads you to very many duties of greatest moment and consequence, such wherein the glory of the most high God, and the honour of your profession, and your own safety and comfort, your own happiness and salvation, is very highly concerned. This truth has in it the force of a powerful motive, to engage you in and for those duties. And the due sense how it obliges soul and conscience therein, will be an effectual means to help you to the performing of them. And I shall endeavour, in the prosecution of this use, to lay both jointly open before you, that you may neither want motives nor means, and may neither be left unwilling nor unable, if you be willing to practise what the Lord hereby calls you to. The first duty I shall instance in is,

1. Thankfulness: a duty so pleasing, so honourable to God, that he will have it continued to eternity; and will have it not only to be the employment of earth, but in heaven, where many other acts, now our duties, will be out of date.

This engages us to thankfulness for all things and at all times, so that our whole life should be made up of acts of gratitude. Whatever we do, should be some way or other a giving thanks to God; otherwise we do not, we cannot answer the engagement which this truth lays upon us, 1 Thes. v. 18. It is his will that you be thankful in everything; it is his will that everything should be an occasion of thankfulness. It is of his good will that everything is so ordered for good, as to minister cause of thankfulness. It might have been otherwise if he would, for everything which obliges you to be thankful was his own, he might have disposed of it as he would; and so, if he had pleased, it might have been worse with you in everything than it is.

But that you may see more distinctly how you are hereby obliged to have your whole life all made up of thankfulness, and that continually, whatsoever we have that is good is from him, of his mere good will and pleasure, and not only the substance, but every degree of it. And we owe it to him as much every moment, as if every instant we did anew receive it of him.

(1.) Whatever is good is from him. Take a survey of all you have: begin at the foundation, at your very being, whatever is added to make it a well-being; the ground-work and the whole structure, the subject and all the accessaries, are wholly from him, for all is his own. How then come you or others to have anything, but merely of his favour and good will, who disposes of his own to whom he pleases? None could constrain him, none could oblige him to part with anything (for by what could they do it, all being his own?), to dispose of his own any otherwise than he would. So that whatever you have, you have it of him, and you have it freely. You have not, you could not have anything, but of his good pleasure. To this you owe all, and so owe thankfulness for everything. All are as free favours (though not so great) as Christ and heaven is. You received everything, and everything *gratis;* so that you have no occasion of glorying in the least, nor in the least an excuse for not being thankful in and for everything, 1 Cor. iv. 7, since there is nothing which thou hast not received, nothing wherein thou canst glory, as if thou hadst it not from his mere bounty. Wherefore art thou not as thankful for everything, as the unworthiest beggar ought to be for the freest alms? Gen. xxxii. 11, the word translated 'not worthy,' is קטנתי, 'I am little, or less, by the least, in respect of thy mercies.' Take away all that Jacob owed to free mercy, and he would have had little left; indeed, he would have been just nothing; he owed all to the mercy or the truth of God, to חסד, or אמת. Some favours he had which were not so much as promised: these were free indeed; the Lord had not obliged himself to bestow them. And some he had by virtue of the promise: these came from the truth and faithfulness of God; but even these were from free mercy too, for this alone moved him to promise, and this moved him to perform the promise, when Jacob's miscarriages might otherwise have disobliged his truth and faithfulness.

And thus are we little, thus have we nothing but we owe to mere bounty, and so should make a thankful acknowledgment of it in everything, if it be but a grain above nothing. All was his own; and it was at his free choice, whether we should have anything of it or nothing.

(2.) Every degree of what is good to us, we have it from him, for all is his own wholly, every degree of it, and wholly at his disposal; and so it was at the choice of his own will, whether we should have it in such a degree or no; and if we have it, we owe it to his good will and pleasure, and therefore owe thankfulness for every the least degree or advance of what we have.

If it be better with us in any degree than it might have been, or than it has been, or than it is with others, we owe it to him who is the owner of all. And so, wherever we look, there will be matter obliging us to thankfulness still in our eye.

If it be better with us than it might have been, for this we should be thankful; it might have been worse, if he would have had it so. We might have been toads or serpents, instead of rational creatures: the matter he made us of was his own; he might have formed it into what shape he pleased. If he had given us the shape of those creatures which we count most ugly, instead of that we have, he had done us no wrong, nor could we have had the least cause to complain; all expostulation had been unjust and unreasonable, Isa. xlv. 9, Jer. xviii. 4–6.

If we had been fools or idiots, without the exercise of reason or the use of senses, he had but done what he had all right to do, in so disposing of us. Could we oblige him any way to make us better, before we were? What we have more desirable than such a lamentable condition, is from the good pleasure of his will. He might have done what he would with his own, and disposed of it in that or a worse condition. The paper cannot oblige the writer; he may put a flourish on it, or make it a blot, as he pleases, no more, &c.

We might have been without common gifts, or without ordinary comforts, without estate, without friends, without ease, without health; we might have consumed our days in want and poverty, in affliction and misery, in languishing sicknesses or torturing pains. What could have hindered the Lord from so disposing of us, his own? Only he would not do it. Not because we could any way engage him to deal better with us, but because he would not do it. We owe every degree of a better condition to his good will; and how much thankfulness do we owe on this account, since every degree of our well-being, in all its latitude, is a free favour?

Yea, he might have cut us off and cast us into hell, before we had got into the way to heaven. You may say his eternal purpose and decree was otherwise: and this is true concerning the elect. But what is his purpose and decree, but his will? And what determines his will but himself? not anything existent or foreseen in us. And might not he who hath right to dispose of his own as he will, both in time and from eternity, have otherwise disposed of thee and me, or any, if he would? Oh what thankfulness does this oblige us to!

(3.) If it be better with us, in any respect or degree, than it has been sometimes, this is from him too who owns all, and to him should it be thankfully ascribed.

If we were sometimes darkness, but are now light in the Lord; if we were dead in sins and trespasses, but are now begotten again to a lively hope; this is from him, and must be gratefully ascribed to the good pleasure of his will, James i. 18.

From whence is this happy change? Might not he, who may do with his own what he will, have left thee still in the gall of bitterness, a state of sin and wrath? If you look for a reason of this, as far as from everlasting, you will find none but his good pleasure. He did this for thee because he would, and if he would, he might have done otherwise. And why may he not do according to his pleasure with his own? And that he deals so graciously with thee, when he had all right to deal otherwise, what heart will it not constrain to all thankfulness!

So if thou hast, in any degree, more comforts, or more health, or more wisdom, or better gifts, or more grace, than heretofore, thou owest it to him who is the owner of all, and owest thankfulness for it. And the more because thou hast it so freely, of his mere good will, when he was not obliged, either by others or by himself, to let thee have so much of his own in these particulars. For as nothing can oblige the Lord to us but his promise, so he has not obliged himself by promise to give any of these, to such or such a degree.

(4.) If it be better with us in any degree than with others; if we have had better education, example, more restraints, means, light. To touch this last a little. Darkness covers the earth, and thick darkness the people. How is it that it does not cover you? Why have you the light of life, that of the gospel, when others have nothing but the light of nature, very dim and obscure, and almost extinct? Are your lines fallen in a pleasant place, in a valley of vision? Why were you not disposed of in some valley of the shadow of death, when such valleys take up far the greatest part of the world? Why did not your lot fall in those dark places of the earth, where Christ is not known, and the way to life not discovered, where they breathe in no air but what is dangerously foggy and pestilential, where is no air for souls but what conveys poison to them, and is infected with the mortal contagion of popery, heathenism, or Mohamedanism? This is the condition of ten to one in the world; and how comes it that your lot is fallen with the fewest, in the light, rather than with the most, in darkness? All places and persons are the Lord's; he disposes of them as he will. What thankfulness do you owe for his disposing of you so mercifully, in comparison of others, so many others, almost all the world? Our Lord Jesus shews how much this obliges to thankfulness by his own practice, Luke x. 21.

(5.) If it be better with you, not only as to that which is good, but, in any degree, as to that which you count not good. Such are afflictions. These are occasions of thankfulness, 1 Pet. iv. 6. The apostle has respect to them, 1 Thes. v. 8. These engage us to glorify and praise God, not only when we are called to suffer for Christ, and have therein a peculiar honour, which the Lord will not vouchsafe to every one of his own, not only because they are sanctified to produce comfortable and blessed effects, but on this account also, because they are easier and more tolerable than they might have been. We never met with any thing grievous in this life, but it might have been heavier. It is never so bad with us in this respect, but it might have been far worse. It is heavy and grievous, but it is not too heavy to be borne; it might have been so. There are very bitter ingredients in it: oh, but they might have been more, and those more bitter; the bitterness of death is not in it. How bad soever it be, it is not hell. So much better as it is than it might have been, so much cause of thankfulness we have; and so in every affliction, thousand and thousand causes of thanks, because it might have been, by many thousand degrees, worse than we suffer.

The Lord has taken away some degrees of our ease, or health, or liberty, some of our friends or dear relatives, some part of our estates, some portion of our comforts; but he might have taken away all, in every degree, for all is his own. And why might he not have taken all that is his own, as well as any part or degree of it? He deals mercifully with us, when he leaves us any thing, when he leaves us so much; when we can challenge nothing as ours, but by his good will and pleasure only. Every good thing, every degree of it left us, is an act, a degree of mercy; and if thankfulness be due for every degree of free mercy and bounty, we have innumerable occasions of thankfulness in the most afflicted condition we meet with.

(6.) We owe him as much thankfulness, every hour or moment, for all we have, as if, every hour or moment, we did receive all; for every moment's continuance thereof is as much a favour, and so as much obliges us to thankfulness, as the first giving of it, because all being his own, he might take what we possess the next instant, and is no more obliged to continue it another hour, than he was at first to let us have it.

As we say, the Lord does as much every moment in preserving the world as he did at first in creating it, the same power and influence which at first made it being put forth every moment to uphold it, so that the preservation of all is no less than a continued creation of all; and all things owe their being to him every minute, as much as if they received it anew of him every minute. Answerably here. The Lord does as much for us, in continuing what we have, as he did at first in giving them, the same favour which at first bestowed it being shewed every moment in not taking it away, so that the continuing of what we have is as much as a continual giving of it; and we owe as much to mercy every hour, in that we lose not what we have, as if every hour we received all from his hand.

God may take away his own when he will; every moment that he does not, the mercy which at first gave them is as good as renewed, and so there is renewed occasion of thankfulness, for all we have, in every moment of our lives; as much cause for it as if we received all by a new gift every hour and moment, so that no part of our lives should be void of thankfulness. We are every moment as much obliged to it, as if every moment we were receiving from him all we have. Let us therefore, as Heb. xiii. 15,—

2. Give up yourselves unto God as your owner, and as to such an owner as indeed he is. This is a great duty, indeed the sum of all that the Lord requires of you. And this truth shews you that there is all reason for it; that you are so strongly obliged to it, that there is no refusing, there can be no pretence for declining. You are his, for all things are his own; and will you not let him have that which is his own? Give unto God the things that are God's. It is most unjust and unreasonable to deny him anything that is his; and if you be not willing yourselves should be his, that which is most in your own power, you will be wholly inexcusable. It is true, the Lord needs not your consent to give him a title to you; you are, and will be his, on a common account, as all other things are, whether you will or no; but by resigning up yourselves to him, you will honour him by acknowledging his title; and this is the way for you to be his in a special manner, and to be owned by him as his peculiarly to be his own, upon an account more for your comfort, advantage, and happiness, than other things and persons are. So, as there is the greatest reason for it, the advantage is answerable; and the danger, in case of refusal, no less. It will prove dreadful in the issue, to put the Lord to distrain for his own, and to make you acknowledge his right and title. Perforce he will secure his honour this way, but you will have nothing left but guilt and misery. And what can they expect better who are not willing the Lord should have his own? If you have any regard of the Lord's honour, or your own happiness; if you would not defraud God, and make yourselves miserable, then resign up yourselves freely to him.

But how must this be done? Wherein does this resigning up of ourselves to God consist?

Ans. It requires an act of the judgment, of the will, and of the life.

(1.) Be apprehensive that you are his, and how much you are so; what clear and full title he has to you, upon the grounds formerly opened; what evidence there is for it in Scripture, and in common reason; and hereupon you must yield a full assent to it, and firmly believe it; and be fully persuaded that you are more his than anything which you count your own is yours; such an act of faith, such a belief and persuasion, of his interest in you, is the foundation of all; and without it nothing will follow to purpose, either in the will or life; but the judgment being fully possessed and convinced hereof, and the apprehension of it being quickened and reinforced with frequent and due thoughts hereof, so as the belief of it be kept firm, actual, and lively; this will facilitate all the rest, and make the will (upon which the acts of the whole life depend) come off more freely to this great work of resigning up ourselves unto God.

(2.) The will must consent, that the Lord shall possess you, and dispose of you, and use you as his own. When the will gives consent to this, thereby we become his own peculiarly; for this is our entering into covenant with God; upon which the Lord owns us, not only as he does all other things, but as his own by covenant, Ezek. xvi. 8; you are his before, but not so as now; not his by covenant till you give consent; you give up yourselves unto him, and effectually acknowledge that you are his, when you consent to the particulars, wherein propriety consists.

[1.] To be possessed by him as his own. You must be willing that he should have possession of mind and heart; that he should have highest place in your minds, the chief place in your hearts. It is fit that the owner should have the best; the best and highest of your thoughts; the best and strongest of your affections, Ps. cxxxix. 13; reins are the seat of desires; the Lord took up his affections, Ps. lxxiii. 25, and his thoughts too, ver. 17. It is not fit that any should be entertained but who the possessor likes; if you yield up your souls to God, as his possession, you must not admit any thoughts, yield to any inclinations, give way to any motions, harbour any affections, but what he allows; none that will take place of him; none that will disturb him in his possession; nor any that will not please and serve him. You yield him not possession, unless you admit him as your King and Lord, for he is so; therefore he must have the throne in your souls; all must be cast out that rebels against him, or any way resists him; nothing must be entertained or tolerated, but under him, or for him; as his footstool, or as his ministers and servants, to observe his will, and do his pleasure; the will must consent to this, if you resign up yourselves unto him.

[2.] To be disposed of by him as his own. You must yield to be ordered by him, as to your condition in this world; to be low as well as high; poor as well as rich; afflicted as well as delivered, if he see fit, so to dispose of you; so was John Baptist, John iii. 30, and the apostle Paul, Philip. iv.

You need not fear that he will dispose otherwise of you than will be for the best; he has given you sufficient security as to that; or if he had not, yet would it be your duty still to yield to be wholly ordered by him; if you do not resign up yourselves to him, you deny, in effect, that you are his own, if you will not be fully at his disposal; you, yourselves, do not count that your own which is not at your disposal.

[3.] To be used by him as his own. Yield soul and body to be put to what use he will; give all powers and members into his hand, to be used his instruments, for what he pleases, and for nothing but what may please him; dedicate them to his use, and his alone; be resolved and ready to be used by him, in any service, active or passive, what suits you, or what suits you not; both in what is easy and what is difficult; not only in what is applauded, but what is reproached; not only in what is gainful, but what is expensive; not only in what is safe, but what is hazardous, and may endanger your outward concernments. You are his own, and if you will acknowledge it, and resign up yourselves to him as his own, you must consent to be used by him as he will; otherwise, you may pretend to give up yourselves to him, but you do it not really. You think it just to allow another to use his own as he will, upon this account, because it is his own; and if you be not willing, the Lord shall put you to what use he will, though you profess to be his own, yet hereby you deny it indeed, and contradict your profession; when there is a sincere resigning of yourselves unto God, the will consents to all this; see it in Paul, Acts ix. 6, 15, 16, a chosen vessel, ready for any use his master would put him to; they were great, and difficult, and hazardous services, and sufferings too, when it came to the trial, Acts xxi. 13.

(3.) You must lay out yourselves for him, in your whole course; employ soul and body, your whole person for him, under a continual sense that they are not your own, but his; an apprehension of his interest in you. No consent is enough without this; indeed, you did never consent enough, *i. e.*, cordially, unless this be the issue of it. The apostle calls for it upon this ground, 1 Cor. vi. 19, 20, employ body and spirit for the interest of his glory; think it not much nor hard to employ both all the members and faculties of both, thus for him, and thus continually. It is not hard, it is no more than is highly reasonable and equal, that both should be thus employed, and thus only; for both, and whatever in either you call your own, is indeed not yours, but his; and for whom should they be laid out, but for their owner? For whom should a servant be employed but him who bought him for his service? His person was part of his master's goods; he had bought it, and paid for it; if he had followed his own employments, or been set a-work by others, instead of doing his master's service, it would not have been endured. We are more the Lord's, not only than mercenary hired servants, but than *mancipia*, bought servants; both our bodies and spirits are his, not our own. If we will let sin, or the world, or self set us a-work, and employ our faculties, senses, or members, the Lord, whose we are, is wronged by it. You may as well work another man's horse without his leave, or command his servant to do your business, as do what these other usurpers would have you; you deny the Lord's interest in you by obeying them, Rom. vi, 16; if we will acknowledge ourselves to be his, we must do his work, and none but that which is some way his; we must be only at his command, ready to do whatever he enjoins, and to undergo what he would have us endure, and to resist what he would have us oppose, and to avoid what he forbids us, and to part with what he would not have us possess.

This may serve to shew you what it is to give up ourselves to him as our owner. This is it which this truth obliges us to. But this is not all; we must give up ourselves to him not only as our owner, but as to such an owner as he is indeed. The particulars you may collect from what was delivered in the explication. I shall instance only in four. We must give up ourselves to him,

[1.] Absolutely, without offering conditions, or making any terms. The Lord is the absolute owner of all; there is no obligation restraining him from disposing of his own as he pleases, but what flows from his own free will. If we will offer to restrain him by any condition as to his disposal or using of us, instead of giving up ourselves to him, we take from him the glory of his absolute dominion.

To say, I will give up myself to him, if he will not urge such a duty, grievous to me, and prejudicial to my wordly interest; if he will allow me in the neglect of this one, or if he will tolerate me in such or such an evil, which is gainful or pleasant, or otherwise endeared to me; this is not to resign up yourselves to him as becomes such a Lord, but to do nothing, yea, that which is far worse than nought; for to make terms with God, and prescribe conditions to him, is an intolerable presumption in the greatest of men, yea, in the highest angels. To make any terms but what himself has made, to offer yourselves to him with an *if*, is to offer him an affront of an unspeakable provocation.

[2.] Principally; for he is the principal owner of all, and of us. Others may have some interest in us as superiors and parents, and so may challenge some observance from us; but we owe none to any but for him, and in subordination to him. They are to have no affection from us but such wherein a greater love is expressed to God. As we love the picture of a dear friend, not for itself, but for something of him in it, so that, even in loving it, we love him more, so are we to love other things and persons, and no otherwise, but for something of God in them; something of his authority, or of his image, or of his goodness, as they resemble him, or as they come from him, or point at him, or lead us to him, or help us in serving him; so that affecting them for him, we may shew even in that affection we more love him.* Likewise they are to have no obedience but such wherein we obey God, and this is to obey in the Lord, Eph. vi. 1, 5–7.

[3.] Entirely; without exception or reservation of anything; for he is the total owner of all, and of us and all wholly. To deny or withhold any one thing is in construction to deny him all; for he has the same title to that one as to any; and so his title, not acknowledged in any one particular, is, by consequence, disclaimed in all; it will hold no more in any than in that. All the superior powers, the mind, conscience, memory, the will and affections; all the inferior faculties, the fancy, appetite, senses, the whole body, with all its parts, must be resigned to him, and given into his hands, to be ordered and disposed of by him, to be used and acted for him, and wholly for him.

No habit or disposition, no inclination or resolution, no intention or motion, no act or word, or thought, must be exempted from his disposal or use; must be ordered or used not as we will, but as he will, as that which is his own. Whatever of these will not serve him must be suppressed, noway tolerated; and what is capable of serving him must be used in his service, and ordered for it.

This is it which the apostle desires for the Thessalonians, and thereby shews it is the duty of all to desire and endeavour it, 1 Thes. v. 23. To be sanctified, is to be given up and dedicated to God, so as to be set apart from all other uses for his use alone, as that which is his own, and

* Our honouring of them must be an honouring God in them, our loving of them a loving of him in and for them, and delighting in them a delighting in God in and by them.

no other's. This is the proper notion of holiness or sanctification. Now thus he would have them sanctified, ὁλοτελεῖς, entirely; wholly as to every part and motion, and the whole of each. He would have ὁλόκληρον ὑμῶν, the all, the whole of them, their body, soul, and spirit; all the parts of the body, all the powers of the soul, both higher and lower, both rational and sensitive; the whole of this thus given up to God, and set apart for his use alone, as the way to be preserved blameless to the coming of Christ.

We are as much concerned in this as they were. We profess Christ to be our Lord, the full owner of us, and he that has a plenary dominion in and over us, and therefore we are obliged to let him have his own; to give up soul, and body, and spirit; to set apart the whole of them wholly for his use, that so, at his coming, we may be found blameless, as those who have effectually acknowledged that he is our Lord, and we wholly his, and have not withheld anything of his own from him.

[4.] Perpetually; for the Lord is the perpetual owner of us, as of all things. His right never ceases, and he is ever actually exercising it; and therefore we should give up ourselves to him by an irrevocable act, such as will never be recalled or repented of; and by a continued act, such as will not admit of any intermission. We must resign up ourselves to be always his own, and always acting as his own. We are hereby obliged to be always his servants, and to be always serving him.

Not only as those husbandmen mentioned in the code, who were to serve their masters, so as all they had and did was his and for him, during the space of thirty years, but afterwards had more freedom and property.

Nor only as those Hebrews, whose service lasted but for seven years, Exod. xxi. 2, but rather like those of them who loved their masters, and would not leave them when the law gave them liberty, and so were to have their ear bored, ver. 5 and 6, and fastened to the door, Deut. xv. 17, whereby was signified, that he was fixed inseparably to his master, and was never to quit his service. He thereby became עבד עלם, a perpetual servant, fastened to his master for ever.

Thus should we give up ourselves to God, to cleave to him inseparably, and continue his servants for ever, as Ruth i. 16, 17.

And as we should be perpetually his servants, so should we be always actually serving him one way or other.

Take care you be always so employed, as if any inquire, at any time, what you are doing, you may be able to answer it, the Lord's work, viz., that which he sets me about, whose I am, and to whose service I am obliged every hour. Be ever doing that which you may be blessed for, if the Lord should come when you are at work, and 'find you so doing.'

But then you need not think that you are only employed in your Lord's work, when you are about acts of worship. For in a due following of your lawful callings, if you sincerely design to employ what you get thereby for the Lord, and to dispose of it, as the Lord, who is owner of you and it, would have it disposed of, you are therein truly serving him. Yea, in eating, sleeping, recreations, if you use these only for this end, to render you more serviceable to the Lord, you may be herein truly said to be serving him. But you must never be employed, but either in that which is his work directly, or that which conduces to it, and is requisite to help you therein; if you will demean yourselves as those who have resigned up themselves unto him, and would effectually acknowledge his interest in you, as those who are his own.

(4.) Improve all you have for God. Your parts, your time, your strength, your estates, all that you have, as well as all that you are, should be laid out for God. The truth in hand leads you directly to this duty, makes it evident that it is your duty, and powerfully obliges you to mind, pursue, and perform it.

For all is his own. All that the world hath, all that you have. And should not all be improved and used for the true and right owner, especially when we are entrusted with all we possess upon these terms, that all of it should be employed for him, whose it is, and for whom we have it in trust? Which is our case, as I shewed you in the explication.

If all be not thus used for God, one way or other, as he has directed you in his word, you will bring great guilt upon your souls, and expose all you have to greater danger than I can easily express, or you apprehend.

Mind this, as to your estates, to instance in that one, where it is so much neglected; and what is said of this, holds proportionably of all, and yourselves may easily apply it to the rest. I must not stay to dilate on severals.

[1.] Let this be your design and end in following your particular callings, to employ what you get for the Lord and owner of all. You should not have the end and design of worldlings in anything; no, not in your earthly affairs; but such ends and intentions as become Christians, if you would approve yourselves to be such really, and not in name and profession only. Your end, in your main course, will shew what you are, whether you have given up yourselves to God or the world. A worldling would be rich. That is his aim in following his calling, therefore is he careful and industrious, therefore sparing and saving, and parts with little to others or himself. But a Christian would be rich in good works, or rich unto God, that is the main end of his care and pains. A worldling would have abundance for him and his. A Christian would have more, that he may do more good, and be more serviceable. A worldling would have the reputation and credit which riches procure, that esteem and respect which a sordid degenerate world almost appropriates to riches. A Christian would honour God with his substance, according to the divine rule, Prov. iii. 9. A worldling would gratify the flesh, or his fancy, with such a garb, state, or accommodation, as a great estate will afford. A Christian would please and glorify God more, and that is his end in desiring and seeking more of the world, that he may be able to lay out more for God. If you be out as to the end of that which is the business of your lives, you are greatly and fearfully out indeed. God will judge of you, not by this or that particular act, but by your whole course, and principally by the end of that. If your end in your callings be that of worldlings, and not of Christians, what portion or reward can you expect from God, but that of worldlings? And if your end be not to employ all you have, all you get, for God, is there any hopes you will so use it? Is it likely you will do that which you never intended to do? When you would express yourselves farthest from doing a thing, you say, You never did intend it. How far are you then from honouring God's dominion, and acknowledging all to be his own, by employing all for him, if it be not your end in possessing or getting what you have, if you do not so much as intend it? Make sure that this be your end in all.

[2.] And that being done, pursue it. Shew that you did sincerely design all for God, by conscientiously employing all for him; that so, when you are thinking to dispose of anything, or actually doing it, and inquiry be made, Who is this expended for? you may be able truly to say, It is for the Lord; I am disposing of it as he, who is the owner of it, and has entrusted me with it, would have it used. Some may say, How can it be our duty to expend all for God? Something must be laid out for ourselves, something for our relatives and families, and something for others. This is true, and yet all may, and must be employed for God principally and ultimately; for no other chiefly, but for him; for others only in subordination to him; for no others, as the last end, without looking further; for others, with respect and reference to his pleasure, and service, and honour; for it, and in subserviency to it, and so only.

Now thus it is not employed,

First, When it is buried; when what we have is kept close to ourselves and ours, as if the Lord had not designed it, or any considerable share of it, for any besides us. Nothing in comparison of what the Lord expects, is laid out for the adorning of their profession, or maintaining of the gospel, or relief of those in want, or comfort of those that suffer. When it should be brought forth freely and plentifully, for these and such uses as the Lord and owner of it would have it employed for, it is hid in the earth, and there they keep it for themselves. This is, with the unprofitable servant, to hide your Lord's money, instead of improving it for him. Consider his dreadful doom, and tremble at being guilty of a crime which the Lord will punish everlastingly with such severity.

Secondly, When it is consumed. When it is laid out for the support of pride, vainglory, earthliness, or sensuality; to nourish the lust of the eye, or the lust of the flesh, or the pride of life; this is not to improve, but consume it, James iv. 3.

Thirdly, When it is thrown away. As it is no better, when used idly, vainly, on such things as will turn to no account; when laid out upon such superfluities, as are not helpful to soul or body, in any way of serviceableness to the great Lord or owner. If the servant entrusted with one talent, had only played with it, or laid it out in trifles, his Lord had got no more advantage by this, than by his hiding it; he had been as unprofitable a servant, and might have met with as much severity.

Fourthly, When no due proportions are observed in employing what you have; but that has all, or very much, which should have little or nothing; and that has little or nothing which should have most; when that which tends, certainly, directly, or advantageously, to the promoting of the Lord's interest, is scanted and pinched, while the main stream of what we possess runs another way; we let but out some drops there, and the sluices not opened but for other occasions.

To clear this a little, and to shew you withal what it is to employ what you have for God, observe these severals.

First, There is a way to lay out what you are entrusted with certainly for God; and that is, when you employ it so as he commands you. That is undoubtedly for his interest, which he himself directs you to. You may have a discovery of this in part from these few scriptures, 1 Tim. vi. 17–19. To do good with what you have, and to do it richly, according to the proportion of your estate; to be as ready to distribute, as willing to communicate, as if it were the way to be rich; so it is indeed to be rich in God's account. What you do thus, you do it for God certainly; for it is by his appointment, Gal. vi. 10, 16, Mat. xxv. 34, 35, 36, 40. You see a way certain, so to employ what you have, as Christ will take it as employed for himself, Heb. xiii. 16. This will be as much for his service, as ever the most acceptable sacrifice was.

These are ways of laying out what we possess for God, who has entrusted us, and that most certainly. Yet many there are, too many, who will expend little this way, in comparison of what they reserve, at great uncertainties, whether ever it will be employed for God or no. Some will be sparing till they have raised their estates to such a pitch, and then they will be free and bountiful; but when this will be, none knows; or whether they will be then of the same mind, all utterly uncertain.

Others will be sparing while they live, but when they come to die, they will leave abundance to good uses; but this is as uncertain as their lives. Others will reserve more for a child, than all the good they have done in their whole life comes to; and it may be for such a child as gives no hopes, much less any certainty, that he will employ what is left him any way for God.

Others, who have no children, will save and spare for they know not who. But all this, and the like, are but wicked attempts of covetous hearts, to defraud God of his own. Those that mean to employ what they have for him, will never neglect those certain ways of his own prescribing, for such ways of their own, as are mere uncertainties. They will rather choose to do nothing at uncertainties (though it be the fashion of the world to do most there), than not to be free and open handed, in a way which they are certain is for God.

Secondly, There is a way to lay out what you have directly for God and his interest, more directly than some other ways which are commanded us. Such is the promoting of his worship, the upholding of his gospel. You cannot lay out what you possess upon any thing that tends more directly to the promoting of God's interests than this; and those that mean to be free for God any way at all, will not be sparing here. The nobles of Israel, upon David's motion in this chapter, contribute more towards the worship of God than the whole estates of all our nobility will amount to. They were sensible it was for the Lord in a special manner, being for his worship; they thought it their duty to return him his own in greatest proportion, when there was so fair an occasion for it. And for the gospel, you cannot expend anything which tends more directly to serve the interest of Christ, than what serves to keep it amongst you, or help others to it; for the several lines of Christ's interest do all, in a manner, centre in the gospel. To uphold that, is to employ what you have to scatter darkness and ignorance, to suppress wickedness and ungodliness, to advance holiness and righteousness, to convert souls, to enlarge Christ's kingdom, and destroy the dominion of Satan; and what can you do which will more directly honour Christ, and serve his interest, than what is of this tendency? Yet many there are (though I hope few, if any, here) who own God and his dominion, yet think a very little to be much, for the upholding of the gospel, for themselves and others. They like ἀδάπανον εὐαγγέλιον, a gospel, a religion that will cost them nothing; but they will make a shift for their souls rather than it shall be chargeable. They will and do lay out far more for superfluities, than for that wherein God and his interest is so directly and highly concerned. They who have devoted what they have unto God will omit no occasions to shew it; but such as more directly concern him, they have a particular respect for; they will not only spare some little out of their superfluities (as one that has little sense of God's interest may do), but will pinch themselves in necessaries, rather than the gospel shall want support amongst themselves or others. As those of Macedonia, in the like case, 2 Cor. viii. 23, and the Galatians before they were seduced, Gal. iv. 18, John xxiii. 12.

Thirdly, There is a way of employing what you have for God advantageously, and that is, by laying it out for a common good. It is obvious to common reason that a public good is to be preferred to a private; it is best, says Plato, both for the whole and each particular, τὸ κοινὸν τίθεσθαι καλῶς μᾶλλον ἢ τὸ ἴδιον, that the common good be regarded more than any particular. And this is evident, not only because therein we do good to more, and do more good at once, than we can do in many particular acts, but because hereby we serve our Lord's interest more advantageously, this being more extensively promoted by a diffusive good than by that which is but personal and particular. This is to act more like God, and to lay out what we have in a way that he likes best. A public spirit is upon this account a more divine and excellent spirit, and most becomes those who would imitate their heavenly Father; it is as far to be preferred before that private spirit which acts too many, and confines them to themselves and relatives, as the sun, which enlightens so much, is to be preferred before a candle, which gives but light in one private room. The Lord would not have our light to shine to ourselves and ours only, but before men, because this is more for his interest, Mat. v. 15, 16. We put that which should make us shine under a bushel when we reserve it for ourselves and ours; when others, far and near, have advantage by it, it is set upon a candlestick, and so it reflects most glory upon God, and best serves his interest. Those who mean to employ what they have for God will be most free where they may do it most advantageously.

This may serve to shew how what you have may be improved for God. What enforcements there are in this truth, to oblige us to improve all we possess for him, I shall next give some account of. From hence we may clearly collect the equity and the advantage of so improving all, and likewise the danger of neglecting it.

1. The equity of employing all for God is hereby apparent. If all be the Lord's, all that is in heaven and in earth, then all that we possess is his. If he be the full and sole owner of all, then is he the owner of all that we have. And if it be his own, is it not equal and reasonable that it should be employed for him?

If he be so much the owner of all, as I have shewed, what we possess, we can have no otherwise than in trust; and the trust, the intent of it, is declared, it is left in our hands for the owner's use, and can it in any equity be employed to other uses? If you should convey any part of your estate to another in trust, and declare for what ends and purposes you did it, you would count it a great iniquity for him who is so entrusted to convert it to other uses. We have our time, opportunities, parts, gifts, graces, health, strength, estates, and all, upon such terms; he is the proprietor, we are but trustees. Is it not equal his own should be used for him according to the trust?

2. The advantage we shall have by employing all for God may be hereby discerned; to use all for him as he would have us, and as all that is his own should be used, is the way to be entrusted longer and entrusted with more.

We need not fear that to improve all for another is the way to have nothing ourselves. To use all for God is the most advantageous improvement thereof for ourselves.

We shall be far from losing anything thereby. He who is owner of the whole world, and all that is in it, has enough to reward us, enough to encourage us, and has declared himself willing and ready to do it. He has so obliged himself, as we have all assurances we shall not have less but more.

It is so with men. If you have a factor that manages your concerns for you to the greatest advantage, you will count it your interest to trust him still, and to commit more to his hands. And thus the Lord represents himself to us in the parable of the talents: he that had improved five talents to the gaining for his lord five more, because he had been faithful in a little, is entrusted with much, Mat. xxv. 22, 23,. 30, 31; for the faithful improvement of one pound for his lord, he is made ruler of ten cities, Luke xix. 16, 17. One that is wise in the world's account, would have thought it more for his advantage to employ the money for himself than for his master, at least to have reserved something of the improvement to himself; but if he had made use of such wisdom he had lost all, it would have undone him. He found that the wisest and surest way to make him a man was to be faithful to his lord. By improving all for him, nothing for himself, he got much more than both stock and improvement came to. And of the like advantage are all assured, ver. 29. To him that uses all he hath for his Lord, though he seem to neglect himself and his particular concernments, yet he shall find it the way both to secure and advance them, to him much shall be given; he shall be entrusted with much more, and shall have abundance. The talent is taken from the unprofitable servant, who would not employ it for his Lord, and given to him who was faithful, ver. 28. Thus the Lord confutes the wretched wisdom of worldlings, who think nothing is to be gained but by serving themselves. Their way of saving and gaining is the direct way to be undone; and his way of improving, by using all for him, and according to his order, though it seem the way to leave ourselves nothing, tends most to the increase of what we have, Lev. xix. 23–25. The three first years they were not to meddle with the fruits of their trees. The Lord was to be first served; he was to have the first-fruits, those being reserved as an acknowledgment that all was his own, and they were not fit for him till they came to full maturity and perfection, which, it seems, in new plantations, was not till the fourth year; so that four years' fruit seem lost to them. Was this the way to make the best advantage of their plantations? Yes; the increase thereof depended on it. It would yield the increase if the Lord had his due and his orders were observed, otherwise they were not to expect it. If you would have anything you possess yield its increase, dedicate it to God, employ it for him. This is not the way to diminish what you have, though it may seem so to carnal and selfish reason, but to have it increased with the increase of God; a blessed increase.

3. The danger of neglecting to improve all for God is hereby discovered; and that both in respect of sin and suffering. It is a dangerous sin, and exposes us to answerable sufferings. The sinfulness of it is great, and the Lord will proceed against it accordingly.

(1.) For the sinfulness:

[1.] There is intolerable unthankfulness in it. It is as if one who had received all that he has in the world from the bounty of another, should, when he has it in his possession, refuse to acknowledge the owner who lent it him, but should call it all his own, and use it accordingly. All that hear of such dealing would cry out of him as a most disingenuous and ungrateful wretch; yet we deal no better with God. Our being, our well-being, all we are and have, he lends us, yet by not employing it for him, we refuse to acknowledge his interest in what we have. We look not upon him, but ourselves as the owners. We say, It is not his, but ours, in using it as we list ourselves, and not as he would have us. And this is all he gets by dealing thus bountifully with us; this is the return we make for all he vouchsafes us, and it is such ingratitude as heaven and earth may condemn. To them the Lord seems to appeal, Isa. i. 2, 3. I have dealt with them as children; they owe their being, their nourishment, their advancement all to me, and yet, as if they owed nothing at all, they do not acknowledge me to be the owner of them and theirs, they are more disingenuous herein than the very beasts. The ox will, according to his capacity, acknowledge his owner, but my people will not consider, not take notice that they are mine, and all they have too, but act as though they had right to dispose of themselves, and all that they have, as their own.

[2.] It is horrid unfaithfulness to God. It is as if a steward, having his master's goods in his hands to be employed for his use, should refuse so to employ them, but challenge them as his own, and convert them to his own use. We are but the Lord's stewards, 1 Peter iv. 10. We have no more right to any gift, grace, enjoyment we are entrusted with, than a steward can claim in his master's goods. We have them but to use and lay out for him, and as he appointed. Now, 1 Cor. iv. 2, 'it is required in a steward that he be found faithful;' but how are we faithful if we observe not the Lord's orders, acknowledging not his propriety, nor him as owner, and employ not all for his use, but as if all were our own, not his, use all as we please, and dispose of all as we list; not for him, but for ourselves and ours, without regard whether therein we serve his interest or not? Oh, what account will be given of such unfaithfulness when the Lord calls us to give an account of our stewardship?

[3.] It is gross theft, and the worst kind of it that any creature can be guilty of; it is a stealing from God, a robbing of God. 'Will a man rob God?' says the prophet, Mal. iii. 8. He is a desperate wretch that will offer to rob a man in the face of death, which the law sets before him. What then is he that will attempt to rob God? Can any such wretch be found out of hell? Alas! they are to be found everywhere. Every one who employs not what he hath for God, is a thief to God, and offers to rob none less than the Almighty. He would take that which is God's, and make it his own, and uses it as if God had no title to it, no right to have it used for him.

By the civil law,* if a man have the use of a thing, if he use it otherwise than the owner allows, *si aliter ea usus fuerit quam acceperit, furti actione tenetur*, he is liable to an action of theft. The Lord is the owner of all, he lets us have the use of what is in our hands, but allows us not to use it any otherwise than for himself, 1 Cor. x., 1 Peter iv. 11. If then we lay it out for ourselves, or ours, in any way which may not justly be accounted an using of it for him, we are no better than thieves, not only to men, but to God, and that even by the determination of human laws, Mal. iii. 8. The Lord charges the Jews for robbing him. They, not imagining themselves guilty of so horrible a crime, ask wherein they had robbed? He answers, 'In tithes and offerings;' in not bringing that which was requisite for the upholding of his worship. To which that in the first chapter may be also reduced, in offering the refuse, that which was of

* Caius. Instit., lib. ii. tit. 10.

small value, to him, and keeping the best for themselves. Now, if we allow not what is necessary for the maintaining of his worship, or give but the Lord the offal of our estate, some crumbs or driblets, something little worth, and of small value in comparison, and reserve the most and best of what we have for ourselves and relatives, will not this in us be proportionably a robbing of God?

And since it is a robbing of God, I need not tell you that it is unrighteousness, that is a dealing most injuriously and unrighteously with God. To deal thus with men was abominable even to the heathen. It is the character of a very odious person to make no conscience of letting others have their own. What is it not to let God have his own? What is it to defraud, to go about to put a cheat upon him, and so act as such cheats in our whole course? To detain from him what is his own, when we know it to be so; to put him off with a little, when we know that all is due; and not to restore, when we are convinced of the fraud; when we profess that all is his, and that we ought to use all as his servants, to use it for ourselves, and as we list, will the Lord endure this? Do we think that he perceives not the fraud of our dealings, the hypocrisy of our pretences? Will he not bring it upon our heads in the issue? Gal. vi. 6, 7. We may deceive and cheat ourselves herein, but God will not be cheated, he will not be abused. We may be sure that as we sow we shall reap; as we deal with God in using what we have for him, or not for him, so will he deal with us.

[4.] It is virtual atheism, and no less in effect than treason against the Most High. We cannot deny that to be his which properly is so, but thereby we shall deny him to be what he is. When we deny his propriety in all, or anything, it is constructively an attempt to dethrone him; it is in effect a denying him to be God. If he be not the owner of all things, if he be not the rightful possessor of heaven and earth, and all things therein, he is not God. Deny his universal propriety and dominion, and you deny him that which is essential to him, viz., to be universal Lord.

But you practically deny his dominion and right to all, when you use what you have as though it were your own, and not his; when you use it not for him, as his own should be employed, you deny in effect that it is his, and thereby deny that he is Lord and owner of all, and consequently that he is God.

Now what a dreadful and dangerous thing is it to go on in practical atheism through the whole course of your life; to be guilty of not owning God in the continued and main concernments of your conversation and actings; to order your improving and using of what you have, so as it will be a disowning of God! And so it is, and will be, if what you have be not improved and used for him as his own.

I need not add that this involves a denial of his infinite power, or wisdom, or justice, which are essential to him, so that, without any one of them, we cannot conceive him to be God. A thief would not adventure to rob a man if he did believe that he was able to resist him, and would be too hard for him; neither would he attempt, if he was sure he should suffer for it according to law. A cheat would not offer to defraud a man, if he perceived that he was aware of him, and discerned all his intents and practices.

And would you neglect to employ what you have for God, which he accounts a defrauding or robbing of him, if you did believe his omniscience, that he is perfectly aware of you in all that you act or design; or his almighty power, that he would certainly be too hard for you; or his justice, that he will undoubtedly have his law executed upon you? If you believe not this, you do not believe that he is God; and you do not believe this to purpose, if you do not resolve and endeavour to employ what you have for God. Though you profess to acknowledge and believe God, yet in works, and that in a continued course, you deny him. You profess yourselves Christians, owners of God and his dominion, but herein you act more like atheists, and deniers of God and his interest in yourselves and in the world.

I beseech you consider these things, and when you are tempted to save or spare what God would have you lay out freely for him, say thus to yourselves, Shall I be such an ungrateful miser as to grudge him anything he calls for, when I owe to him all that ever I have? Shall I be such an unfaithful wretch as to reserve and convert my master's goods to my own use? Shall the world prevail with me to be so desperate as to offer to rob or defraud God of what is his own? Shall I act so atheistically under the profession and vizard of a Christian, as to disown God in the improvement and use of what I have? Oh far be this from me; far be this from any of us. It would be incomparably better, and more tolerable, that we and ours should be utterly beggars, than that we should involve ourselves, under any pretence whatsoever, in such horrible guilt. And this they will one day acknowledge, and be sensible of as a real truth, who are now farthest from believing or considering it.

(2.) You see the danger in respect of guilt, how great it is. Let me shew you also the hazard, in respect of suffering, in a few particulars.

[1.] You forfeit all you have if you employ it not for God. You are by him entrusted with it upon these terms; upon these you hold all; and upon the observing of the terms your right of holding what you have depends. If you observe them not, your right is gone, and all you have is forfeited. What right soever may continue in respect of men, yet you leave yourselves no right at all in respect of God. And to hold what you have without any such right, is a lamentable tenure. You are but as usurpers in the sight of God, though human laws do allow your title.

If a tenant pay not his rent, observe not conditions, his lease is void; he has no right to what he holds. So in the feudal laws,* *negato servitio amittitur feudum;* he loses his land, who denies the homage he is obliged to for it. And there is an instance of the emperor Frederick, who, holding a dukedom of another, and denying fealty for it because he was sovereign, yet, by the judgment of his peers, for the refusal, he forfeited the dukedom.

The homage and fealty which we owe to God for what we have, is the employing it for him for his honour and interest. Upon these terms we hold it; and if they be neglected, what we have is forfeited. He shews, when he will, that no right remains to the possessors, by turning them out, and taking what is in their hands away. He does it not always, but he may do it when he will; and Israel is threatened accordingly, Hos. ii. 8, 9. She did not acknowledge that she had them from God, and that they were his own; she did not employ them for him, but as her own inclination led her; thereby she forfeited them; and the Lord will take the forfeiture, and strip her of all, ver. 10–12; 'She forgat me,' ver. 13. So by those ancient laws,† if one acknowledge not the interest of the lord in his estate,

* Lib. ii. tit. 100, *vid.* lib. ii. tit. 24, sect. 'Non est alia justior causa,' &c.
† Gothofr., L. ii., p. 510.

si propriâ autoritate capiat, if he hold it as his own, *feudum amittit*, he loses it. So we hold it; when we employ it not for God, we extinguish what right we have, and provoke the Lord to take the forfeiture, and to deal with us as with Israel, ver. 8.

[2.] That which you have, if you employ it not for God, will never prosper, nor will a blessing attend it. If he takes it not away, he will some way or other blast it; and you will find it, or yourselves, blasted for it sooner or later. When one gets or increases what he has fraudulently or unrighteously, it is the common sense of mankind, and we are wont to express it by saying confidently, It will never prosper. And why? But because we think (as we have reason) that the righteous God will never encourage unjust and unrighteous practices with his blessing; he will not let that fraud and injustice to prosper whereby others suffer; and can we think he will be more favourable, where himself, in his honour and interest, suffers? Doth he curse us, when we cheat men? And will he bless us, when we defraud God? Will he bless us in unrighteously withholding his own from his own use, that which he has given and designed it for? No, sure, you may make account, that what you spare or save, when it should be laid out for God, will be followed with a curse; which will seize either upon your estate, or souls, or other concerns, or all together. You may expect either a visible, or (which is far worse and more dangerous) an insensible curse: Mal. iii. 9, 'Cursed with a curse;' *i. e.*, exceedingly, superlatively cursed. Why so? Ye have robbed God. Wherein? In not giving that which was due to his worship, and his officers employed in it, ver. 8. They may think that the sparing of so much, and keeping it to themselves, was the way to be rich; but the Lord confuted their vain imaginations with a curse. He cursed what they had, and cursed what might have supplied them with more. A blessing did neither attend their possessions nor their hopes.

If they had laid out all which was due to God, in his worship and servants, they might have thought this the way to impoverish them, lessen their estates, and keep them low. But their worldly hearts did befool and delude them; it was quite otherwise: this had been the way to all plenty and abundance, ver. 10, 11. Their hands and hearts were shut, so that God could have little or nothing of what was due to him; this shut the windows of heaven: whereas large hearts for God would have set them wide open, and made way for more than they had room for, and, what was more than all, his blessing with it. If you would not have what you possess cursed of God, and blasted from heaven, employ it faithfully for God.

[3.] God will judge for this. He will have an account of you for all his own wherewith he entrusted you. It may be, you hope to make shift, as to the curse here (as some seem to do, when it falls especially upon the soul, and there is not taken notice of, though the fall of it there is heaviest and most dreadful), but what will you do hereafter, when God will reckon with you for all that you have had of his?

The day is coming when he will say, 'Give an account of thy stewardship, for thou mayest be no longer steward.' He will then mind you of that which it may be now you forget, for he has a book of remembrance; and then the books will be opened, and there you may find what has been done with all you had, and how and for whom it has been disposed of; so much to please my humour, my fancy, my appetite, my vanity, my curiosity; so much for the excess of my garb, my table, my other accommodations, to please myself, or answer the vain expectation of others; great sums for these: and for some there will be so much to satisfy pride, or revenge, or lust, or vain-glory, no small quantity, the rest left to my children or relatives. For what? To educate them so, as they might be more serviceable: it may be some respect to that; but principally to make them rich, or great, to bear up my name and family, or that they may live like the children of one who had a better estate than others.

Well; but what in all this for God? what for his worship? what for his gospel? what for his suffering messengers? what for his poor members? what for others in need and distress? what for the adorning of your profession, and winning others to a good opinion of the ways of Christ? what for any public good? Why, something for these, or some of them, what little I could spare from those other uses, wherein myself alone, or myself multiplied, was so much concerned.

Or another, who loved the world too much to be expensive any way, will have nothing to say, but, 'There was that which is thine.' I did no good with it while I lived, and when I died I know not what became of it. The napkin I carefully hid it in was opened when I was gone; I left it amongst them, and if they have squandered it away, I cannot help it.

But, may the Lord say, all that you had was mine own, and should have been all employed for me, How comes it then to pass that so little account was made of me, and of my interest, and so very little laid out for me, in comparison of the great sums expended otherwise, whenas it should have been all for me? More for a costly garment, or a needless ornament, or a modish excrement, in one day sometimes, than for me directly in a whole year. And, upon the whole, more for mere superfluities and excesses, than for the special concerns of my interest in your whole life. Is this the account you will give God of all his own you have had? Is this to be faithful stewards, or not more like to unfaithful and unprofitable servants?

What will be answered for these things? What can be expected but confounded silence? what but shame, and remorse, and confusion? what but that dreadful sentence which Christ, at the last day, will pronounce against, and execute upon, those who have not been faithful in using what they were entrusted with for him? Mat. xxv. You see those who employ not what they have for Christ, will at the last day be counted goats, useless and odious creatures, in comparison of the sheep; they will be set at his left hand, as those that are castaways, rejected by him; they will be cursed, as he who turned what was set apart for God to another use was *anathema*, cursed, Lev. xxvii. 28. They will be separated from the blessedness of the divine presence, as those who had not given up what they had to him, and separated it for other uses from him. They will be cast into everlasting fire, and there tormented with the devil and his angels, and that for ever. And why all this severity, in so fearful a sentence and so terrible an execution? It is plainly upon this account, because they laid not out what they had, so as it might be accounted laid out for Christ. Oh that you would avoid the wrath of the Lamb, and of him that sits upon the throne! If you have been guilty herein, yield to conviction. Break off this dangerous evil without delay, persist not in such wickedness. Take warning before it be too late. Employ what you have so as, when you stand before the tribunal of Christ, you may give an account thereof with joy, and not with grief, and shame, and terror, and a fearful expectation of judgment and fiery indignation, which will then devour those who continue in such ungrateful, unfaithful, injurious dealing with God, and will be devouring of them for ever and ever.

[4.] I might add, as another inducement, the comfort we may have thereby. This is the way to make all we have, and all we do, to be holy, holy unto the Lord, and used holily. How acts of worship, and what is set apart thereto, are holy, we easily apprehend; but how our particular callings, our earthly business and worldly enjoyments, should be made so holy, and those pursued, and these used, in a holy manner, is the difficulty, and yet a most necessary duty, for otherwise we cannot be holy in all manner of conversation, which is required of us indispensably, 1 Pet. i. 15. Not only in that part of our conversation which immediately respects God in duties of worship, but that part of it which respects the world, and the business and enjoyments of it. How may these be made holy, or we shew ourselves holy in them? Why, plainly, thus: that is holy which is set apart to God, and used for him. That which you design and really resolve shall be for God, you consecrate it, and make it holy, and what you use (as so set apart) for him, you use as a holy thing; so that if God be your end and design in your particular callings, if you follow your business for him, and employ what you get for God, all thus become holy, and you use them as becomes holy persons to use holy things. If your intention in all be to please, and serve, and honour God, and you employ all in a subserviency to these ends, and no otherwise, you are holy, even in this part of your conversation, and not only in that part of it which is taken up with his worship, Heb. xiii. 16, Philip. iv. 16–18.

The art* of sacrificing was a holy employment, and the sacrifice offered to God was a holy thing, and so are you employed, when you are doing good with what you have; and that portion of your estates which you do good with, which you employ to please, and serve, and honour God with, it assumes, as it were, the nature of a sacrifice, and is offered to God as a holy thing.

You see the way that holiness to the Lord may be upon all you have and do in the world. Use it as that which is God's, and as he who is the owner would have it used; use it not for yourselves or others, but so as God may be served, and pleased, and honoured by it, and then it is employed for God. It is as it were offered to him; it will be holy and acceptable to him, as the sacrifices of his own appointing were.

And how comfortable will it be for you to have the Lord look upon the use and employment of what you have in the world, as the odour of a sweet smell, a sacrifice acceptable and well-pleasing to him, and to make it the end of your callings, and the business of your lives, to be (when others are sacrificing all to their lusts, or themselves) still offering to him (in the use), or preparing for him (in your care and industry) such holy offerings.

[5.] What you have will hereby be better secured. The Lord will be particularly interested in the preservation of it as that which is his own, not only by a common right which he has in all things, but by a particular right, such as he has in things dedicated to him.

If our end and design be, if we sincerely intend to employ what we have for God, we have thereby given it up, dedicated it to God; and so it is his own peculiarly, and those that wrong us therein, wrong God himself, not as common transgressors only, but as those who should steal away that which was provided and prepared for a sacrifice for God. This would not only be a wrong to the person who provided it, but to the Lord for whom

* Qu. 'act'?—ED.

it was designed, and to whom it was to be offered. God is herein more particularly concerned than in common injuries, and will shew it by taking special vengeance for it. Those that will oppose or defraud you, or by deceit or violence take anything from you, when you have given up all to God, and are accordingly employing all, run a more dreadful hazard than any other deceivers or oppressors, they shall not escape so well as others. He will make them know they had better have employed their fraud or violence anywhere than upon such, they shall feel what it is to attempt upon that which is God's own, Jer. ii. 3. 'Israel was consecrated or set apart to me, and the first-fruits of my revenues, all that devour him shall offend,' not as common offenders, but as those which devoured that which was God's, as such who attempt to rob the exchequer of the Most High; 'evil shall come upon them,' some grievous evil answerable to the offence. They shall not escape without exemplary punishment.

Hereby you have assurance, that the Lord will secure what you have as he will secure his own. All you have is his, and so should be given up to him, and used for him; hereby it becomes his own peculiarly. And so this is the way to engage him to take care of your concerns as his own. But enough of this; though indeed never enough of it, till it lead you effectually to the practice of this most important duty, of employing all for God.

4. Another duty that this truth leads us to is patience, and the continual exercise of it, as there is occasion. It will help us, being duly considered and effectually believed, in patience to possess our souls, whatever our condition or the circumstances of it be. It will serve both as a motive and a means to keep our souls in a submissive, quiet, composed, undisturbed temper, even in such cases which are most like to disturb and discompose us, to make us yield submissively to the disposal of God when others rise up against it, and to silence and quiet our hearts when they are tempted to grumble and murmur and shew themselves unsatisfied. This will shew us that the least degree of impatience is most unreasonable, very sinful, and exceeding dangerous, that it reflects untowardly upon the universal dominion and propriety of God as to all things, and either denies it, or questions whether he duly exercise it towards us, and by such guilt very much endangers us, and tends to make our condition far worse, when we think it too bad already. Let me instance, in three particulars, when impatience has the greatest advantage, and usually most prevails.

(1.) In wants and necessities. When we have not what we desire, or so much of it as we would have, this brings us into impatience. But how unreasonable it is to yield to it, whatever our wants be, how heinous and dangerous it is, hereby appears evidently.

The Lord is the owner of all: that which we would have, as well as that which we have, is his own, and so he has all right to dispose of it as he will. No, says impatience (this is the voice and language of it, though we are apt to put a better construction on it), it ought to be disposed otherwise; I should have more than I have, I have not enough, my share is too little in this, or that, or many degrees. And what is the meaning of this, but a denying that God is the owner of what we would have, or that he has not the right to dispose of his own as he pleases? And how intolerable is this, for a poor worthless creature, who has nothing at all but what he owes to the mere bounty of God, thus to rise up against the Lord of heaven and earth, and question his interest, and impeach his undoubted right, and prescribe to him how he should order that which is his own! If a beggar, when you have given him what you think fit, should murmur and repine, and say you gave him not enough, he wants this, and that, and so much of it, and ought to have it of you, you would take him up as saucy and impudent, for challenging more than you think fit to give, and prescribing to you how you should dispose of what is your own, you would tell him if he were not satisfied with what you think fit to give, he should have nothing at all, as he deserved. A greater sauciness in such a beggar would be nothing to that of our impatience in God's account; the absoluteness of his dominion and right, with the infiniteness of the distance betwixt us, raises the provocation inconceivably higher.

It were more tolerable if that which we are impatient to have were our own, or any way due to us; but this truth leaves us no plea nor pretence for that. God is the true and sole owner of all; and therefore this should hush and quell all the stirrings of impatience, and quiet our hearts when our needs would disturb us, as it silenced those in the parable, who murmured that they had no more, Mat. xx. 11, 13, 15. Is it not most intolerable not to allow the absolute Lord of all that right which we challenge ourselves, to do what we will with our own, when that we call our own is nothing so much ours as all are his? If any say, the Lord has promised what I would have, and so, though it be not otherwise due, yet by virtue of his promise it is; for that creates some right;—

Ans. The Lord has nowhere promised earthly blessings in such a degree to thee or any; he has promised in general what is good for his people in temporal enjoyments, but not such or such a degree thereof, or so much as they may desire, no, nor spiritual blessings in such a degree, though we are in little danger of impatient desires after these (alas! we do not so much value them, we are not so sensible of our want of them, the Lord encourages importunate eagerness after these), our danger is in respect of temporal enjoyments; and the degrees of these he has nowhere promised, and so he has not, as to these, any way restrained his own right of disposing of them in what degree and proportion soever he will. His dominion herein continues fully absolute, and altogether unlimited and unrestrained, so that we cannot challenge this or that degree of them as any way due to us, no, not so much as by his promise. He is at liberty to give less or more, as he thinks fit. And if we will impatiently desire this or that, or more of it, which he has reserved to his free disposal, we exalt ourselves against the dominion of God, as though he were not the owner of all, and might not distribute them as he pleases.

(2.) In losses. When we lose much, or that which is dear to us, we are apt to be impatient at the loss. But to arm us against the assaults of this evil, let us consider whose it is we part with, and who it is that takes it from us. It is the Lord that takes, whoever be the instrument, and it is he that is the owner of it, for he is the owner of all. He takes but his own; and should we repine, or think much that the Lord should have his own when he calls for it? Is this reasonable? Is this tolerable? Should you not rather be thankful that you had it at all, and that he would let you have it so long, than grudge that he should have liberty to take his own when he sees fit? Job had as great temptations to impatience as any we are like to meet with, considering how much he lost, and how dear some of it was to him, and in what way he was bereaved thereof, and yet by such considerations became an example of patience to the world. He was so far from repining at his losses as he blesses God under the pressure of them, Job i. 21. It is the Lord of it who gave it; it is the Lord, the owner of it, who took it: blessed be his name in both, adored and admired be his dominion both in giving and taking away.

If you should, in kindness, lend a friend what he needs; and he, after he has had the use and advantage, should think much to let you have your own again, when you have occasion to call for it; what a heavy censure would you think he deserves! We are worthy of a heavier censure ourselves, when we give way to the least impatience, when the Lord calls for anything in our possession. He did not give, but lend us what we have. He lets us not have the propriety, but the use of it. Our estates, outward comforts, dearest relatives, they are but lent us; when we have them, he is the proprietor, not we ourselves. And shall we think much to part with his own to him, when he will? Do we think ourselves the owners, because we have been so long entrusted with what is truly his? Will we deny his universal right and interest in all, because he has been so kind and bountiful to us? Is not this shameful, and to be abhorred by a temper that has the least tincture of ingenuousness? Let it then make us ashamed to give way to any impatience in such a trial.

(3.) In troubles and afflictions; when they are many, or grievous, or smarting, or tedious, then we have need of patience; and this truth, duly considered, that the Lord is the owner of all, may help us to it. He who is the owner of all things, is the owner of us. We are more his own than anything is ours, which we think we may use as we please, because it is ours. And has not he, then, all right to deal with us as he will? May he not do all his pleasure with that which is so much his own? And shall we be any ways impatient, when he does us no wrong at all, nor can do? Shall we repine, when we have not the least cause to complain; as we have not, when we are not at all wronged. And can he do us any wrong, who has all right to do with us what he will? And so he has, if we be his own; and so we are, if he be the owner of all: Job ii. 10, 'Shall we receive good at the hands of God, and shall we not receive evil?' so Job checks the impatience of his wife. Shall we think ourselves wronged in one more than the other, when the Lord has equal right to do both?

When all those grievous things were threatened Eli, which the Lord declared he would inflict upon him and his, what says he, but that which expresses a great patience? And this is the ground of it, 1 Sam. iii. It is the Lord, he who has all dominion over me and mine; he has right to inflict on us whatever seems good to him; it will be good and righteous, whatever it seem to be; he will herein do us no wrong. And so we shall have no cause to complain, not the least excuse, not the least reason for any touch of impatience. It hereby appears to be a most unreasonable evil, and that which those who have the use of reason should be ashamed of, and blush at, as if it transformed them into the state of brutes.

5. This will serve, as a powerful means, to help us to humility. It may be improved, as one of the best expedients to make us humble, and to keep us so; to cast down all high thoughts and imaginations of ourselves, and to keep them under. All that we are, all that we have, may, by this consideration, be converted into the nourishment of humility, a grace which nourishes all other graces. This will teach you to make use of everything which others are proud of, to lay you low, and make you humble. There is nothing more tends to 'hide pride from man,' and to make ashamed, and afraid of it, as a most shameful, and one of the worst of evils. For hereby it appears,

(1.) That it is a most absurd and ridiculous evil. If God be the owner of all, we have nothing of our own. And, therefore, whoever is proud of anything, he is proud of that which is not his own. Now we count it matter of scorn and laughter, to see one proud of that which is another's; to see one strut or look big, because he wears a jewel or a rich garment, when we know it is but lent him, is occasion of derision or indignation to any that observe it. Such a person is counted a fool, as being proud, when there is not the least occasion, nor any shadow of reason for it. And this is our case; we have nothing to lift us up, nothing to set us off in our own eyes, or in the eyes of others, which is truly and properly our own. We have no accomplishments, no enjoyments, which we can call our own. God is the owner of all we are and have. And to think better of ourselves for that which is not our own, is to shew ourselves fools, and to make ourselves ridiculous, and worthy of all scorn and indignation. Upon this account, that may be ackowledged as true, which passes for a rule amongst the masters of reason; so far as any man is proud, so far he is a fool. If he wants not reason, yet herein he wants the use of it; he has not judgment enough to discern what is nearest him, or to understand himself in that which is most obvious. If we have a high opinion of ourselves, when there is not the least reason for it, we are unreasonably, absurdly, ridiculously proud; and no person on earth can be proud at a more intolerable rate, because he has nothing of his own, and so no reason in the world to give way to the least stirring of pride, 1 Cor. iv. 7. If thou art exalted upon the account of anything thou hast, it is without reason. As if the madman at Athens, who fancied all the ships which came into the port were his own, should have been proud upon this conceit. There is as little reason, as much madness, in all the pride of the world; it is all for that which is not their own.

(2.) That it is a perverse and desperate malady. Pride feeds itself by that which should starve it; turns that into poison which should cure it; is swelled and puffed by that which should take down the tumour. We are proud of something which we have; whereas everything we have should humble us, because we have nothing of our own. What a desperate malady is this, which is enraged and heightened by that which is most proper to assuage and heal it! How incurable by any art, by any hand, but that of the great Physician! How impossible the cure of it by anything but infinite wisdom and power! How dreadful to us should that distemper be, which is so hard to cure!

(3.) That it is a transcendent wickedness. You could not be proud, if you did effectually believe that you were nothing, that you had nothing at at all of your own. If you do not believe this, you disown God; you do not acknowledge his universal dominion, his propriety and interest in all things. And what a horrid and monstrous wickedness this is, I need not tell you. Yet when you give way to pride, you harbour such a monster, which rises up against God, opposes his dominion, and denies him to be the Lord and owner of all.

Make use of this to make and keep you humble; to suppress and quell all the stirrings of pride; to repel and baffle all temptations to it.

When you are in danger to be proud of gifts, or parts, or any accomplishments wherein you seem to excel others, ask yourselves, From whom had I these? Whose are they? Wherefore are they in my possession? Did I receive them? If I be any way before others, who made the difference betwixt them and me? did I make myself to differ? And when he let me have them, did he part with his propriety? Is he not the owner still?

Are not all these my master's talents? Have I them otherwise than in trust? And shall I be proud of that which is another's, and put a greater value on myself, for that which is not my own, or have higher thoughts of my own condition, because I have more of another's in my hands? If all those feathers which set me off, and make so fair a show, were plucked away, and none left me but what I might truly call mine own, what should I have left, for any to be proud of?

Some are in danger to be lifted up with a conceit of their *beauty* and comeliness. Now what would you think of one that is proud of a painted face? You would judge her worthy of scorn and laughter. It is not her own beauty, you will say, she owes it to the art and colours of another. And do not you more owe what comeliness you have to the hand of God? And does not this make it as little your own as that which you deride is hers? Native and painted beauty differ not in this respect; neither is your own; it is equally groundless and ridiculous to be proud of either.

Some are so vain as to be proud of what they *wear*, if it be finer and richer than others have. This seems some pre-eminence, and may possibly puff up a mind that has no better ballast than mere vanity. They think better of themselves for it, and think others will do so too. Now if you should see one adorned exactly according to the mode, with all the art and cost that might set her off to the eye of the beholders, and while she is shewing how proud she is thereof, by looks and gesture, one should declare, in the hearing of her, and all about her, that nothing of this was her own; that all from top to toe was stolen or borrowed; this would be enough to prick the bladder, and make the empty thing fall lank, and blush at her folly. Why, whatever you were, it is no more your own than that which is borrowed; nay, many times it is stolen, as it is always, when it should have been employed to better uses. At the best, he that clothes the lilies affords you clothes; you owe it to another as well as they, and have no more reason than they to be proud of it. If you were stripped of all that is not your own, you would be left, not only without your ornaments, but without your being. And should he be high-minded, who is as much in debt as all that he has comes to?

Others are in danger to be proud of their *estates*. The apostle will have those that are rich warned that they be not high-minded, 1 Tim. vi. Something in them apt to lift up the mind. Riches are apt to puff men up. There is some venom attends them, which if those who have them be not aware of, will make them swell. And the world is ready to feed the poisonous humour, which being not acquainted with the precious things of heaven, and the treasures above its reach, will have that most valued which is visible and sensible. Many are apt to be raised in their conceits, and to look upon others as below them, because they have more than others; they value themselves more, because they have much.

Well, but whose is that which you have? Is it your own? 'The land is mine,' saith the Lord to Israel. 'The silver and the gold is mine,' saith he to the Jews, Haggai ii. All the riches in the world is his, Ps. civ. 24, 25. If all the riches in the earth and in the sea be his, what is there that is properly yours? What has any to be proud of, unless they will be proud of nothing? You have more in your hands than others, but whose is it, and wherefore have you it? Is it not the Lord's, since he is the owner of all? And are you not to improve it for him? And were you not entrusted with it for this end, and upon these terms? And will you think better of yourselves, because you have more than others in your hands, whenas nothing of it is your own? yours only in trust, and for the use of him who is the true owner. You will count that steward little better than a changeling, who will be proud because his master is rich. It is true, the more his lord has, the more the steward may be entrusted with; but what is that to him, since he cannot call justly one penny of it his own, nor can otherwise employ any of it but for his master's use, unless he will play the knave, and be false to his master and his trust?

Those that have most have no more of their own than such stewards who have nothing but their master's goods. What the richest have, they have but in trust, and the Lord entrusts them with it for this end, that it may be wholly employed for his use, and according to his appointment. And what occasion in the least to be high-minded for what they have, when it is not theirs properly, nor at their disposal, but according to the Lord's appointment?

So that those that have most have no more of their own than they that have least; and so no more reason to be high-minded in respect of their estates than the poorest; only one is more in trust than the other. And if it be said, It is more honour to be entrusted with more; and he that is more honoured may be more valued by others, and may have some sense of it himself; I answer, It is more honour to be entrusted with more, if the faithfulness be answerable to the trust; otherwise it is no more honour than to be a greater cheat and deceiver than to be a less. The greater fraud, the greater infamy and reproach. And such is the fraud of those that are unfaithful in the employing of great estates. And if they be faithful, this also is from him from whom they receive what they are faithful in, 1 Cor. vii. 25. So that they owe both what they have, and their faithfulness in it, to him who is the Lord and owner of all; and therefore have no occasion for anything, but a great humility in all.

6. Another great duty which this truth teaches us is self-denial. It leads us to it directly, and strongly obliges us to the continual exercise of it. If God be the owner of all things, he is the owner of us; and if he be the owner of us, we are not to own ourselves, and not to own ourselves is to deny ourselves; to deny ourselves is to make account we are not our own, but belong to another as our owner; and to demean ourselves as in the condition of such a one who is not *sui juris*, his own man; as children in respect of their parents, or more fully, as bond-servants in respect of their master. They are not their own, but pertain to another as their owner. If they look upon themselves as their own, they wrong the true proprietor.

So the Lord being our owner, we wrong him if we account ourselves our own. If we deny not ourselves, we deny his right and interest in us. So far as we own ourselves, we deny him; and his universal dominion, we acknowledge it not in all things, because not in ourselves. If we will give him the honour to be the owner of all things, we must not own, we must deny ourselves. You see what a necessary connection self-denial has with the acknowledging of this truth. Let us shew how it obliges us to the exercise of this grace, in some particulars, wherein self-denial consists.

(1.) As to our own *judgments*. He that is not his own man, must not follow his own judgment, must submit to be ordered by the discretion of his owner. Children must be guided by their parents, and servants must be ordered at the discretion of their master: δοῦλος πέφυκας, οὐ μέτεστί σοι λόγου. Thou art a servant, what hast thou then to do with reason? The master's reason must conclude the servant; for why, he is not his own man, and so not to be ordered by his own judgment, but give up himself to the conduct of his owner. We are no more our own, the Lord is more our owner; therefore we must quit our own mind and judgment, and be guided by the wisdom of him who is our Lord and owner. We must give up ourselves to the conduct of that judgment which is laid down in Scripture, that which is called the mind of the Lord.

(2.) As to our *wills*. He that is not his own man, must not be ruled by his own will; he is to be disposed of at the will of him in whose power he is. The will of his owner must be his will. Since the Lord is our owner so fully, so absolutely, so transcendently, we must have no will of our own. This must be denied, crossed, laid down; and the will of the Lord must take its place, and be our will.

(3.) As to our *ends*. We own ourselves in that which is of greatest moment, that which influences our whole course, and moves all the wheels of it, if we pursue our own ends and designs. We are far from acknowledging ourselves to be wholly the Lord's, if we mind our own ends instead of his. Unless we deny ourselves herein, we deny his propriety and interest in us. If we be wholly his, we should give up ourselves wholly to serve his end, an end higher than our own, and that in all things. The pleasing, and honouring, and enjoying of God is the end, the only end, that they should propose to themselves, either in holy duties or worldly business, who look upon themselves as entirely the Lord's, and not their own. Whatever is not subservient to this, is wholly excluded, &c.

(4.) As to our *interests*. That which is God's must be ours, and that only, if we own him, and none else, as our owner. He acts as if he were his own man, and not his master's servant, who minds his own interests, and not his master's, as Ziba did, 2 Sam. xvi. 3. He shewed that he had more mind to be a master than a servant, and acted as a traitor, not like one faithful to his lord, when he did Mephibosheth that disservice to serve his own turn.

If the Lord be your owner, you ought to own and mind his interest, and none else. You must disclaim the interest of the flesh and of the world, as inconsistent with the interest of your Lord; you must espouse that.

(5.) As to our *business* and employments. He that is not his own man must not do his own work, but that which his owner sets him about. So did the Israelites when they were bond-servants in Egypt, they did what work Pharaoh would have them. A servant, says Aristotle, is δεσπότου ὄργανον, his master's instrument; so must we be in the hand of God as living tools, to act as he moves us, to do what he would have us, to follow that business, and that only, which he employs us about. Our Lord Jesus, when he took upon him the form of a servant and acted in our stead, gave us an example what we should be always doing, Luke ii. 49, John iv. 34, and ix. 4. We must be followers of him, making it the business of our lives not to do our own work, but the work of him that sent us, and that only. We must not do what our own humour, or inclination, or interest leads us to; nor what Satan, or the world, or the flesh, would have us. None should set us a-work, but our Lord and owner. We shall shew whom we acknowledge ourselves to belong to, by the work we busy ourselves about. If we let Satan employ us, we shall thereby confess he has interest in us, John viii. 41, 44. If we do Satan's work, we shall thereby declare that we own his interest in us, rather than God's.

If we follow the world, for the world's sake, and do its drudgery, we shall thereby shew that we are the children τοῦ αἰῶνος τούτου, of this world, and that we belong to it of choice, and to no other than this present world.

If we do what the flesh would have us, that is our master, and we can expect no other reward but what such a lord and owner can give us, Gal. vi. 8; Rom. vi. 20, 21; Rom. viii. 13.

If we do our own work, that which seems good in our own eyes, self prevails, and we shew hereby, that we think we are our own, and acknowledge not the Lord to be our owner. We own not God and his propriety and interest in us, unless it be the business of our lives to do his work, unless it be of that nature as it may be some way truly counted his.

(6.) As to our *possessions*. If the Lord be the owner of all, and of us, we ought to deny ourselves so far as to look upon what we possess as his, not ours.

Self-denial includes a denial that we are owners of ourselves. And he that is not the owner of himself, can call nothing his own. A bought servant, as I told you, being his master's possession, could neither count his person, nor anything he had, his own. Yea, whatsoever fell to him while a servant, it was his master's, and that by law, Lev. xxv. 45, 46, Exod. xxi. 21. And if a woman had a child while in service, and that by a freeman, the child was as much the master's as the mother, as much his servant, and part of his possession, as she. The Lord is more the owner of us, than any lord is of his servant. And we do not acknowledge his dominion and propriety in all, or in us, unless we look upon what we have as not our own but his, and so use it. But of this before.

We are not the disciples of Christ, unless we endeavour to live in the practice of self-denial. And how much this truth engages us to it, and how far the belief and due consideration of it may help us herein, you may discern by the premises.

7. This may be improved as a powerful means to wean us from the world. To bring us to a holy indifferency as to the riches and plenty of it; to make us contented with what the Lord has allotted us, though it be or seem but little; to take down the immoderate esteem we are apt to have of earthly enjoyments, a large portion of them; to moderate our affections towards them; to help us against an excess of love to, or delight in, or desires after them, or care to get, fear to lose them, or grief when they are lost; and so to crucify our hearts to the world, and the world to them; and likewise to take us off from that eagerness in pursuing the world, which engrosses the time, strength, endeavours, of so many, and leaves so little of this for heaven and their souls; and so dry up both the spring and the stream of those excesses and inordinacies towards the world, which are so common, and bear down the most that meddle with it, and are too hard for the best, both to cure this reigning disease, and to remove the symptoms and ill consequences of it.

Those who mind their souls, and are sensible how much they are endangered by the world, will look upon that, which may effect such a cure, as a receipt of sovereign virtue, and exceeding great value. Now such is the truth before us; if it be duly improved, there is that in which it may be effectual to cure this deadly distemper where it is working, and to prevent it where it is not. There are several considerations which flow from it, that are powerful for this purpose. For hereby it appears that,

(1.) Whatever you have of the world, how much soever you can get more of it, yet you will be nothing the richer for it all. Now if men were fully convinced of this, that if they could get as much as they would have, if they could compass all that is in the large grasp of their worldly designs, yet they would not be in any degree richer than they are at present, or than such are, who have but a very little for their earthly portion; if we could make them believe this, that all their care and pains, and affectionate industry, would nothing increase their riches, this would do much to quench that feverish thirst wherewith so many are distempered; for this is manifest, that it is eagerness to be rich that sets all the wheels a-going, and whirls them into disorderly motions; and had they no hopes to grow richer, they would drive on more heavily; they would be more moderate in their pursuit of the world.

Now if you believe this truth, that God is the owner of all things; the absolute, the total, the sole owner of all, as I have explained and proved it; it will not be hard to convince you, unless the love of the world have left no use of reason, that whatever you get more will make you nothing the richer; for if God be the owner, the sole owner of all things, then he is and will be the owner of all that you have already, and of all that you can get hereafter; and if so, you are not, you cannot be the true owner of it; it will not be your own, but his (whatever your title be in reference to men), and that which is not your own, how much soever it be, cannot make you rich, how much soever it be increased, cannot make you richer; how much soever you have in your hands, if it be all another man's, you count yourselves no richer for it. Now whatever you have, or can get into your hands, it is and will be another's. God is still the owner of it, and not you yourselves; and will you count yourselves the richer, for that which is none of your own? When you have done all you can to raise and enlarge your estates, yet he that has the least, and is the poorest, will have as much of his own as you, and so will be as rich as you. Men may count you rich, and human laws may give you title to more than others, and in reference thereto the Scripture calls you rich, speaking according to common apprehension; but, in respect of God and his dominion and propriety, all that you can get will make you no richer than those who have least, unless more of that which is not your own can make you richer.

You count not a tenant rich for having much land in his hand, because it is none of his own; nor is he like to be rich, if he be tied to let his landlord have all the improvement of it, all that he can make of it; such a tenure there was once in England; and we hold all we have of God by no other tenure; the Lord lets to us all that we have, he continues Lord and owner of it, and has obliged us to improve it all for him; both the estate and the improvement is his, not ours. If, then, we have never so much in our hands, what shall we be the richer, since nothing of it is our own?

You count not a man the richer, because he has much in his possession; if he have borrowed it all, and be bound to restore it when the owner calls for it; so it is with those that have most; the Lord has but lent them what they have; he parts not with the propriety, though he lets you have the use and possession; he is still the owner of it; and you are obliged to part with it whenever he calls for his own; and will that which is but borrowed, how much soever it be, make you richer? Joseph had a great trust, when Potiphar, a great officer of Pharaoh's, put all he had in his hand, Gen. xxxix. 4–6; but Joseph counted himself not the richer for all this; because all in his hand was his master's, not his own; and answerably, some understand that passage, 'and he knew not aught that he had,' referring it to Joseph; he converted none of all that he was entrusted with to his own use. What was he the richer for it, when it was not his own, nor might he turn any of it to his own use? So it is with those that have most, and with those that are industrious to get more; they are but labouring to get more of their master's goods into their hands; and when they have got all they can, they will be no richer for it; it will not be their own, nor for their own use, if they mean to be honest and faithful to the owner of it, as Joseph was. They have as much of their own already, as ever they will have; nor will they be richer, do what they can, unless that which is not their own will make them so.

If riches be that which you so highly esteem, so much affect, so eagerly labour for, this may be sufficient to moderate and restrain you herein; since God is the owner of all, more of the world will not make you richer, nor rich at all, how much soever you have, unless you could call it your own; which you cannot call it, nor account it, since it is his who is the Lord of all. Much of the world is (whether for this I do not now examine) in the account of Christ, riches but falsely so called and accounted, Luke xvi. 11. 'True riches' are put in opposition to that which is riches in the world's account, which therefore is not true riches.

You see also by this, what reason we have to be contented with what we have already, though it seem little, since we can have no more that will be our own; and what a strange humour is it not to be satisfied, unless we have more in our hands that is not our own!

(2.) You will have no more to spend than you have already, if you should get more of the world; no more to lay out, as it is the guise and custom of the world to lay it out; and this is it which endears a large share of earthly things unto us; this makes us put so high a value on it, and affect it so much, and follow it so keenly, even with the neglect of better things; this is counted the great privilege and advantage of having much; they who have it may lay out more than others in ways that please them; but this truth will let us see that those who have much have no more to expend in the way expressed. For God being the owner of all things, and so of all we have, we have no right to use it, but as he would have us; we are obliged to employ it so (and no otherwise, but) as he has appointed us; and so, how much soever you have, you will have nothing to expend, as the world is wont to do it; those that have most, have no more to spend upon their lusts than those that have least; no more for pride, or lust, or revenge, or intemperance, or sensuality, or ostentation, or the maintaining of factions and parties, or the countenance of any evil whatsoever. If they expend anything of their abundance in any such way, they are thieves to God, and thieves to men also, viz., to those for whose relief and refreshment that was due, which runs into such a sink. The employing great estates and revenues this way is no better than unjust wars are called, *magna latrocinia*, great robberies, and persons so spending them, the greatest robbers; they have no more to spend idly and vainly, so as no way tends to serve the Lord's interest, than those who have least; they have not a penny to spend this way, more than the poorest have; and if they venture to do it, it is at their peril; they do it against the express order of him who is the Lord and owner of it, and has entrusted them in it for no such purposes. But have they not more to lay out for themselves and relatives? No; not for themselves simply and precisely, but only for God upon themselves; only in such ways, and such a manner, as the laying it out on themselves may be justly said to be an employing it for God, the owner of it.

As for their relatives and children, they may have more, if thereby the Lord's interest may be best served; but if they be such as give no hopes that they will employ what is left them for God, but rather against him, they ought to have no more, from those that have most, than what will serve them with mere necessaries, and keep them from being chargeable to others. And that seems to be all intended in that text, which is much abused otherwise in favour of worldly designs, 1 Tim. v. 8. He is speaking of poor widows whom the church relieved. Those of them who belonged to families, and had relatives that could maintain them, they were to be provided for by their pains and industry, so as they might not be chargeable to the church.*

Now if those that have more than others have no more to spend, in ways desirable to a carnal heart and a worldly temper, than those that have less, as it is plain they have not, because the Lord, who is the owner of all they have, allows them no more to expend in any such way, why are we not content with less? why not more indifferent whether we have more or no? why do we so much value, so much affect more of the world, and take so much care and pains for it? Is it because we would have more to lay out for God? He, who is the owner of it, and all, approves of no end but this, or what may be reduced to this. Indeed, when we see any so eager after the world, singly and sincerely because they would have more to expend for God, and manifest it by so employing it, they should be so far from being discouraged or pulled back, that they ought to be greatly admired, as those who have attained such a high degree of holiness and love to God, and zeal for his interest, as is rarely to be found amongst the children of men.

For those who cannot say they desire more of the world for this end, because they would have God to have more from them, here is all reason to abate this keenness. They have no right from God, the owner of all, to spend any of it in the other ways they propose to themselves; though they be worth many thousands, they have not one penny to spend in their own ways more than the poorest beggar. And if they take the liberty to do it, they do it in opposition to God's dominion and right in themselves and the world.

(3.) The more you have, the more you are in debt; and where is the advantage then of a great estate, if the more it be increased the farther you run in debt? But so it is, and by the truth in hand it appears to be so: for the Lord is the owner of all, you owe to him all you have, and he that has most owes most; and you owe to all those to whom the Lord and owner orders you to pay it; and the debt to these is proportionable to your estate, and rises higher as the estate is raised; for 'to whom much is given, of him shall much be required,' Luke xii. 48.

The more you get, the more you owe to God, the more for the upholding of his gospel and worship, the more to his messengers, the more to his suffering servants, the more to all in want, especially those of the household of faith, the more to the common good; the more for the honouring your profession, the more for the promoting of his interest here and abroad. And the debt grows vastly and insensibly through the neglect of payment, yea, or for the improvement of every parcel which was due, but not discharged, ever since it was neglected. None so much in debt as those that

* So the provision there urged comes to no more than what would keep them from being chargeable to the church, when it was not in a condition to be charged with them.

have most in their hands: it sometimes eats them up, and they owe more than they are worth before they are aware, because they employed that otherwise which should have discharged it. What a hole would be made in many men's estates, if their debts were paid, if all were deducted which they owe even in God's account? The Lord will not dispense with their neglect of payment, though they have so little conscience as to dispense with themselves. He would have the people of old so just in paying what they owed, that he allowed them and their children to be sold for satisfaction of their creditors, if they had not otherwise wherewith to satisfy: Lev. xxv. 39, 41, 2 Kings iv. 1, Mat. xviii. 25. Now did the Lord admit of such a course for the discharge of what was due to men? What course then will he take with those who neglect to discharge what is due to him and his? The best plea that can be used, in excuse of such neglects, is a great charge of children, many poor relatives to be provided for. But he was so far from allowing they should be provided for out of what was due to men, as he would rather let them be sold for slaves or servants; and will he allow provision to be made for them out of that which is due to himself?

You owe much of what you have; and the more you have the more you owe, and the Lord keeps an exact account of it, and will not think (as you may) that the great sums which you owe can be discharged with a trifle. Till what you owe be faithfully paid, you hoard up or spend that which is another's, that which should pay your debts. You eat that which should feed others, and wear that which should clothe others, and make yourselves fine, and fare deliciously, with that which you owe to others' necessities, and live upon the estate of your creditors. Those whom the Lord has made such, you eat their meat, and wear their clothes, and lay up that for yourselves which should be in their purses, if you would be so just as to pay your debts. In like manner does Basil* express this wickedness, Τοῦ πεινῶντος ἐστιν ὁ ἄρτος ὃν συ κατέχεις, it is the bread of the hungry that thou eatest; Τοῦ γυμνητεύοντος, &c., the garment of the naked which thou wearest; Τοῦ χρήζοντος τὸ ἀργύριον, &c., the money of the needy which thou hoardest up. And the ground of it, which Augustine† thus delivers: What the Lord lets us have, above what we need, he doth not give it to us, but transfers it, that we may lay it out for others; *et si non dederimus, res alienas invasimus*, which, if we give them not, we invade other men's goods. This is no better than to defraud our creditors, σὺ δὲ οὐκ ἀποστερητὴς, ἃ πρὸς διχονομίαν ἐδέξω, ταῦτα ἴδια σεαυτοῦ ποιούμενος; art not thou a defrauder, which keepest that to thyself which thou receivedst to be distributed to others? If you should see one sumptuous in his habit, diet, and accommodations, and designing great portions for his children or relations, when you know him to be over head and ears in debt, would not this move your indignation? Would you not judge him void of all conscience and honesty? Alas! this is the case of many who little think of it. None are more in debt than those who have much of the world. You can scarce look anywhere but you may see something they are indebted to some persons whom the Lord has made their creditors; and many times deal with them, as the unjust steward did with his master's debtors, Luke xvi. 5–7. They deal worse with those they are indebted to on the Lord's account; when they owe eighty or an hundred, they set down not eighty or fifty, but put him off with one or two, and so make a shameful composition, when they have more than enough to pay all. The Lord and

* Serm. de Avarit, page 155.

† Serm. 29. de Temp.

Owner of all will not thus be put off: he will not be so defrauded, though men may.

And since the having of more will put you more in debt, and the Lord will see it paid, or have satisfaction for it here or hereafter, what is it that men propose to themselves? What is it that they expect? What makes them so greedy after more? You use to count that no great or desirable advantage which will put you as much in debt as it comes to.

(4.) The more you have, the greater charge is upon you; and the greater charge, the heavier burden; and we care not in other cases to be burdened. Every one cannot bear a great burden, and to those who can make a shift to bear it, yet is it heavy and troublesome; and they are wont to desire rather to be eased of some of it than to have more weight laid on.

To have children is counted a charge, as the world now goes. Those that have very many are said to have a great charge of children; their condition is not thought to be so easy, there is more lies upon them. A great estate is as truly a great charge. If all that is required of those that have it were duly minded, it would be so accounted. They have more to maintain proportionably to what they have; there is far more lies upon them than upon others.

And it is not an easy burden that lies upon them, if we believe the Scripture, where riches are called thorns, Mat. xiii. 22.

It would be a wonder to see one forward to take up a burden of thorns on his back; an astonishment to see him eager for more and more, unless he be void of sense, and feel neither weight nor smart. Who else would be earnest to pierce himself through and through with so sharp a load? 1 Tim. vi. 9, 10. He that would bear such a wounding weight, and that too not for himself, but another, might well be counted a person of rare self-denial. And if you count it your own, you wrong God, deny him to be the owner of all; and if you would have it for yourselves principally, you would not have it in God's way, nor upon his terms, nor as becomes those who profess they are his. Yet it is selfish aims and respects most commonly, which makes all seem easy and light, and takes away sense of smart or burden, and digests all those fears, cares, perplexities, sorrows, cumber, trouble, which otherwise would make much of the world an uneasy burden and a burdensome charge, if at all tolerable.

Consider it as a trust (as it is no more indeed); the more you are entrusted with, the greater is your charge. A man in a journey would not choose to have along with him a great charge of money, especially if it were another's, and himself responsible for it; nay, he would be loath to have much treasure that is not his own long in his own house, if he had no other meaning but to be honest and faithful to the owner.

If we look upon what we have as no otherwise ours than in trust (and this truth allows us to look upon it no otherwise), why are we so importunate to be still charged with more, and to have more of that which is another's in our hands, unless we think to defeat the true owner, and convert what we are entrusted with for another to our own use?

If you observed one to make it his business to be entrusted with all that he could any way compass, and to get into his hands of other men's all that possibly he could, you would suspect he had some dishonest design for himself therein, and that he did not intend only the advantage of those that trusted him, because none are wont to be so desirous of more trust and charge. We have cause to suspect ourselves, that our ends are not right, and such as become our profession, when we are still earnest for more of the world, which, when we have it, we know will not be our own, but his who is the owner of all; since in other cases we rather decline a mere trust and charge, the benefit and fruit whereof not we, but others, must reap. If we intend our own advantage thereby, we are unfaithful to our trust, and to the Lord of all, whom we would have to trust us. If we intend not our own pleasure or profit, and design not to serve ourselves of it, why are we not content without a greater trust and charge? Even self will be content with less, when more does not tend to serve it.

(5.) The more you have, the more is your danger. And great danger is enough to those who are apprehensive of it, to take them off from that which they have otherwise a mind to. Those that have most are in most danger, not only of cumber and trouble, and those torturing affections which attend much, nor only of losing more, fraud and violence being most levelled against such; those who live by preying upon others being most eager upon the richest prey; such men being set in slippery places, and they being in most danger to fall who stand highest, when the place is slippery, and the fall from such a height being more dangerous, such tumbling, *lapsu graviori*, with a more terrible fall.

Nor only of losing that which is more valuable than all the world, of losing their souls, and heaven, and eternal life, and of being drowned in perdition. Those who are cast into a depth, with a greater weight about them, sinking lower and most irrecoverably, and those who have more, having more to obstruct their way to heaven, and make the passage so difficult, as it will be next to impossible, Mat. xix. 23, 24. But also in most danger of that which is worse than the loss of all the world, yea, worse than the loss of heaven, yea, worse than hell itself. What is that? Why, they are in more danger of sin, 1 Tim. vi. 9. They fall into temptation, and the most dangerous temptation, a snare; and such a snare as makes them sure, entangles them in not one, but divers, lusts; and such lusts as are not only foolish and hurtful, but most destructive, βυθίζουσι, such as engulf or plunge them deep, past recovery, in utter perdition.

More particularly, to insist upon that which is most pertinent, he that has more is in danger of greater unfaithfulness. He is entrusted with more, and so, if not faithful, he is false to the greater trust, which is to be most heinously false.

He that is trusted is thereby tried; so he that has more is, all the time he has it, under the greater trial: Ταῦτα δοκιμασίας ἕνεκα πολλάκις δίδοται. Outward enjoyments, says Isidore,* are for the most part given us for trial's sake, just as afflictions are frequently called trials in Scripture. Riches are not counted afflictions; but they are no better in this respect, they are trials no less than afflictions; and the more dangerous trials, because the danger of them is not so well discerned, nor so much feared, and so not so easily avoided. Both are trials or temptations; for the import of πειρασμος, which is rendered temptation, is no more than a trial. But much of the world is the more dangerous trial or temptation. And so the apostle, when he says it leads men into temptation, adds, 'and into a snare;' the danger of which is the greater, because it is laid secretly, so as those for whom it is laid do not see it, and so may not fear, and consequently take no care to escape it, but be fast in it before they are aware.

Such a trial or temptation, and, in the issue, such a snare, is a plentiful estate. The Lord tries those with whom he trusts it, whether they will employ it for him who is the owner of it. He tries whether they will be

* Ep. ccxiv. lin. 5.

faithful in seeking, and possessing, and using it for him as his own ought to be, or whether they will be unfaithful, in doing this for themselves only or principally.

Now, here is the danger, the world minds not the end of getting, nor the rule in keeping, nor the proportion which is to be observed in disposing of what they possess. It is the custom of the world (so far has the temptation prevailed) to look upon what they have, and what they can get, as their own; and so make account they have right to dispose of it as they think fit, forgetting that God is the owner of it, and not they themselves; and that they have no right to dispose of any of it, but some way or other for him, and according to his order, who is the Lord and owner of all. And accordingly they do actually use it as if God had actually parted with the propriety, and made them the owners.

This, being so common, taints professors also, whose apprehensions and actions should be conformed to the word, and not to the world; and so they become guilty in not acknowledging the Lord to be the owner of what they have, and not employing it for him; and the more they have, the greater the guilt, the greater the danger.

(6.) The more you have, the more you are to give an account for, and the more difficult will it be to give a good account of it, Eccles. xii. 14, Rom. xiv. 10, 2 Cor. v. 10. If you must give account to God of all you get, of all you possess, of all you do dispose of, you are highly concerned to look after it. There is nothing can possibly come into your thoughts that is of more weight and consequence than such an account, nothing that should strike your souls with a more awful regard than how you may acquit yourselves therein, as being your very greatest concernment. Those who look no further than the present world, judge it their great concernment to mind whether they or theirs be poor or rich. Poverty is a dreadful thing to them, and wealth a principal, a highly-valued attainment. Oh but riches or poverty are but trifles, no more to be regarded than children's playthings, in respect of the consequence of that last account! In that you are infinitely concerned, for all eternity depends on it; in comparison of which this life is but as a moment, and all the enjoyments of it are but as bubbles of one or two minutes. The consequence of that account is the eternal state of your persons hereafter; the everlasting happiness, or everlasting misery, of soul and body. No less are you concerned in such an account, and it is certain such an account you will be called to; it is evident by this truth; for if he be the Lord of all, and the true owner of all you have, he will certainly reckon with you for his own. If he be the right proprietor, and what you possess you have but from him, and hold but of him in trust, he will undoubtedly examine whether you have been true to him and your trust or no. If he be the chief Lord, and you but stewards, he will have an account of your stewardship. It would be blasphemy to imagine him like those careless lords who never look after what they have, or those whom they trust with it; that is not for his honour, nor consistent with his perfections. His dominion over all, and his wise and righteous exercise of it, requires an account, and obliges us to look and prepare for it. He who is Lord and owner of all you have, will have an account of all you have, why you sought it, and how and wherefore you kept it, and how you employed and disposed of it, and every parcel of it, to whom, and upon what, and in what manner, and for what end, and in what proportions.

And so much for the considerations which this truth affords to secure us against the most ensnaring temptations of the world. They are such as (if duly believed and weighed) may be helpful to wean us from earthly enjoyments, to satisfy us that they are not so highly to be valued, or so much affected, or so eagerly pursued with any neglect of heaven and our souls, and to help us against those excesses and inordinances, wherein the men of the world are quite drowned, and worldly professors are dangerously overwhelmed.

Use III. For encouragement. Here is great encouragement to all sorts.

1 (1.) To those who have not yet given up themselves to God; to those that are yet in their sins, and engaged in the service of other lords, that have hitherto continued in the service of sin, or of the world, or of themselves; what encouragement is here to relinquish these, and to make choice of God to be your Lord! If you will be his, he will be yours, and so all will be yours; for all that is in heaven and earth is his.

(2.) He will be your friend. And what an infinite advantage will it be to have such a friend, one so rich, and who can do so much for you! If you were a friend, a favourite of some prince of great dominions, you would think you had enough, having such interest in one that had so much, and would deny you nothing. Why, but all the dominions of earthly princes are but mole hills, compared with the possessions of that great Lord. The greatest kings are but stewards to him, who will be your friend, if you will but enter into covenant with him. You may be his favourite, if you will but set your hearts upon him; you may have such interest in him, as he will deny you nothing that the greatest favour and friendship can afford, nothing of all that is in heaven, and all that is in earth, that is good for you. He were not a friend if he would let you have that which is not good; but all that is good you may be sure of, for all is his own, and he can dispose of it to whom he will, and to whom so soon as his friends and favourites? And such you may be, if you will relinquish his enemies, and make choice of him, and reserve yourselves for him only.

(3.) He will be your Father. And what will it be to have him for your Father, who is the Lord and owner of all things! 'We have Abraham to our father,' said the Jews. That was an honour, a privilege which they were proud of. We have a king to our father, say others. They think they have much to boast of who can say that. But both these are nothing in comparison of what you may say, if you will give up yourselves to God. If you will make choice of him, he will adopt you, own you as his children; you may say, he is my Father, to whom Abraham was a servant, and few kings are so much as subjects, so good as servants to him; he is my Father, who is absolute King and Lord of all kings, and their dominions, who can say, All that is in heaven and earth is mine: 'Thine is the kingdom, and majesty, and thou art exalted as head above all.'

Oh, what can they want who have such a Father! Is not all that is in heaven, and all that is on earth, enough to supply you, enough to provide for his children? What need you fear? Has not your Father all things in his hands? Are they not his own, so as he can and may dispose of them as he will? And can he not dispose of what you fear, so as it may prove a comfort and security to you, instead of what you fearfully expect from it? Can he not do it? And who more ready to do it than a father? So he will be, if you be but heartily willing to be his.

(4.) He will be your portion. Do but make choice of God for your portion, and he will be so. And what a portion will this be! What is it to have him for your inheritance, who is the owner of all things, who possesses and disposes of all that is in heaven, and all that is in earth, as his own! Interest in him will give you interest in all, insomuch that all the wealth which the men of the world possess will be but as the drop of a bucket, and as the small dust of the balance in comparison of it.

Then may it be truly said, all are yours, as 1 Cor. iii. 21, 22. Not only ordinances and offices, spiritual things and enjoyments, but the world, so far as it is good, so much of it as is truly desirable; not only things present, but things to come, which are so much greater and better than this present world can afford, as eye hath not seen, nor ear heard, nor hath it entered into the heart of man to conceive how much greater and better they are; life also for the enjoyment of things present, and death to convey you to the enjoyment of things to come. Oh where will you have such a rich possession? or, who will make you such an offer, or can make good any considerable part of it? Can you gain any such thing by serving sin, or following the world, or seeking yourselves? 1 Sam. xxii. 7.

What can sin, or Satan, or the world offer to move you to continue in their service, comparable to what the Lord offers you, if you will come over to him?

Oh how great will the condemnation of the children of men be, who will be tempted from God with a trifle, while he is offering them, what he will really give, himself and all. These deluders promise you much, but they are cheats and deluders; they cannot, they will not make good anything. But the Lord can make it good; for all that is in heaven and earth is his own.

2. To those who have interest in God.

What comfort is it, what ground of rejoicing, to have interest in him who is the owner of all things; to be able to call him yours, who can, and who only can, call all that is in heaven, and all that is in earth, his own. What reason have you to rejoice in the Lord, and to rejoice in him always, and to say with joyful hearts, 'My lines are fallen in a pleasant place,' &c. What a goodly heritage have you! What comparable to it, when you can lay claim to him who is Lord and owner of all!

What cause have you to be contented in every condition, to be well satisfied, though your share of earthly things seem small! You have enough in God, if all in heaven and earth be enough. All is his, who allows you to call himself your own. What if all be not in your hands, is it not better for you that it is in his hands, who vouchsafes to call himself your Father, your Husband? You are richer, and it is more for your advantage that it is in his hands than if all were in your own. He is able, he is willing to manage it more for your advantage than if it were in your possession. Be satisfied then, and say, as you have reason, 'Return to thy rest, O my soul.'

What support is here to your faith! What encouragement to expect the accomplishment of all those great and precious promises which he has given you! This leaves no occasion to doubt of it in the least. When men promise many and great things to us, the multitude or greatness of them may make us apt to question the performance, especially if it be delayed. But though the Lord has promised more and greater things to us than men or angels could have expected, or can make good, yet, since the Lord hath promised, there can be no doubt but he will perform all, if he be able; and that he is able to make good all to a tittle, there can be no doubt, if all in heaven and earth can make it good; for all that is in the heavens and in the earth is his own, and fully, absolutely at his disposal.

Unless that which you expect to be performed be more than heaven and earth, and all that is therein amount to, this truth leaves you not the least occasion of unbelief or doubting.

More particularly, this truth affords you encouragement in those special cases which are most apt to trouble and deject you.

(1.) In wants and necessities, whatever they be, whether they concern your inward or outward estate. If the Lord be both able and willing to supply you, you need not be careful, you need not be troubled. But hereby it is evident that the Lord is both able and willing to supply you.

[1.] That he is able. For what are your needs? Are they such as anything in heaven or anything in earth can relieve? Why, then, no doubt but he can relieve you; for all heaven and earth is his own, and he can give any of it to whom he will.

Want you wealth, or what you judge a competency? ver. 12. All the riches of the world are in his hands, and he can dispose thereof to whom and what proportion he see good, 2 Cor. ix. 8, Philip. iv. 19.

Want you authority to countenance and secure you? All the authority in the world is his; the greatness, and the power, and the majesty, and the kingdom, ver. 11. He has the disposing of it all.

Want you victory over enemies, those that afflict and oppress your souls? The Lord can give it you; it is his own.

Want you strength outward or inward, to do, or to suffer, or to resist? This he can also help you, for it is all his own, ver. 12.

Want you wisdom? This is his too: thine is the wisdom, James i. 5.

Want you gifts or graces, or a greater measure of them? These he can help you to; they are his, even as light is the sun's, James i. 17. He can give them as easily as the sun gives light.

Want you comfort? He is the owner of that too, 2 Cor. i. 3.

Want you friends? That cannot be, if you want not God. All the friends in the world are but cyphers to him. He is the best, the most powerful friend, who has all, and can dispose of all, in heaven and earth. You see hereby he is able; he is all-sufficient for your relief, whatever your necessities be. And,

[2.] That he is willing also, is manifest by this truth, divers ways. For,

First, You are his, since he is the owner of all. And who is the Lord willing to provide for, if not for his own? You see him ready to supply all that any way pertain to him. He makes provision for the ravens, the young lions, the wild beasts, the grass of the field, the lilies. His hand is open, and he is ready to satisfy every living thing, Ps. civ. 10, and xxi. 24, 27, 28. He provides for all; he neglects nothing that is any way his. But if you have given up yourselves to him, you are his own peculiarly; and since he is ready to provide for all that are but his by common title, can you think him unwilling to supply those that are his own by special interest?

Will not he who provides for the very dogs of his great family, and takes care of the least thing that any way pertains to it, be more ready to make provision for his own children? There is little faith indeed, where there is any doubt of this, Mat. vi. 26, 28, 29, 30.

For whom does a father design the best share of his possessions? Is it not for those whom he counts most his own, his children? And will your heavenly Father deal worse with those whom he counts most his own? Mat. vii. 9–11.

Secondly, The Lord has nothing the less, for what he affords to relieve and supply you, how much soever your necessities require. For he continues ever the owner of all, whatever is transferred into other hands; it remains still as much his own, as if none else were the possessor of it. The words of the text are eternally true, 'All that is in the heavens, &c., is thine.'

If the Lord lost anything by supplying your needs, there might be some question whether he were willing to afford you all supplies. But how much soever you have of him, he loses nothing; he has nothing the less than if you had it not, for he parts not with the propriety; that and all is his own still, and he is as much in possession of it, as if it were not in your hands. It is not with him as with men, who, the more they give, the less they have. But he gives all things, as the sun gives light; and accordingly the apostle, in reference to his gifts, calls him 'the Father of lights,' as the sun is called the fountain of lights, James i. 17. The sun, when it communicates its light to the whole world, and diffuses it through heaven, and air, and earth, yet has not one jot the less light for all this; in what place soever, or how much soever it shine, it is all the light of the sun still; so how much soever the Lord communicates to you, he has nothing the less, it is all his own still. And why should you doubt of his willingness to supply all his children's needs, when all those supplies will not in the least impair his own stores?

Thirdly, The more the Lord does for your supply, the more he gives, the more he shews himself to be the owner of all; the more conspicuous does he hereby make the glory of his riches, and the greatness of his dominion.

As the sun is so far from losing anything, by communicating its light to the world, that the more it shines, the more glorious it appears; so the Father of lights, by expressing his bounty in relieving his people, gets himself more glory; he makes it appear that all is his own, in that there is no wants whatsoever but he can supply them. And you do not doubt but he is willing to be glorified.

(2.) Here is encouragement, to undergo or undertake anything for God which he calls you to; to offer yourselves willingly to the most difficult, or expensive, or hazardous services, for his name's sake; for why? He is the owner of all things, and so has enough to requite you, to reward you, if all that is in heaven and in earth be enough to do it.

Why do men venture themselves freely for princes or great persons, but because they know such can do far more for them than all their hazards or expenses in their behalf come to; and because they hope that those that are able will be effectually mindful of such eminent services? And shall any be more free to venture themselves and what they have for men, than we are for God? Does not he take more notice of all you do, or suffer, or expend for him? And is not he infinitely more able to recompense you, when he has all things in the world at his disposing, for that purpose? This made Moses contemn the greatest things on earth, and prefer sufferings, before the honours, and pleasures, and riches of a flourishing kingdom, Heb. xi. 24–26. Let this make all difficulties in the work of God seem easy. You are working for him who has all in heaven and earth at his disposal to reward. Let this make all sufferings for him seem light. You are suffering for him who is the Lord and owner of all things. Are you like to lose anything by suffering for such a God? Rom. viii. 18.

Let this make all expenses for him seem small. You understand not your own interest, when you will be saving or sparing in anything wherein God is specially concerned. If you had assurance to receive an hundred-fold for all you lay out, either in hand or that which is equivalent, you would think it the best improvement you could possibly make of what you had, to lay out all you could spare in such a way. The Lord has given you assurance of this, as to all you part with for him, Mat. xix. 29. And since he has promised, nothing can hinder you from this hundred-fold advantage, unless the Lord be not able to make it good. But who can question that, since he is Lord and owner of all things?

Particularly, [1.] In losses for God. When anything is taken from you because you will not sin against God, the case, as this truth directs us to state it, is this: they take that which is the Lord's out of their hands, whom he has made his stewards, because they will not be unfaithful to their Lord. You need not question but the Lord, in due time, will take order with such wretches as dare attempt this. And in the mean time, you ought to be sensible that he suffers more by it than you, it being more his than yours. Nor need you to fear that you shall lose anything by such a loss, if you had assurance that you should receive an hundredfold.

[2.] In banishment. In case you should be forced to leave your country, and your enjoyments in it. This is great encouragement. None can ever send you out of your Father's dominions. You will be still there, where he is the owner and disposer of all. If a child were sent from one of his father's houses to another, what great affliction would that be, so long as he is still in his father's house, and amongst no persons nor things but such as he is the owner and disposer of! This was Chrysostom's support, when he was threatened by Eudoxia the empress, εἰ θέλει ἐξορίζειν, if she will banish me, ἐξοριζέτω, let her banish me; the earth is the Lord's, and the fulness of it; every part of it is part of his dominion. What matter is it to be sent out of the emperor's dominion? You can be sent to no place but where the Lord is the owner of all, for all is his own; and so can dispose of all as easily for your comfortable subsistence, as much for your satisfaction, in any place, as in that which you most affect. He could not be counted the owner of all if he could not so dispose of all, and that everywhere.

[3.] In fears and dangers. If the Lord be the owner of all, then you are his own; and if you have resigned up yourselves to him, to be possessed, and disposed of, and used as his own, then are you his by a special title. And will not the Lord secure and take care of that which is his own? This may encourage you to call upon him in the day of distress, and to expect relief from him.

The people of God of old did find support upon this ground. This has encouraged them to pray, and to pray in faith. This hath strengthened the weak hands and the feeble knees under great pressures, Ps. cxix. 49, Ps. xliv. 4, Jer. xiv. 8, 9. Thy name is put upon us, as men mark what is their own with their name. This encouraged to hope the Lord would not leave them unregarded, undelivered in their distress, Jer. ii. 2. Israel being set apart to God as his own, he looked upon that people as part of his revenue; this he would not suffer to be spoiled and devoured. He would make them examples, that would so provoke him by devouring that which was his own.

[4.] In reference to your children. We are apt to be solicitous about them, how they shall be disposed of, how they may be provided for when we are gone, when they are many, and but a little to leave them. As

Andrew said, John vi. 9, so we are ready to say, What will my little be, divided amongst so many? Well, but if the Lord be the owner of all, then sure he has enough both for thee and thine. Though thou hast not, yet he has sufficient for them, if all that is in heaven and in earth be sufficient; for all this is his. True, you may say, he is all-sufficient, but will he take care of mine? For this, too, look again upon the truth before us. If the Lord be the owner of all, then he is the owner of your children. If he have a transcendent interest in all, then those children are more his than they are yours. And whom will the Lord take care of, whom will he provide for, if not for his own?

You have given them up unto God; let it be your greatest care that they may give up themselves unto him, as becomes those who are in covenant; and then remember what he says to Abraham, Gen. xvii. 7. If he will be a God to thy seed after thee, he will own them when thou art gone; he will dispose of them, and provide for them as his own. And what can you desire more?

HEARING THE WORD.

Take heed therefore how ye hear.—Luke VIII. 18.

In the former part of this chapter we have the parable of the sower, which is propounded, explained, confirmed, applied.

1. Propounded, from ver. 5 to 8, 'A sower went out to sow his seed: and as he sowed, some fell by the way-side; and it was trodden down, and the fowls of the air devoured it. And some fell upon a rock; and as soon as it was sprung up, it withered away, because it lacked moisture. And some fell among thorns; and the thorns sprang up with it, and choked it. And other fell on good ground, and sprang up, and bare fruit an hundred-fold.'

2. Explained. The occasion, ver. 9, 'The disciples asked him, saying, What might this parable be?' The preface to it, ver. 10, 'He said unto them, Unto you it is given to know the mysteries of the kingdom of God: but to others in parables; that seeing they might not see, and hearing might not understand.' To you it is given to know savingly, effectually, &c.; to others no further than to make them inexcusable. The explication itself from ver. 11 to 16, what by 'seed,' ver. 11, what by the 'way-side,' ver. 12, on the 'rock,' ver. 13, 'among thorns,' ver. 14, 'good ground,' ver. 15.

3. Confirmed, by the causes of the several events. The cause of the unfruitfulness of that by the way-side was, 1. 'It was trodden down;' 2. 'The fowls of the air,' *i.e.*, the devil, 'devoureth, takes it away;' 3. He 'understands it not,' Mat. xiii. 19. The unfruitfulness of that on the rock was, 1. Because 'it lacked moisture,' ver. 6; 2. It 'had no root,' ver. 13; 3. 'Temptation,' ver. 13; 'affliction,' 'persecution for the word's sake,' Mark iv. 17; called the sun, Mat. xiii. That among thorns was unfruitful, because the cares, riches, pleasures of this life choked it: Mark iv. 19, 'The cares of this world, and deceitfulness of riches, and the lusts of other things.' That on the good ground was fruitful: 1. Because 'an honest and good heart receives it;' 2. 'Understands it,' Mat. xiii.; 3. 'Keeps it;' 4. 'Brings forth with patience,' ver. 15.

4. Applied. Makes use of it by exhortation and admonition; exhorts to manifest fruitfulness; urges it by a similitude, ver. 16, and a proverb, ver. 17. 2. By an admonition, 'Take heed therefore how ye hear.'

Obs. Those to whom the gospel is preached must take heed how they hear; take heed as to the act, matter, manner.

1. As to the act: Take heed *that* ye hear. This is implied, and neces-

sarily supposed. The *modus* supposes the act; and expressed, ver. 8, 'He that hath ears to hear, let him hear.'

2. As to the object or matter: So take heed *what* ye hear. *How* with Luke is *what* with Mark. He concludes the parable with this admonition, chap. iv. 24, 'Take heed what you hear.' That it be good seed, as well as good ground; that this seed be the seed of God, his who sows wheat, not tares.

3. As to the manner, *How*. This is principally intended, though the other be necessary. If we hear not at all, take not heed what we hear, neglect the means, the duty, no hopes to be fruitful. If we receive not seed, we can bring forth nothing but briars and thorns, cursed fruits, destined to the fire. If you hear, but take not heed what, you miscarry. If you receive not good seed, you cannot bring forth good fruit. If tares be sown only, no reason to expect wheat. If you take heed what, but not how, all is in vain. If you receive good seed, but not in a right manner, if you hear that which is good, but not as those that are good; you must receive good seed as good ground, not as the highway, else no good will come of it. If ever you would reap benefit by hearing, you must take heed how you hear. It is in vain to hear, in vain to hear that which is good, except we hear it well.

The manner being principally intended, I shall principally insist on it. I need not go far for reasons, this chapter affords abundance.

1. Few hear well. There are not many good hearers; the most miscarry; therefore there is need to take heed. Of four sorts of hearers in the parable, three are naught, but one good. There is but one sort of good ground; the seed is lost upon three; they are barren, fruitless. Nay, in every of those three sorts there are many more bad than those that are good: 'Many are called, few chosen.' Many have common, rocky, worldly hearts, few good and honest. Though the multitude of hearers be as the sand of the sea, yet but a remnant hear well, Is. x. 22. Those that are planted by the rivers of waters are for multitude as the trees of a vast forest, yet those that bear fruit are so few as a child may write them, ver. 19. Good ground is but as a little island to the large continents of Africa, Asia, and America. The most that hear perish; few hear savingly. This should be a strong argument to take heed. If you were to shoot a gulf where millions had been drowned, not hearkening to the pilot, and but a few escaped, would you not take heed? If one should have told the Israelites, when they came out of Egypt, that if they would not hearken to Moses, all those hundred thousands should perish in the wilderness, and only two or three enter into Canaan, would they not have taken heed how they hearkened to him? The Lord gives us warning beforehand.

2. There are many enemies to oppose, and many impediments to hinder you in hearing. Where there is great danger, and much difficulty, there is reason to take heed. Here are enemies within, without, many, powerful, active, implacable; difficulties insuperable, but by almighty power, from ourselves, Satan, the world, afflictions, allurements; blindness, ignorance in the mind, no suitableness betwixt the faculty and objects, averseness to the word, 'will not see,' it is holy, just, good; the heart unclean, evil, desperately so, evil beyond knowledge; hardness, rocky, resists the word; it can take no impression, find no root; fulness, multitude of lusts, no room for the word. *Intus existens prohibet alienum*, 1 Pet. ii. 1, overgrown with weeds.

Satan opposes hearing with all his strength and craft, this being the principal means of salvation, ver. 12, he is resolute and able too; a multitude, the fowls of the air; nimble, can pick it up in an instant, immediately, Mark iv. 15. It is his meat to do it, as fowls feed on corn. He is a bird of prey; therefore, Job i. 6, 'When the sons of God came to present themselves before the Lord, Satan comes also among them.'

The world, this opposes on the right hand and left; on the left hand with afflictions, tribulation, persecution, hot and scorching like the sun, Mark xvi. 17; on the right hand riches, pleasures, honours, cares, for these to get them, to keep them, and lusting after them, Luke viii. 14. These are as thorns to choke it, leave no room for it to root in, no moisture to nourish it. These overtop it, crush it down; no good engrafting among thorns. The soul spends its strength and spirits upon these; no power to conceive the word, no strength to bring forth.

3. The advantage or disadvantage. This in the text, 'For whosoever hath, to him shall be given; but from him that hath not, shall be taken away even that which he hath.' Mark explains and applies it to the purpose: Mark iv. 24, 25, 'With what measure ye mete, it shall be measured to you; and unto you that hear shall more be given, for he that hath,' &c. According as you measure to God in hearing, so will he measure to you in blessing or cursing. The gospel continued, increased in light and glory, more of God's presence, Spirit, workings, motions, inclinings, more light, knowledge increased. Light to you, which is darkness to others. Comfort more refreshing; it shall be as marrow and fatness; grace more strengthening and nourishing; you shall grow up as calves of the stall. Else the candlestick shall be removed, a famine of hearing, Amos viii. 11; your pastors shall be removed into corners, Isaiah xxx. 20; the Spirit withdraw, no longer strive; light end in darkness, stench, delusions, 2 Thes. ii. 11; joy in terror, despair, lie down in sorrow, Isaiah l. 10, 11; seeming graces, fair appearances vanish, he will take away what he seemed to have; outward blessings removed, and turned into war and desolation, Satan loosed. Then no balm in Gilead, no physician, no bread of life for the dying soul, no support for the sinking sinner, no hopes, no Christ, no pool for the diseased soul, or no Spirit to trouble the waters; no manna, or no stomach; no strength or sweetness, as in the quails, 'He gave them their request, but sent leanness into their souls,' Ps. cvi. 15.

And when the gospel is gone, all outward judgments rush in. After the white horse, Christ with the gospel, neglected, comes the red horse of war, the black horse of famine, and the pale horse of pestilence, and other judgments, Rev. vi.

4. The gospel, according as it is heard, is a great mercy or a great judgment, a blessing or a curse, therefore great reason to take heed. The abuse of the greatest mercy may curse it. It lifts up to heaven or casts down to hell; it is the savour of life or of death, 2 Cor. ii. 15, 16; advances salvation or aggravates condemnation. The cords of love or the snares of death; mollifies or hardens, Mat. xiii. 14, 15, Isa. vi. 9, 10; enlightens or darkens their eyes, Rom. xi. 10, John xii. 40, ix. 39; opens the heart to Christ, or shuts it against him. If one should tell you this diet, according as you use it, will be life or death, would you not take heed? The gospel is like the water of jealousy. A bad hearer is like the adulteress, to him it is bitter water, which causeth a curse, Num. v. 19; her belly shall swell, and thigh rot; it causes tumours and rottenness, and

makes him a curse among the people. To a good hearer it is sweet, blessed, the water of life, fruitfulness, causes him to conceive seed, ver. 28. The word brings nearer heaven or further from it, it does good or hurt, makes better or worse, it is *medicamen* or *venenum*, a quickening spirit or killing letter. It returns not in vain, Isa. lv. 10, 11; it shall accomplish that which I please, and prosper in the thing whereto I sent it. Now he appoints his servants, as Jer. i. 10, not only to build, but to pull down; not only to plant, but to root out and destroy; and puts his words in their mouths for that end, ver. 9. It blasts those who blossom not, flourish not under it; overthrows where it edifies not; consumes, where it refines not as fire; it is a sword, either lances imposthumes, or pierces the heart savingly or mortally.

They are in a more desperate condition who hear amiss, take not heed how they hear, than those who cannot hear, those who never had the gospel. Their sin is more heinous, against clearest light, the gospel added to the law, John ix. 41, the greatest mercy, more inexcusable: John xv. 22, 'If I had not come and spoke to them, they had not had sin,' &c. The punishment is more grievous, more severe, sudden, certain. 'Under the whole heavens hath not been done as hath been done upon Jerusalem,' Dan. ix. 12. The reason is often given, 'We obeyed not his voice,' ver. 10, 14. The dregs of God's wrath was poured upon them because they had tasted the quintessence of his mercy, the gospel. No people like them in gospel enjoyments, which they not heeding, no people like them in grievous sufferings. What caused that fearful desolation, see 2 Chron. xxxvi. 15, 16, 'They despised his words, and the wrath of the Lord came on them without remedy.' 'How shall we escape if we neglect so great salvation?' Heb. ii. 3. The nearer to heaven any are lifted up by gospel preaching, the lower will they sink into hell if they heed it not. 'It shall be more tolerable for Sodom and Gomorrah,' Luke x. 12; 'for Tyre and Sidon,' the most heathenish, the most abominable people in the world, those who have been most notorious both for vile abominations and dreadful sufferings, these shall fare better in the day of judgment, and suffer less in hell than gospel despisers; cords for them, scorpions for these; the finger of justice will lie heavier on these than it lies on them, those everlasting burnings will be made seven times hotter. These shall rise up in judgment against them, Luke xi. 31. The queen of the South, 'Woe be to thee, Bethsaida,' Luke x. 12, 13, 'And thou, Capernaum,' ver. 15.

6. It is the eternal concernment of souls. Hearing is the provision made for the soul's eternal well-being, its everlasting welfare depends upon it; if you fail here, your souls perish without remedy. For salvation comes by faith, and faith comes by hearing. It is an act of eternal consequence. According to our hearing, so shall the state of our souls be to eternity. It is not a temporal interest, but eternal. As you hear in time, so shall you be to everlasting. It is not the concernment of credit, body, or estate, but of your souls immortal. If a friend should say, Take heed to my advice, and you shall live in credit, and preserve your reputation unstained, but if you will not hearken to me, you will live in perpetual disgrace and contempt, who would not diligently observe what such a friend suggests? Is there not more reason to take heed how we hear God? His word concerns eternal glory, theirs but temporary opinion and repute. If a skilful physician should come to a patient desperately sick, and assure him if he hearken to his advice he would recover, if not, he should certainly die, who would not in that case take heed to his advice? The great

Physician of souls prescribes hearing as the only way to recover our sick, desperately diseased souls. Shall we not take heed how we hear? The gospel preached holds forth a sovereign receipt for a dying soul; shall we not hear and take heed how? There is no hope for your souls but in Christ, no benefit by Christ but by faith, no faith but by hearing. If we miscarry in hearing, not only our estate, or bodies, but souls miscarry, and perish eternally without recovery. Is it not reason to take heed how we hear? Shall we be heedful to advice for body and estate, and not for our souls; for temporals, and not for eternals?

7. The gospel preached is the word of God, not of man, though by man; God is the fountain, man but the conduit-pipe; he the author, man the instrument; it is the sun his light, they the medium. The word of God is not that only which is written, but that which is equivalent to it, as the translations, *verbum*, though not *verba Dei.* That which is agreeable to it, if not expressed in the same words which are in Scripture, yet if in others, so as to express the mind of God, his intention; it is his word if it be his sense and meaning, though not tied to the form of words in which it is written. An ambassador sent from a king to a foreign state with short instructions to transact public affairs, though he do not tie himself to the words and letters of his instructions, if he express the meaning, and prosecute the intentions of his master in words of his own at large, yet are they received as the words or message of his master. Ministers are Christ's ambassadors, 2 Cor. v. 20, who speak the word of God, Heb. xiii. 7. That which is deducible from it by just consequence, that which is drawn from Scripture by necessary consequence, is Scripture. That which follows from the word of God is the word of God, if not directly, yet by consequence. Christ justifies consequences by his own practice; being to prove the resurrection by Scripture, he proves it by consequence: 'God is the God of the living,' Mat. xxii. 32, Luke xx. 37. That which we draw from the words of men by consequence is not always their judgment, for man is short-sighted, of a narrow understanding, and therefore cannot see all that may be drawn from his words; but the Lord's understanding is infinite and immensely comprehensive; when he spoke and inspired his word, he foresaw all possible consequences, and will own them which are just to be his word as well as the letter from whence they are drawn. If he should have spoke at large, and expressed all that is consequent, the world would not have contained the books. He expressed his mind in brief for our convenience, and has appointed, and enabled, and authorised his servants, his deputies, to explain, to enlarge, to deduce, apply, what would have been impossible or inconvenient to have delivered at large. He gives his word in Scripture as a lump of precious metal, more precious than gold, appoints ministers to beat it out into large plates; and as gold is the same in the lump and mass and in the plate, so is the word the same word of God as it is read and as it is preached; he gives us his word in the Scriptures as honey in the comb, he appoints the ministers of the gospel to squeeze it out, it is the same honey in the comb and out. Only take this caution, that the gospel preached be received as the word of God, it is required he that preaches it should be sent by God, invested with his authority, appointed to be his vicegerent, sent as ambassador from him, otherwise doctrine agreeable to God's word cannot be delivered authoritatively as the word of God; it is like silver, though precious in itself, yet not current, not money, without the magistrate's stamp and impression. A private man may deliver things agreeing with the instructions of an ambassador, yet

no state will look upon them as the words of a king, because he is not authorised by him to deliver them.

Now ministers are sent by Christ: 'Go, teach,' Mat. xxviii., made Christ's vicegerents, have the honour and authority of ambassadors; they are Christ's mouth, χεῖλη τοῦ Χριστοῦ, deputies, *vice-Christi*, as they are called. 'No man takes this honour to himself, but he that is called' to it. They are furnished with abilities, 'I am with you,' 'in you,' Mat. x. 40, Luke x. 16, John xiii. 20.

That therefore is the word of God which is equivalent, agreeable to, deducible from it, when delivered by those who are sent with authority from Christ to preach it. Such is the gospel which has long and is daily preached to you. Take heed, then, how ye hear, for it is the word of God.

It is more than if it were the word of a king, the greatest potentate. Yet in the word of a king there is power; it is as the roaring of a lion, strikes dead,* reverence into hearers. What heed would one take to hear a king; how composed, how reverent, attentive, obsequious; but what is it then to hear the King of kings, Lord of hosts, Prince of the kings of the earth, in comparison of whom all kings are not so much as worms!

It is more than if one from the dead should speak to us, as is plain in the parable, Luke xvi. 31, 'They have Moses and the prophets,' who, being authorised to speak from God, and as God, do deserve so much reverence, obedience, attention, as if they will not hear them, if they do not respect my word from them, my authority in them, it cannot be expected they should mind one from the dead; though one from the dead might tell them his experience, yet this might be as soon questioned, and more easily evaded than those sent by me.

It is more than if an angel from heaven should speak, Gal. i., if not sent; if he spoke never so heavenly, seraphically, yet if it do not agree with the word, the word of God in the mouth of the meanest worm would be better entertained, Gal. i., Heb. ii. 1–3. How attentive and heedful would we be if an angel should speak with the tongue of angels; much more when God speaks, when it is the tongue of God.

Nay, it is better far, than if God himself should appear and speak immediately: his glory, his majesty would affright us. None can see him and live. Israel at Sinai, Exod. xx. 18, 19, and xxiv. 17. The sight of the glory of the Lord was like devouring fire. Shall we despise this treasure, because in an earthen vessel; this light, because it appears in an elementary body; this water of life, because it passeth through a leaden pipe?

However we receive it, he looks upon it, accounts it his word; and he will resent it more heinously, in some respect, as he speaks by men, than if it were spoke by himself; for he condescends to our weakness, speaking to us by one of ourselves. So we contemn not only his word, but his mercy, in delivering his word in such a familiar way. We might pretend fear if he should speak immediately, durst not hear; but now, speaking by one of us, there is no excuse. If we will not take heed how and what we hear, it is because we will not. Hearers, generally, are guilty of a sin proportionable to the sin of the Jews. There is a like mistake about *verbum Domini* with us, as there was about *Verbum Dominum* with them. They took not the Word for God, because it appeared in flesh; we receive not the gospel as the word of God, because delivered by flesh. Their mistake was fatal and woeful. They crucified the Lord of life, because in the

* Qu. 'dread'?—ED.

likeness of sinful flesh; we trample under foot the word of life, because it proceeds from sinful flesh. The mistake was their ruin, and so it will be to us. Come to hear, as expecting God to speak, hear it as the word of the great God.

8. It is that by which you must be judged at the last day: Judge, &c., according to this gospel, Rom. ii. 16, John xii. 48. The sentence is already passed in the gospel: 'He that believes shall be saved,' &c. The execution accordingly will be at the last day; evidence will be brought in by the gospel. Herein, will Christ say, was laid open the way of life; herein discovered the paths of death; herein unbelief, impenitency, disobedience, were noted as damning sins, yet you would not avoid them, Luke viii. 17. 'Nothing is secret that shall not be made manifest, neither any thing hid that shall not be made known.' At the day of judgment, an account of every sermon will be required, and of every truth in each sermon: of every idle word we must give account, Mat. xii. 36. If of every idle word, much more of every idle act; if accountable of what we speak to others, much more of what God speaks to us; if of unedifying speaking, much more of unprofitable hearing. The books will be opened, all the sermons mentioned which you have heard, and a particular account required, why you imprisoned such a truth revealed, why you committed such a sin threatened, why neglected such duties enjoined. The gospel, at the last day, if neglected, will plead you inexcusable. 'If I had not come,' &c., 'you had no sin.' You cannot say, *Si scissem, fecissem*. Oh what a fearful account! So many sermons slept, not regarded, prejudiced, hated, forgotten, unpractised.

We must give account of all talents, all enjoyments, how improved, time, parts, riches. If of common mercies, much more of special, extraordinary. None like the gospel, no account therefore so exact. Other mercies are but as one talent, the gospel as five in proportion to one. If he that improved not one, received such a heavy sentence, what shall he expect who neglects, hides, improves not five? 'If every transgression and disobedience,' in the use of less mercies, 'receive a just recompence of reward, how shall we escape if we neglect' the gospel, 'which at first began to be spoken by the Lord, and was confirmed unto us by those that heard him?' Heb. ii. 'Therefore we ought to give the more earnest heed to the things which we hear.' No wrath so fierce as God's for the contempt of mercy, and of the greatest mercy in the gospel; no plea, no excuse, no escaping.

Use. Reproof to those that will not hear, neglect opportunities, make light of it. If it be a duty to hear well, it is a sin not to hear. If it be a sin not to hear right, it is a great sin not to hear at all; it is a common sin, national sin, threatens ruin to the gospel. Heathens and savages more forward than we! Manna is loathed, light hated. The sin of this place! A thin congregation makes me jealous with a godly jealousy, out of love to your souls. Are not you absent upon small occasions? A little rain, cold season, small employments, prejudice against God's messengers, keep you at home. Is not this to make light of the gospel? Others compass sea and land, run from sea to sea, to hear; you will not stir out of doors. Read the parable, Mat. xxii. A king made a feast at the marriage of his son, sent his servants to invite guests: they made excuses; one had married a wife, &c. What was the issue? The king was wroth, sent out his armies to destroy and burn their city, not one of them should taste of his supper. God in the gospel offers to espouse us to his Son, to feast us with fat things, the pleasures of his house; invites us. If we neglect, we shall never taste of Christ. The children of the kingdom shall be cast out. It will be with you in this nation, and this place, as with the Jews: he turned from them to the Gentiles. He will take Christ and the gospel from you and give it to Americans; and when the gospel is gone, then look for destruction and desolation. The Lord convince you of the sinfulness of this sin!

1. It is a high contempt of God, of Christ. Contempt is the highest degree of dishonour; God is jealous of this. Men cannot endure it, much less God; he is infinitely above us, we are worms; he stands in no need of us. It is for our good, our happiness: it is God contemned in his dearest and most glorious manifestation, mercy, bowels. If a great king should send an ambassador to a poor impotent man lying on a dunghill, a stranger, an enemy to him, to offer reconciliation, to adopt him, to make him heir of his kingdom, if this wretch should refuse to hear him, would it not highly exasperate him? So it is here; the Lord sends to us lying in our blood, poor, blind, &c. Mercy slighted, turns into the greatest fury. The arm of God's vengeance will fall heavier upon gospel-slighters than upon any persons in the world. 'It shall be more tolerable for Sodom,' Luke x. Why, might they say, it is but man that delivers it; if it were God, we might expect severity. Nay, it is all one: he adds, 'He that hears you, hears me.'

2. If you will not hear God now, God will not hear you in the time of distress, though you may make many prayers, Isa. i. 15. He will send you to the gods whom ye have served: Isa. lxvi. 4, 'I will bring their fears upon them; because when I called, none did answer; when I spake, they did not hear: but they did evil before mine eyes,' &c. Isa. lxv. 12–14, 'I will number you to the sword, and ye shall all bow down to the slaughter: because when I called, ye did not answer,' &c. 'He will laugh at your destruction,' Prov. i. 24–31, Jer. vii. 14–16. The time may come, when all outward refuges and supports will fail, at least on your deathbed, when it will be in vain to call to men and angels. If you then cry for pardon, mercy, the Lord will stop his ears; you heard not him in health, life, and he will not then hear you. Nay, at the day of judgment, when you, with the foolish virgins, knock at the gate of heaven, and say, Lord, open, deliver me from these everlasting burnings; Oh save me from these tormentors who are ready to hale me into endless torture. Nay, Christ will say, You would not hear me when I invited, beseeched, nay, and wept over you; now I will not hear you. Then you shall hear nothing but that dreadful sentence, 'Depart from me, ye cursed, into everlasting burnings,' &c. If this terrible sentence must be denounced and executed upon wretches, because they did not feed, clothe, and visit Christ, much more against those who would not so much as hear him. Lord, hear me, or I perish, I sink into the bottomless pit, I shall be haled into outer darkness. Nay, you would not hear: he will hear no plea, no excuse.

3. Consider the state of the damned, those who, for neglecting the light, are cast into outer darkness. With what torture and anguish do they look upon their neglect of the gospel! Read the parable of Dives, Luke xvi. Lay your ear to hell, and hear those forlorn creatures cry out against this sin, as that which has damned them, sunk their souls into endless miseries. Suppose you heard them say, Oh that we had esteemed the gospel! Oh that we had more regarded the Lord's messengers! Oh that we had hearkened to the voice of Christ in them! Then might we have escaped

that wrath which was once to come, but now is upon us; but now it is too late; alas, it is too late, the day of our visitation is shut up in eternal night! But oh if it were possible that time might be recalled, and a revenging God appeased, oh what would we give to hear the word of reconciliation from the most despised minister! We would give our estates; our health, our liberty, would be thought a small matter to part with for such advantage. Oh what would we do to hear but the least hope offered in the gospel! We would run from sea to sea, watch night and day, spend time, and strength, and means, upon condition we might but hear one gospel sermon, Christ once more offer peace to us! Oh what would we suffer, to redeem one of those many neglected opportunities! We would endure a thousand years' torments for one hour's time; a thousand years' darkness for one minute of gospel light; a thousand years' burning for one encouraging word from Christ, ten thousand of which we formerly slighted.

But there is no hope for them, despair is part of their torture: yet can they not choose but be astonished at the desperate carelessness of men on earth, who will not hear, though this sin have sunk millions into hell; who will take any excuse, any occasion to be absent, when Christ is offering life and reconciliation; for hopes of a little gain, hazard the loss of their souls; for a little ease, expose themselves to eternal torments. It is too cold to hear the word, but you will find an alteration in hell; that will be hot enough, seven times hotter for you then. A little rain or snow will keep you at home when Christ speaks; but how will you endure that horrible tempest, which the Lord will rain upon gospel contemners? A flood of brimstone will be poured on you, kindled by the Lord's fiery indignation.

Use II. Exhortation to this duty. It is a duty of Christ's enjoining, and to his disciples.

To further the practice of it, I shall, 1, remove impediments that hinder; 2, prescribe means to facilitate and direct.

1. The impediments are ignorance, contempt, distractions, prejudice, obduration, bad ends or principles.

(1.) *Ignorance* in the mysteries of the gospel, the principles of religion: 'Without knowledge the heart is naught,' Prov. xix. 2. Now the seed of the word is not well received, but into a good and honest heart, ver. 15. This is one of the defects in those who receive the seed, as the high-way, they understand it not, Mat. xiii. 19; and therefore are more obnoxious to the wiles of that wicked one: none so fit a subject for Satan to delude, to work upon, as ignorants; we are easily deceived in that, and deprived of that, of which we have not knowledge. Ignorance is darkness spiritual, and darkness is Satan's element; he is the prince of darkness; he has most advantages to act there, most nimbly, dexterously, and advantageously. Ignorance hinders the operation of the word upon conscience, will, affections; it is a thick, gross medium, which either much weakens, or quite obstructs the influence of the gospel. Conscience, not awakened, sleeps on, darkness serves the sleepy temper. On the will; will not yield to he knows not what, nor admit he knows not who. On the affections; a blind man is not affected with colours, how rare and orient soever; set before him the most exquisite pictures, the most curious pieces, that art can frame, they move him not. In the gospel, Christ and sin, grace and the world, are set out in their own colours, but to no effect, till the eye be opened, and the scales of ignorance removed: 'The God of this world has blinded the minds of them which believe not,' 2 Cor. iv. 4; 'My people are destroyed for lack of knowledge,' Hos. iv. 6; the mind is not opened but by the key of knowledge, Luke xi. 52; be sensible of it, bewail it, use all means to get knowledge, reading, conference; dig for it as for hidden treasures, above all for the knowledge of Christ, as Paul.

(2.) *Contempt* of the gospel. That which we despise, we heed not. If we think it not worth hearing, we will not take heed how we hear; say not you are innocent, the best are incident to it: 2 Sam. xii. 9, Nathan to David, 'Wherefore hast thou despised the commandment of the Lord, to do evil in his sight?' Not hearing, is evil doing, either initially, or causally, or formally; it is the beginning, or cause, or the same with evil. Contempt is the natural issue of pride, and pride is the enemy of hearing, Jer. xiii. 15–17, 'Hear ye, &c., be not proud;' Jer. v. 5, 'Broken the yoke, and burst the bonds.' We must deny our own excellencies and understandings, and in the apprehension of the glory of the gospel, and the glory of that God who delivers it, lie low and tremble: Ezra x. 3, 'Tremble at the commandment of our God;' and ix. 4, 'Every one that trembled at the words of the God of Israel,' Isa. lxvi. 2; a sweet promise, 'To this man will I look, that is poor, and of a contrite spirit,' &c.; 'Though heaven be his throne,' &c.; and ver. 5, 'Hear the word of the Lord, ye that tremble at his word.' Others will not.

Nor is this a legal temper; see it in the gospel, 2 Cor. vii. 15. The Corinthians received Titus with fear and trembling; not Christ, nor Paul, but Titus, an inferior teacher; and the Corinthians did it out of awful apprehensions of God, and not eye the instrument alone, having high raised thoughts of the gospel, 2 Cor. iii. The most glorious manifestation that ever was vouchsafed, which the angels desire to pry into, παρακύψαι, 1 Pet. i. 12. Principalities and powers think it not below them to be taught by the gospel, Eph. iii. 10; look on it as the gospel of peace, the word of reconciliation, of life, nothing but death without it; of salvation to those who would otherwise perish; of glory, else hell. What low condescensions of God in the gospel! What high exaltation of man, promises, privileges, relations.

(3.) *Distractions.* Wanderings, rovings of mind, will, affections, senses, caused by the cares of the world and lusts of the flesh; carefulness of other things makes careless of the word. It is hard to hit a moving object, a bird in flight; as well, to as much purpose, sow the waves in a tempest, or cast seed upon branches tossed with the wind, as preach to a distracted, wandering hearer; nothing fixes, sinks, abides; his soul is like a highway, every man or beast has free passage. What encouragement has the husbandman to sow there? It is impossible, while it is crowded; and if clear, yet being open, it would be trodden down.

Fix your whole soul on God. *Hoc age.* Let there be no thoughts, projects, motions, affections, but what is suitable to, or raised by the word; summon the whole soul to wait, to attend to God; watch, that ye be not surprised; if any intrude, cast them out, drive them away: 'Keep thy heart with all diligence,' Prov. iv. 23. What an affront would it be to turn your back on a king, or to discourse with others while he is speaking to you! The postures and motions of your souls are as visible to God as your outward one to another. Deal with wandering thoughts, extravagant motions, as Abraham did with the fowls which came down upon his sacrifice, Gen. xv. 11, he drove them away; wandering thoughts, like these fowls, would spoil our sacrifices; they are a progeny of devils, Satan has that name in the parable; they are his emissaries; bid them as Christ, 'Avoid, thou art an offence to me;' drive these fowls away. We must serve God with our whole heart, not suffer it to be divided, distracted, especially in the act of worship: 'My heart is fixed,' says David, Ps. ix. 1; Ps. cxix. 10, 'I will praise the Lord with my whole heart;' 'Unite my heart to fear thy name,' Ps. lxxxvi. 11.

(4.) *Prejudice.* An ill conceit of the gospel; the matter, or the manner of delivery, plainness, simplicity; or ministers, their persons, conversation, office, or execution of it. This was the ruin both of Jews and Gentiles, hindered them from hearing, or made the hearing ineffectual, though preached by Christ himself, or the apostles extraordinarily assisted. The gospel, and the prime subject of it, Christ, was 'to the Jews a stumbling-block, to the Greeks foolishness;' the gospel, when preached by extraordinary agents, when confirmed by miracles; much more now. The Jews were prejudiced against Christ his person; he answered not their expectation. They looked for a glorious monarch, not one in the form of a servant; his calling, not sent of God, an impostor, deceiver, blasphemer; his conversation, his country: 'Can any good come out of Nazareth?' His doctrine, too plain, too severe, taxing abuses. Paul was a babbler to the Athenians.

To remove it, consider there is no reason, no room for prejudice against the gospel; those that despise it never saw its glory, nor tasted its sweetness: 'If our gospel be hid, it is hid to them that are lost,' 2 Cor. iv. 3; shall we think worse of the sun, because a blind man speaks against it, because an owl cannot behold it? and for ministers, there is glory enough in the gospel to gild them, how mean soever. To neglect the gospel, for their weakness or infirmities, is to refuse to take up manna because it falls on the ground; if there be any fault in them, they must bear it, it will be no excuse to you. Those who would not hear Judas, were no less guilty than those who would not hear the other disciples; Christ makes no distinction, either in his commission or sanction; those were equally threatened who received not him as the rest. Prejudice, when there is some ground for it, does not excuse; but for the most part it is groundless. I am apt to think, where there is a call, there can be no ground of prejudice; therefore, if there be any ground of prejudice, it must be something that may make the calling questionable.

Now those things from which we raise prejudice, are not sufficient to make a minister's calling questionable; for those objections, which are ordinarily made use of to this end, Christ or the apostles themselves are liable to.

Meanness, or despicableness of the person. Christ a carpenter's son, no beauty in him, &c. The apostles fishermen.

Ambition, affectation of superiority. Christ's disciples contend who shall be greatest.

Hypocrisy, covetousness. These were in Judas, yet he was called.

Weakness. The disciples had no acquired parts, their education would not admit it, they were ignorant of many truths.

Difference in judgment and affections. The stumbling-block in these times, yet visible in Peter and Paul, Gal. ii. 11, and Barnabas and Paul, Acts xv. 39. The contention so sharp as they parted asunder.

Carnalness, looking for a temporal kingdom and preferment thereby. Fear of suffering, all forsook him. Intemperate zeal, they call for fire from heaven.

(5.) *Obduration:* hardness of heart. 'To-day if ye will hear his voice, harden not your hearts,' Heb. iii. 7, 8; Pharaoh heard not Moses, for his heart was hardened. We sow upon rocks; no hopes of fruit, where neither root nor moisture; it should be an 'engrafted word,' James i. 21; can one engraft upon stone? It should 'dwell in us richly,' Col. iii, 16; the heart is hardened by sinning against light. When the gospel reveals this to be sin, and that a duty, and no regard to practise this, or avoid that, the first brings the first degree; and after the more neglects, the more hardness, till the conscience grow senseless, and, as it were, cauterized. The Lord for this sin hardens judicially, withdraws mollifying influence, and exposes to occasions that harden.

Take heed of sinning against light, disobeying the gospel. Be not disobedient to the heavenly vision. Urge the covenant, whereby God is engaged to take away the heart of stone, Ezek. xxxvi. 26. Plough up the fallow-ground, Jer. iv. 3, Hos. x. 12. Make use both of law and gospel, that to break, this to melt. The heart must be softened, then broken, then melted, that it may be cast into the mould of the word. The image of Christ is stamped on the word, it must leave impressions of Christ on us; therefore we must be cast, delivered into it, Rom. vi. Hereby it transforms, Rom. vi. 17, obeyed from the heart. Observe what considerations do soonest affect, judgment or mercy, promise or threatening, and make use of that which is most effectual.

Look upon hardness as the greatest judgment, more fearful than any temporal sickness, poverty, blindness, sword, &c., a sign of reprobation, an earnest of hell. Desire, with all importunity, a tender, melting, bleeding heart, trembling, yielding to every stroke, receiving every impression, running into the mould, complying, obeying.

(6.) Bad *ends and principles*, motives or reasons inducing to hear, these make every act good or bad. Take heed to these. We take not heed how we hear, when we hear.

[1.] Out of custom, because others do it. It is the fashion of the nation, and he that runs not with the stream hazards his reputation. He that hears but thus, will never take heed how he hears. Yet, which is lamentable, this is the ground upon which the greatest part found both their religion and the exercises of it. Why are most protestants? Their parents, their magistrates, the major part are so; not weight of reason, but number of professors. So for religious exercises, hearing, praying, singing; not for any necessity, excellency, or spiritual advantage, but because others do it. And this is the cause of inconstancy in religion, and negligence and formality in the duties of it. He that will be religious, hear, &c., only because the most do so, shall receive that reward which the most do.

[2.] To carp, cavil, ensnare, take advantages. So the Pharisees to Christ. Make a man an offender for a word. It is the practice of the devil, he hears, observes, that he may accuse, disquiet, ensnare. To pervert it in such a horrid way makes you worse than the devil, the word was never intended for his advantage.

[3.] To please the fancy, perfect intellectuals, to get notions, to satisfy itching ears; *placere*, not *sanare*; neat expressions, apt similes, quaint notions, please more than wholesome words. This is to abase the gospel, and bring it down to base ends, which was appointed for the highest.

[4.] To satisfy conscience, if convinced it be a duty enjoined under penalty, and conscience not asleep, dare not omit. Or to pacify conscience, to expiate a week's sin with one act of service.

Get right principles. Propound the best, the highest motives. Act upon spiritual grounds. Be armed by spiritual reasons.

God's glory, Jer. xiii. 16. Hearing brings glory to God, acknowledges many of his attributes, authority, truth, mercy, our subjection to him. It is an act of worship naturally engaging.

Our good. Our necessity of it as new-born babes. Come as the Israelites to gather manna. It is the bread of life, water of life. Come as to the pool. Consider the excellency of it. Hear the word out of love and delight: Ps. cxix. 127, 'I love thy commandments above gold.' 'Oh how I love thy law!' Ps. cxix. 97. If the law, much more should we love the gospel. It is 'sweeter than honey,' Ps. xix. 10. 'As the hart panteth after the water brooks, so panteth my soul after thee, O God, &c. Oh when shall I come and appear before God?' Ps. xlii. 1, 2. Ps. lxxxiv. 10, 'A day in thy courts is better than a thousand.' Consider the spiritual advantages of it, light, life, strength, growth, comfort, peace, glory. It is an inestimable treasure and mine, an universal remedy, πανφάρμακον, the choicest dainties, an all-sufficient magazine, an infallible oracle.

2. Directions how to hear.

(1.) Get a punctual knowledge of the state of your souls in reference to God. Every man is either in a state of nature or grace, regenerate or unregenerate, either in the faith or in his sins. Now before you can hear aright, you should know in which of these states you are. The reason is this, we must take heed how we hear, that we may hear fruitfully, that the word may be profitable. It is most profitable when it is seasonable. It cannot be seasonable to you (whatever it be in itself), except you be acquainted with your soul's condition. It is seasonable in itself when it is suitable to a hearer's condition, but it is not seasonable to him, except he know it to be suitable, which he cannot do except he know what his condition is. 'A word in due season, is like apples of gold in pictures of silver,' Prov. xxv. 11. It is precious, lovely, excellent, profitable, adorning, and enriching. It requireth the tongue of the learned to speak seasonably, Isa. l. 4. It requireth a learned heart to hear seasonably. Indeed, this is requisite to every spiritual service, whether we pray, read, receive, else we offer the sacrifice of fools. Paul in another sense, 1 Cor. xiv. 8, 'If the trumpet give an uncertain sound, who shall prepare himself to the battle?' It is uncertain, when it is not known what it means, or whom it concerns. The sound of the gospel is uncertain, when hearers know not whom it concerns, know not whether them or no. Ministers speak in the air, to no purpose. And ver. 11, 'If I know not the meaning of the voice, he that speaks is a barbarian,' &c.

It is dangerous. If a man, not knowing his temper and constitution, come into an apothecary's shop, where are receipts of all sorts, he might, through ignorance of his complexion, take that which would be poison to him, though healthful to another. The word offers that which is proper to every condition. That which is not proper is destructive. If you know not your condition, you may undo your souls, apply promises for threatenings, persuade yourselves of God's love when in a state of enmity, conclude for heaven when heirs of wrath. As you love your souls, follow the apostle's advice, 2 Cor. xiii. 5: 'Examine yourselves whether ye be in the faith, prove your own selves.' The duty is ingeminated and enforced with a reason, 'Know you not your own selves, how that Christ is in you, except ye be reprobates.'

(2.) Before you hear, endeavour to get your souls into a capacity of hearing fruitfully, to get spiritual advantage by hearing. Take pains with your hearts in private before ye come, make them tender, fit to receive impressions. Set them open, that Christ may come in. Make room, empty them of sin and vanity, that the Spirit may work freely, with liberty, without interruption. Get them melted in prayer, sublimated, raised by meditation. If you seek the Lord there, he will find you here. If you meet him in private, he will come along and continue with you.

You expect no increase from seed if it be cast into the ground before it be ploughed and broken up. You must get the fallow-ground of your hearts broken up before you come to receive the seed of the word: Hos. x. 12, 'Sow to yourselves in righteousness, reap in mercy, break up the fallow ground; for it is time to seek the Lord, till he come and rain righteousness upon you.' If you would sow rightly, and reap in mercy, you must break up, &c. How is that? Seek the Lord by heart-breaking, heart-melting prayer; then he will rain righteousness, rain peace and holiness; not in drops, but showers, Jer. iv. Sow not among thorns, pluck them up, cast them out, cares, pleasures, lusts; else no room for the good seed; they will choke it. Say to them, as Abraham to his young men going to sacrifice, Gen. xxii. 5, 'Abide you here, and I will go yonder and worship, and come again to you,' if lawful. Let not your hearts be as the highway; that seed prospered not which fell there. Enclose your hearts with holy thoughts, awful apprehensions of God. He is a jealous God, and will be sanctified. Common hearts are profane hearts; there must be a separation; you must fence your hearts against the inroads of the world.

Let not your hearts continue rocky; if they are, though the seed may abide there, yet it cannot take root. Get them mollified, melted, that they may receive impressions from the mould of the word. By conversing in the world, we contract hardness and pollution; though it make us not altogether incapable of fruitful and familiar converse with God in ordinances, yet it many times leaves but a remote capacity. To remove this requires extraordinary presence and working, which we have no reason to expect. Green wood will not quickly nor easily take fire if we would kindle it suddenly; the matter must be dry. We must get our hearts warmed in private, that we may be kindled in public, so as our hearts may burn within us when he speaks to us. Those who have experience of the Lord's presence and workings, find there is a vast difference, as to the efficacy of the word, when they come negligently and preparedly. When they step immediately out of the world into God's presence, their interviews are not so delightful, so advantageous, the word not so powerful, melting, inflaming, as when they have endeavoured to dispose their hearts for so great a work.

(3.) Receive the word, and every part of it, as concerning thee in particular. Set thyself as in God's presence, and persuade thyself that he speaks to thee; hear it, as believing that God designed it, cut it out for thee. God aims at thee, intended it and put it into the mouth of his messenger on purpose for thee. It is Satan's policy to persuade, that he may render it ineffectual, the word belongs to others, not to me. It is certain there is no truth delivered, no sin threatened, no duty enjoined, no state discovered, but it concerns every one, and therefore thee in particular, and God sends it on purpose to thee; for if a sparrow do not fall to the ground but by God's appointment, surely there is no word proceeds from the mouth of God but out of design. If providence reach less things, much more greater. If thou must give an account for every word thou hearest, sure every word concerns thee; for God is not imprudent or unjust, &c. Hear it then as spoke to thee, as sent to thee.

The word never is effectual but when it is particularly applied; when thy soul is opened to receive it, as Lydia's; when thy heart is pricked, as Peter's hearers. Now *generalia non pungunt*, generals affect not. Now ministers, in public auditories, can but speak generals; they must not name men, and say, as Nathan to David, 'Thou art the man.' Though it be their duty, and they endeavour to speak punctually to every man's condition, which is ὀρθοτομεῖν τὸν λόγον, yet that which is most particular as from them is but a general notion to thee; if thou apply it not, receive it not as spoken to thee. If there be not a receptive faculty in every particular soul, in every member of the mystical body, as there is in every part of the natural body, this spiritual food will never nourish. A chirurgeon bids apply a salve to a sore hand; the hand casts it off as fitter for the head; is there any hopes of a cure? A physician prescribes physic to a sick man; he refuses to take it, and says his neighbour stands in more need of it; so if you, when threatenings are denounced, say such a man indeed is a great sinner, this may belong to him, but I thank God I am not so bad, I am not as other men, &c., this is a dangerous stratagem of Satan, to make the word unprofitable. The word, whenever it does good, enters into the heart, Acts xvi. 14; Ps. xl. 9, 'Thy law is within my heart;' Ps. cxix. 11, 'Thy word have I hid in my heart;' Jer. xxxi. 33, 'I will put my law in their inward parts.' Now by those means the word is kept out.

Some truths are more seasonable than others, yet all seasonable in some respect. That is seasonable which is suitable to our condition. Our condition is past, present, future, or possible. That is most seasonable which concerns the present state, others as they have an influence upon it.

Present. If in the state of nature, it is seasonable to shew the misery of it, and the necessity of a change.

Past. This may be useful to one regenerate, to make him thankful, fearful of relapsing into former sins, pitiful to others, affectionate to Christ.

Future. I am now in health and prosperity; but sickness and persecution will come, and it will be seasonable now to prepare for them.

Possible. You hear some grievous sin threatened, you are not guilty of it, but it is possible you may be; the seeds of that sin are in you. Therefore it is useful to make you watchful and dependent upon Christ, and sad for the sinfulness of your nature.

Get knowledge of your greatest wants, weakest graces, strongest lusts, worst distempers, coldest affections, difficultest encumbrances, that so you may know how to apply the word. All must be applied, but those more especially that are most seasonable. There is prudence required, to discern 'what is that good, perfect, acceptable will of God,' Rom. xii. 2. The word, if you apply it not, will no more profit than meat not eaten.

(4.) Be not satisfied with anything in hearing, but the presence of God. That special presence, when operative, makes the word effectual to the ends appointed. The presence of the Lord his glory filled the tabernacle under the law; and his presence is as abundant and glorious under the gospel. He fills now the tabernacle with his presence, when the glorious effects of his presence are sensible in the hearts of the hearers, convincing, enlightening, terrifying, humbling, melting, inflaming, comforting, strengthening, quickening. These are the signs of this glorious presence. It is a greater glory than the other, though not visible; it is liker to that of heaven, and more suitable to the spiritual and elevated estate of gospel spirits.

The efficacy of all ordinances, and of this in special, depends upon God's co-operating presence, their light, life, power, sweetness. No healing virtue in these waters, but when the angel of God's presence descends, and troubles the waters, whoever steps in after the troubling is made whole of whatsoever disease, John v. 4.

It is a popish delusion to expect anything, *ex opere operato*, from the work done, without respect to the manner of doing. It is a great provocation to expect *ex opere operantis*, from the preparation of the hearer or endeavours of the speaker without looking higher. All that we have to depend on, or expect from, is *opus co-operantis*, the concurrence of God. If an angel from heaven should preach, or a man with the tongue of men and angels, it would be ineffectual without co-operation. If Christ himself should again exercise his prophetical office on earth, and preach the gospel, it would have no better success than on the Jews, without divine concurrence. The word, though light in itself, is darkness to you, except the glorious presence of God scatter the clouds which benight the faculty, clear the medium, discover the object. The word, though spirit and life in itself, yet will be a dead letter to thee, except his Spirit and presence quicken it. It is as a body without a soul; it is his presence that informs, acts, enlivens. It is quick and powerful in itself, but it moves not the soul, conscience, will, or affections; these weapons are mighty through God. The affections are like the wheels in Ezekiel's vision, God's presence like the spirit of those living creatures: Ezek. i. 21, 'Whithersoever the spirit was to go, they went: for the spirit of the living creatures was in the wheels; when they go, these go; when they stood, these stood; when they were lifted up from the earth, these were lifted up.'

What is the reason that a truth sometimes breaks in with rays of light and evidence, which was always darkness before, though oftentimes before propounded? What is the reason some passage doth sometimes affect, move, inflame; at other times, though pressed with as much power, moves not at all? God's presence. The heart is sometimes as brass, sometimes as oil. Seek God's presence above all, avoid what hinders; mourn and lament after him. If thou goest not with us, we will not go. 'She called his name Ichabod, saying, The glory is departed,' 1 Sam. iv. 21. Cry after him, 'Oh that thou wouldst bow the heavens, and come down,' Isa. lxiv. 1.

(5.) Take heed of suppressing any good motions raised by the word. Constant hearers have experience of some convictions of sin, and resolve to leave it and mind the soul. Nourish these, take heed of smothering them. They are the blessed issues of heaven; will you stifle, murder them in the conception, make them like an untimely birth? They are buds springing from the immortal seed; will you nip them? They are sprigs planted by the hand of Christ, which would grow into a tree of life; will ye pluck them up by the roots, expose them to the frosts, break them while young and tender? They are sparks kindled by the breath of God, heavenly fire; will you quench it? They are the Spirit's breathings, strugglings, he will not always strive. They are Christ's knockings, you know not how long he will stand; will you send him away without admission? They are the Bridegroom's wooings; will you repulse him, and cause him to make no more motions? They are Christ's messengers; he sends these for trial, prepare the way before him. What became of them who stoned and killed the messengers? Mat. xxi. 35, 41–43.

Nourish these, encourage them; the children are come to the birth, get strength to bring forth, concur with the Lord. Overwhelm them not with worldly employments, choke them not with cares, quench them not with pleasures. Drown not the voice, as the Israelites the noise of the sacrificed children; nor, as Cain, run to build cities, busy yourselves in the world, stop your ears, till God's voice be heard and accomplished. Go not from this place into worldly company, &c.; retire to your closet, blow up the sparks into a flame with prayer; digest it with meditation, cast it not up till concocted.

(6.) Come with resolution to do whatever ye shall hear, to comply with the whole will of God without reserves. There must be no more respect of truths than respect of persons. You must not deal with duties as Nebuchadnezzar with his subjects, Dan. v. 19, which you will set up, and which you will pull down. This is to exalt yourselves above God. There is a concatenation of truths and duties; if you take one link out of the golden chain, you break the whole, James ii. 10. Obedience is the sweetest harmony the Lord can hear on earth, the perfection of it is a consonancy to the divine will; if every string, every act be not screwed up thereto, there can be no concert, nothing but discord, harsh and unpleasing in his ear. You must present yourselves before the Lord as Cornelius and his company: Acts x. 33, 'We are all here present before God, to hear all things that are commanded thee of God;' to hear all things commanded, and to do all things we hear. You must believe every truth revealed, avoid every sin forbidden, practise every duty commanded, without exceptions; you must not pick and choose. Every fruitful hearer has a good and honest heart, and this is a heart after God's own heart. The character of such a heart we have in David, he fulfilled πάντα τὰ θελήματα, Acts xiii. 22.

Resolve to do what the people promised the prophet: Jer. xlii. 5, 6, 'The Lord be a true and faithful witness between us, if we do not even according to all things for which the Lord thy God shall send thee to us. Whether it be good, or whether it be evil, we will obey the voice of the Lord our God;' whether it seem good or bad to us, great or little, difficult or easy, pleasing or harsh; though it cross carnal reason, lusts, interests.

Say not, Is it not a little one? the Lord will dispense, he is not so precise as the minister. There is nothing little which the great God commands. His pure eye sees atoms, the least will damn. He is jealous; he that offends in one of these little ones, better a mill-stone were tied about his neck.

Think not anything difficult: to avoid all sin and the occasions, to exercise every grace, to keep a constant watch over heart and ways. Is anything too hard for God? He is engaged: Isa. xl. 31, 'They that wait upon the Lord shall renew their strength,' &c. The more difficulty, the more honour. Abraham is ready to obey in that which was grievous. Did not Christ suffer more grievous things than you can do? Is not the penalty more intolerable? Would the damned think anything too hard?

What if it cross reason? Paul consulted not with flesh and blood. Say not as the Jews, σκληρός λόγος: 'It is a hard saying, who can bear it?' John vi. 60. 'O man, who art thou that repliest against God?' Rom.

ix. 20. Art thou wiser than he? Is not infinite understanding the rule of his will? Captivate reason, bend the understanding to his mind.

What if it ruin thy lusts, pluck out thy right eye? Is it not better, 'more profitable, that one member should perish, than that the whole body be cast into hell?' Mat. v. 29. An honest heart counts that word most pleasant which wounds his lusts: Ps. cxli. 5, 'Let the righteous smite me, it shall be a kindness; let him reprove me, it shall be an excellent oil, which shall not break my head.' He says to the word, to the minister preventing sin, as David to Abigail, 1 Sam. xxv. 32, 33, 'Blessed be the Lord God of Israel, which sent thee this day to meet me: and blessed be thy advice, and blessed be thou, who hast kept me this day from coming to shed blood.' Lay thy conscience bare; say, Speak, Lord; smite, Lord, with a deadly wound these thine enemies that would not have thee to rule.

What if it comport not with thy interests, profit, pleasure, credit? Is any interest dearer than thy soul's? Is it not better to deny thyself than that Christ should deny thee? What lost Zaccheus by restitution? Ask him now in heaven. What lost Moses by choosing afflictions rather than the pleasures of sin? What lost the apostles by exposing themselves to contempt? περικαθάρματα. They are so far from repenting, as, if they were on earth again, they would say with David, 2 Sam. vi. 22, 'I will yet be more vile than thus.' If thou make exceptions against any command, God will except thee when he dispenses eternal rewards.

It is not enough to promise God to the half of the kingdom; halting obedience will never come to heaven; all, or none. Say not, 'The Lord be merciful to me in this.' The Lord will never be merciful to any allowed disobedience: 'If any man shall take away from the words of the book of this prophecy,'—from the words expressing God's will,—'God shall take away his part out of the book of life, and out of the holy city,' &c., Rev. xxii. 19.

(7.) Mix it with faith: Heb. iv. 2, 'The word preached did not profit them, not being mixed with faith in them that heard it.' Faith is a necessary ingredient to all spiritual services. Without faith it is impossible to please God; and that which does not please him cannot profit us. Get faith, and exercise it. Believe, 1, that God speaks; 2, to you; 3, that which is true; and, 4, good. Of the first and second I spoke formerly.

Believe the truth and goodness of what you hear; true in itself, good to you. There are two acts of faith, assent, consent; that in the mind, this in the will; the object of *that*, truth, of *this*, goodness; both necessary; that ineffectual, insufficient without this. Get to be assured of the truth and goodness of the word; all truth is excellent, this transcendent, of a higher descent; *chara Dei soboles*, it is divine, derives its original from God; comprises all other truths, and adds, *de proprio*, unspeakable excellency to them. Not only logical or moral, but divine; consists in a conformity not only with the mind of men and angels, but of the mind of God; divine intellect, infinite understanding.

So is its goodness in consonancy to the divine will; it is appetible, ὀρεκτὸν, to God, so convenient and agreeable to his will, as it is called directly the will of God.

It has all degrees of goodness: καλὸν, ἡδὺ, χρήσιμον.

[1.] Holy and just, perfectly so; the rule of all holiness and justice in the world; *primum et perfectissimum in unoquoque genere, mensura reliquorum.*

[2.] Sweet: honey, manna, bread of life, water of life. It is to the soul as these would be to one dying, ready to expire for hunger or thirst.

[3.] Profitable: to make perfect, happy. Both these are applicable to assertions, commandments, promises, threatenings. The truth none but an atheist can deny. The goodness is unquestionable, if that which seems most doubtful be certain, viz., that the threatenings are good. That is clear in Hezekiah, 2 Kings xx. 19. Hezekiah said unto Isaiah, 'Good is the word of the Lord which thou hast spoken;' notwithstanding, we may take up the prophet's complaint, Isa. liii. 1, 'Who hath believed our report?' If we did believe 'the wages of sin is death,' 'Except a man be born again, he cannot see the kingdom of God,' 'Except we repent, we shall perish,' 'He that is not in Christ is a reprobate,' we should follow Jehoshaphat's advice: 2 Chron. xx. 20, 'Believe in the Lord your God, so shall ye be established; believe his prophets, so shall ye prosper.' Let it dwell in your hearts by faith.

(8.) Receive the truth in the love of it: 2 Thes. ii. 10, 'Because they received not the love of the truth,' *i. e.*, truth in love, 'that they might be saved.' He that would hear savingly, must hear it with love; not out of fear, custom, not for by-ends, for credit, profit, preferment; but out of love to the naked truth, for its own native loveliness, without extrinsecal consideration; as the truth is in Jesus, of him, from him.

If you are moved by base ends, when these are removed, the word will be rejected. But if you are moved by the intrinsecal excellency of the word; that being eternal, your actings for, and affections to, the word will be constant.

This was the cause of the inconstancy, the apostasy of the stony ground; they believed, received the word with joy while the word was in credit, while they might do it with safety, applause, and outward advantage; but when persecution arose, they fell away.

It is love that gives the word rooting. Love would have made the rock open, not content to receive it in the superficies. It unites the word to us, us to it; it is *affectus unionis*, Ps. cxix. 81; it incorporates it, it transforms us into its likeness, assimilates us to it.

Some truths challenge a special love, evangelical, spiritual, above those common to us with heathens; such as discover our happiness or misery, moral virtues; the excellency of Christ, necessity of him, way to him, privileges by him. Practical, not notional; only such as may awaken sin, nourish grace, and teach us to order our conversation. Searching; such as discover our condition, pierce conscience, unmask the soul, detect hypocrisy, and offer to our view the more refined and less visible stains of the spirit: pride, selfishness, earthliness, and other secret and little discerned evils.

OF TAKING UP THE CROSS.

Whosoever doth not bear his cross, and come after me, cannot be my disciple.
—LUKE XIV. 27.

THESE are the words of Christ. The occasion of them you may see, ver. 25. He seeing multitudes following him, takes occasion to tell them upon what terms they must follow him, if they would follow him to purpose. Lest any of them should deceive themselves, and think that a bare outward profession of Christ would be sufficient, a safe, easy, external following him would serve their turn, he tells them what he did expect from every one that would be his follower and disciple. It was not so safe and easy a thing to be a Christian as they might suppose. It would cost them more than they did imagine. He deals plainly with them, and lets them know the worst of it. If they would be his disciples, his followers, Christians indeed, they must be so upon these and these terms, which he expresses in two propositions.

1. They must leave all for him. They could not follow him, unless they were content to forsake all to follow him, ver. 26. If any man seem willing to be a disciple of mine, he must have such an affection to me as to hate all other things for my sake, otherwise I will never own him, he is but a pretender; he is not, he cannot be a Christian indeed.

But has Christ no disciples but such as these? Are none Christians but upon these terms? Alas! who then is a Christian? Who then can be saved? Can none be disciples of Christ but those that will hate their dearest relations, their best worldly enjoyments, yea, their own lives, for Christ's sake? Will he own none, will he admit none to follow him, but upon these terms? Sure this is σκλῆρος ὁ λόγος, this is a hard saying indeed, who can bear it?

Why, but thus it is, Christ will admit none to be his disciples, he will own none for Christians, upon other terms than he here expresses. Only you must not mistake. He requires not that you should hate these relations absolutely; for that would be to contradict his own law, the law of God and nature, which requires natural affection. But this is it which he requires, you must hate them,

(1.) In effect. You must as freely part with them for Christ's sake, as if you did hate them. You must be as willing to relinquish them, when he requires it, as you are to part with a thing that you hate. You will part with a hated thing freely, readily, cheerfully; even so must you part with your relations, enjoyments, and life too, not out of hatred to them, but leave them all as readily, when Christ calls, as if you did hate them. To hate them here, is freely to forsake them for Christ's sake. And so it is expressed, Mat. xix. 29. Part with them as freely for Christ, that the world may judge you do hate them, because you quit them so easily, without murmuring, repining, reluctancy.

(2.) Comparatively. You must love Christ more than all these, more than the dearest of these, and shew you do so indeed by quitting all of them, rather than forsake, or dishonour, or displease Christ. If you do not, you love these more than Christ: Mat. x. 37, 'He that loveth father or mother more than me, is not worthy of me.' And to love anything more than Christ, is to hate him. A less degree of love is called hatred in Scripture, Gen. xxix. 30, 31. Because he loved Leah less than Rachel, he is said to hate her. Even as you may be said to hate your relations, enjoyments, lives, when you love them less than Christ, so much less as you will be content to part with them for his sake, whenever he requires it. And in this sense you must be able to hate them, or else you cannot be the disciples of Christ, or else you are not Christians; for upon these terms, and no other, will he own you for such.

The second proposition, wherein he expresses upon what terms we must be disciples, is in the text, ver. 27. It is not enough to part with all, but you must be willing to suffer all; to undergo sufferings not only privative, but positive: the cross includes the former, and something more. It signifies all afflictions for Christ's sake. It denotes all sufferings, calamities, torments, even those that are most ignominious and most grievous; in allusion to those sorrows and tortures which Christ on the cross suffered for his people. Whoever does not bear these, he is not, he cannot be, a disciple; *i. e.*, he that does not actually bear the cross when it is laid upon him, or he that is not fully resolved to bear it, how heavy and grievous soever it may be, whenever it shall be laid upon him, he is not, he cannot be, a disciple of Christ.

A disciple, what is that? Why, he cannot be a Christian. A disciple and a Christian are all one, Acts xi. 26. A disciple of Christ is one that gives up himself to be wholly at Christ's disposing; to learn what he teacheth, to believe what he reveals, to do what he commands, to avoid what he forbids, to suffer what is inflicted by or for him, in expectation of that reward which he hath promised. Such a one is a disciple of Christ, and he, and none else, is a Christian. Such as these, who give up themselves to be taught and governed by Christ in all things, were at first called disciples, and afterwards at Antioch they were called Christians; they are two names of the same persons. Many descriptions you have of them in Scripture, and here you have them described by one of their essential properties. *Christiani sunt cruciani*, says Luther, Christians are cross-bearers. So they are always, though they be not always in a suffering condition; they ever bear the cross, either *quoad actum* or *quoad propositum*. It is in their hearts to bear the cross, whatever it be, whensoever Christ shall require it; and they do actually bear it whenever they are called to it. They do not flinch from it, nor decline it, nor turn from it, by any indirect or unlawful course. They had rather lose all they have in the world, and suffer all that an enraged world can inflict on them, than deny any truth of Christ, or decline any way of Christ, or commit any sin against Christ. This is their temper, their practice, who are Christians.

And those who are otherwise disposed, let them call themselves what they will, they are not Christians. Nor can they be Christians upon any other terms. They have not given up themselves to him, they have no interest in him, they can have no benefit by him, they shall have no reward from him.

So that you see the words contain the terms upon which you must be Christians, if you will be Christians indeed, and not in name, and show, and profession only. They afford us this

Obs. He that doth not, will not bear the cross, he is not, he cannot be, a Christian. He that is not ready to suffer for Christ, he is none of Christ's disciple. You cannot be Christians upon lower, upon easier terms, than bearing the cross, and undergoing sufferings for him. So Christ himself tells us over and over: Mat. x. 38, 'He that taketh not his cross and followeth after me, is not worthy of me.' 'Not worthy of me,' *i. e.*, he is not for my turn. If he pretend to be one of mine, he does but disparage me, he deals unworthily with me. It was never my intention, nor is it for my honour, to own any who are not content to undergo the sorest and heaviest afflictions and calamities for my sake. He speaks again, Mat. xvi. 24, 'If any man will come after me, let him deny himself, and take up his cross and follow me.' Let no man offer to follow me unless he be resolved to follow me in this posture, unless he will follow me under the cross. A third evangelist tells us the same thing: Mark viii. 34, 'Whosoever will come after me, let him deny himself, and take up his cross, and follow me.' And once more we have it, Luke ix. 23. To follow Christ, and to be a disciple of Christ, is all one; for scholars or disciples do not go before, but follow their masters. And to be a Christian is all one as to be a follower of Christ. As the scholars or disciples of Plato, Aristotle, Galen, Paracelsus, are called their followers, so the disciples of Christ, or Christians, are the followers of Christ, those that follow his doctrine, and are as ready to follow him in his sufferings. And those that will be Christians indeed must thus follow him daily, take up the cross daily, always, continually, every day. But how can this be? (Let this be noted, lest any of you should think this truth unseasonable at this time.) How can the cross be taken up daily, since every day does not trouble us with the cross? The people of God have some *lucida intervalla*, some times of joy and peace. The rod of the wicked doth not always lie upon them. Though a great part of their voyage through the world be stormy and tempestuous, yet now and then they may have calm, and serene, and halcyonian times. This is true, and yet the cross must be taken up daily. It must be taken up actually every day when providence brings it to us. And those days of peace and security, when it is not brought to us, we cannot take it up actually indeed; but even every of those days must the cross be taken up in the preparation and disposition of the mind; it must be in your hearts to bear the cross every day, even when it is not actually laid upon you. So that this concerns you every day while you are in this world, if you be concerned every day to shew yourselves Christians.

Let me a little more particularly explain to you what is meant by the cross, and what by bearing of it.

1. The cross includes loss and damage, the greatest losses as well as the least; the loss of all outward things, as well as the loss of any. When Christ was nailed to the cross, he was bereaved of all, and fastened to it naked; he had not so much as his garments left; they who brought him to the cross divided these amongst them. He that is not willing to part

with all, to follow Christ, when he cannot fully and faithfully follow him without quitting all, he is not worthy of him, unworthy the name of a Christian.

He that is not content, when he is called to it, to be separated from nearest friends and dearest relations, to part with his country and habitation, to be stripped of his estate and outward accommodations, to be deprived of his liberty, and what else is dear to him in this world, he is not for Christ's turn, he cares for no such followers. The foregoing verse leads us to this particular: ver. 26, 'If any man come to me, and hate not his father, and mother, and wife, and children, and brethren, and sisters, yea, and his own life also, he cannot be my disciple.' He that is not content to follow Christ, so as to leave all these behind him, he does not follow him as a disciple, as a Christian; for he that is a Christian indeed, he loves Christ above all, but he that will not part with relations, estate, country, liberty, for Christ's sake, he loves them better than he loves Christ; for that a man loves most which he will least part with. He that will not part with them all rather than sin against Christ, has not the love of a disciple for Christ, and so is not indeed a Christian.

2. It speaks shame and reproach. It was *servile supplicium*, a base, ignominious suffering, to which none were exposed but the vilest of men. It was a suffering proper to slaves and fugitives; there was not the meanest freeman amongst the Romans but was above it. Hence shame and the cross are joined together, Heb. xii. 2. Hence that expression, Heb. xiii. 13, 'bearing his reproach,' *i. e.*, bearing the cross. No coming to Christ but in this posture, when the Lord calls to it. He that is not content to bear the scorn and contempt of an insolent world; he that cannot be content to be jeered and derided, to be vilified and set at nought even by vile persons, to be abused and reviled, even for doing good to those that so abuse him, to be made the scorn of men, and reproach of the people, as Christ was, to be counted as the filth and off-scouring of all things, *περιψήματα* and *περικαθάρματα*, as the apostles were; he that cannot, will not digest this when he meets with it in the world for Christ's sake, he is not fit to be a disciple of Christ; for we cannot be his disciples upon other terms.

3. It imports pain and torture. The cross was a most grievous and painful suffering. Ausonius calls it *pœnæ extremum*, the extremity of torture. And Cicero, *crudelissimum teterrimumque supplicium*, the most cruel and horrid suffering. If you be not content to bear the hatred and cruelty of an enraged world, to endure any pains and tortures, the most exquisite torments that the malice of man can invent, or their cruelty execute, rather than deny Christ or his truth, rather than leave his ways and worship, never think of being Christians, never take on you the name of his followers, you cannot be his disciples upon other or easier terms. When Ignatius was going to be exposed to the fury of wild beasts for the name of Christ, he cries, *νῦν ἄρχομαι μαθητὴς εἶναι*, Now I begin to be a disciple.

4. It imports death itself. The cross was *ultimum supplicium*, the last thing that could be suffered. Cruelty was herein terminated, and could go no further, at least to the sense of the sufferer. It was the worst kind of death. *Illa morte nihil pejus inter omnium mortium genera.* Of all kinds of death there was none worse than this: Phil. ii. 8, 'That humbled himself to the death of the cross.' To no less than death, and the worst kind of death. If you be not willing to die for Christ, and to die the worst kind of death, to drink up this cup, and to be baptized with this baptism when his cause, and honour, and interest requires it; to drink up the cup of

death, and to be baptized in your own blood, rather than be disobedient or unfaithful to him; if your hearts cannot say as the apostle, 'Neither count I my life dear, that I may win Christ.' Acts xx. 24; I am not only ready to be bound, but, Acts xxiv. 13, to die, whenever and wherever he shall require it; not only ready to sacrifice my name and reputation, but my person for Christ; not only ready to suffer some pain and torment, but to suffer death, rather than the honour, and truths, and worship of Christ should suffer by me; not only ready to part with relations, liberty, country, enjoyments, but to part with my life whenever he calls for it;—if this be not the resolution of your hearts, you are not his disciples; for this he requires of all, ver. 26, 'He that does not hate his life,' *i. e.*, is not as free to part with it for Christ as if he hated it, he loves his life more than Christ; and he will never count them Christians, whatever they may count themselves, who love anything, though it be life itself, more than him, or equally with him.

Thus you see what the cross is. Let us inquire what it is to bear it. Bearing the cross supposes or includes these four things:

1. You must make account of it. If you will follow Christ indeed, make account you will meet with the cross. This Christ presseth and illustrates by two similitudes in the verses following the text, from 28 to 34. To taking upon you the profession of Christ, without casting up what it is like to cost, that which is like to prove both shameful and dangerous in the issue. If you make account of better fare in following Christ than you are like to meet with, you will go near to repent your bargain, to tack about to save yourselves, and so come off with shame and ruin in the issue; and make it appear that whatever you did profess, you were never Christians in reality.

Sit down, then, and cast up what it is like to cost you. If you will give up yourselves to Christ entirely, to follow him in all his ways seriously, and closely, and faithfully, you are like to meet with all the hatred, and opposition, and hard usage that he expected from the implacable enmity of hell and the world. I must look to meet with many a bitter taunt and jeer. I am like to be hated, scorned, reviled, and reproached, and trampled on in the world. I may have trial of cruel mockings and scourgings, yea, moreover, of bonds and imprisonment. It may cost me the loss of all that is dear to me in the world, relations, liberty, country, estate, yea, life and all. You must make account of this beforehand, if you mean to be Christians indeed. And then see what your hearts say to it. Can you endure this, or can you not? If not, your profession of Christ is vain. If you promise yourselves ease, safety, respect, plenty, and a quiet enjoyment of what is grateful to the flesh, and think the cross will not come near you, or at least fall so heavy on you, but you may be able by one shift or other to avoid it well enough; if this be your temper, though you may make fair shows, you are never like to hold out, and so had better never pretend to be Christians. He is far from following Christ under the cross, who does not so much as make account of it.

2. A resolution to bear the cross, whatever it be, how heavy, or grievous, or tedious soever it may prove; a firm, and hearty, and settled resolution to bear it, is a virtual bearing of it beforehand, ver. 33. Whosoever he be that is not resolved to part with all that is dear to him, to undergo all that is grievous to him, rather than flinch from Christ his cause, truth, worship, interest, whatever he seem to be, he is no disciple indeed; he is far from bearing the cross as becomes a follower of Christ, who is not yet come to

a point so as so resolve to bear it without dispute, doubting, or hesitation, whatever come of it.

When the account is cast up, this and this it will cost thee, this and this thou must part with, these and these things thou must suffer, if thou wilt be Christ's disciple; and then the question is put, Wilt thou give up thyself to him on these terms? Wilt thou take him for better and worse? Wilt thou follow him through good report and evil report? Wilt thou make after him, though stripped, and wounded, and overwhelmed with shame and reproach? Wilt thou follow him through fire and water, yea, through the valley of the shadow of death? Wilt thou follow him alone, though all forsake thee, though no friends or relations may accompany thee? When the question is put, he that is a Christian indeed will resolve on it fully and freely. *In re tam necessaria non est deliberandum.* I need not take time to think upon this; I am at a point; I will follow Christ whatever befall me, though my way lie through poverty, and banishment, and prisons, and solitude, and pains, and tortures, and scorn, and contempt, or death itself. I will never leave him, I will never turn aside from him, let Satan and the world do their worst. He resolves to follow him as Ruth did Naomi, when her mother-in-law tried to divert her by so many arguments, and such as prevailed with her sister to turn back, Ruth i. 16–18. She was stedfastly minded to cleave to her in her poor, forlorn, desolate condition. Such a resolution is, by interpretation, a bearing the cross before it come. So Abraham is said to offer up his son Isaac, though he was not actually sacrificed, Heb. xi, 17, because he did fully purpose and resolve to do it; it was in his heart to do it. Though he was not sacrificed upon the altar, yet he was already offered up in his heart. To be fully, heartily resolved to bear it, is a kind of bearing it before it comes. And in this sense there may be many martyrs who never suffered death for Christ. If they be so resolved to die for Christ as nothing hinders but want of opportunity, they are martyrs in heart, though not in act; the Lord accepts the will for the deed in such cases. When the mind is so resolved on it as nothing hinders the deed but want of a call or an occasion, the Lord looks on it as if it were done. A disciple thus resolved to bear the cross, will be accepted as one that bears it, though it be not actually laid on him. But he that is not come up to this full and sincere resolution to part with all, to suffer all for Christ, he is not so much as a Christian intentionally; he is not, he does not intend to be, a disciple of Christ, whatever he may pretend to.

8. You must be always ready for the cross, always preparing for it, whether it seem near, or whether it seem further off. One paraphraseth the words thus, 'Whosoever doth not come to me with a preparation of mind to suffer anything rather than part with me, he is not for my turn.'

This is to bear the cross daily, as Christ requires, Luke ix. Though every day do not afford a cross, yet every day we bear the cross by daily preparing for it, 1 Cor. xv. 31. I protest by that which I take most joy in of anything in the world, viz., my fidelity to Christ; which appeared not only in that he every day ran the hazard of death for Christ, but in that he was every day ready to die, 2 Tim. iv. 6. *ἐγὼ γὰρ ἤδη σπένδομαι*, I am now offered up. He speaks of it as done, not only because it was near, but because he had made himself ready to be sacrificed for Christ whenever he should call him to it. Gen. xxii. 9, 10, Abraham was prepared, had made all things ready to sacrifice his son, and therefore, though he was hindered from doing of it, yet the Lord accepted of it, and spoke of it as done, ver. 16; James ii. 21.

Even when the cross seems far off, much more when it is in view, you must be preparing for it, if you be Christians indeed; and the Lord will take your readiness to bear it for a bearing of it, when he sees good to prevent it. A man that is ingenuous, if his friend have made all things ready to entertain him, though he come not, will take it as kindly as if he had partaken of the entertainment. Christ will resent your faithfulness to him, as if you were always bearing the cross for his sake, if you be always preparing for it. If you be still loosening your hearts more and more from the world, your relations and enjoyments; if you be still dragging the flesh, with its affections and lusts, unto the cross; still fortifying your souls against a day of trial; still crucifying the world, and crossing your carnal and worldly inclinations; it may be the cross you expect will not be laid upon you, but whether it be or no, you shall not lose the reward of those who are faithful in bearing it, because you are as ready to do it as those that are actually under it. Christ looks on you as taking up the cross, because you are so ready to take it up; whereas those who mind it not, prepare not for it, put the thoughts of it far from them, they are so far from bearing the cross before it come, as they are never like to touch it (though it may be heavy on them) as becomes the followers of Christ. They are like to deal unworthily with him.

4. It speaks actual undergoing it when it is laid on us. The followers of Christ, whether the cross be far off, or whether it be near, they must make account of it, resolve on it, prepare for it. There is no bearing the cross without these; these are included, and are, as it were, some offers at it at a distance. But when the Lord brings it to us, we must actually take it up. He is no disciple for Christ that will not do it. He whose heart is so linked, glued to his relations and outward enjoyments, that he cannot tell how to part with them; who must have the flesh pleased and gratified in its inclinations and desires; who must have the ease, and plenty, and respect, and favour of the world; he is not of a temper fit for a Christian, he is not for Christ's turn. He will not own him for a disciple who will not endure the cross, whatever it be, when he is called to it. But when are we called to take up the cross? Why, when it cannot be avoided without sin, then are you clearly called to it. When you cannot shun the cross without dishonouring Christ, deserting his cause, or betraying his interest, or denying his truth, or declining his way, or transgressing his will one way or other, then are you called to shew yourselves disciples by taking up the cross. When this *dilemma* is before you, either you must suffer, or sin; if, then, you decline suffering, whatever it be, you are unworthy the name of Christians.

And so I have explained the object, and shewed what is meant by the cross; and the act, as to the substance of it, what is meant by bearing. Let me inquire a little into the manner: how does he who is a Christian bear the cross? He endeavours to bear it,

1. *Patiently*. That while the cross oppresses his outward man, he may possess his soul in patience. Not the patience of the Stoics, a senseless stupidness; nor the patience of the heathen, a mere yielding to necessity; but a due sense of the pressure, with a quiet submission to the hand of God, whoever be the instrument, without murmuring, repining, disquietment, or despondency. 'Good is the word of the Lord,' though that word bring a real cross. So the judgment submits, takes it kindly that it is no worse, Isa. xxxix. 9, accepting the punishment of their iniquity. So the will submits, as knowing it may be from sin, though it be for Christ too.

And the inward man being thus possessed does influence the outward, Lev. x. 3, Ps. xxxix. 9. This is to bear the cross, so as to come after Christ, to tread in his steps, to imitate him 'who was led as a lamb to the slaughter,' &c., 1 Peter ii. 21, 23.

He that follows Christ in bearing the cross will 'let patience have its perfect work,' James i. 4. The perfect work of patience is its most eminent act, *i. e.*, a submissive but resolute perseverance, holding out, and bearing up, notwithstanding the sharpness, the tediousness, the variety of crosses and calamities. 'That you may be perfect and entire, wanting nothing;' *i. e.*, defective in no part, in no grace, which is requisite to a soul that is entirely Christian. It is a perfection of parts here spoken of. When a Christian has all the graces of the Spirit in exercise, he has all the parts of a Christian; and having all his parts, he is entire, and so is wanting in nothing necessary to his Christian constitution. But if patience be wanting, he wants a necessary, an essential part, and so is not entire and complete. And therefore as you have other graces, so be sure you get also the grace of patience. This is essential to a disciple of Christ. If this be not exercised under the cross, you bear it not as Christians, you do not come after Christ in bearing it. Patience is the noblest piece of valour; that which those who have been most cried up for their valour in the world have not attained to; they were indeed daring rather than valiant. True valour appears more in bearing pressures and sufferings without disturbance, than in attempting dangers or encountering difficulties. The world places valour in a resolute attempting of dangers, the Scripture places valour in patient enduring of sufferings. 2 Tim. ii. 13, κακοπάθησον. Endure patiently the cross, so shalt thou shew thyself an excellent soldier: ὡς καλὸς στρατιώτης. He is a good soldier that will follow his leader close, whatever come of it. So doth he follow Christ who runs after him with patience, Heb. xii. 1, 2. He that endures the cross with patience, runs after Christ, follows him closely.

2. He endeavours to bears it *cheerfully*. That which is bearing the cross here is taking up the cross, chap. ix. Now, to take up the cross, imports not only a patient bearing of it when it is laid upon us, but also a ready and voluntary undergoing it. Christ bore his cross willingly; Simon of Cyrene was compelled to bear that cross. Christ would have us come after him, imitate him, bear it as he did. It should not be a forced, but a voluntary act. Not that we are to pull crosses upon ourselves, as some of the primitive martyrs did—whom yet we should not censure, because we know not by what spirit they were acted—but we should cheerfully undergo it, when the Lord imposeth it. When the honour and interest of Christ requires it, we should take up the cross as we would take up a crown. We should receive it as a gift: 'To you it is given.' We should meet it with joy, look on it as our glory, Gal. That cross may denote not only the sufferings which Christ endured for him, but also those sufferings which he endured for Christ; for in these he gloried, Rom. v. 3, 2 Cor. vii. 4, ὑπερπερισσεύομαι. He was more than full, he did more than overflow with joy; it did run over into glorying in all his tribulations. We may glory in them as in a triumph, the greatest occasion of joy and glorying in this world, Rom. viii. 37. We may glory in them as our happiness, a greater happiness than all the victories and triumphs in the world can afford us, being the beginnings and pledges of an eternal triumph in heaven, Mat. v. When those who suffer for Christ sink into sorrow, dejection, despondency under the cross, they deal unworthily

with Christ, they shew themselves no way worthy to bear his name, Mat. x. 38.

3. He endeavours to bear it *fruitfully*. The cross is dry wood, and so was Aaron's rod; but as that blossomed, so does this bring forth fruit, when improved, Heb. xii. 11. It is no miracle for honey to be found in the carcase of this lion; the goodness of God has made it ordinary, the promise of God gives assurance of it; and this puts the followers of Christ upon seeking the sweet fruits of peace and holiness in the bowels of devouring calamities: to get spiritual gain and advantage by outward loss; to grow richer unto God by worldly impoverishment; to converse more with God when separated from friends and relations; to value more the love of Christ when they smart by the world's hatred; to partake more of holiness when he partakes less of the ease, peace, plenty of the world; to make use of the cross for the crucifying of the flesh; to make sin more hateful and dreadful, the conscience more tender, the world less tempting, more contemptible, grace more active and lively, the word more sweet and effectual, prayer more fervent and affectionate, the appearing of Christ more lovely and desirable, the conversation more heavenly. To bear the cross as a disciple of Christ, is to bring forth more fruit in bearing of it.

So much for explication; we shall confirm this truth by these three propositions:

I. The cross is the ordinary lot of Christians.

II. A Christian cannot ordinarily avoid the cross without sinning against Christ.

III. He that will ordinarily sin against Christ to avoid the cross, cannot be a Christian. This being proved, it will appear an evident truth, that he that doth not, will not, bear the cross, is not, cannot be a Christian.

I. For the first, the cross is ordinarily the lot of Christians. The cross is so inseparable from a Christian, as he seems to be nailed to it, Ps. xxxiv. 19, John xvi. 33, Acts xiv. 22, Mat. x. 34. So it was under the Old Testament. The prophets and people of God had not troubles and persecutions only from the heathen—the Egyptians, the Philistines, the Assyrians, the Babylonians—but from those who professed themselves to be of the church, Mat. xxiii. 31, 34, Acts vii. 51, 52. And so it hath been under the New Testament, not only in the time of Christ and the apostles and primitive Christians, but in all ages. Search the records of all times, and you shall find that persecution and troubles have always attended the people of God. And so it will be while there is rage and malice in Satan, and enmity in the world, and necessity even from the sufferers that it should be so.

The first three hundred years after Christ, to go no higher, are divided into ten persecutions. It was no less than death to bear the name of a Christian. And though there were some *lucida intervalla*, some breathing times, yet were they usually short, always uncertain; they had rather some truce than any firm peace, and the longer respite they had, the more grievous was the cross when it came. Witness the last of those ten persecutions, which succeeded an intermission of about forty years; but was so cruel when it came, that lasting ten years, there was in thirty days no less than seventeen thousand put to death for the name of Christ. So for the three first ages, the Christians were seldom from under the cross.

The fourth century is accounted more peaceable and favourable to the Christian name, Constantine the emperor being a Christian. Yet were not the people of Christ free from the cross all his time, much less in the time of his successors. In the beginning of his reign they suffered grievous things from Maxentius, Maximinus, and Licinius, who of a professor turned a persecutor, alleging the Christians prayed for Constantine and not for him. And in the latter end of his reign, great troubles were raised by the Arians; so that Eustathius, Athanasius, and others suffered persecution even to banishment in the time of Constantine.

After his decease, his son Constantius, seduced by the Arians, persecutes the orthodox Christians; and therein survived his brethren, who were of a better temper.

After him the apostate Julian shewed all the enmity to the Christian name that his subtilty could devise, and sought to root it out by fraud, which he saw had been in vain attempted by force.

After him, Valens opposes them as much in the east as Valentinian favoured them in the west. And so far did violence prevail in that and the other Arian persecutions, that the sincere professors of Christ were driven from the public meetings into dens, and caves, and solitudes. *Nam si alicubi sunt pii, &c.* If there be any that are godly, says Athanasius, and affectionate to Christ, they are hid with Elias the prophet; they secure themselves in dens and caves, *in cavernas et speluncas terræ se abscondunt;* or they continued wandering about in exile and solitude, *aut in solitudine oberrantes commorantur.* So Hilary complains, and Augustine after him: *qui erant firmiores reliquis,* those that were stedfast and faithful; *illi partim pro fide fortiter exulabant, partim toto orbe latitabant;* they were either banished or hid themselves, and that was their condition through the whole world. So heavy did the cross lie upon the people of Christ, in the fourth age, which seemed to promise the greatest freedom from it. It is almost incredible, which the ancients affirm of those times, that there were scarce five pastors left in the whole world that were true Christians, truly Christian; and those in banishment too, and the church laid thus desolate by those who professed themselves to be of the church.

In the fifth and sixth ages the Goths, and other barbarous nations in the west, the Vandals in the south, the Persians in the east, made havoc of the church.

And in the seventh, Mahomet riseth in the east, and Antichrist appears in the west, under which character Gregory, a pope himself, describes Antichrist; and these have made it their business in the following ages, that the faithful followers of Christ should be always under the cross.

Thus it has been, and thus it will be. And the reasons of it are evident.

[1. The malice of Satan, who knowing himself to be cast off by God, he hates God with an implacable hatred; and since the Lord is above the reach of his malice, he falls upon those who are dearest to him, the people of God. Christ having excluded those apostate spirits from any benefit of his redemption, they are filled with rage against him, but being not able to reach the head, they let out their rage upon his members: Gen. iii. 15, 'I will put enmity between thee and the woman, and between thy seed and her seed: it shall bruise thy head, and thou shalt bruise his heel.' His commission, or rather permission, is no larger, and he will not fail to go as far as he can; he will be always bruising the heel, since the head is above him. It is his business to multiply crosses, and to make them as heavy and piercing as may be. All his fury, for which he is called a lion, and all his subtilty, for which he is called a serpent, will be employed to this purpose, 1 Peter v. 8. He is watchful upon all occasions to let out his wrath upon the woman, Rev. xii. 4. He would have stifled Christianity in the birth, but being then prevented, he makes another attempt, ver. 13. And when this succeeds not, he will cross her another way, ver. 15. He pours whole floods of calamities upon her. And when these do not the execution he desires, yet he desists not, his wrath still boils up, ver. 17.

2. The enmity of the world. The world will be sure to cross, to afflict and persecute what it hates; and the disciples of Christ are hated by the world, John xv. 19. Not only that part of the world, which evidently lies in wickedness, but the more refined part of it, which dresseth up itself in a form of godliness. Those who have no more but the form, hate those that have the power, because this is a real reproof and conviction of the vanity and insufficiency of outward forms, how specious soever; and that which detects them is hated by them, 1 John v. 19. Open wickedness makes open war with the people of Christ, but the form of godliness will not persecute the power of it openly, but under some disguise or other, which may afford some plausible excuse for its hatred and violence. But enmity there is in all the seed of the serpent, Gen. iii. 15. And this enmity will find vent one way or other; sometimes openly, so as the devil may be plainly seen in it; sometimes covertly and subtilly, so as Satan conceals himself, as he did in the form of a serpent, and acts in the shape and form of innocent creatures. But however it act, the tendency of it is to keep the people of Christ always under the cross.

3. There is a necessity of the cross upon a manifold account.

(1.) To distinguish true disciples from hypocrites and pretenders. When Christ may be professed and followed with ease, and safety, and credit, multitudes will follow him, even many will profess him, whose hearts are not with him. But when the cross comes, that makes a distinction. When it comes to this, if you will stick to the truth of Christ, if you will worship him according to his own rule, if you will be true to your engagements, the cross will be upon you; you are sure to suffer for it; you cannot escape hatred, reproach, poverty, imprisonment, exile, or death itself. Will you be at such cost and hazard for a small truth, a rite, a circumstance, a disputable point? No; this is counted folly with those who are wiser for the world than for their soul. Here the formal professor, how forward soever he was before, plucks in his horns. Now will it appear who are really for Christ, and who are but pretenders, Mat. xiii. 20, 21. Before the storm, the chaff and the corn lie together in one heap, but when the wind riseth it blows away *paleas levis fidei*, the chaff, and makes the heap less in the garner.

The cross is expressed by a fiery trial. Now it is the property of fire and heat, *segregare heterogenea*, to separate those things which, though they be of differing natures, yet are congealed together in one heap; but when the heat comes, that dissolves and separates them. This is the property of the cross. It separates false-hearted professors from faithful Christians, and makes it appear they are of different natures and tempers, though before the trial they lay together in one lump. As the apostle says of heresies, 1 Cor. xi. 19, 'There must be heresies, that they which are approved may be made manifest.'

(2.) To try his disciples, that he may have an experiment of their affection and faithfulness to him: 'Who is on my side? Who?' says Jehu, 2 Kings ix. 33. So says Christ, when he brings out the cross; let me now see who is for me, let me see who it is that will bear the cross for me. The sharper, the heavier, the more grievous it is, the more love will he shew that takes it up cheerfully for my name's sake; the more faithfulness will he shew that will continue under it, that will not use shifts, and excuses, and distinctions, and pretences, to keep it off, or throw it off, when the interest of my truth, and worship, and honour requires him to bear it. You profess you love Christ above all, that you love him more than father, and mother, and wife, houses, ease, plenty, life; well, but how shall it be known that you have such an affection for him indeed? Why, hereby shall it be known that you love him more than all, if you will part with any of these, with all of these, for his sake. That is the clearest way to decide the question, and to give Christ, and the world, and your own consciences a convincing evidence, that you have such a transcendent affection for Christ. 'Lovest thou me more than these?' says Christ to Peter. So he asks you in the day of trial, Lovest thou me more than these? Every one will be ready to answer, Yes, God forbid but I should love Christ more than all the world. Oh but the heart is deceitful, how shall this be discovered? Why, Christ has a trial for you; when the cross comes, he brings you to the test. You have often said you love me so and so, let me now see it; I shall now perceive what is in your hearts. If you love me more than relations, come follow me into exile or solitude, and leave them all behind you. If you love me more than riches, be content with want and poverty for my sake. This and this you must do, or else you are like to be ruined and undone in the world, and this you cannot do without offending me. Now shall I see whether you love me better than your estates. If you love me more than liberty, you will freely go to prison for me; if you love me more than life, you will freely die for me, when you cannot have liberty or life but upon such terms as will dishonour me. Hereby it will be known whether you love Christ indeed, or whether you do but talk of it. The cross is to try your sincerity, faithfulness, affection, it is needful upon this account, Dan. xi. 35, Rev. ii. 10. That is true love indeed, which all the waters will not quench.

(8.) For the advantage of grace. A Christian is not complete unless he have on his whole armour; and it is the cross puts us upon putting of it on; it would lie rusting by us, if we were not roused to the use of it by the frequent approaches of the cross. We should be at a loss as to suffering graces, and a great part of the whole armour is wanting, we are far from being complete and entire when these graces are to seek. Samson roused up himself when he heard that the Philistines were upon him. The soul would grow drowsy, and grace would lose it strength for want of use, were we not awakened by the cross. Grace gets or loses as it is more or less exercised. 'To him that hath shall be given,' &c. We have no more grace, in effect, than what we use, and the more we use the more we shall have. He that is much in the exercise of what he hath, be it little or much at first, he shall have abundance in a little time. Nothing more strengthens and increases holiness than the frequent exercise of it, and the cross calls it forth into exercise in all the means of grace. What a difference is there betwixt the prayers of one at ease, and the prayers of one under the cross? Isa. xxvi. 16. The soul is melted and runs forth in every such prayer. And the word makes a far greater impression upon a soul under trouble, it has more sweetness, and power, and efficacy.

It is not out of love to our souls that we are so much in love with outward prosperity; it is hard and rare for the soul to prosper in such a condition. It does so much befriend our corruption, and yields it such advantages, that grace would be borne down and overpowered thereby, did not the Lord prevent it by frequent mixtures of the cross. The heart would be overgrown with weeds were it not often ploughed up by sufferings. And hence is it that men are suffered to make long furrows upon the backs of his people. Those crosses which seem to threaten our ruin do often prevent our ruin; so that one may say of the cross, as Themistocles in his banishment, *Periissem nisi periissem*, I had been undone unless they had undone me. It had fared ill with my soul if I had fared better in the world.

(4.) To take us off from the world. The cross embitters the world to us, and confutes those vain conceits which make us fond of it. The visard falls off by which it had deluded us, and now we may perceive what an impostor it was, when, for all its fair promises, we meet with nothing but vanity, and enmity, and vexation, and hard usage. And will it not seem lovely? Or can we doat on it any longer? The cross lets us not only see, but feel what the world is. When we find that while we are in it our souls are amongst lions, and we dwell with briars and thorns, which tear away what we have from us, and pierce us besides, how can we be in love with it any longer? Those, Heb. xi. 37, 38, 'who wandered in deserts, and in mountains, and in dens and caves of the earth; who wandered in sheep-skins, and goat-skins, being destitute, afflicted, tormented;' I warrant they were as willing to be rid of the world as the world was to be rid of them. The cross is the best instrument to crucify the world, Gal. vi. 14. The crosses that we meet with from the world may be made use of for the crucifying of the world itself. It would go near to ruin us if the cross did not help us against it. If we were not emptied from vessel to vessel, our hearts would settle here upon the lees.

(5.) To tame the flesh, and keep it under, which otherwise would grow headstrong, and bear down all the restraints of grace, and hurry us into carnal excess: John xv., 'Every branch that beareth fruit he purgeth it.' He lops off the luxuriances of natural corruption. And how is this done? Why, a sharp cross will be effectual to do it, when the Lord takes it into his hand and useth it for this purpose! Isa. xxvii. 9, Nothing will better hinder corruption from taking its course than a hedge of thorns, Hos. ii. 6. A condition of ease, and peace, and plenty in the world cherishes our lusts; it thrives best when we thrive most in the world. There would be no dealing with it were it not curbed, and taken down by the cross; it then pines away and languishes when it is fastened with us to the cross.

(6.) To endear heaven to us. The ark was more acceptable to Noah's dove, when she found no rest to the soles of her feet on the face of the earth. The thoughts of the promised kingdom were sweeter to David when he was hunted as a partridge upon the mountains. Canaan was more acceptable to the children of Israel when their burdens, oppressions, and sufferings increased in Egypt. There remains a rest for the people of God: with what joy will they think of that, when they find no rest here below! How sweet will the thoughts of that eternal rest be to those who are still labouring under the cross; how sweet will it be to think of a day of redemption for those who are still oppressed with the hatred and malice and insolence of the world, Rom. viii. 23. How sweet will those days of refreshment from the presence of the Lord be to them who are vexed, and troubled, and harassed here below! how sweet the thoughts of approaching glory to those who are here reviled, and abused, and covered with shame and reproach! how sweet the thoughts of an eternal triumph to those who are still conflicting under the cross! 2 Tim. iv. 7, 8. A sharp sight of afflictions is an effectual means to make us in love with the appearing of Christ; whereas when all things succeed with us in the world as we desire, heaven is neglected, the thoughts of it are not so sweet, our desires after it are more faint and cold, we are apt to forget that we are pilgrims and strangers here below.

II. Proposition. The cross cannot ordinarily be avoided without sinning against Christ: 2 Tim. iii. 12, 'All that will live godly in Christ Jesus shall suffer persecution.' He must suffer, even when the times are peaceable, as well as when they are troublesome. He will suffer persecution, either of the hand, or of the tongue, or of the heart; he will be hated if he be not reproached; he will be reproached if he be not smitten; he will be smitten if he be not slain. He is sure of it if he will live godly. Indeed, if he will comply, or dissemble, or swim with the stream, or soothe men in their sinful humours, or stretch his confidence to serve his worldly interests, he may shift it off; but if he will live godly in Christ Jesus, if live like a Christian, he shall suffer persecution.

III. Proposition. Those that will sin ordinarily, to avoid the cross, they are no Christians. I say not he that does at any time sin, for we see Peter did it, but it was against his resolution, and upon surprisal; and he recovered himself by a quick and deep repentance, and we hear no more of any such fall afterwards. But the case is otherwise with those who sin ordinarily to avoid sufferings; ordinarily, *i.e.* as often as temptation comes, whether it come frequently or seldom. Those that will sin, to avoid danger, as often as their relations, estates, or lives are in danger, they are no Christians; for to sin ordinarily is to commit sin. And he that commits sin is the servant of sin, not the servant of Christ, John viii. 34.

Those that will sin, rather than suffer, Christ renounceth them here, and he will do it solemnly hereafter. Though they may possess, and pretend to the name of Christ, he will have nothing to do with them; he will express himself ashamed of them, Mark viii. 8, Luke ix. 26, whether they be the words of faith or obedience. He that, to avoid shame or reproach from a wicked generation, forbears to give his testimony to any truth of Christ, or forbears to yield obedience to any command of Christ, Christ will be ashamed to own such a man for a Christian, he will renounce him as one that has no part in him, Math. x. 33; 2 Tim. ii. 12.

Christ is denied either when faith or obedience is denied. Faith is denied either expressly or tacitly: expressly when any truth of Christ is disclaimed, to avoid sufferings, when the party knows it to be a truth, and is called to bear witness to it; tacitly, when the truth is betrayed by our silence. So he denies Christ, says Fulgentius, *qui silendo non adstruit veritatem*, who, by holding his peace, does not assert the truth when his testimony is required. Christ is denied too when obedience is denied him: Tit. i. 16, they 'profess to know God, but in works they deny him, being abominable and disobedient.' He that will disobey Christ ordinarily, rather than venture suffering for obeying him, he is no Christian; Christ will disown him. He looks upon such not as Christians, but as enemies, Phil. iii. 18. Many there are who bear the name of Christ and yet are of a most unchristian temper; such as will not suffer anything for Christ, will not stand by any truth or practice that may bring sufferings on them, but will comply with Jews or Gentiles to avoid persecution. The Christians in the apostles' times were in danger of suffering, both from the Jews and from the Gentiles. Now, some that professed themselves to be Christians, but, indeed, preferred the accommodations of this life, ease, safety, credit, plenty, before Christ, rather than they would be exposed to sufferings, they did comply with both.

They complied with the Gentiles, to escape persecution from them, by sitting with them at their feasts in their temples, and there eating things sacrificed unto idols; pleading, this was a thing indifferent, ἀδιαφορεῖν εἰδωλοθύτων, as Eusebius tells us the Gnostics did.

They complied with the Jews, to avoid persecution from them, by being circumcised themselves, and urging others to be circumcised, Gal. vi. 12. And yet they made a fair show of a profession; but they would comply rather than suffer persecution. And for this they are branded by the apostle as false teachers, and false Christians, and, indeed, whatever they pretend, enemies to the cross of Christ. Those that will sin, though under never so fair and specious pretences, rather than suffer, rather than bear the cross, they are no Christians, Christ and his apostles disclaim them.

Quest. What is it to suffer for Christ? How may I know that I suffer for him, that my suffering is the cross of Christ? The resolution of this is necessary, both for the comfort of the sufferers and for the explication of the doctrine. For the cross is properly a suffering for Christ; and, therefore, that we may know what the cross is here mentioned, and when we bear it, we must understand what it is to suffer for Christ. *Non pœna, sed causa facit martyrem.*

Ans. In general. The Scriptures describe this to us in several expressions. It is to suffer for the gospel, Mar. x. 29; 'for Christ' and 'for the gospel' are joined together as terms explaining one another. To suffer for the truths of the gospel, for the profession, the promoting, the maintaining of, adhering to the gospel, is to suffer for Christ.

It is to suffer for the kingdom of God, Luke xviii. 29. For acknowledging and promoting the kingdom of Christ inwardly or outwardly, in those ways and means whereby he exercises his regal office in his church under the gospel. It is to suffer for righteousness, Mat. v. 10. This is suffering for his name's sake, ver. 11; so 1 Pet. iii. 14; for doing that which is righteous; for obedience to any of Christ's commands, in observance of any law of God. It is to suffer for the discharging of a good conscience, 1 Pet. ii. 19. It is to suffer for well-doing, 1 Pet. iii. 17; explained by another expression, 1 Pet. iv. 19. To suffer according to the will of God, is to suffer for doing anything that he would have us do, whatever the will and judgment of men be concerning it.

Now these general grounds being laid down before us in Scripture, we may by the light and help thereof proceed to a more particular resolution of the question, and such as may tend more to remove the doubts and scruples whereby Satan has been wont (and will be ready) to rob sufferers of their comfort under the cross. We shall attempt this, 1, negatively; 2, positively. In the negative observe these rules:

1. It cannot be concluded that sufferings are not for God, because those who profess themselves to be the people of God are the instruments of them; or that it is not the cross of Christ which is borne, because it is laid on by those who profess Christ. Abel is called the protomartyr, the first sufferer for God; and he suffered by the hand of one who worshipped the same God, with the same kind of worship: both Abel and his persecutor

offered sacrifice. Isaac suffered by Ishmael, Gal. iv. 29; yet Ishmael was Abraham's son, and by him circumcised, and so admitted to the church and its privileges. Who were those that persecuted the prophets of old, but they who professed themselves to be the peculiar people, and true worshippers of the true God? Jerusalem, the chosen city, killed the prophets, and stoned God's messengers, Mat. xxiii. 37. Amongst this people, though there was no other people that owned the true God in the world, some persecutors were found in every generation. Even when they utterly disclaimed this, as thinking themselves far enough from being persecutors, yet then are they charged with this guilt by Christ himself, ver. 30, 31. Christ himself suffered by those who took themselves peculiarly to be the people of God. And since the profession of Christ became general, ordinarily a man's enemies are those of his own house. The bitterest persecutors are those of the same profession.

2. It cannot be concluded that sufferings are not for Christ, because those who inflict them will not acknowledge it; for they will always plead it is for evil-doing, though it be really for Christ and righteousness. If persecutors may state the cause of those whom they persecute, none amongst Christians will ever suffer for Christ; for though they love the thing, yet they hate the name of persecutor, and therefore will pretend always some other cause of their hatred and violence. They think themselves concerned, not to let it appear that they persecute any for Christ's sake, or for righteousness, or for the gospel, though that be the cause indeed.

As it is said of the heathens in primitive times, they covered the Christians with beasts' skins, so that the wild beasts, to whom they exposed them, might with more fury seize on them; so it is, and has been with persecutors in all ages. They shew the people of Christ in an odious habit, state their cause otherwise than it is, that so they may let out their malice and cruelty more freely upon them.

Thus Ahab persecuted Elijah, not for his faithfulness in reproving his wickedness, and calling back the people from their idolatry and apostasy to the sincere worship of God: no, that had been odious; but he falls upon him as a troubler of Israel, 1 Kings xviii. 17. He charges him as one that brought trouble upon the church and state, as one who dissuaded the people from the religion established, and so disturbed the peace of the land, Ezra iv. 12, Esth. iii. 8.

Thus Jeremiah was persecuted as a seditious preacher, an enemy to king and state, when, indeed, he sought to secure them from ruin, by bringing them back to God, from whom they had revolted, Jer. xxxvii. 12, 13, and xxxviii. 4. And upon such an account must Paul and Silas suffer, as disturbers of the peace, breakers of ancient customs, and opposers of Cæsar, as evil-doers, if their persecutors may be judges, Acts xvi. 20, and xvii. 6, 7.

Yea, Christ himself must suffer for sedition, and as an enemy to Cæsar, if Pilate and the Jews may state his cause. The Jews thus accuse him: Luke xxiii. 2, 'We found this fellow perverting the nation, and forbidding to give tribute to Cæsar, saying, That he himself is Christ, a King.' And they cry out, John xix. 12, 'If thou let him go, thou art not Cæsar's friend; whosoever maketh himself a king, speaketh against Cæsar.' And the cross was the punishment in use for that crime. *Authores seditionis aut tumultus, pro qualitatis dignitate, aut in crucem tollentur, &c.* But because he died the death of a seditious person, shall we judge he died for no better cause?

The primitive Christians were persecuted as incendiaries, enemies of the emperor and empire, *κατεψεύσαντο ἡμῶν Θυέστεια δεῖπνα καὶ Οἰδιποδείους μίξεις*, as the French churches in those times complain (Euseb. lib. 5), accused of inhumanity and horrible uncleanness, as causes of all the evils that befell the empire: and, therefore, when any calamity befell them, they were wont to cry out, *Christianos ad leones*; for this they must be cast to wild beasts, as though they suffered for no other cause, but as being causes of the world's calamities. No people ever suffered more clearly for Christ than the Christians in those times; and yet their persecutors fasten on them for other causes of their sufferings.

3. It cannot be concluded that their sufferings are not for Christ, because their sins have provoked God to leave them to sufferings. Though sin should raise the storm, yet he who is ready, in that tempest, to have himself, and what is dear to him, cast overboard, rather than Christ should be further dishonoured, will not want the comfort and honour of suffering for Christ.

Cyprian tells the elders and deacons in an epistle, lib. 4, that the persecution came upon them for their sin. *Intelligendum est enim et confitendum, secundum peccata nostra venisse.* And yet then such multitudes suffered for Christ, that the persecution, *Gregem nostram maxima ex parte populata est, et usque populatur*, had even laid their churches desolate. Eusebius, in the beginning of lib. 8, going to describe the tenth persecution, gives an account of those sins which brought those sufferings upon them; yet never was there greater multitudes in any age who gave up themselves to be sacrificed for the name of Christ. Though the sins of God's people may provoke him to let loose the rage of hell, and the world upon them, and to bring them into a suffering condition, yet, if in this case they humble themselves, and return to him, and in the day of trial part with all, rather than flinch from him, they will be owned as sufferers for him.

Nor need it seem strange that the same suffering should be both for sin and for righteousness. Here is no contradiction: these are very well consistent in different respects. The same suffering may be for sin in reference to God, who may leave his people to sufferings, because they have sinned against him; for pride, worldliness, slothfulness, security, lukewarmness; for their contentions, divisions, want of brotherly love; or for their backsliding, declinings, or their non-proficiency and unfruitfulness, or other sinful miscarriages. And yet these very sufferings may be for righteousness, in reference to their persecutors, who afflict them, not because they have sinned against God, but because they will not sin more; not because they have been unfaithful to Christ, but for their faithfulness to him, because they will not further provoke him by complying with their sinful impositions, or serving their wicked designs. The hard measures which the believing Hebrews met with from the unbelieving Jews, when they were reproached, and their goods spoiled, were sufferings for Christ, else they could not have endured this joyfully, and yet the apostle speaks of these sufferings under the notion of chastisements, Heb. xii. Now chastisings are properly for sin; take the word in a proper sense, and none are chastened but in reference to some miscarriage.

The two last particulars I shall a little more insist on, adding what the time would not then permit me to offer to you. And the rather because I find I am apt to be mistaken, and such constructions put upon my words as the expressions will not bear, and my thoughts were never guilty of.

It may be of some use to take notice of those sins which Cyprian and

Eusebius mention, as the provocations which brought the Christians in their times into a suffering condition.

Eusebius tells us that the Christians, under some of the governors before Diocletian, had much liberty, many encouragements, and some of them great preferments. But *ἐκ τῆς ἐπὶ πλέον ἐλευθερίας*; they as it were surfeiting of too much liberty, grew wanton and slothful, contented themselves with a specious outside holiness, fell into divisions and contentions, envying and reproaching one another, and strove who should get uppermost to lord it over their brethren, *οἷα τε τυραννίδας τὰς φιλαρχίας ἐκθύμως διεκδικοῦντες*. That which he most insists on, and repeats over and over, is their divisions and contentions amongst themselves, *ταῖς πρὸς ἀλλήλους ἀνεφλέγοντο φιλονεικίαις*. The fire of contention broke out amongst them; discord, threatening, emulation, and mutual hatred did increase among them. For these sins did the Lord wax angry, and involved them in that dreadful persecution. Yet afterwards he gives an account of hundreds and thousands that suffered for Christ. So that hence it is clear that men may suffer for sin, and for righteousness too.*

The sins that Cyprian tells us brought the Christians in his time under persecution, were their too much minding their estates and riches, *patrimonio et lucro studentes;* pride, *superbiam sectantes;* emulation and dissension, *emulationi et dissentioni vacantes;* neglecting the faith and simplicity of the gospel, *simplicitatis fidei negligentes;* worldliness, *seculo verbis solis, et non factis, renunciantes;* self-pleasing, and offensiveness to others, *unusquisque sibi placentes, et omnibus displicentes.* These sins brought them into a suffering condition; for he adds, *vapulamus itaque ut meremur,* we have deserved these scourges, *cum scriptum sit, servus,* &c., Luke xii. Yea, he instances in the confessors themselves, who were already under sufferings, that were also under guilt, and yet owns them as confessors, *i.e.*, sufferers for Christ, though they had not yet resisted unto blood.

But it may be you will be better satisfied with a domestic instance. Let me give you one nearer home, and which some of you are better acquainted with. In Edward the VI. his time a reformation was happily begun, the main body of popery was cast out, and the gospel had a free passage. Yet the reformation being so opposed as it could not be perfected, and the gospel not being duly esteemed, and obeyed, and improved, these and other sins, as the martyrs confess, brought those black and dreadful days of Queen Mary's government; so that sin brought those suffering times, and yet those times afforded many hundred martyrs. The martyrs acknowledge that their sins had some hand in kindling those flames wherein so many were sacrificed for the testimony of Jesus; so that it is clear to any one that will not shut their eyes that men may suffer for their sins, and yet for Christ too.

4. It cannot be concluded, they do not suffer for Christ, who have some sin mixed with that which is made the cause of their sufferings, if it be the cause of God indeed, for the substance of it, and they sincere in it for the main. When the people of God are ready to offer up themselves, and what they have for him, he will not reject such a sacrifice for every blemish. Christ had something against the church of Ephesus, something to charge her with as matter of provocation, even when he is speaking of her sufferings, Rev. ii. 4. And yet he owns her as one that had suffered and laboured for his name's sake, verse 3.

Nor can this be concluded, because of some miscarriage under their suf-

* *Vid.* Spondanum.

ferings. David, while he was persecuted by Saul, miscarried divers ways, as you may see 1 Sam. xxi. 2, 12, 13, and elsewhere; yet this did not hinder him from being a sufferer for righteousness.

As the Lord has provided a way, that what his people do for him may be accepted as done for him, though there be too many sinful mixtures therein, so he has provided an expedient, that what they suffer for him may be accepted as suffered for him, though there be many flaws therein, both for matter and manner. The Lord Jesus, the advocate of and sacrifice for his people, is effectual for both. When they apply themselves to him, in the exercise of faith and repentance, through his mediation, that which is therein evil shall not be remembered, that which is good therein will be accepted, Rom. xii. 1. How acceptable, see Eph. i. 6, 7.

Licinius, as you may read, Eusebius *De vita Constantini*, makes an edict, that whosoever did relieve the imprisoned and distressed Christians should suffer the same things that were inflicted upon them. Now, suppose some, out of love to Christ and his afflicted members, should have ventured (as many did indeed) to have relieved them, and yet should have done it too sparingly, or too fearfully, or with some selfish reflections, and should, according to the edict, have suffered for relieving them, here had been some sin mixed with the cause of their sufferings. And yet in this case, since their cause was good, and the cause of Christ, for the substance of it, who would deny but they suffered for Christ?

Or suppose one should suffer because he would not leave praying (which was Daniel's case, Dan. vi.), and yet in his prayer should have some mixture of unbelief, and lukewarmness, and other distempers, which the best cannot always escape, here would be some sin mixed with the cause of sufferings; yet who would deny but that, suffering for doing his duty, he is a sufferer for God?

To proceed a little further: suppose some godly Lutherans should suffer for those great truths of the gospel, which they maintain against the papists, and together with them should suffer for consubstantiation, which indeed is an error, here would be a sin mixed with the cause of their suffering; yet I suppose their laying down their lives for those other great truths of Christ, notwithstanding this sinful mixture, would be accounted a suffering for Christ.

So much for the negative rules. Proceed we now to the positive.

1. They suffer for Christ, who suffer for the truths of Christ. He suffers for Christ who suffers for the gospel, who will part with all, rather than deny any truth of the gospel, Rev. ii. 13. To 'hold fast Christ's name,' and 'not to deny the faith,' are all one. So that to suffer, as Antipas did, rather than deny the faith, is to suffer for Christ's name, Philip. i. 27. To stand striving for the faith of the gospel, συναθλοῦντες τῇ πίστει, striving as combatants, resolving to uphold the truth, or to fall for it, is to suffer for Christ; for he adds, ver. 29, 'To you it is given, not only to believe, but to suffer for his name.' Jude, ver. 3, ἐπαγωνίζομαι, struggling for it, as with the pangs of death. It is taken *pro luctu in morte*, says Gerard. Those that strive for the truth as for life, being ready to part with life and all rather than quit it, in such contests they are suffering for Christ. He that parts with all, rather than deny the least truth, for the name of Christ is concerned in all, and he is faithful indeed who will not be unfaithful in a little. So the Christians in the fourth age would suffer rather than yield a title, an ἰῶτα, to the prejudice of the truth they were then called to contend for, viz., the divinity of Christ; rather than they would put ὁμοιούσιος for ὁμοούσιος, in their confessions of faith (though there be

but the difference of the least letter in the alphabet), they would be exposed to the rage and cruelty of the Arians.

Some think that which is said here of the church of Pergamos is a prophetical description of the state of the church under popish corruptions, that apostasy being a falling from the faith; so suffering for the truths corrupted or subverted by the papists will be a suffering like Antipas, which wants but a syllable of Antipapas.

2. They that suffer for the worship of Christ. The name of Christ is put for his worship, 2 Tim. ii. 19. To suffer for his worship is to suffer for his name's sake, to suffer because they will not neglect the worship of Christ. So Daniel, because he would not forbear praying, though there was a law to the contrary, Dan. vi. 7, was cast into the den of lions; he suffered for God. Or because they will not give the worship of God to any other, so the three faithful Jews would be cast into the furnace rather than fall down before an image; they would not give outward adoration to an image, though they were free to keep their hearts and inward man for the true God, Dan. iii.

So those that have suffered by the papists' cruelty, for not bowing to altars, and images, and crucifixes, have suffered for Christ. 'Mine honour will I not give to another,' Isa. xlii. 8. He is jealous of it, and takes it as a kindness to himself when others are jealous of it too.

So the primitive Christians that suffered, not only for not sacrificing, but rather than they would throw a little incense into the fire with respect to an idol, as those did who are called by the ancients *Thurificati*; yea, rather than they would receive a ticket signifying they had done so, though indeed they had not, thereby to escape suffering as those did whom they call *Libellatici*.

Or because they will not worship God otherwise than he has prescribed, according to the devices and inventions of men, who are so presumptuous as to think their own inventions may take place of God's institutions, and will not be content to serve God as the apostles and primitive Christians served him. Those that have suffered for opposing the superstitions and will-worship of papists, and popish innovators, have suffered for God; they are amongst the number of those who, as the apostle expresses it, 'suffer according to the will of God,' 1 Pet. iv. 15, when they run all hazards rather than not worship God according to his will. The children of Israel, while they retained their integrity, are ready to hazard their lives, even against their brethren, upon an apprehension that they had innovated upon the service of God by setting up an altar, Joshua xxii. 11, 12, as the apostles did for not observing the Jewish ceremonies.

Or because they will not be present at false worship, though they do not join in it. So the Reformed divines determined upon the question, that those who would be faithful should suffer rather than be present at the mass, though their hearts were against it, Dan. iii. They might have directed their inward worship to the true God, and to him they might have referred their outward adoration too, without intending to give either to the image. But such relative worship they did not know, or could not swallow, though modern idolaters and their advocates think theirs sufficiently excused and justified upon this pretence, that what honour they seem to give the image is directed and referred to God in Christ.

3. Those that suffer for the discipline of Christ. For hereby Christ exercises his kingly office in the church; and to suffer for his kingdom is to suffer for himself, Luke xviii. 29. Christ has left us not only ordi-

nances of worship, but ordinances of discipline, probation, and trial of officers and members, ordination, admonition, excommunication, that the societies of Christians may be visibly holy, and their administrations not profane. They that suffer for observing the orders Christ has left us, for keeping out those who have no visible right to church-membership and privileges, or casting out those who are scandalous and impenitent, lest the church of Christ should become a nest of unclean birds, to the profaning of his ordinances and the dishonour of the Christian name, they suffer for the name of Christ, Rev. ii. 2, 3. He owns what they had done or suffered in trying pretenders, and not enduring those that were evil amongst them, as done for his name's sake. Those who are acquainted with the practice of the churches in the first three hundred years after Christ, may observe a remarkable strictness and severity both in their admissions and censures.* Nor were they deterred therefrom by all the sufferings in those times.

4. Those that suffer for acts of mercy or justice. These in Scripture pass frequently under the name of righteousness, and so to suffer for them is to suffer for righteousness' sake; and that is all one as to suffer for Christ's sake, Mat. v. To suffer for such acts as those of the two famous virgins Prazidis and Potentiana, who hazarded themselves to bury the bodies of the martyrs, and laid out their estates to relieve those that were in distress: Mat. xxv. 40, 'Inasmuch as ye have done it to one of the least of these my brethren, ye have done it unto me;' consequently, inasmuch as they suffer for doing this for the least of Christ's members, they suffer for him. Such an act was that of Obadiah, 1 Kings xviii. 34. Now if he had suffered for this act of mercy and charity, he had suffered, not only for relieving men, but fearing God, for that was the rise of it.

So for acts of justice. Elijah causes the priests of Baal to be slain. For this cause Jezebel persecutes him, 1 Kings xix. 1, 2, and puts him to fly for his life. Now, herein he suffered for God, and so he apprehends it: ver. 10, 'I have been very jealous for the Lord God of hosts.' This will be more evident and unquestionable when those acts are done out of love to Christ, or in obedience to him, or with respect to his honour, or in subserviency to his interest; for acts of a lower nature thus done, are done for Christ, and to suffer thus is to suffer for Christ. Elijah had warrant to do thus by the law of God; for, by the judicial law, idolaters and seducers were to be put to death, Deut. xvii. 2. And this was done with the concurrence of the elders and the people; for there was met in Carmel a general assembly of all Israel by Ahab's order, so that, if the prophet was not a magistrate, we need not have recourse to special and extraordinary instinct to justify the act. He, according to the law of God, requires the assembly, consisting of magistrates and people, to do execution, and they do it; but for this Jezebel threatens and persecutes him.

5. You may suffer for Christ, though the cause for which you suffer be a civil act. That a person may suffer for God, it is not always requisite that the cause for which he suffers be merely and strictly religious. The cause of David's sufferings from the hand of Saul was his title to the kingdom, and that was a civil thing; yet when for this he was hunted as a partridge upon the mountains, he is counted as one that was persecuted for righteousness' sake. A man may suffer for God when he is persecuted for a civil act, if that act be his duty, if he was called to it by God, if it was that which God would have him do; for in this case he suffers for

* *Vid.* Spondan. in Cypr.

well-doing. He suffers according to the will of God, he suffers for righteousness, which expressions are all one in Scripture with suffering for God. He that is persecuted for doing the will of God, whether it be in a matter religious or civil, he is a sufferer for God. And so he may be more comfortably when the cause is mixed; when, for the matter of it, it is civil, but the end of it is religious (and so indeed it should be always), when the end is the advancement of Christ, promoting his gospel, depressing of wickedness, encouraging of holiness; when it has a special tendency to these or like ends, and is undertaken in order thereto, then is their suffering for it more evidently for God. I say, it will more evidently be a suffering for Christ if the civil act be directed further, and so is of a higher tendency than otherwise in its own nature it would be. For substance, the choice of officers or magistrates in a corporation is a civil act. Now, suppose a man should endeavour, in his place and station, so far as lawfully he may, to get such chosen as will oppose popery, give free passage to the gospel, discourage wickedness, decline persecuting, and be true to the interest of Christ, and the nation, and the people of Christ in it, if he should suffer for such endeavours, though he act but in his civil capacity, yet he would constructively and really suffer for Christ; and so far as he acts sincerely with such intention, Christ will own him as one that suffers for his name's sake, and he may have the comfort of such a sufferer. And those that decline such endeavours, for fear it should expose them to suffering, they thereby decline the cross when they are called to take it up, and are so far guilty of disobedience and unfaithfulness to Christ.

6. A man may suffer for Christ in refusing to do that which in itself is lawful to be done; and that in two cases, to instance in no more.

(1.) When the doing of that which is lawful in itself may be an offence to others; *i. e.*, an occasion of sin to one or other, either to weak brethren or to false brethren. The apostle is an example to us in both, 1 Cor. viii. 13. Though it was lawful for him to eat this or that, yet rather than he would lay a stumbling-block before those whose weakness was not satisfied of the lawfulness of it, he would not eat, whatever came on it, whatever he suffered for it.

And as careful he was not to lay an occasion of sin before false brethren, as appears in another instance. Circumcision was in his time lawful; and so being in such circumstances wherein it might be done without offence, he circumcised Timothy, Acts xvi. 3. But when it was like to prove an occasion of sin, he refused to circumcise Titus, Gal. ii. 4, 5. He saw, if he should then have used that rite, which otherwise was lawful, it would have confirmed the unbelieving Jews in their opinion of the necessity of it, when indeed it was not necessary, and it would have encouraged them to impose and obtrude it as necessary upon others. The case being thus, rather than he would do it, he exposed himself to the malice and rage of those false brethren who persecuted him upon this account. Yet, Gal. v. 11, what he suffered for this cause he suffered for Christ, insomuch as he glories in his sufferings.

Obj. Whereas it may be objected, that there is a twofold offence, *scandalum acceptum et datum*, an offence taken, and an offence given; it is the offence given that is of pernicious consequence, when a dangerous occasion is offered, such as tends to the prejudice of another's soul. This offence the apostle condemns, and would have avoided; and we ought to suffer (as he would have done) rather than offer it to any. But an offence taken is another thing; when one takes occasion when no just occasion is offered;

when he is scandalised, stumbles, and falls, because another does that which he may lawfully do.

Ans. It is an eating to this latter sort of offence which the apostle forbids and condemns (that which seems more innocent and more tolerable), the meat which he speaks of, the eating of it was lawful in itself; he declares it so, and was persuaded of it by the Lord Jesus, Rom. xiv. 14; and yet he would have it forborne when thereby a weak brother is offended, though the meat being not forbidden, and so the eating of it innocent in itself, the weak brother had no just occasion of offence offered; nor could he reasonably take it, it was merely his mistake to judge it unlawful. He would have every one avoid occasion of such offence, this tending to destroy him who takes it, Rom. xiv. 15, 20. And we ought rather to suffer than do what is otherwise lawful, when it may prove destructive to another's soul.

(2.) When the thing is lawful, yet he who is put upon the doing it is doubtful whether it be lawful or no, Rom. xiv. 23; while he doubts of its lawfulness, if he should do it, he would sin; and therefore if he should suffer for not doing of it, he suffers for avoiding sin, and consequently suffers for conscience towards God, which indeed is a suffering for God, Rom. xviii. 23. He that eateth or does anything not of faith, *i. e.*, as he explains it, while he doubteth of the lawfulness of it, if he be not fully persuaded that he may do it lawfully, as verse 5, he sins. He does that for which he may be damned, that which exposes him to condemnation; and therefore he ought to suffer anything rather than to venture on anything with a doubting conscience, for any suffering from man is far more tolerable than condemnation by God. And those who enjoin anything, not only apparently sinful, but which is suspected and doubtful, and those under penalties, instead of that love they should have for souls, take the course to damn them.

7. Whatever be alleged as the cause of good men's sufferings, whether it be a matter religious or civil, whether it be a duty or a thing indifferent, yea, though it be some sin or miscarriage that is pretended to be the cause why they are hated, and reproached, and persecuted, yet if the great motive, the main inducement, be their godliness, their strictness in following Christ, their zeal for his interest, their severity against sin, their endeavours for reformation, and the like, though their persecutors would have it believed that they suffer as evil doers, yet Christ will own them as suffering for him.

Polybius tells us that statesmen have their *causas justificantes*, some plausible reasons, which they publish as the cause of their actings, to put the fairer colours upon them; and some *causas reales*, which though they conceal, yet really set them a-work, and are the true reason of their proceedings. Just so have persecutors something specious, which they give out to be the cause of their acting against the people of Christ, whenas they conceal that which has the greatest influence on them, and is the true cause indeed. It would not be for their credit to let it be known that they are so fierce against any that profess Christ for their strictness, and holiness, and faithfulness to Christ.

Now, whatever be alleged as the cause of any man's sufferings, if the *causa realis*, the true reason, and the great inducement, that sets them against him, be his strictness, holiness, faithfulness in discharge of his place, &c., endeavours to reform what provokes God; so that were it not for this, notwithstanding anything alleged against him, he might be passed by, he might escape hatred, reproach, persecution as well as others; in this case, however the cause of his sufferings may be disguised, yet is it for Christ that he suffers indeed, 2 Tim. ii. 9. When the panther flies upon a picture, and tears it, because it has some resemblance of a man, the picture suffers, but it is for the man's sake. If persecutors fly upon you for the image of Christ in you, for any resemblance you have of him, whatever you suffer, it is for Christ's sake.

Whatever Cain might pretend why he fell upon his brother, the Scripture tells us the true cause: 1 John iii. 12, 'Because his works were evil, and his brother's righteous.' And upon this account Cain passeth for a murderous persecutor, and Abel for a martyr.

Whatever the wicked Jews pretended of old for their persecuting the prophets, and fair pretences they had to delude their own consciences and justify their actions before others, yet the true cause was because the prophets reproved them for their backsliding, and corrupting the worship of God, and endeavouring their reformation. And upon this account Christ brands the Jews as persecutors, and honours the prophets as sufferers for his name's sake, Mat. v.

The primitive Christians, as Eusebius and others tell us, were accused of sedition, sacrilege, murder, meeting privately to conspire against the emperor, putting out the lights and committing filthiness together, &c.; and by these and the like pretended crimes the persecutors sought to justify their rage against them, whereas the true cause was because they were Christians, worshippers, and followers of Christ, and would not join with them in their worship of idols. And now the other odious and false aspersions being wiped off, the true cause of their sufferings appears, and is acknowledged; and they are, and will be in all generations, honoured as the martyrs of Jesus, as sufferers for Christ, even by those who otherwise follow the steps of those persecutors in their false accusations of the people of God, and in their real enmity to purity and holiness.

To go a little further: suppose one should speak or act something without due cautiousness, such as prudence requires, and thereby occasion be taken to draw him within the compass, or make him obnoxious to some law, rigidly and so injuriously interpreted, and thereupon he suffer grievously; if there be sufficient ground to believe that this advantage would not have been taken against him, it might have been overlooked, but that he had before appeared steady for the interest of Christ, or in opposition to mischievous designs and attempts against it; in such a case, though this be never alleged, nor so much as mentioned, as the cause of his sufferings, yet he may be justly reputed to suffer for Christ, though another occasion was taken to make him suffer.

This and the other I thought it requisite to insist on for the ends forementioned. Other doubts and scruples that perplex any under the cross may be reduced to these, and so hereby be removed. It concerns you to take notice of them, and remember them, against any hour of trial and temptation, when Satan, and subtile and malicious persecutors, would rob you of the comforts you may have in suffering for Christ; or want of a clear understanding of the true cause of suffering may hide them from you, and render a suffering condition dreadful. Nothing can hinder it from being formidable, unless you be satisfied that you suffer for Christ.

Use. Information. If he that will not suffer for Christ is no Christian, this shews us that Christianity is another thing than many take it to be; a harder thing to be a Christian than it is supposed to be. Many (it is to be feared) take themselves to be Christians who are not so indeed, think themselves complete Christians when they want that which Christ himself hath made essential to a Christian.

That thou mayest be a Christian indeed, it is not enough to be baptized into the name of Christ, nor to take up the profession of Christ, nor to believe the truths of Christ, nor to partake of the outward privileges of Christians, nor to expect the reward of Christians, nor to do the acts and perform some duties of Christians, to pray, hear, communicate with them, and minister to their necessities, &c.,—these are some things indeed that belong to Christians; but these are not all, all this is not enough.

When the young man told Christ that he had observed all the commandments, 'All these,' says he, 'have I kept from my youth,' Mark x. 20, one would have thought this had been enough. No, says Christ; for all this, 'One thing thou lackest,' ver 21, 'sell whatsoever thou hast, and give to the poor, and thou shalt have treasure in heaven.' So say I, or rather Christ in the text says it to you, notwithstanding all the truths which you believe as Christians, notwithstanding all the duties you perform as Christians, yet one thing you lack; and for all the good conceit you have of yourselves, if this one thing be wanted, indeed, all that you profess you have will be nothing to prove you Christians. This one thing will try what your professions and pretences are. And what is this one thing upon which so much depends? Why, it is the cross. What think you of that? Here is the test. Are you willing to take it up? Are you willing to be hated, and reproached, and impoverished, and tortured, and ruined for Christ? What say you to this? Do you think it a hard saying? Must you hate* the ease, and the plenty, and the credit, and the friendship of the world, or else no bargain? You like not to be Christians upon other terms; you are ready, with the young man, to go away sorrowful when you hear that it is like to cost you so much; or, you will not believe that Christ is so strict, or that it is so dangerous a thing to be a Christian. Well, I know not upon what grounds you go, but I am sure these are the words of Christ, and such as you will find true hereafter, however you may evade them now. He that taketh, &c. He that is not willing, ready, resolved to part with all that is dear to him in this world, to suffer all that is grievous to the flesh for Christ's sake whenever he shall be called to it, let him please himself with what fancies he will, Christ will never own him for a Christian. If you be not ready to entertain the cross for the name of Christ, whatever you are, or do, or believe, you are but almost Christians; what progress soever you seem to have made in Christianity, you are not so much as fully persuaded to be Christians if you be not resolved upon the cross, Acts xxvi. 28, 29. Except these bonds, says Paul. We may wish, indeed, that there were such an exception, that the sufferings which attend the faithful profession of Christ might not deter any from being Christians; but, whatever we may wish, Christ has made no such exception. He tells us plainly, if we will have him, we must have him with the cross; if we will take him we must take him with bonds, and imprisonment, and poverty, and disgrace, or whatever we may be put to suffer for his sake. He would not have us mistaken in promising ourselves better usage than we are like to find: Mat. x. 34, 'Think not that I am come to send peace on earth; I came not to send peace, but a sword.' Do not deceive yourselves with a conceit that I came into the world with any design to secure those that follow me in a quiet and peaceable possession of outward prosperity. No; if you will follow me indeed, you must rather

* Qu. 'have'?—ED.

expect the sword; not only lesser sufferings, but death itself, ver. 35. No bonds, sacred or civil, shall restrain those from whom you might expect better usage, from exercising their malice and cruelty against you; the nearer they are to you the more bitterly will they persecute you. These are the terms which Christ makes known to you. Now are you Christians upon these terms? Can you welcome Christ with the cross? Will you bear it for him? Are you ready to be nailed, to be fastened to it, for his sake, whenever you have a call to it? If not, delude not yourselves, you are no Christians. *Qui timet pati, non est ejus qui passus est*, says Tertullian; he that will not suffer for Christ is none of his who suffered so much. And by this it is too manifest that there are few Christians indeed, how many soever take up the profession. And we shall endeavour to convince you of it in some particulars, since such conviction is exceeding necessary; for while men persuade themselves they are what they really are not, they will never seek to be what indeed they should be.

(1.) What shall we think of those, who are so far from bearing the cross themselves, that they are ready to lay it upon others; those who hate, and revile, and reproach, and persecute the servants and ministers of Christ; whose hearts are possessed with hatred, and malice, and bitterness against them; who are so far from bewailing and resisting these unchristian distempers, and striving to suppress them and root them out, as they nourish them, and are pleased with them, and encourage one another therein, and desire more power and liberty to let them out more freely, and take all occasions to express their malice and enmity against them? What think you, are these Christians? Another question may resolve this. Were they Christians who persecuted Christ himself? Were those Jews Christians who cried out, 'Crucify him, crucify him'? If they were not, no more are these; for those who hate, and reproach, and persecute the members of Christ, they, in Christ's account, do this against himself. 'Saul, Saul, why persecutest thou me?' And upon inquiry it will appear they have little more to excuse themselves from this guilt than those wretched Jews had; for if some should plead that they do not hate, or reproach, or persecute any, because they are Christians, or ministers, but because they are hypocrites, and pretend to be what indeed they are not, why, just this did the Jews: they did not persecute Christ because he was the Messiah (they abhorred the thought of such a crime), but because (as they wretchedly alleged) he was an impostor, one that deceived the people, and pretended to be the Christ, the Messiah, when they could not believe he was any such person.

And if any should plead that they are far from persecuting any, they abhor the name, the thing; they detest those wretches who burnt the martyrs in Queen Mary's days; if they had lived in those times, they would have used those faithful people otherwise. Why, but just this did those Jews, who persecuted Christ and his followers; even while they were eagerly persecuting, they detest the name of persecutors. They condemn their forefathers for killing the prophets; if they had lived in their days, they would have been far from so abusing the Lord's messengers, Mat. xxiii. 29, 30. This they said, whenas they were walking in the steps of their fathers, ready to express the same persecuting spirit which possessed them. Yet they would have been taken for the people of God, as persecutors since would be accounted the people of Christ. But he tells them what they are indeed: ver. 33, 'Ye serpents, ye generation of vipers, how can ye escape the damnation of hell?' The poison of malice and hatred which fills their hearts, the sting which these put forth in their words and actings, shews what they are: not Christians, but a generation of vipers; not the seed of the woman, but the seed of the serpent; not the disciples of Christ, but the followers of those who persecuted Christ and the prophets of old.

(2.) What shall we think of those who will not part with their lusts, will not forsake their sins for Christ, will live in them, however he forbid them, however he threaten them? Are these Christians? No, certainly; whatever they may think themselves, whatever others may account them, Christ will never own them as his disciples. Are they no Christians, who will not part with father and mother?' &c. And are they Christians who will not so much as part with their lusts for Christ? Will they take up their cross for Christ, who will not lay aside their cursed sins for his sake? Will they obey Christ, when he calls them to lay down their lives for him, who will not obey him, when he commands them to leave their swearing, and drunkenness, and Sabbath-breaking, and worldliness, and uncleanness, and revengefulness, and malice, for his sake?

Can you think that servant will go an hundred miles for you, who will not so much as stir out of doors for you, when you command him? Will they suffer so much for Christ as the bearing of the cross amounts to, who will not do so little for him as the leaving of a sin comes to? Will they suffer all extremities for the name of Christ, who will not forbear profaning that blessed name by their oaths, and irreverent use of it in common discourse? Will they endure to be tortured for Christ, who will not deny their carnal ease and sensual pleasures, who will not cross their carnal appetite and inclination for his sake? Will they part with all in the world for Christ, who will not be restrained, at the command of Christ, from such an immoderate pursuit of the world, as makes them neglect heaven and their souls? Will they drink up the bitter cup of death for Christ, who will not leave their intemperate cups at his command?

What clear convincing evidence is here, that those who allow themselves in any known sin are no Christians! If men were not under a strong delusion, they would never think themselves Christians while they go on in any sin. But, alas! the God of this world has blinded their minds. What clearer reason than this? Those that will not bear the cross of Christ are no Christians; but they who will not leave their sins for Christ, will never bear the cross for him; (Are they like to suffer for Christ, who daily make him suffer by their sins?) *Ergo*, those that will not leave their sin for Christ are no Christians.

(3.) Others there are who will bear but some part of the cross. The whole weight of it is too heavy, too grievous, they must be excused if they will not endure that.

Some cannot endure to be vilified, and reviled, and reproached for Christ. They will decline those ways that are covered with shame and reproach. They forbear good company, and neglect good duties, lest their wretched acquaintance should jeer and deride them. That way, which is everywhere spoken against, shall have none to walk in it for them. But are they Christians who will not bear the lightest part of the cross? What lighter than the froth and spawn of malicious hearts and tongues? Are they worthy the name of Christians, who will not endure to be abused and reviled for his sake, who gave his back to the smiters, and his cheeks to the nippers, and withheld not his face from shame and smiting?* That was a Christian temper in David, who, when he was jeered for

* Qu. 'spitting'?—ED.

his zeal for God, could answer, 2 Sam. vi. 22, 'I will be yet more vile than thus.' Others can better bear reproach; but to lose their estates, their places, their livelihood, to have their relations ruined, to be brought to a low, poor, necessitous condition, this they cannot bear. They will stoop to unworthy shifts, and stretch their consciences, and not stick at a small matter, to prevent this. Why, but if you have given up yourselves to Christ, you give up your estates, and all you have, to be at his disposing. You promised to be content with him alone, so you might but have him for your portion. If, therefore, when it comes to the trial, you will not part with all rather than offend him, it signifies you did never heartily enter into covenant with him, yea, but did flatter with your lips. That was a temper truly Christian in the Hebrews, who, as the apostle testifies, did suffer the spoiling of their goods with joy, Heb. x. 34.

Others can better endure the loss of outward comfort; but when life is endangered, when a shameful or cruel death is before them, though they have been forward before, yet then they recoil, they relent, they comply, here they will be excused. 'Skin for skin, and all that a man hath will he give for his life.' Why, but Christ himself tells you, in the verse before the text, that life itself must be hated if you will be Christians. If you love life itself more than him, you are none of his. If you be Christians, you are not your own, neither your estates, nor your bodies, nor your spirits; all that are called yours before are now his, 1 Cor. vi. 19, 20. Now, if they be all his, you are no more true Christians, if you do not part with life and all when the honour and interest of Christ requires it, than he is a truly honest man who will not give every one his own. You are his, all you have is his, not your own; and do you deal as Christians, do you deal honestly, if, when he calls for it, you will not give up that which is his own? An honest heathen would not deal thus with you. And can they be counted Christians who will deal thus with Christ.

(4.) Others are confident that they will be ready to suffer for Christ, whenas there is not any probability that ever they will suffer for the truth of Christ. This is too evident in those who are ignorant of the main truths of the gospel, and will not spare time, nor take pains to get a competent knowledge thereof, for all the means of knowledge which are at hand. Is there any probability that such will suffer for the truth? Is it likely that men will suffer for they know not what? Or count that worth the dying for which they count not worth the knowing? or endure the pains of death for that which they will not take the pains to understand? Is it likely they will take up the cross, rather than deny the truth, who count it a cross to labour for the knowledge of it? How far are these from being Christians, if none be Christians but those that take up the cross, since there is no likelihood that such will ever take up the cross whatever become of the truth.

Others presume they will suffer for Christ and the gospel in the gross; suffer rather than turn Turks, or Jews, or papists. But single out any particular truth, and rather than they will suffer for it, they will deny it, or yield it up for peace' sake, or overlook it as a point of small consequence, or give half of it away by some distinction, or betray it by concealment, when it requires a plain and open confession; this argues more fear of the cross than love to the truth, this is not to deal with it as Christians. Christ will not own these as his disciples, he will be ashamed of them who are afraid or ashamed to bear witness to his truth: Mark viii. 38, 'My words;' whatever he hath delivered to us.

(5.) How few are there who would suffer for the worship of Christ! How manifest is this, since there are so many who wilfully neglect the worship of God in their families, are so far from instructing them, that they do not pray with them, though they have all liberty and encouragement to do it, no danger yet of suffering for it, these are more like heathens than Christians. The prophet makes it the character of heathens, Jer. x. 25. Though some would suffer rather than yield to gross and palpable idolatry, yet how few would suffer for that which is only probably and in appearance such?

How few would take up the cross rather than yield to superstition and will-worship, since so many run into it of their own accord! How few would suffer for the purity and spirituality of gospel-worship, as freed from carnal rites and ceremonies, and from the mixtures of man's devices and inventions! And yet this is the character of true worshippers, *i. e.*, of true Christians, John iv. 23, 24.

(6.) How few would suffer for avoiding of sin, unless some gross and notorious abominations!

[1.] How few would suffer rather than offend in a little? The general looseness of men's lives, and largeness of their consciences, gives occasion of jealousy in this particular. How few of the temper and tenderness of that famous sufferer Marcus of Arethusa, who would die rather than give a halfpenny for the repairing of an idol temple! *Ne obolum quidem.* He would be tortured to death rather than give two farthings for such an unlawful use, Sozomen. lib. 5, cap. 9. How far are many from the temper of Valentinian, that great captain under Julian, and afterwards emperor, who, having a drop of water sprinkled upon his garment, which was cast about by their priest in their heathenish services (much like the papists' holy water), to shew how far he was from approving their superstition, cut off that piece of his garment upon which the drop fell, and that in the sight of the heathenish emperor, *αὐτίκα περιτεμεῖν καὶ ἀποῤῥίψαι σὺν αὐτῇ τῇ ψεκάδι ὅσον ἐβράχη τῆς ἐσθῆτος*, and hereupon was afterwards banished by Julian, pretending (says Sozomen. lib. 6, cap. 6) that he was negligent in looking to his soldiers; for he would not seem to punish him for his religion, lest he should have the honour of a martyr or confessor, p. 371.

In the primitive times, they excluded such from the communion of Christians who had yielded to an officious lie that they might avoid suffering; nor would they re-admit them till they had satisfied the church by an exemplary repentance. This was the case of those who, in Cyprian's phrase, did *libellis conscientiam suam maculare*, purchase tickets, signifying that they had complied with the heathen in their worship, when indeed they had not, and so avoided suffering by a kind of officious lie. Those that did thus they looked upon as *lapsi*, such as had fallen from the faith, and therefore they would not own them as Christians, nor admit them to the privilege of the church without a deep and solemn repentance; yea, they would not look upon them as Christians who would make use of a lie for the avoiding of the greatest extremities.

[2.] How few would suffer for avoiding the appearance of evil! Not only for shunning apparent evils, but the appearance of them; apparent sins, but sins in appearance. The ancient Christians would not conform to the rites and customs of the heathens when abused by them to idolatry, though they might have been otherwise lawfully used; they would suffer rather than do this, because there was an appearance of evil in it, viz., a seeming compliance with the heathen.

It was lawful in itself to set up lights and bays at their doors, but because the heathen did this out of respect to their idols, therefore the Christians would rather suffer than do it, *in gratiam magistratus*, though the magistrate enjoined it. *Igitur quia lucernæ præ foribus, et laurus in postibus, ad dæmones pertinent; accendantur lucernæ quibus lux nulla est: Affigant postibus lauros, postmodum arsuras, quibus ignes imminent.**

It was lawful in itself to wear garlands upon their heads, yet because the pagans did it, the Christians, to avoid the appearance of that evil, would suffer rather than do it. Hence the soldier, for whom Tertullian pleads, *in lib. de Corona Militis*, when he came to the tribune for his donative, would not wear the garland upon his head, but brought it in his hand, by which, discovering himself to be a Christian, he was haled to prison and executed. How far are they from this temper and tenderness, how far from suffering upon such accounts, who are zealous for a conformity to the papists in those rites, ceremonies, and gestures which they apparently abuse to idolatry!

Diocletian, having a design to root out the Christian religion, gave order that the Scriptures should everywhere be burned, whereupon multitudes suffered in that tenth persecution because they would not deliver their Bibles to the flames. Amongst the rest, Secundus being commanded to deliver his Bible, makes answer, *Christianus sum, non traditor*, I am a Christian, I cannot do it. Then he is required to give up some riff-raff, *aliqua ecvola*, to be burnt instead of his Bible; this also he refused, and would rather suffer than do it; for though it was lawful, yet it had some appearance of that evil which they were guilty of who are called *Traditores;* he would die to avoid the appearance of sin (Park. p. 11).

[3.] How few would suffer for avoiding that which is evil by construction and interpretation; for avoiding that which others put an ill construction on, though themselves see no hurt therein. Julian, above others, infamous for endeavouring by subtilty to overthrow Christianity, used many artifices in a cunning way to ensnare Christians, and to debauch their consciences. He would dress up that which he required them to do in the fair shows of innocency and lawfulness; but, when he had drawn them to do it, then he would construe it to be a compliance with him in his idolatrous services. And since they could comply in one thing, why not in another? Thus, like an angler, he hid the hook till he could catch them. And some indeed he did ensnare. But when the hook was discerned, his design discovered, they would suffer anything rather than be tempted by the fairest baits he could lay before them. To give some instances pertinent to our purpose. The Christians thought it lawful to give some honour to the emperor in his picture; Julian taking an advantage by this to ensnare them, together with his own picture, sets up some of the images of the heathen gods, *ἐκέλευσε*, &c., says Sozomen, lib. v. cap. 16, *παραμίγνυσθαι ταῖς εἰκόσι*. Now the Christians, while they suspected no hurt, continued their civil reverence to the emperor in his resemblance; but some of them understanding that he accounted this an adoring of his heathenish images, *οὐκ ἀνέχοντο προσκυνεῖν*, would give him that reverence no longer, when so ill a construction was put upon it; but rather chose to suffer, though he made them suffer upon this account, *ὡς καὶ εἰς πολιτείαν καὶ βασιλέα ἐξαμαρτάνοντες*, as offenders against king and state, for so are the historian's words.

Theodoret gives us another instance. When the soldiers were to receive donatives from Julian, he had ready before his throne a fire with incense; and those who would receive the gold from him, must first throw some

* Tertul. 'De Idololatria.'

incense into the fire. This divers of them did, looking on it as a civil custom, and suspecting no hurt in it, τὴν δὲ τὴν πάγην οἱ πλεῖστοι μὲν ἠγνόησαν παντελῶς, lib. iii. chap. 15. They understood not that it was a snare. But when it was told them that this was not agreeable to the Christian profession, ταῦτα γὰρ τῆς χριστιανικῆς ὁμολογίας ἀντίπαλα, they lamented bitterly, and tore their hair, and cried out in the streets, that they were ensnared by the emperor's fraud, βασιλικοῖς παρακεκροῦσθαι τεχνάσμασι; and run to the palace, and desired that they might be cast into the fire, since they had dishonoured Christ by casting incense into the fire, chap. 16.

It is to be feared, then, many amongst us would not be so ready to suffer for such a thing, as to excuse it, and plead its lawfulness, as Marcellinus did, *non Diis sacrificavi;* that which I did was no sacrificing unto idols, *sed tantum grana thuris*, &c., but only throw a grain of frankincense into the fire. But this excuse did not hinder Marcellinus, the Bishop of Rome, from being condemned as an apostate. Nor is he worthy the name of a Christian, who, to avoid suffering, will do anything (howsoever excusable by fair pretences) which may be interpreted to be a denial or dishonour of Christ.

Another pernicious device of Julian's to ensnare the Christians was this, all the meat which was to be sold in the market at Constantinople, he mixeth secretly with that which had been offered to idols (as Baronius relates it) that so the Christians might either perish by famine, or else eat that which might be interpreted an honouring of his idols. This they perceived, abstaining from buying any meat in the market, and contented themselves *cocto frumento*, with boiled corn. And though some may think this a nicety, and more scrupulousness than was needful, yet if that of Augustine be allowed, it will justify them; for he determines that it is better to die by famine than to eat an idolothyte.

It is to be feared that many who bear the name of Christians would make use of the Nicolaitans' plea, rather than suffer in such a case: Though I eat the idols' meat, yet my heart is free from all idolatry and superstition; though I do thus and thus, &c., as papists and superstitious persons do, yet, &c. Ay, but there is something else to be minded, if you will demean yourselves as Christians indeed; not only what the act is in itself, or what you intend in it, but what others may judge of it, and suffer rather than do that which is like to be judged evil. He that sees thee eat meat dedicated to idols, *existimabit te nonnihil idolorum cultus deferre*, says Chrysostom. And we must suffer rather than do that which may be judged a countenancing of idolatry.

[4.] How few would suffer for avoiding of that which is but accidentally evil? In itself lawful, but by accident evil, as it may be an occasion of sin to others; because it is *ædificans ad delictum*, as Tertullian defines scandal, may build up others either in erroneous opinions or unlawful practices. We think it enough if we are ready to suffer rather than sin ourselves; but the apostle thought it a sufficient ground to suffer rather than give occasion of sin to others; he would take up the cross, and bear it, rather than venture upon a thing lawful in itself, in case of scandal. In the interval betwixt the death of Christ and the destruction of the temple, the ceremonies of the law were indifferent, and in themselves lawful; yet the apostle would rather suffer than use them, when the use of them was like to prove an occasion of sin to others, viz., when the Jews were like thereby to be confirmed in their opinion of their necessity, which was an error; or encouraged to press them as necessary upon others, which was a sin to the prejudice of Christian liberty. In such cases the apostle would suffer persecution rather than use them, Gal. v. 11. As if he had said, Some report that I am for the urging of circumcision, but this report appears to be evidently false, because I suffer persecution for this very thing. If I would use circumcision as others do, I should be no more troubled with the cross; the wrath of the Jews would be appeased, and the cross would cease. I should escape it as well as others. The main cause why the apostle was persecuted and suffered so much from the Jews was his non-conformity to the ceremonial law; because he would not practise himself, and press upon others, those ceremonies which were indifferent in themselves, but could not be ordinarily used without offence, *i.e*, without being occasion of sin.

It was sometimes lawful to eat that which had been sacrificed to idols, viz., in case the party that ate thereof did not know it had been idolatrously abused; for so it could not be countenancing idolatry. Or in case none present with him knew it to have been so abused; for so it could not prove a scandal. But in case of scandal, however otherwise it might be lawful, it was no ways allowable, 1 Cor. viii. 9, 1 Cor. x. 25, 28. If it be a Gentile that tells thee, avoid it, lest thou confirm him in his idolatry. Or if it be a weak Christian that tells thee, one not satisfied of the lawfulness of it, avoid it for his sake, lest by thy example he be drawn to eat thereof with a doubting conscience, and so be betrayed to sin. Or if it be one in the way to Christianity, not fully taken off from his idols, avoid it for his sake, lest by thy example he be turned back again to his idolatrous practices, *καὶ ὁδὸς ἐπὶ εἰδωλολατρείαν τὸ πρᾶγμα ἐγίνετο*, Chrysost. in 1 Cor. x. He would have them avoid even that which in itself is lawful in such cases as these, though they suffer for it; for he more than intimates that, ver. 13. Though some motives you meet with may tempt you to comply herein with idolaters, viz., the persecution of the heathen, yet let not this fright you into such a compliance; for this is the common lot of Christians to be persecuted, and God will moderate their rage, and deliver you. And therefore avoid this evil, and fear not, whatever may befall you for so doing.

And to be brief, those who, to avoid persecution and the cross, would eat things sacrificed to idols, whatever offence came thereby, Christ himself thinks them unfit and unworthy to be continued in the fellowship of Christians, and reproves the church of Pergamos for not casting them out, Rev. ii. 14. There was some amongst them who bare the name of Christians, and after ages called them Gnostics, whose principle it was that they might comply with idolaters, to avoid persecution; and therefore rather than suffer, they would eat things offered to idols, though thereby they laid a stumbling-block (like Balaam) in the way of others, and occasioned their falling into sin. He reproves the church for tolerating such among them; he would not have them owned as Christians.

Many who now profess Christ are too much of this temper, as far from taking up the cross of Christ, since they shew themselves so ready to comply with things that have been as much abused to popish idolatry as those meats that were offered to heathenish idols.

To conclude this use, since it is essential to a Christian to bear the cross rather than offend Christ, to suffer rather than sin, how few true Christians are there to be found, since so many who bear the name will rather sin, in one kind or other, than bear the cross, and undergo anything grievous for the name of Christ.

Use II. For Exhortation. Let this stir you up to prepare for the cross. He is not a Christian that will not bear the cross; and he that doth not prepare for it never means to bear it.

The disciples of Christ are always liable to the cross, and that which we are always liable to we should be always ready for. Christians should always make account of the cross; so the apostle, Acts xx. 22, 23. And what we should always make account of, we should always prepare for. Christ would have his disciples take up his cross daily. Now you do not, in the remotest sense, take it up daily, if you do not daily prepare for it. It is certain the cross will be upon you if you will be faithful to Christ, but when it will fall upon you is uncertain; you cannot promise yourselves one day's exemption from it, and therefore you should be every day ready. Christ having discoursed of the troubles which were like to befall his disciples in the general calamities that were coming upon that generation, concludes it with this use, 'Watch ye therefore,' 'be ye always ready,' Mat. xxiv. 42, 44; Mark xiii. 33, 35–37; Luke xxi. 34–36.

Obj. But some may say, I see no danger of the cross, no danger of persecution, and therefore what need so much talking of it? What need so much preparing for it?

Ans. 1. Is there no danger because you do not see it? Did no evil ever befall you but what you foresaw? Has nothing fallen out in your days but what you saw beforehand? or rather, has anything remarkable fallen out in these times which you did expect a year before it came?

It does not become a Christian to say he need prepare for no danger but what he sees. He is in most danger who sees least. If you be Christians, you are engaged in a spiritual warfare. Now if a soldier should tell his captain that he will not prepare, he will not be ready for danger till he see it, he would think him more fit to be cashiered than to be trusted. Even so may Christ, the Captain of our salvation, deal with such secure professors. What, are there no ambuscades, no surprisals in your spiritual warfare, nothing that may be upon you before you are aware of it? You run quite counter to Christ's advice. He would have his disciples watch always, be always ready, because they know not at what hour the master of the house will come, at what hour a calamity will come. He will have them always ready, because it may come at such an hour when they are not aware of it. You think it needless to be ready, because you know not the hour; needless to prepare for it, till you see it and be aware of it. *Nec tamen remittendæ sunt excubiæ, si quando hostis simulabit tranquillitatem.* If you will demean yourselves as Christians indeed, you must not neglect your watch; you must not neglect to be in readiness, when there is fairest show of tranquillity; that is the way to be surprised.

Ans. 2. Grant you see no danger of public and open persecution, yet there may be much still of the cross, and much persecution where it is not open and public, and by authority. You may meet with enough of the cross, enough of persecution, in a private way, if authority do discountenance it. You may, said I; nay, you must, says the apostle, either of the heart, or the countenance, or the tongue, or the head. There was no persecution by public authority till the latter end of Nero's reign, above thirty years after Christ's death; yet in that time of connivance and indulgence the Christians had a heavy share of the cross, escaped no kind of sufferings, as you may see in the Acts of the Apostles, and in the catalogue of Paul's sufferings, 2 Cor. xi. 23-25.

Ans. 3. If you will not prepare for the cross till it come, you will not prepare for it till it be too late. What, prepare to take up the cross when it is upon you! Preparation is a readiness beforehand. If it be upon you before you are ready, preparation comes too late. Then it is most necessary, most seasonable, before the cross comes; and because it ordinarily comes before men can or will see it, it will be necessary to prepare for it before it be seen.

It may be, some of you feel not the pressure of the cross. Oh, but if you be Christians, this in general you must make account of, that it will be upon you one time or other, and when, or how soon that time will be, you know not; and therefore, if you would not be surprised, you should always watch, *i. e.*, as Christ himself explains it, you should be always ready, always prepared. It may come as a thief in the night, who chooses to come when his coming is least looked for, least feared or suspected. It may come as a snare which is laid out of sight, and catches him who thinks he treads safe and discerns no danger. Therefore be always watchful, always prepared.

The watchful soldier will stand upon his guard, and have all things ready, even when he sees no danger, because there may be danger when there is none seen, he may be surprised; but if he perceive danger near, and see an enemy approaching, even though he be disposed to sleep, he will not then give way to it, he will not then need any warning to have all things ready for his defence. You should be always preparing for the cross, even when you see no danger of it; much more when it is visible, and the approaches of it are apparent.

But how shall we prepare for the cross? I shall give some directions.

1. Make your peace with God. Rom. v. 1, 'Being justified by faith, we have peace with God, through our Lord Jesus Christ.' What follows? ver. 2, 3, 'We glory in tribulations,' &c. Peace with God will enable you not only to bear the cross, but to triumph under it. John xvi. 33, Christ promises peace as the best means to bear up his disciples under the cross. Without this, tribulation will be unsupportable, the cross will be intolerable.

Now, though Christ promise peace, yet this, as all other promises, will have its accomplishment in his own way. You must use the means that he has prescribed, walk in the way that he has directed you to, if you will have the peace he has promised. And therefore, if there be any controversy betwixt God and you, make haste to get it taken up; fly to the blessed Umpire, the great Mediator betwixt God and you. Mourn that you have given him any offence; apply the blood of Christ by faith; beseech him with all importunity that he would interpose and make your peace, and rest on him for that purpose as the great peace-maker.

If your conscience check you for any act, or any neglect, which may be the matter of a controversy betwixt God and your soul, bewail it with grief and anguish of spirit, humble yourselves for it to the dust, get your hearts filled with hatred and indignation against it, and yourselves for it; get your souls raised to strong and vigorous resolutions against it. Shew the sincerity hereof, by avoiding all occasions, by watching against all temptations, by diligence in the use of all appointed means, that you may never return to it. Or if it be some secret corruption which hath not broken forth into open act, but disturbs your peace by its inward motions and solicitations, engrossing your thoughts, or drawing your hearts to inclinations towards it, why then rise up with all your might for the subduing of it, fly unto Christ for more strength, be diligent in the use of all means to get it mortified. Shew that you look upon it as an enemy (though it be in your quarters, and you cannot get it dislodged), by making a hearty, a constant, a resolute resistance. Let the Lord see that you look upon it as a greater grievance than any outward pressure or suffering.

Or if your conscience do not check you for outward acts, or inward corruption, take heed it be not because conscience is asleep. And therefore be diligent in searching conscience, lest anything escape you that may make a difference between God and your souls. It will be sad to have conscience asleep, till it be awakened by the cross. The pressure of the cross and the pressure of guilt falling on you together, is like to prove a burden too heavy for you. The cross, when it falls upon a guilty soul, it is like a heavy burden upon a galled shoulder, the pain and anguish of it will scarce be tolerable. If conscience be not pacified, if God be not at peace with you when the cross comes, the coming of it will be terrible. Jer. xvii. 17.

If men accuse, and reproach, and revile you, and conscience accuse you too; if they frown, and through guilt you can expect no smile from God; if they threaten, and you find yourselves under the Lord's threatenings also; if the world's rage and hatred break out against you, and the Lord withdraw the sense of his love; if the world smite and wound you while conscience is lashing you; if the Lord be a terror to you while the terrors of sufferings are before you; if you have no peace with the world, nor no peace with God neither, what will bear you up in such a condition? If the cross lie heavy on you, and, through guilt, you cannot with any confidence expect support from God, the pressure will be unsupportable. And therefore, if you would not sink under the burden, get this laid as the foundation to bear up all: whatever you do, mind this above all, your peace with God. Whatever you neglect, neglect not to do this, for so the cross may undo you. No matter how much water there may be without the ship, the more sea-room it hath, the safer it is in the storm; but if water get within the vessel, then it is in danger of sinking. It will be less matter how many troubles soever you meet with from without, if there be peace within. And therefore keep the way of peace, if the Lord have continued you in it; or if you have swerved, make haste to recover it. Search out your sins, especially those that have had any influence upon the public, that have contributed anything to the loss of gospel liberties, or the bringing of national judgments. Apply yourselves seriously to the exercises of repentance and the actings of faith upon Christ, for we have peace, being justified, and are justified through Christ, and that is by faith, which acts not in this case without the exercise of repentance.

2. Get much love to Christ. A strong affection will carry you after Christ when you cannot follow him but under the cross, will make you follow him wherever he goes, though the way be deep, and rugged, and thorny, though it lead directly to the cross, and bring you to mount Calvary.

Much love will make you willing, ready, resolute to suffer for Christ; and it is want of will, more than want of strength, that disables us from bearing the cross. Christ uses not to deny strength to those who are resolutely willing to suffer for his name's sake. There is a strength in love which is too hard for death itself; love is strong as death.

Much love will make you suffer much, for it is *affectus unionis*, that which makes the soul cling to Christ; and the more it is, the faster it cleaves to him, and the more hardly will it part from him; no small matter will part them. A servant that has some affection to his master will suffer something for him, but an affectionate wife will suffer far more for her husband, because the conjugal love is stronger.

If you mean to suffer much, you must learn to love much. A little love will go but a little way under the cross. If love be weak, get it strengthened; if it be cooling, get it inflamed; if it be declining, get it repaired. A declining love is a step to apostasy, and will be in danger to end there in a day of trial. When the Church of Ephesus has lost her first love, Christ speaks of her as fallen, Rev. ii. 4, 5. There are some amongst these churches who professed Christ, but, for want of love to him, gave way to a principle which was more for their own safety than his honour. They would hold all those things indifferent for which they were like to suffer, that so none might condemn them for yielding in things indifferent, rather than be ruined. These held it indifferent to be circumcised, to escape sufferings from the Jews; indifferent to eat things offered to idols, to escape sufferings from the Gentiles; and, when they had no other way to escape, they would hold it indifferent to deny the faith. So Eusebius, lib. vi. chap xi., tells us, it was the opinion of their followers, ὅτι τὸ ἀρνήσασθαι ἀδιάφορον ἐστί, indifferent ἐν ἀνάγκαις, in great necessities, to deny with the mouth, provided they do it not with the heart. Now it is probably thought that this principle had made some impression upon the church of Ephesus. Hereupon she is charged with losing her first love, because she was not so ready to suffer for Christ as at first. This principle, inclining her more to comply than suffer, she was not so disposed to do her first works, and undergo her first sufferings, for which she is commended, ver. 3. And why? Her first love was lost, she was fallen. If you would not decline the cross, or fall under it, keep up your first love; or, if it be declined, make haste to get it repaired. Follow Christ's advice to Ephesus, ver. 5, 'Remember from whence thou art fallen, and repent,' &c.

Content not yourselves with some small degree of love to Christ; that will not serve you when a day of trial and suffering comes. A little water will quench a spark; it must be a flame, indeed, that all the waters will not quench, nor the floods drown and extinguish, Cant. viii. 6, 7. Get your love kindled into a vehement flame, and then you will follow Christ, and may safely do it, though all the waves and the billows go over you.

Labour by all means to raise your affections to a higher pitch. That love, which will make a fair show, and makes a shift to go after Christ, while it is encouraged by outward prosperity, will not serve your turn when the cross comes. The apostle, 1 John iv. 18, speaks of a perfect love; not that there is any love in this life free from imperfection, but there is one degree of love perfecter than another; a love which will embolden a man to appear for Christ in the face of discouragements and dangers. Such a love he calls perfect, as being nearer to perfection than that which startles at the cross. And thus he describes it, ver. 17, 'Herein is our love made perfect, that we may have boldness in the day of judgment;' that we may have boldness, viz., in confessing Christ and his truth. It is παρρησία, a bold, and open, and fearless confessing of Christ in the face of dangers. He had been speaking of confessing Christ before, ver. 18; not every one that professeth this upon any terms, for every professor dwelleth not in God, and God in him, but he that thus confesseth Jesus when he hazards the loss of all by so confessing him. The perfection of this love expresseth itself in such a boldness for Christ, ἐν ἡμέρᾳ κρίσεως, in the day of judgment, i. e., not the final judgment, but when we are brought before the tribunal of men, to be judged or sentenced for faithfulness to Christ, because as he is, so are we in this world; as he was exposed to sufferings in this world, so are we; and our love to him should carry us through these sufferings, as his love to us did him. He adds, ver. 18, 'There is no fear in love, but perfect love casteth out fear.' Such a degree of love makes us fearless of sufferings, renders the soul bold and valiant for Christ, so as he will not shrink from him and his interest for any danger; he will not think any cross so dreadful as to decline it when Christ calls him to bear it. So Tertullian fourteen hundred years since explained this text. John denies, says he, that there is fear in love: *Quem timorem intelligi præstat, nisi negavimus authorem?* What fear may we here best understand but that which is the cause of denying Christ? *Quam dilectionum perfectionem,* what perfect love, *nisi fugatricem timoris, et animatricem confessionis,* but that which banisheth fear and animates to a confession of Christ. So that love, thus freeing the heart from the fear of the cross, is an excellent preparative to the bearing of it.

But how shall our hearts be raised to such a degree of love? Why, I know nothing more effectual in the world than frequent and fixed thoughts of the love of Christ. If that will not kindle your hearts into flames, vehement flames, I know not what in heaven or earth will do it, 1 John iv. 19. Set some time apart frequently to meditate on the love of Christ, and the wonderful transporting expressions of it.

Say to thy soul, Was he, in whom there dwelt the fulness and riches of the Godhead, content to become so poor for my sake, as he had not whereon to lay his head? And shall I think much to hazard my estate and outward enjoyments for his sake? Oh what had become of my soul if he had stood upon such terms!

Was he, who was the brightness of the Father's glory, content to become the scorn of men and reproach of the people; to be jeered, and buffeted, and spit upon? Was he willing, when he was the King of glory, to be reviled and abused, as the vilest of men, for me? And shall I think much to be vilified, and scorned, and reproached for his sake?

Was he content to leave the delights and joys of heaven, that he might become a man of sorrows? Was he willing to be scourged, and nailed, and wounded, and endure such grievous things for me, as made his soul heavy unto death, and forced him to cry out to heaven, 'My God, my God, why hast thou forsaken me?' and to cry out to earth, 'Have ye no regard, all ye that pass by?' &c. And shall I think much to endure any pain or torture for him?

Was he content to bear the wrath of God, and the rage of men and devils for me? And shall I think much to endure the rage and malice of men for him?

Was he content to suffer a cruel, a shameful, a cursed death for me? And shall I refuse to suffer a blessed death, a death that himself hath blessed, for his sake?

Oh what had become of me! in what a hopeless and helpless condition had my soul been in, if he had stood on the honour, and ease, and plenty, and respect of the world, yea, or his own life! And shall I stand upon these, when his honour and interest requires me to forego them?

Make such use of the love of Christ to provoke your hearts to a more ardent and vehement affection. 'The love of Christ constrains us,' says the apostle. There is something in it that is irresistible; a sweet and powerful force therein, when the Spirit of God impresseth the sense thereof upon the heart, to constrain you to such a love as will compel you to take up the cross, and bear it for his sake, notwithstanding any reluctancy of flesh and blood.

3. Learn to deny yourselves. Be still practising of self-denial. It is self that is pinched by the cross, and so makes us loath to take it up, and impatient to bear it. Till self be renounced, the cross will not be endured, Mat. xvi. 24, Mark viii. 34, Luke ix. 23. The order and connection of these in all the evangelists shews us plainly that self must be first denied before ever we will take up the cross. Self-denial is the first letter (as you see in these texts) in the Christian's alphabet; he that hath not learnt this is far from the highest form, which in the school of Christ is the place of sufferers. When the cross comes, Christ and self are brought into competition, either self must be denied or Christ will be denied. He that cannot deny himself, rather than take up the cross, will deny Christ, either in point of faith or obedience. If ever you would bear the cross, as becomes the disciples of Christ, you must learn to deny,

(1.) Your own worth and excellency, the apprehensions and conceits thereof, whether the ground of it be your accomplishments or enjoyments. If this be not denied, you will think yourselves too good to suffer for Christ. He that is high in his own apprehension will never stoop to the cross; he will count it intolerable, to be vilified, and set at nought, and trampled on, and reproached, and counted (as the apostles were) the refuse and off-scouring of all things: Mat. xi. 29, 'Take my yoke, &c., for I am lowly.' If you will follow Christ, and take up the cross as he did, you must be qualified as he was, meek and lowly.

(2.) Your own judgment and wisdom; else you will be too wise to suffer for Christ. You will think it foolishness to be undone in this world, rather than yield in a small matter, offend Christ in a little; you will think it folly to suffer, when you may avoid it by straining conscience a little. The cross is foolishness to the wisdom of the world, 1 Cor. i. 18, 22, 23.

(3.) Your own reasonings, else you will reason yourselves out of the reach of the cross. This is too small a matter (will carnal reason say) to lose all for; and this is not clear, it is controverted amongst great names, persons of great learning and judgment; and this is yielded to by men of great repute for piety and strictness; and this few stick at, the whole stream runs against it. Which was the great reasoning against Luther of late, and Athanasius of old; what pertinacy, for one man to hold against the whole world! Or this may be connived at now, it may be retrieved hereafter. To tack about is not to go backward (not to backslide), but to make our way so well as the wind will serve; when it serves fairer, we will keep a more direct course; but now we must do as we can, though we do not what we should. If such reasonings had not been renounced heretofore, the world would have had but few instances of such as would follow him under the cross.

(4.) Your own wills. 'Not my will, but thine be done,' says Christ, and yields up all when the question was about his suffering. He that cannot follow Christ in this, will never take up the cross, unless per force, will never bear it as a Christian. Accustom yourselves daily to make yourselves yield to God when his will lies cross to yours, which if you will not do now you are not like to do it when the cross comes, when it cannot be done but upon harder terms, and more contrary to flesh and blood. If your wills be flexible now, and you are accustomed to submit at every beck, at every intimation of the Lord's pleasure in the way of obedience, there is no such danger that they will be stiff and inflexible when the Lord tries you in a way of suffering.

(5.) Your own inclinations. If you give way to these, they will carry you far from the cross, even when Christ calls you to it. He that cannot endure to cross his own natural inclinations will never endure the cross.

(6.) Your own ease and contentments. The cross of Christ and your own ease are inconsistent; if you cannot forego these, you are never like to bear this as becomes the followers of Christ. If respect to your ease make you neglect holy duties, or cut them short, so that you do not watch to them, and continue in them; if the exercise of repentance and duties of mortification be waived, or slightly passed over, because they cross your ease, how will the cross be endured, which is more inconsistent with your ease? As the prophet, Jer. xii. 5, 'If thou hast run with the footmen, and they have wearied thee, then how canst thou contend with horses?' &c. The apostle would have Timothy to inure himself unto hardship, 2 Tim. ii. 3. If it seem a hardship, and contrary to the ease which the flesh would have, to be much in prayer, meditation, self-examining, watchfulness, the exercise of repentance, the duties of mortification, if this seem a hardship, inure yourself to it; forego your own ease herein, and that will be a good preparative to greater hardships. It will not go so much against the hair, to quit your ease when the cross will not give way to it, if you have been accustomed to it before. He that has found his inclinations commonly denied, will not think much to be denied upon special and extraordinary reasons.

(7.) Your own interest. When the question is, Whether you shall bear the cross or no? the question is indeed, Whether the interest of Christ shall be preferred before your own interest? For a carnal heart counts it his interest to have ease, plenty, safety, which the cross would bereave him of; but the interest of Christ is, that we should suffer rather than displease or dishonour him. Now he that can deny his own interest will readily take up the cross and bear it; but he that is wedded to his own interest, and will not be divorced from it, will deny Christ one way or other, expressly or implicitly, directly or by consequence, less or more, rather than let his own interest be crucified, as it must be if he yield himself up to the cross.

The more you can deny yourselves in all respects, the more are you prepared for the cross, the more ready for sufferings; and therefore, if you would bear the cross as followers of Christ, be much in the practice of self-denial. If you be to seek here, Christ will have you to seek when he calls you to suffer.

4. Die to the world. Get your minds and affections disentangled, your hearts loosened more and more from worldly relations and enjoyments. An inordinate affection to the things of the world, arising from an over-valuing of them, is a main reason which keeps men from following Christ in bearing the cross, and puts them upon sinful shifts to avoid suffering: 2 Tim. iv. 10, 'Demas hath forsaken me, having loved this present world.' He left him, and would not partake with him in his sufferings, which he is there speaking of, because he loved this present world. A man who is in love with the world will run into the embraces of that strumpet, far more readily than follow Christ in a way of suffering. Hence worldlings are called adulterers and adulteresses for their excess of love to the world, James iv. 4. This friendship is enmity to God, enmity to Christ, especially to the cross of Christ. Die to the world; for he that is alive to

it must needs look upon the cross as dreadful. Now he is alive to the world whose mind and heart is upon the riches, and delights, and splendour of it; whose soul, by a high esteem of these, and an immoderate affection to them, is linked and united to the world. For as natural life is from an union of soul and body, and spiritual life from an union of the soul with Christ, so this moral life is from an union of the soul with the world; which union is affected by love to worldly things; for love is *affectus unionis*, and this love is begat and nourished by a high esteem of worldly things. So far as you overvalue and overlove the world, so far you are alive to it; and so far as your esteem thereof is taken down, and your love thereto is taken off, so far you die to the world. So far as you are dead to the world, so far you will less fear or regard the cross, as that which only can bereave you of what your heart hath already quitted, and from which your soul is already separated and divorced, which you have inwardly relinquished as a worthless, unlovely object, as a dead thing.

The more you are dead to the world, the less sensible will you be of sufferings in your worldly concernments; the loss of them will but be as the removing the dead out of your sight. It would have been a great affliction to Abraham to have been bereaved of Sarah while she was alive, but when she was dead, 'Give me a burying-place,' says he, 'that I may bury my dead out of my sight.'

While you are alive to the world, riches, and honours, and the pleasant things of the world will be lovely and amiable, you will be apt to doat upon them, know not how to be without them, cannot bear the loss of them, count that an insupportable cross; but you being dead to them, and they to you, you will not then think much to have them removed, to have them buried out of your sight.

It was an evident symptom of this death in the apostle, when he was so indifferent as to outward things, indifferent whether he did abound or was in want, Philip. iv. 11, 12. Make this your business, your great endeavour, so far to die to the world, to get mind and heart so far separated from it, as to be indifferent whether you be high or low, whether you want or abound, whether you have much or little, whether you be respected or despised; and then you will be fit indeed to bear the cross, yea, and ready to welcome it. 'I can do all things,' as he adds, ver. 13. No cross will be too heavy for you if you could once come to this. The apostle could not only bear the cross, but triumph under it, glory in it, yea, and in nothing so much, Gal. vi. 14. But how was he enabled thus to entertain the cross with triumph and glorying? Why, the following words shews us: 'By whom I am crucified,' &c. He was dead to the world, and the world was as a dead thing to him. Now what means you should use to this purpose, I have shewed at large on another subject.

5. Get freed from fears of the cross and the instruments of it. Fear not men, fear not sufferings, if you would bear them like Christians. Give not way to diffident, distracting, perplexing, discouraging fears. There is no one thing that you have more frequently from the mouth of God in Scripture than this, 'Fear not,' 'Be not afraid.' Labour to be obedient to this heavenly call, to the command of God, if you would not decline the cross, or sink under it, or under something worse than any cross can be; for such fear makes the cross worse than it is, and makes a Christian less than he is, and exposeth him to that which is far worse than the cross.

(1.) Fear makes the cross worse than it is. Many a man has sunk under his fears, who might have been otherwise able to have stood upright upon the cross. When we look upon suffering through our fear, it is like a magnifying glass, which represents it greater than it is, makes a mole-hill seem a mountain. And besides, fear often troubles us more than the troubles that we fear. A man suffers more by his fears than by the sufferings he is afraid of. Fear many times proves the heaviest part of the cross, so that he that gets his fears removed is already freed from the weightiest part of the cross, that which is often most oppressive. Many have been more oppressed with the fears of a low afflicted condition than with the condition itself when they have come to try it; many more afflicted with fear of a prison and exile than with imprisonment and banishment itself, when the Lord has vouchsafed them his presence in such a state; many more troubled with fears of death before it came than with death itself when they have come to it, which occasioned that saying, *Mortis timor est morte pejor*, the fear of death is worse than death.

This is a remarkable difference betwixt the enjoyments of the world and sufferings for Christ. Those enjoyments promise more than ever they perform, these sufferings threaten more to a fearful heart than they ordinarily execute. Those enjoyments prove not so good as we expect, these sufferings prove not so bad as we fear. Our fears are often the worst part of them, and tortures a man more than what he suffers. 'Fear has torment,' says the apostle. Get fear removed, and the sting and torment of the cross is in a great part gone, you will more easily bear it.

(2.) Fear makes a Christian less than he is, less fit to bear the cross than a weaker person whose fears are less. It makes him both unable and unwilling either to take up the cross or to bear it; it makes him unable, it deprives him of his strength, or makes his strength useless. Fear dispirits and discourages him; and when his courage and spirits are down, the strongest Christian is like Samson when his locks were cut, he becomes like other men, no more fit to bear the cross than if he had no strength to bear it. A strong and numerous army, when they are under fears, and their courage gone, are easily routed, a small matter will put them to flight. A weak Christian, when he has a spirit of courage raised above fears, will venture more, and may undergo more for Christ, than a Christian, otherwise strong, when his spirits are sunk under the burden of his fears; even as a stout stripling may shew more gallantry than a fearful, cowardly giant. Fear weakens the hands, and makes the knees feeble, so that he can neither take up the cross nor undergo it.

And as it disables, so it makes unwilling. The more fearful any one is, the more loath to venture upon anything hazardous; it makes him draw back when the cross approaches. No greater obstacle in the way of sufferings than fear: 1 John iv. 18, 'Fear hath torment.' The expression may be three ways taken, and so may serve to illustrate all the three particulars before us; κόλασις may be as much as κώλυσις, an impediment or hindrance. Fear stops a man, and keeps him back from suffering; and it is an impediment, because it is tormenting; there is a kind of rack in it which awes men, so as they will not, dare not venture upon anything noble and heroical for the name of Christ. You will never be able, never be willing, never dare to venture on the cross further than you prevail against the fears of it.

(3.) Fear exposeth you to that which is far worse than any cross you can meet with; Jer. i. 8, 'I am with thee,' that is one motive. But he adds another kind of inducement, ver. 17, 'Fear not their faces,' their stern countenances, their wrathful dispositions, which are wont to appear in the face. Fear not to deliver my message to them, fear not when thou shalt be convented before them for delivering it. Why so? Lest I confound thee; or, as the word signifies, lest I break thee to pieces before them, lest I destroy thee utterly; and that will be worse than anything which they can inflict on thee. So Mat. x. 28, Luke xii. 4, 5. To fear what you may suffer from man, to fear the cross which they may lay on you, so as to offend God by shifting it off, is as if a man should fear the sting of a wasp, whenas a dagger is at his heart, or as if he should fear the wetting of his clothes, when he is in apparent danger of drowning. If you will be unfaithful out of fear to suffer, there is something more to be feared in such a case, and that which is so dreadful, as should swallow up the sense of your other fear, 1 John iv. 18, κόλασιν. Fear hath punishment. The Lord will dreadfully punish that fear which keeps you from taking up the cross when he calls you to it. What punishment, says Tertullian, *Nisi quam negator relaturus est*, but that which he that denies Christ shall suffer; *cum corpore et anima occidendus in Gehennam*, when he shall be destroyed body and soul in hell. This is the portion of the fearful, of those whose fears make them unfaithful to Christ, Rev. xxi. 8, δειλοῖς, the cowardly. Those that are so cowardly and fearful as to deny Christ rather than suffer, so fearful as to be ἄπιστοι, unfaithful to Christ in the day of trial, have something worse to fear than the cross, viz., their part in the second death. *Inter reprobos, imo ante omnes*; amongst others, nay, before others, says Tertullian, *Timidis particula in stagno ignis*.

But how shall we get above these fears, which are so dangerous in themselves, and such heavy aggravations of the cross, and such great impediments to the bearing of it? Why, briefly, if you would be freed from fears of man, set God before you; it is the means which himself does everywhere direct us to. How often do we meet with that, 'Fear not, for I am with thee'? Let your eye be much and often upon the infinite greatness of God, and man's nothingness; upon the absolute sovereignty and power of God, and man's impotency; upon the unlimited goodness of God, and the restraints of man's mischievousness, Isa. li. 12, 13. Man is not much feared but when God is out of sight and not remembered.

[1.] View much the greatness of God, and man's nothingness in comparison. See how the Lord describes himself, and how inconsiderable all the world is when set before him, Isa. xl. 15, 17, 22, 23, 24. What proportion do they whom you are apt to be afraid of bear to this drop, to this dust! How little are they, how little to be feared, when all nations are so little, of which they are but a small part, and, as it were, the thousand part of this drop! What fear of such a thing as this! What, be afraid of that which is not so much as nothing, be afraid of that which is less than nothing and vanity, be afraid of those which are not so much as grasshoppers compared with that great God who is your security!

[2.] Upon the sovereignty and power of God, who has all things at his beck, and rules the hearts, and tongues, and hands of all men, so as they cannot so much as move without him, nor move any farther, nor any otherwise than he will give leave, no more than the rod can move without the hand; and therefore the hand of God should be feared, and not men, who are but as a rod in his hand, and cannot stir without him, Isa. x. 5, 24.

[3.] Upon the unlimited goodness of God, who is so good that he can turn evil into good, and none can hinder him; let the actings and intentions of men be never so mischievous, the issue of them, in despite of hell and the world, shall be good to his people; a greater good than the friendship of the world could do them, or the enmity of the world can deprive them of; a good that will more than countervail all the evil that men can bring upon them, Rom. viii., Jer. xxiv. 5, Gen. l. 20. Now, if all they can do shall turn to good, why are they so much feared? A wise man does not use to fear a good turn. But these things I must but point at.

6. Get corruption mortified. The mortified Christian is the best suffering Christian, the willingest to take up the cross, and the ablest to bear it, so as to honour Christ in bearing of it. Carry on the work of mortification with all speed, with all diligence, for mortification affords many advantages for enduring the cross.

(1.) There will be less reluctancy to the cross the more you are mortified. When corruption is subdued, there will be little left to lift up itself against the will of Christ, calling you to the cross; for though nature not corrupted would be averse to that which is afflictive to it, yet corruption very much strengthens this reluctancy. And though outward prosperity would be desirable to innocent nature, yet corruption desires it excessively, doats upon it, knows not how to be without it. And no wonder, for this brings in provision to the flesh, and cherishes corruption, and gratifies our lusts; whereas the cross rather straitens, and pinches, and starves them. So that the voice of the flesh is always that of Peter's to Christ, when he was speaking of his suffering, 'Master, spare thyself.' It cannot endure to hear of the cross. An unmortified soul is like an untamed heifer, a bullock unaccustomed to the yoke; it will not be brought to the cross without much struggling, it will fling every way to avoid it; and when it cannot be avoided, will fling it off as soon as may be, whatever come on it. But so far as corruption is mortified, there is a quiet submission to take the cross when Christ calls to it, and to bear it, whatever it be, during his pleasure. You see it eminently in the apostle: he being dead to sin, could die daily for Christ, and could rejoice in so doing.

(2.) There will be more strength to bear the cross, for corruption is the soul's sickness and distemper; and the stronger a distemper is, the weaker is the subject. A soul little mortified is in a sickly, and weakly, and languishing condition, not able to support itself, much less to bear a cross, a heavy cross. Where corruption is unsubdued, there is but little spiritual strength; and a little strength will be apt to sink or faint under an oppressing cross, Prov. xxiv. 10. A soul of small strength will be ready to faint in the day of adversity; and where corruption is strong, spiritual strength is small. A mortified soul is of a healthy, strong constitution, having purged out those distempers under which others languish, and so is the more able to bear up under the cross. The more you are mortified, the more strength you have both to do and suffer.

(3.) Mortification is a kind of martyrdom, it has some resemblance of it, and the expressions which represent it to us in Scripture import as much; for our natural corruption is called our old man, and a body of death, Rom. vii. 24; a body of sin, Rom. vi. 6, Col. ii. 11. And our lusts are called the members of that our body, Col. iii. 5; and naturally are as dear to us, and we as tender of them, as of the members of our bodies. And then to mortify them, as the word tells us, is to kill them, to lay them dead, νεκρώσατε, Col. iii. 5; to put them to death, θανατοῦτε, Rom. viii. 13; to put them to the worst kind of death, to crucify them. So that he who is daily mortifying his lusts is daily suffering for Christ's sake; and so it will be no new, no strange thing for him to suffer; he has this lesson ready, he daily learns and practises it. Hence when Christ calls him to part with relations, or estate, or liberty, he can say he hath parted with that already which he loved as much as these; he hath parted with the life of his lusts, which naturally are as dear to us as our lives. When Christ calls him to suffer pains, or tortures, or death, why, he hath suffered some such things as these long since, he daily suffers it; he is cutting off his right hand, and plucking out his right eye, and wounding the members of his body of sin; yea, he has sacrificed his Isaac, his darling sin, for Christ's sake. And he that has suffered thus much, what will he stick to suffer for Christ? He has parted with one life already, the life of his lusts, and so has learned the better to part with the other life too when Christ requires it. You are dead, says the apostle, Col. iii. 4; and I am crucified, says he of himself, Gal. ii. 20. He hath suffered one death already, the death of his body of sin, which is indeed another self, and so is the readier to suffer the other death when he shall be called to it. He has given up his old man within him to be crucified for Christ's sake, and so will not think much to give up his whole man to be crucified, or otherwise martyred, if the honour and interest of Christ should require it. None so ready, so fit, so willing, so able to suffer for Christ, as he that is most mortified; and therefore if you would be thoroughly prepared to bear the cross, get thoroughly mortified. The book which goes under the name of Cyprian, *De duplici Martyrio*, is express in this: *Si deest tyrannus, si tortor, si spoliator, non deerit concupiscentia, martyrii materiam quotidianam nobis exhibens*: if there be no tyrant, no tormentor, no spoiler, yet concupiscence (our natural corruption) will be present always to afford us a continual occasion of martyrdom, p. 365. And afterward: *Apud Deum tamen quicunque carnem suam crucifixerunt, &c., martyres sunt, nec martyrum corona fraudabuntur*. In God's account, those who crucify the flesh, *quicunque Christo vere commortui sunt*, those who are truly dead with Christ, they are martyrs, and shall not be deprived of the crown of martyrdom.

7. Keep conscience tender. Be tender of his truths, of his worship, of all his ways, of every part of his will, so as not to offend in the least; to avoid the appearance of evil, to hate the garments spotted with the flesh; not only the flesh, and the spot of it, but the garment that is spotted with it. He that is fearful of all sin, afraid of the least, will be ready to suffer rather than offend in a little. Fear sin more than suffering, and then you will welcome the cross rather than give way to any sin.

Want of this tenderness has made way for many to make shipwreck of faith and a good conscience, cast these over board to save themselves from suffering. Want of this tenderness is the highway to apostasy, the highway to deny Christ, and betray his cause, and renounce his truth; for he that will be drawn to sin in a small matter, to escape suffering, may by degrees be drawn to yield to anything rather than suffer. We may observe it in experience: some, by bending their consciences to comply in less things, by degrees have made them so flexible as to yield to anything; by admitting of small evils, have made way for the greatest. For every degree of evil brings a degree of hardness with it; so the conscience in a little while becomes as it were paved, so that anything may pass it without scruple, when it would have scrupled a little thing at first. By often swallowing, the passage becomes wider and wider, so that anything will down at last, especially when fear of suffering enforceth it. *Qui modica contemnit, &c.*, says Augustine; he that slights smaller evils, by little and little falls into greater; and he instanceth in his mother Monica, who by sipping of a little wine at first, came by degrees to take large draughts. Turn but a bowl down a steep hill with the least touch, and you will scarce be able to stop it till it comes to the bottom.

Thus the ancients, by giving too much way to ceremonies and human inventions in the worship of God, made by degrees a way for popery, as protestant divines observe; and by giving way to an exorbitant prelate in a particular church, made a way for a pope in the universal church. Though they saw no harm in prelacy to make them scruple it, but thought it a prudential expedient to prevent divisions in the church, as Jerome tells, yet the premises being laid by them, after ages thought such a conclusion did necessarily follow as they little dreamed of: if a prelate be necessary to prevent divisions in a particular church, then a pope is necessary to prevent divisions in the universal church. This consequence had never been swallowed, if men had been so tender as not to yield the antecedent. And to this day the papists rely upon the connection of these, and thereupon ground some hopes and expectation of prevailing; insomuch as Contren the Jesuit is bold to say, in his Politics, lib. ii. cap. xviii., that were all England once brought to approve of bishops, it were easy to reduce it to the Church of Rome.

The want of this tenderness, too, has let in idolatry amongst those who profess the name of Christ; and has made them so far from being sufferers, as the primitive Christians were, for not yielding to the appearances of idolatry, that they are transformed into persecutors of those who will not join with them in their idol worship. At first there was such tenderness, as they thought themselves greatly defiled by the touch of an idol: *seque putant contactu simulacri vehementer contaminari.* They would rather suffer death, as the supposed Cyprian tells us, than to defile themselves: *Ut mortem oppetant citius*, &c., p. 364. *Non est dubium*, says Lactantius, *quum nulla religio sit, ubicunque simulacrum:* without all doubt there is no religion where there are images. And the Council of Eliberis, Can. 36: *Placuit picturas in ecclesia esse non debere:* let there be no pictures at all in the church. And Epiphanius, when he found a picture in a hanging at a church door, he tore it in pieces. But by degrees this tenderness was remitted; pictures were admitted into the church for ornament, and, in Gregory's time, in the seventh century, for instruction. And then in the eighth century the second Council of Nice decrees that images should be adored, and those that opposed this decree were persecuted. So that when at first they would suffer rather than touch or see an image in their churches, this tenderness being lost by degrees, it came to this in the conclusion, they must suffer who would not adore those images which the primitive innocency detested and abhorred.

Those that will not preserve their consciences tender, so as to avoid the occasions, the beginnings, the appearance of evil; instead of suffering for Christ, are in danger to prove persecutors of such who are faithful to him; instead of taking up the cross themselves, are in the highway to lay it upon others. If you would be faithful to Christ in bearing the cross, preserve that tenderness of conscience, which will be alarmed at the first approaches of any corruption, either in doctrine, worship, or daily practice.

8. Acquaint yourselves more with God. Get effectual apprehensions of him, what he is in himself, and what he is to his people. Walk in the sight, in the view of God; have him often in your eye. This enabled Moses to endure the cross, Heb. xi. 24–28. Study much the all-sufficiency, the power, the goodness, the unchangeableness of God.

(1.) The all-sufficiency of God. What fulness there is in him to make up all you can lose for him; what refreshments there are in him to sweeten all you can suffer for him.

What fulness. You may as well doubt that all the waters of the ocean cannot fill a spoon, as that the divine fulness cannot be enough to you, if you should have nothing left in this world; for all the waters that cover the sea are not so much as a spoonful, compared with the boundless and infinite fulness of all-sufficiency.

What refreshments in him, &c. One drop of divine sweetness is enough to make one in the very agony of the cruellest death to cry out with joy, The bitterness of death is past. Now in him there are not only drops, but rivers; not a scanty sprinkling, but an infinite fulness.

What is there you can want under the cross, but all-sufficiency can supply! What is there you can fear under the cross, but all-sufficiency can secure you! And that which can secure you from all wants, and from all fears, is enough, well considered, duly improved, to make you willing to take up the cross, and make you able to bear it.

(2.) Eye much the power of God, how it can support under the cross, what it can bring to pass for you by the cross. No cross so sharp and grievous, but he can make it sweet and comfortable. No cross so heavy and intolerable, but he can make it light and easy. No cross so ignominious and reproachful, but he can turn it to your honour. No cross so fastened to you, but he can easily remove it: Eph. iii. 20, he is 'able to do exceeding abundantly above what we can ask or think.' A man may ask much, so much as men and angels cannot give; but how much soever he ask, he can think more than he may think fit to ask. Yea, but let him ask or think as much as ever he can, the Lord can do more than he can either ask or think, abundantly more, exceeding abundantly more, ὑπὲρ πάντα ὑπερεκπερισσοῦ, more than superabundantly more.

You may be apt to think, Oh if such a cross befall me, such disgrace, or poverty, or imprisonment, or such tortures as the primitive Christians suffered, I shall never endure it, I shall sink under it, it will be my utter ruin. Oh but look to the power of God. He can make the cross prove quite another thing than you imagine it to be; far more easy, far more comfortable, far more advantageous, than you can imagine; far better to you every way, than that part of your life wherein you have fared best in the world.

He can make a ruining, impoverishing cross, the way to the greatest riches and advancement. See it in Joseph: what a grievous cross was that for him, who was his father's darling, to be sold by his own brethren for a slave; to be slandered by his mistress as a rogue; to be thrust into the worst dungeon as the vilest malefactor, where his feet were hurt in the stocks, and he laid in irons! Would you think this a way to preferment? Yet so the Lord ordered, as thereby he was advanced to be lord of Egypt, and, which was more, the preserver of Israel.

Nay, which is stranger and better too, he can make the cross a means to advance the soul nearer heaven. Never was David's soul in a more gracious and heavenly temper, never nearer to God, nearer to heaven on earth, than when he was bereaved of all that was dear to him, not only outward comforts, but public ordinances, and hunted as a partridge upon the mountains; which plainly appears by the psalms he penned in that condition.

He can make a poor and indigent estate most rich in inward comforts and sweet contentments, as you see in Paul.

He can turn a prison into a most delightful paradise. So Pomponius Algerius found it, who, being imprisoned for the gospel, dates his letter from thence, *ex delectabili carcere*, from my delightful paradise.

Finally, What more terrible to flesh and blood than fire? What more dreadful to nature than a tormenting flame? Yet this the Lord can make as full of ease as a bed of down, as full of delight as a bed of roses. So our English martyr found it, and tells the papists out of the midst of the fire, when his body was all of a light flame, I feel no more pain in this fire, than if I were in a bed of down; it is as pleasant to me as a bed of roses.

Look to the power of God; if you would be encouraged to take up the cross, if you would be enabled to bear it, he can make it as tolerable, as comfortable, as that condition which most likes you.

(3.) His goodness. His all-sufficiency and power make him able, his goodness makes him willing to do for his people under the cross what his all-sufficiency and almighty power can afford. His goodness sets his mighty power a-work for his suffering saints. His goodness sets his all-sufficiency, his fulness, abroach for them, so that it runs freely upon them; and never more freely than when they are under the cross: Ps. xxvii. 13, 'I had fainted, unless I had believed to see the goodness of the Lord,' &c. What is it that makes you ready to faint under the cross, or thoughts and foresight of it? Look to the goodness of God, there is support.

[1.] Fear you the pain of the cross, the weight, the pressure, the tediousness of it? Why, but the Lord is too good to lay more on you than you are able to bear. He will not suffer you to be tempted above what you are able. He knows your frame, he remembers that you are but dust. He spares you, as a father spares his son that serves him. He stays the rough wind in the day of the east wind: he afflicts in measure; and though the wicked know no measure, nor no end, he will make them know both; the rod of the wicked shall not always lie upon the back of the righteous. He will not contend for ever, lest the spirit should fail. He is too good to let the cross lie too heavy, or to let it lie too long. He is so good, as he will suffer with you, and as it were, bear his part of the cross. In all their afflictions he was afflicted. He cries out, as touched with the sense of the pressure, 'Saul, Saul, why persecutest thou me?' As though it were not goodness enough for Christ to admit us to the fellowship of his sufferings, he is so good as to come himself into the fellowship of our sufferings. As we suffered in him then, so he suffers with us now, and so head and members are all along fellow-sufferers. And fear you to suffer, when Christ will suffer with you? Will you not take up that cross, whereof Christ himself will bear a part? Oh what honour, what happiness is this, to suffer for Christ, nay, to suffer with him! Who had not rather have a share in such a cross, than in all the glory of the world?

Or [2.] do you fear want under the cross? Why, but hear what Goodness itself says to this: Mat. vi. 26, 'Behold the fowls of the air: for they sow not, neither do they reap, nor gather into barns; yet your heavenly Father feedeth them. Are ye not much better than they?' If you have a servant that works for you, you will think yourselves obliged to provide for him, much more if he suffer for you. Why, but here is a greater engagement the Lord lays upon himself. Those that take up the cross for him, he looks on them as children, as children suffering for him. Now will not he who provides for his ordinary servants, yea, for the very birds, provide for children when under the cross for his sake? Sure, if ordinary means fail, he will provide for them in an extraordinary way: he that feeds the ravens, will send the ravens to feed his children, as he did the prophet, rather than that they shall not be provided for. What special care may not they be confident of, since he sometimes feeds the ravens in a way little less than miraculous, if we may believe what some good authors report. They tell us, that when the young ravens are forsaken of their dams, and so in danger to be starved, out of their own dung there ariseth a worm, which creepeth to their mouths, and becomes nourishment to them. Has the Lord such a care of ravens? will common goodness do so much for them? what then may children, suffering children, expect from the special goodness of a heavenly Father? Are ye not much better, much dearer to him than they? If you would be encouraged to take up the cross, and bear it, look to the goodness of God.

(4.) The unchangeableness of God. He is the same God to you, though your condition be not the same, and therefore you may have as much peace and contentment, as much joy and comfort, under the cross, as in a prosperous condition; and if so, there will be no reason to dread the cross, or to decline it. This may make you as ready to embrace the cross as to embrace outward prosperity.

Those exhortations, whereby the apostle calls us to rejoice evermore, and to rejoice always, may seem strange. What, rejoice in poverty, disgrace, in losses and sufferings, in wants and dangers, when destitute, afflicted, tormented! What, can we rejoice as much then as when all things succeed with us in the world according to our desires? Why, yes; if your joys and contentments be those of Christians, and not those of wordlings, you may have as much joy and contentment in a suffering as in a prosperous condition, because the Lord, who is the ground of your joy, is still the same. Where there is the same ground of contentment, contentment may be the same, but the Lord is the same in every condition. Indeed, if your joys and contentments arise from earthly things, they will alter as those things suffer alteration. But if they arise from God, as they do if they be such as become Christians, they may be the same under the cross, because God is the same still; though your condition be changed, yet the Lord, who is the ground of your comfort and contentment, is not changed. 'I the Lord change not.' His all-sufficiency, his power, his love, his goodness, is without variableness or shadow of change. If there be any change, it is not in his nature, but in some outward expressions; and even in these, when you come under the cross, there will be no change unless for the better. The Lord may be better to you in a suffering condition than in any other condition; and indeed so he is wont to be far better to his people under the cross than in outward prosperity; they find him then a thousand times better than ever. And this we may expect from that promise, whereby he engages himself to return an hundredfold for whatever they suffer or part with for his name's sake. He will be an hundred times better to them under reproach for his sake, than when they are cried up by the world; an hundred times better in wants and losses for his sake than when they have the greatest abundance; an hundred times better in prison and sufferings than at ease and liberty. To be still looking thus upon God is an effectual way to prepare you for the cross. Such a view of God will make you ready to take it up, and willing to bear it.

9. Get more spiritual strength. Make it your business, before the cross comes, to strengthen yourselves for it. Be diligent in the use of all means

to get all the strength that may be; and the more, to use the apostle's expression, as you see the day approaching.

There is an habitual strength, which consists in the grown and confirmed habits of grace, strengthen that which is weak, Rev. iii. 2. And there is an actual strength, which consists in the exercise of grace, which the Scripture expresseth by girding up the loins, denoting agility. And there is an auxiliary strength, which consists in divine influences and assistances, Eph. vi. 10. And there is an external strength, which consists in extrinsecal advantages, such as a staff is to a man under a burden, and such as wind, and sun, and armour, and fortifications, are to a soldier. And there is a strength proper for a suffering condition, which consists more peculiarly in suffering graces, faith, and patience, &c.

Now, if you would be prepared for the cross, you must endeavour to strengthen yourselves every way; all will be little enough to enable you to demean yourselves as the followers of Christ, and so as you may honour your leader.

The less strength you have, the less will you be able, as to do, so to suffer for Christ. *Nihil agit ultra vires.* A little cannot do much, suffer much, 1 Cor. xvi. 13. If you will 'quit yourselves like men, be strong.'

The less strength, the more danger sinfully to decline the cross, or shamefully to sink and fall under it. You know what befell Peter when he encountered the cross in his weakness.

The less strength, the more afflictive, the more painful, will any cross be. A man of strength will carry that with ease which will be a grievous oppression to a child or a weakling.

The less strength, the more weaknesses and distempers will you shew under any cross whatsoever, so as Christ and his cause and interest may hereby come to suffer by you when you are called to suffer for him.

(1.) Get more habitual strength. Get the habits and principles of grace strengthened and confirmed. The cross will try your strength.

[1.] Content not yourselves with the infancy of grace, with the first beginnings of it. Think not that enough which will barely give you a title to heaven. If you will come there, you must keep the way, and the way lies through many tribulations; and it will require more than the strength of an infant, to hold on in deep and rugged paths, to bear up under many and heavy crosses, Eph. iv. 14. As there is a wind of temptation from the sleight and cunning craftiness, so there is a temptation from the hatred, malice, and violence of men; those that are but like children will be in danger to be tossed to and fro with every wind. It must be a strong cable that will ride out a storm. Labour to be rooted and grounded in every grace. A weak plant, not well rooted, will hardly bear up against a fierce blast, Mat. xiii. 21. Those that have no root, when tribulation and persecution ariseth, will never stand; those that are but weakly rooted will be in danger to fall.

[2.] Take heed of inward consumptions and declinings, which waste the strength already attained. Take heed there be no carnal, or worldly, or spiritual distemper insensibly consuming the inward man. A languishing consumptive soul is very unfit to bear a cross, Rev. iii. 1, 2. Some of them had already fallen under persecution. Though they seemed to be alive, yet when the cross came they appeared to have no more strength than dead men. Others of them were ready to die, ready to fall; their weakness was not like to bear up under the cross. To prevent the danger, he calls upon them to strengthen that which was weak and languishing.

Make this your great business, to grow in grace. While others make it their business to grow rich and great, or to entrench themselves so as their worldly interest may be secured; while they trouble themselves about the many things of this life, mind you this, as that one thing needful, to grow in grace.

Keep up eager desires after the increase of grace. The hungry soul is, above all other, the growing and thriving soul. 'He filleth the hungry with good things.' He is wont to do it, to fill them that hunger with the strength and riches of grace. And he is engaged to do it, Mat. v. Never look to thrive and grow strong, if you keep not up an eager appetite after more and more spiritual strength. 'The rich he sends empty away.' Who are the rich? Those who think themselves rich, who demean themselves as though they had enough already. Be diligent in the use of all appointed means for the increase of grace. It is the diligent hand that makes rich. Spiritual riches is spiritual strength. Be the more diligent, because the time is short and your opportunities may be shorter. Suck in the word, as those that know your life, and strength, and growth, depends on it, 1 Peter. ii. 2. Labour to retrieve what you have lost by former sloth and negligence, and be much at the throne of grace; there it is you may find grace to help in time of need, Heb. iv. 16. Come with faith, with fervency, with importunity. You are encouraged by the promise of God and the experience of his people, Ps. cxxxviii. 3, תרהבני, Thou shalt strengthen me. He hath done it, and he will do it. Let this encourage you, and provoke you, not only to pray, but to cry as he did.

(2.) Get more actual strength. Be much in the exercise of grace. A man that hath strength and useth it not, loseth it for want of use; he will be able to do less when the trial comes than he that hath less and useth it more. A soul well furnished with grace is like a good instrument, but if grace be not kept in exercise, it is out of tune. He that hath a worse instrument may play a lesson in less time and with less pains than the other can tune a neglected instrument. When Christ would have his disciples prepared for the troubles he had been foreshewing them, he calls upon them to have their loins girt and their lights burning, Luke xii. 35, *i. e.*, keep your graces still in exercise. No matter how much match soever a soldier have, if his match be out when danger is upon him, he is not like to do any service. If grace be not kept in exercise, your light is not burning, your match is out; you are more like to run than stand to it when danger comes. 'I sleep, but my heart waketh,' says the spouse. 'I have put off my coat, how shall I put it on?' Cant. v. 2, 3. That is the posture and condition of a soul that hath not grace in exercise; how much soever he be furnished with, yet it is as it were put off and laid aside when it is not used and exercised; and in that case he will be unready to entertain Christ, when he comes with a visit of love, much more when he comes with the cross. The strongest man, when he is asleep, may be more easily mastered and baffled than a weaker person upon his guard. If the cross surprise you when you are asleep, *i. e.*, when grace is unexercised and laid down in a sluggish rest, it will find you unprepared, unable, unfit to bear it.

(3.) Get more auxiliary strength. Look up to God for divine assistance and influences. The strength of inherent grace, though it be necessary, yet it is not sufficient to support you under the cross, unless it be continually empowered and influenced from above. We are not sufficient of ourselves, 2 Cor. iii. 5. Who had more inward strength than the apostle? And yet that was not sufficient, without a further aid, to think of bearing the cross, to resolve on it, much less actually to endure it. But our sufficiency is of God. It is the name of God, 1 Sam. xv. 29. He is 'the strength of Israel.' And so he is, not only by planting strength in the soul, but by a continued conveyance of strengthening influences. For the strength implanted in the soul is but a dependent strength, something like a staff in a man's hand, which depends upon the hand both for its support and motion. Remove the hand, and the staff falls, and will stand him in no stead who formerly leaned on it. If you rely upon inherent grace, without looking higher, it will prove like a broken reed; it will fail you when the pressure of the cross is upon you.

The earth hath a vegetative power in itself, whereby it brings forth herbs, and flowers, and fruit; but without the heat and influence of the sun, this power will be fruitless. Even so will the power of inherent grace. It will be fruitless, and stand you in no stead, unless it be excited, and quickened, and fortified by renewed aids and influences from above: Eph. vi. 10, 'Be strong in the Lord, and in the power of his might.' There is the fountain of your strength. That which you have in the cistern has no virtue nor power otherwise than by a secret intercourse betwixt it and the fountain. Apply yourselves then to the Lord for those divine aids and influences: engage him to vouchsafe and continue them, by a continual dependence on him for them. 'Those that wait on the Lord shall renew their strength.'

Take heed you provoke not God, by high conceits or self-confidence, neglects of him, or any otherwise, to suspend these influences of assisting grace. Not only Peter, a man compassed with like infirmities as we, but Adam in the state of innocency, of perfection, and the angels in a higher state both of grace and glory than he, when they were left to themselves, found all their strength to be mere weakness, not able to support them a moment. They fell by a less temptation than the cross may prove; for the impressions of fear, proper to the cross, are more forcible than those of the other affections wherewith they were overpowered.

(4.) Make use of strengthening advantages. I shall name some of them, which will contribute much strength and support under the cross.

[1.] Keep the sense of former comforts. To comfort is *confortari*, to strengthen, as the word imports. The joy of the Lord is your strength, Nehem. viii. 10. Comfort is that strength which the object contributes to the heart, as one describes it; and the strength is proportionable to the object. The Lord being the best object, brings most strength to the heart. He that can comfort himself in the Lord, will be thereby so strengthened as he will not faint under the cross.

[2.] Make use of former experiences, both your own and others'. Remember what the Lord hath been, and what he hath done for yourselves and others under the cross. Experiments are great encouragements, and that which encourageth the heart doth strengthen it. When the psalmist was ready to sink under the pressure of his troubles, he fetches strength and support from hence, Ps. lxxvii. 10–12. From the experience of times past, he draws encouraging presages of future mercies, and had thereby strength and relief under the infirmity and weakness he there mentions.

[3.] Stay yourselves on the word, the promises of God. No such cordials in a fainting fit. Treasure up those promises which are suited to the cross. No condition hath so many promises, nor any of a sweeter import. Let these be your delight, and they will be your strength,

Ps. cxix. 92. He had fainted and sunk under the weight of his afflictions, but that the promise was his support, and that which he delighted to stay upon.

[4.] Keep in God's way. The strength of a soldier is in his intrenchments and fortifications. While he [is] within his works he is in his strength, whenas a straggler may be easily cut off. While you straggle not, but keep God's way, you are within your fortifications; 'The way of the Lord is strength,' Prov. x. 29. If a cross meet you there, it may trouble you, but it cannot easily hurt you. If a storm rise while you are at anchor in the channel, or in the harbour, you may ride it out more safely; but if it take you while you are amongst rocks and shelves (as you are always when you leave the way of God), you will be in danger to be wrecked. When a man is under a heavy burden, it is a great advantage to him if his way be fair; but if he be upon a bog, the weight of his burden will go near to sink him. Every step out of God's way is over a quagmire. There is no bearing a heavy cross where you can have no sure footing; but the way of God is firm; it will bear you up under any pressure.

(5.) Labour for that strength especially which will serve in a more peculiar manner to fortify you under the cross, that strength which consists in suffering graces. Let me insist a little upon two, faith and patience. Every grace may contribute something to enable you for the cross, but these two more than any of the rest, more especially, more immediately.

[1.] For faith. The apostle commends this to us above all the rest, with an ἐπὶ πᾶσιν, as that which above all the rest will enable us to stand in a day of trial, Eph. vi. 13, 14, 16. Above all, get the shield of faith, if you would stand. Get faith strengthened, get it exercised; act it upon the attributes, upon the promises of God; encourage it by your relations to him, by your experiences of him, by the acts of his providence for you and others under the cross in all ages. Those worthies of whom we have a catalogue, Heb. xi., were by faith enabled both to do wonders, and to endure wonderfully. All that they acted, all that they suffered, is by name ascribed to faith, ver. 24, 25. By faith Moses took up the cross out of choice; he did choose it, rather than all the pleasures, riches, and honours of Egypt. And by faith, when he had taken it up, he bare it, he endured it, ver. 27; and others were enabled thereby to endure things more grievous, ver. 35–38. And all by faith. This enabled them to encounter death in all shapes, to bear all kinds of crosses, even those that seem most intolerable to flesh and blood; and so to endure them, as they were not only admired by men, but the Lord himself breaks forth into their praises, ver. 39. If you would tread in their steps under the cross, you must get their faith; for faith affords the greatest advantages to fortify you for bearing the cross. Let me instance in some briefly.

First, Faith engages the strength of God with you; and they are strong indeed who are fortified with his strength. What cross is there that the strength of the Almighty will not enable you to bear? Now faith will make you sure of this. It will oblige the everlasting arm to bear you up, and to keep you upright under the cross, how heavy and oppressing soever it be, 1 Pet. i. 5–7. What kept them in such a temper under the cross, as they could rejoice under manifold sufferings, so as they lost no more by their sufferings than the gold loseth by the fire, which comes out more bright and precious and orient than it goes in; yea, so as their manifold crosses, and their undergoing them, was to the praise and honour and glory of God, exceedingly every way to his glory? What is there that could keep flesh and blood thus under the cross? Why, it was the power of God, to which nothing is impossible, nothing difficult, being kept by the power of God. And how came this power of God to be engaged with them? Why, through faith. Never fear the heaviest cross, if there be the power of God to bear it. And this will not be wanting if faith be not wanting. Faith is a relying upon God for strength. Now those that rely on him oblige him; he will not fail them, Ps. ix. 18, עֲנִיִּים. The oppressed, those that are ready to sink under their pressure, if they expect the Lord's strength to bear them up (and faith doth expect it), he will not disappoint them. That would be a great dishonour to him, to disappoint those whom he has encouraged to depend on him. Honest and ingenious men will not deal thus, much less the faithful God. If you believe, the Lord and his power is engaged.

Secondly, Faith stays itself upon God, Isaiah l. 10. Believing is a leaning on him, Cant. viii. 5. The words סמך and שׁען, whereby faith is ordinarily expressed in the Old Testament, signify to stay or lean upon. One of them is used when Saul is said to lean upon his spear. And from שׁען comes משׁען, a staff, such a staff as a man leans upon, and supports himself by, when any pressure is upon him; so that the words which the Holy Ghost makes use of to express faith clearly teach us thus much, that by trusting God, by believing on him, the Lord himself becomes our stay, our staff, our support. And what cross can be too heavy when there is such a support under it? when the Almighty becomes, as it were, your staff, your stay, to bear you up? Ps. lv. 22. The burden of the cross is too heavy for thee; why, but it is not too heavy for the Lord, and he would have thee cast both thyself and thy burden upon him. He can and will sustain both; and so sustain it, that how heavy soever it be, it shall not so much as move thee. He will bear it himself, rather than it shall move; only cast it upon him. That is the way to be eased of the pressure, to cast it upon God. But how is this done? Why, by believing. It is cast upon God by trusting him. So it is explained, Ps. xxxvii. 5, 53. And the same word is rendered trusting, Ps. xxii. 8; so that faith is a compendious way to give you ease under the cross. When it grows heavy, you may relieve yourselves by rolling it upon God, which is done by believing. And he commands you thus to ease yourselves, by casting the burden upon him. You can never be oppressed, let the cross be what it will, if faith be thus employed.

Thirdly, Faith brings strength from heaven into the soul, fetches supplies from above for the strengthening of the soul under the cross, Ps. xxvii. 13; faith strengthened his heart, kept him from fainting, ver. 14; so Ps. lix. 9, because of his strength עֻזּוֹ; because of the strength which I have from God, I will wait upon him; for that is the way to have it; thereby God becomes my strength and defence. It was by faith that the suffering saints, Heb. xi., out of weakness were made strong; so strong, as nothing was too hard, too heavy for them, Isa. xl. 31. Those that rest upon God for his aid, and rely on him for the accomplishment of his promise, they shall have new supplies of strength, enabling them to bear up and hold out when they seem to be quite spent; they shall as easily surmount all the grievances and difficulties that encounter, as if they were carried above them upon eagles' wings; they shall be above the cross even while they are under it; they shall run when the cross lies heaviest on them; it shall not weary nor retard them; they shall walk with it and not faint. Such are the wonderful effects of faith, and the efficacy of that strength wherewith it empowers a believing soul.

Fourthly, Faith strengthens by its representations, Heb. xi. 1; it makes those things visible and evident which are not seen, gives the believer a clear prospect of them, and represents those things as present which are yet to come, gives them, as it were, a present subsistence, and consequently shews him those things as past which at present are grievous; represents to him the crown as though it were present, and the cross that is upon him as though it were already past.

First, Faith represents Christ to one under the cross, as though he were standing by him, as though he saw and heard him, and felt him. It shews him Christ, as though he saw him before his eyes smiling on him, and expressing himself highly pleased that he will express such love to his Saviour as to suffer for him.

It sets Christ before him as though he felt him putting under his almighty arm to ease and support him under the pressure; as though he felt him holding his head and wiping off the sweat or blood, as one of the martyrs testified, and embracing him with all affectionateness and tenderness.

It sets Christ before him as though he heard him speaking in his ear, Well done, good and faithful servant; I see thy love, thy faithfulness to me, and I will never forget it. Oh if you did but see Christ standing by you, and hear him with an audible voice speaking so to you, you would think nothing too grievous to suffer for him! Why, faith will represent him as effectually as if your eye saw him, and your ears heard him, as though you heard him whisper in your ears those sweet words, Mat. v. 11, 12, 'Blessed are ye, when men shall revile you, and persecute you, and shall say all manner of evil against you falsely for my sake. Rejoice, and be exceeding glad; for great is your reward in heaven.' It was such a representation of faith that enabled Moses to endure, Heb. xi. 27; by faith he saw him, and so endured, as 'seeing him who is' otherwise 'invisible.'

Secondly, Faith represents heaven to him, as though it were set open to his eye; shews him all the glory that is approaching, as though it were already present; helps him to such a prospect of heaven in a promise, as Moses had of Canaan from mount Pisgah: 'If we suffer with him, we shall also reign with him.' 'Henceforth is laid up for me a crown,' 2 Tim. iv. 8. 'The sufferings of this present life are not worthy to be compared to the glory which shall be revealed in us,' Rom. viii. 18. It is already revealed to faith, though not to sense. Faith can draw the veil, and get such a sight of glory as will make the sense of sufferings to vanish. Faith sees the crown, as though he were already crowned; sees the kingdom, as though he were already reigning; sees the glory of it, as though he were already shining in it: looks upon these things as matters of as great reality and certainty, as any thing that he hears, or sees, or actually enjoys.

Faith gave Moses such a sight of heaven, as enabled him both to take up the cross and bear it, Heb. xi. 28, ἀπέβλεπε γὰρ; he looked upon it, he had a sight of it. And so had the apostle; and that made him think light of all the crosses that befell him, 2 Cor. iv. 17, 18. How came the apostle to such a sense of glory as made him speak so slightly of all his afflictions and sufferings; to make nothing of them, as light, momentary, and inconsiderable? Why, ver. 18, he looked at things not seen: he saw the exceeding greatness and eternity of an unseen glory. And nothing but faith could give him such a sight.

Thirdly, Faith represents the cross as if it were past, looks upon it as that which is but for a moment, and can easily overlook a moment when the boundless length and breadth of eternity is before it. 'These light afflictions, which are but for a moment,' says the apostle, when the eye of faith was upon that unseen eternity. Faith compares the time of suffering with the time of reigning, and sees that that is but as the twinkling of an eye, when it is set against an infinite duration. 'Mine age is nothing before thee,' says David of his life, compared with God's everlastingness, Ps. xxxix. 5. If the cross should lie upon us while we live, yet that is nothing to the eternity of glory with which it shall be recompensed, and faith will not think much to endure that which it looks upon as nothing.

If you would be prepared for the cross, get such a faith as this, and thus exercise it. Let it represent to you Christ and heaven as if they were present, crosses and sufferings as if they were past; since it is but a moment, and they will be no more. Make use of it to engage the strength of God with you; though a small cross may be grievous to you, yet nothing can be too heavy for that. Make God your stay, your support; lean on him by faith; and if the cross grow too weighty, cast it, roll it upon him: he is ready to sustain you, if you will but trust him. At what an easy rate may you be eased of all your pressures!

And when you are ready to faint, make use of faith to bring in new supplies of strength. If you have not such trials now, yet you cannot want occasions to exercise it every day; and the more you exercise it now, the readier will it be to serve your turn in greater necessities, under heavier pressures. This will hold the head above water in the fiercest storms: no cross will ever sink you while faith bears up.

[2.] Patience. Get yourselves stored with this: a quiet submission to the hand of God, without disturbance or discomposure, without murmuring or repining; not thinking it too heavy, or too tedious; not giving way to a thought of revenge, or of making the least ill return to the instruments of your sufferings. This is a grace, serving in a special manner to fit you for the cross. There is no bearing it like the followers of Christ, unless in patience you possess your souls. Hence it is so frequently required, and so highly extolled. The apostle glories in the Thessalonians: 2 Thes. i. 4, 'We glory in you in the churches of God, for your patience and faith in all your persecutions and tribulations that ye endure.' And indeed, it is a great advantage under the cross: it makes the cross far more easy. *Levius fit quicquid corrigere est nefas*: that which is otherwise intolerable, is easily endured by a patient soul. A weak Christian, armed with patience, will better bear a heavier cross than one that has more strength and less patience. This secures the soul against that inward disturbance and discomposure, which is the very sting and malignity of any outward suffering.

But how shall we compass this patience? Why, briefly, follow the apostle's advice: Heb. xii. 1, 2, 'Let us run with patience the race set before us, looking unto Jesus, the author and finisher of our faith,' &c. Look upon Jesus, see with what patience he bore the cross in all forms, and endured all kinds of persecution.

First, The persecution of the heart, that is hatred. He was hated, and hated with cruel hatred, as the effects of it shewed; and hated without cause. David therein was a type of Christ, and hated by those to whom he expressed the greatest love, John xv. 18; and yet he was the greatest expression of love to the world that ever the world saw, John iii.

Secondly, The persecution of the countenance, when scorn and derision appears in it. For this is Ishmael branded as a persecutor, Gal. iv. And how did he persecute him? Gen. xxi. 9. By mocking. The word is *metsahhak*, which signifies derision, or laughing to scorn. And with this, as some conceive, begin the four hundred years of the Egyptian affliction. Such persecution Christ endured. They fleered at him, and derided him; they scorned him when he preached against their wickedness; Luke xvi. 14, ἐξεμυκτήριζον, they blew their noses at him, as the word signifies; they nodded their heads at him when he was in the greatest extremity.

Thirdly, The persecution of the tongue. He was reviled and vilified, falsely accused, and horribly reproached. They called him a glutton, a wine-bibber, a friend of publicans and sinners, Mat. xi. 19; a Sabbath-breaker, John v. 16, 18; an impostor, a deceiver, John vii. 12; a Samaritan, and one that had a devil, John viii. 48; a conjuror, and one that cast out devils by the help of the prince of devils; Mat. xii. 24, Βεελζεβούλ, a blasphemer; Matth. xxvi. 65, a traitor, an enemy to Cæsar. And upon these accusations he suffered, and all this falsely. He infinitely abhorred the very thought of what they laid to his charge. They might as well have charged the sea with want of moisture, or accused the sun itself of darkness.

Fourthly, The persecution of the hand. They thrust him out of their synagogues, and out of their city, Luke iv. 29. They apprehended him as a thief, Mat. xxvi. 55; arraigned him as a malefactor; they stripped him, and buffeted him, and smote him with the palms of their hands, ver. 67. They tore his flesh with scourges, and pierced his head with thorns, and wounded his side and heart with a spear, and drove great nails through his hands and feet, thereby fastening him to the cross, and putting him to a painful, a cruel, a lingering death.

Now how did he demean himself under all these sufferings and abuses, which were the more provoking and the less sufferable with any patience, because they were offered to a person of perfect innocency, of infinite worth and excellency. Could he endure this with patience? Could the Lord of glory put up such things, when vile worms thus used him? Why, yes; the prophet shews us how he endured: Is. liii. 7, 'He was oppressed, and he was afflicted, yet he opened not his mouth; he is brought as a lamb to the slaughter, and as a sheep before the shearers is dumb, so he openeth not his mouth.' Not an impatient word, not an impatient motion; and the apostle, 1 Pet. ii. 22, 23, 'Who, when he was reviled, reviled not again,' &c. And thus he suffered, that he might teach us thus to suffer, ver. 20, 21. If you would learn patience, look upon Jesus; if his example will not teach it, there is nothing in heaven or earth can help you to learn it.

Thus much for direction. Let me now remove some pleas which carnal reason is apt to make use of, and flesh and blood, when it is consulted with, will be ready to lay hold of, to excuse itself from bearing the cross, and to decline it when Christ calls for the taking of it up.

Some may be ready to say, I would willingly take up the cross, rather than deny Christ, or renounce the religion I profess; I would suffer rather than quit the substantial and fundamental truths of the gospel.

Obj. But when the question is about circumstantials and smaller matters, about rites and ceremonies, gestures and postures, this or that form of worship or discipline,—here I must be excused,—these are not worth the contending about; no wisdom to run any great hazard for such small matters as the Arians of old. What needs so much stir, *propter duas vocales*, for two small words, and those not found anywhere expressly in the Scripture?

In answer to this, let me present to your consideration these four things.

1. He that is a Christian indeed, and follows Christ fully and faithfully, will not, in the day of trial, inquire whether the matter be small or great that is imposed on him, but whether it be lawful or unlawful. If it be unlawful, not warranted by the law of God, how small soever it may seem, he counts it an occasion great enough to suffer anything rather than yield to it; he will submit to anything, how great soever it be, provided it be lawful; he will yield to nothing, how small soever it be, if it be a sin against God. In this case, *nihil obstinacius Christiano* (as the ancient says), nothing more obstinate than a Christiam. Let the thing be never so small, if he discern but the least sin in it, do what you will with him, he will never yield to it while he acts like himself.

He counts no sin small, whatever the world may judge of it. Though one sin be less than another, yet no sin to him is little absolutely; as the earth, though it seem but a small point compared with the heavens, yet absolutely, and in itself considered, it is of a vast bigness. So are those sins to him which the world counts little. He sees something of infiniteness in every sin, as that which is committed against an infinite majesty, as that which makes him obnoxious to infinite justice, as that which deserves infinite or eternal torments, as that which cannot be expiated without a satisfaction of infinite value. Let them make light of sin who never saw its sinfulness, who never felt its weight and grievousness. The true Christian has seen and felt that in sin which will not suffer him to look upon it as a light matter, in what diminutive shape soever it appear; and therefore, when it comes to this, either you must do such a thing, forbear such a thing, or suffer for it; he inquires not whether this thing be small or great, but whether it be sin or no; as a man that is careful of his life will not inquire whether a suspected potion be less or more, but whether it be poison or no; if it be deadly poison, he knows a drop is too much, and may destroy him as well as a large draught, and therefore will not meddle with a drop of it. A true Christian looks upon every sin as deadly poison, how finely soever it be gilded over; in how small quantity soever it be offered him, he dare not venture his soul to take it, he will rather venture body and all outward things under the cross.

Thus Daniel would hazard his life rather than not open his window towards Jerusalem; though this was but a circumstance, and the main duty might have been done unobserved, and so without danger, if this had been omitted, Dan. vi. 10.

So Laurentius the deacon, in the primitive times, would die rather than discover the church's treasure to those that would have seized on it, though it is like the church would have been willing to lose their treasure to have saved the life of such a person.

So the man of Berne, that Melancthon speaks of, would be martyred rather than observe a fast in the popish manner, though that may seem a small matter.

So divers Christians, in Diocletian's persecution, would suffer rather than yield to the appearance of evil; they would not redeem their lives by giving a piece of paper at the command of the officers, lest thereby they should have seemed to have delivered their Bibles to the fire.

And the Christians in Tertullian's time would suffer rather than use the rites, and ceremonies, and customs of idolaters, though they might have used them to another end, and with another mind, than they did.

They thought these sinful, and therefore, though they might seem small matters to others, they counted them matter sufficient to suffer. And so is the smallest matter which is but in the leastwise sinful to every true Christian; he that will be faithful to Christ must choose the greatest sufferings rather than the smallest sin, and take up the heaviest cross rather than offend in the least.

There may be great evil in that which passes for a little sin, a small matter. Vain thoughts are counted the smallest sins, but the Scripture otherwise represents them: ver. 4, 14, 'Wash thine heart from wickedness, that thou mayest be saved; how long shall vain thoughts lodge within thee?' There is pernicious wickedness in vain thoughts, such as may hinder those who allow it from being saved. An idle word passes for a slight fault, many will count it none at all; but we are told, Mat. xii. 36, 'Every idle word that men shall speak they shall give account thereof in the day of judgment.' Is it not better to be condemned at man's tribunal for avoiding of that which, how small soever, may be matter of condemnation at the judgment-seat of Christ? The apostle would have us avoid all appearance of evil, 1 Thes. v. 22. He would have us avoid nothing but what we may comfortably suffer for, yet would have us avoid not only apparent evils, but the appearance; so Jude 23, 'hating the garment spotted with the flesh.'

2. A small evil in itself may become a great evil in consequence; by giving way to the least we may make way for the greatest. He that will yield to small evils, rather than endure the cross, may thereby lay the foundation of the greatest mischiefs. *Solent et minima paulatim despecta in malum magnum trahere.* The least evils slighted are wont to draw us into the greatest.

This is evident in all experience. The greatest abominations in the Christian world have had their rise from small beginnings, and such as it would be counted a nicety to scruple at. What greater abomination was there ever amongst Christians than the popish mass, as we find it now in the Roman missal? Pursue this to its original, and the first step to it will appear to have been a stinted, imposed liturgy. No such thing as a common prescribed liturgy can be found in the first and purest ages of the church. Nay, Socrates the historian tells us, that in his time (and he lived about the middle of the fifth century), lib. v. cap. xxi, page 698, παρὰ πάσαις θρησκείαις τῶν εὐχῶν οὐκ ἐστιν εὑρεῖν (ἀλλήλαις) συμφωνούσας δύο ἐπὶ τὸ αὐτό, that amongst all the sorts of worshippers there were not two to be found that used the same prayers. But in the beginning of the seventh century Gregory the Great, who is called the last bishop and the first pope of Rome, imposed the Gregorian form upon the Church of Rome,* thrusting into it the invocation of saints.† And in the ninth century it was urged upon the other western churches by Charles the Great: and in the eleventh century upon the churches of Spain by Alphonsus the VI. And still, as it pro-

ide Field, Append. † *Vide* Chemnit.

ceeded, some additions were made, the additions bringing in new corruptions, and the universal imposition making the corruptions generally received, till at last it came up to that height of superstition, idolatry, and error, which we see it now consists of, and which all true protestants cannot but greatly abhor and detest. And so we perceive what a mischief may arise from a small and seemingly innocent thing.

Nor can any deny, but if way had not been given to a stinted, imposed form, the popish mass had never taken place in the world. So that hence it is manifest that a small and seemingly innocent thing may make way for a dreadful mischief. Let me add another instance.

The first step to the pope's throne was the inequality introduced amongst ministers, by one degree after another, rising to a papal height. There was granted to one person, first a presidency over others, then a sole power of ordination, then a sole power of jurisdiction over the rest; and that first over all in a city or diocese, then over all in a province, then over all in divers provinces, and at last over all through the whole world.

If this inequality, in the former degrees of it, had not been yielded to, the man of sin could never have advanced himself above all that is called God. If that egg had never been laid, or had been crushed when it first appeared, this cockatrice had never been hatched; it had never become a dragon, or such a fiery flying serpent as we now find it.

The papists' invocation of saints is apparently idolatrous, and yet the beginnings of it seemed modest. They first began with a commemoration of the saints, naming them, and praising God for them. From thence they proceeded to the suffrages of the saints, beseeching God that they might have the benefit and advantage of the prayers and supplications of the saints departed. And so, in fine, they came to direct their prayers immediately to the saints, making them mediators of intercession. Now if they had at first scrupled those commemorations, they had never gone so far as intercession; but yielding to the one as harmless, made a more easy way to the other, though grossly idolatrous.

Nay further, some words, though less material than things, being incautiously used, have been the foundation of pernicious errors. The ancients using the words *merit* and *satisfaction* in a tolerable sense, the papists upon those words have hatched their blasphemous opinions of the merit of condignity and human satisfactions, challenging heaven as that which they have deserved, and presuming they can make God a recompence for the injury sin has done him.

There is danger in words, not only in rites and actions. Change in words may occasion some change in religion; which the Jesuits apprehend, and therefore advise their followers not to use the words of protestants. So the Rhemists, 'While they say ministers, let us say priests; and when they call it a communion-table, let us call it an altar. Let us,' say they, 'keep our old words, and we shall keep our old things, our religion.' So jealous are they of their religion, indeed their superstition, as they will not hazard it by the change of a word; whenas both names and things as hazardous to our religion, are swallowed down freely by many who are accounted protestants.

Basil was more cautious, who would not abate one syllable to keep his place and purchase the emperor's favour. It is remarkable what Theodoret relates of him, lib. iv. cap. xvii. The emperor Valens being desirous to win Basil over to a compliance with the Arians, sends a governor to him, with instructions, either to prevail with him or cast him out of his place. The governor applies himself to Basil with all persuasive words, exhorting him to yield to the time, εἶξαι τὶ τῷ καιρῷ, and not to run so great a hazard for so small a matter, δι' ὀλίγην δογμάτων ἀκρίβειαν; promises him the emperor's favour, and great advantages thereby, both to himself and others. Basil answers him, 'These words are fitter for children, whose weakness is apt to be taken with such things; but those who are nourished up with the word of God, οὐδὲ μίαν ἀνέχονται συλλαβὴν, will not quit so much as one syllable of divine truth; nay rather, they will suffer, πάσας τοῦ θανάτου τὰς ἰδέας, all kinds of death. As for the emperor's favour (says he) μέγα γὰρ ἡγοῦμαι μετ' εὐσεβείας, I value it highly when it is consistent with piety; but without this I count it pernicious, ὀλεθρίαν ἀποκαλῶ.

If the ancients had foreseen that their incautiousness in some smaller matters would have been of such pernicious consequence to after-ages, they would have kept closer to the rule, both in rites and words, though they had suffered for it. And we, being warned by such experiences, will be left inexcusable, if we do not endure the cross rather than yield to the least thing which may be of dangerous consequence either to present or future generations.

8. Small things may be accompanied with such circumstances, effects, and attendants, as may swell them into a monstrous and very formidable bigness. Those things which seem small, when you consider them in themselves simply, yet behold them in their concomitants, and you may discern them to be exceeding great evils. As,

(1.) If we stand obliged against them under sacred and solemn bonds, if we be engaged against them by solemn oath and covenant, in that case there is no yielding to them without perjury and perfidiousness to God and men. And that is no small thing which involves us in the guilt of perjury, and that vengeance which will follow it. 'It is a fearful thing to fall into the hands of the living God.' And such perfidiousness will bring us under the hand and stroke of divine vengeance; for the Lord threatens he will avenge the quarrel of his covenant, and avenge it with the dreadfullest judgments, sword, and famine, and pestilence, Lev. xxvi. 25, 26. And you may see one part of the threatening executed with severity in David's time: 2 Sam. xxi. 1, 2, Saul had slain some of the Gibeonites, and thereby violated the covenant made with them some hundred years before, in the days of Joshua. And for the breaking of that solemn league, though it was rashly made, and the Israelites were drawn into it by fraud and dissimulation; and it was questionable whether it was lawfully made, since the Lord had commanded to destroy the Canaanites, part of whom by this oath escaped the sentence of destruction; nevertheless the Lord's wrath broke forth against Israel, nor would he be atoned till David had punished that perfidiousness upon Saul's house by the sword, as he had punished it upon all Israel by famine.

There is some comfort, if we fall into the hands of men for our faithfulness; but what comfort can there be if we fall under the hand of God for perfidiousness? The faithful found some comfort and support in a desolate condition, upon this account, because they had been faithful in the covenant, Ps. xliv. 17, 19. Though they were brought into the most desolate condition of horror and darkness, the very next degree to death itself, yet this supports them, they had not dealt falsely, &c. But perfidiousness will leave us under the revenging hand of God, without support. That is no small thing which will bring us under such a horrid guilt, and under such a dreadful danger.

(2.) If they make us like idolaters. It is no small evil to be like those whom God abhors, in small matters. The Lord will not have the Jews to use the rites of the idolatrous nations. Because the Gentiles worshipped towards the east, he will have his temple built westward. He forbids the shaving of their heads, because he would not have them like the Gentiles. *Longum divortium mandat Deus ab idololatria* (says Tertullian, *de cor. Mil.*) The Lord commands us to keep the greatest distance from idolatry. *In nullo proxime agendum*, We must not in any thing come near it. *Draco etiam terreus de longinquo hominis spiritum absorbet*, The dragon can kill a man at a distance, and therefore need to keep far off. The idolatry of the papists is as odious to God as the idolatry of the Gentiles, and in many respects more abominable; and therefore it is dangerous to borrow their rites, and habits, and forms, lest in imitating them we partake with them, Rev. xviii. 4. To have fellowship with them in their ceremonies and manner of worship, may be ill resented, 2 Cor. vi. 14–17. The Lord is a jealous God: he will have the relics of idolatry to be abolished; those that will retain them, provoke him to jealousy. Though the brazen serpent was set up by his own appointment, yet when it was once abused to idolatry, Hezekiah breaks it down, and is commended for it by the Lord. How much more should the inventions of men be cashiered, after an apparent abuse, when the Lord will not have his own appointments spared, after once they have been idolatrously abused? Hosea ii. 17. Though the names Baali and Ishi signify both of them an husband, and Baali is an appellation of God himself, Isa. liv. 4, yet since it had been abused and given to idols, he would have it no more used. The Lord is so jealous of his service, that he will not endure an abused name to be made use of in his worship. And will it not provoke the Lord to jealousy, to use not only names, but things, which have been popishly and idolatrously abused? Or is it a small matter to provoke the Lord to jealousy?

(3.) If they give scandal, and lay a stumbling-block in the way of others; if they induce others to sin, or confirm them in sin, or hinder their spiritual edification and comfort, they are scandalous. That which hardens the papists in their way, and makes them apt to think, that those who have left them are again returning to them. That which disposeth others to a better liking of popery, and abates their detestation of the Roman antichrist, which is a principal means to secure them against his impostures; that which confirms any in their superstitious, formal, and heartless devotions; as though the worship of God were but a bodily exercise, a lip-labour, or a ceremonious complimenting with God: that which is of this tendency is scandalous, and that which is scandalous is no small matter. The apostle makes it murder, Rom. xiv. 15; and Christ burdens it with dreadful woes, Mat. xviii. 7, Luke xvii. 1, 2.

(4.) If they tend to corrupt the doctrine of the gospel. Rites, and ceremonies, and forms of worship, borrowed from the papists, in use amongst them, seem small things; but the Reformed churches abandon them all, lest the doctrine of the gospel should be hereby endangered. *Utinam vidissent* (says P. Martyr) *qui hæc conservanda censuerunt;* I would they had seen, who would have these things retained, *evangelium, iis manentibus, non satis esse firmum*, that while they continue, the gospel is not secure. The divines of Hamburgh, in their epistle to Melancthon, call the popish mixtures in the German *Interim*, though they passed under the name of indifferent things, *semina corruptelæ*, the seeds of Romish corruption; intimating, that in time they were like to bring forth a large popish crop. They looked upon them as *cuniculi*, as secret mines, through which the papists would convey themselves under their foundations, and so overthrow their churches. (*Vid.* Park. of the Cross, page 67.)

The divines of Saxony looked upon it as a design of Satan, *qui ab his parvis initiis ceremoniarum*, &c., who, from those small ceremonious beginnings, was making his way to corrupt their doctrine. Now that is no small evil, how small soever it may seem, which tends to corrupt the doctrine of the gospel.

If any ask, why we may not imitate the papists in their ceremonious worship, what hurt, what danger in that? We may have an answer from Augustine: *In multitudine ceremoniarum periclitatur fides*, the faith itself is endangered by such ceremoniousness. We shall be put to borrow Roman principles, that we may defend Romish practices. Why may we not imitate them in the government and discipline of the church, rather than tie ourselves strictly to primitive rules? Why, that of Cyprian may deter us from it: 'It cannot be,' says he, 'that Novatus should keep the doctrine of the church, if he break the discipline.'

(5.) If they be a hindrance to the gospel, and the powerful preaching of it, they are no small things; for that which is an impediment to the gospel strikes at the interest of Christ: for this is the main instrument to advance him in the world, by casting out Satan, and beating down sin, and promoting holiness. Yet so have these small things been managed heretofore, to the great prejudice of the gospel; being made use of for the thrusting out, or keeping out many able and faithful labourers, and making many congregations desolate, leaving them in darkness, or without any more light than some stinking snuff would afford them, like those Gileadites, Judges xii. 6. They have served, like those Gileadites, to keep the passages of the church, so as no minister, how able or worthy soever, could pass, unless he could pronounce this Shibboleth. That is no small thing which has been the cause of so great mischief to the souls of men, as the want of the gospel comes to. Boniface, the martyr, wished for the golden preachers which were in the church when they had but wooden chalices; he would have counted it an ill bargain to have exchanged golden preaching for wooden ceremonies.

It is the observation of learned and moderate Bucer, one of the principal reformers both here and in Germany, 'That the ceremonies and the preaching of the word, do mutually for the most part expel one another. Where knowledge prevaileth through the preaching of the gospel, there the love of them withereth; and where the love of these prevail, there knowledge decayeth.' And therefore, in his judgment, though they were small things, they were great mischiefs.

To conclude this, Bellarmine himself is forced to confess this much, that when a man hath more care to adorn the church with outward ornaments than with a preacher, though his mind be not Jewish, yet doth he *repræsentare Judaicam superstitionem*, he acts as superstitiously as a Jew. To hinder the preaching of the gospel, or to discourage or disable the ministers of it for rites and forms, is the way to make these small things intolerable mischiefs, and such as we had better suffer any thing than yield to.

(6.) If they be made engines of persecution; if they be made use of to vex, and afflict, and oppress, and ruin those that are truly conscientious.

And this is no new or strange thing either here or in other parts. Such small things have been made the instruments of great oppression and cruelty. You may see it in the persecution of the *Interim* by Charles the Fifth in Germany. I instance so far off, because some men see better afar off than near at hand. There divers popish rites were urged as *adiophora*, under the notion of things indifferent. And though they called them small, yet they made them heavy, imposing them under great penalty. And the pressure lay heaviest upon those who were most conscientious, especially the ministers, who, for a modest refusal of what their consciences could not digest, were reproached as turbulent and seditious, deprived of their places and estates, driven out of the country; and so many congregations were laid waste, and left as sheep without a shepherd; and the shepherds were scattered, or left to wolves in priests' habits.

Now let such things as these be counted never so small, they will be found grievous things in the conclusion, which involve men in the guilt of persecution; especially since Christ counts himself persecuted in the sufferings of his people. He resents it, as though himself were reproached, indicted, arraigned, banished, imprisoned, when his servants are thus used for conscience towards God: 'Inasmuch as you did it to one of the least of these my brethren, you did it unto me.' It holds as well in doing them hurt as in doing them good.

And thus you see everything is not small that is so accounted. That which seems little may be exceedingly big with guilt. He that will not bear the cross, rather than yield to things thus aggravated, under a pretence that they are matters of small moment, never intends to bear the cross at all.

(7.) When they are instruments of division, and engines to make breaches amongst Christians, as they are, and will be, when they are generally and rigorously imposed. And hence it comes to pass that those are the greatest dividers who most cry out against divisions, and the greatest enemies to unity who are most violent for uniformity. For when they will not be content to worship God, and order the churches, as the apostles did, and will not satisfy themselves with the primitive simplicity, with those few plain things which the Scriptures make necessary, but will urge such things, and so many, as no general concurrence can be expected, they must needs cause a falling off of many particulars, and so they become the greatest schismatics who most declaim against schism; for they are the schismatics, not who withdraw when they have just cause, but who give the cause of withdrawing. As our divines justify themselves against the papists, when they charge them with separating from Rome. We are not *fugitivi*, but *fugati;* they stirred not till they were chased away, and had just cause given of withdrawing from them. When a necessity is laid upon things which are not necessary, and such small things are rigorously imposed, they make great breaches; and if that be a great evil, these things so urged are not a little guilty.

4. The less the evils are for which any bear the cross, the more faithful they are in following Christ. This is to follow him fully, when you will rather suffer than swerve from him in a small matter. He is faithful indeed who will bear a heavy cross rather than yield to the least evil. He is exactly faithful who will not be unfaithful in a little.

This is the greatest trial, and he that quits himself well here will give a signal testimony that he is a good and faithful servant. This shews the greatest love to Christ, gives the greatest encouragement to others, and will have the greatest reward. For what Christ promises in another case he will make good in this: Luke xix. 17, 'Because thou hast been faithful in a very little, have thou authority over ten cities;' Mat. xxiv. 23, 'Thou hast been faithful in a little, I will make thee ruler over much,' ἐπὶ ὀλίγα ἦς πιστός.

END OF VOL. I.

CPSIA information can be obtained
at www.ICGtesting.com
Printed in the USA
LVHW101337160422
716387LV00003B/76

9 783752 591637